Praise for John Joseph Adams

For *Wastelands*

"This harrowing reprint anthology of 22 apocalyptic tales reflects the stresses of contemporary international politics, with more than half published since 2000. All depict unsettling societal, physical and psychological adaptations their authors postulate as necessary for survival after the end of the world."

—*Publishers Weekly* (Starred Review)

"Arguably my favorite anthology of all time—just packed with speculative masterworks."

—Paul Goat Allen, *Barnes & Noble.com*

For *The Living Dead*

"Believe the hype. *The Living Dead* is absolutely the best zombie anthology I've ever read (and I've read many).... If you have even a vague interest in zombie fiction, you MUST buy this book."

—*HorrorScope*

"A superb reprint anthology that runs the gamut of zombie stories. Great storytelling for zombie fans as well as newcomers."

—*Publishers Weekly* (Starred Review)

For *By Blood We Live*

"The reigning king of the anthology world is John Joseph Adams....Yet another masterful—dare I say perfect—anthology."

—*Barnes & Noble.com*

"As he's done on *Wastelands* and *The Living Dead*, John Joseph Adams has given readers another definitive anthology."

—*SFF World*

Cover design by John Coulthart
Interior design by Elizabeth Story

Tachyon Publications
1459 18th Street #139
San Francisco, CA 94107

Series Editor: Jacob Weisman
Project Editor: Jill Roberts

ISBN 10: 1-61696-084-1
ISBN 13: 978-1-61696-084-1

Printed in the United States by Worzalla
First Edition: 2012
9 8 7 6 5 4 3 2 1

EPIC

LEGENDS OF FANTASY

TACHYON | SAN FRANCISCO

EPIC

Legends of Fantasy

Other anthologies edited by John Joseph Adams

Armored
Brave New Worlds
By Blood We Live
Federations
The Improbable Adventures of Sherlock Holmes
Lightspeed: Year One
The Living Dead
The Living Dead 2
Other Worlds Than These
Seeds of Change
Under the Moons of Mars: New Adventures on Barsoom
Wastelands
The Way of the Wizard

Forthcoming anthologies edited by John Joseph Adams

Dead Man's Hand
The Mad Scientist's Guide to World Domination
Robot Uprisings (co-edited with Daniel H. Wilson)

For Robert Barton Bland,
the most epic guy I know.

CONTENTS

Foreword

Brent Weeks

ALL FICTION IS LIES, varying only in scope and audacity. Epic fantasy is lies turned up to eleven. It is the outcast, living in the margins of our literary maps where fearful scribes have written, "Here be dragons."

Perhaps this explains the persistent resistance it finds among critics. Have you ever met an inveterate liar, full of sound and fury? Entertaining for ten minutes, twenty maybe. But why would you spend a thousand pages poring over the froth of a fevered imagination? Even Tolkien faced this—critics who wished to hang literature on a wall and bracket it with thick frames that might cover up the embarrassment of that silliness at the edges.

But every genre is a contract. There are demands made of an audience, and expectations of an author. If you write historical fiction, and you set your story in New York City on September 12, 2001, there are certain events you simply cannot ignore. If you write romance, and the girl decides to become a nun, you've betrayed expectations. If you write mystery, and it turns out no one died—that instead, dastardly, twice-divorced CEO Tom is really merely vacationing happily in Fiji—you've given your audience a stone when they asked for bread. If you write police procedural, and the suspect is beaten senseless by the cops in a Seattle alley and never read his rights, you'd better have a great reason why this doesn't get him off the hook. (Whereas the same scene wouldn't raise an eyebrow, even if set in the same city, if the novel were a Western set in 1860.)

That contract is simply broadest in epic fantasy: Tell me a great story, the audience says. I'll work to remember lots of names and foreign terms and odd cultures and strange ways if you sweep me away.

And these authors oblige.

There is, as you will see even within this volume, enormous range within epic fantasy. From conciliatory stories that show the good guys winning (though often at great cost) in a Tolkienesque tenor to the challenging "there are no good guys, much less winning" in an Abercrombian argot, all seek to tell moving stories in immersive worlds.

When an author of grand imagination who is capable of adroit explication meets a perspicacious reader, something magical happens: the scale of the story changes the experience of the story qualitatively. What we worked so hard to digest now swallows us. Epic fantasy is uniquely immersive. We enter a new world, and all too often, we don't want to leave. (Part of why it tends to such length.)

But doesn't that very immersive quality simply prove that fantasy is escapist? Best suited for children and those unable to face the real world?

In "On Fairy Stories," Tolkien said that those who dismiss fantasy as escapist are confusing "the Escape of the Prisoner with the Flight of the Deserter....Why should a man be scorned, if, finding himself in prison, he tries to get out and go home? Or if, when he cannot do so, he thinks and talks about other topics than jailers and prison-walls?"

The frame focuses the whole painting, and when you set the frame too narrowly, so that the frame covers up that "nonsense" at the edges of the map where it says, "Here be dragons," you've excluded an essential element. Not only would we lose everything from Homer to Virgil to Dante to Beowulf from our literature, but we also would lose some of the range of human creativity. It would be as if we told artists that no True Art could feature violet. Doubtless a lot of great art could be created without violet, but why accept such a limitation?

If we can accept a map beyond our traditional critical frames, fantasy can take us on a journey beyond our traditional frames of reference. It can give us respite and consolation; it can challenge; it can tell us the truth by slipping right past our prejudices. It is often only in hindsight, as we have absorbed a story and been absorbed by it, that we recognize how it is molding us. When we read a story that sticks with us, it becomes part of our frame of reference. A small Jewish kid trying out for a sports team might feel like David facing Goliath—and take consolation from the fact that David won! The Lord of the Rings isn't a novel about the environment, but Saruman's defilement of the natural world has struck millions with horror. The Odyssey isn't about drug abuse, but Odysseus's encounter with the Lotus Eaters has been warning audiences about the dangers of narcotics for 2,800 years.

Great stories don't change minds, they change hearts.

G. K. Chesterton said it whimsically: "Fairy tales do not tell children that dragons exist. Children already know that dragons exist. Fairy tales tell children that dragons can be killed."

There are dragons. And here they be.

Enjoy.

Brent Weeks

Introduction

John Joseph Adams

EPIC FANTASY HAS BECOME the literature of *more*. We equate it with more pages than the average book, more books than the average series. There are more characters, more maps, more names, and more dates. The stories and the worlds are bigger to contain all of this *more*. And when all the books have been devoured, the fans want more.

Fifty years ago, there was precious little. Modern epic fantasy was non-existent in the early twentieth century until J. R. R. Tolkien's Lord of the Rings came along. A few scattered classics would be added to the pantheon in subsequent years, but notable exceptions aside, few believed epic fantasy was a viable commercial genre. Publications within this field were rare. That all changed in 1977, when *The Sword of Shannara* by Terry Brooks became the first work of fantasy ever to appear on the *New York Times* bestseller list, and the rest is history.

But that is only *modern* history. Epic fantasy has extremely deep roots. Drawing on the traditions of the great extended poems and oral tales that are the origins of literature, epics represent some of the most beloved tales in human culture. Even in these ancient stories, we can see the trappings of the modern epic: exotic fantastical settings peopled with larger-than-life characters, where fates of entire worlds often rest on the shoulders of protagonists who are forced to become heroes or crumble under the pressure.

The oldest existing written literature is the *Epic of Gilgamesh*, from ancient Mesopotamia, about a king who uses his power to harm his own people. His adventure causes him heartbreak, conflict with the gods, and even forces him to face his own mortality...until he returns home and realizes the virtue and beauty of the civilization he should have been ruling and protecting. He is changed into a better man by his quest. This cycle, of a simple or flawed man facing peril in order to preserve his world, appears over and over in literature. Mythology scholar Joseph Campbell called this cycle the *monomyth*, or more aptly, The Hero's Journey. He argued that stories about figures in many religions and myths all follow the same cycle of the hero rising to the occasion to save his people or his civilization.

Along with modern epic fantasy's growth into the all-powerful *more*, the literature has evolved in ways that would have fascinated Campbell. While the genre exploded during the 1980s, much of that decade's output—at least in book form—followed the model set down by Tolkien: an ancient all-powerful evil, usually a Dark Lord, is stirring and will destroy a secondary world filled with magic and wonder, unless a small band of heroes can recover a powerful artifact to aid the armies of good in the final battle. This model, right down to the same races of mythical creatures, flooded the shelves as publishers churned out bestseller after bestseller.

Although epic fantasy exploded in the '80s, with most of it following the above-described template, there were some other notable earlier entries in the genre that broke the Tolkien mold. Ursula K. Le Guin's protagonist Ged, in *A Wizard of Earthsea* (1968), hearkened back to the ancient stories of a prideful, flawed protagonist who causes great harm with his powers, and must learn to master his magic and his values before he can resemble anything like a hero. And then fantasy anti-heroes like Stephen R. Donaldson's Thomas Covenant (1977) and Michael Moorcock's Elric of Melniboné (1961) were precursors to the morally ambiguous protagonists many twenty-first-century readers have come to prefer in their epic fantasies.

Tyrion Lannister in George R. R. Martin's A Song of Ice and Fire series has become the poster-boy for morally ambiguous or "gray" protagonists in the genre, and Martin's books—consisting of sprawling, thousand-page doorstoppers—are the epitome of the all-powerful *more*, though it was Robert Jordan's Wheel of Time books that first shattered the trilogy model established by Tolkien and was instrumental in shaping the contemporary epic fantasy marketplace.

In addition to the above-mentioned moral complexity, today's epics are also usually founded on strong worldbuilding and deep insight into the human condition. Another popular component is the struggle against overwhelming odds and/or an overwhelming power(s), which results in significant changes to the world. While this final element often makes for good epic fantasy, the monumental struggle is not absolutely essential, as some of these stories will demonstrate. Tad Williams's "The Burning Man," George R. R. Martin's "The Mystery Knight," and Robin Hobb's "Homecoming" all take place in epic fantasy worlds their respective authors have written about in multiple books; these stories take place on a smaller scale, but setting them in the same world makes them feel just as epic. (Longtime fans of the genre will also note several other stories in the anthology that take place in the same milieus as their respective author's novel series.) Carrie Vaughn's standalone tale "Strife Lingers in Memory," meanwhile, provides another twist to the monumental struggle argument, presenting a tale that begins after such a battle is over. There are also stories in here without connections or allusions to apocalyptic battles, but somehow they are no less epic.

The stories in this anthology are epic because of exotic worldbuilding and the remarkable humanity of the characters as they struggle with their situations. Every epic begins and ends in the hero's heart. When we know what forces in the world have formed that heart, and learn what pushes that character to his or her very limit, we learn the shape of his or her own personal crucible.

Any story that can show us that is truly epic, regardless of page counts or whether or not sweeping battles are rocking the realm…and when we find something truly epic, it should be no surprise so many of us want *more*.

Homecoming

Robin Hobb

Robin Hobb *(a/k/a Megan Lindholm) is the author of The Realm of the Elderlings epic fantasy series, which is comprised of several subseries, including The Farseer Trilogy, The Liveship Traders, The Tawny Man, and The Rain Wilds Chronicles. Her most recently published book is* City of Dragons, *the third volume of The Rain Wilds Chronicles, published in February 2012. Her recent publications include* The Inheritance and Other Stories, *incorporating shorter pieces of fiction published under both of her pseudonyms.* Blood of Dragons *is the concluding volume of The Rain Wilds Chronicles. It will be published in March of 2013. Robin Hobb currently resides in Tacoma, Washington.*

Day the 7th of the Fish Moon

Year the 14th of the reign of the Most Noble and Magnificent Satrap Esclepius

CONFISCATED FROM ME this day, without cause or justice, were five crates and three trunks. This occurred during the loading of the ship *Venture*, setting forth upon Satrap Esclepius' noble endeavor to colonize the Cursed Shores. Contents of the crates are as follows: One block fine white marble, of a size suitable for a bust, two blocks Aarthian Jade, sizes suitable for busts, one large fine soapstone, as tall as a man and as wide as a man, seven large copper ingots, of excellent quality, three silver ingots, of acceptable quality, and three kegs of wax. One crate contained scales, tools for the working of metal and stone, and measuring equipment. Contents of trunks are as follows: Two silk gowns, one blue, one pink, tailored by Seamstress Wista and bearing her mark. A dress-length of mille-cloth, green. Two shawls, one white wool, one blue linen. Several pairs hose, in winter and summer weights. Three pairs of slippers, one silk and worked with rosebuds. Seven petticoats, three silk, one linen and three wool. One bodice frame, of light bone and silk. Three volumes of poetry, written in my own hand. A miniature by Soiji, of myself, Lady Carillion Carrock, nee Waljin, commissioned by my mother, Lady Arston Waljin, on the occasion of my 14th birthday. Also included were clothing and bedding for a baby, a girl of four years and two boys, of six and ten years, including both winter and summer garb for formal occasions.

I record this confiscation so that the thieves can be brought to justice upon my return to Jamaillia City. The theft was in this manner: As our ship was being loaded for departure, cargo belonging to various nobles aboard the vessels was detained upon the docks. Captain Triops informed us that our possessions would be held, indefinitely, in the Satrap's custody. I do not trust the man, for he shows neither my husband nor myself proper deference. So I make this record, and when I return this coming spring to Jamaillia City, my father, Lord Crion Waljin, will bring my complaint before the Satrap's Court of Justice, as my husband seems little inclined to do so. This do I swear.

Lady Carillion Waljin Carrock

Day the 10th of the Fish Moon
Year the 14th of the reign of the Most Noble and Magnificent Satrap Esclepius

Conditions aboard the ship are intolerable. Once more, I take pen to my journal to record the hardship and injustice to preserve a record so that those responsible may be punished. Although I am nobly born, of the house of Waljin, and although my lord husband is not only noble, but heir to the title of Lord Carrock, the quarters given us are no better than those allotted to the common emigrants and speculators, that is, a smelly space in the ship's hold. Only the common criminals, chained in the deepest holds, suffer more than we do.

The floor is a splintery wooden deck, the walls are the bare planks of the ship's hull. There is much evidence that rats were the last inhabitants of this compartment. We are treated no better than cattle. There are no separate quarters for my maid, so I must suffer her to bed almost alongside us! To preserve my children from the common brats of the emigrants, I have sacrificed three damask hangings to curtain off a space. Those people accord me no respect. I believe that they are surreptitiously plundering our stores of food. When they mock me, my husband bids me ignore them. This has had a dreadful effect on my servant's behavior. This morning, my maid, who also serves as a nanny in our reduced household, spoke almost harshly to young Petrus, bidding him be quiet and cease his questions. When I rebuked her for it, she dared to raise her brows at me.

My visit to the open deck was a waste of time. It is cluttered with ropes, canvas and crude men, with no provisions for ladies and children to take the air. The sea was boring, the view only distant foggy islands. I found nothing there to cheer me as this detestable vessel bears me ever farther away from the lofty white spires of Blessed Jamaillia City, sacred to Sa.

I have no friends aboard the ship to amuse or comfort me in my heaviness. Lady Duparge has called on me once, and I was civil, but the differences in our station make conversation difficult. Lord Duparge is heir to little more than his title, two ships and one estate that borders on Gerfen Swamp. Ladies Crifton and Anxory appear content with one another's company and have not called upon me at all. They are both too young to have any accomplishments to share, yet their mothers should have instructed them in their social responsibility to their betters. Both might have profited from my friendship upon our return to Jamaillia City. That they choose not to court my favor does not speak well of their intellect. Doubtless they would bore me.

I am miserable in these disgusting surroundings. Why my husband has chosen to invest his time and finances in this venture eludes me. Surely men of a more adventurous nature would better serve our Illustrious Satrap in this exploration. Nor can I understand why our children and myself must accompany him, especially in my condition. I do not think my husband gave any thought to the difficulties this voyage would pose for a woman gravid with child. As ever, he has not seen fit to discuss his decisions with me, no more than I would consult him on my artistic pursuits. Yet my ambitions must suffer to allow him to pursue his! My absence will substantially delay the completion of my "Suspended Chimes of Stone and Metal." The Satrap's brother will be most disappointed, for the installation was to have honored his thirtieth birthday.

Day the 15th of the Fish Moon

Year the 14th of the reign of the Most Noble and Magnificent Satrap Esclepius

I have been foolish. No. I have been deceived. It is not foolishness to trust where one has every right to expect trustworthiness. When my father entrusted my hand and my fate to Lord Jathan Carrock, he believed he was a man of wealth, substance, and reputation. My father blessed Sa's name that my artistic accomplishments had attracted a suitor of such lofty stature. When I bewailed the fate that wed me to a man so much my senior, my mother counseled me to accept it and to pursue my art and establish my reputation in the shelter of his influence. I honored their wisdom. For these last ten years, as my youth and beauty faded in his shadow, I have borne him three children, and bear beneath my heart the burgeoning seed of yet another. I have been an ornament and a blessing to him, and yet he has deceived me. When I think of the hours spent managing his household, hours I could have devoted to my art, my blood seethes with bitterness.

Today, I first entreated, and then, in the throes of my duty to provide for my children, demanded that he force the captain to give us better quarters. Sending our three children out onto the deck with their nanny, he confessed that we were not willing investors in the Satrap's colonization plan but exiles given a chance to flee our disgrace. All we left behind, estates, homes, precious possessions, horses, cattle...all are forfeit to the Satrap, as are the items seized from us as we embarked. My genteel respectable husband is a traitor to our gentle and beloved Satrap and a plotter against the Throne Blessed by Sa.

I won this admittance from him, bit by bit. He kept saying I should not bother about the politics, that it was solely his concern. He said a wife should trust her husband to manage their lives. He said that by the time the ships re-supply our settlement next spring, he would have redeemed our fortune and we would return to Jamaillian society. But I kept pressing my silly woman's questions. All your holdings seized? I asked him. All? And he said it was done to save the Carrock name, so that his parents and younger brother can live with dignity, untarnished by the scandal. A small estate remains for his brother to inherit. The Satrap's Court will believe that Jathan Carrock chose to invest his entire fortune in the Satrap's venture. Only those in the Satrap's innermost circle know it was a confiscation. To win this concession, Jathan begged many hours on his knees, humbling himself and pleading forgiveness.

He went on at great length about that, as if I should be impressed. But I cared nothing for his knees. "What of Thistlebend?" I asked. "What of the cottage by the ford there, and the monies from it?" This I brought to him as my marriage portion, and humble though it is, I thought to see it passed to Narissa when she wed.

"Gone," he said. "All gone."

"But why?" I demanded. "I have not plotted against the Satrap. Why am I punished?"

Angrily, he said I was his wife and of course I would share his fate. I did not see why, he could not explain it, and finally told me that such a foolish woman could never understand, and bid me hold my tongue, not flap it and show my ignorance. When I protested that I am not a fool, but a well-known artist, he told me that I am now a colonist's wife, and to put my artistic pretenses out of my head.

I bit my tongue to keep from shrieking at him. But within me, my heart screams in fury against this injustice. Thistlebend, where my little sisters and I waded in the water and plucked lilies to pretend we were goddesses and those our white and gold scepters... Gone for Jathan Carrock's treacherous idiocy.

I had heard rumors of a discovered conspiracy against the Satrap. I paid no attention. I thought it had nothing to do with me. I would say that the punishment was just, if I and my innocent babes were not ensnared in the same net that has trapped the plotters. All the confiscated wealth has financed this expedition. The disgraced nobles were forced to join a Company composed of speculators and explorers. Worse, the banished criminals in the hold, the thieves and whores and ruffians, will be released to join our company when we disembark. Such will be the society around my tender children.

Our Blessed Satrap has generously granted us a chance to redeem ourselves. Our Magnificent and Most Merciful Satrap has granted each man of the company two hundred leffers of land, to be claimed anywhere along the banks of the Rain Wild River that is our boundary with barbarous Chalced, or along the Cursed Shores. He directs us to establish our first settlement on the Rain Wild River. He chose this site for us because of the ancient legends of the Elder Kings and their Harlot Queens. Long ago, it is said, their wondrous cities lined the river. They dusted their skin with gold and wore jewels above their eyes. So the tales say. Jathan said that an ancient scroll, showing their settlements, has recently been translated. I am skeptical.

In return for this chance to carve out new fortunes for ourselves and redeem our reputations, Our Glorious Satrap Esclepius asks only that we cede to him half of all that we find or produce there. In return, the Satrap will shelter us under his protective hand, prayers will be offered for our well-being, and twice yearly his revenue ships will visit our settlement to be sure we prosper. A Charter for our Company, signed by the Satrap's own hand, promises this.

Lords Anxory, Crifton and Duparge share in our disgrace, though as lesser lords, they had less far to fall. There are other nobles aboard the other two ships of our fleet, but no one I know well. I rejoice that my dear friends do not share my fate yet I mourn that I enter exile alone. I will not count upon my husband for comfort in the disaster he has brought upon us. Few secrets are kept long at court. Is that why none of my friends came to the docks to bid me farewell?

My own mother and sister had little time to devote to my packing and farewells. They wept as they bade me farewell from my father's home, not even accompanying me to the filthy docks where this ship of banishment awaited me. Why, oh Sa, did they not tell me the truth of my fate?

At that thought, a hysteria fell upon me, so that I trembled and wept, with occasional shrieks bursting from me whether I would or no. Even now, my hands tremble so violently that this desperate scrawl wanders the page. All is lost to me, home, loving parents, and most crushing, the art that gave me joy in life. The half-finished works I left behind will never be completed, and that pains me as much as a child still-born. I live only for the day that I can return to gracious Jamaillia by the sea. At this moment, forgive me Sa, I long to do so as a widow. Never will I forgive Jathan Carrock. Bile rises in my throat at the thought that my children must wear this traitor's name.

Day the 24th of the Fish Moon
Year the 14th of the reign of the Most Noble and Magnificent Satrap Esclepius

Darkness fills my soul; this voyage to exile has lasted an eternity. The man I must call husband orders me to better manage our household, but I scarcely have the spirit to take up my pen. The children weep, quarrel and complain endlessly, and my maid makes no effort to amuse them. Daily her contempt grows. I would slap her disrespectful scowl from her face if I had the strength. Despite my pregnancy, she lets the children tug at me and demand my attention. All know a woman in my condition should experience a serene existence. Yesterday afternoon, when I tried to rest, she left the children napping beside me while she went out to dally with a common sailor. I awoke to Narissa crying and had to arise and sing to her until she calmed. She complains of a painful belly and a sore throat. No sooner was she settled than both Petrus and Carlmin awoke and started some boyish tussling that completely frayed my spirit. I was exhausted and at the edge of hysteria before she returned. When I chided her for neglecting her duties, she saucily replied that her own mother reared nine children with no servants to aid her. As if such common drudgery were something I should aspire to! Were there anyone else to fulfil her duties, I would send her packing.

And where is Lord Carrock through all of this? Why, out on deck, consulting with the very nobles who led him into disgrace.

The food grows ever worse and the water tastes foul, but our cowardly captain will not put into shore to seek better. My maid says that her sailor has told her that the Cursed Shore is well named, and that evil befalls those who land there as surely as it befell those who once lived there. Can even Captain Triops believe such superstitious nonsense?

Day the 27th of the Fish Moon
Year the 14th of the reign of the Most Noble and Magnificent Satrap Esclepius

We are battered by storm. The ship reeks of the vomit of the miserable inhabitants of its bowels. The constant lurching stirs the foul waters of the bilge, so that we must breathe their stench. The captain will not allow us out on the deck at all. The air down here is damp and thick, and the beams drip water on us. Surely, I have died and entered some heathen afterlife of punishment.

Yet in all this wet, there is scarcely enough water for drinking, and none for washing. Clothing and bedding soiled with sickness must be rinsed out in seawater that leaves it stiff and stained with salt. Little Narissa has been most miserable of the children. She has ceased vomiting but has scarcely stirred from her pallet today, poor little creature. Please, Sa, let this horrid rocking and sloshing end soon.

Day the 29th of the Fish Moon
Year the 14th of the reign of the Most Noble and Magnificent Satrap Esclepius

My child is dead. Narissa, my only daughter, is gone. Sa, have mercy upon me, and visit your justice upon treacherous Lord Jathan Carrock, for his evil has been the cause of all my woe! They wrapped my little girl in canvas and sent her and two others into the waters, and the sailors scarce paused in their labors to notice their passing. I think I went a little mad then. Lord Carrock seized me in his arms when I tried to follow her into the sea. I fought him, but he was too strong for me. I remain trapped in this life his treachery has condemned me to endure.

Day the 7th of the Plow Moon
Year the 14th of the reign of the Most Noble and Magnificent Satrap Esclepius

My child is still dead. Ah, such a foolish thought to write, and yet still it seems impossible to me. Narissa, Narissa, you cannot be gone forever. Surely this is some monstrous dream from which I will awake!

Today, because I sat weeping, my husband pushed this book at me and said "Write a poem to comfort yourself. Hide in your art until you feel better. Do anything, but stop weeping!" As if he offered a squalling baby a sugar teat. As if art took you away from life rather than plunging you headlong into it! Jathan reproached me for my grief, saying that my reckless mourning frightens our sons and threatens the babe in my womb. As if he truly cared! Had he cared for us as a husband and a father, never would he have betrayed our dear Satrap and condemned us to this fate.

But, to stop his scowl, I will sit here and write for a time, like a good wife.

A full dozen of the passengers and two crewmen have died of the flux. Of one hundred sixteen who began this voyage, ninety-two now remain. The weather has calmed but the warm sunlight on the deck only mocks my sorrow. A haze hangs over the sea and to the west the distant mountains smoke.

Day the 18th of the Plow Moon

Year the 14th of the reign of the Most Noble and Magnificent Satrap Esclepius

I have no spirit to write, yet there is nothing else to occupy my weary mind. I, who once composed the wittiest prose and most soaring poetry, now plod word by word down a page.

Some days ago we reached the river mouth; I did not note the date, such has been my gloom. All the men cheered when we sighted it. Some spoke of gold, others of legendary cities to plunder, and still others of virgin timber and farmland awaiting us. I thought it marked an end to our voyage, but still it drags on.

At first the rising tide aided our upriver progress. Now the crew must labor at their oars for every ship-length we gain. The prisoners have been taken from their chains and utilized as rowers in tiny boats. They row upriver and set anchors and drag us against the current. By night, we anchor and listen to the rush of the water and the shrieks of unseen creatures from the jungle on the shore. Daily the scenery grows both more fantastic and threatening. The trees on the banks stand twice as tall as our mast, and the ones behind them are taller still. When the river narrows, they cast deep shadows over us. Our view is a near impenetrable wall of greenery. Our search for a kindly shore seems folly. I see no sign that any people have ever lived here. The only creatures are bright birds, large lizards that sun themselves on the tree roots at the water's edge, and something that whoops and scuttles in the treetops. There are no gentle meadows or firm shores, only marshy banks and rank vegetation. Immense trees root stilt-like in the water and dangling vines festoon them, trailing in the chalky water. Some have flowers that gleam white even in the night. They hang, fleshy and thick, and the wind carries their sweet, carnal breath. Stinging insects torment us and the oarsmen are subject to painful rashes. The river water is not potable; worse, it eats at both flesh and wood, softening oars and ulcerating flesh. If left to stand in vessels, the top layer of the water becomes drinkable, but the residue swiftly eats into leaks in the bucket. Those who drink it complain of headaches and wild dreams. One criminal raved of "lovely serpents" and then threw himself overboard. Two crewmen have been confined in chains because of their wild talk.

I see no end to this horrid journeying. We have lost sight of our two companion vessels. Captain Triops is supposed to put us off at a safe landing that offers opportunity for a settlement and farming. The company's hope of open sunny meadows and gentle hills fades with every passing day. The captain says that this fresh water is bad for his ship's hull. He wishes to put us ashore in the swamp, saying that the trees on the shore may be concealing higher land and open forest. Our men argue against this, and often unroll the charter the Satrap has given us and point out what was promised to us. He counters by showing the orders the Satrap gave him. It speaks of landmarks that don't exist, navigable channels that are shallow and rocky, and cities where only jungle crawls. Sa's priests made this translation and they cannot lie. But something is very wrong.

The entire ship broods. Quarrels are frequent, the crew mutters against the captain. A terrible nervousness afflicts me, so that tears are never far away. Petrus suffers from nightmares and Carlmin, always a reclusive child, has become near mute.

Oh, Fair Jamaillia, city of my birth, will I ever again see your rolling hills and graceful spires? Mother, father, do you mourn me as lost to you forever?

And this great splotch is Petrus jostling me as he climbs upon my lap, saying he is bored. My maid is next to useless. She does little to earn all the food she devours, and then she is off, to slink about the ship like a cat in heat. Yesterday, I told her that if she got with child from her immoral passions, I would immediately turn her out. She dared to say she did not care, for her days in my service were numbered. Does the foolish slat forget that she is indentured to us for another five years?

Day the 22nd of the Plow Moon

Year the 14th of the reign of the Most Noble and Magnificent Satrap Esclepius

It has happened as I feared. I crouch on a great knee of root, my writing desk a chest of my meager possessions. The tree at my back is as big around as a tower. Strands and tangle of roots, some as big around as barrels, anchor it in the swampy ground. I perch on one to save my skirts from the damp and tussocky earth. At least on the ship, in the middle of the river, we were blessed with sunlight from above. Here, the foliage over-shadows us, an eternal twilight.

Captain Triops has marooned us here in the swamp. He claimed that his ship was taking on water, and his only choice was to lighten his load and flee this corrosive river. When we refused to disembark, there was violence as the crew forced us from the ship. After one of our men was thrown overboard and swept away, our will to resist vanished. The stock that was to sustain us they kept. One of our men frantically seized the cage of messenger birds and fought for it. In the tussle, the cage broke, and all our birds rose in a flock to disappear. The crew threw off the crates of tools, seed and provisions that were supposed to aid us in establishing our colony. They did it to lighten the ship, not to help us. Many fell in deep water, out of reach. The men have salvaged what they could of those that fell on the soft riverside. The muck has sucked the rest down. Now we are seventy-two souls in this forsaken place, of which forty are able-bodied men.

Great trees tower over us. The land trembles under our feet like a crust on a pudding, and where the men marched over it to gather our possessions, water now seeps, filling their footprints.

The current swept the ship and our faithless captain swiftly from our sight. Some say we must stay where we are, beside the river, and watch for the other two ships. Surely, they say, they will help us. I think we must move deeper into the forest, seeking firmer land and relief from the biting insects. But I am a woman, with no say in this.

The men hold council now, to decide leadership of our company. Jathan Carrock put himself forward, as being of the noblest birth, but he was shouted down by others, former prisoners, tradesmen and speculators who said that his father's name had no value here. They mocked him, for all seem to know the "secret" that we are disgraced in Jamaillia. I walked away from watching them, feeling bitter.

My own situation is a desperate one. My feckless maid did not leave the ship with us, but stayed aboard, a sailor's whore. I wish her all she deserves! And now Petrus and Carlmin cling to me, complaining that the water has soaked their shoes and their feet sting from the damp. When I shall have a moment to myself again, I do not know. I curse the artist in me, for as I look up at the slanting beam of sunlight slicing through the intervening layers of branch and leaf, I see a wild and dangerous beauty to this place. Did I give in to it, I fear it could be as seductive as the raw glance of a rough man.

I do not know where such thoughts come from. I simply want to go home.

Somewhere on the leaves above us, it is raining.

Day the 24th of the Plow Moon
Year the 14th of the reign of the Most Noble and Magnificent Satrap Esclepius

I was jolted from sleep before dawn, thrown out of a vivid dream of a foreign street festival. It was as if the earth leaped sideways beneath us. Then, when the sun was fairly up in the unseen sky, we again felt the land tremble. The earthquake passed through the Rain Wild about us like a wave. I have experienced earthquakes before, but in this gelid region, the tremor seemed stronger and more threatening. It is easy to imagine this marshy ground gulping us down like a yellow carp swallowing a breadcrumb.

Despite our inland trek, the land remains swampy and treacherous beneath our feet. Today, I came face to face with a snake hanging down from a tangle of green. My heart was seized both by his beauty and my terror. How effortlessly he lifted himself from his perusal of me to continue his journey along the intertwining branches overhead. Would that I could cross this land as effortlessly!

Day the 27th of the Plow Moon
Year the 14th of the reign of the Most Noble and Magnificent Satrap Esclepius

I write while perched in a tree like one of the bright parrots that share the branch with me. I feel both ridiculous and exhilarated, despite hunger, thirst and great weariness. Perhaps my headiness is a side effect of starvation.

For five days, we have trekked ponderously through soft ground and thick brush, away from the river, seeking dryer ground. Some of our party protest this, saying that when our promised ship comes in spring, it will not be able to find us. I hold my tongue, but I doubt that any ship will come up this river again.

Moving inland did not improve our lot. The ground remains tremulous and boggy. By the time our entire party has passed over it, we leave a track of mud and standing water behind us. The damp inflames our feet and rots the fabric of my skirt. All the women go draggle hemmed now.

We have abandoned whatever we could not carry. Every one of us, man, woman and child, carries as much as possible. The little ones grow weary. I feel the child inside me grow heavier with each sucking step.

The men have formed a Council to rule us. Each man is to have one vote in it. I regard this ignoring of the natural order as perilous, yet there is no way for the outcast nobles to assert their right to rule. Jathan told me privately that we do best to let this happen, for soon enough the company will see that common farmers, pickpockets and adventurers are not suited to rule. For now, we heed their rules. The Council has gathered the dwindling food supplies into a common hoard. We are parceled out a pittance each day. The Council says that all men will share the work equally. Thus Jathan must stand a night watch with his fellows as if he were a common soldier. The men stand watch in pairs, for a sole watchman is more prone to the strange madness that lurks in this place. We speak little of it, but all have had strange dreams, and some of our company seem to be wandering in their minds. The men blame the water. There is talk of sending out exploring parties to find a good dry site for our settlement.

I have no faith in their brave plans. This wild place does not care for our rules or Council.

We have found little here to sustain us. The vegetation is strange, and the only animal life we have seen moves in the higher reaches of the trees. Yet amidst this wild and tangled sprawl, there is still beauty, if one has an eye for it. The sunlight that reaches us through the canopy of the trees is gentle and dappled, illuminating the feathery mosses that drape from the vines. One moment I curse it as we struggle through its clinging nets, and in the next, I see it as dusky green lace. Yesterday, despite my weariness and Jathan's impatience, I paused to enjoy the beauty of a flowering vine. In examining it, I noticed that each trumpet-like flower cupped a small quantity of rainwater, sweetened by the flower's nectar. Sa forgive me that I and my children drank well from many of the blossoms before I told the others of my find. We have also found mushrooms that grow like shelves on the tree trunks, and a vine that has red berries. It is not enough.

It is to my credit that we sleep dry tonight. I dreaded another night of sleeping on the damp ground, awakening wet and itching, or huddled atop our possessions as they slowly sink into the marshy ground. This evening, as the shadows began to deepen, I noticed bird nests dangling like swinging purses from some of the tree limbs. Well do I know how cleverly Petrus can climb furniture and even drapes. Selecting a tree with several stout branches almost at a level, I challenged my son to see if he could reach them. He clung to the vines that draped the tree while his little feet found purchase on the rough bark. Soon he sat high above us on a very thick limb, swinging his feet and laughing to see us stare.

I bade Jathan follow his son, and take with him the damask drapes that I have carried so far. Others soon saw my plan. Slings of all kinds now hang like bright fruit in these dense trees. Some sleep on the wider branches or in the crotches of the trees, others in hammocks. It is precarious rest, but dry.

All praised me. "My wife has always been clever," Jathan declared, as if to take the credit from me, and so I reminded him, "I have a name of my own. I was Carillion Waljin long before I was Lady Carrock! Some of my best known pieces as an artist, 'Suspended Basins' and 'Floating Lanterns' required just such a knowledge of balance and support! The difference is one of scale, not property." At this, several of the women in our party gasped, deeming me a braggart, but Lady Duparge exclaimed, "She is right! I have always admired Lady Carrock's work."

Then one rough fellow was so bold as to add, "She will be just as clever as Trader Carrock's wife, for we will have no lords and ladies here."

It was a sobering thought to me and yet I fear he has the right of it. Birth and breeding count for little here. Already they have given a vote to common men, less educated than Lady Duparge or I. A farmer has more say in our plans than I do.

And what did my husband mutter to me? "You shamed me by calling attention to yourself. Such vanity to boast of your 'art accomplishments.' Occupy yourself with your children's needs, not bragging of yourself." And so he put me in my place.

What is to become of us? What good to sleep dry if our bellies are empty and our throats dry? I pity so the child inside me. All the men cried "Caution!" to one another as they used a hoist and sling to lift me to this perch. Yet all the caution in the world cannot save this babe from the wilderness being his birthplace. I miss my Narissa still, and yet I think her end was kinder than what this strange forest may visit upon us.

Day the 29th of the Plow Moon
Year the 14th of the reign of the Most Noble and Magnificent Satrap Esclepius

I ate another lizard tonight. It shames me to admit it. The first time, I did it with no more thought than a cat pouncing on a bird. During a rest time, I noticed the tiny creature on a fern frond. It was green as a jewel and so still. Only the glitter of its bright eye and the tiny pulse of life at its throat betrayed it to me. Swift as a snake, I struck. I caught it in my hand, and in an instant I cupped its soft belly against my mouth. I bit into it, and it was bitter, rank and sweet all at once. I crunched it down, bones and all, as if it were a steamed lark from the Satrap's banquet table. Afterwards, I could not believe I had done it. I expected to feel ill, but I did not. Nevertheless, I felt too shamed to tell anyone what I had done. Such food seems unfit for a civilized human, let alone the manner in which I devoured it. I told myself it was the demands of the child growing in me, a momentary aberration brought on by gnawing hunger. I resolved never to do it again, and I put it out of my mind.

But tonight, I did. He was a slender gray fellow, the color of the tree. He saw my darting hand and hid in a crack of the bark, but I dragged him out by his tail. I held him pinched between my finger and thumb. He struggled wildly and then grew still, knowing it was useless. I looked at him closely, thinking that if I did so, then I could let him go. He was beautiful, his gleaming eyes, his tiny claws and lashing tail. His back was gray and rough as the tree bark, but his soft little belly was the color of cream. There was a blush of blue on the soft curve of his throat and a pale stripe of it down his belly. The scales of his belly were tiny and smooth when I pressed my tongue against them. I felt the pattering of his tiny heart and smelled the stench of his fear as his little claws scrabbled against my chapped lips. It was all so familiar somehow. Then I closed my eyes and bit into him, holding both my hands over my mouth to be sure no morsel escaped. There was a tiny smear of blood on my palm afterward. I licked it off. No one saw.

Sa, sweet Lord of all, what am I becoming? What prompts me to behave this way? The privation of hunger or the contagious wildness of this place? I hardly know myself. The dreams that plague my sleep are not those of a Jamaillian lady. The waters of the earth scald my hands and sear my feet, until they heal rough as cobs. I fear what my face and hair must look like.

Day the 2ⁿᵈ of the Greening Moon
Year the 14ᵗʰ of the reign of the Most Noble and Magnificent Satrap Esclepius

A boy died last night. We were all shocked. He simply did not wake up this morning. He was a healthy lad of about twelve. Durgan was his name, and though he was only a tradesman's son, I share his parents' grief quite strongly. Petrus had followed him about, and seems very shaken by his death. He whispered to me that he dreamed last night that the land remembered him. When I asked what he meant by that, he could not explain, but said that perhaps Durgan had died because this place didn't want him. He made no sense to me, but he repeated himself insistently until I nodded and said perhaps he was right. Sweet Sa, do not let the madness be taking my boy. It frightens me so. Perhaps it is good that my boy will no longer seek the companionship of such a common lad, yet Durgan had a wide smile and a ready laugh that we will miss.

As fast as the men dug a grave, it welled full of murky water. At last his mother had to be taken away while his father condemned his son's body to the water and muck. As we asked Sa's peace on him, the child inside me kicked angrily. It frightened me.

Day the 8ᵗʰ of the Greening Moon (I think. Marthi Duparge says it is the 9ᵗʰ.)
Year the 14ᵗʰ of the reign of the Most Noble and Magnificent Satrap Esclepius

We have found a patch of drier ground and most of us will rest here for a few days while a chosen party of men scouts for a better place. Our refuge is little more than a firmer island amidst the swamp. We have learned that a certain type of needled bush indicates firmer ground, and here it is quite dense. It is resinous enough to burn even when green. It produces a dense and choking smoke, but it keeps the biting insects at bay.

Jathan is one of our scouts. With our child soon to be born, I thought he should stay here to help me care for our boys. He said he must go, to establish himself as a leader among the Company. Lord Duparge is also to go as a scout. As Lady Marthi Duparge is also with child, Jathan said we could help one another. Such a young wife as she cannot be of much use at a birthing, and yet her company will be preferable to none at all. All of us women have drawn closer as privation has forced us to share our paltry resources for the good of our children.

Another of the women, a weaver's wife, has devised a way to make mats from the abundant vines. I have begun to learn this, for there is little else I can do, so heavy have I become. The mats can be used as bed-pallets and also laced together into screens for shelter. All the nearby trees are smooth-barked, with the branches beginning very high, so we must contrive what shelter we can on the ground. Several women joined us and it was pleasant and almost homey to sit together and talk and work with our hands. The men laughed at us as we raised our woven walls, asking what such frail barriers can keep out. I felt foolish, yet as dark fell, we took comfort in our flimsy cottage. Sewet the weaver has a fine singing voice, and brought tears to my eyes as she sang her youngest to sleep with the old song of Praise to Sa in Tribulation. It seems a lifetime since last I heard music. How long must my children live with no culture and no tutors save the merciless judgment of this wild place?

As much as I disdain Jathan Carrock for bringing about our exile, I miss him this evening.

Day the 12ᵗʰ or 13ᵗʰ of the Greening Moon
Year the 14ᵗʰ of the reign of the Most Noble and Magnificent Satrap Esclepius

A madness came upon our camp last night. It began with a woman starting up in the darkness, shouting, "Hark! Hark! Does no one else hear their singing?" Her husband tried to quiet her, but then a young boy exclaimed that he had heard the singing for several nights now. Then he plunged off into the darkness as if he knew where he was going. His mother ran after him. Then the woman broke free of her husband, and raced off into the swamp. Three others went after her, not to bring her back but crying, "Wait, wait, we will go with you!"

I rose and held onto both my sons, lest the madness take them. A peculiar undark suffuses this jungle by night. The fireflies are familiar, but not an odd spider that leaves a glob of glowing spittle in the middle of its web. Tiny insects fly right into it, just as moths will seek a lantern's fire. There is also a dangling moss that gleams pale and cold. I dare not let my lads know how gruesome I find it. I told them I shivered because of the chill, and in concern for those poor benighted wretches lost in the swamp. Yet it chilled me even more to hear little Carlmin speak of how lovely the jungle was by night, and how sweet the scent of the night blooming flowers. He said he remembered when I used to make cakes flavored with those flowers. We never had such flowers in Jamaillia City, yet as he said it, I almost recalled little brown cakes, soft in the middle and crispy brown at the edges. Even as I write the words, I almost recall how I shaped them into blossoms before I cooked them in hot bubbling fat.

Never have I done such cooking, I swear.

As of midday, there is no sign of those the night madness took. Searchers went after them, but the search party returned wet and insect-bitten and disconsolate. The jungle has swallowed them. The woman left behind a small boy who has been wailing for her most of the day.

I have told no one of the music that haunts my dreams.

Day the 14th or 15th of the Greening Moon
Year the 14th of the reign of the Most Noble and Magnificent Satrap Esclepius

Our scouts still have not returned. By day, we put a fine face on it for the children, but by night Marthi Duparge and I share our fears while my boys sleep. Surely our men should have returned by now, if only to say that they found no better place than this boggy island.

Last night Marthi wept and said that the Satrap deliberately sent us to our deaths. I was shocked. Sa's priests translated the ancient scrolls that told of cities on this river. Men dedicated to Sa cannot lie. But perhaps they erred, and grievously enough to cost our lives.

There is no plenty here, only strangeness that lurks by day and prowls amongst our huts by night. Almost every night, one or two folk awake shrieking from nightmares they cannot recall. A young woman of easy virtue has gone missing for two days now. She was a whore for coin in Jamaillia's streets, and continued her trade here, asking food from the men who used her. We do not know if she wandered off or was killed by one of our own party. We do not know if we harbor a murderer in our midst, or if this terrible land has claimed another victim.

We mothers suffer the most, for our children beg us for more than the meager rations allotted us. The supplies from the ship are gone. I forage daily, my sons at my side. I found a heaped mound of loosened earth a few days ago, and poking through it, discovered eggs with brown speckled shells. There were almost fifty of them, and though some of the men refused them, saying they would not eat snake or lizard eggs, none of the mothers did. One lily-like plant is difficult to pull from the shallows, for inevitably I am splashed with stinging water and the roots are long and fibrous. There are nodules on the roots, no bigger than large pearls, and these have a pleasantly peppery flavor. Sewet has been working with the roots themselves, making baskets and recently a coarse cloth. That will be welcome. Our skirts are in tatters up to our calves, and our shoes grow thin as paper. All were surprised when I found the lily pearls. Several people asked how I knew they were edible.

I had no answer to that. The flowers looked familiar somehow. I cannot say what made me pull up the roots nor what prompted me to pick the pearly nodules and put them in my mouth.

The men who stayed here constantly complain of standing watches by night and keeping our fires alight, but in truth I think we women work as hard. It is taxing to keep our youngsters safe and fed and clean in these circumstances. I confess I have learned much of managing my boys from Chellia. She was a laundress in Jamaillia, and yet here she has become my friend, and we share a little hut we have built for the five children and ourselves. Her man, one Ethe, is also amongst the explorers. Yet she keeps a cheerful face and insists that her three youngsters help with the daily tasks. Our older boys we send out together to gather dry dead wood for the fire. We caution them never to go beyond the sounds of the camp, but both Petrus and Olpey complain that no dry wood remains nearby. Her daughters Piet and Likea watch Carlmin while Chellia and I harvest the water from the trumpet flowers and scavenge whatever mushrooms we can find. We have found a bark that makes a spicy tea; it helps to stave off hunger as well.

I am grateful for her company; both Marthi and I will welcome her help when birth comes upon us. Yet her boy Olpey is older than my Petrus and leading him into bold and reckless ways. Yesterday the two were gone until dusk, and then returned with only an armful of firewood each. They told of hearing distant music and following it. I am sure they ventured deeper into this swampy forest than is wise. I scolded them both, and Petrus was daunted but Olpey snidely asked his mother what else should he do, stay here in the mud and grow roots? I was shocked to hear him speak so to his mother. I am sure that he is the influence behind Petrus' nightmares, for Olpey loves telling wild tales full of parasitic specters that float as night fogs and lizards that suck blood. I do not want Petrus influenced by such superstitious nonsense and yet, what can I do? The boys must fetch wood for us, and I cannot send him alone. All of the older boys of our company are given such chores. It grieves me to see Petrus, the descendent of two illustrious bloodlines, put to such work alongside common boys. I fear he will be ruined long before we return to Jamaillia.

And why has Jathan not returned to us? What has become of our men?

Day the 19ᵗʰ or 20ᵗʰ of the Greening Moon
Year the 14ᵗʰ of the reign of the Most Noble and Magnificent Satrap Esclepius

Today three muddy men and a woman walked into our campsite. When I heard the hubbub, my heart leapt in excitement, for I thought our men had returned. Instead, I was shocked to discover that this party was from one of the other ships.

Captain, crew and passengers were flung into the river one evening when the ship simply came apart. They had little opportunity to salvage supplies from the foundering ship. They lost more than half the souls aboard it. Of those that made it to shore, many took the madness, and in the days following the shipwreck, ended their own lives or vanished into the wilds.

Many of them died in the first few nights, for they could find no solid ground at all. I covered my ears when they spoke of people falling and literally drowning in the mud. Some woke witless and raving after experiencing strange dreams. Some recovered, but others wandered off into the swamp, never to be seen again. These three were the vanguard of those who remained alive. Minutes later, others began to arrive. They came in threes and fours, bedraggled and bug-bitten, and horribly scalded from prolonged contact with the river water. There are sixty-two of them. A few are disgraced nobles, and others are commoners who thought to find a new life. The speculators who invested wealth in this expedition in the hope of making fortunes seem the most bitter.

The captain did not survive the first night. Those sailors who did are distressed and bewildered by their sudden plunge into exile. Some of them hold themselves apart from the "colonists" as they call us. Others seem to understand they must claim a place amongst us or perish.

Some of our party drew apart and muttered that we had little enough shelter and victuals for ourselves, but most of us shared readily. I had never thought to see people more desperate than we were. I feel that all profited from it, and Marthi and I perhaps most of all. Ser, an experienced midwife, was of their party. They also had a thatcher, their ship's carpenter, and men with hunting skills. The sailors are fit and hearty creatures and may adapt enough to be useful.

Still no sign of our own men.

Day the 26ᵗʰ of the Greening Moon

Year the 14ᵗʰ of the reign of the Most Noble and Magnificent Satrap Esclepius

My time came. The child was born. I did not even see her before the midwife took her away. Marthi and Chellia and Ser the midwife all say she was born dead, yet I am sure I heard her wail once. I was weary and close to fainting, but surely I recall what I heard. My babe cried out for me before she died.

Chellia says it is not so, that the babe was born blue and still. I have asked why I could not have held her once before they gave her to the earth? The midwife said I would grieve less that way. But her face goes pale whenever I ask about it. Marthi does not speak of it. Does she fear her own time, or do they keep something from me? Why, Sa, have you taken both my daughters from me so cruelly?

Jathan will hear of it when he returns. Perhaps if he had been here, to help me in my last heavy days, I would not have had to toil so hard. Perhaps my little girl could have lived. But he was not with me then and he is not with me now. And who will watch my boys, find food for them and make sure they return safe each night while I must lie here and bleed for a babe that did not live?

Day the 1ˢᵗ of the Grain Moon
Year the 14ᵗʰ of the reign of the Most Noble and Magnificent Satrap Esclepius

I have risen from my lying in. I feel that my heart is buried with my child. Did I carry her so far and through such hardship for nothing?

Our camp is now so crowded with newcomers that one can scarce thread a path through the makeshift shelters. Little Carlmin, separated from me for my lying-in, now follows me like a thin little shadow. Petrus has made fast his friendship with Olpey and pays no mind to my words at all. When I bid him stay close to camp, he defies me to venture ever deeper into the swamps. Chellia tells me, let him go. The boys are the darlings of the camp for discovering dangling bunches of sour little berries. The tiny fruits are bright yellow and sour as bile, but even such foul food is welcome to folk as hungry as we are. Still, it infuriates me that all encourage my son to disobey me. Do not they listen to the wild tales the boys tell, of strange music, distantly heard? The boys brag they will find the source of it, and my mother's heart knows it is nothing natural and good that lures them ever deeper into this pestilential jungle.

The camp grows worse every day. Paths are churned to muck, and grow wider and more muddy. Too many people do nothing to better our lot. They live as best they can today, making no provision for tomorrow, relying on the rest of us for food. Some sit and stare, some pray and weep. Do they expect Sa himself to swoop down and save them? Last night a family was found dead, all five of them, huddled around the base of a tree under a pitiful drape of mats. There is no sign of what killed them. No one speaks of what we all fear: there is an insidious madness in the water, or perhaps it comes up from the ground itself, creeping into our dreams as unearthly music. I awaken from dreams of a strange city, thinking I am someone else, somewhere else. And when I open my eyes to mud and insects and hunger, sometimes I long to close them again and simply go back to my dream. Is that what befell that hapless family? All their eyes were wide open and staring when we discovered them. We let their bodies go into the river. The Council took what little goods they had and divided them, but many grumble that the Council only distributed the salvage to their own friends and not to those most in need. Discontent grows with this Council of few who impose rule on all of us.

Our doubtful refuge is starting to fail us. Even the paltry weight of our woven huts turns the fragile sod to mud. I used to speak disdainfully of those who lived in squalor, saying, "they live like animals." But in truth, the beasts of this jungle live more graciously than we do. I envy the spiders their webs suspended in the shafts of sunlight overhead. I envy the birds whose woven nests dangle over our heads, out of reach of mud and snakes. I envy even the splay-footed marsh-rabbits, as our hunters call the little game animals that scamper so elusively over the matted reeds and floating leaves of the shallows. By day, the earth sucks at my feet with every step I take. By night, our sleeping pallets sink into the earth, and we wake wet. A solution must be found, but all the others say, "Wait. Our explorers will return and lead us to a better place."

I think the only better place they have found is the bosom of Sa. So may we all go. Will I ever see balmy Jamaillia again, ever walk in a garden of kindly plants, ever again be free to eat to satiation and drink without regard for the morrow? I understand the temptation to evade my life by dozing away the hours in dreams of a better place. Only my sons keep me anchored in this world.

Day the 16th of the Grain Moon
Year the 14th of the reign of the Most Noble and Magnificent Satrap Esclepius

What the waking mind does not perceive, the heart already knows. In a dream, I moved like the wind through these Rain Wilds, skimming over the soft ground and then sweeping through the swaying branches of the trees. Unhindered by muck and caustic water, I could suddenly see the many-layered beauty of our surroundings. I balanced, teetering like a bird, on a frond of fern. Some spirit of the Rain Wilds whispered to me, "Try to master it and it will engulf you. Become a part of it, and live."

I do not know that my waking mind believes any of that. My heart cries out for the white spires of Jamaillia, for the gentle blue waters of her harbor, for her shady walks and sunny squares. I hunger for music and art, for wine and poetry, for food that I did not scavenge from the crawl and tangle of this forbidding jungle. I hunger for beauty in place of squalor.

I did not gather food or water today. Instead, I sacrificed two pages of this journal to sketch dwellings suitable for this unforgiving place. I also designed floating walkways to link our homes. It will require some cutting of trees and shaping of lumber. When I showed them, some people mocked me, saying the work is too great for such a small group of people. Some pointed out that our tools have rapidly corroded here. I retorted that we must use our tools now to create shelters that will not fail us when our tools are gone.

Some willingly looked at my sketches, but then shrugged, saying what sense to work so hard when our scouts may return any day to lead us to a better location? We cannot, they said, live in this swamp forever. I retorted they were right, that if we did not bestir ourselves, we would die here. I did not, for fear of provoking fate, utter my darkest fear: That there is nothing but swamp for leagues under these trees, and that our explorers will never return.

Most people stalked away from my scorn, but two men stood and berated me, asking me what decent Jamaillian woman would raise her voice in anger before men. They were only commoners, as were the wives that stood and nodded behind them. Still, I could not restrain my tears, nor how my voice shook as I demanded what sort of men were they, to send my boys into the jungle to forage food for them while they sat on their heels and waited for someone else to solve their problems? They lifted their hands and made the sign for a shamed woman at me, as if I were a street girl. Then all walked away from me.

I do not care. I will prove them wrong.

Day the 24th of the Grain Moon
Year the 14th of the reign of the Most Noble and Magnificent Satrap Esclepius

I am torn between elation and grief. My baby is dead, Jathan is still missing, and yet today I feel more triumph than I did at any blessing of my artwork. Chellia, Marthi and little Carlmin have toiled alongside me. Sewet the weaver woman has offered refinements to my experiments. Piet and Likea have gathered food in my stead. Carlmin's small hands have amazed me with their agility and warmed my heart with his determination to help. In this effort, Carlmin has shown himself the son of my soul.

We have floored a large hut with a crosshatching of mats atop a bed of reeds and thin branches. This spreads the weight, so that we float atop the spongy ground as gently as the matted reeds float upon the neighboring waters. While other shelters sink daily and must be moved, ours has gone four days without settling. Today, satisfied that our home will last, we began further improvements. Without tools, we have broken down small saplings and torn their branches from them. Pieces of their trunks, woven with lily root into a horizontal ladder, form the basis for the walkways around our hut. Layers of woven matting to be added tomorrow will further strengthen our flimsy walkways. The trick, I am convinced, is to spread the weight of the traffic out over the greatest possible area, much as the marsh-rabbits do with their splayed feet. Over the wettest section, behind our hut, we have suspended the walkway, anchoring it like a spider-web from one tree to its neighbors as best we can. It is difficult, for the girth of the trees is great and the bark smooth. Twice it gave way as we struggled to secure it, and some of those watching jeered, but on our third effort, it held. Not only did we cross over it several times in safety, we were able to stand upon our swaying bridge and look out over the rest of the settlement. It was no lofty view, for we were no more than waist high above the ground, but even so, it gave me a perspective on our misery. Space is wasted with wandering paths and haphazard placement of huts. One of the sailors came over to inspect our effort, with much rocking on his heels and chewing on a twig. Then he had the effrontery to change half our knots. "That'll hold, madam," he told me. "But not for long and not under heavy use. We need better rigging to fasten to. Look up. That's where we need to be, rigging onto all those branches up there."

I looked up to the dizzying heights where the branches begin and told him that, without wings, none of us could reach those heights. He grinned and said, "I know a man, might could do it. If anyone thought it worth his trying." Then he made one of those ridiculous sailor bows and wandered off.

We must soon take action, for this shivering island diminishes daily. The ground is over trodden and water stands in our paths. I must be mad to try; I am an artist, not an engineer nor a builder. And yet if no one else steps forward, I am driven to the attempt. If I fail, I will fail having tried.

Day the 5th or 6th of the Prayer Moon
Year the 14th of the reign of the Most Noble and Magnificent Satrap Esclepius

Today one of my bridges fell. Three men were plunged into the swamp, and one broke a leg. He blamed his mishap upon me and declared that this is what happens when women try their knitting skills as construction. His wife joined in his accusations. But I did not shrink before them. I told them that I did not demand that he use my walkways, and that any who had not contributed to them and yet dared to walk upon them deserved whatever fate Sa sent them for laziness and ingratitude.

Someone shouted "blasphemy" but someone else shouted "Truth is Sa's sword." I felt vindicated. My work force has grown enough to be split into two parties. I shall put Sewet in charge of the second one, and woe betide any man who derides my choice. Her weaving skills have proven themselves.

Tomorrow we hope to start raising the first supports for my Great Platforms into the trees. I could fail most spectacularly. The logs are heavier, and we have no true rope for the hoisting, but only lines of braided root. The sailor has devised several crude block-and-tackles for us. He and my Petrus were the ones who scaled the smooth trunk of a tree to where the immense limbs branch overhead. They tapped in pegs as they went, but even so, my heart shook to see them venture so high. Retyo the sailor says that his tackles will make our strength sufficient for any task. I wait to see that. I fear they will only lead to our woven lines fraying all the more. I should be sleeping and yet I lie here, wondering if we have sufficient line to hoist our beams. Will our rope ladders stand up to the daily use of workers? What have I undertaken? If any fall from such a height, they will surely die. Yet summer must end, and when winter rains come, we must have a dry retreat.

←—✦—→

Day the 12th or 13th of the Prayer Moon
Year the 14th of Satrap Esclepius

Failure upon failure upon failure. I scarce have the spirit to write of it. Retyo the sailor says we must count as a success that no one has been injured. When our first platform fell, it sank itself into the soft earth rather than breaking into pieces. He cheerfully said that proved the platform's strength. He is a resourceful young man, intelligent despite his lack of education. I asked him today if he felt bitter that Fate had trapped him into building a colony in the Rain Wilds instead of sailing. He shrugged and grinned. He has been a tinker and a share-farmer before he was a sailor, so he says he has no idea what fate is rightfully his. He feels entitled to take any of them and turn it to his advantage. I wish I had his spirit.

Idlers in our Company gawk and mock us. Their skepticism corrodes my strength like the chalky water sears the skin. Those who complain most about our situation do the least to better it. "Wait," they say, "wait for our explorers to return and lead us to a better place." Yet daily our situation worsens. We go almost in rags now, though Sewet experiments daily with what fibers she can pull from the vines or rub from the pith of reeds. We find barely enough food to sustain us daily, and have no reserves for the winter. The idlers eat as much as those who work daily. My boys toil alongside us each day and yet receive the same ration as those who lie about and bemoan our fate. Petrus has a spreading rash at the base of his neck. I am sure it is due to poor diet and the constant damp.

Chellia must feel the same. Her little daughters Piet and Likea are no more than bones, for unlike our boys who eat as they gather, they must be content with what is handed to them at the end of the day. Olpey has become a strange boy of late, so much so that he frightens even Petrus. Petrus still sets out with him each day, but often comes home long before Olpey. Last night, I awoke to hear Olpey softly singing in his sleep. It was a tune and a tongue that I swear I have never heard, and yet it was haunting in its familiarity.

Heavy rains today. Our huts shed the most of it. I pity those who have not made any effort to provide shelter for themselves, even as I wonder at their lack of intelligence. Two women came to our hut with three little children. Marthi and Chellia and I did not want to let them crowd in with us, yet we could not abide the pitiful shivering of the babes. So we let them in, but warned them sternly that they must help with the construction tomorrow. If they do, we will help them build a hut of their own. If not, out they must go. Perhaps we must force folk to act for their own benefit.

◆—╬—▶

Day the 17th or 18th of the Prayer Moon
Year the 14th of Satrap Esclepius

We have raised and secured the first Great Platform. Sewet and Retyo have woven net ladders that dangle to the ground. It was a moment of great triumph for me to stand below and look up at the platform solidly fixed amongst the tree limbs. The intervening branches almost cloaked it from sight. This is my doing, I thought to myself. Retyo, Crorin, Finsk and Tremartin are the men who have done most of the hoisting and tying, but the design of the platform, how it balances lightly on the branches, putting weight only where it can be borne and the selection of the location was my doing. I felt so proud.

It did not last long, however. Ascending a ladder made of vines that gives to each step and sways more the higher one goes is not for the faint of heart nor for a woman's meager strength. Halfway up, my strength gave out. I clung, half swooning, and Retyo was forced to come to my rescue. It shames me that I, a married woman, wrapped my arms about his neck as if I were a little child. To my dismay, he did not take me down, but insisted on climbing up with me, so that I could see the new vista from our platform.

It was both exhilarating and disappointing. We stood far above the swampy land that has sucked at our feet for so long, yet still below the umbrella of leaves that screens out all but the strongest sunlight. I looked down on a deceptively solid-appearing floor of leaves, branches and vines. Although other immense trunks and branches impeded our view, I could suddenly see a distance into the forest in some directions. It appears to go on forever. And yet, seeing the branches of adjacent trees nearly touching ours filled me with ambition. Our next platform will be based in three adjacent trees. A cat-walk will stretch from Platform One to Platform Two. Chellia and Sewet are already weaving the safety nets that will prevent our younger children from tumbling off Platform One. When they are finished with that, I will put them to stringing our catwalks and the netting that will wall them.

The older children are swiftest to ascend and the quickest to adapt to our tree-dwelling. Already, they are horribly careless as they walk out from the platform along the huge branches that support it. After I had warned them often to be careful, Retyo gently rebuked me. "This is their world," he said. "They cannot fear it. They will become as sure-footed as sailors running rigging. The branches are wider than the walkways of some towns I've visited. The only thing that prevents you from walking out along that branch is your knowledge of how far you may fall. Think instead of the wood beneath your feet."

Under his tutelage, and gripping his arm, I did walk out along one of the branches. When we had gone some way and it began to sway under our weight, I lost my courage and fled back to the platform. Looking down, I could only glimpse the huts of our muddy little settlement below. We had ascended to a different world. The light is greater here, though still diffuse, and we are closer to both fruit and flowers. Bright colored birds squawk at us, as if disputing our right to be there. Their nests dangle like baskets hung in the trees. I look at their suspended homes and wonder if I cannot adapt that example to make a safe "nest" for myself. Already I feel this new territory is mine by right of ambition and art, as if I inhabit one of my suspended sculptures. Can I imagine a town comprised of hanging cottages? Even this platform, bare as it is right now, has balance and grace.

Tomorrow I shall sit down with Retyo the sailor and Sewet the weaver. I recall the cargo nets that lifted heavy loads from the dock onto the deck of the ship. Could not a platform be placed inside such a net, the net thatched for privacy, and the whole hung from a sturdy branch, to become a lofty and private chamber here? How, then, would we provide access to the Great Platforms from such dwellings? I smile as I write this, knowing that I do not wonder if it can be done, but only how.

Both Olpey and Petrus have a rash on their scalps and down their necks. They scratch and complain and the skin is rough as scales to the touch. I can find no way to ease it for either of them, and fear that it is spreading to others. I've seen a number of the children scratching miserably.

Day the 6th or 7th of the Gold Moon
Year the 14th of Satrap Esclepius

Two events of great significance. Yet I am so weary and heartsick I scarce can write of either of them. Last night, as I fell asleep in this swinging birdcage of a home, I felt safe and almost serene. Tonight, all that is taken from me.

The first: Last night Petrus woke me. Trembling, he crept under my mats beside me as if he were my little boy again. He whispered to me that Olpey was frightening him, singing songs from the city, and that he must tell me even though he had promised he would not.

Petrus and Olpey, in their ranging for food, discovered an unnaturally square mound in the forest. Petrus felt uneasy and did not wish to approach it. He could not tell me why. Olpey was drawn to it. Day after day, he insisted that they return to it. On the days when Petrus returned alone, it was because he had left Olpey exploring the mound. At some point in his poking and digging, he found a way into it. The boys have entered it several times now. Petrus describes it as a buried tower, though that made no sense to me. He said the walls are cracked and damp seeps in, but it is mostly solid. There are tapestries and old furniture, some sound, some rotted, and other signs that once people lived in it. Yet Petrus trembled as he spoke, saying that he did not think they were people like us. He says the music comes from it.

Petrus had only descended one level into it, but Olpey told him it went much deeper. Petrus was afraid to go down into the dark, but then by some magic, Olpey caused the tower to blossom with light. Olpey mocked Petrus for being fearful, and told tales of immense riches and strange objects in the depths of the tower. He claimed that ghosts spoke to him and told him its secrets, including where to find treasure. Then Olpey began to say that he had once lived in the tower, a long time ago when he was an old man.

I did not wait for morning. I woke Chellia, and after hearing my tale she woke Olpey. The boy was furious, hissing that he would never trust Petrus again and that the tower was his secret and the treasures all his, and he did not have to share it. While the night was still dark, Olpey fled, running off along one of the tree branches that have become footpaths for the children, and thence we knew not where.

When morning finally sifted through the sheltering branches, Chellia and I followed Petrus through the forest to his tower-mound. Retyo and

Tremartin went with us, and little Carlmin refused to stay behind with Chellia's girls. When I saw the squared mound thrusting up from the swamp, my courage quailed inside me. Yet I did not wish Retyo to see me as a coward and so I forced myself on.

The top of the tower was heavily mossed and draped with vinery yet it was too regular a shape to blend with the jungle. On one side, the boys had pulled away vines and moss to bare a window in a stone wall. Retyo kindled the torch he had brought, and then, one after another, we cautiously clambered inside. Vegetation had penetrated the room as tendrils and roots. On the grimy floor were the muddy tracks of the boys' feet. I suspect they have both been exploring that place for far longer than Petrus admits. A bedframe festooned with rags of fabric was in one corner of the room. Insects and mice had reduced the draperies to dangling rags.

Despite the dimness and decay, there were echoes of loveliness in the room. I seized a handful of rotted curtain and scrubbed a swath across a frieze, raising a cloud of dust. Amazement stilled my coughing. My artist's soul soared at the finely shaped and painted tiles and the delicate colors I had uncovered. But my mother's heart stood still at what was revealed. The figures were tall and thin, humans rendered as stick insects. Yet I did not think it was a conceit of the artist. Some held what might have been musical instruments or weaponry. We could not decide. In the background workers tended a reed-bed by a river like farmers harvesting a field. A woman in a great chair of gold overlooked all and seemed pleased with it. Her face was stern and yet kind; I felt I had seen her before. I would have stared longer, but Chellia demanded we search for her son.

With a sternness I did not feel, I bade Petrus show us where they had been playing. He blanched to see that I had guessed the truth, but he led us on. We left the bedchamber by a short flight of downward stairs. On the landing, there was heavy glass in two windows, but when Retyo held our torch close to one, it illuminated long white worms working in the wet soil pressed against it. How the glass has withstood the force of earth, I do not know. We entered a wide hall. Rugs crumbled into damp thread under our tread. We passed doorways, some closed, others open archways gaping with dark maws, but Petrus led us on. We came at last to the top of a stair, much grander than the first. As we descended this open staircase into a pool of darkness, I was grateful to have Retyo at my side. His calmness fostered my poor courage. The ancient cold of the stone penetrated my worn shoes and crept up my legs to my spine as if it reached for my heart. Our torch illuminated little more than our frightened faces and our whispers faded, waking ghostly echoes. We passed one landing, and then a second, but Petrus neither spoke nor faltered as he led us down. I felt as if I had walked into the throat of some great beast and was descending to its belly.

When at last we reached the bottom, our single torch could not penetrate the blackness around us. The flame fluttered in the moving air of a much larger chamber. Even in the dimness, I knew this room would have dwarfed the great ballroom of the Satrap's palace. I slowly groped my way forward, but Carlmin suddenly strode fearlessly beyond the reach of both my hand and the torchlight. I called after him, but his pattering footsteps as he hurried away was my only answer. "Oh, follow him!" I beseeched Retyo, but as he started to, the room suddenly lit around us as if a horde of spirits had unhooded their lanterns. I gave one shriek of terror and then was struck dumb.

In the center of the room, a great green dragon was up-reared on its hind legs. Its hind claws were sunk deep in the stone and its lashing tail stretched halfway across the room. Its emerald wings were unfurled wide and supported the ceiling high overhead. Atop its sinuous neck was a head the size of an oxcart. Intelligence glittered in its shining silver eyes. Its smaller forelimbs clutched the handle of a large basket. The basket itself was elaborately beribboned with bows of jade and streamers of ivory. And within the basket, reclining serenely, was a woman of preternatural authority. She was not beautiful; the power expressed in her made beauty irrelevant. Nor was she young and desirable. She was a woman past her middle years; yet the lines the sculptor had graved in her face seemed wisdom furrows on her brow, and thought lines at the corners of her eyes. Jewels had been set above her brow lines and along the tops of her cheeks to mimic the scaling of the dragon. This was no expressionless representation of Sa's female aspect. I knew, without doubt, that this statue had been fashioned to honor a real woman and it shocked me to my bones. The dragon's supple neck was carved so that he twisted to regard her, and even his reptilian countenance showed respect for her that he carried.

I had never seen such a representation of a woman. I had heard foreign tales of Harlot Queens and woman rulers, but always they had seemed fabrications of some barbarous and backward country, seductive women of evil intent. She made such legends lies. For a time, she was all I could see. Then my mind came back to me, and with it my duty.

Little Carlmin, all his teeth showing in a wide smile, stood some distance from us, his hand pressed against a panel attached to a column. His flesh looked like ice in the unnatural light. His smallness put the huge chamber into perspective, and I suddenly saw all that the dragon and woman had obscured.

The light flowed in pale stars and flying dragons across the ceiling. It crawled in vines across the walls, framing four distant doorways to darkened corridors. Dry fountains and statuary broke up the huge expanse of dusty floor. This was a great indoor plaza, a place for people to gather and talk or idly stroll amongst the fountains and statuary. Lesser columns supported twining vines with leaves of jade and carnelian blossoms. A sculpture of a leaping fish denied the dry fountain basin below it. Moldering heaps of ruin scattered throughout the chamber indicated the remains of wooden structures, booths or stages. Yet neither dust nor decay could choke the chilling beauty of the place. The scale and the grace of the room left me breathless and woke a wary awe in me. Folk who created such a chamber would not perish easily. What fate had over-taken a people whose magic could still light a room years after their passing? Did the danger that destroyed them threaten us? What had it been? Where had they gone?

Were they truly gone?

As in the chamber above, it felt as if the people had simply departed, leaving all their goods behind. Again, the boys' muddy tracks on the floor betrayed that they had been here before. Most led toward a single door.

"I did not realize this place was so big." Petrus' small voice seemed shrill in the vastness as he stared up at the lady and her dragon. He turned round in a slow circle, staring at the ceiling. "We had to use torches here. How did you light it, Carlmin?" Petrus sounded uneasy at his small brother's knowledge.

But Carlmin didn't answer. My little one was trotting eagerly across the vast chamber, as if called to some amusement. "Carlmin!" I cried, and my voice woke a hundred echoing ghosts. As I gawked, he vanished through one of the archways. It lit in a murky, uncertain way. I ran after him, and the others followed. I was breathless by the time I had crossed the plaza. I chased him down a dusty corridor.

As I followed him into a dim chamber, light flickered around me. My son sat at the head of a long table of guests in exotic dress. There was laughter and music. Then I blinked and empty chairs lined both sides of the table. The feast had dwindled to crusty stains in the crystal goblets and plates, but the music played on, choked and strained. I knew it from my dreams.

Carlmin spoke hollowly as he lofted a goblet in a toast, "To my lady!" He smiled fondly as his childish gaze met unseen eyes. As he started to put it to his lips, I reached him, seized his wrist and shook the glass from his grasp. It fell to shatter in the dust.

He stared at me with eyes that did not know me. Despite how he has grown of late, I snatched him up and held him to me. His head sagged onto my shoulder and he closed his eyes, trembling. The music sagged into silence. Retyo took him from me, saying sternly, "We should not have allowed the boy to come. The sooner we leave this place and its dying magic, the better." He glanced about uneasily. "Thoughts not mine tug at me, and I hear voices. I feel I have been here before, when I know I have not. We should leave this city to the spirits that haunt it." He seemed shamed to admit his fear, but I was relieved to hear one of us speak it aloud.

Then Chellia cried that we could not leave Olpey here, to fall under whatever enchantment had seized Carlmin. Sa forgive me, all I wanted to do was seize my own children and flee. But Retyo, carrying both our torch and my son, led us on. His friend Tremartin smashed a chair against the stone floor and took up one of the legs for a club. No one asked him what use a club could be against the spider-webs of alien memory that snagged at us. Petrus moved up to take the lead. When I glanced back, the lights in the chamber had winked out.

Through a hall and then down another flight of stairs that wound down to a smaller hall we went. Statues in niches lined the walls, with the dwindled remnants of dust-grimed candle stubs before them. Many were women, crowned and glorified like kings. Their sculpted robes glittered with tiny inset jewels, and pearls roped their hair.

The unnatural light was blue and uncertain, flickering with the threat of utter darkness. It made me oddly sleepy. I thought I heard whispering and once, as I brushed through a doorway, I heard two women singing in the distance. I shuddered with fear, and Retyo glanced back as if he, too, had heard them. Neither of us spoke. We went on. Some passages blossomed into light around us as we entered. Others remained stubbornly dark and made our failing torch seem a lie. I do not know which was more daunting to me.

We found Olpey at last. He was sitting in a little room on an opulently carved chair before a gentleman's dressing table. The gilt had fallen from the wood to scatter in flakes all round it. He looked into a mirror clouded with age; black spots had blossomed in it. Shell combs and the handle of a brush littered the table before him. A small chest was open on his lap, and looped around his neck were many pendants. His head drooped to one side but his eyes were open and staring. He was muttering to himself. As we drew near, he reached for a scent bottle and mimed dabbing himself with its long dried perfume as he turned his face from side to side before his hazy reflection. His motions were the preening of a lordly and conceited man.

"Stop it!" his mother hissed in horror. He did not startle and almost I felt that we were the ghosts there. She seized him and shook him. At that he woke, but he woke in a terror. He cried out as he recognized her, glanced wildly about himself, and then fell into a faint. "Oh, help me get him out of here," poor Chellia begged.

Tremartin put Olpey's arm across his shoulders and mostly dragged the lad as we fled. The lights quenched as we left each area, as if pursuing darkness were only a step behind us. Once music swelled loudly around us, subsiding as we fled. When we finally clambered out of the window into open air, the swamp seemed a healthful place of light and freshness. I was shocked to see that most of the day had passed while we were below.

Carlmin recovered quickly in the fresh air. Tremartin spoke sharply to Olpey and shook him, at which he angrily came back to his senses. He jerked free of Tremartin, and would not speak sensibly to us. By turns sullen or defiant, he refused to explain why he had fled to the city or what he had been doing. He denied fainting. He was coldly furious with Petrus and extremely possessive of the jeweled necklaces he wore. They glittered with bright gemstones of every color, and yet I would no more put one around my neck than I would submit to a snake's embrace. "They are mine," he kept exclaiming. "My lover gave them to me, a long time ago. No one will take them from me now!"

It took all of Chellia's patience and motherly wiles to convince Olpey to return with us. Even so, he dawdled grudgingly along. By the time we reached the outskirts of camp, the dwindling light was nearly gone and insects feasted on us.

The platforms high above were humming with excited voices like a disturbed beehive. We climbed the ladders, and I was so exhausted I thought only of my own shelter and bed. But the moment we reached the Platform, cries of excitement greeted us. The explorers had returned. At the sight of my husband, thin, bearded and ragged, but alive, my heart leaped. Little Carlmin stood gawking as if at a stranger, but Petrus rushed to greet him. And Retyo gravely bid me farewell and vanished from my side into the crowd.

Jathan did not recognize his son at first. When he did, he lifted his eyes and looked over the crowd. When his eyes had passed me twice, I stepped forward, leading Carlmin by the hand. I think he knew me by the look on my face rather than by my appearance. He came to me slowly, saying, "Sa's mercy, Carillion, is that you? Have pity on us all." By which I judged that my appearance did not please him. And why that should hurt so much is something I do not know, nor why I felt shamed that he took my hand but did not embrace me. Little Carlmin stood beside me, staring blankly at his father.

And now I shall leave this wallowing in self-pity and sum up their report. They found only more swamp. The Rain Wild River is the main drainage of a vast network of water that straggles in threads through a wide valley on its way to the sea. The water runs under the land as much as over it. They found no sound ground, only bogs, marshes and sloughs. They never had clear sight of a horizon since they had left us. Of the twelve men who set out, seven returned. One drowned in quicksand, one vanished during a night and the other three were over-taken by a fever. Ethe, Chellia's husband, did not return.

They could not tell how far inland they had traveled. The tree cover hampered their efforts to follow the stars and eventually they must have made a great circle, for they found themselves standing at the riverside again.

On their journey back to us, they encountered the remnants of those who had been on the third ship. They were marooned downriver from where we were abandoned. Their captain gave up on his mission when he saw wreckage from a ship float past them. Their captain was more merciful than ours, for he saw that all their cargo was landed with them, and even left them one of the ship's boats. Still, their lives were hard and many wished to go home. The jewel of good news was that they still had four messenger birds. One had been dispatched when they were first put ashore. Another was sent back with news of their hardship after the first month.

Our explorers dashed all their hopes. They decided to abandon their effort at a settlement. Seven of their young men came back with our explorers to help us evacuate as well. When we join them, they will send a message bird to Jamaillia, begging for a rescue ship. Then we will journey down the river and to the coast, in hopes of rescue.

When Chellia, Retyo and I returned, our company was sourly predicting that no ship would be sent. Nonetheless, all were packing to leave. Then Chellia arrived with her jewel-draped son. As she tried to tell her story to a crowd of folks too large to hear it, a riot near broke out. Some men wanted to go immediately to the buried tower, despite the growing dark. Others demanded a chance to handle the jewels, and as young Olpey refused to let anyone touch them, this set off a scuffle. The boy broke free, and leaping from the edge of the Platform, he sprang from one branch to another like a monkey until his shape was lost in the darkness. I pray he is safe tonight, but fear the madness has taken him.

A different sort of madness has taken our folk. I huddle in my shelter with my two sons. Outside, on the platforms, the night is full of shouting. I hear women pleading to leave, and men saying, yes, yes, we will, but first we will see what treasure the city will offer us. A messenger bird with a jewel attached to its leg would bring a ship swiftly, they laugh. Their eyes are bright, their voices loud.

My husband is not with me. Despite our long separation, he is in the thick of these arguments rather than with his wife and sons. Did he even notice that my pregnancy had passed, yet my arms were empty? I doubt it.

I do not know where Chellia and her daughters have gone. When she discovered that Ethe had not returned, it broke her. Her husband is dead and Olpey may be lost, or worse. I fear for her, and mourn with her. I thought the return of the explorers would fill me with joy. Now I do not know what I feel. But I know it is not joy or even relief.

Day the 7th or 8th of the Gold Moon
Year the 14th of Satrap Esclepius

He came to me in the dark of the night, and despite the soreness of my heart and our two sons sleeping nearby, I let him have what he sought. Part of me hungered only for a gentle touch; part of me mocked myself for that, for he came to me only when his more pressing business was done. He spoke little and took his satisfaction in darkness. Can I blame him? I know I have gone to skin and bones, my complexion rough and my hair dry as straw. The rash that has afflicted the children now crawls like a snake up my spine. I dreaded that he would touch it, mostly because it would remind me that it was there, but he did not. He wasted no caresses. I stared past his shoulder into the darkness and thought not of my husband, but of Retyo, and he a common sailor who speaks with the accents of the waterfront.

What have I become here?

Afternoon

And so I am Lord Jathan Carrock's wife again, and my life is his to command. He has settled our fate. As Olpey has vanished, and neither Retyo nor Tremartin can be found, Jathan has declared that his son's discovery of the hidden city gives him prime claim to all treasure in it. Petrus will lead him and the other men back to the buried tower. They will search it systematically for treasure that will buy our way back into the Satrap's graces. He is quite proud to claim that Petrus discovered the tower and thus the Carrocks merit a larger share of the treasure. It does not disturb him that Olpey is still missing, and that Chellia and her daughters are distraught with worry. He talks only of how the treasure will secure our glorious return to society. He seems to forget the leagues of swamp and sea between Jamaillia City and us.

I told him that the city was a dangerous place and he should not venture into it thinking only of spoils. I warned him of its unhealthy magic, of lights that brighten and fade, of voices and music heard in the distance, but he disdains it as a "woman's overwrought fancy." He tells me to stay out of danger here in my "little monkey nest" until he returns. Then I spoke bluntly. The Company does not have reserves of food or the strength to make a trek to the coast. Unless we better prepare, we will die along the way, treasure or not. I think we should remain here until we are better prepared, or until a ship comes here for us. We need not admit defeat. We might prosper if we put all our men to gathering food and found a way to trap rainwater for our needs. Our tree city could be a thing of grace and beauty. He shook his head as if I were a child prating of pixies in flowery bowers. "Ever immersed in your art," he said. "Even in rags and starving, you cannot see what is real." Then he said he admired how I had occupied myself in his absence, but that he had returned now and would take charge of his family.

I wanted to spit at him.

Petrus did not wish to lead the men. He believes the tower took Olpey and we shall never see him again. He speaks of the underground with deep dread. Carlmin told his father he had never been to a buried city, and then sat and sucked his thumb, as he has not since he was two.

When Petrus tried to warn Jathan, he laughed and said, "I'm a different man than the soft noble who left Jamaillia. Your silly mama's goblins don't worry me." When I told him sharply that I, too, was a different woman than the one he had left alone to cope in the wilds, he stiffly replied that he saw that too clearly, and only hoped that a return to civilization would restore me to propriety. Then he forced Petrus to lead them to the ruins.

No amount of treasure could persuade me to return there, not if there were diamonds scattered on the floor and strands of pearls dangling from the ceiling. I did not imagine the danger, and I hate Jathan for dragging Petrus back to it.

I shall spend the day with Marthi. Her husband returned safely, only to leave her again to hunt treasure. Unlike me, she is overjoyed with his plans, and says that he will return them to society and wealth again. It is hard for me to listen to such nonsense. "My baby will grow up in Sa's blessed city," she says. The woman is thin as a string, with her belly like a knot tied in it.

Day the 8th or 9th of the Gold Moon
Year the 14th of Satrap Esclepius

A ridiculous date for us. Here there will be no golden harvest moon, nor does the Satrap mean anything to me anymore.

Yesterday Petrus showed them to the tower window, but ran away when the men entered, leaving his father shouting angrily after him. He came back to me, pale and shaking. He says the singing from the tower has become so loud that he cannot think his own thoughts when he is near it. Sometimes, in the corridors of black stone, he has glimpsed strange people. They come and go in flashes, he says, like their flickering light. I hushed him, for his words were upsetting Marthi. Despite Jathan's plans, I spent yesterday preparing for winter. I put a second thatch on both our hanging huts, using broad leaves laced down with vines. I think our shelters, especially the smaller hanging cottages and the little footbridges that connect them to the Great Platforms will require reinforcement against winter winds and rain. Marthi was little help to me. Her pregnancy has made her ungainly and listless, but the real problem was that she believes we will soon go home to Jamaillia. Most of the women are now only waiting to leave.

Some of the treasure hunters returned last night, with reports of a vast buried city. It is very different from Jamaillia, all interconnected like a maze. Perhaps some parts of it were always underground, for there are no windows or exits in the lowest chambers. The upper reaches of the buildings were homes and private areas and the lower seemed to have been shops and warehouses and markets. Toward the river, a portion of the city has collapsed. In some chambers, the walls are damp and rot is well at work on the furnishings but others have withstood time, preserving rugs and tapestries and garments. Those who returned brought back dishes and chairs, rugs and jewelry, statues and tools. One man wore a cloak that shimmered like running water, soft and supple. They had discovered amphorae of wine, still sealed and intact in one warehouse. The wine is golden and so potent that the men were almost instantly drunk. They returned laughing and spirit-breathed, bidding us all come to the city and celebrate with wine the wealth that had come to us. There was a wild glitter in their eyes that I did not like.

Others returned haunted and cringing, not wishing to speak of what they had experienced. Those ones began immediately to plan to leave tomorrow at dawn, to travel down river and join the other folk there.

Jathan did not return at all.

Those obsessed with plunder talk loudly, drunk with old wine and mad dreams. Already they gather hoards. Two men came back bruised, having come to blows over a vase. Where will greed take us? I feel alone in my dismal imaginings.

That city is not a conquered territory to be sacked, but more like a deserted temple, to be treated with the respect one should accord any unknown god. Are not all gods but facets of Sa's presence? But these words come to me too late to utter. I would not be heeded. I feel a terrible premonition, that there will be a consequence to this orgy of plundering.

My tree settlement was almost deserted earlier today. Most of our folk had been infected with a treasure fever and gone underground. Only the infirm and the women with the smallest children remain in our village. I look around me and I am suffused with sorrow, for I am seeing the death of my dreams. Shall I wax more eloquent, more dramatic, more poetic as I once would have thought it? No. I shall simply say I am engulfed in disappointment. And shocked to feel it.

It is hard for me to confront what I mourn. I hesitate to commit it to paper, for the words will remain here, to accuse me later. Yet art, above all, is honesty, and I am an artist before I am a wife, a mother or even a woman. So I will write. It is not that there is now a man that I would prefer over my husband. I admit that freely. I care not that Retyo is a common sailor, seven years my junior, without education or bloodlines to recommend him. It is not what he is but who he is that turns my heart and eyes to him. I would take him into my bed tonight, if I could do so without risking my sons' future. That I will write in a clear hand. Can there be shame in saying I would value his regard above my husband's, when my husband has so clearly shown that he values the regard of the other men in this company over his wife's love?

No. What turns my heart to rust this day is that my husband's return, and the discovery of treasure in the buried city and the talk of returning to Jamaillia dismantles the life I have built here. That grieves me. It is a hard thing to contemplate. When did I change so completely? This life is harsh and hard. This country's beauty is the beauty of the sunning snake. It threatens as it beckons. I fancy that I can master it by giving it my earnest respect. Without realizing it, I had begun to take pride in my ability to survive and to tame some small part of its savagery. And I have shown others how to do that. I did things here, and they were significant.

Now that will be lost to me. I become again Lord Jathan Carrock's wife. My caution will be discarded as a woman's foolish fear, and my

ambitions for a beautiful abode built amongst the trees will be dismissed
as a woman's silly fancy.

Perhaps he would be right. Nay, I know he is right. But somehow, I
no longer care for what is right and wise. I have left behind the life where
I created art for people to admire. Now my art is how I live and it daily
sustains me.

I do not think I can set that aside. To be told I must abandon all that
I have begun here is more than I can bear. And for what? To return to his
world, where I am of no more consequence than an amusing songbird in
a filigreed cage.

Marthi was with me today when Chellia came to ask Petrus to help
her look for Olpey. Petrus would not look at her. Chellia began to plead,
and Petrus covered his ears. She nagged him until he began to weep,
frightening Carlmin. Chellia shrieked as if mad, accusing Petrus of not
caring anything for his friend, but only for the riches of the city. She lifted
a hand as if to strike my boy, and I rushed in and pushed her. She fell, and
her girls dragged her to her feet and then pulled her away, begging her
simply to "come home, Mother, come home." When I turned around,
Marthi had fled.

I sit by myself on the limb above my cottage while my boys sleep
within tonight. I am ashamed. But my sons are all I have. Is it wrong for
me to keep them safe? What good would it do to sacrifice my sons to save
hers? We might only lose them all.

←—✦—→

5th day of the City
Year the 1st of the Rain Wilds

I fear we have come through many trials and tribulations, only to perish
from our own greed. Last night, three men died in the city. No one
will say how; they brought the unmarked bodies back. Some say it was
the madness, others speak of evil magic. In the wake of the gruesome

development, seventeen people banded together and bid the rest of us farewell. We gave them ropes and woven mats and whatever else we could spare and wished them well as they left. I hope they reach the other settlement safely, and that someday, someone in Jamaillia may hear the tale of what befell us here. Marthi pleaded with them to tell the other folk to wait a day or two longer before they depart for the coast, that soon her husband will be bringing her to join them.

I have not seen Retyo since my husband returned. I did not think he would go to hunt treasure in the city, but it must be so. I had grown accustomed to being without Jathan. I have no claim to Retyo, and yet miss him the more keenly of the two.

I visited Marthi again. She has grown paler and is now afflicted with the rash. Her skin is as dry as a lizard's. She is miserable with her heaviness. She speaks wildly of her husband finding immense wealth and how she will flaunt it to those who banished us. She fantasizes that as soon as the message bird reaches Jamaillia, the Satrap will send a swift ship to fetch us all back to Jamaillia, where her child will be born into plenty and safety. Her husband returned briefly from the city, to bring her a little casket of jewelry. Her dull hair is netted with chained jewels and gleaming bracelets dangle from her thin wrists. I avoid her lest I tell her that she is a fool. She is not, truly, save that she hopes beyond hope. I hate this wealth that we can neither eat nor drink, for all have focused upon it, and willingly starve while they seek to gather ever more.

Our remaining company is divided into factions now. Men have formed alliances and divided the city into claimed territories. It began with quarrels over the heaps and hoards, with men accusing each other of pilfering. Soon it fostered partnerships, some to guard the hoard while the others strip the city of wealth. Now it extends to men arming themselves with clubs and knives and setting sentries to guard the corridors they have claimed. But the city is a maze, and there are many routes through it. The men fight one another for plunder.

My sons and I remain with the infirm, the elderly, the very young and the pregnant here at the Platform. We form alliances of our own, for while the men are engrossed in stealing from each other, the gathering of food goes undone. The archers who hunted meat for us now hunt treasure. The men who had set snares for marsh rabbits now set traps for one another. Jathan came back to the hut, ate all that remained of our supplies, and then left again. He laughed at my anger, telling me that I worry about roots and seeds while there are gems and coins to be gathered. I was glad when he went back to the city. May he be devoured by it! Any food I find now, I immediately give to the boys or eat myself. If I can think of a secret place to cache it, I'll begin to do so.

Petrus, forbidden the city, has resumed his gathering duties, to good end. This day he returned with reeds like the ones we saw peasants cultivating in that mosaic in the city. He told me that the city people would not have grown them if they did not have some use, and that we should discover what it was. It was more disturbing to me when he told me that he remembered that this was the season for harvesting them. When I told him that he could not possibly remember any such thing, he shook his head at me, and muttered something about his "city memories."

I hope that the influence of that strange place will fade with time.

The rash has worsened on Carlmin, spreading onto his cheeks and brows. I slathered a poultice onto it in the hopes of easing it. My younger son has scarcely spoken a word to me this day, and I fear what occupies his mind.

My life has become only waiting. At any time, my husband may return from the city and announce that it is time for us to begin our trek down the river. Nothing I build now can be of any consequence, when I know that soon we will abandon it.

Olpey has not been found. Petrus blames himself. Chellia is near mad with grief. I watch her from a distance, for she no longer speaks to me. She confronts any man returning from the city, demanding word of her son. Most of them shrug her off; some become angry. I know what she fears, for I fear it, too. I think Olpey returned to the city. He felt entitled to his treasures, but fatherless as he is and of common birth, who would respect his claim? Would they kill the boy? I would give much not to feel so guilty about Olpey. What can I do? Nothing. Why, then, do I feel so bad? What would it benefit any of us to risk Petrus in another visit to the city? Is not one vanished boy tragedy enough?

8th Day of the City
Year the 1st of the Rain Wilds

Jathan returned at noon today. He was laden with a basket of treasure, jewelry and odd ornaments, small tools of a strange metal and a purse woven of metal links and full of oddly minted gold coins. His face was badly bruised. He abruptly said that this was enough, there was no sense to the greed in the city. He announced that we would catch up with the others who had already left. He declared that the city holds no good for us and that we are wiser to flee with what he has than to strive for more and die there.

He had not eaten since he last left us. I made him spice bark tea and lily-root mush and encouraged him to speak of what is happening underground. At first he spoke only of our own company there and what they did. Bitterly he accused them of treachery and betrayal. Men have come to bloodshed over the treasure. I suspect Jathan was driven off with what he could carry. But there is worse news. Parts of the city are collapsing. Closed doors have been forced open, with disastrous results. Some were not locked, but were held shut by the force of earth behind them. Now slow muck oozes forth from them, gradually flooding the corridors. Some are already nearly impassable, but men ignore the danger as they try to salvage wealth before it is buried forever. The flowing muck seems to weaken the city's ancient magic. Many chambers are subsiding into darkness. Lights flash brightly, then dim. Music blares forth and then fades to a whisper.

When I asked him if that had frightened him, he angrily told me to be quiet and recall my respect for him. He scoffed at my notion that he would flee. He said it was obvious that the ancient city would soon collapse under the weight of the swamp, and he had no wish to die there. I do not believe that was all of it, but I suppose I am glad he was intelligent enough to leave. He bade me get the children ready to travel and gather whatever food we had

Reluctantly, I began to obey him. Petrus, looking relieved, sprang to the meager packing. Carlmin sat silently scratching the poultice off his rash. I hastily covered it afresh. I did not want Jathan to see the coppery scaling on his son's skin. Earlier I had tried picking the scab loose, but when I scrape it off, he cries and the flesh beneath is bloody. It looks as if he is growing fish scales. I try not to think of the rash down my spine. I make this entry hastily, and then I will wrap this small book well and add it to my carry basket. There is precious little else to put in it.

I hate to leave what I have built, but I cannot ignore the relief in Petrus' eyes when his father said we would go. I wish we had never ventured into the city. But for that haunted place, perhaps we could have stayed here and made it a home. I dread our journey, but there is no help for it. Perhaps if we take Carlmin away from here, he will begin to speak again.

Later

I will write in haste and then take this book with me into the city. If ever my body is found, perhaps some kind soul will carry this volume back to Jamaillia and let my parents know what became of Carillion Waljin and where she ended her days. Likely it and I will be buried forever in the muck inside the hidden city.

I had finished our packing when Chellia came to me with Tremartin. The man was gaunt and his clothing caked with mud. He has finally found Olpey, but the lad is out of his wits. He has barricaded a door against them, and will not come out. Retyo and Tremartin had been searching the city for Olpey all this time. Retyo has remained outside the door, striving to keep it clear of the relentlessly creeping muck filling the passageway. Tremartin does not know how long he can keep up with it. Retyo thinks that Petrus could convince Olpey to open the door. Together, Tremartin and Chellia came to us to beg this favor.

I could no longer ignore the desperation in my friend's eyes, and felt shamed that I had so long. I appealed to Jathan, saying that we could go directly to where the boy is, persuade him to come out, and then we could all leave together. I even tried to be persuasive, saying that such a larger party would do better in facing the Rain Wilds than if we and our sons went alone.

He did not even call me apart or lower his voice as he demanded why he should risk his son and his heir for the sake of a laundress' boy, one we would not even employ as a servant were we still in Jamaillia. He berated me for letting Petrus become attached to such a common lad and then, in a clear voice, said I was very much mistaken if I thought him such a fool that he did not know about Retyo. Many a foul thing he said then, of what a harlot I was to take a common man into a bed by right a Lord's, and treacherously support a low sailor as he made his bid to claim leadership of the company.

I will not record any more of his shameful accusations. In truth, I do not know why he still has the power to make me weep. In the end, I defied him. When he said I must follow him now or not at all, I told him, "Not at all. I will stay and aid my friend, for I care not what work she used to do, here she is my friend."

My decision was not without cost to me. Jathan took Petrus with him. I saw that my elder son was torn, and yet wished to flee with his father. I do not blame him. Jathan left Carlmin behind, saying that my poor judgment had turned his son into a moron and a freak. Carlmin had scratched the poultice from his face, baring the scales that now outline his brows and upper cheeks. My little boy did not even wince to his father's words. He showed no reaction at all. I kissed Petrus goodbye and promised him that I would follow as soon as I could. I hope I can keep that promise. Jathan and Petrus took with them as much as they could carry of our goods. When Carlmin and I follow, we will not have much for supplies until we catch up to them.

And now I shall wrap this little book and slip it, pen and inkpot into the little carry basket they left to me, along with materials for torches and fire starting. Who knows when I shall write in it again? If you read this, my parents, know that I loved you until I died.

Day the 9th of the City, I think
Year the 1st of the Rain Wilds

How foolish and melodramatic my last entry now looks to me.

I pen this hastily before the light fails. My friends wait for me patiently, though Chellia finds it foolish that I insist on writing before we go on.

Less than ten days have passed since I first saw this city, but it has aged years. The passage of many muddy feet was evident when we entered, and everywhere I saw the depredations of the treasure seekers. Like angry boys, they had destroyed what they could not take, prying tiles out of mosaics, breaking limbs off statues too big to carry, and using fine old furniture for firewood. As much as the city frightens me, still I grieve to see it plundered and ravaged. It has prevailed against the swamp for years, only to fall prey to our greed in days.

Its magic is failing. Only portions of the chamber were lit. The dragons on the ceiling had dimmed. The great woman-and-dragon statue bears marks from errant hammers. The jade and ivory of the woman's basket remain out of the reach of the treasure hunters. The rest of the pavilion had not fared so well. The fish fountain was being used as a great dish to hold someone's hoard. A man stood atop the heap of plunder, knife in one hand and club in the other and shouted at us that he would kill any thieves who came near. His appearance was so wild, we believed him. I felt shamed for him, and looked aside as we hurried past. Fires burn in the room, with treasure and a guard by each one. In the distance we could hear voices, and sometimes challenging shouts and hammering. I caught a glimpse of four men ascending the steps with heavy sacks of loot.

Tremartin kindled one of our torches at an abandoned fire. We left that chamber by the same passage we had used before. Carlmin, mute since morning, began to hum a strange and wandering tune that stood up the hair on the back of my neck. I led him on, while Chellia's two girls wept silently in the dimness as they followed us, holding hands.

We passed the shattered door of a chamber. Thick mud-water oozed from the room. I glanced inside the chamber; a wide crack in its back wall had allowed mud to half-fill the room. Still, someone had entered and sought treasure. Moldy paintings had been pulled loose from the walls and discarded in the rising muck. We hastened on.

At an intersection of corridors, we saw a slowly advancing flow of mud, and heard a deep groaning in the distance, as of timbers slowly giving way. Nonetheless, a guard stood at that juncture, warning us that all behind him belonged to him and his friends. His eyes gleamed like a wild animal's. We assured him that we were only seeking a lost boy and hurried on. Behind him, we heard hammers begin and surmised that his friends were breaking down another door.

"We should hurry," Tremartin said. "Who knows what will be behind the next door they break? They won't leave off until they've let in the river. I left Retyo outside Olpey's door. We both feared others might come and think he guarded treasure."

"I just want my boy. Then I shall gladly leave this place," Chellia said. So we still hope to do.

I can write little of what else we saw, for the light flickers. We saw men dragging treasure they could never carry through the swamp. We were briefly attacked by a wild-eyed woman shrieking, "Thieves, thieves!" I pushed her down, and we fled. As we ran, there was first damp, then water, then oozing mud on the floor. The mud sucked at our feet as we passed the little dressing chamber where we had found Olpey the first time. It is wrecked now, the fine dressing table hacked to pieces. Tremartin took us down a side corridor I would not have noticed, and down a narrow flight of stairs. I smelled stagnant water. I tried not to think of the sodden earth ever pressing in, as we descended another, shorter flight of steps and turned down a wide hall. The doors we passed now were metal. A few showed hammer marks, but they had withstood the siege of the treasure seekers.

As we passed an intersection, we heard a distant crack like lightning, and then men shouting in terror. The unnatural veins of light on the walls flickered and then went out. An instant later, men rushed past us, fleeing back the way we had come. A gush of water that damped us to the ankles followed them, spending itself as it spread. Then came a deep and ominous rumbling. "Come on!" Tremartin ordered us, and we followed, though I think we all knew we were running deeper into danger, not away from it.

We turned two more corners. The stone of the walls suddenly changed from immense gray blocks to a smooth black stone with occasional veins of silver in it. We went down a long flight of shallow steps, and abruptly the corridor was wider and the ceiling higher, as if we had left behind the servants area and entered the territory of the privileged. The wall niches had been plundered of their statues. I slipped in the damp on the floor. As I put my hand on a wall to catch myself, I suddenly glimpsed people swarming all around us. Their garb and demeanor were strange. It was a market day, rich with light and noise of conversation and the rich smells of baking. The life of a city swirled around me. In the next moment, Tremartin seized my arm and jerked me away from the wall. "Do not touch the black stone," he warned us. "It puts you in the ghosts' world. Come on. Follow me." In the distance, we saw the brighter flare of a fire gleaming, shaming the uneasily flickering light.

The fire was Retyo's torch. He was grimed from head to foot. Even when he saw us, he continued to scoop mud away from a door with a crude wooden paddle. The watery ooze was a constant flow down the hall; not even a dozen men could hope to keep up with it. If Olpey did not open the door soon, he would be trapped inside as the mud filled the corridor.

I stepped down into the shallow pit Retyo had been keeping clear. Heedless of the mud on him, heedless that my son and friend watched me, I embraced him. If I had had the time, I would have become what my husband had accused me of being. Perhaps, in spirit, I am already a faithless wife. I care little for that now. I have kept faith with my friends.

Our embrace was brief. We had little time. We called to Olpey through the doors, but he kept silent until he heard his little sisters weeping. Then he angrily bade us to go away. His mother begged him to come out, saying that the city was giving way and that the flowing mud would soon trap him. He retorted that he belonged here, that he had always lived here and here he would die. And all the while that we shouted and begged, Retyo grimly worked, scraping the advancing muck away from the doorsill. When our pleas did not work, Retyo and Tremartin attacked the door, but the stout wood would not give to boots or fists, and we had no tools. In a dull whisper, Tremartin said we must leave him. He wept as he spoke. The mud was flowing faster than both men could contain, and we had three other children to think of.

Chellia's voice rose in a shriek of denial, but was drowned by an echoing rumble behind us. Something big gave way. The flow of the muck doubled, for now it came from both directions. Tremartin lifted his torch. In both directions, the corridor ended in blackness. "Open the door, Olpey!" I begged him. "Or we all perish here, drowned in muck. Let us in, in Sa's name!"

I do not think he heeded my words. Rather it was Carlmin's voice, raised in a command in a language I've never heard that finally won a reaction. We heard latches being worked, and then the door grated grudgingly outward through the muck. The lit chamber dazzled our eyes as we tumbled into it. Water and flowing muck tried to follow us onto the richly tiled floor, but Tremartin and Retyo dragged the door shut, though Retyo had to drop to his knees and push mud out of the way to do so. Mud-tinged water crept determinedly under the closed door.

The chamber was the best preserved that I had seen. We were all dazzled by the richness of the chambers and the brief illusion of safety amidst the strangeness. Shelves of gleaming wood supported exquisite vases and small stone statues, intricate carvings and silver ornaments gone black with time. A little winding staircase led up and out of sight. Each step of it was lined with light. The contents of the room could have ransomed our entire company back into the Satrap's good will, for the objects were both fine and strange. Olpey stooped down protectively to roll back a carpet in danger of being overtaken by the ooze. It was supple in his hands, and as he disturbed the dust, bright colors peeped out. For a few moments, none of us spoke. As Olpey came to his feet and stood before us, I gasped. He wore a robe that rippled with colors when he moved. About his forehead he had bound a band of linked metal disks, and they seemed to glow with their own light. Chellia dared not embrace him. He blinked owlishly, and Chellia hesitantly asked her son if he knew her.

His reply came slowly. "I dreamed you once." Then, looking about the room he said worriedly, "Or perhaps I have stepped into a dream. It is so hard to tell."

"He's been touching that black wall too much," Tremartin growled. "It wakes the ghosts and steals your mind. I saw a man two days ago. He was sitting with his back to the wall, his head leaned against it, smiling and gesturing and talking to people who weren't there."

Retyo nodded grimly. "Even without touching them, it takes a man's full will to keep the ghosts at bay after a time down here in the dark." Then, reluctantly, he added, "It may be too late to bring Olpey all the way back to us. But we can try. And we must all guard our minds as best we can, by talking to one another. And get the little ones out of here as quickly as we can."

I saw what he meant. Olpey had gone to a small table in a corner. A silver pot awaited beside a tiny silver cup. As we watched in silence, he poured nothing from the pot to the cup, and then quickly quaffed it. He wiped his mouth on the back of his hand and made a face, as if he had just drunk liquor too strong for him.

"If we're going to go, we must go now," Retyo added. He did not need to say, "Before it's too late." We were all thinking it.

But it was already too late. There was a steady seepage of water under the door, and when the men tried to open it, they could not budge it. Even when all the adults put our shoulders to it, it would not move. And then the lights began to flicker dismally.

Now the press of muck against the door grows heavier, so that the wood groans with it. I must be short. The staircase leads up into absolute darkness and the torches we have contrived from the articles in the room will not last long. Olpey has gone into a daze, and Carlmin is not much better. He barely responds to us with a mutter. The men will carry the boys, and Chellia will lead her two girls. I will carry our supply of torches. We will go as far as we can, hoping to discover a different way back to the dragon-woman chamber.

◄—✦—►

Day—I do not know
Year the 1ˢᵗ of the Rain Wilds

So I head this account, for we have no concept of how much time has passed. For me, it seems years. I quiver, but I am not certain if it is from cold, or from striving to remain who I am. Who I was. My mind swims with the differences, and I could drown in them, if I let go. Yet if this account is to be of any use to others, I must find my discipline and put my thoughts into order.

As we ascended the stairs, the last breath of light in the chamber sighed out. Tremartin lifted our torch bravely but it barely illuminated his head and shoulders in the engulfing blackness. Never have I experienced darkness so absolute. Tremartin gripped Olpey's wrist and compelled the boy to follow him. Behind him went Retyo, carrying Carlmin, then Chellia leading her trembling daughters. I came last, burdened with the crude torches created from the furniture and hangings in the chamber. This last act had infuriated Olpey. He attacked Retyo and would not stop until Retyo struck him a hard open-handed blow to the face. It dazed the boy and horrified his mother and sisters, but he became compliant, if not co-operative.

The stair led to a servant's room. Doubtless the privileged noble in the comfortable chamber below would ring a bell, and his servants would spring to satisfy the master's wish. I saw wooden tubs, perhaps for washing, and glimpsed a worktable before Tremartin hurried us on. There was only one exit. Once outside, the corridor offered blackness in both directions.

The noise of the burning torch seemed almost loud; the only other sound was the dripping of water. I feared that silence. Music and ghostly voices lingered at the edge of it.

"The flame burns steadily," Chellia observed. "No drafts."

I had not thought of that, but she was right. "All that means is that there is a door between us and the outside." Even I doubted my words. "One we must find and open."

"Which way shall we go?" Tremartin asked all of us. I had long ago lost my bearings, so I kept silent.

"That way," Chellia answered. "I think it goes back the direction we came. Perhaps we will see something we recognize, or perhaps the light will come back."

I had no better suggestion to offer. They led and I followed. Each of them had someone to hold tight, to keep the ghosts of the city at bay. I had only the bundled torches in my arms. My friends became shadows between me and the unsteady torch light. If I looked up, the torch blinded me. Looking down, I saw a goblin's dance of shadows around my feet. Our hoarse breathing, the scuff of our feet on the damp stone and the crackling of the torch were the only sounds I perceived at first. Then I began to hear other things, or to think that I did: the uneven drip of water and once a sliding sound as something in the distance gave way.

And music. It was music thin as watered ink, music muffled by thick stone and time, but it reached out to me. I was determined to take the men's advice and ignore it. To keep my thoughts my own, I began to hum an old Jamaillian lullaby. It was only when Chellia hissed, "Carillion!" at me that I realized my humming had become the haunting song from the stone. I stopped, biting my lip.

"Pass me another torch. We'd best light a fresh one before this one dies completely." When Tremartin spoke the words, I realized he'd spoken to me twice before. Dumbly I stepped forward, presenting my armload of makeshift torches. The first two he chose were scarves wrapped around table legs. They would not kindle at all. Whatever the scarves were woven from, they would not take the flame. The third was a cushion tied crudely to a chair leg. It burned smokily and with a terrible stench. Still, we could not be fussy, and holding aloft the burning cushion and the dwindling torch, we moved slowly on. When the torch had burned so close to Tremartin's fingers that he had to let it fall, we had only the smoldering glow of the cushion to light our way. The darkness pressed closer than ever and the foul smell of the thing gave me a headache. I trudged along, remembering the annoying way the long coarse hair tangled on my rough skinned fingers when I bundled the coiled hair in amongst the pith to make the cushion more springy and longer lasting.

Retyo shook me, hard, and then Carlmin came into my arms, sniffling. "Perhaps you should carry your son for a while," the sailor told me, without rebuke, as he stooped to gather the spare torches that I had dropped. Ahead of us in the dark, the rest of our party was shadows in shadow, with a red smear for our torch. I had just stopped in my tracks. If Retyo had not noted my absence, I wonder what would have happened to me. Even after we spoke, I felt as if I were two people.

"Thank you," I told him ashamedly.

"It's all right. Just stay close," he told me.

We went on. The punishing weight of Carlmin in my arms kept me focused. After a time, I set him down and made him walk beside me, but I think that was better for him. Having once been snared by the ghosts, I resolved to be more wary. Even so, odd bits of dreams, fancies, and voices talking in the distance drifted through my mind as I walked, eyes open, through the dark. We trudged on endlessly. Hunger and thirst made themselves known to us. The seeping runnels of water tasted bitter, but we drank sparingly from them anyway.

"I hate this city," I said to Carlmin. His little hand in mine was becoming chill as the buried city stole our body warmth from us. "It's full of traps and snares. Rooms full of mud waiting to crush us, and ghosts trying to steal our minds."

I had been speaking as much to myself as him. I didn't expect a response. But then he said slowly, "It wasn't built to be dark and empty."

"Perhaps not, but that is how it is now. And the ghosts of those who built it try to steal our minds from us."

I heard more than saw his scowl. "Ghosts? Not ghosts. Not thieves."

"What are they, then?" I asked him, mostly to keep him talking.

He was silent for a time. I listened to our footsteps and breathing. Then he said, "It's not anyone. It's their art."

Art seemed a far and useless thing to me now. Once I had used it to justify my existence. Now it seemed an idleness and a ploy, something I did to conceal the insignificance of my daily life. The word almost shamed me.

"Art," he repeated. He did not sound like a little boy as he went on, "Art is how we define and explain ourselves to ourselves. In this city, we decided that the daily life of the people was the art of the city. From year to year, the shaking of the earth increased, and the storms of dust and ash. We hid from it, closing our cities in and burrowing under the earth. And yet we knew that a time would come when we could not prevail against the earth itself. Some wished to leave, and we let them. No one was forced to stay. Our cities that had burgeoned with life faded to a trickle of souls. For a time, the earth calmed, with only a shiver now and then to remind us that our lives were daily granted to us and could be taken in a moment. But many of us decided that this was where we had lived, for generations. So this would be where we perished. Our individual lives, long as they were, would end here. But not our cities. No. Our cities would live on and recall us. Recall us...would call us home again, whenever anyone woke the echoes of us that we stored here. We're all here, all our richness and complexity, all our joys and sorrows..." His voice drifted away in contemplation once more.

I felt chilled. "A magic that calls the ghosts back."

"Not magic. Art." He sounded annoyed.

Suddenly Retyo said unsteadily, "I keep hearing voices. Someone, talk to me."

I put my hand on his arm. "I hear them, too. But they sound Jamaillian."

With pounding hearts our little party hastened toward them. At the next juncture of corridors, we turned right and the voices came clearer. We shouted, and they shouted a reply. Through the dark, we heard their hurrying feet. They blessed our smoky red torch; theirs had burned out. There were four young men and two women from our company. Frightened as they were, they still clutched armloads of plunder. We were overjoyed to find them, until they dashed our relief into despair. The passage to the outside world was blocked. They had been in the dragon-and-woman chamber when they heard heavy pounding from the rooms above. A great crash was followed by the slow groan of timbers giving way. As a grinding noise grew in volume, the lights in the big chamber flickered and watery mud began to trickle down the grand staircase. They had immediately tried to escape, only to find the stairway blocked by collapsed masonry oozing mud.

Perhaps fifty folk had gathered in the dragon-and-woman chamber, drawn back there by the ominous sound. As the lights dimmed and then went out, some had gone one way and some another, seeking for escape. Even in this danger, their suspicion of one another as thieves had prevented them from joining forces. I was disgusted with them, and said as much. To my surprise, they sheepishly agreed. Then, for a time, we stood uselessly in the dark, listening to our torch burn away and wondering what to do.

When no one else spoke, I asked, "Do you know the way back to the dragon chamber?" I fought to speak steadily.

One man said he did.

"Then we must go back there. And gather all the people we can, and pool what we know of this maze. It is our only hope of finding a way out before our torches are gone. Otherwise, we may wander until we die."

Grim silence was their assent. The young man led our way back. As we passed plundered rooms, we gathered anything that might burn. Soon those who had joined us must abandon their plunder to carry more wood. I thought they would part from us before surrendering their treasure, but they decided to leave it in one of the rooms. They marked their claim upon the door, with threats against any thieves. I thought this foolishness, for I would have traded every jewel in the city simply to see honest daylight again. Then we went on.

We reached at last the dragon-woman chamber. We knew it more by its echoes than by the view that our failing torch offered. A small fire still smouldered there, with a few hapless folk gathered around it. We added fuel to wake it to flames. It drew others to join us, and we then raised a shout to summon any who might hear us. Soon our little bonfire lit a circle of some thirty muddy and weary people. The flames showed me frightened white faces like masks. Many of them still clutched bundles of plunder, and eyed one another suspiciously. That was almost more frightening than the slow creep of thick mud spreading from the staircase. Heavy and thick, it trickled inexorably down, and I knew that our gathering place would not long be a refuge from it.

We were a pitiful company. Some of these folk had been lords and ladies, and others pick-pockets and whores, but in that place, we finally became equals and recognized one another for what we were: desperate people, dependent on each other. We had convened at the foot of the dragon statue. Now Retyo stepped up onto the dragon's tail and commanded us, "Hush! Listen!"

Voices ebbed away. We heard the crackling of our fire, and then the distant groans of wood and stone, and the drip and trickle of watery muck. They were terrifying sounds and I wondered why he had made us listen to them. When he spoke, his human voice was welcome as it drowned out the threats of the straining walls.

"We have no time to waste in worrying about treasure or theft. Our lives are the only things we can hope to carry out of here, and only if we pool what we know, so we don't waste time exploring corridors that lead nowhere. Are we together on that?"

A silence followed his words. Then a grimy, bearded man spoke. "My partners and I claimed the corridors from the west arch. We've been exploring them for days now. There are no stairs going up and the main corridor ends in collapse."

It was dismal news but Retyo didn't let us dwell on it.

"Well. Any others?"

There was some restless shifting.

Retyo's voice was stern. "You're still thinking of plunder and secrets. Let them go, or stay here with them. All I want is a way out. Now. We're only interested in stairways leading up. Anyone know of any?"

Finally, a man spoke up reluctantly. "There were two from the east arch. But...well, a wall gave way when we opened a door. We can't get to them anymore."

A deeper silence fell on us and the light from the fire seemed to dwindle.

When Retyo spoke again, his voice was impassive. "Well, that makes it simpler for us. There's less to search. We'll need two large search parties, one that can divide at each intersection. As each group goes, you'll mark your path. On your way, enter every open chamber, and seek always for stairs leading up, for doubtless that is our only way out. Mark every path that you go by, so that you may return to us." He cleared his throat. "I don't need to warn you. If a door won't open, leave it alone."

"This is a pact we must make: that whoever finds a way out will risk their lives again to return and guide the rest of us out. To those who go out, the pact we make is that we who stay here will try to keep this fire burning, so that if you do not find a way out, you can return here, to light and another attempt." He looked around carefully at all the upturned faces. "To that end, every one of us will leave here whatever treasure we have found. To encourage any that find a way out to come back, for gain if not to keep faith with us."

I would not have dared to test them that way. I saw what he did. The mounded hoard would give hope to those who must stay here and tend the fire, as well as encourage any who found an escape to return for the rest of us. To those who insisted they would take their treasure with them, Retyo simply said, "Do it. But remember well what you choose. No one who stays here will owe you any help. Should you return and find the fire out and the rest of us gone, do not hope that we will return for you."

Three men, heavily burdened, went aside to heatedly argue amongst themselves. Other people began to trickle back to the dragon pavilion, and were quickly informed of the pact. These folk, having already tried to find a way out, quickly agreed to the terms. Someone said that perhaps the rest of our company might dig down to free us. A general silence greeted that thought as we all considered the many steps we had descended to reach this place, and all the mud and earth that stood between us and outside air. Then no one spoke of it again. When finally all agreed to abide by Retyo's plan, we counted ourselves and found that we numbered fifty-two bedraggled and weary men, women and children.

Two parties set out. Most of our firewood went with them, converted to torches. Before they left, we prayed together, but I doubted Sa could hear us, so deep beneath the ground and so far from sacred Jamaillia. I remained with my son, tending the fire. We took turns making short trips to nearby rooms, to drag back whatever might burn. Treasure seekers had already burned most of the close fuel, but still we found items ranging from massive tables it took eight of us to lift to broken bits of rotted chairs and tatters of curtain.

Most of the children had remained by the fire. In addition to my son and Chellia's children, there were four other youngsters. We took it in turns to tell stories or sing songs to them, trying to keep their minds free of the ghosts that clustered closer as our small fire burned lower. We begrudged every stick of wood we fed to it.

Despite our efforts, the children fell silent one by one and slipped into the dreams of the buried city. I shook Carlmin and pinched him, but could not find the will to be cruel enough to rouse him. In truth, the ghosts plucked at my mind as well, until the distant conversations in an unknown language seemed more intelligible than the desperate mutterings of the other women. I dozed off, then snapped awake as the needs of the dying fire recalled me to my duty.

"Perhaps it's kinder to let them dream themselves to death," one of the women said as she helped me push one end of a heavy table into the fire. She took a deeper breath and added, "Perhaps we should all just go to the black wall and lean against it."

The idea was more tempting than I liked to admit. Chellia returned from a wood foraging effort. "I think we burn more in torch than we bring back as fuel," she pointed out. "I'll sit with the children for a while. See what you can find to burn."

So I took her stub of torch and went off seeking firewood. By the time I returned with my pitiful scraps, a splinter group of one of the search parties had returned. They had swiftly exhausted their possibilities and their torches and returned hoping that others had had better luck.

When a second party returned shortly afterward, I felt more discouragement. They brought with them a group of seventeen others whom they had discovered wandering in the labyrinth. The seventeen were the "owners" of that section of the city, and said that days ago they had early discovered that the upper stories in that section were collapsed. In all the days they had explored it, always the paths had led outward and downward. Any further explorations in that direction would demand more torches than we presently had.

Our supply of wood for the bonfire was already dwindling, and we weren't finding much in the pillaged rooms that we could use for torches. Hunger and thirst were already pressing many of us. Too soon we would have to confront an even more daunting shortage. Once our fire failed, we would be plunged into total darkness. If I dared to think of it, my heart thundered and I felt faint. It was hard enough to hold myself aloof from the city's lingering "art." Immersed in blackness, I knew I would give way to it.

I was not the only one who realized this. Tacitly, we let the fire die down and maintained it at a smaller size. The flow of mud down the grand stair brought damp that chilled the air. People huddled together for warmth as much as companionship. I dreaded the first touch of water against my feet. I wondered which would overtake me first; total darkness or rising muck.

I don't know how much time passed before the third party returned to us. They had found three staircases that led up. All were blocked before they reached the surface. Their corridor had become increasingly ruined the further they had gone. Soon they had been splashing through shallow puddles and the smell of earth had grown strong. When their torches were nearly exhausted and the water growing deeper and colder about their knees, they had returned. Retyo and Tremartin had been members of that party. I was selfishly glad to have him at my side again, even though it meant that our hope was now whittled to a single search party.

Retyo wished to shake Carlmin out of his daze, but I asked him, "To what end? That he might stare into the darkness and know despair? Let him dream, Retyo. He does not seem to be having bad dreams. If I can carry him out of here into daylight once more, than I will wake him and try to call him back to me. Until then, I will leave him in peace." I sat, Retyo's arm around me and thought silently of Petrus and my erstwhile husband Jathan. Well, he had made one wise decision. I felt oddly grateful to him that he had not allowed me to squander both our sons' lives. I hoped he and Petrus reached the coast safely and eventually returned to Jamaillia. At least one of my children might grow to adulthood.

And so we waited, our hopes dwindling as swiftly as our firewood. Our men had to venture further and further into the darkness in search of fuel. Finally Retyo lifted his voice. "Either they are still exploring, in hope of finding a way out, or they have found a way out and are too fearful to return for us. In either way, we gain nothing more by sitting here. Let us go where they went, following their marks, while we still have light to see them. Either we will find the same escape route they did, or die together."

We took every splinter of firewood. The more foolish among us gathered treasure to carry out. No one remonstrated with them, though many laughed bitterly at their hopeful greed. Retyo picked up Carlmin without a word; it moved me that my son was treasure to him. In truth, weakened as I was by hunger, I do not know if I could have carried my son. I do know that I would not have left him there. Tremartin took Olpey slung across his shoulders. The boy was limp as a drowned thing. Drowned in art, I thought to myself. Drowned in memories of the city.

Of Chellia's two daughters, Piet still clung to wakefulness. She stumbled piteously along beside her mother. A young man named Sterren offered to carry Likea for Chellia. She was so grateful, she wept.

And so we trudged off. We had one torch to lead us, and one at the tail of our procession, so that no one would fall victim to the city's allure and be left behind. I walked in the middle of the company, and the darkness seemed to pluck and snag at my senses. There is little to say of that endless walk. We took no rest, for our fire ate our torches at an alarming rate. There was dark, and wet, the mutter of hungry and thirsty and weary folk all around me, and more darkness. I could not really see the halls we walked through, only the smudge of light that we followed. Bit by bit, I gave up my burden of wood to our light-bearers. The last time I moved forward to offer a new torch, I saw that the walls were of shining black stone veined with silver. They were elaborately decorated with silhouettes of people, done in some shining metal. Curious, I reached out a hand to touch one. I had not even realized that Retyo was at my side. He caught my wrist before I could touch the silhouette. "Don't," he warned me. "I brushed against one once. They leap into your mind if you touch them. Don't."

We followed the marks of the missing search party. They had marked off the dead ends and drawn arrows as they progressed, and so we trudged on, hoping. Then, to our horror, we caught up with them.

They were huddled in the middle of the corridor. Torches exhausted, they had halted there, paralyzed by the complete blackness, unable to either go on or to come back to us. Some were insensible. Others whimpered with joy at the sight of us and clustered around our torch as if light were life itself flowing back into them.

"Did you find a way out?" they asked us, as if they had forgotten that they were the searchers. When they finally understood that they had been our last hope, the life seemed to go out of them. "The corridor goes on and on," they said. "But we have not yet found one place where it leads upward. The chambers we have been able to enter are windowless. We think this part of the city has always been underground."

Grim words. Useless to dwell on them.

And so, we moved on together. We encountered few intersections, and when we did, we made our choice almost randomly. We no longer had torches to explore every possibility. At each intersection, the men in the lead debated and then chose. And we followed, but at each one we had to wonder if we had made a fatal error. Were we walking away from the passage that would have led to light and air? We gave up having a torch at the end of our procession, instead having folk hold hands and come behind us. Even so, too swiftly we had but three torches, and then two. A woman keened as the final torch was kindled. It did not burn well, or perhaps the dread of the dark was so strong in us that no light would have seemed sufficient. I know we crowded closer around our torch-bearer. The corridor had widened and the ceiling retreated. Every now and then, the torchlight would catch a silver silhouette or a vein of silvery mineral in the polished black wall and it would blink beckoningly at me. Still we marched hopelessly on, hungry, thirsty and ever more weary. We did not travel fast, but then, we did not know if we had any destination save death.

The lost spirits of the city plucked at me. Ever stronger grew the temptation to simply let go of my puny life and immerse myself in the beckoning remembrance of the city. Snatches of their music, conversation heard in a distant mutter, even, it seemed to me, whiffs of strange fragrances assailed me and tempted me. Well, was not that what Jathan had always warned me? That if I did not take a firmer grip on my life, my art would immerse and then devour me? But it was so hard to resist; it tugged at me like a hook in a fish's lip. It knew that it had me; it but waited for darkness to pull me in.

The torch burned lower with every step we took. Every step we took might be one more step in the wrong direction. The passage had widened around us into a hall; I could no longer see the gleaming black walls, but I could feel them commanding my attention. We passed a still fountain flanked by stone benches. We watched in vain for anything that might fuel our fire. Here, these elder folk had built for eternity, from stone and metal and fired clay. I knew that these rooms now were the repository of all they had been. They had believed they would always live here, that the waters of the fountains and the swirling beams of light would always dance at their touch. I knew that as clearly as I knew my own name. Like me, they had foolishly thought to live forever through their art. Now it was the only part of them that lingered still.

And in that moment, I knew my decision. It came to me so clearly that I am not sure it was solely my own. Did some long dead artist reach out and tug at my sleeve, begging to be heard and seen one last time before we tumbled into the dark and silence that had consumed her city?

I put my hand on Retyo's arm. "I'm going to the wall now," I said simply. To his credit, he immediately knew what I meant.

"You would leave us?" he asked me piteously. "Not just me, but little Carlmin? You would drown yourself in dreams and leave me to face death alone?"

I stood on tiptoe to kiss his whiskery cheek and to press my lips briefly against my son's downy head. "I won't drown," I promised him. It suddenly seemed so simple. "I know how to swim in those waters. I have swum in them since my birth, and like a fish, I will follow them upstream to their source. And you will follow me. All of you."

"Carillion, I don't understand. Are you mad?"

"No. But I cannot explain. Only follow me, and trust, as I followed you when I walked out on the tree limb. I will feel the path surely; I won't let you fall."

Then I did the most scandalous thing I've ever done in my life. I took hold of my weary skirts, long tattered halfway up my calf, and tore them free of my stained waistband, leaving only my pantaloons. I bundled them up and pushed them into his shocked hands. Around us, others had halted in their shadowy trudging to watch my strange performance. "Feed these to the torch, a bit at a time, to keep it alive. And follow me."

"You will walk near naked before all of us?" he asked me in horror, as if it were of great concern.

I had to smile. "While my skirts burn, no one will notice the nakedness of she who stripped to give them light. And after they have burned, we will all be hidden in the darkness. Much like the art of these people."

Then I walked away from him, into the engulfing darkness that framed us. I heard him shout to our torch-bearer to halt, and I heard others say that I had gone mad. But I felt as if I had finally plunged myself into the river that all my life had tantalized my thirst. I went to the city's wall willingly, opening my mind and heart to their art as I approached it, so that by the time I touched the cold stone, I was already walking among them, hearing their gossip and corner musicians and haggling.

It was a market square. As I touched the stone, it roared to life around me. Suddenly my mind perceived light where my closed eyes did not, and I smelled the cooking river fish on the smoky little braziers, and saw the skewers of dripping honeyed-fruit on the tray of a street hawker. Glazed lizards smoked on a low brazier. Children chased one another past me. People paraded the streets, dressed in gleaming fabrics that rippled color at their every step. And such people, people that befitted such a grand city! Some might have been Jamaillian, but amongst them moved others, tall and narrow, scaled like fish or with skin as bronzed as polished metal. Their eyes gleamed too, silver and copper and gold. The ordinary folk made way for these exalted ones with joy rather than cold respect. Merchants stepped out from their stalls to offer them their best and gawking children peeped from around their mothers' trousered legs to glimpse their royalty passing. For such I was sure they were.

With an effort, I turned my eyes and my thoughts from this rich pageantry. I groped to recall whom and where I truly was. I dragged Carlmin and Retyo back into my awareness. Then, I deliberately looked around myself. Up and sky, I told myself. Up and sky, into the air. Blue sky. Trees.

Fingers lightly touching the wall, I moved forward.

Art is immersion, and good art is total immersion. Retyo was right. It sought to drown me. But Carlmin was right, too. There was no malice in the drowning, only the engulfing that art seeks. And I was an artist, and as a practitioner of that magic, I was accustomed to keeping my head even when the current ran strongest and swiftest.

Even so, it was all I could do to cling to my two words. Up and sky. I could not tell if my companions followed me or if they had abandoned me to my madness. Surely, Retyo would not. Surely, he would come behind me, bringing my son with him. Then, a moment later, the struggle to remember their names became too great. Such names and such people had never existed in this city, and I was a citizen of the city now.

I strode through its busy market time. Around me people bought and sold exotic and fascinating merchandise. The colors, the sounds, even the smells tempted me to linger, but Up and Sky were what I clung to.

They were not a folk who cherished the outside world. Here they had built a hive, much of it underground, lit and warm, clean and immune to wind and storm and rain. They had brought inside it such creatures as appealed to them, flowering trees and caged song birds and little glittering lizards tethered to potted bushes. Fish leaped and flashed in the fountains, but no dogs ran and barked, no birds flew overhead. Nothing was allowed that might make a mess. All was orderly and controlled, save for the flamboyant people who shouted and laughed and whistled in their precisely arranged streets.

Up and Sky, I told them. They did not hear me, of course. Their conversations buzzed uselessly around me, and even once I began to understand them, the things they spoke of did not concern me. What could I care about the politics of a queen a thousand years gone, for society weddings and clandestine affairs noisily gossiped about? Up and Sky I breathed to myself, and slowly, slowly, the memories I sought began to flow to me. For there were others in this city for whom art was Up and Sky. There was a tower, an observatory. It rose above the river mists on foggy nights, and there learned men and women could study the stars and predict what effect they might have on mortals. I focused my mind on it, and soon "remembered" where it was. Sa blessed us all, in that it was not far from their marketplace.

I was halted once, for though my eyes told me that the way ahead of me was well lit and smoothly paved, my groping hands found a cold tumble of fallen stone and earth seeping water. A man shouted by my ear and restrained my hands. Dimly I recalled my other life. How strange to open my eyes to blackness and Retyo gripping my hands in his. Around me in the darkness, I heard people weeping or muttering despairingly that they followed a dreamer to their deaths. I could see nothing at all. The darkness was absolute. I had no idea how much time had passed, but I was suddenly aware of thirst that near choked me. Retyo's hand still clutched at mine, and I knew then of the long chain of people, hands clasped, that trustingly followed me.

I croaked at them. "Don't give up. I know the way. I do. Follow me."

Later, Retyo would tell me that the words I uttered were in no tongue he had ever known, but my emphatic shout swayed him. I closed my eyes, and once more the city surged to life around me. Another way, there had to be another way to the observatory. I turned back to the populous corridors, but now as I passed the leaping fountains, they taunted me with their remembered water. The tantalizing memories of food smells lingered in the air and I felt my belly clench on itself in longing. But Up and Sky were my words, and I walked on, even as I became aware that moving my body was becoming more and more taxing to me. In another place, my tongue was leather in my mouth, my belly a cramped ball of pain. But here, I moved with the city, immersed in it. I understood now the words that flowed past me, I smelled familiar foods, even knew all the words to the songs the corner minstrels were singing. I was home, and as the city as art flowed through me, I was home in a deeper way than ever Jamaillia had been home to me.

I found the other stairs that led to the observatory, the back stairs for the servants and cleaners. Up these stairs, humble folk carried couches and trays of wine glasses for nobles who wished to recline and gaze up at the stars. It was a humble wooden door. It swung open at my push. I heard a murmured gasp behind me, and then words of shouted praise that opened my eyes.

Daylight, thin and feeble, crept down to us. The winding stair was wooden, and rickety, but I decided we would trust it. "Up and Sky," I told my company as I set my foot to the first creaking step. It was a struggle to recall my precious words and speak them aloud. "Up and Sky." And they followed me.

As we ascended, the light came stronger, and we blinked like moles in that sweet dimness. When at last I reached the stone-floored upper chamber, I smiled so that my dry lips split.

The thick glass panels of the observatory windows had given way to cracks, followed by questing vines that faded to pale writhing things as they left the daylight behind. The light through the windows was greenish and thick, but it was light. The vines became our ladder to freedom. Many of us were weeping dry tears as we made that last painful climb. Unconscious children and dazed people were passed up and out to us. I took a limp Carlmin in my arms and held him in the light and fresh air.

There were rain flowers awaiting us, as if Sa wished us to know it was her will we survive here, enough rain flowers for each of us to wet our mouths and gather our senses. The wind seemed chill and we laughed joyfully to shiver in it. We stood on top of what had been the observatory, and I looked out with love over a land I had once known. My beautiful wide river valley was swamp now, but it was still mine. The tower that had stood so high above all was only a mound now, but around us were the hunched and mossy remains of other structures, making the land firm and dry beneath our feet. There was not much dry land, less than a leffer, and yet after our months in the swamp, it seemed a grand estate. From atop it, we could look out over the slowly moving river where slanting sunlight fell on the chalky waters. My home had changed, but it was still mine.

Every one of us who left the dragon chamber emerged alive and intact. The city had swallowed us, taken us down and made us hers, and then released us, changed, in this kindlier place. Here, by virtue of the city buried beneath us, the ground is firmer. There are great, strong-branched trees nearby, in which we can build a new platform. There is even food here, a plenitude by Rain Wild standards. A sort of climbing vine festoons the trunks of the trees, and is heavy with pulpy fruit. I recall the same fruit sold in the vendor stalls of my city. It will sustain us. For now, we have all we need to survive this night. Tomorrow will be soon enough to think on the rest of it.

Day the 7th of Light and Air
Year the 1st of the Rain Wilds

It took us a full six days to hike down river to our original settlement. Time in the light and air have restored most of us to our ordinary senses, though all of the children have a more detached air than they used to have. Nor do I think I am alone in my vivid dreams of life in the city. I welcome them now. The land here has changed vastly since the days of the city; once all was solid ground, and the river a silver shining thread. The land was restless in those days, too, and sometimes the river ran milky and acid. Now the trees have taken back the meadows and croplands, but still, I recognize some features of the land. I recognize, too, which trees are good for timber, which leaves make a pleasantly stimulating tea, which reeds can yield both paper and fabric when beaten to thread and pulp, and oh, so many other things. We will survive here. It will not be lush or easy living, but if we accept what the land offers us, it may be enough.

And that is well. I found my tree city mostly deserted. After the disaster that sealed us in the city, most of the folk here gave up all for lost and fled. Of the treasure they collected and mounded on the platform, they took only a pittance. Only a few people remained. Marthi and her husband and her son are among them. Marthi wept with joy at my return.

When I expressed my anger that the others could go on without her, she told me, quite seriously, that they had promised to send back help, and she was quite sure that they would keep their word, as their treasure is still here.

As for me, I found my own treasure. Petrus had remained here, after all. Jathan, stony-hearted man that he is, went on without the boy when Petrus had a last-moment change of heart and declared that he would wait here for his mother to return. I am glad that he did not wait for me in vain.

I was shocked that Marthi and her husband had remained, until she put in my arms her reason. Her child was born, and for his sake, they will dwell here. He is a lithe and lively little thing, but he is as scaled as a snake. In Jamaillia, he would be a freak. The Rain Wilds are where he belongs.

As we all do, now.

I think I was as shocked at the changes in Marthi as she was in the change in me. Around her neck and wrists where she had worn the jewelry from the city, tiny growths have erupted. When she stared at me, I thought it was because she could see how much the city memories had changed my soul. In reality, it was the beginning of feathery scales on my eyelids and round my lips that caught her eye. I have no looking glass, so I cannot say how pronounced they are. And I have only Retyo's word that the line of scarlet scaling down my spine is more attractive than repellent.

I see the scaling that has begun to show on the children, and in truth, I do not find it abhorrent. Almost all of us who went down into the city bear some sign of it, either a look behind the eyes, or a delicate tracing of scales or perhaps a line of pebbled flesh along the jaw. The Rain Wilds have marked us as their own, and welcome us home.

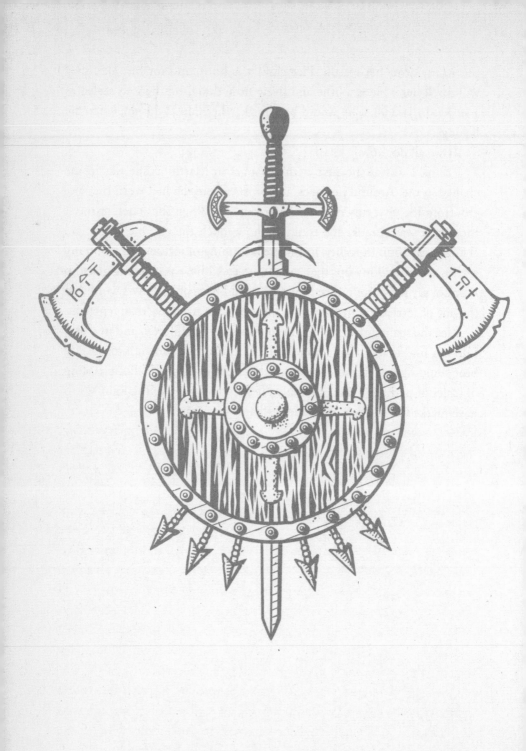

The Word of Unbinding

Ursula K. Le Guin

Ursula K. Le Guin is the author of innumerable SF and fantasy classics, such as The Left Hand of Darkness, The Lathe of Heaven, The Dispossessed, *and* A Wizard of Earthsea *(and the others in the Earthsea Cycle). She has been named a Grand Master by the Science Fiction Writers of America, and is the winner of five Hugos, six Nebulas, two World Fantasy Awards, and twenty Locus Awards. She's also a winner of the Newbery Honor, the National Book Award, the PEN/Malamud Award, and was named a Living Legend by the Library of Congress.*

WHERE WAS HE? The floor was hard and slimy, the air black and stinking, and that was all there was. Except a headache. Lying flat on the clammy floor Festin moaned, and then said, "Staff!" When his alderwood wizard's staff did not come to his hand, he knew he was in peril. He sat up, and not having his staff with which to make a proper light, he struck a spark between finger and thumb, muttering a certain Word. A blue will o' the wisp sprang from the spark and rolled feebly through the air, sputtering. "Up," said Festin, and the fireball wobbled upward till it lit a vaulted trapdoor very high above, so high that Festin projecting into the fireball momentarily saw his own face forty feet below as a pale dot in the darkness. The light struck no reflections in the damp walls; they had been woven out of night, by magic. He rejoined himself and said, "Out." The ball expired. Festin sat in the dark, cracking his knuckles.

He must have been overspelled from behind, by surprise; for the last memory he had was of walking through his own woods at evening talking with the trees. Lately, in these lone years in the middle of his life, he had been burdened with a sense of waste, of unspent strength; so, needing to learn patience, he had left the villages and gone to converse with trees, especially oaks, chestnuts, and the grey alders whose roots are in profound communication with running water. It had been six months since he had spoken to a human being. He had been busy with essentials, casting no spells and bothering no one. So who had spellbound him and shut him in this reeking well? "Who?" he demanded of the walls, and slowly a name gathered on them and ran down to him like a thick black drop sweated out from pores of stone and spores of fungus: "Voll."

For a moment Festin was in a cold sweat himself.

He had heard first long ago of Voll the Fell, who was said to be more than wizard yet less than man; who passed from island to island of the Outer Reach, undoing the works of the Ancients, enslaving men, cutting forests and spoiling fields, and sealing in underground tombs any wizard or Mage who tried to combat him.

Refugees from ruined islands told always the same tale, that he came at evening on a dark wind over the sea. His slaves followed in ships; these they had seen. But none of them had ever seen Voll... There were many men and creatures of evil will among the islands, and Festin, a young warlock intent on his training, had not paid much heed to these tales of Voll the Fell. "I can protect this island," he had thought, knowing his un-tried power, and had returned to his oaks and alders, the sound of wind in their leaves, the rhythm of growth in their round trunks and limbs and twigs, the taste of sunlight on leaves or dark groundwater around roots.—Where were they now, the trees, his old companions? Had Voll destroyed the forest?

Awake at last and up on his feet, Festin made two broad motions with rigid hands, shouting aloud a Name that would burst all locks and break open any man-made door. But these walls impregnated with night and the name of their builder did not heed, did not hear. The name re-echoed back, clapping in Festin's ears so that he fell on his knees, hiding his head in his arms till the echoes died away in the vaults above him. Then, still shaken by the backfire, he sat brooding.

They were right; Voll was strong. Here on his own ground, within this spell-built dungeon, his magic would withstand any direct attack; and Festin's strength was halved by the loss of his staff. But not even his captor could take from him his powers, relative only to himself, of Projecting and Transforming. So, after rubbing his now doubly aching head, he transformed. Quietly his body melted away into a cloud of fine mist.

Lazy, trailing, the mist rose off the floor, drifting up along the slimy walls until it found, where vault met wall, a hairline crack. Through this, droplet by droplet, it seeped. It was almost all through the crack when a hot wind, hot as a furnace-blast, struck at it, scattering the mist-drops, drying them. Hurriedly the mist sucked itself back into the vault, spiraled to the floor, took on Festin's own form and lay there panting. Transformation is an emotional strain to introverted warlocks of Festin's sort; when to that strain is added the shock of facing unhuman death in one's assumed shape, the experience becomes horrible. Festin lay for a while merely breathing. He was also angry with himself. It had been a pretty simpleminded notion to escape as a mist, after all. Every fool knew that trick. Volt had probably just left a hot wind waiting. Festin gathered himself into a small black bat, flew up to the ceiling, retransformed into a thin stream of plain air, and seeped through the crack.

This time he got clear out and was blowing softly down the hall in which he found himself towards a window, when a sharp sense of peril made him pull together, snapping himself into the first small, coherent shape that came to mind—a gold ring. It was just as well. The hurricane of arctic air that would have dispersed his air-form in unrecallable chaos merely chilled his ring-form slightly. As the storm passed he lay on the marble pavement, wondering which form might get out the window quickest.

Too late, he began to roll away. An enormous blank-faced troll strode cataclysmically across the floor, stopped, caught the quick-rolling ring and picked it up in a huge limestone-like hand. The troll strode to the trapdoor, lifted it by an iron handle and a muttered charm, and dropped Festin down into the darkness. He fell straight for forty feet and landed on the stone floor—clink.

Resuming his true form he sat up, ruefully rubbing a bruised elbow. Enough of this transformation on an empty stomach. He longed bitterly for his staff, with which he could have summoned up any amount of dinner. Without it, though he could change his own form and exert certain spells and powers, he could not transform or summon to him any material thing—neither lightning nor a lamb chop.

"Patience," Festin told himself, and when he had got his breath he dissolved his body into the infinite delicacy of volatile oils, becoming the aroma of a frying lamb chop. He drifted once more through the crack. The waiting troll sniffed suspiciously, but already Festin had regrouped himself into a falcon, winging straight for the window. The troll lunged after him, missed by yards, and bellowed in a vast stony voice, "The hawk, get the hawk!" Swooping over the enchanted castle towards his forest that lay dark to westward, sunlight and sea-glare dazzling his eyes, Festin rode the wind like an arrow. But a quicker arrow found him. Crying out, he fell. Sun and sea and towers spun around him and went out.

He woke again on the dank floor of the dungeon, hands and hair and lips wet with his own blood. The arrow had struck his pinion as a falcon, his shoulder as a man. Lying still, he mumbled a spell to close the wound. Presently he was able to sit up, and recollect a longer, deeper spell of healing. But he had lost a good deal of blood, and with it, power. A chill had settled in the marrow of his bones which even the healing-spell could not warm. There was darkness in his eyes, even when he struck a will o' the wisp and lit the reeking air: the same dark mist he had seen, as he flew, overhanging his forest and the little towns of his land.

It was up to him to protect that land.

He could not attempt direct escape again. He was too weak and tired. Trusting his power too much, he had lost his strength. Now whatever shape he took would share his weakness, and be trapped.

Shivering with cold, he crouched there, letting the fireball sputter out with a last whiff of methane—marsh gas. The smell brought to his mind's eye the marshes stretching from the forest wall down to the sea, his beloved marshes where no men came, where in fall the swans flew long and level, where between still pools and reed-islands the quick, silent, seaward streamlets ran. Oh, to be a fish in one of those streams; or better yet to be farther upstream, near the springs, in the forest in the shadow of the trees, in the clear brown backwater under an alder's roots, resting hidden...

This was a great magic. Festin had no more performed it than has any man who in exile or danger longs for the earth and waters of his home, seeing and yearning over the doorsill of his house, the table where he has eaten, the branches outside the window of the room where he has slept. Only in dreams do any but the great Mages realize this magic of going home. But Festin, with the cold creeping out from his marrow into nerves and veins, stood up between the black walls, gathered his will together till it shone like a candle in the darkness of his flesh, and began to work the great and silent magic.

The walls were gone. He was in the earth, rocks and veins of granite for bones, groundwater for blood, the roots of things for nerves. Like a blind worm he moved through the earth westward, slowly, darkness before and behind. Then all at once coolness flowed along his back and belly, a buoyant, unresisting, inexhaustible caress. With his sides he tasted the water, felt current-flow; and with lidless eyes he saw before him the deep brown pool between the great buttress-roots of an alder. He darted forward, silvery, into shadow. He had got free. He was home.

The water ran timelessly from its clear spring. He lay on the sand of the pool's bottom letting running water, stronger than any spell of healing, soothe his wound and with its coolness wash away the bleaker cold that had entered him. But as he rested he felt and heard a shaking and trampling in the earth. Who walked now in his forest? Too weary to try to change form, he hid his gleaming trout-body under the arch of the alder root, and waited.

Huge grey fingers groped in the water, roiling the sand. In the dimness above water vague faces, blank eyes loomed and vanished, reappeared. Nets and hands groped, missed, missed again, then caught and lifted him writhing up into the air. He struggled to take back his own shape and could not; his own spell of homecoming bound him. He writhed in the net, gasping in the dry, bright, terrible air, drowning. The agony went on, and he knew nothing beyond it.

After a long time and little by little he became aware that he was in his human form again; some sharp, sour liquid was being forced down his throat. Time lapsed again, and he found himself sprawled face down on the dank floor of the vault. He was back in the power of his enemy. And, though he could breathe again, he was not very far from death.

The chill was all through him now; and the trolls, Voll's servants, must have crushed the fragile trout-body, for when he moved, his ribcage and one forearm stabbed with pain. Broken and without strength, he lay at the bottom of the well of night. There was no power in him to change shape; there was no way out, but one.

Lying there motionless, almost but not quite beyond the reach of pain, Festin thought: Why has he not killed me? Why does he keep me here alive?

Why has he never been seen? With what eyes can he be seen, on what ground does he walk?

He fears me, though I have no strength left.

They say that all the wizards and men of power whom he has defeated live on sealed in tombs like this, live on year after year trying to get free....

But if one chose not to live?

So Festin made his choice. His last thought was, If I am wrong, men will think I was a coward. But he did not linger on this thought. Turning his head a little to the side he closed his eyes, took a last deep breath, and whispered the word of unbinding, which is only spoken once.

This was not transformation. He was not changed. His body, the long legs and arms, the clever hands, the eyes that had liked to look on trees and streams, lay unchanged, only still, perfectly still and full of cold. But the walls were gone. The vaults built by magic were gone, and the rooms and towers; and the forest, and the sea, and the sky of evening. They were all gone, and Festin went slowly down the far slope of the hill of being, under new stars.

In life he had had great power; so here he did not forget. Like a candle flame he moved in the darkness of the wider land. And remembering he called out his enemy's name: "Voll!"

Called, unable to withstand, Voll came towards him, a thick pale shape in the starlight. Festin approached, and the other cowered and screamed as if burnt. Festin followed when he fled, followed him close. A long way they went, over dry lava-flows from the great extinct volcanoes rearing their cones against the unnamed stars, across the spurs of silent hills, through valleys of short black grass, past towns or down their unlit streets between houses through whose windows no face looked. The stars hung in the sky; none set, none rose. There was no change here. No day would come. But they went on, Festin always driving the other before him, till they reached a place where once a river had run, very long ago: a river from the living lands. In the dry streambed, among boulders, a dead body lay: that of an old man, naked, flat eyes staring at the stars that are innocent of death.

"Enter it," Festin said. The Voll-shadow whimpered, but Festin came closer. Voll cowered away, stooped, and entered in the open mouth of his own dead body.

At once the corpse vanished. Unmarked, stainless, the dry boulders gleamed in starlight. Festin stood still awhile, then slowly sat down among the great rocks to rest. To rest, not sleep; for he must keep guard here until Voll's body, sent back to its grave, had turned to dust, all evil power gone, scattered by the wind and washed seaward by the rain. He must keep watch over this place where once death had found a way back into the other land. Patient now, infinitely patient, Festin waited among the rocks where no river would ever run again, in the heart of the country which has no seacoast. The stars stood still above him; and as he watched them, slowly, very slowly he began to forget the voice of streams and the sound of rain on the leaves of the forests of life.

The Burning Man
Tad Williams

Tad Williams *is the bestselling author of the* Memory, Sorrow & Thorn *series, the* Otherland *series, and the* Shadowmarch *series. He has also written several other novels, such as* Tailchaser's Song, The War of the Flowers, *and* The Dragons of Ordinary Farm, *which was co-written with his wife, Deborah Beale. His short fiction has appeared in such venues as* Weird Tales, The Magazine of Fantasy & Science Fiction, *and in the anthologies* Legends *and* Legends II. *A collection of his short work,* Rite, *was released in 2006. He has also written for D.C. Comics, first with the miniseries* The Next, *and then doing a stint on* Aquaman.

YEARS AND YEARS LATER, I still start up in the deepest part of night with his agonized face before me. And always, in these terrible dreams, I am helpless to ease his suffering.

I will tell the tale then, in hope the last ghosts may be put to rest, if such a thing can even happen in this place where there are more ghosts than living souls. But you will have to listen closely—this is a tale that the teller herself does not fully understand.

I will tell you of Lord Sulis, my famous stepfather.

I will tell you what the witch foretold to me.

I will tell you of the love that I had and I lost.

I will tell you of the night I saw the burning man.

Tellarin gifted me with small things, but they were not small to me. My lover brought me sweetmeats, and laughed to see me eat them so greedily.

"Ah, little Breda," he told me, "it is strange and wonderful that a mere soldier should have to smuggle honeyed figs to a king's daughter." And then he kissed me, put his rough face against me and kissed me, and that was a sweeter thing than any fig that God ever made.

But Sulis was not truly a king, nor was I his true daughter.

Tellarin was not wrong about everything. The gladness I felt when I saw my soldier or heard him whistling below the window was strange and wonderful indeed.

My true father, the man from whose loins I sprang, died in the cold waters of the Kingslake when I was very small. His companions said that a great pikefish became caught in the nets and dragged my father Ricwald to a drowning death, but others whispered that it was his companions themselves who murdered him, then weighted his body with stones.

Everyone knew that my father would have been gifted with the standard and spear of Great Thane when all the thanes of the Lake People next met. His father and uncle had both been Great Thane before him, so some whispered that God had struck down my poor father because one family should not hold power so long. Others believed that my father's companions on the boat had simply been paid shame-gold to drown him, to satisfy the ambition of one of the other families.

I know these things only from my mother Cynethrith's stories. She was young when my father died, and had two small children—me, not yet five years old, and my brother Aelfric, two years my elder. Together we went to live in the house of my father's father because we were the last of his line, and among the Lake People of Erkynland it was blood of high renown. But it was not a happy house. Godric, my grandfather, had himself been Great Thane for twice ten years before illness ended his rule, and he had high hopes that my father would follow him, but after my father died, Godric had to watch a man from one of the other families chosen to carry the spear and standard instead. From that moment, everything that happened in the world only seemed to prove to my grandfather that the best days of Erkynland and the Lake People had passed.

Godric died before I reached seven years, but he made those years between my father's death and his own very unhappy ones for my mother, with many complaints and sharp rebukes at how she managed the household and how she raised Aelfric and me, his dead son's only children. My grandfather spent much time with Aelfric, trying to make him the kind of man who would bring the spear and standard back to our family, but my brother was small and timid—it must have been clear he would never rule more than his own household. This Godric blamed on my mother, saying she had taught the boy womanish ways.

Grandfather was less interested in me. He was never cruel to me, only fierce and short-spoken, but he was such a frightening figure, with bristling white beard, growling voice, and several missing fingers, that I could never do anything but shrink from him. If that was another reason he found little savor in life, then I am sorry for it now.

In any case, my mother's widowhood was a sad, bitter time for her. From mistress of her own house, and wife of the Great Thane, she now became only one of three grown daughters in the house of a sour old man, for one of my father's sisters had also lost her husband, and the youngest had been kept at home, unmarried, to care for her father in his dotage.

I believe that had even the humblest of fishermen courted my mother, she would have looked upon him kindly, as long as he had a house of his own and no living relatives. But instead a man who has made the entire age tremble came to call.

"What is he like?" Tellarin once asked me. "Tell me about your stepfather."

"He is your lord and commander," I smiled. "What can I tell you that you do not know?"

"Tell me what he says when he is in his house, at his table, what he does." Tellarin looked at me then, his long face suddenly boyish and surprised. "Hah! It feels like sacrilege even to wonder!"

"He is just a man," I told him, and rolled my eyes. Such silly things men feel about other men—that this one is so large and important, while they themselves are so small! "He eats, he sleeps, he breaks wind. When my mother was alive, she used to say that he took up more room in a bed than any three others might, because he thrashed so, and talked aloud in his sleep." I made my stepfather sound ordinary on purpose, because I did not like it when Tellarin seemed as interested in him as he was in me.

My Nabbanai soldier became serious then. "How it must have grieved him when your mother died. He must have loved her very much."

As if it had not grieved me! I resisted the temptation to roll my eyes again, and instead told him, with all the certainty of youth, "I do not think he loved her at all."

My mother once said that when my stepfather and his household first appeared across the meadowlands, riding north toward the Kingslake, it was as though the heavenly host itself had descended to earth. Trumpets heralded their approach, drawing people from every town as though to witness a pilgrimage passing, or the procession of a saint's relic. The knights' armor and lances were polished to a sparkle, and their lord's heron crest gleamed in gold thread on all the tall banners. Even the horses of the Nabban-men were larger and prouder than our poor Erkylandish ponies. The small army was followed by sheep and cattle in herds, and by dozens and dozens of wagons and oxcarts, a train so vast that their rutted path is still visible on the face of the land three score years later.

I was a child, though, and saw none of it—not then. Within my grandfather's hall, I heard only rumors, things whispered by my aunts and my mother over their sewing. The powerful lord who had come was a Nabbanai nobleman, they reported, called by many Sulis the Apostate. He claimed that he came in peace, and wanted only to make a home for himself here beside the Kingslake. He was an exile from his own country—a heretic, some claimed, driven forth by the Lector under threat of excommunication because of his impertinent questions about the life of Usires Aedon, our blessed Ransomer. No, he had been forced from his home by the conniving of the escritors, said others. Angering a churchman is like treading on a serpent, they said.

Mother Church still had an unsolid grip on Erkynland in those days, and even though most had been baptized into the Aedonite faith, very few of the Lake People trusted the Sancellan Aedonitis. Many called it "that hive of priests," and said that its chief aim was not God's work, but increasing its own power.

Many still think so, but they no longer speak ill of the church where strangers can hear them.

I know far more of these things today than I did when they happened. I understand much and much, now that I am old and everyone in my story is dead. Of course, I am not the first to have traveled this particular sad path. Understanding always comes too late, I think.

Lord Sulis had indeed fallen out with the church, and in Nabban the church and the state were so closely tied, he had made an enemy of the Imperator in the Sancellan Mahistrevis as well, but so powerful and important was the family of my stepfather-to-be that he was not imprisoned or executed, but instead strongly encouraged to leave Nabban. His countrymen thought he took his household to Erkynland because any nobleman could be king in that backward country—my country—but Sulis had his own reasons, darker and stranger than anyone could guess. So it was that he had brought his entire household, his knights and kerns and all their women and children, a small city's worth of folk, to the shores of the Kingslake.

For all the sharpness of their swords and strength of their armor, the Nabbanai treated the Lake People with surprising courtesy, and for the first weeks there was trade and much good fellowship between their camp and our towns. It was only when Lord Sulis announced to the thanes of the Lake People that he meant to settle in the High Keep, the deserted castle on the headlands, that the Erkynlanders became uneasy.

Huge and empty, the domain only of wind and shadows, the High Keep had looked down on our lands since the beginnings of the oldest tales. No one remembered who had built it—some said giants, but some swore the fairy-folk had built it themselves. The Northmen from Rimmersgard were said to have held it for a while, but they were long gone, driven out by a dragon from the fortress the Rimmersmen had stolen from the Peaceful Ones. So many tales surrounded that castle! When I was small, one of my mother's bondwomen told me that it was now the haunt of frost-witches and restless ghosts. Many a night I had thought of it standing deserted on the windy clifftop, only a half-day's ride away, and frightened myself so that I could not sleep.

The idea of someone rebuilding the ruined fortress made the thanes uneasy, but not only for fear of waking its spirits. The High Keep held a powerful position, perhaps an impregnable one—even in their crumbling condition, the walls would be almost impossible to storm if armed men held them. But the thanes were in a difficult spot. Though the men of the Lake People might outnumber those of Sulis, the heron knights were better armed, and the discipline of Nabbanai fighting men was well-known—a half-legion of the Imperator's Sea Wolves had slaughtered ten times that number of Thrithings-men in a battle just a few years before. And Osweard, the new Great Thane, was young and untested as a war leader. The lesser thanes asked my grandfather Godric to lend his wisdom, to speak to this Nabbanai lord and see what he could grasp of the man's true intention.

So it was that Lord Sulis came to my grandfather's steading, and saw my mother for the first time.

When I was a little girl, I liked to believe that Sulis fell in love with my mother Cynethrith the moment he saw her, as she stood quietly behind her father-in-law's chair in Godric's great hall. She was beautiful, that I know—before my father died, all the people of the household used to call her Ricwald's Swan, because of her long neck and white shoulders. Her hair was a pale, pale gold, her eyes as green as the summer Kingslake. Any ordinary man would have loved her on sight. But "ordinary" must be the least likely of all the words that could be used to describe my stepfather.

When I was a young woman, and falling in love myself for the first time, I knew for certain that Sulis could not have loved her. How could anyone who loved have been as cold and distant as he was? As heavily polite? Aching then at the mere thought of Tellarin, my secret beloved, I knew that a man who acted as my stepfather had acted toward my mother could not feel anything like love.

Now I am not so sure. So many things are different when I look at them now. In this extremity of age, I am farther away, as though I looked at my own life from a high hilltop, but in some ways it seems I see things much more closely.

Sulis was a clever man, and could not have failed to notice how my grandfather Godric hated the new Great Thane—it was in everything my grandfather said. He could not speak of the weather without mentioning how the summers had been warmer and the winters shorter in the days when he himself had been Great Thane, and had his son been allowed to succeed him, he as much as declared, every day would have been the first day of Maia-month. Seeing this, Sulis made compact with the bitter old man, first by the gifts and subtle compliments he gave him, but soon in the courting of Godric's daughter-in-law as well.

While my grandfather became more and more impressed by this foreign nobleman's good sense, Sulis made his master stroke. Not only did he offer a bride price for my mother—for a widow!—that was greater than would have been paid even for the virgin daughter of a ruling Great Thane, a sizeable fortune of swords and proud Nabban horses and gold plate, but Sulis told Godric that he would even leave my brother and myself to be raised in our grandfather's house.

Godric had still not given up all hope of Aelfric, and this idea delighted him, but he had no particular use for me. My mother would be happier, both men eventually decided, if she were allowed to bring at least one of her children to her new home on the headlands.

Thus it was settled, and the powerful foreign lord married into the household of the old Great Thane. Godric told the rest of the thanes that Sulis meant only good, that by this gesture he had proved his honest wish to live in peace with the Lake People. There were priests in Sulis' company who would cleanse the High Keep of any unquiet spirits, Godric explained to the thanes—as Sulis himself had assured my grandfather—and thus, he argued, letting Sulis take the ancient keep for his own would bring our folk a double blessing.

What Osweard and the lesser thanes thought of this, I do not know. Faced with Godric's enthusiasm, with the power of the Nabbanai lord, and perhaps even with their own secret shame in the matter of my father's death, they chose to give in. Lord Sulis and his new bride were gifted with the deserted High Keep, with its broken walls and its ghosts.

Did my mother love her second husband? I cannot answer that any better than I can say what Sulis felt, and they are both so long dead that I am now the only living person who knew them both. When she first saw him in the doorway at Godric's house, he would certainly have been the light of every eye. He was not young—like my mother, he had already lost a spouse, although a decade had passed since his widowing, while hers was still fresh—but he was a great man from the greatest city of all. He wore a mantle of pure white over his armor, held at the shoulder by a lapis badge of his family's heron crest. He had tucked his helmet under his arm when he entered the hall and my mother could see that he had very little hair, only a fringe of curls at the back of his head and over his ears, so that his forehead gleamed in the firelight. He was tall and strongly made, his unwhiskered jaw square, his nose wide and prominent. His strong, heavy features had a deep and contemplative look, but also a trace of sadness—almost, my mother once told me, the sort of face she thought God Himself might show on the Day of Weighing-Out.

He frightened her and he excited her—both of these things I know from the way she spoke of that first meeting. But did she love him, then or in the days to come? I cannot say. Does it matter? So many years later, it is hard to believe that it does.

Her time in her father-in-law's house had been hard, though. Whatever her deepest feelings about him, I do not doubt that she was happy to wed Sulis.

In the month that my mother died, when I was in my thirteenth year, she told me that she believed Sulis had been afraid to love her. She never explained this—she was in her final weakness, and it was difficult for her to speak—and I still do not know what she meant.

The next to the last thing she ever said to me made even less sense. When the weakness in her chest was so terrible that she would lose the strength to breathe for long moments, she still summoned the strength to declare, "I am a ghost."

She may have spoken of her suffering—that she felt she only clung to the world, like a timid spirit that will not take the road to Heaven, but lingers ever near the places it knew. Certainly her last request made it clear that she had grown weary of the circles of this world. But I have wondered since if there might be some other meaning to her words. Did she mean that her own life after my father's death had been nothing more than a ghost-life? Or did she perhaps intend to say that she had become a shade in her own house, something that waited in the dark, haunted corridors of the High Keep for her second husband's regard to give it true life—a regard that would never come from that silent, secret-burdened man?

My poor mother. Our poor, haunted family!

I remember little of the first year of my mother's marriage to Lord Sulis, but I cannot forget the day we took possession of our new home. Others had gone before us to make our arrival as easeful as possible—I know they had, because a great tent had already been erected on the green in the Inner Bailey, which was where we slept for the first months—but to the child I was, it seemed we were riding into a place where no mortals had ever gone. I expected witches or ogres around every corner.

We came up the cliff road beside the Kingslake until we reached the curtain wall and began to circle the castle itself. Those who had gone before had hacked a crude road in the shadow of the walls, so we had a much easier passage than we would have only days before. We rode in a tunnel cut between the wall and forest. Where the trees and brush had not been chopped away, the Kingswood grew right to the castle's edge, striving with root and tendril to breach the great stones of the wall.

At the castle's northern gate we found nothing but a cleared place on the hillside, a desolation of tree stumps and burn-blackened grass—the thriving town of Erkynchester that today sprawls all around the castle's feet had not even been imagined. Not all the forest growth had been cleared. Vines still clung to the pillars of the shattered gatehouse, rooted in the cracks of the odd, shiny stone which was all that remained of the original gateway, hanging in great braids across the opening to make a tangled, living arbor.

"Do you see?" Lord Sulis spread his strong arms as if he had designed and crafted the wilderness himself. "We will make our home in the greatest and oldest of all houses."

As he led her across that threshold and into the ruins of the ancient castle, my mother made the sign of the Tree upon her breast.

I know many things now that I did not know on the first day we came to the High Keep. Of all the many tales about the place, some I now can say are false, but others I am now certain are true. For one thing, there is no question that the Northmen lived here. Over the years I have found many of their coins, struck with a crude "F" rune of their King Fingil, and they also left the rotted remains of their wooden longhouses in the Outer Bailey, which my stepfather's workmen found during the course of other diggings. So I came to realize that if the story of the Northmen living here was a true one, it stood to reason that the legend of the dragon might also be true, as well as the terrible tale of how the Northmen slaughtered the castle's immortal inhabitants.

But I did not need such workaday proofs as coins or ruins to show me that our home was full of unquiet ghosts. That I learned for myself beyond all dispute, on the night I saw the burning man.

Perhaps someone who had grown up in Nabban or one of the other large cities of the south would not have been so astonished by their first sight of the High Keep, but I was a child of the Lake People. Before that day, the largest building I had ever approached was the great hall of our town where the thanes met every spring—a building that could easily have been hidden in any of several parts of the High Keep and then never discovered again. On that first day, it was clear to me that the mighty castle could only have been built by giants.

The curtain wall was impressive enough to a small girl—ten times my own height and made of huge, rough stones that I could not imagine being hauled into place by anything smaller than the grandest of ogres—but the inner walls, in the places where they still stood, were not just vast but also beautiful. They were shaped of shining white stone which had been polished like jewelry, the blocks of equal size to those of the outer wall but with every join so seamless that from a distance each wall appeared to be a single thing, a curving piece of ivory or bone erupting from the hillside.

Many of the keep's original buildings had been burned or torn down, some so that the men from Rimmersgard could pillage the stones to build their own tower, squat as a barrel but very tall. In any other place the Northmen's huge construction would have loomed over the whole landscape and would certainly have been the focus of my amazement. But in any other place, there would not have been the Angel Tower.

I did not know its name then—in fact, it had no name, since the shape at its very peak could scarcely be seen—but the moment I saw it I knew there could be nothing else like it on earth, and for once childish exaggeration was correct. Its entrance was blocked by piles of rubble the Northmen had never finished clearing, and much of the lower part of its facade had cracked and fallen away in some unimaginable cataclysm, so that its base was raw stone, but it still thrust into the sky like a great white fang, taller than any tree, taller than anything mortals have ever built.

Excited but also frightened, I asked my mother whether the tower might not fall down on us. She tried to reassure me, saying it had stood for a longer time than I could imagine, perhaps since before there had even been people living beside the Kingslake, but that only made me feel other, stranger things.

The last words my mother ever spoke to me were, "Bring me a dragon's claw."

I thought at first that in the final hours of her illness she was wandering in her thoughts back to our early days at the castle.

The story of the High Keep's dragon, the creature who had driven out the last of the Northmen, was so old it had lost much of its power to frighten, but it was still potent to a little girl. The men of my stepfather's company used to bring me bits of polished stone—I learned after a while that they were shards of crumbled wall-carvings from the oldest parts of the castle—and tell me, "See, here is a broken piece of the great red dragon's claw. He lives down in the caves below the castle, but sometimes at night he comes up to sniff around. He is sniffing for little girls to eat!"

The first few times, I believed them. Then, as I grew older and less susceptible, I learned to scorn the very idea of the dragon. Now that I am an old woman, I am plagued by dreams of it again. Sometimes even when I am awake, I think I can sense it down in the darkness below the castle, feel the moments of restlessness that trouble its long, deep sleep.

So on that night long ago, when my dying mother told me to bring her a dragon's claw, I thought she was remembering something from our first year in the castle. I was about to go look for one of the old stones, but her bondwoman Ulca—what the Nabbanai called her handmaiden or body servant—told me that was not what my mother wanted. A dragon's claw, she explained to me, was a charm to help those who suffered find the ease of a swift death. Ulca had tears in her eyes, and I think she was Aedonite enough to be troubled by the idea, but she was a sensible young woman and did not waste time arguing the right or wrong of it. She told me that the only way I could get such a thing swiftly would be from a woman named Xanippa who lived in the settlement that had sprung up just outside the High Keep's walls.

I was barely into womanhood, but I felt very much a child. The idea of even such a short journey outside the walls after dark frightened me, but my mother had asked, and to refuse a deathbed request was a sin long before Mother Church arrived to parcel up and name the rights and wrongs of life. I left Ulca at my mother's side and hurried across the rainy, nightbound castle.

The woman Xanippa had once been a whore, but as she had become older and fatter she had decided she needed another profession, and had developed a name as a herbwife. Her tumbledown hut, which stood against the keep's southeast curtain wall, overlooking the Kingswood, was full of smoke and bad smells. Xanippa had hair like a bird's nest, tied with what had once been a pretty ribbon. Her face might have been round and comely once, but years and fat had turned it into something that looked as though it had been brought up in a fishing net. She was also so large she did not move from her stool by the fire during the time I was there— or on most other occasions, I guessed.

Xanippa was very suspicious of me at first, but when she found out who I was and what I wanted, and saw my face as proof, she accepted the three small coins I gave her and gestured for me to fetch her splintered wooden chest from the fireplace corner. Like its mistress, the chest had clearly once been in better condition and more prettily painted. She set it on the curve of her belly and began to search through it with a painstaking care that seemed at odds with everything else about her.

"Ah, here," she said at last. "Dragon's claw." She held out her hand to show me the curved, black thing. It was certainly a claw, but far too small to belong to any dragon I could imagine. Xanippa saw my hesitation. "It is an owl's toe, you silly girl. 'Dragon's claw' is just a name." She pointed to a tiny ball of glass over the talon's tip. "Do not pull that off or break it. In fact, do not touch it at all. Do you have a purse?"

I showed her the small bag that hung always on a cord around my neck. Xanippa frowned. "The cloth is very thin." She found some rags in one of the pockets of her shapeless robe and wrapped the claw, then dropped it into my purse and tucked it back in my bodice. As she did so, she squeezed my breast so hard that I murmured in pain, then patted my head. "Merciful Rhiap," she growled, "was I ever so young as this? In any case, be careful, my little sweetmeat. This is heartsbane on the tip of this claw, from the marshes of the Wran. If you are careless, this is one prick that will make sure you die a virgin." She laughed. "You don't want that, do you?"

I backed to the door. Xanippa grinned to see my fright. "And you had better give your stepfather a message from me. He will not find what he seeks among the womenfolk here or among the herbwives of the Lake People. Tell him he can believe me, because if I could solve his riddle, I would—and, oh, but I would make him pay dearly for it! No, he will have to find the Witch of the Forest and put his questions to her."

She was laughing again as I got the door open at last and escaped. The rain was even stronger now, and I slipped and fell several times, but still ran all the way back to the Inner Bailey.

When I reached my mother's bed, the priest had already come and gone, as had my stepfather, who Ulca told me had never spoken a word. My mother had died only a short time after I left on my errand. I had failed her—had left her to suffer and die with no family beside her. The shame and sorrow burned so badly that I could not imagine the pain would ever go away. As the other women prepared her for burial, I could do nothing but weep. The dragon's claw dangled next to my heart, all but forgotten.

I spent weeks wandering the castle, lost and miserable. I only remembered the message Xanippa had given me when my mother had been dead and buried almost a month.

I found my stepfather on the wall overlooking the Kingslake, and told him what Xanippa had said. He did not ask me how I came to be carrying messages for such a woman. He did not even signify he had heard me. His eyes were fixed on something in the far distance—on the boats of the fisher-folk, perhaps, dim in the fog.

The first years in the ruined High Keep were hard ones, and not just for my mother and me. Lord Sulis had to oversee the rebuilding, a vast and endlessly complicated task, as well as keep up the spirits of his own people through the first bleak winter.

It is one thing for soldiers, in the initial flush of loyal indignity, to swear they will follow their wronged commander anywhere. It is another thing entirely when that commander comes to a halt, when following becomes true exile. As the Nabbanai troops came to understand that this cold backwater of Erkynland was to be their home forever, problems began— drinking and fighting among the soldiers, and even more unhappy incidents between Sulis' men and the local people...my people, although it was hard for me to remember that sometimes. After my mother died, I sometimes felt as if I were the true exile, surrounded by Nabbanai names and faces and speech even in the middle of my own land.

If we did not enjoy that first winter, we survived it, and continued as we had begun, a household of the dispossessed. But if ever a man was born to endure that state, it was my stepfather.

When I see him now in my memory, when I picture again that great heavy brow and that stern face, I think of him as an island, standing by himself on the far side of dangerous waters, near but forever unvisited. I was too young and too shy to try to shout across the gulf that separated us, but it scarcely mattered—Sulis did not seem like a man who regretted his own solitude. In the middle of a crowded room his eyes were always on the walls instead of the people, as though he could see through stone to some better place. Even in his happiest and most festive moods, I seldom heard him laugh, and his swift, distracted smiles suggested that the jokes he liked best could never truly be explained to anyone else.

He was not a bad man, or even a difficult man, as my grandfather Godric had been, but when I saw the immense loyalty of his soldiers it was sometimes hard for me to understand it. Tellarin said that when he had joined Avalles' company, the others had told him of how Lord Sulis had once carried two of his wounded bondmen from the field, one trip for each, through a storm of Thrithings arrows. If that is true, it is easy to understand why his men loved him, but there were few opportunities for such obvious sorts of bravery in the High Keep's echoing halls.

While I was still young, Sulis would pat me on the head when we met, or ask me questions that were meant to show a paternal interest, but which often betrayed an uncertainty as to how old I was and what I liked to do. When I began to grow a womanish form, he became even more correct and formal, and would offer compliments on my clothes or my stitchery in the same studied way that he greeted the High Keep's tenants at Aedonmansa, when he called each man by his name—learned from the seneschal's accounting books—as he filed past, and wished each a good year.

Sulis grew even more distant in the year after my mother died, as though losing her had finally untethered him from the daily tasks he had always performed in such a stiff, practiced way. He spent less and less time seeing to the matters of government, and instead sat reading for hours—sometimes all through the night, wrapped in heavy robes against the midnight chill, burning candles faster than the rest of the house put together.

The books that had come with him from his family's great house in Nabban were mostly tomes of religious instruction, but also some military and other histories. He occasionally allowed me to look at one, but although I was learning, I still read only slowly, and could make little of the odd names and devices in the accounts of battle. Sulis had other books that he would never even let me glance at, plainbound volumes that he kept locked in wooden boxes. The first time I ever saw one go back into its chest, I found the memory returning to me for days afterward. What sort of books were they, I wondered, that must be kept sealed away?

One of the locked boxes contained his own writings, but I did not find that out for two more years, until the night of Black Fire was almost upon us.

It was in the season after my mother's death, on a day when I found him reading in the gray light that streamed into the throne room, that Lord Sulis truly looked at me for the one and only time I remember.

When I shyly asked what he was doing, he allowed me to examine the book in his lap, a beautiful illuminated history of the prophet Varris with the heron of Honsa Sulis worked in gilt on the binding. I traced with my finger an illustration of Varris being martyred on the wheel. "Poor, poor man," I said. "How he must have suffered. And all because he stayed true to his God. The Lord must have given him sweet welcome to Heaven."

The picture of Varris in his agony jumped a little—I had startled my stepfather into a flinch. I looked up to find him gazing at me intently, his brown eyes so wide with feelings I could not recognize that for a moment I was terrified that he would strike me. He lifted his huge, broad hand, but gently. He touched my hair, then curled the hand into a fist, never once shifting that burning stare from me.

"They have taken everything from me, Breda." His voice was tight-clenched with a pain I could not begin to understand. "But I will never bend my back. Never."

I held my breath, uncertain and still a little frightened. A moment later my stepfather recovered himself. He brought his fist to his mouth and pretended to cough—he was the least able dissembler I have ever known—and then bade me let him finish his reading while the light still held. To this day I do not know who he believed had taken everything from him—the Imperator and his court in Nabban? The priests of Mother Church? Or perhaps even God and His army of angels?

What I do know was that he tried to tell me of what burned inside him, but could not find the words. What I also know is that at least for that moment, my heart ached for the man.

My Tellarin asked me once, "How could it be possible that no other man has made you his own? You are beautiful, and the daughter of a king."

But as I have said before, Lord Sulis was not my father, nor was he king. And the evidence of the mirror that had once been my mother's suggested that my soldier overspoke my comeliness as well. Where my mother had been fair and full of light, I was dark. Where she was long of neck and limb and ample of hip, I was made small, like a young boy. I have never taken up much space on the earth—nor will I below it, for that matter. Wherever my grave is made, the digging will not shift much soil.

But Tellarin spoke with the words of love, and love is a kind of spell which banishes all sense.

"How can you care for a rough man like me?" he asked me. "How can you love a man who can bring you no lands but the farm a soldier's pension can buy? Who can give your children no title of nobility?"

Because love does not do sums, I should have told him. Love makes choices, and then gives its all.

Had he seen himself as I first saw him, though, he could have had no questions.

It was an early spring day in my fifteenth year, and the sentries had seen the boats coming across the Kingslake at first light of morning. These were no ordinary fishing-craft, but barges loaded with more than a dozen men and their war-horses. Many of the castle folk had gathered to see the travelers come in and to learn their news.

After they had brought all their goods ashore on the lakefront, Tellarin and the rest of the company mounted and rode up the hill path and in through the main gates. The gates themselves had only lately been rebuilt—they were crude things of heavy, undressed timbers, but enough to serve in case of war. My stepfather had reason to be cautious, as the delegation that arrived that day was to prove.

It was actually Tellarin's friend Avalles who was called master of these men, because Avalles was an equestrian knight, one of the Sulean family nephews, but it was not hard to see which of the two truly held the soldiers' loyalty. My Tellarin was barely twenty years old on the first day I saw him. He was not handsome—his face was too long and his nose too impudent to grace one of the angels painted in my stepfather's books—but I thought him quite, quite beautiful. He had taken off his helmet to feel the morning sun as he rode, and his golden hair streamed in the wind off the lake. Even my inexperienced eye could see that he was still young for a fighting man, but I could also see that the men who rode with him admired him too.

His eyes found me in the crowd around my father and he smiled as though he recognized me, although we had never seen each other before. My blood went hot inside me, but I knew so little of the world, I did not recognize the fever of love.

My stepfather embraced Avalles, then allowed Tellarin and the others to kneel before him as each swore his fealty in turn, although I am sure Sulis wanted only to be finished with the ceremony so he could return to his books.

The company had been sent by my stepfather's family council in Nabban. A letter from the council, carried by Avalles, reported that there had been a resurgence of talk against Sulis in the imperatorial court at Nabban, much of it fanned by the Aedonite priests. A poor man who held odd, perhaps irreligious beliefs was one thing, the council wrote, but when the same beliefs belonged to a nobleman with money, land, and a famous name, many powerful people would consider him a threat. In fear for my stepfather's life, his family had thus sent this carefully picked troop and warnings to Sulis to be more cautious than ever.

Despite the company's grim purpose, news from home was always welcome, and many of the new troop had fought with other members of my stepfather's army. There were many glad reunions.

When Lord Sulis had at last been allowed to retreat to his reading, but before Ulca could hurry me back indoors, Tellarin asked Avalles if he could be introduced to me. Avalles himself was a dark, heavy-faced youth with a fledgling beard, only a few years Tellarin's elder, but with so much of the Sulean family's gravity in him that he seemed a sort of foolish old uncle. He gripped my hand too tightly and mumbled several clumsy compliments about how fair the flowers grew in the north, then introduced me to his friend.

Tellarin did not kiss my hand, but held me far more firmly with just his bright eyes. He said, "I will remember this day always, my lady," then bowed. Ulca caught my elbow and dragged me away.

Even in the midst of love's fever, which was to spread all through my fifteenth year, I could not help but notice that the changes which had begun in my stepfather when my mother died were growing worse.

Lord Sulis now hardly left his chambers at all, closeting himself with his books and his writings, being drawn out only to attend to the most pressing of affairs. His only regular conversations were with Father Ganaris, the plain-spoken military chaplain who was the sole priest to have accompanied Lord Sulis out of Nabban. Sulis had installed his old battle-field comrade in the castle's newly built chapel, and it was one of the few places the master of the High Keep would still go. His visits did not seem to bring the old chaplain much pleasure, though. Once I watched them bidding each other farewell, and as Sulis turned and shouldered his way through the wind, heading back across the courtyard to our residence, Ganaris sent a look after him that was grim and sad—the expression, I thought, of a man whose old friend has a mortal illness.

Perhaps if I had tried, I could have done something to help my stepfather. Perhaps there could have been some other path than the one that led us to the base of the tree that grows in darkness. But the truth is that although I saw all these signs, I gave them little attention. Tellarin, my soldier, had begun to court me—at first only with glances and greetings, later with small gifts—and all else in my life shrank to insignificance by comparison.

In fact, so changed was everything that a newer, larger sun might have risen into the sky above the High Keep, warming every corner with its light. Even the most workaday tasks took fresh meaning because of my feelings for bright-eyed Tellarin. My catechisms and my reading lessons I now pursued diligently, so that my beloved might not find me lacking in conversation...except on those days when I could scarcely attend to them at all for dreaming about him. My walks in the castle grounds became excuses to look for him, to hope for a shared glance across a courtyard or down a hallway. Even the folktales Ulca told me over our stitchery, which before had been only a means to make the time pass pleasantly, now seemed completely new. The princes and princesses who fell in love were Tellarin and me. Their every moment of suffering burned me like fire, their ultimate triumphs thrilled me so deeply that some days I feared I might actually faint.

After a time, Ulca, who guessed but did not know, refused to tell me any tale that had kissing in it.

But I had my own story by then, and I was living it fully. My own first kiss came as we were walking in the sparse, windy garden that lay in the shadow of the Northmen's tower. That ugly building was ever after beautiful to me, and even on the coldest of days, if I could see that tower, it would warm me.

"Your stepfather could have my head," my soldier told me, his cheek touching lightly against mine. "I have betrayed both his trust and my station."

"Then if you are a condemned man," I whispered, "you may as well steal again." And I pulled him back farther into the shadows and kissed him until my mouth was sore. I was alive in a way I had never been, and almost mad with it. I was hungry for him, for his kisses, his breath, the sound of his voice.

He gifted me with small things that could not be found in Lord Sulis' drab and careful household—flowers, sweetmeats, small baubles he found at the markets in the new town of Erkynchester, outside the castle gates. I could hardly bring myself to eat the honeyed figs he bought for me, not because they were too rich for his purse, although they were—he was not wealthy like his friend Avalles—but because they were gifts from him, and thus precious. To do something as destructive as eat them seemed unimaginably wasteful. "Eat them slowly, then," he told me. "They will kiss your lips when I cannot."

I gave myself to him, of course, completely and utterly. Ulca's dark hints about soiled women drowning themselves in the Kingslake, about brides sent back to their families in disgrace, even about bastardy as the root of a dozen dreadful wars, were all ignored. I offered Tellarin my body as well as my heart. Who would not? And if I were that young girl once more, coming out of the shadows of her sorrowful childhood into that bright day, I would do it again, with equal joy. Even now that I see the foolishness, I cannot fault the girl I was. When you are young and your life stretches so far ahead of you, you are also without patience—you cannot understand that there will be other days, other times, other chances. God has made us this way. Who knows why He chose it so?

As for me, I knew nothing in those days but the fever in my blood. When Tellarin rapped at my door in the dark hours, I brought him to my bed. When he left me, I wept, but not from shame. He came to me again and again as autumn turned to winter, and as winter crept past we built a warm, secret world all our own. I could not imagine a life without him in it every moment.

Again, youth was foolish, for I have now managed to live without him for many years. There has even been much that was pleasing in my life since I lost him, although I would never have been able to believe such a thing then. But I do not think I have ever again lived as deeply, as truly, as in that first year of reckless discovery. It was as though I somehow knew that our time together would be short.

—•—

Whether it is called fate, or our weird, or the will of Heaven, I can look back now and see how each of us was set onto the track, how we were all made ready to travel in deep, dark places.

It was a night in late Feyever-month of that year when I began to realize that something more than simple distraction had overtaken my stepfather. I was reeling back down the corridor to my chamber—I had just kissed Tellarin farewell in the great hall, and was mad with the excitement of it—I nearly stumbled into Lord Sulis. I was first startled, then terrified. My crime, I felt sure, must be as plain as blood on a white sheet. I waited trembling for him to denounce me. Instead he only blinked and held his candle higher.

"Breda?" he said. "What are you doing, girl?

He had not called me "girl" since before my mother died. His fringe of hair was astrew, as though he had just clambered from some assignation of his own, but if he had, his stunned gaze suggested it had not been a pleasant one. His broad shoulders sagged, and he seemed so tired he could barely hold up his head. The man who had so impressed my mother on that first day in Godric's hall had changed almost beyond recognizing.

My stepfather was wrapped in blankets, but his legs showed naked below the knee. Could this be the same Sulis, I wondered, who as long as I had known him had dressed each day with the same care as he had once used to set his lines of battle? The sight of his pale bare feet was unspeakably disturbing.

"I...I was restless and could not sleep, sire. I wished some air."

His glance flicked across me and then began to rove the shadows again. He looked not just confused but actually frightened. "You should not be out of your chamber. It is late, and these corridors are full of..." He hesitated, then seemed to stop himself from saying something. "Full of draughts," he said at last. "Full of cold air. Go on with you, girl."

Everything about him made me uneasy. As I backed away, I felt compelled to say, "Good night, sire, and God bless you."

He shook his head—it almost seemed a shudder—then turned and padded away.

A few days later the witch was brought to the High Keep in chains.

I only learned the woman had been brought to the castle when Tellarin told me. As we lay curled in my bed after lovemaking, he suddenly announced, "Lord Sulis has captured a witch."

I was startled. Even with my small experience, I knew this was not the general run of pillow talk. "What do you mean?"

"She is a woman who lives in the Aldheorte forest," he said, pronouncing the Erkylandish name with his usual charming clumsiness. "She comes often to the market in a town down the Ymstrecca, east of here. She is well-known there—she makes herbal cures, I think, charms away warts, nonsense such as that. That is what Avalles said, anyway."

I remembered the message that the once-whore Xanippa had bade me give my stepfather on the night my mother died. Despite the warm night, I pulled the blanket up over our damp bodies. "Why should Lord Sulis want her?" I asked.

Tellarin shook his head, unconcerned. "Because she is a witch, I suppose, and so she is against God. Avalles and some of the other soldiers arrested her and brought her in this evening."

"But there are dozens of root peddlers and conjure-women in the town on the lakeshore where I grew up, and more living outside the castle walls. What does he want with her?"

"My lord does not think she is any old harmless conjure-woman," Tellarin said. "He has put her in one of the deep cells underneath the throne room, with chains on her arms and legs."

I had to see, of course, as much out of curiosity as out of worry about what seemed my stepfather's growing madness.

In the morning, while Lord Sulis was still abed, I went down to the cells. The woman was the only prisoner—the deep cells were seldom used, since those kept in them were likely to die from the chill and damp before they had served a length of term instructive to others—and the guard on duty there was perfectly willing to let the stepdaughter of the castle's master gawk at the witch. He pointed me to the last cell door in the underground chamber.

I had to stand on my toes to see through the barred slot in the door. The only light was a single torch burning on the wall behind me, so the witch was mostly hidden in shadows. She wore chains on wrists and ankles, just as Tellarin had said, and sat on the floor near the back of the windowless cell, her hunched shoulders giving her the shape of a rain-soaked hawk.

As I stared, the chains rattled ever so slightly, although she did not look up. "What do you want, little daughter?" Her voice was surprisingly deep.

"Lord...Lord Sulis is my stepfather," I said at last, as if it explained something.

Her eyes snapped open, huge and yellow. I had already thought her shaped like a hunting bird—now I almost feared she would fly at me and tear me with sharp talons. "Do you come to plead his case?" she demanded. "I tell you the same thing I told him—there is no answer to his question. None that I can give, anyway."

"What question?" I asked, hardly able to breathe.

The witch peered at me in silence for a moment, then clambered to her feet. I could see that it was a struggle for her to lift the chains. She shuffled forward until the light from the door slot fell on her squarely. Her dark hair was cut short as a man's. She was neither pretty nor ugly, neither tall nor short, but there was a power about her, and especially in the unblinking yellow lamps of her eyes, that drew my gaze and held it. She was something I had not seen before and did not at all understand. She spoke like an ordinary woman, but she had wildness in her like the crack of distant thunder, like the flash of a deer in flight. I felt so helpless to turn away that I feared she had cast a spell upon me.

At last she shook her head. "I will not involve you in your father's madness, child."

"He is not my father. He married my mother."

Her laugh was almost a bark. "I see."

I moved uneasily from foot to foot, face still pressed against the bars. I did not know why I spoke to the woman at all, or what I wanted from her. "Why are you chained?"

"Because they fear me."

"What is your name?" She frowned but said nothing, so I tried another. "Are you really a witch?"

She sighed. "Little daughter, go away. If you have nothing to do with your stepfather's foolish ideas, then the best you can do is stay far from all this. It does not take a sorceress to see that it will not end happily."

Her words frightened me, but I still could not pull myself away from the cell door. "Is there something you want? Food? Drink?"

She eyed me again, the large eyes almost fever-bright. "This is an even stranger household than I guessed. No, child. What I want is the open sky and my forest, but that is what I will not get from you or anyone. But your father says he has need of me—he will not starve me."

The witch turned her back on me then and shuffled to the rear of the cell, dragging her chains across the stone. I climbed the stairs with my head full to aching—excited thoughts, sorrowful thoughts, frightened thoughts, all were mixed together and full of fluttering confusion, like birds in a sealed room.

My stepfather kept the witch imprisoned as Marris-month turned into Avrel and the days of spring paced by. Whatever he wished from her, she would not give it. I visited her many times, but although she was kind enough in her way, she would speak to me only of meaningless things. Often she asked me to describe how the frost on the ground had looked that morning, or what birds were in the trees and what they sang, since in that deep, windowless cell carved into the stone of the headland, she could see and hear nothing of the world outside.

I do not know why I was so drawn to her. Somehow she seemed to hold the key to many mysteries—my stepfather's madness, my mother's sorrow, my own growing fears that the foundations beneath my new happiness were unsolid.

Although my stepfather did feed her, as she had promised he would, and did not allow her to be mistreated in anything beyond the fact of her imprisonment, the witch woman still grew markedly thinner by the day, and dark circles formed like bruises beneath her eyes. She was pining for freedom, and like a wild animal kept in a pen, her unhappiness was sickening her. It hurt me to see her, as though my own liberty had been stolen. Each time I found her more drawn and weak than the time before, it brought back to me the agony and shame of my mother's last, horrible days. Each time I left the cells, I went to a spot where I could be alone and I wept. Even my stolen hours with Tellarin could not ease the sadness I felt.

I would have hated my stepfather for what he was doing to her, but he too was growing more sickly with each day, as though he were trapped in some mirror version of her dank cell. Whatever the question was that she had spoken of, it plagued Sulis so terribly that he, a decent man, had stolen her freedom—so terribly that he scarcely slept in the nights at all, but sat up until dawn's first light reading and writing and mumbling to himself in a kind of ecstasy. Whatever the question, I began to fear that both he and the witch would die because of it.

The one time that I worked up the courage to ask my stepfather why he had imprisoned her, he stared over my head at the sky, as though it had turned an entirely new color, and told me, "This place has too many doors, girl. You open one, then another, and you find yourself back where you began. I cannot find my way."

If that was an answer, I could make no sense of it.

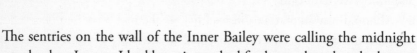

I offered the witch death and she gave me a prophecy in return.

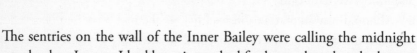

The sentries on the wall of the Inner Bailey were calling the midnight watch when I arose. I had been in my bed for hours, but sleep had never once come near. I wrapped myself in my heaviest cloak and slipped into the hallway. I could hear my stepfather through his door, talking as though to a visitor. It hurt to hear his voice, because I knew he was alone.

At this hour, the only guard in the cells was a crippled old soldier who did not even stir in his sleep when I walked past him. The torch in the wall-sconce had burned very low, and at first I could not see the witch's shape in the shadows. I wanted to call to her, but I did not know what to say. The bulk of the great, sleeping castle seemed to press down on me.

At last the heavy chains clinked. "Is that you, little daughter?" Her voice was weary. After a while she stood and shuffled forward. Even in the faint light, she had a terrible, dying look. My hand stole to the purse that hung around my neck. I touched my golden Tree as I said a silent prayer, then felt the curve of that other thing, which I had carried with me since the night of my mother's death. In a moment that seemed to have its own light, quite separate from the flickering glow of the torch, I pulled out the dragon's claw and extended it to her through the bars.

The witch raised an eyebrow as she took it from me. She carefully turned it over in her palm, then smiled sadly. "A poisoned owl's claw. Very appropriate. Is this for me to use on my captors? Or on myself?"

I shrugged helplessly. "You want to be free," was all I could say.

"Not with this, little daughter," she said. "At least, not this time. As it happens, I have already surrendered—or, rather, I have bargained. I have agreed to give your stepfather what he thinks he wants in exchange for my freedom. I must see and feel the sky again." Gently, she handed me back the claw.

I stared at her, almost sick with the need to know things. "Why won't you tell me your name?"

Another sad smile. "Because my true name I give to no one. Because any other name would be a lie."

"Tell me a lie, then."

"A strange household, indeed! Very well. The people of the north call me Valada."

I tried it on my tongue. "Valada. He will set you free now?"

"Soon, if the bargain is honored on both sides."

"What is it, this bargain?"

"A bad one for everyone." She saw my look. "You do not want to know, truly. Someone will die because of this madness—I see it as clearly as I see your face peering through the door."

My heart was a piece of cold stone in my breast. "Someone will die? Who?"

Her expression became weary, and I could see that standing with the weight of her shackles was an effort for her. "I do not know. And in my weariness, I have already told you too much, little daughter. These are not matters for you."

I was dismissed, even more miserable and confused. The witch would be free, but someone else would die. I could not doubt her word—no one could, who had seen her fierce, sad eyes as she spoke. As I walked back to my bedchamber, the halls of the Inner Bailey seemed a place entirely new, a strange and unfamiliar world.

My feelings for Tellarin were still astonishingly strong, but in the days after the witch's foretelling I was so beset with unhappiness that our love was more like a fire that made a cold room habitable than a sun which warmed everything, as it had been. If my soldier had not had worries of his own, he would certainly have noticed.

The cold inside me became a chill like deepest winter when I overheard Tellarin and Avalles speaking about a secret task Lord Sulis had for them, something to do with the witch. It was hard to tell what was intended—my beloved and his friend did not themselves know all that Sulis planned, and they were speaking only to each other, and not for the benefit of their secret listener. I gathered that my stepfather's books had shown him that the time for some important thing had drawn close. They would build or find some kind of fire. It would take them on a short journey by night, but they did not say—or perhaps did not yet know—on what night. Both my beloved and Avalles were clearly disturbed by the prospect.

If I had feared before, when I thought the greatest risk was to my poor, addled stepfather, now I was almost ill with terror. I could barely stumble through the remaining hours of the day, so consumed was I with the thought that something might happen to Tellarin. I dropped my beadwork so many times that Ulca took it away from me at last. When dark came, I could not get to sleep for hours, and when I did I woke up panting and shuddering from a dream in which Tellarin had fallen into flames and was burning just beyond my reach.

I lay tossing in my bed all the night. How could I protect my beloved? Warning him would do no good. He was stubborn, and also saved his deepest beliefs for those things he could grasp and touch, so I knew he would put little stock in the witch's words. In any case, even if he believed me, what could he do? Refuse an order from Lord Sulis because of a warning from me, his secret lover? No, it would be hopeless to try to persuade Tellarin not to go—he spoke of his loyalty to his master almost as often as he did of his feelings for me.

I was in an agony of fearful curiosity. What did my stepfather plan? What had he read in those books, that he now would risk not just his own life, but that of my beloved as well?

Not one of them would tell me anything, I knew. Even the witch had said that the matter was not for me. Whatever I discovered would be by my own hand.

I resolved to look at my stepfather's books, those that he kept hidden from me and everyone else. Once it would have been all but impossible, but now—because he sat reading and writing and whispering to himself all the night's dark hours—I could trust that when Sulis did sleep, he would sleep like the dead.

I stole into my stepfather's chambers early the next morning. He had sent his servants away weeks before, and the castle-folk no longer dared rap on his doors unless summoned. The rooms were empty but for my stepfather and me.

He lay sprawled across his bed, his head hanging back over the edge of the pallet. Had I not known how moderate most of his habits were, I would have thought from his deep, rough breathing and the way he had disordered the blankets that he had drunk himself stuporous, but Sulis seldom took even a single cup of wine.

The key to the locked boxes was on a cord around his neck. As I tugged it out of his shirt with as much care as I could, I could not help but see how much happier he appeared with the blankness of sleep on him. The furrows on his brow had loosened, and his jaw was no longer clenched in the grimace of distraction that had become his constant expression. In that moment, although I hated what he had done to the witch Valada, I pitied him. Whatever madness had overtaken him of late, he had been a kind man in his way, in his time.

He stirred and made an indistinct sound. Heart beating swiftly, I hurried to draw the cord and key over his head.

When I had found the wooden chests and unlocked them, I began to pull out and examine my stepfather's forbidden books, leafing quickly and quietly through each in turn, with one ear cocked for changes in his breathing. Most of the plainbound volumes were written in tongues I did not know, two or three in characters I could not even recognize. Those of which I could understand a little seemed to contain either tales of the fairy-folk or stories about the High Keep during the time of the Northmen.

A good part of an hour had passed when I discovered a loosely bound book titled "Writings of Vargellis Sulis, Seventh Lord of Honsa Sulis, Now Master of the Sulean House in Exile." My stepfather's careful hand filled the first pages densely, then grew larger and more imperfect as it continued, until the final pages seemed almost to have been scribed by a child still learning letters.

A noise from the bed startled me, but my stepfather had only grunted and turned on his side. I continued through the book as swiftly as I could. It seemed to be only the most recent of a lifetime's worth of writings—the earliest dates in the volume were from the first year we had lived in the High Keep. The bulk of the pages listed tasks to be performed in the High Keep's rebuilding, and records of important judgements Sulis had made as lord of the keep and its tenant lands. There were other notations of a more personal nature, but they were brief and unelaborated. For that terrible day almost three years earlier, he had written only "Cynethrith Dead of Chest Fever. She shall be Buried on the Headland."

The sole mention of me was a single sentence from several months before—"Breda happy Today." It was oddly painful to me that my somber stepfather should have noticed that and made a record of it.

The later pages held almost no mention of the affairs of either home or governance, as in daily life Sulis had also lost interest in both. Instead, there were more and more notes that seemed to be about things he had read in other books—one said "Plesinnen claims that Mortality is consumed in God as a Flame consumes Branch or Bough. How then..." with the rest smudged—one word might have been "nails," and further on I could make out "Holy Tree." Another of his notes listed several "Doorways" that had been located by someone named Nisses, with explanations next to each that explained nothing at all—"Shifted," read my stepfather's shaky hand beside one, or "from a Time of No Occupation," or even "Met a Dark Thing."

It was only on the last two pages that I found references to the woman in the cell below the throne room.

"Have at Last rec'd Word of the woman called Valada," the scrawl stated. "No one else Living North of Perdruin has Knowledge of the Black Fire. She must be Made to Speak what she knows." Below that, in another day's even less disciplined hand, was written, "The Witch balks me, but I cannot have another Failure as on the Eve of Elysiamansa. Stoning Night will be next Time of Strong Voices beneath the Keep. Walls will be Thin. She will show me the Way of Black Fire or there is no other Hope. Either she will answer, or Death."

I sat back, trying to make sense of it all. Whatever my stepfather planned, it would happen soon—Stoning Night was the last night of Avrel, only a few days away. I could not tell from his writings if the witch was still in danger—did he mean to kill her if she failed, or only if she tried to cheat his bargain with her?—but I had no doubt that this search for the thing called Black Fire would bring danger to everyone else, most importantly and most frighteningly my soldier, Tellarin. Again my stepfather murmured in his sleep, an unhappy sound. I locked his books away and stole out again.

All that day I felt distracted and feverish, but this time it was not love that fevered me. I was terrified for my lover and fearful for my stepfather and the witch Valada, but what I knew and how I had discovered it I could not tell to anyone. For the first time since my soldier had kissed me, I felt alone. I was full up with secrets, and unlike Sulis, had not even a book to which they could be confided.

I would follow them, I decided at last. I would follow them into the place my stepfather spoke of, the place beneath the keep where the walls were thin and the voices strong. While they searched for the Black Fire, I would watch for danger. I would protect them all. I would be their angel.

━━◆━━

Stoning Night came around at last.

Even had I not read my stepfather's writings, I think I would have known that the hour had come in which they meant to search for Black Fire, because Tellarin was so distracted and full of shadows. Although he admitted nothing to me as we lay together in my bedchamber, I could feel that he was anxious about what would happen that night. But he was bound to my stepfather by honor and blood, and had no choice.

He snapped at me when I kissed his ear and curled my fingers in his hair. "Give a man some peace, girl."

"Why are you a man and I am a girl?" I teased him, pretending a lightness I did not truly feel. "Is there such a difference in our ages? Have I not given to you already that which makes me a woman?"

My soldier was short-tempered and did not hear the love in what I said. "Anybody who will not leave off when she is asked proves herself still a child. And I am a man because I wear a soldier's badge, and because if my master asks, I must give my life."

Tellarin was five years my elder, and in those long-ago days I was almost as impressed by the difference as he was, but I think now that all men are younger than their women, especially when their honor has been touched.

As he stared at the ceiling his face turned from angry to solemn, and I knew he was thinking of what he must do that night. I was frightened too, so I kissed him again, softly this time, and apologized.

When he had gone, full of excuses meant to hide his actual task, I prepared for my own journey. I had hidden my thickest cloak and six fat candles where Ulca and the other serving-women would not find them. When I was dressed and ready, I touched my mother's golden Tree where it lay against my heart, and said a prayer for the safety of all who would go with me into darkness.

Stoning Night—the last night of Avrel, on the eve of Maia-month, the black hours when tales say spirits walk until driven back to their graves by dawn and the crowing cock. The High Keep lay silent around me as I followed my beloved and the others through the dark. It did not feel so much that the castle slept as that the great keep held its breath and waited.

There is a stairwell beneath the Angel Tower, and that was where they were bound. I learned of it for the first time on that night, as I stood wrapped in my dark cloak, listening from the shadows of the wall opposite the tower. Those I followed were four—my stepfather, Tellarin and his friend Avalles, and the woman Valada. Despite the bargain she had made, the witch's arms were still chained. It saddened me to see her restrained like an animal.

The workmen who had been repairing the tower had laid a rough wooden floor over the broken stones of the old one—perhaps to make certain no one fell down one of the many holes, perhaps simply to close off any openings into the castle's deepest places. Some had even suggested that all the old castle floor should be sealed under brick, so that nothing would ever come up that way to trouble the sleep of God-fearing folk.

Because of this wooden floor, I waited a long time before following them through the tower's outer portal, knowing it would take some time for my stepfather and his two bondmen to shift the boards. As I lurked in the shadows by the tower wall while the wind prowled the Inner Bailey, I thought about the Angel who stood at the top of the tower, a figure black with the grime of centuries that no rain could wash away, tipped sideways as though about to lose her balance and fall. Who was she? One of the blessed saints? Was it an omen—did she watch over me as I meant to look over Tellarin and the rest? I looked up, but the tower's high top was invisible in the night.

At last I tried the latch of the tower door and found the bolt had not been shot. I hoped that it meant the Angel was indeed looking out for me.

Inside the tower the moonlight ended, so while still in the doorway I lit my first candle from the hidden touchwood, which had nearly burnt down. My footsteps seemed frighteningly loud in the stony entry hall, but no one appeared from the shadows to demand my business in that place. I heard no sound of my stepfather or the rest.

I paused for a moment in front of the great, upward-winding staircase, and could not help but wonder what the workmen would find when they cleared the rubble and reached the top—as I still wonder all these years later, with the painstaking work yet unfinished. I suppose I will not see it in my lifetime. Will they discover treasures left by the fairy-folk? Or perhaps only those ancient beings' frail bones?

Even were it not for the things that happened on that fateful night, still the Angel Tower would haunt me, as it haunts this great keep and all the lands beneath its long shadow. No mortals, I think, will ever know all its secrets.

Once, long ago, I dreamed that my stepfather gave me the Angel herself to clean, but that no matter how I tried, I could not scrub the black muck from her limbs and face. He told me that it was not my fault, that God would have lent me the strength if He truly wanted the Angel's face to be seen, but I still wept at my failure.

I moved from the entry hall to a place where the floor fell away in great broken shards, and tried to imagine what could smash stones so thoroughly and yet leave the tower itself still standing. It was not easy to follow where my stepfather and my beloved had already gone, but I climbed down the rubble, leaning to set my candle before me so that I could have both my hands free. I wished, not for the last time, that I had worn something other than my soft shoes. I clambered down and down, hurting my feet, tearing my dress in several places, until I reached the jumble of smaller broken stones which was the floor, at least a half-dozen times my own height below the level of the Inner Bailey. In the midst of this field of shards gaped a great, black hole bigger than the rest, a jagged mouth that waited to swallow me down. As I crunched closer to it, I heard what I knew must be the voices of the others floating up from the depths, although they sounded strange to me.

More stones had been pushed aside to reveal the entrance to the stairwell, a lip of shiny white with steps inside it that vanished into shadow. Another voice floated up, laughing. It belonged to no one I knew.

Even with all that had happened in the previous days, I had never yet felt so frightened, but I knew Tellarin was down there in the dark places. I made the sign of the Tree upon my breast, then stepped onto the stairway.

At first I could find no trace of them.

As I descended, the light of my single candle served only to make the stairwell seem more than ever like a shadowy throat waiting to swallow me, but fear alone could not keep me from my beloved—if anything, it sped my steps. I hurried downward until it seemed I must have gone as far beneath the castle as the Angel Tower loomed above it, but still I had not caught up with them.

Whether it was a trick of sound, or of the winds that are said to blow through the caves of the Kingslake cliffs, I continued to hear unfamiliar voices. Some seemed so close that if I had not had a candle, I would have been certain I could reach out and touch the person who whispered to me, but the flickering light showed me that the stairwell was empty. The voices babbled, and sometimes sang, in a soft, sad tongue I did not understand or even recognize.

I knew I should be too frightened to remain, that I should turn and flee back to moonlight and clean air, but although the bodiless murmurs filled me with dismay, I felt no evil in them. If they were ghosts, I do not think they even knew I was there. It was as though the castle talked to itself, like an old man sitting beside the fire, lost in the memories of days long past.

The stairwell ended in a wide landing with open doorways at either end, and I could not help thinking of the doorways mentioned in my stepfather's book. As I paused to consider which way I should go, I examined the carvings on the walls, delicate vines and flowers whose type I had never seen before. Above one doorframe a nightingale perched on a tree bough. Another tree bough was carved above the far doorway—or rather, I saw as I moved my candle, they were both boughs from one single tree, which had been carved directly above me, spreading across the ceiling of the stairwell as though I myself were the tree's trunk. On the bough above the second doorway twined a slender serpent. I shuddered, and began to move toward the nightingale door, but at that moment words floated up out of the darkness.

"...if you have lied to me. I am a patient man, but..."

It was my stepfather, and even if I had not recognized his faint voice, I would have known him by the words, for that is what he always said. And he spoke the truth—he was a patient man. He had always been like one of the stones of the hilltop rings, cool and hard and in no hurry to move, growing warm only after the sun of an entire summer has beat upon him. I had sometimes felt I would like to break a stick upon him, if only to make him turn and truly look at me.

Only once did he ever do that, I had believed—on that day when he told me that "they" had taken everything from him. But now I knew he had looked at me another time, perhaps seen me smile on a day when my lover had given me a gift or a kiss, and had written in his book, "Breda happy Today."

My stepfather's words had drifted up through the other doorway. I lit another candle and placed it on top of the first, which had burned almost to the holder, then followed the voice of Sulis through the serpent door.

Downward I went, and downward still farther—what seemed a journey of hours, through sloping, long-deserted corridors which twisted like yarn spilled from a sack. The light of the candles showed me stone that, although I knew it was even more ancient, seemed newer and brighter than that which I had seen farther above. In places the passageways opened into rooms choked with dirt and rubble, but which must have been massive, with ceilings as high as any of the greatest halls I have ever heard of in Nabban. The carvings I could see were so delicate, so perfect, that they might have been the actual things of nature—birds, plants, trees—frozen into stone by the sort of magical spells so often part of my mother's and Ulca's stories.

It was astonishing to think that this entire world had lain in its tomb of earth below us as long as we had lived in the High Keep, and for generations before that. I knew I was seeing the ancient home of the fairy-folk. With all the stories, and even with the evidence of the tower itself, I had still never imagined they would have such a way with stone, to make it froth like water and shimmer like ice, to make it stretch overhead in slender arcs like the finest branches of a willow tree. Had the Northmen truly killed them all? For the first time, I understood something of what this meant, and a deep, quiet horror stole over me. The creators of all this beauty, slaughtered, and their houses usurped by their slayers—no wonder the darkness was full of unquiet voices. No wonder the High Keep was a place of haunted sadness for everyone who lived in it. The castle of our day was founded on ancient murder. It was built on death.

It pulled at me, that thought. It became tangled in my mind with the memory of my stepfather's distracted stare, of the witch in chains. Good could not come from evil, I felt sure. Not without sacrifice. Not without blood and atonement.

My fear was growing again.

The Peaceful Ones might have been gone, but I was learning that their great house remained lively.

As I hurried downward, following the tracks of my stepfather and his company in the dust of centuries, I found suddenly that I had taken a wrong turning. The passage ended in a pile of broken stone, but when I returned to the last cross-corridor, there was no sign of footprints, and the place itself was not familiar, as though the ruins themselves had shifted around me. I closed my eyes, listening for the sound of Tellarin's voice, for I felt sure that my heart would be able to hear him through all the stone in Erkynland, but nothing came to me but the ghost-murmurs, which blew in like an autumn breeze, full of sighing, rustling nonsense.

I was lost.

For the first time it became clear to me what a foolish thing I had done. I had gone into a place where I should not be. Not one person knew I was there, and when my last candle burned out, I would be lost in the darkness.

Tears started in my eyes, but I wiped them away. Weeping had not brought my father back, or my mother. It would do me no good now.

I did my best to retrace my steps, but the voices flittered around me like invisible birds, and before long I was wandering blindly. Confused by the noises in my head and by the flickering shadows, twice I almost tumbled into great crevices in the passageway floor. I kicked a stone into one that fell without hitting anything until I could not bear to listen any longer.

The darkness seemed to be closing on me, and I might have been lost forever—might have become another part of the whispering chorus—but by luck or accident or the hand of fate, I made a turning into a corridor I did not recognize and found myself standing at the lip of another stairwell, listening to the voice of the witch Valada drift up from the deeps.

"...Not an army or a noble household that you can order about, Lord Sulis. Those who lived here are dead, but the place is alive. You must take what you are given..."

It is as though she had heard my very thoughts. Even as I shuddered to hear my forebodings spoken aloud, I hurried toward the sound, terrified that if it faded I would never again hear a familiar voice.

What seemed another hour went by, although I had been so long in the haunted dark that I was no judge. My lover and the rest seemed almost to have become phantoms themselves, floating ahead of me like dandelion seeds, always just beyond my reach.

The stairs continued to curl downward, and as my third and fourth candles burned I could see glimpses of the great spaces through which we all descended, level upon level, like a pilgrimage down the tiers of Heaven. At times, as the candles flickered on the wooden base, I thought I could see even more. From the corner of my eye the ruins seemed to take on a sort of life. There were moments when the ghost-voices swelled and the shadows seemed to take on form. If I half-closed my eyes, I could almost see these bleak spaces full of bright, laughing folk.

Why did the Northmen kill such beauty? And how could a people who built such a place be defeated by any mortals, however bloodthirsty and battle-hungry?

A light bloomed in the depths, red and yellow, making the polished stone of the stairwell seem to quiver. For a moment I thought it only another wisp of my imagination, but then, from so close it seemed we could kiss if we wished, I heard my beloved's voice.

"Do not trust her, Sire," Tellarin said, sounding more than a little fearful. "She is lying again."

Intensely happy, but with my caution abruptly restored, I shaded the candle with my palm and hurried down the stairs as quietly as I could. As their voices grew louder, and I saw that the light blooming in the darkness came from their torches, I pinched the flame to extinguish my candle completely. However glad I was to find them, I guessed they would not feel the same about me.

I crept closer to the light, but could not see Tellarin and the others because something like a cloud of smoke blocked my view. It was only when I reached the base of the curving stair and stepped silently onto the floor of the great chamber that I could actually see the four shapes.

They stood in the middle of a room so cavernous that even the torches my lover and Avalles held could not carry light to its highest corners. Before them loomed the thing I had thought was smoke. I still could not see it clearly, despite the torch flames burning only an arm's length from it, but now it seemed a vast tree with black leaves and trunk. A shadow cloaked it and hid all but the broadest outline, a dark shroud like the mist that hid the hills on a winter morning, but it was not mist in which the tree-shape crouched, I felt sure. It was pure Darkness.

"You must decide whether to listen to me or a young soldier," the witch was saying to my stepfather. "I will tell you again—if you cut so much as a leaf, you will mark yourselves as ravagers and it will not go well with you. Can you not feel that?"

"And I think Tellarin is right," Avalles proclaimed, but his voice was less sure than his words. "She seeks to trick us."

My stepfather looked from the tree-shadow to the witch. "If we may not take any wood, then why have you brought us here?" he asked slowly, as though it cost great effort just to speak.

I could hear the sour smile in Valada's answer. "You have held me captive in your damp pile of stones for two moons, seeking my help with your mad questions. If you do not believe that I know what I know, why did you shackle me and bring me here?"

"But the wood...?"

"I did not say you could not take anything to burn, I said that you would be a fool to lift axe or knife to the Great Witchwood. There is deadfall beneath, if you are bold enough to search for it."

Sulis turned to Avalles. "Go and gather some dead wood, nephew."

The young knight hesitated, then handed his torch to my stepfather and walked a little unsteadily toward the great dark tree. He bent beneath the outer branches and vanished from sight. After an interval of silence, Avalles stumbled back out again.

"It is...it is too dark to see," he panted. His eyes were showing white around the edges. "And there is something in there—an animal, perhaps.

I...I can feel it breathing." He turned to my stepfather. "Tellarin's eyes are better than mine..."

No! I wanted to scream. The tree-thing sat and waited, cloaked in shadows no torchlight could penetrate. I was ready to burst from hiding and beg my beloved not to go near it, but as if he had heard my silent cry, Lord Sulis cursed and thrust the torch back into Avalles' hand.

"By Pelippa and her bowl!" my stepfather said. "I will do it myself."

Just before he stepped through the branches, I thought I heard the leaves whisper, although there was no wind in the chamber. The quiet hiss and rattle grew louder, perhaps because my stepfather was forcing his way beneath the thick branches. Long moments trudged past, then the rustling became even more violent. At last Sulis emerged, staggering a little, with what seemed a long bar of shadow clasped under each arm. Tellarin and Avalles stepped forward to help him but he waved them off, shaking his head as though he had been dealt a blow. Even in the dark room, I could see that he had gone very pale.

"You spoke the truth, Valada," he said. "No axe, no knife."

While I watched, he bade Avalles and my beloved make a ring on the ground from the broken stones that littered the chamber. He crossed the two pieces of wood he had gathered in the center of the circle, then he used kindling from a pouch on his belt and one of the torches to set the witchwood alight. As the strange fire sputtered into life, the room seemed to become darker, as though the very light from the torches bent toward the firepit and was sucked away. The flames began to rise.

The rustle of the shadowy tree stilled. Everything grew silent—even the flames made no sound. My heart pounded as I leaned closer, almost forgetting to keep myself hidden. It was indeed a Black Fire that burned now in that deep, lost place, a fire that flickered like any blaze, and yet whose flames were wounds in the very substance of the world, holes as darkly empty as a starless sky.

It is hard to believe, but that is what I saw. I could look through the flames of the Black Fire, not to what stood on the other side of the fire, but to somewhere else—into nothingness at first, but then color and shape began to expand outward in the space above the firepit, as though something turned the very air inside-out.

A face appeared in the fire. It was all I could do not to cry out.

⊸⊹⊸

The stranger surrounded by the black flames was like no man I had ever seen. The angles of his face were all somehow wrong, his chin too narrow, the large eyes slanted upward at the corners. His hair was long and white, but he did not look old. He was naked from the waist up, and his pale, glossy skin was marked with dreadful scars, but despite the flames in which he lay, his burns seemed old rather than new.

The Black Fire unshaped even the darkness. All that was around it bent, as though the very world grew stretched and shivery as the reflection on a bubble of river water.

The burning man seemed to slumber in the flames, but it was a horribly unquiet sleep. He pitched and writhed, even brought his hands up before his face, as though to protect himself from some terrible attack. When his eyes at last opened, they were dark as shadow itself, staring at things that I could not see, at shadows far beyond the fire. His mouth stretched in a silent, terrible scream, and despite his alien aspect, despite being so frightened I feared my heart would stop, I still ached to see his suffering. If he was alive, how could his body burn and burn without being consumed? If he was a ghost, why had death not ended his pain?

Tellarin and Avalles backed away from the firepit, wide-eyed and fearful. Avalles made the sign of the Tree.

My stepfather looked at the burning man's writhing mouth and blind eyes, then turned to the witch Valada. "Why does he not speak to us? Do something!"

She laughed her sharp laugh. "You wished to meet one of the Sithi, Lord Sulis—one of the Peaceful Ones. You wished to find a doorway, but some doorways open not on elsewhere, but elsewhen. The Black Fire has found you one of the fair folk in his sleep. He is dreaming, but he can hear you across the centuries. Speak to him! I have done what I promised."

Clearly shaken, Sulis turned to the man in the flames. "You!" he called. "Can you understand me?"

The burning man writhed again, but now his dark unseeing eyes turned in my stepfather's direction. "Who is there?" he asked, and I heard his voice in the chamber of my skull rather than in my ears. "Who walks the Road of Dreams?" The apparition lifted a hand as though he might reach through the years and touch us. For a moment, astonishment pushed the agony from his odd face. "You are mortals! But why do you come to me? Why do you disturb the sleep of Hakatri of the House of Year-Dancing?"

"I am Sulis." The tremble in my stepfather's voice made him seem an old, old man. "Called by some 'the Apostate,' I have risked everything I own—have spent years studying—to ask a question which only the Peaceful Ones can answer. Will you help me?"

The burning man did not seem to be listening. His mouth twisted again, and this time his cry of pain had sound. I tried to stop my ears, but it was already inside my head. "Ah, it burns!" he moaned. "Still the worm's blood burns me—even when I sleep. Even when I walk the Road of Dreams!"

"The worm's blood...?" My stepfather was puzzled. "A dragon? What are you saying?"

"She was like a great black snake," Hakatri murmured. "My brother and I, we followed her into her deep place and we fought her and slew her, but I have felt her scorching blood upon me and will never be at peace again. By the Garden, it pains me so!" He made a choking sound, then fell silent for a moment. "Both our swords bit," he said, and it was almost a chant, a song, "but my brother Ineluki was the fortunate one. He escaped a terrible burning. Black, black it was, that ichor, and hotter than even the flames of Making! I fear death itself could not ease this agony..."

"Be silent!" Sulis thundered, full of rage and misery. "Witch, is this spell for nothing? Why will he not listen to me?"

"There is no spell, except that which opens the doorway," she replied. "Hakatri perhaps came to that doorway because of how the dragon's blood burned him—there is nothing else in all the world like the blood of the great worms. His wounds keep him always close to the Road of

Dreams, I think. Ask him your question, Nabban-man. He is as like to answer it as any other of the immortals you might have found."

I could feel it now—could feel the weird that had brought us here take us all in its grip. I held my breath, caught between a terror that blew like a cold wind inside my head, that screamed at me to leave Tellarin and everything else and run away, and a fierce wondering about what had brought my stepfather to this impossibly strange meeting.

Lord Sulis tilted his chin down toward his chest for a moment, as though now the time had come, he was uncertain of what he wished to say. At last he spoke, quaveringly at first, but with greater strength as he went on.

"Our church teaches us that God appeared in this world, wearing the form of Usires Aedon, performing many miracles, singing up cures for the sick and lame, until at last the Imperator Crexis caused him to be hung from the Execution Tree. Do you know of this, Hakatri?"

The burning man's blind eyes rolled toward Sulis again. He did not answer, but he seemed to be listening.

"The promise of the Aedon the Ransomer is that all who live will be gathered up—that there will be no death," my stepfather continued. "And this is proved because he was God made flesh in this world, and that is proved because of the miracles he performed. But I have studied much about your own people, Hakatri. Such miracles as Usires the Aedon performed could have been done by one of your Sithi people, or even perhaps by one of only half-immortal blood." His smile was as bleak as a skull's. "After all, even my fiercest critics in Mother Church agree that Usires had no human father."

Sulis bowed his head again for a moment, summoning up words or strength. I gasped for air—I had forgotten to breathe. Avalles and Tellarin still stared, their fear now mixed with astonishment, but the witch Valada's face was hidden from me in shadow.

"Both my wives have been taken from me by death, both untimely," my stepfather said. "My first wife gave me a son before she died, a beautiful boy named Sarellis who died himself in screaming pain because he stepped on a horseshoe nail—a nail!—and caught a death fever. Young men I have commanded were slaughtered in the hundreds, the thousands, their corpses piled on the battlefield like the husks of locusts, and all for a small stretch of land here or there, or sometimes merely over words. My parents are dead, too, with too much unspoken between us. Everyone I ever truly loved has been stolen from me by death."

His hoarse voice had taken on a disturbing force, a cracked power, as though he meant to shout down the walls of Heaven itself.

"Mother Church tells me to believe that I will be reunited with them," he said. "They preach to me, saying, 'See the works of Usires our Lord and be comforted, for his task was to show death should hold no fear,' they told me. But I cannot be sure—I cannot simply trust! Is the Church right? Will I see those I love again? Will we all live on? The masters of the Church have called me a heretic and declared me apostate because I would not give up doubting the divinity of the Aedon, but I must know! Tell me, Hakatri, was Usires of your folk? Is the story of his godhood simply a lie to keep us happy, to keep priests fat and rich?" He blinked back tears, his stolid face transfigured by rage and pain. "Even if God should damn me forever to hell for it, still I must know—is our faith a lie?"

He was shaking so badly now that he took a staggering step back from the fire and almost fell. No one moved except the man in the flames, who followed Sulis with his blank, dark eyes.

I realized that I was weeping too, and silently rubbed the tears away. Seeing my stepfather's true and terrible pain was like a knife twisted inside me, and yet I was angry too. All for this? For such unknowable things he left my mother lonely, and now had nearly destroyed his own life?

After a long time in which all was silent as the stone around us, Hakatri said slowly, "Always you mortals have tortured yourselves." He blinked, and the way his face moved was so alien that I had to turn away and then look at him anew before I could understand what he said. "But you torture yourself most when you seek answers to things that have none."

"No answers?" Sulis was still shaking. "How can that be?"

The burning man raised his long-fingered hands in what I could only guess was a gesture of peace. "Because that which is meant for mortals is not given to the Zida'ya to know, any more than you can know of our Garden, or where we go when we leave this place.

"Listen to me, mortal. What if your messiah were indeed one of the

Dawn Children—would that prove somehow that your God had not chosen that to happen? Would that prove your Ransomer's words any the less true?" Hakatri shook his head with the weird, foreign grace of a shorebird.

"Just tell me whether Usires was one of your folk," Sulis demanded raggedly. "Spare me your philosophies and tell me! For I am burning too! I have not been free of the pain in years!" As the echoes of my stepfather's cry faded, the fairy-lord in his ring of black flames paused, and for the first time he seemed truly to see across the gulf. When he spoke, his voice was full of sadness.

"We Zida'ya know little of the doings of mortals, and there are some of our own blood who have fallen away from us, and whose works are hidden from us as well. I do not think your Usires Aedon was one of the Dawn Children, but more than that I cannot tell you, mortal man, nor could any of my folk." He lifted his hands again, weaving the fingers in an intricate, incomprehensible gesture. "I am sorry."

A great shudder ran through the creature called Hakatri then— perhaps the pain of his burns returning, a pain that he had somehow held at bay while he listened to my stepfather speak. Sulis did not wait to hear more, but stepped forward and kicked the witchwood fire into a cloud of whirling sparks, then dropped to his knees with his hands over his face.

The burning man was gone.

After a march of silence that seemed endless, the witch called out, "Will you honor your bargain with me now, Lord Sulis? You said that if I brought you to one of the immortals, you would free me." Her voice was flat, but there was still a gentleness to it that surprised me.

My stepfather's reply, when it came, was choked and hard to understand. He waved his hand. "Take off her chains, Avalles. I want nothing more from her."

In the midst of this great bleak wilderness of sorrow, I felt a moment of sharp happiness as I realized that despite my foreboding, the witch, my beloved, even my tortured stepfather, all would survive this terrible night. As Avalles began to unlock the witch's shackles, shivering so that he could hardly hold the key, I had a moment to dream that my uncle would return to health, that he would reward my Tellarin for his bravery and loyalty, and that my beloved and I would make a home for ourselves somewhere far away from this ghost-riddled, windswept headland.

My stepfather let out a sudden, startling cry. I turned to see him fall forward onto his belly, his body ashake with weeping. This seizure of grief in stern, quiet Sulis was in some ways the most frightening thing I had yet seen in that long, terrifying night.

Then, even as his cry rebounded in the invisible upper reaches of the chamber and provoked a dim rustle in the leaves of the shadowy tree, something else seized my attention. Two figures were struggling where the witch had stood. At first I thought Avalles and the woman Valada were fighting, but then I saw that the witch had stepped back and was watching the battle, her bright eyes wide with surprise. Instead, it was Avalles and Tellarin who were tangled together, their torches fallen from their hands. Shocked, helpless with surprise, I watched them tumble to the ground. A moment later a dagger rose and fell, then the brief struggle was ended.

I screamed, "Tellarin!" and rushed forward.

He stood, brushing the dust from his breeks, and stared at me as I came out of the shadows. The end of his knife was blackened with blood. He had a stillness about him that might have been fear, or simply surprise.

"Breda? What are you doing here?"

"Why did he attack you?" I cried. Avalles lay twisted on the ground in a spreading puddle of black. "He was your friend!"

He said nothing, but leaned to kiss me, then turned and walked to where my stepfather still crouched on the ground in a fit of grief. My beloved put his knee in my stepfather's back, then wrapped his hand in the hair at the back of the older man's head and pulled until his tearstained face was tilted up into the torchlight.

"I did not want to kill Avalles," my soldier explained, in part to me, in part to Sulis. "But he insisted on coming, fearing that I would become closer in his uncle's favor if he were not there too." He shook his head. "Sad. But it is only your death that was my task, Sulis, and I have been waiting long for such a perfect opportunity."

Despite the merciless strain of his position, my stepfather smiled, a ghastly, tight-stretched grin. "Which Sancellan sent you?"

"Does it matter? You have more enemies in Nabban than you can count, Sulis Apostate. You are a heretic and a schismatic, and you are dangerous. You should have known you would not be left here, to build your power in the wilderness."

"I did not come here to build power," my stepfather grunted. "I came here to have my questions answered."

"Tellarin!" I struggled to make sense where there could be none. "What are you doing?"

His voice took on a little of its former gentle tone. "This is nothing to do with you and me, Breda."

"Did you...?" I could scarcely say it. My tears were making the chamber as blurry as the black fire ever did. "Did you...only pretend love for me? Was it all to help you kill him?"

"No! I had no need of you, girl—I was already one of his most trusted men." He tightened his grip on Sulis then, until I feared my stepfather's neck would break. "What you and I have, little Breda, that is good and real. I will take you back to Nabban with me—I will be rich now, and you will be my wife. You will learn what a true city is, instead of this devilish, backward pile of stone."

"You love me? Truly, you love me?" I wanted very much to believe him. "Then let my stepfather go, Tellarin!"

He frowned. "I cannot. His death is the task I was given to do before I ever met you, and it is a task that needs doing. He is a madman, Breda! Surely after tonight's horrors, after seeing the demon he called up with forbidden magic, you can see why he cannot be allowed to live."

"Do not kill him, please! I beg you!"

He lifted his hand to still me. "I am sworn to my master in Nabban. This one thing I must do, and then we are both free."

Even an appeal in the name of love could not stop him. Confused and overwhelmed, unable to argue any longer with the man who had brought me so much joy, I turned to the witch, praying that she would do something—but Valada was gone. She had taken her freedom, leaving the rest of us to murder each other if we wished. I thought I saw a movement in the shadows, but it was only some other phantom, some flying thing that drifted above the stairwell on silent wings.

Lord Sulis was silent. He did not struggle against Tellarin's grip, but waited for slaughter like an old bull. When he swallowed, the skin on his neck pulled so tight that watching it made tears spill onto my cheeks once more. My beloved pressed his knife against my stepfather's throat as I stumbled toward them. Sulis looked at me, but still said nothing. Whatever thought was in his eyes, it had gone so deep that I could not even guess what it might be.

"Tell me again that you love me," I asked as I reached his side. As I looked at my soldier's frightened but exultant face, I could not help thinking of the High Keep, a haunted place built on murder, in whose corrupted, restless depths we stood. For a moment I thought the ghost-voices had returned, for my head was full of roaring, rushing noise. "Tell me again, Tellarin," I begged him. "Please."

My beloved did not move the blade from Sulis throat, but said, "Of course I love you, Breda. We will be married, and all of Nabban will lie at your feet. You will never be cold or lonely again." He leaned forward, and I could feel the beautiful long muscles of his back tense beneath my hand. He hesitated when he heard the click of the glass ball as it fell to the tiles and rattled away.

"What...?" he asked, then straightened suddenly, grabbing at the spot at his waist where the claw had pricked him. I took a few staggering steps and fell, weeping. Behind me, Tellarin began to wheeze, then to choke. I heard his knife clatter to the stone.

I could not look, but the sound of his last rattling breaths will never leave me.

Now that I am old, I know that this secretive keep will be the place I die. When I have breathed my last, I suppose they will bury me on the headland beside my mother and Lord Sulis.

After that long night beneath the castle had ended, the Heron King, as the Lake People called my stepfather, came to resemble once more the man he had been. He reigned over the High Keep for many more years, and gradually even my own brawling, jealous folk acknowledged him as their ruler, although the kingship did not outlive Sulis himself.

My own mark on the world will be even smaller.

I never married, and my brother Aelfric died of a fall from his horse without fathering any children, so although the Lake People still squabble over who should carry the standard and spear of the Great Thane, none of my blood will ever lead them again. Nor, I expect, will anyone stay on in the great castle that Lord Sulis rebuilt after I am dead—there are few enough left of our household now, and those who stay only do so for love of me. When I am gone, I doubt any will remain even to tend our graves.

I cannot say why I chose to keep this bleak place as my home, any more than I could say why I chose my stepfather's life over that of my beautiful, deceitful Tellarin. Because I feared to build something on blood that should have been founded on something better, I suppose. Because love does not do sums, but instead makes choices, and then gives its all.

Whatever the reasons, I have made those choices.

After he carried me out of the depths and back to daylight, my stepfather scarcely ever mentioned that terrible night again. He was still distant to the end of his days, still full of shadows, but at times I thought I sensed a peace in him that he had not had before. Why that might be, I could not say.

As he lay at last on his deathbed, breath growing fainter and fainter, I sat by his side for hours of every day and spoke to him of all that happened in the High Keep, talking of the rebuilding, which still continued, and of the tenants, and the herds, as if at any moment he might rise to resume his stewardship. But we both knew he would not.

When the last moment came, there was a kind of quiet expectancy on his face—no fear, but something more difficult to describe. As he strained for his final breath of air, I suddenly remembered something I had read in his book, and realized that I had made a mistake on that night so long ago.

"...She will show me the Way of Black Fire or there is no other Hope," he had written. "Either she will answer, or Death."

He had not meant that he would kill her if she did not give him what he needed. He had meant that if she could not help him find an answer, then he would have to wait until death came for him before he could learn the truth.

And now he would finally receive an answer to the question that had tormented him for so long.

Whatever that answer might be, Sulis did not return to share it with me. Now I am an old, old woman, and I will find it soon enough myself. It is strange, perhaps, but I find I do not much care. In one year with Tellarin, in those months of fierce love, I lived an entire lifetime. Since then I have lived another one, a long, slow life whose small pleasures largely balanced the moments of suffering. Surely two lives are enough for anyone—who needs the endless span of the immortals? After all, as the burning man made clear, an eternity of pain would be no gift.

And now that I have told my tale, even the ghosts that sometimes still startle me awake at midnight seem more like ancient friends than things to be feared.

I have made my choices.

I think I am content.

As the Wheel Turns

Aliette de Bodard

Aliette de Bodard lives in Paris. She shares a flat with more computers than warm bodies, and with two Lovecraftian plants gradually taking over the living room. She has a day job as a Computer Engineer, and writes speculative fiction in her spare time, indulging in her love of mythology and history: her trilogy of Aztec noir fantasies, Obsidian and Blood, is published by Angry Robot, and her short fiction has appeared in venues such as Asimov's and Interzone, garnering her nominations for the Hugo and Nebula Awards.

Prologue: the Wheel

IN THE TENTH COURT OF HELL, stands the Wheel of Rebirth.

Its spokes are of red lacquered wood; it creaks as demons pull it, dragging its load of souls back into the world.

And before the Wheel stands the Lady.

Every soul who goes to the Wheel must endure her gaze. Every soul must stop by her, and take from her pale hands the celadon cup, and drink.

The drink is herbs gathered from the surfaces of ponds, tears taken from the eyes of children, scales shed from old, wise dragons. To drink is to forget; for no soul can come back into the world remembering past lives, or the punishments meted out to it within the other Courts of Hell.

No soul.

Save one.

1. Yaoxin (Wen-Min Empire), 316 years after the Founding

The old beggar was a sorry sight squinting through rheumy eyes. One of his legs was missing, and he leant on his crutch to make his slow, unsteady way on the road.

Dai-Yu, in spite of herself, watched him. There was something about him that drew the eye; something that made her forget the tea leaves and spices her mother had asked her to get from the market in Yaoxin.

He seemed somehow more real, more sharply defined than the rest of the world. Dai-Yu couldn't explain the feeling, not even to herself.

As he passed by her, she drew a string of copper coins from her sleeve, and held it out to him.

The beggar's hand brushed hers, sending a tingle of heat up her arm. He stopped, then raised her palm to the light, staring at the darker patch on her skin.

"I've had it all my life," Dai-Yu said, apologetically. "It's just a birth-mark."

"I know that mark," the beggar said. "So you're the one, the child they were promised."

"What are you talking about?"

His fingers almost distractedly traced the outline of her mark. "Choice-maker. That's what the sign in your hand says."

He was crazy. He had to be. "It's just a birthmark," Dai-Yu protested. "I'm nothing."

He looked up at her, his face deadly serious. "You are the arbiter. You will have to choose between them."

The worst thing about the beggar wasn't his crazy talk; it was the single-mindedness, the way he kept tracing until Dai-Yu stared at the mark in her hand, trying to see the characters he'd spoken of. "Who—?"

"Tiger," the beggar said. "Crane."

The words he used weren't the names of animals, but rather their archaic forms. Even to Dai-Yu, who at fourteen had received no education other than the arts of housekeeping, they could only mean one thing. "The Founders?" She laughed, then stopped when she saw his eyes. The rheuminess was peeling away, revealing a keen gaze trained on her.

"Yes," the beggar said. "You will have to choose."

"Choose between what? The Founders have been dead for centuries! Demons take you, you've told me nothing!"

"There is a...an argument," the beggar said. "A question they could not solve."

"What question?" Dai-Yu asked, but he shook his head, and began walking away.

"Wait!" she shouted, but he wasn't shuffling any more—he was running towards the gates of Yaoxin as fast as one leg and his crutch could carry him.

Dai-Yu ran, too, steadily catching up to him—but then he passed through the gate, and she lost him in the marketplace. She stood shaking in the midst of the crowd, knowing she should have outrun him easily.

Later that night, she crept into the shrine of her ancestors, and stared at the very earliest tablet: the one that bore, entwined, the names of the warrior philosophers who had founded the Empire. Tiger. Crane.

The beggar's words would not leave her.

Choice-maker. You are the arbiter.

2. Yaoxin (Wen-Min Empire), 321 years after the Founding

They came a few years later. By then, Dai-Yu had married, and moved into the house of the wealthy merchant He En-Lai as his second wife. She spent her days running the household and helping to raise the three children of the first wife.

One hot, stormy summer evening, Dai-Yu was sitting alone in the wives' quarters, playing a mournful tune on the zither, when a gust of wind sent rain into her face. Startled, she got up to close the shutters.

And, slowly, became aware she was no longer alone.

She did not move. Guards, she knew, watched the house, and every door was barred.

"Dai-Yu," a voice chanted, and it was the lament of the wind. Another voice took up the words of her name, and whispered, "Choice-maker."

She moved, then, trembling, to face them.

They stood in darkness, both of them: vague silhouettes whose faces she could not see. They smelled of old, musty things, books left too long untended.

"What are you doing here?" she asked.

One of them smiled. Teeth glittered in the shadows. "You are the child of the promise, Dai-Yu. You must choose."

Choose choose choose, whispered the other voice, a raucous, rhythmical chant like the calls of birds.

"You're dead," Dai-Yu whispered. "The Annals say you died in the Imperial Palace."

"We cannot die," the first voice said. "We became something else."

"It does not matter," said the second voice. "She must choose."

"You're crazy," Dai-Yu said, trying to deny the fear that clenched her chest. "Go away. I wasn't born to choose anything."

The first voice laughed. The sound echoed on and on under the lacquered ceiling, taking strength from the walls. "Do you truly think so?"

And Dai-Yu, shocked, saw that the birthmark in her hand glowed red, like maple leaves, like the lanterns of New Year's Eve. "No," she whispered.

"This is the choice laid before you." The first voice was the drawl of a large feline, one that would toy with its prey until exhaustion brought death. Tiger. "When we founded the Empire three hundred years ago, we argued over what would keep it together."

"Duty," Crane said. "Homage to one's ancestors, and respect of the law. Those are the things that will make us last."

"Man knows no duty," Tiger said, breathing into the room the humid smell of jungles. "Man knows no respect. Only fear will keep the Empire intact. Fear of our neighbours to unite us. Fear of death and chaos to keep us from crumbling."

Dai-Yu, poised near the open window, said, "This is..." *a philosophers' argument,* she wanted to say. Children's words, without meaning. It's not ideas that will keep us together, that will keep the Hsiung Nu from our frontiers.

Crane whispered, "It is no game. The loser will renounce. No longer shall he guide the destiny of the Empire."

"Because you decide anything? What about the Emperor? What about the Imperial Court?"

A dry bout of laughter, from Crane. "Everyone listens to their ancestors, child. We cannot die. We still rule. Now choose."

Dai-Yu stared, trying to see their faces through the darkness. "I know nothing." They were each as vast and terrible, both as unfathomable. "This is ridiculous. Just find someone else."

"There is no-one else." The shadows behind Crane drew the darker hint of wings the colour of obsidian. "Choose."

"I can't," Dai-Yu whispered, the words forced out of her before she could think.

In the darkness, she could feel their combined gaze, assessing her, judging her. The hollow in her stomach would not go away.

"Very well," Crane said. "You are not ready."

"Think on it," Tiger whispered. "We will come back."

There was no noise when they left, but Dai-Yu could breathe more easily; she no longer had the sense that every word she said was being set apart and weighed.

The shadows returned to those of the wives' quarters.

She could not stop shaking. What did they think she was, to be embroiled in their vast, unknowable games? She was human. She had a husband, and soon would have children of her own. She was no prophet, no wise woman.

All she wanted was to sleep, and to forget. To forget that they had ever been there, or that they would ever return.

In silence she moved through the house, her sandals making no noise on the slats of the floor. She was almost at the door of her own room when something stopped her.

She could not have told what. Like with the beggar, it was a sense that something was more real than it ought to have been.

The door to the nursery was ajar, as it had been earlier in the evening. And yet...

Gently, Dai-Yu slid the door open, then entered the room. Through the gaps in the shutters fell the white light of the moon, tracing the outlines of three beds.

Dai-Yu could feel nothing. Not even fear, nor anger. She moved towards the furthest bed, where Pao, the youngest son, was sleeping.

A ray of light lay across his face, throwing into relief what they had done to him. There were scars, like claw-marks: three swipes on each cheek, bleeding in the white light.

And it was a claw-swipe, too, that had opened his chest, laying the heart bare amidst its cage of ribs.

The wind whispered, in Tiger's voice: *A reminder, Dai-Yu. Until we return.*

She screamed, then: a sound torn out of her lungs that echoed throughout the house, a scream of rage and grief and despair. It woke the other two boys, who huddled in their beds, their faces frozen in shock. It summoned the servants, and then her husband and his first wife.

"Dai-Yu?" En-Lai, her husband, said. He was shaking her, but she could not answer him; she could not banish the image of the dead boy in his bed. The more he insisted, the more she withdrew within herself, until she hovered at the edge of a chasm in her mind, knowing that if she fell into it there would be no return.

"Lin Dai-Yu," another voice said.

She looked up. This was the district magistrate, with his jade robes of office and his velvet cap. Three militiamen had taken position at the entrance of the room, their staffs at the ready.

"What happened here?" The magistrate's face was stern.

"That slut killed my boy," the first wife said, quivering with anger.

Dai-Yu, still struggling to remain focused, could only shake her head. *No no no. Not I. He did that.*

The magistrate looked at her, his grey gaze expressionless. She looked back.

The magistrate's gaze moved to the bed, then back to Dai-Yu. "No. It could not have been her. What weapon would she have used?" He raised Dai-Yu's hands, displayed their shorn nails. "See," he said. "These are not claws."

"Then who did this?" En-Lai demanded in anger, and grief.

The magistrate's gaze rested on the servants for a moment. "Who indeed." And now his look was trained on the first wife, and on the long, lacquered fingernails that were her pride. Each of them was protected by an elegant bronze sheath—a sheath that tapered to a sharp, clawlike point.

The first wife was still standing near Dai-Yu, ready to accuse her again. Her gaze met the magistrate's, and her face pinched in anger. "You accuse me?" she said, drawing herself to her full height. "Of killing my own son?"

The magistrate smiled without joy. "I have seen mothers do worse than that."

"No," Dai-Yu whispered, understanding that the nightmare was not over. But no-one was listening to her.

"You're making a mistake," En-Lai said, as the militiamen came into the room, and bound the first wife's wrists. "That accusation is ludicrous."

Dai-Yu found her voice from some remote place. "This wasn't done by human hands."

The magistrate turned to her. The light falling on his robes bleached them white for a moment, like a coat of feathers; a moment only, but in that moment Dai-Yu looked into his eyes, and saw the ageless, malicious gaze of Crane.

No.

"The law must be honoured," the magistrate said, with a tight smile, and they were not his words, but something far older, far more vicious. "A crime cannot go unpunished. We will find out the truth."

Tiger's voice in her mind, endlessly whispering its promise: *A reminder, Dai-Yu. Until we return.*

Crane's voice: *A crime cannot go unpunished.*

A dead boy in his bed, his face slashed, his chest yawning with the heart inside.

The first wife, struggling as they dragged her out of the room, screaming, calling them names. In vain.

The chasm in Dai-Yu's mind opened wider, and she tumbled into the darkness, screaming all the while.

Her husband En-Lai, seeing her face go slack, shook her again, but she no longer had speech.

The doctor, summoned to the scene, found the body of the boy, the husband protesting his wife's innocence, and Dai-Yu standing tall and straight, yet silent.

He listened to the voice of her heart, but could find nothing wrong. In the end, he prescribed a calming brew to En-Lai, whose sickness he could understand, then left the house, glad to be away from Dai-Yu's stare.

The first wife admitted to the murder of her son under torture, and was executed.

En-Lai had Dai-Yu moved to a dark room at the back of the house, where two very old servants tended her. For seven years she spoke little, only dwindled away, the skin over her bones as translucent as rice paper, the gestures she made more and more sluggish.

In the end, she caught the lung sickness, and died.

Thus ended her first life.

Interlude: Tenth Court of Hell

The soul comes before the Wheel for its first rebirth. But the Lady does not move. Her hands are empty.

"Why?" the soul asks, and its voice is a mere whisper.

"You cannot drink. You must remember," the Lady says. Her face is emotionless. "You must answer them."

The soul's face is indistinct; if it had any expression, it would be anger. "Never," it says.

"You have no choice." The Lady's yellow sleeves billow in the wind, beckoning the soul onwards. "Come, child. There is another life awaiting you."

3. Wen-Min Empire, 343-631 years after the Founding

Thus, in every life, Dai-Yu was born knowing everything, from her first birth to her last. No more childhoods of innocence, no more days free from fear. In every life, she dreaded that Tiger and Crane would come back and ask the question.

They did not always come, but, when they did, they destroyed everything. Tiger killed her family. Crane had them arrested, or aroused in them the desire to fight on the border: they took up the swords of soldiers, and came back wounded and silent, or not at all.

A reminder, Tiger said.

Think of the Empire, Crane whispered. *Can you leave it to crumble because of a caprice?*

And they had been right—they were everywhere: in the eyes of merchants in the marketplace; in the faces of priests as they said their devotions; in the judges and clerks at the tribunal, passing through all of them like dark, beating shadows.

She could not escape.

But she would not yield.

4. Shunliu (Wen-Min Empire), 650 years after the Founding

When she was fourteen, Yi-Sen, who had once been Dai-Yu, was given in marriage to Zheng Lei, first clerk of the tribunal in Shunliu.

She had two sons, and obsessively watched each of them in his cradle. And when the hot storms of summer came, she moved to the nursery and spent the nights watching over her children.

Her husband Lei had his own quarters, but servants' gossip did reach him, in the end.

He asked her into his study one night. Yi-Sen came hesitantly, tiptoeing past the shelves crammed with books—her husband's study was his preserve, a scholar's haven in which women had no place.

Lei was sitting at his reading table, which was bare save for a writing brush and a lantern. He raised his gaze to her. "You must be wondering why I've asked you here."

"Yes," Yi-Sen said. Bluntness, her parents had told her more than once, was no quality for a woman. But even an army of tutors had not been able to take it out of her.

"Sit down," Lei said.

She pulled over a chair, and sat before him, waiting for him to speak. At last he said, "Yi-Sen. I'm no fool. What do you fear?"

Her heart missed a beat. "What do you mean?"

"Don't toy with me. I've seen the way you watch shadows. Men guilty of some unpunished offence look the same when the militia passes their way."

"I—" Yi-Sen hesitated. She had kept the secret of her past lives, of the mark in her hand, like a miser hoards his gold and jade.

In Lei's eyes was nothing but a mild curiosity.

"You won't believe me," she said.

"I'm a scholar. Let me be the judge of what to believe."

"My name is Dai-Yu," she said. "I was born in the year three hundred and one. I am the child of the promise."

It all came spilling out of her, then, the stories of Tiger and Crane, of the boy dead in his bed, the gaping wound in his chest, of the other dead in her past.

Lei's grey eyes watched her, judged her, just as Tiger's and Crane's eyes had. He said, finally, "I would like to believe you've invented all of this."

"But you don't?" Yi-Sen asked. She had expected many things, but not that.

Lei said, slowly, "You can't read. You're no scholar. And yet...yet you've told me things from the past. Details that are true. I've read them in books."

"I didn't learn them," Yi-Sen said. "I remember. Always."

His gaze was on her, and did not waver. "I believe you do."

"Thank you."

"It's not an easy fate. Nor an easy choice."

"You don't understand," Yi-Sen said. "Why should I choose? Why should I grant anything to them?" Her voice was rising, spinning out of control: she heard herself say the words from a faraway place. "They bring nothing but pain and sorrow."

"The Founders lived in a harsh time. I'm not excusing them," Lei added, raising a hand to check her. "I'm just giving you information to understand them."

"I don't. They're not human."

"Not any more," Lei said. "There are tales about the things that do not die, that keep ageing, that never descend into Hell. They're not pleasant stories." He rose, came behind her. His arm settled around her shoulders. She rose in turn, faced him in silence.

"Yi-Sen...This is where I'll fail you. I'm a minor scholar, not a warrior or a conjuror. I can't help you."

"It doesn't matter. No-one can stand against them, can they?"

"It would take an equal to resist them. But there is no-one in Wen-Min who has their power. Yet I would stand by your side, if need be."

"Why?" she asked. "Why would you go to such trouble?"

He spun her round to face him. "Haven't you guessed?" His voice was mild, seemingly emotionless, but a bare quiver betrayed him.

"No," Yi-Sen said. "No. Please don't. They—they take everything I love. They use it against me."

"You said it yourself. No-one can stand against them. If that's the case, then nothing truly matters."

She raised her hand, traced the outline of his face, both familiar yet utterly alien to her. "I won't lie to you," she said, softly. "It matters to me. To know I'm not alone."

"You'll never be alone again. I promise."

She stared away from him, knowing this was a promise he could not keep. "Tell me. What would you choose, if you had to?"

"Neither," Lei said. "And yet how we need them, to keep us together. Duty. Fear. But what they have become... Can you choose between the storms and the flood?"

She had no answer.

After a while, he moved away to extinguish the lantern. "I'll look in my books. I may find some things in the old Annals, something you can use against them."

Although she did not believe he would find anything, Yi-Sen nodded. "You're a good man."

He gave a bitter laugh. "No. I know all my flaws. Do not flatter me."

"I don't flatter," she protested, but he was already leading her away from the reading table.

"Come," he said. "For this night at least, let us forget them."

5. Shunliu (Wen-Min Empire), 657 years after the Founding

Yi-Sen stood on the highest floor of the house, watching the streets go up in flames. Peach blossoms fell everywhere like rain, and she wondered whether she saw truly, or only mistook embers for flowers.

A shadow fell across the doorway. "Dai-Yu," a deep voice said.

Crane. She did not turn around. She knew what he had come for. "That's not my name."

"It was your first name. It is your true one." Crane came closer to her. He smelled old, like dead books, the same smell the magistrate had had, all those years ago. "Your husband is dead, Dai-Yu."

She had known it as soon as she heard his voice. But still, cold flared in her chest, then spread to every part of her until she felt nothing any more. "And his blood is on your hands. You sent him to defend the tribunal, knowing the mob would kill him."

"He only did his duty," Crane said, his voice heavy with malice. "He was first clerk of the tribunal. He had to bar the mob's entry, to stop the riots."

"He chose nothing," she said. "He was your toy."

"Had you chosen, he would still be alive."

Rage filled her. "If I had chosen? Did you think to force my hand? Did you think I would tell you that you were in the right, and Tiger wrong?"

Beady eyes shone in the shadows: amused, perhaps. "It is time to choose. Your husband is dead. Will you leave your children to inherit this world, this mad world where rioters can take everything away from you?"

"Do you think I care?" she asked, softly.

Softer footsteps echoed under the ceiling of the room. She heard Tiger's voice behind her. "Your husband is dead, Dai-Yu. Do you wish to meet the same fate?"

She said nothing. There was no longer room in her for fear. Below her, the city glowed red with fire, resounded with the cries of the mob as they lynched every clerk they could find.

"Choose," Tiger said.

Crane's hand on her shoulder tightened its grip. "Choose."

Storms and floods, Lei had said. How can you choose between them? *Choose.*

Lei was dead, trampled by the mob, all because he had fallen in love with her. She could have wept, but it was not what she needed. She needed to fuel her rage. She needed to gather her courage.

"I told you," she said. "I won't choose. I won't let you force me."

"You have nowhere to go," Crane said.

"Give us our answer," Tiger added.

No escape. There was no escape from them, not ever.

But there was a place where neither of them could go.

"Find someone else," Yi-Sen said. And, before she could lose her courage, she leapt in one fluid gesture from the open window.

It was only three floors, but her fall seemed to have no end. When she did land, splayed like a puppeteer's broken doll, pain spread everywhere, in her arms, in her chest, through her heart. Her face was turned towards the sky, and the peach blossoms fell over her like rain.

She could not see Tiger or Crane.

When the darkness came for her, she was smiling.

Interlude: Tenth Court of Hell

The Lady watches the soul come, and stop before her.

"Another life," she says.

The soul does not move. This time it says nothing, which, of course, does not mean it feels nothing.

"You should know you cannot stay forever in Hell," the Lady says. "You committed no sin. You did not cheat, or lie, or abuse your power. You earned nothing but a brief respite."

"Even a few years is enough."

"You cannot escape forever," the Lady says.

"No," the soul says. "It doesn't matter. Just don't send me where Lei went."

"Child, he is not here. He was a virtuous man, and he has earned a stay in the Southern Paradise before his next life."

The soul remains silent for a while. The Wheel turns.

"I am glad. Our paths won't cross again. Things are as they should be."

For the first time, there is pity in the Lady's voice, barely audible. "Dai-Yu. Give them what they want. You are nothing."

"I'm the child of the promise," the soul says. "My power is in making a choice. Or in failing to make it. I won't relent. Life after life, they destroy me. They kill those I love, as they killed Lei. I owe them nothing."

"They are fighting," the Lady says. "In Laijing, the policies from the Imperial Palace are growing more incoherent."

"So?"

"There are those," the Lady says, "who will know how to take advantage of strife. Those who have waited long enough to topple Wen-Min."

"Yes. But I don't care."

"You should," the Lady says. A wind blows, carrying her words away. "It is time, child. Come."

And then it starts again, all of it.

6. Wen-Min Empire, 701-987 years after the Founding

She ran. She did not allow herself to love, or even care for anyone. There had been enough deaths.

She became a hermit, endlessly travelling the roads of the Empire. On her travels, she made acquaintances, never keeping them for more than a few moons: merchants on their way to make a fortune; soldiers going to the boundaries to defend against the Hsiung Nu; families made homeless by famines, floods. As the outer edges of the Empire became lost to the Hsiung Nu hordes, she met refugees flung on the roads with nothing but their clothes, people with haunted faces who would not speak about their past.

Even if she made the choice between Tiger and Crane, it would not help them. That would merely replace the Emperor with a tyrant, a power unchecked by any other. She had seen what Tiger and Crane could do. She had learnt to fear them. She hardened her heart, and moved on.

But, no matter how far she went, Tiger and Crane always found her, always pressed her for an answer. And always she took her own life rather than choose.

A brief respite, the Lady had said. But even that was better than nothing.

Interlude: Tenth Court of Hell

The souls meet before the Wheel.

They do not come from the same place. One, the elder, has come through the Nine Courts of Hell. The other has had fewer lives: for, in a former incarnation, it was found so virtuous it earned a stay in the Southern Paradise. And now the stay has ended, and it must be reborn. It has asked for only one thing, and this request was granted.

The Lady knows this should not be happening. But where there are rules, there are exceptions. Not many things can sway the Judges of Hell, but devotion and virtue always find their reward.

"Dai-Yu," the younger soul says.

The elder of the souls does not move. It looks at the other soul, trying to make out its features. Finally it says, its voice shaking, "Lei? You shouldn't be here. You should have forgotten."

"I am where I need to be," the younger soul says. "Listen, Dai-Yu."

"No—stay away from me. Crane killed you the last time, just for being my husband. How can you even think of coming here?"

"Dai-Yu," Lei's soul says. It reaches out with a translucent finger, tenderly. "I made a promise. I am here."

"You can do nothing. Stay away. Please. Be reborn in some place where I won't have to meet you."

"I did something for you," Lei's soul says. "In the Southern Paradise is a library that holds every book ever printed in Wen-Min. I went there, and searched. You are the child of the promise. But did you ever ask yourself who promised you to the Founders?"

The silence, this time, has an almost palpable quality.

"We have forgotten," Lei's soul says. "Tiger and Crane rewrote the histories to make us forget." Its voice takes on a singsong quality. "'Three philosophers founded the Empire, in a time so far removed that all that remains are myths written on crumbling bamboo strips. And, as philosophers are wont to do, they fell out.'"

"Three..." Her soul's voice is a mere whisper.

"Crane, Tiger," Lei's soul says. "And Tortoise. He wouldn't choose, Dai-Yu. He wouldn't be the arbiter between Tiger and Crane. So he withdrew to the highest mountain in Wen-Min, but not before promising them there would be a child."

"I," Dai-Yu says.

Lei says nothing.

"I need to find him."

"You won't. Because he would not take part in the future of the Empire, he was thrown out of it. He became a hermit, wandering on the roads of Wen-Min: a monk answering to no-one—"

"A beggar," Dai-Yu's soul whispers.

"What?"

"It's nothing. Thank you, Lei."

"You don't have to thank me," Lei's soul says. "Dai-Yu—"

Their souls brush, part. Something has been exchanged: a kiss, if souls could kiss. A promise, perhaps.

Lei's soul takes the celadon cup from the Lady's hands, and drinks. Its light is fading away now, its memories scattering. Dai-Yu's soul stands by the side, quivering. It does not drink from the cup. It never drinks. For the first time, it occurs to Dai-Yu that it is a blessing, this remembrance.

The Wheel turns, taking its load of souls back into the world of flesh.

7. Mount Xu (Wen-Min Empire), 1021 years after the Founding

There was a temple on Mount Xu. It was not one of the Five Great Temples, not a place where pilgrims would endlessly flock, seeking salvation amidst clouds of incense.

The temple at Mount Xu was a mere pagoda of three storeys. Its slanted roof was made of lacquered wood, ungilded.

It was to this temple that Dai-Yu came, after years of searching; years spent on the roads, from her native city of Yaoxin to fertile Shandong in

the south, from windy, arid Menzhou in the east to Laijing, the capital at
the centre of the Empire.

The air was warm, promising the sweetness of summer, and pink
cherry blossoms littered the path. Dai-Yu, pausing on the last rise,
inhaled, and felt the serenity of the place fill her bones, as if all her life
had been leading her here.

There was no-one within the pagoda. The path went on, into the
gardens, and then deeper into the mountains.

The beggar was waiting for her at the end, sitting in meditation before
a waterfall in the shadow of pine trees. It was the same man Dai-Yu had
met so many years ago: the same man, with the missing leg and iron
crutch, with the rheumy eyes that pierced her soul.

"Dai-Yu," he said, when she came closer. "Child of the promise."

"You knew I would come," Dai-Yu said, angrily. Had she been led
here, manipulated since the beginning like a puppet on its strings?

"There are not many mountains in Wen-Min," the beggar said. "And
I have not moved for many years." He rose. "Come, child. Let us walk."

"How could you?" Dai-Yu said. "How could you promise me to them,
to make the choice you didn't have the courage to make yourself?"

"They were children. Grasping for what they couldn't have." Tortoise's
eyes turned to the waterfall endlessly pouring its water into the misty
pool. "There is no choice."

"Not choosing is a choice."

"So is running away," Tortoise said. "So is suicide."

These references angered her. "You accuse me?"

Tortoise shrugged. "I don't know, child. I can't tell you what to do, for
I never could find out. There isn't much time left."

The sun had sunk below the cover of the trees; already the forest was
darkening. Cold spread within Dai-Yu's bones. "They are coming," she
said.

"Yes," Tortoise said.

"Why?"

"They knew you would come to me, eventually. They knew the
moment you entered this temple, the moment we finally met. For you
are the child of the promise," Tortoise said. "My child."

It rang true. And yet it was impossible. "No—I have...I have parents. I have a human soul. I remember well enough."

Tortoise reached out, traced the mark on her hand. It sent a tingle of heat up her arm, as it had done, an eternity ago, on the road to Yaoxin. "I made you," he said. "Who else could have chosen in my stead? Who else would not have to drink the Brew of Oblivion in the Courts of Hell?"

"No—"

"You are the breath from my breath, the flesh from my flesh, the seed from my seed. Dai-Yu—"

The darkness was almost complete. A cold wind rose, scattering the pine needles on the ground, whispering words of mourning. And Dai-Yu, staring at her maker in the dim light, saw fear in his eyes, and the sallow cast of his skin, and understood that he would not help her, that he had long since forgotten his power. That he, too, was nothing compared to Tiger and Crane.

"No," she whispered, but the wind carried the word away.

Two shadows coalesced at the heart of the darkness. Dai-Yu watched them take on substance, transfixed.

"Dai-Yu," Tiger said, in a feline growl. "It is time."

"Choose," Crane said.

Wind whipped at Dai-Yu's sleeves.

Tortoise still stood frozen beside her. "Leave her."

Tiger laughed. "Too late, brother. You relinquished your mantle to her. Now she must do what you could not."

"Tiger—" Tortoise said, moving to stand in front of Dai-Yu.

A hand flashed, shining like metal in the darkness. Tortoise fell back, one hand going to his chest, then rising to his face. Blood dripped from it onto the ground, one drop at a time, a soft patter, like rain.

Dai-Yu felt the cut as if it were in her own chest; she stumbled, gasping, then tried to stand.

"My child," Tortoise whispered. Time slowed, stopped; in that single moment when Tortoise reeled back, she heard the words he was not saying.

Not choosing is a choice.

So is running away.

Fear is a choice.

Dai-Yu, staring at Tortoise's shocked face, felt a cold certainty rise within her. She moved until she stood before him, seeing the gaping hole in his chest, the same hole Tiger had once opened in Pao's chest.

She remembered Lei's words: *It would take an equal to resist them. There is no-one in Wen-Min who has their power.*

Yet Tortoise had been their equal, once. The power was still within him, but fear prevented him using it.

"Breath from my breath," she whispered. "Flesh from my flesh." And, more slowly, "You have relinquished your mantle."

She laid a hand on Tortoise's chest, plunged it deep into the wound until she felt the heart beating under her fingers, the sticky heat of it on her skin. Warmth spread up her arm, into her chest, through her whole body, until she shivered with the same rhythm.

Flesh from my flesh.

The warmth rose within her, stronger and hotter. Under her spread fingers, Tortoise was fading, crumbling away to nothing, to dust carried by the wind.

Breath from my breath.

There was nothing where he had been: only dust; only a memory, already fading.

Seed from my seed.

Every part of her tingled now. She turned, slowly, and made her way to Tiger and Crane, facing them for the first time in centuries.

"Tiger," she said. "Crane."

All her lives she had run away from the darkness, never once thinking that shadows, undispelled, only grow. She stared at both of them now, shivering, but not with fear. She was their equal.

She raised her hand.

Light sprang up, throwing into sharp relief their faces: the lined, wizened masks of old men; the pale skins of things forever living in shadows.

There was a smell, a musty smell like books left too long untended.

"You are children," she said.

"No," Tiger growled, but in the light he was no longer as frightening as he had been.

"Think of the Empire," Crane sighed.

They were smaller, now, as if the light had robbed them of their majesty; smaller, and ever dwindling.

What would you choose? she had once asked Lei.

She could still remember his answer. *Neither. And yet how we need them, to keep us together.*

He had been wrong.

Old, dead things. Things that do not die, that keep ageing. Things no longer needed.

"I choose," Dai-Yu said. And, bending, caught both of them in her hands. "None of you. Let the Empire rise or fall on its own terms."

They weighed nothing: a leaf; a breath; a length of silk. They shrank under her touch, shrieking their rage in tinny voices, dwindling ever more until they finally fell silent.

In Dai-Yu's hand was nothing but coldness, and then even that was gone.

She stared at her trembling palm, then at the darkness all around her that distorted the pine trees into demon shadows.

"It is ended," she whispered, and did not know whether to smile or laugh. Tortoise's power coursed within her, begging to be used, to shape things as they should be. But she, who had seen what power could do, quelled it.

She saw, for the first time, the life that would be hers: free from the shadow of fear; free to make her own choices, to love and be loved in return; to raise her children in peace. Free at last, she thought, with a smile.

She walked away from the pool, her hands as empty as when she came, seeing the paths of her future before her, like so many flowers she could pick.

Epilogue: the Wheel

In the Tenth Court of Hell, the Lady waits before the Wheel. To every soul that passes she hands the celadon cup, and watches them drink until every memory has scattered away.

There is no exception.

Not any more.

The Alchemist
Paolo Bacigalupi

Paolo Bacigalupi's debut novel, The Windup Girl, *took the science fiction field by storm, winning the Hugo, Nebula, Locus, Compton Crook, and John W. Campbell Memorial awards. He is also the author of the young adult novel,* Ship Breaker, *which won the Michael L. Printz Award and was a finalist for the National Book Award. His latest novel is* The Drowned Cities, *a companion novel to* Ship Breaker. *He's also the author of several short stories, most of which can be found in his award-winning collection,* Pump Six and Other Stories. *"The Alchemist" shares its setting with the novella "The Executioness" by Tobias S. Buckell, and the two stories first appeared as an audiobook published by Audible.com called* The Alchemist and the Executioness. *Paolo currently lives in Western Colorado with his wife and son, where he is working on a new novel.*

1

It's DIFFICULT TO SELL your last bed to a neighbor. More difficult still when your only child clings like a spider monkey to its frame, and screams as if you were chopping off her arms with an axe every time you try to remove her.

The four men from Alacan had already arrived, hungry and happy to make copper from the use of their muscles, and Lizca Sharma was there as well, her skirts glittering with diamond wealth, there to supervise the four-poster's removal and make sure it wasn't damaged in the transfer.

The bed was a massive piece of furniture. For a child, ridiculous. Jiala's small limbs had no need to sprawl across such a vast expanse. But the frame had been carved with images of the floating palaces of Jhandpara.

Cloud dragons of old twined up its posts to the canopy where wooden claws clutched rolled nets and, with a clever copper clasp, opened on hinges to let the nets come tumbling down during the hot times to keep out mosquitoes. A beautiful bed. A fanciful bed. Imbued with the vitality of Jhandpara's lost glory. An antique made of kestrel-wood—that fine red grain so long choked under bramble—and triply valuable because of it.

We would eat for months on its sale.

But to Jiala, six years old and deeply attached, who had already watched every other piece of our household furniture disappear, it was another matter.

She had watched our servants and nannies evaporate as water droplets hiss to mist on a hot griddle. She had watched draperies tumble, seen the geometries of our carpets rolled and carried out on Alacaner backs, a train of men like linked sausages marching from our marbled halls. The bed was too much. These days, our halls echoed with only our few remaining footfalls. The porticos carried no sound of music from our pianoforte, and the last bit of warmth in the house could only be found in the sulphurous stink of my workshop, where a lone fire yet blazed.

For Jiala, the disappearance of her vast and beautiful bed was her last chance to make a stand.

"NOOOOOOOO!"

I tried to cajole her, and then to drag her. But she'd grown since her days as a babe, and desperation gave her strength. As I hauled her from the mattress, she grabbed hold of one huge post and locked her arms around it. She pressed her cheek against the cloud dragon's scales and screamed again. "NOOOOOOOO!"

We all covered our ears as she hit a new crystal-shattering octave.

"NOOOOOOOO!"

"Please, Jiala," I begged. "I'll buy you a new one. As soon as we have money."

"I don't want a new one!" she screamed. "I want this one!" Tears ran down her reddening face.

I tugged at her, embarrassed under the judging gaze of Mistress Lizca and the workmen behind me. I liked Lizca. And now she saw me at my most reduced. As if the empty house wasn't enough. As if this sale of my child's last belonging was not humiliating in the extreme, I now begged a child for cooperation.

"Jiala. It's only for a little while. And it will just be down the narrows at Mistress Lizca's. You can visit if you like." I looked to Lizca, hoping desperately that she wouldn't contradict. "It will be just next door."

"I can't sleep next door! This is mine! You sold everything! We don't have anything! This is mine!" Jiala's shrieks rose to new levels, and this brought on her coughing, which alternated with her screams as I tried to pry her arms free.

"I'll buy you a new one," I said. "One fit for a princess."

But she only screamed louder.

The workmen kept their hands over their ears as the gryphon shrieks continued. I cast about, desperate for a solution to her heartbreak. Desperate to stop the coughing that she was inflicting on herself with this tantrum.

Stupid. I'd been stupid. I should have asked Pila to take her out, and then ordered the workmen to come stealthy like thieves. I cast about the room, and there on the workmen's faces, I saw something unexpected. Unlike Lizca, who stood stonily irritated, the workmen showed nothing of the sort.

No impatience.

No anger.

No superiority nor disgust.

Pity.

These refugee workmen, come across the river from Lesser Khaim to do a bit of labor for a few coppers, pitied me. Soiled linen shirts draped off their stooped shoulders and broken leather shoes showed cold mudcaked winter toes, and yet they pitied me.

They had lost everything fleeing their own city, their last portable belongings clanking on their backs, their hounds and children squalling and snot-nosed, tangled around their ankles. Flotsam in a river of refugees come from Alacan when their Mayor and Majisters accepted that the city could not be held and that they must, in fact, fall back—and quickly—if they wished to escape the bramble onslaught.

Alacan men, men who had lost everything, looked at me with pity. And it filled me with rage.

I shouted at Jiala. "Well, what should I do? Should I have you starve? Should I stop feeding you and Pila? Should we all sit in the straw and gnaw mice bones through the winter so that you can have a kestrel-wood bed?"

Of course, she only screamed louder. But now it was out of fear. And yet I continued to shout, my voice increasing, overwhelming hers, an animal roar, seeking to frighten and intimidate that which I could not cajole. Using my size and power to crush something small and desperate.

"Shut up!" I screamed. "We have nothing! Do you understand? Nothing! We have no choices left!"

Jiala collapsed into sobbing misery, which turned to deeper coughing, which frightened me even more, because if the coughing continued I would have to cast a spell to keep it down. Everything I did led only to something worse.

The fight went out of Jiala. I pried her away from the bed.

Lizca motioned to the Alacaners and they began the process of disassembling the great thing.

I held Jiala close, feeling her shaking and sobbing, still loud but without a fight now. I had broken her will. An ugly solution that reduced us both into something less than what the Three Faces of Mara hoped for us. Not father and daughter. Not protector and sacred charge. Monster and victim. I clutched my child to me, hating what had been conjured between us. That I had bullied her down. That she had forced me to this point.

But hating myself, most of all, for I had placed us in this position.

That was the true sickness. I had dragged us into danger and want. Our house had once been so very fine. In our glory days, when Merali was still alive, I made copper pots for rich households, designed metal and glass mirrors of exquisite inlay. Blew glass bargaining bulbs for the great mustached merchants of Diamond Street to drink from as they made their contracts. I engraved vases with the Three Faces of Mara: woman, man, and child, dancing. I etched designs of cloud dragons and floating palaces. I cast gryphons in gold and bronze and copper. I inlaid forest hunts of stags and unicorns in the towering kestrel forests of the East and sculpted representations of the three hundred and thirty-three arches of Jhandpara's glorious waterfront. I traded in the nostalgic dreams of empire's many lost wonders.

And we had been rich.

Now, instead of adornments for rich households, strange devices squatted and bubbled and clanked in my workroom, and not a single one of them for sale. Curving copper tubes twisted like kraken tentacles. Our impoverished faces reflected from the brass bells of delivery nozzles. Glass bulbs glowed blue with the ethereal stamens of the lora flower, which can only be gathered in summer twilight when ember beetles beckon them open and mate within their satin petals.

And now, all day and all night, my workroom hissed and steamed with the sulphurous residues of bramble.

Burned branches and seeds and sleep-inducing spines passed through my equipment's bowels. Instead of Jhandpara's many dreams, I worked now with its singular nightmare. The plant that had destroyed an empire and now threatened to destroy us as well. Our whole house stank day and night with the smell of burning bramble and the workings of my balanthast. That was the true cause of my daughter's pitched defense of her kestrel-wood bed.

I was the one at fault. Not the girl. I had impoverished us with every decision I had made, over fifteen years. Jiala was too young to even know what the household had looked like in its true glory days. She had arrived too late for that. Never saw its flowering rose gardens and lupine beds. Didn't remember when the halls rang with servants' laughter and activity, when Pila, Saema and Traz all lived with us, and Niaz and Romara and— some other servant whose name even I have now forgotten—swept every corner of the place for dust and kept the mice at bay. It was my fault.

I clutched my sobbing child to my breast, because I knew she was right, and I was wrong, but still I let Mistress Lizca and her Alacan workmen break the bed apart, and carry it out, piece by piece, until we were alone in an empty and cold marble room.

I had no choice. Or, more precisely, I had stripped us of our choices. I had gone too far, and circumstances were closing upon us both.

2

Jiala kept from me for several days after I sold her bed. She went out, and disappeared for hours at a time. She was resentful, but she spoke no more to me, and seemed willing to let me bribe her back to forgiveness with syrup crackers from Sugar Alley. She disappeared into the cobbled streets of Khaim, and I took advantage of the peaceful time to work.

The sale of the bed, even if it was a fabulously rare piece of art, even if it did come from kestrel-wood which no one had been able to harvest in more than five decades as the bramble sprawl overwhelmed its cathedral forests, would only last so long. And after the money ran out, I would have no more options.

I felt as if I was trapped in the famous torture room of Majister Halizak, who liked to magic his victims into a closed cell, without door or window, and then slowly spell the whole room down from the size of an elephant to the size of a mouse. It was said that Halizak took great pleasure listening to people's screams. And then, as their prison shrank beyond their ability to bear, he would place a goblet below the tiny stone box, to catch the juices of his dying enemies and drink to his own long health.

But I was close.

Halizak's Prison was closing down on me. But unlike Halizak's victims, I now spied a door. A gap in my squeezing prison. We would not go without a home. Jiala and I would not be forced across the river to Lesser Khaim to live with the refugees of bramble spread.

I would be a hero. Recognized through the ages. I was going to be a hero.

Once again, I primed my balanthast.

Pila, my last faithful servant, watched from beside the fireplace. She had gone from a smiling young girl to a grown woman who now looked at me with a cocked head and a thoughtful expression as if I was already mad. She had brought in the final bits of my refashioned device, and my workshop was a new disaster of brass nails, armatures, and iron filings. The debris of inspiration.

I smiled at Pila. "This time it will work," I said.

The reek of burnt neem and mint filled the air. In the glass chamber atop the balanthast, a few sprigs of mint lay with bay and lora flower and the woody shavings of the neem.

I struck a match. Its flame gleamed. I was close. So very close. But Pila had seen other failures...

Pounding on the door interrupted my preparation.

I turned, annoyed. "Go answer," I told Pila. "Tell them I am busy."

I prepared again to ignite the balanthast, but premonition stayed my hand. Instead, I listened. A moment passed. And then a shriek echoed through the halls. Anguish and loss. I dropped the match and ran for the door.

Falzi the butcher stood at the threshold, cradling Jiala in his huge arms. She dangled limp, head lolling.

"I found her in a bramble," he said. "Deep in. I had to use a hook to pull her out, it was closing on her." Pila and I both reached for her, but Falzi pulled away from us. "You don't have the clothes for it." And indeed, his own leather shirt and apron were covered in pale thready bramble hairs. They fairly seemed to quiver with wormy malevolence. Even a few were dangerous, and Jiala's body was furred with them.

I stared, horrified. "But what was she doing there?" Jiala knew enough of bramble from my own work to avoid its beckoning vines. "She shouldn't have been anywhere near bramble."

"Street urchins..." Falzi looked away, embarrassed at the implication, but plunged on. "The Mayor offers a reward for bramble seeds collected in the city. To prevent the spread. A copper for a sack. Better pay than catching rats. Some children...if they are hungry enough, will go to the big brambles in the fields and burn it back. Then gather the seeds when the pods explode."

"My workshop," I said. "Quickly!"

Falzi carried Jiala's small body easily. Set her on the stones by the fire. "What will you do?" he asked. "The poison's already in her."

I shook my head as I used a brush to push away the bramble threads that clung to her. Redness stained her flesh wherever they touched. Poison and sleep, coursing beneath her skin. When I'd cleared a place on her throat, I pressed my fingers to her pulse, feeling for the echo of her heart.

Slow. So very slow.

"I have supplies that may help," I said. "Go. Thank you. But go!"

Falzi touched his heart in farewell. Shaking his head, he left us alone.

"Close the doors, Pila." I said. "And the windows."

"But—"

"Do it! And don't come within. Lock the doors."

When I first thought that I might have a method of killing bramble, it was because I noticed how it never grew around the copper mines of Kesh. Even as Alacan fell and landholders retreated all along the line of bramble's encroach, the copper mines remained pristine.

Of course, over time it became impossible to get to the mines. Bramble surrounded that strange island of immunity and continued its long march west into Alacan. The delicate strand of road that led through the bramble forest to the copper mines became impossible to defend.

But the copper mines remained safe, long after everything else was swallowed. I noticed the phenomenon on my trips there to secure new materials for my business. Keshian copper made fine urns that were much in demand from my patrons and so I made the journey often. I remember making my careful way down that long bramble tunnel when workers still fought to keep the road to the mines open. Remember the workers' faces sooty and sweaty with the constant chopping and burning, their leather bladder sacks and brass-nozzled burners always alight and smoking as they spread flaming paste upon the poisonous plant.

And then the copper mines, opening before me. The deep holes and scrapings of mine work, but also grasslands and trees—the huge bramble growing all around its perimeter, but none inside. An oasis.

A few majisters and scholars also noticed the Keshian copper mines' unique qualities, but by the time anyone sought the cause of the place's survival, the bramble was coming strong, and soon no one could hack their way back to that isolated place of mining tools and tailings ponds for more investigation.

Of course, people experimented.

A few people thought to beat copper into our roads, or created copper knives to cut through the bramble, thinking that the metal was bramble's bane. And certainly some people even started to call it that. Copper charms sold well for a brief time. I admit that I even trafficked in such baubles, casting amulets and beating fine urns to ward off its encroach. But soon enough, people discovered that copper gave root to bramble as easily as a farmer's tilled field and the mortar of Alacan's massive city walls. Granite was better at warding off the plant, but even that gave root eventually.

Even so, the Keshian copper mines remained in my mind, much as they likely remained in the deep bramble forest, a dream of survival, if only we could puzzle it out. And so now, from memory, I sought to reconstruct the conditions of Kesh in the environs of my workshop, experimenting with the natural interactions of flora and ore, seeking that singular formula which had stalled bramble in its march.

The door closed behind Pila. I felt again for Jiala's pulse. It was nearly gone. The drug of bramble has been used by assassins and thwarted lovers. Its poison produces an overwhelming sleep that succumbs to deeper darkness. It squeezes the heart and slows it until blood flows like cold syrup, and then stops entirely, frozen, preserving a body, sometimes for years, until rats and mice and flies burrow deep and tear the body apart from within.

And now bramble's poisonous threads covered Jiala's skin. I took a copper rod and ran it over her arms. Then touched mint to her flesh. With a pair of brass pincers, I began plucking the threads from her skin. Setting them in a pottery bowl beside me so that I wouldn't carelessly touch them myself. Working as quickly as I could. Knowing that I couldn't work fast enough. There were dozens of them, dozens and dozens. More coated her clothing but they didn't matter. Her skin was covered. Too many, and yet still I plucked.

Jiala's eyelids fluttered. She gazed up from under heavy lashes, dark eyes thick with bramble's influence.

"Do I have enough?" she murmured.

"Enough what, child?" I continued plucking threads from her skin.

"Enough...seeds...to buy back my bed."

I tried to answer, but no words came. My heart felt as if it was squeezed by Halizak's Prison, running out liquid and dead.

Jiala's eyes closed, falling into the eternal sleep. I frantically felt after her heart's echo. A slow thud against my fingertip, sugar syrup running colder. Another thud. Thicker. Colder. The sluggish call of her heart. A longer pause, then...

Nothing.

I stumbled away from my dying girl, sick with my failures.

My balanthast lay before me, all its parts bubbling and prepared. In desperation, I seized it and dragged it over to my dying daughter. I aimed its great brass bell at her inert form. Tears blurred my vision. I swept up a match, and then...paused.

I don't know why it came to me. It's said that the Three Faces of Mara come to us and whisper wisdom to us in our hour of need. That inspiration comes from true desperation and that the mysteries of the world can be so revealed. Certainly, Mara is the seed of life and hope.

I knelt beside Jiala and plucked a strand of hair from her head, a binding, a wish, a... I did not know, but suddenly I was desperate to have something of hers within the workings of the balanthast, and the bramble, too. All with the neem and mint... I placed her hair in the combustion chamber, and struck the match. Flame rose into the combustion chamber, burning neem and mint and bramble and Jiala's black hair, smoking, blazing, now one in their burn. I prayed to Mara's Three Faces for some mercy, and then twisted the balanthast's dial. The balanthast sucked the burning embers of her hair and the writhing threads of bramble and all the other ingredients into its belly chamber.

For a moment, nothing happened. Then blue flame exploded from the bell, enveloping Jiala.

Wake up, Papa.
  Wake up.
  Wake.
  Up.

Dim echoing words, pokes and proddings.

Wake up, Papa.
Papa?
Papa papa papapapapapa.

I opened my eyes.

Jiala knelt over me, a haziness of black hair and skinny brown limbs and blue skirts. Blurred and ethereal. Limned in an uncertain focus as light bound around her. A spirit creature from within the Halls of Judgment. Waiting for Borzai the Judge to gather her into his six arms, peer into her soul, and then pass her on to the Hall of Children, where innocents live under the protective gaze of dog-headed Kemaz.

I tried to sit up, couldn't. Lay back. The spirit creature remained, tugging at me. The workshop was a shambles, all of it blurry and unsteady, as if it lay on the plane of clouds.

All of us dead, then.

"Papa?"

I turned to her echoing voice. Stared at her. Stared again at the ravaged workroom. Something cold and sharp was pressing against my back. Not spirit-like at all.

Slowly, I dragged myself upright, leaning against the stone wall. I was lying far across the room from the fireplace. The balanthast lay beside me, its glass chambers shattered, its vacuum bulbs nothing but jagged teeth in their soldered sockets. Bent copper tubes gleamed all around me, like flower petals scattered to Mara during the planting march.

"Are you alright, Papa?" Jiala stared at me with great concern. "Your head is bloody."

I reached up and touched her small worried face. Warm. Alive. Not a spirit creature.

Whole and alive, her skin smoking with the yellow residue of bramble's ignition. Blackened threads of bramble ash covered her, her hair half-melted, writhing with bramble thread's death throes still. Singed and scalded and blistery but whole and miraculously alive.

I ran my hand down her scorched cheek, wonder-struck.

"Papa?"

"I'm alright, Jiala," I started to laugh. "More than alright."

I clutched her to me and sobbed. Thanking Mara for my daughter's salvation. Grateful for this suspended execution of my soul.

And beyond it, another thought, a wider hope. That bramble, for the first time in all my experiments, had truly died, leaving not even its last residue of poison behind.

Fifteen years is not too long to seek a means to save the world.

3

Of course, nothing is as simple as we would wish.

After that first wild success, I succeeded in producing a spectacular string of failures which culminated in nearly exploding the house. More worrying to me, even though Jiala survived her encounter with the bramble, her cough was much worsened by it. The winter damp spurred it on, and now she hacked and coughed daily, her small lungs seemingly intent on closing down upon her.

She was too young to know how bad the cough had been before—how much it had greatly concerned me. But after the bramble, blood began staining her lips, the rouge of her lungs brought forth by the evils that bramble had worked upon her body as it sought to drive her down into permanent sleep.

I avoided using magic for as long as possible, but Jiala's cough worsened, digging deeper into her lungs. And it was only a small magic. Just enough spelling to keep her alive. To close the rents in her little lungs, and stop the blood from spackling her lips. Perhaps a sprig of bramble would sprout in some farmer's field as a result, fertilized by the power released into the air, but really it was such a small magic, and Jiala's need was too great to ignore.

The chill of winter was always the worst. Khaim isn't like the northern lands, where freezes kill every living plant except bramble and lay snow over the ground in cold drifts and wind-sculpted ice. But still, the cold ate at her. And so, I took a little time away from my alchemy and the perfecting of the balanthast to work something within her.

Our secret.

Even Pila didn't know. No one could be allowed to know but us.

Jiala and I sat in the corner of my workshop, amidst the blankets where she now slept near the fire, the only warm room I had left, and I used the scribbled notes from the book of Majister Arun to make magic.

His pen was clear, even if he was long gone to the Executioner's axe. His ideas on vellum. His hand reaching across time. His past carrying into our future through the wonders of ink. Rosemary and pkana flower and licorice root, and the deep soothing cream of goat's milk. Powdered together, the yellow pkana flower's petals all crackling like fire as they touched the milk. Sending up a smoke of dreams.

And then with my ring finger, long missing all three gold rings of marriage, I touched the paste to Jiala's forehead, between the thick dark hairs of her eyebrows. And then, pulling down her blouse, another at her sternum, at the center of her lungs. The pkana's yellow mark pulsed on her skin, seeming wont to ignite.

As we worked this little magic, I imagined the great majisters of Jhandpara healing crowds from their arched balconies. It was said that people came for miles to be healed. They used the stuff of magic wildly, then.

"Papa, you mustn't." Jiala whispered. Another cough caught her, jerking her forward and reaching deep, squeezing her lungs as the strongman squeezes a pomegranate to watch red blood run between his fingers.

"Of course I must," I answered. "Now be quiet."

"They will catch you, though. The smell of it—"

"Shhhh."

And then I read the ancient words of Majister Arun, sounding out the language that could never be recalled after it was spoken. Consonants burned my tongue as it tapped those words of power. The power of ancients. The dream of Jhandpara.

The sulphur smell of magic filled the room, and now round vowels of healing tumbled from my lips, spinning like pin wheels, finding their targets in the yellow paste of my fingerprints.

The magic burrowed into Jiala, and then it was gone. The pkana flower paste took on a greenish tinge as it was used up, and the room filled completely with the smoke of power unleashed. Astonishing power, all around, and only a little effort and a few words to bind it to us. Magic. The power to do anything. Destroy an empire, even.

I cracked open the shutters, and peered out onto the black cobbled streets. No one was outside, and I fanned the room quickly, clearing the stench of magic.

"Papa. What if they catch you?"

"They won't." I smiled. "This is a small magic. Not some great bridge-building project. Not even a spell of fertility. Your lungs hold small wounds. No one will ever know. And I will perfect the balanthast soon. And then no one will ever have to hold back with these small magics ever again. All will be well."

"They say that the Executioner sometimes swings wild, doesn't chop a man in half with kindness. But makes him flop instead. That the Mayor pays him extra to make an example of the people who use magic."

"It's not true."

"I saw one."

"No, you didn't."

"It was last week. At the gold market. Right in the square. I was with Pila. And the crowd was so thick we couldn't leave. And Pila covered my eyes, but I could see through her fingers. And the Executioner chopped and chopped and chopped and chopped and the man yelled so loud and then he stopped, but still he didn't do a good job. Not a clean cut at all, the pig lady said. Said she does better with her swine."

I made myself smile. "Well, that's not our problem. Everyone does a little magic. No one will mind us. As long as we don't rub anyone's nose in it."

"I wouldn't want to see you chopped and chopped and chopped."

"Then make sure you drink Pila's licorice tea and stay out of the cold. It's a hard thing to keep secrets. But secrets are best when there are only two to know." I touched her forehead. "You and I."

I pulled my mustaches. "Tug for luck?"

But she wouldn't. And she wasn't consoled.

A month later, as the muddy rags of cruel spring snow turned to the sweet stink of wet warming earth, I made the last adjustments to the balanthast and set it loose on the bramble wall.

We left the city deep in the night, making our way east over muddy roads, the balanthast bundled on my back. Jiala, Pila and I. With the embrace of darkness, the women of the bramble crews with their fire and hatchets were gone, and the children who gathered seeds behind them in careful lines had given up. There would be no witnesses to our experiment. The night was chill and uncomfortable. We held our torches high.

It took only two hours to reach the bramble wall, much to my surprise.

"It's moved," I muttered.

Pila nodded. "The women who sell potatoes say they've lost more fields. Some of them before they had a chance to dig up the last of their crop."

The bramble loomed above us, many tangled layers, the leading edge of an impenetrable forest that stretched all the way to fabled Jhandpara. In the light of the torches the bramble threw off strange hungry shadows, seeming eager to tug us into its sleep-inducing embrace. I thrust my torch amongst its serpent vines. Tendrils crackled and curled in the heat, and a few seed pods, fat as milkweed, burst open, spilling new seeds onto the ground.

Tender green growths showed all along the edge where the bramble crews had been burning and pruning, but deep within, the bramble had turned woody, impenetrable, and thick. Sharp blood-letting thorns glinted in the torchlight, but more troublesome were the pale fine hairs shimmering everywhere, coating every vine's length, the venomous fibers that Jiala had so nearly succumbed to.

I took a breath, unnerved despite myself in the presence of our implacable enemy.

"Well," Pila said. "You wanted to show us."

My faith faltered. Small experiments in the workshop were one thing. But out in the open? Before my daughter and Pila? I cursed myself for my pride. I should have come to test the balanthast in private. Not like this where all my failures could be mocked or pitied.

"Well?" Pila said.

"Yes," I said. "Yes. We'll get started."

But still I delayed.

Pila gave me a look of disgust and started setting out the kestrel-wood tripod. She had grown insolent over the years, as her salary had been reduced and her responsibilities increased. Not at all the young shy girl she had been when she first came to the house. She now carried too much authority, and too much of a skeptical eye. Sometimes I suspected that I would have given up long ago on my experimentations, if not for Pila watching me with her silent judgments. It's easy to fail yourself, but failing before another, one who has watched you wager so much and so mightily on an uncertain future—well, that is too much shame to bear.

"Right," I murmured. "Of course."

I unbound the balanthast from my back. Set it upon the kestrel-wood to brace it. Since my first wild success, I had managed to dampen much of the balanthast's explosive reaction, venting it from rows of newly designed chimneys that puffed like a cloud dragon's nostrils. The balanthast now held fast and didn't topple and didn't blow one across the room to leave a body lying bruised and dazed. I crouched and made sure that the tripod was well set in the muddy earth.

To be honest, the tripod could have been made of anything, certainly something less extravagant. But kestrel-wood I loved. So hard and strong that even fire couldn't take it. The northmen of Czandia used to forge swords of kestrel-wood. Lighter than steel. Just as strong. The tripod seemed to say to me that we still had a future, that we might once again stand strong, and grow the wonders of old.

Or, if you were Pila, you called it the expensive affectation of a foolish man, even as she helped me fashion its sturdy base.

I straightened and unlimbered the rest of the balanthast's components. Pila and Jiala helped me assemble its many pieces.

"No," I whispered, and then realized that I was doing so and cleared my throat. "Jiala, put the vacuum chamber so that it faces forward, toward the mouth. And please be careful. I don't have enough fire to blow another."

"I'm always careful, Papa."

At last we were ready, the brass belly chamber and curling copper tubes and glass bulbs gleamed in the silver of the moon, a strange and unearthly thing.

"It looks like something that would have come out of Jhandpara," Pila said. "So much fine artistry, put into this one object."

I primed the combustion bulb of the balanthast. Neem and bay, and mint and twilight lora flower and a bramble clipping. By torchlight, we dug into the earth, seeking the root bundle. There were many. With leather-gloved hands, I scooped out a bit of earth, bramble's vessel.

Mara's fertile womb. The necessary ingredient that would contain the alchemical reaction and channel it into the deeply embedded bramble, much as Jiala's hair had bound the reaction deep into her body. Saltpeter and sulphur and charcoal to drive the concoction home, poured into the belly chamber. I slid closed the combustion bulb, twisted the brass latches tight.

With a target now chosen, I thrust the balanthast's three newly constructed nozzles into the earth beside it. Jiala covered her mouth with a tiny hand as I lit the match. I almost smiled. I set the match under the combustion bulb, and the assembled ingredients caught fire. It glowed like a firefly in its glassine chamber. Slowly the flame died. We watched. Breaths held.

And then as if the Three Faces of Mara had inhaled all at once, the entire careful wad disappeared, sucked into the belly chamber. The primed balanthast quivered with power, elements coming together.

The reaction was so sudden that we had no chance to brace. The very earth tossed us from our feet. Yellow acrid smoke billowed over us. A desperate animal shriek filled the air, as if the swine women were amongst the pigs in a sty, wounding and bleeding a great herd and not killing a single one. We gained our feet and ran, coughing and tearing, stumbling over muddy furrows. Jiala was worst taken. Her cough ripped deep into her lungs, making me fear I'd need to use the healing magic on her again before the night was over.

Slowly the smoke dispersed, revealing our work. The balanthast quivered on its tripod, steady still where it had been jammed into the earth, but now, all around it, there was a seething mass of bramble tendrils, all writhing and smoking. The vines hissed and burned, flakes of ash falling like scales from a dragon. Another shudder ran through the earth as deep roots writhed and ripped upward—and then, all at once, the vines collapsed, falling all to soot, leaving clear earth behind.

We approached cautiously. The balanthast had not only killed the root I had chosen, but destroyed horse-lengths of bramble in every direction. It would have taken workers hours to clear so much. I held up my torch, staring. Even at the perimeter of the balanthast's destruction, the bramble growth hung limp like rags. I stepped forward, cautious. Struck a damaged plant with a gloved hand. Its vines sizzled with escaping sap, and collapsed.

I swung about, staring at the ground. "Do you see any seeds?"

We swept our torches over the earth, straining to make out any of the pods which should have sprung out and burst open in the blaze of fire's heat.

Jiala squatted in the cold damp earth, turning it over and running it through her little gloved fingers.

"Well? Is there anything?"

Jiala looked up, amazed. "No, Papa."

"Pila?" I whispered. "Do you see any?"

"No." Astonishment marked her voice. "There are none. Not a single one."

Together, we continued our hunt. Nothing. Not a single seed disbursed from a single pod. The bramble vine had died, and left nothing of itself behind to torment us another day.

"It's magic," Pila whispered. "True magic."

I laughed at that. "Better than magic. Alchemy!"

4

The next morning, despite the previous late night, we all woke with the first crowing of roosters. I laughed to find Pila and Jiala already clustered in the workroom, peering out the shutters, waiting for enough sunlight to see the final result.

As soon as the sun cracked the horizon, we were out in the fields again, headed across the muddy furrows to the bramble wall. The first of the bramble crews were already at work, with axes and long chopping knives, wearing leather aprons to protect themselves from the sleeping spines. Smoke from bramble's burn rose into the air, coiling snakes, black and oily. Dirty children walked in careful lines through the fields with shovels and hoes, uprooting new incursions. In the dawn light, with the levee labor all at the wall, it looked like the scene of some recent battle. The smoke, the hopeless faces. But as we approached the site of my balanthast firing, a small knot of workers huddled.

We slipped close.

"Have you come to see it?" they asked.

"See what?" Pila asked.

"There's a hole in the bramble." A woman pointed. "Look how deep it goes."

Several children squatted in the earth. One of them looked up. "It's clean, Mama. No seeds at all. It's like the bramble never came at all."

I could barely restrain my glee. Pila had to drag me away to keep me from blurting out my part. We rushed back to Khaim, laughing and skipping the whole way.

Back in our home, Pila and Jiala brought out my best clothes. Pila helped me work the double buttons of my finest vest, pursing her lips at the sight of how skinny I had become since I last wore the thing in my wealth and health.

I laughed at her concern.

"Soon I'll be fat again, and you'll have your own servants and we'll be rich and the city will be saved."

Pila smiled. Her face had lost its worry for the first time in years. She looked young again, and I was struck with the memory of how fine she had been in youth, and how now, despite worry and years, she still stood, unbent and unbroken by the many responsibilities she had taken on. She had stuck with our household, even as our means had faltered, even as other, richer families offered a better, more comfortable life.

"It's very good that you are not mad, after all," Pila said.

I laughed. "You're very sure I'm not mad?"

She shrugged. "Well, not about bramble, at least."

The way to Mayor's House must pass around Malvia Hill, through the clay market and then down along the River Sulong, which splits Khaim from Lesser Khaim.

Along the river, the spice market runs into the potato market runs into the copper market. Powdered spices choke the air, along with the calls of spice men with their long black mustaches that they oil and stretch with every child. Their hands are red with chilies and yellow with turmeric, and their lungs give off the scents of clove and oregano. They sit under their archways along the river, with their big hemp bags of spice out front, and the doorways to their storehouses behind, where piled spices reach two stories high. And then on to the women in the potato market, where they used to sell only potatoes, but now sell any number of tubers, and then the copper families, who can beat out a pot or a tube, who fashion brass candlesticks for the rich and cooking pots for the poor.

When I was young, there was only Khaim. At that time, there was still a bit of the old Empire left. The great wonders of the East and the great capital of Jhandpara were gone, but still, there was Alacan and Turis and Mimastiva. At that time, Khaim was a lesser seat, valued for its place on the river, but still, a far reach from Jhandpara where great majisters had once wielded their power and wore triple diamonds on their sleeves. But with the slow encroachment of the bramble, Khaim grew. And, across from it, Lesser Khaim grew even faster.

When I was a child, I could look across the river and see nothing but lemon trees and casro bushes, heavy with their dense fruits. Now refugees squatted and built mud huts there. Alacaners, who had destroyed their own homes and now insisted on destroying Khaim as well. Turis, of course, is nothing but ash. But that wasn't their fault. Raiders took Turis, but Alacaners had only themselves to blame.

Jiala hurried along the river with me, her hand in mine. Small. So small. But now with a future. Not just a chance at life and wealth, but a chance that she would not run like the Alacaners from her home as bramble swallowed her childhood and history.

Out on the Sulong, tiny boats made their way back and forth across the water, carrying workers from Lesser Khaim into the main city. But now, something else marred the vista.

A great bridge hung in the air, partially constructed. It floated there, held down by ropes so that it would not fly free. Magic. Astonishing and powerful magic coming into play. The work of Majister Scacz, the one man in the city who wielded magic with the sanction of the Mayor, and so would never fear the Executioner's axe.

I paused, staring across the water to the floating bridge. Magic such as had not been seen since Jhandpara fell. Seeing it there, rising, it filled me with a superstitious dread. So much magic in one place. Even the balanthast couldn't protect against that much magic.

A spice man called out to me. "You want to buy? Or are you going to block my trade?"

I tipped my velvet hat to him. "So sorry, merchantman. I was looking at the bridge."

The man spat. Eyed the floating construction. "Lot of magic, there." He spat again. Tobacco and kehm root together. Narcotic. "I hear they're already chopping bramble on the far bank. Hardly any bramble on the west side at all, and now it's growing in the wagon ruts. Next thing, we'll be like Alacan. Swallowed by bramble because our jolly Mayor wants to connect here with there. Bad enough that all these new Alacaners use their small magics. Now we have big magic too. Scacz and the Mayor pretending Khaim should be another Jhandpara with majisters and diamonds and floating castles."

He spat more kehm root and tobacco, and eyed the bridge. "Executioner will be busy now. Sure as bramble creep, we'll have new heads spiked on city gates. Too much big magic to let the little magics run wild."

"Maybe not," I started, but Jiala pinched my hand and I fell silent.

The spice man eyed me as if I was mad. "I had to burn an entire sack of cloves, today. Whole sack I couldn't sell. Full of bramble seeds and sprout. Someone makes his little magic, ruins my business."

I wanted to tell him that the bundle on my back would change the balance, but Jiala, at least, had sense, and so I kept my words to myself. Magic brings bramble. A project like the bridge had an inevitable cost.

I hefted my bag of implements and we carried on, around the edge of the hill and then up its face to where Mayor's House looked down over Khaim.

We were ushered into the Mayor's gallery without fuss. Marble floors and arches stretched around us. My clothes felt poor, Jiala's as well. Even our best was now old and worn.

In the sudden cool of the gallery, her cough started. A dry hacking thing that threatened to build. I knelt and gave her a sip of water. "Are you well?"

"Yes, Papa." She watched me, solemn and trusting. "I won't cough." And then immediately her dry cough started again. It echoed about, announcing our presence to all the other petitioners.

We sat in the gallery, waiting with the women who wanted to change their household tax and the men who were petitioning to escape levee labor. After an hour, the Mayor's secretary came to us, his medallion of office gleaming gold on his chest, the Axe of the Executioner crossed over the Staff of the Majister, the twin powers that the Mayor wielded for the benefit of the city. The secretary led us across another marble gallery, and thence into the Mayor's offices, and the door was shut behind us.

The Mayor wore red velvet and his own much larger medallion on a chain of gold around his neck. His fingers touched the medallion every so often, a needy gesture. And with him, the Majister Scacz. My skin prickled at the sight of one who used magic as a daily habit, passing the consequences of his activities onto the bramble crews and the children of the city who dug and burned the minor bits of bramble from between mortar stones and cobbles.

"Yes?" the Mayor asked. "You're who, then?"

"Jeoz, the alchemist," the secretary announced.

"And he reeks of magic," Majister Scacz murmured.

I made myself smile. "It is my device."

The Mayor's eyebrows rose, fuzzy gray caterpillars arching over his ruddy face. His mustache was short, no child in his history at all. An old scar puckered one side of his cheek, pulling his mouth into a slight smile. "You practice magic?" he asked sharply. "Are you mad?"

I made a placating gesture. "I do not practice, Excellency. No. Not at all." A nervous laugh escaped my lips. "I practice alchemy. It does not bring bramble. I have no dealings with the curse of Jhandpara." It was unbelievable how nervous I had become. "No need for the Executioner, here. None at all." I untied my bag and began pulling out the pieces of the balanthast. "You see..." I screwed one of the copper ends into its main chamber. Unwrapped the combustion bulb, breathing a sigh of relief that it had survived the trip. "You see," I repeated myself, "I have created something, which your Excellency will appreciate. I think."

Beside me, Jiala coughed. Whether from sickness, or nervousness, I couldn't say. Scacz's eyes went to her. Held. I didn't like the way he stared at her. His thoughtful expression. I plunged on.

"It is a balanthast."

The Mayor examined the device. "It looks more like an arquebus."

I made myself smile. "Not at all. Though it does use the reactants of fire. But my device has properties most extraordinary." My hands were shaking. I found the mint. The neem bark. Lora flower. Set them in the chamber.

Scacz was watching closely. "Am I watching sorcery, sir. Right before myself? Unsanctioned?"

"N-no." I shook under his examination. Tried to load the balanthast.

Jiala took it away. "Here, Papa."

"Y-yes. Good. Thank you, child." I took a deep breath. "You see, a balanthast destroys bramble. And not just a little. The balanthast reaches for a bramble's root and poisons it utterly. Place it within a yard or two of a heart root, and it will destroy more than a bramble crew can destroy in half a day."

The Mayor leaned close. "You have proof of this?"

"Yes. Of course. I'm sorry." I pulled a small clay pot shrouded in burlap out of my bag and put on my leather gloves before unwrapping it.

"Bramble," I explained.

They both sucked in their breath at the sight of the potted plant. I looked up at their consternation. "We use gloves."

"You carry bramble into the city?" the Mayor asked. "Deliberately?"

I hesitated. Finally I said, "It was necessary. For the testing. The science of alchemy requires much trial and error." Their faces were heavy with disapproval. I lit my match, and touched it to the glass bulb. Clamped it closed.

"Hold your breath, Jiala." I looked apologetically at the Mayor. "The smoke is quite acrid."

Mayor and Majister also sucked in their breaths. The balanthast shivered as its energy discharged. A ripple of death passed into the soil. The pot cracked as the bramble writhed and died.

"Magic!" Scacz cried, lunging forward. "What magic is this?"

"No, Majister! Alchemy. Magic has never been able to affect bramble. It does not sap bramble's poison, nor kill its seeds, nor burn back its branches. This is something new."

Scacz grabbed for the balanthast. "I must see this."

"It's not magic." I yanked the balanthast back, afraid that in his hurry he would destroy it. "It uses the natural properties of the neem," I said. "A special species, loved by majisters, yes, but this is merely the application of nature's principles. We vaporize the neem with a few other ingredients, force it through the tube, and with the aid of sulphur and saltpeter and charcoal, we send its essence into the earth. Even a small application does wonders. The neem essence binds with the root of the bramble. Kills it, as you see. Attracted like a fly to honey."

"And what causes neem to seek bramble?"

I shrugged. "It's difficult to say. Perhaps some magical residue or aura from the plant. I tried thousands of substances before the neem. Only the neem bark works so well."

"The neem is attracted to magic, you think?"

"Well," I hedged. "It is certainly attracted to bramble. Oil and water never mix. Neem and bramble seem the opposite. What causes the affinity..." I could feel myself starting to sweat under their combined gazes, not liking how Scacz obsessed with magic. "I hesitate to say that it's magic the neem essence finds so attractive..."

"You talk all around the root of the issue." Scacz said. "Worse than a priestess of Ruiz."

"Forgive me," I stammered. "I don't want you to think that I've been unwary in my investigations."

"He's worried we're about to send him off to the Executioner," the Mayor said.

I gave the man a sickly smile. "Quite. Bramble is unique. It has qualities that we may think of as magical—its astonishing growth, its resilience, the way that magic seems to fertilize its flourishing—but who can say what unique aspect causes the neem's essence to bind with it? These questions are beyond me. I experiment, I record my results, and I experiment again.

"The alchemical response to neem is bramble death. What causes that reaction, whether it is some magical residue that leeches from the bramble root and somehow makes it vulnerable to neem, or some other quality, I can't say. But it works. And works well. There is a plot of earth that I myself have cleared into the bramble wall. In the time it takes you to clap your hands three times, I cleared more land than this office occupies."

Mayor and Majister both straightened at the news.

"So quickly?" the Mayor asked.

I nodded vigorously. "Even today, it still shows no sign of regrowth. No seeds, you understand? Not a single one. With my device, you can arm the people and take back farmland. Push back the bramble wall. Save Khaim."

"Extraordinary," Scacz said. "Not just push the bramble back. Perhaps even reclaim the heart of the empire. Return to Jhandpara."

"Exactly." I couldn't help feeling relief as their expressions lost their skepticism.

The Mayor had begun to smile widely. He stood. "By the Three Faces of Mara, man, you've done something special!"

He motioned for Jiala and me. "Come! The two of you must have a glass of wine. This discovery is worth celebrating."

He laughed and joked with us as he guided us to a room with great windows that looked out over the city. Khaim jumbled down the hill below us. On the horizon, the sun was slowly sinking. Red sunlight filtered through the smoke and cookfires of Lesser Khaim. The half-constructed floating bridge arched across the river like a leaping cat, held in place by great hemp ropes to keep it from sailing away as they worked to extend its skeleton.

"This couldn't come at a better time," the Mayor said. "Look out there, alchemist. Lesser Khaim grows every day. And not just from the refugees of Turis and Alacan. Others too, small holders who have been overwhelmed by the bramble. And they bring their magics with them.

"Before they came, we were nearly in balance. We could still cut back enough bramble to offset the bits of magic use. Even the bridge would have been acceptable. But the Alacaners are profligate with their magic, and now the bramble comes hard upon us. Their habits are crushing us. Everyone has some little magic that he or she believes is justified. And then when a bit of bramble roots in a neighbor's roof beams, who can say who caused it?"

He turned to me. "You know they call me the Jolly Mayor over there? Make fun of me for my scar and my poor humor." He scowled. "Of course I'm in a poor humor. We fight bramble every day, and every day it defeats us. If this keeps on, we'll be run out of here in three sixes of years."

I startled at his words. "Surely it's not that bad."

The Mayor raised his caterpillar brows. "Oh yes." He nodded at Jiala. "Your girl will be part of a river of refugees twice the size of the one we took in from Alacan." He turned again to look west. "And where will they go then? Mpaias? Loz? Turis is gone to raiders." He scowled. "Lesser Khaim is just as vulnerable. We barely fought off the raiders' last attack. Without the bridge, I cannot have a hope of defending that side of the river. And so we spend magic where we would prefer not to, and add to the problem. We're caught in Halizak's Prison, for certain."

His steward arrived with wine and goblets. I looked at the stemmed glasses with curiosity, wondering if I myself had long ago blown their shapes, but then recognized the distinctive mark of Saara Solso. She had improved since I used to compete with her. Another reminder of how long I had been at my project.

The steward paused on the verge of uncorking the wine bottle. "Are you certain about this, Excellency?" he asked.

The Mayor laughed and pointed at me. "This man comes to us with salvation, and you worry about an old vintage?"

The steward looked doubtful, but he uncorked the bottle anyway. A joyful scent filled the room. The Mayor looked at me, eyes twinkling. "You recognize it?" he asked. "The happy bouquet of history."

I was drawn by the scent, like a child to syrup crackers. Astonished and intoxicated, wide-eyed. "What is it?"

"Wine from the hillsides of Mount Sena, the summer vineyards of the old empire," Majister Scacz said. "A rare thing, now that those hillsides are covered with bramble. Perhaps a score of bottles still exist, of which our Jolly Mayor possesses, now, two."

"Don't call me that."

Scacz bowed. "The name suits you today, Excellency."

The Mayor smiled. "For once."

The steward poured the wine into the glassine bulbs.

"Currant and cinnamon and joy." Majister Scacz was watching me. "You're about to taste one of the finest pleasures of the Empire. Served at spring planting, for harvest and for flowering-age ceremonies. The richest merchants had fountains of it in their floating castles, if you can credit such a thing. Magic, make no mistake. The vintner's genius bound with the majister's craft."

He caught Jiala watching, her eyes shining at the scent. "Come, girl. Taste our lost history." He poured a splash into a glass. "Not too much. You're too small to do more than taste, but I promise you, you will not forget this thing."

The Mayor held up his glass, ruby and black in the setting sun. "A toast, then, gentlemen. To our future, refound."

We drank, and the blood of the old empire coursed through our veins and made us giddy. We examined my instrument again, with the Majister and the Mayor making exclamations at the workmanship, at my methods for joining glass to copper, of metallurgy that had yielded a combustion chamber that would not crack with the power of the flames released. We talked of the difficulties of making more balanthasts and speculated how many miles we might clear of the surrounding countryside.

"It takes a great deal of trouble to make one," Scacz observed.

"Oh yes," I said fondly, patting the venting tubes that ran along its outer surface and collected the gases of the burning neem.

"How many do you think you can make?"

"At first?" I shrugged. "Perhaps it will take me a month to make another." The Mayor and Scacz both showed their consternation, and I rushed on. "But I can train other metal workers, other glassblowers. I need not do every piece of work. With others working to my specification. With a larger workshop, many more could be made."

"We could train the crafters who make the new arquebus," Scacz said. "Their work is obviously pointless. A weapon that can only be fired once and is so fussy, does not even pack the power of a decent crossbow and is slower still. But this?"

The mayor was nodding. "You're right. This is worth our effort. Those silly weapons are nothing to this."

Scacz took another sip of his wine, running his hand over the balanthast. A slow caress. "The potential here...is astonishing." He looked up at me, inquiring. "I think I would like to test it for a little while. See what it does."

"Majister?"

Scacz patted me on the back. "Don't worry. We'll be very careful with it. But I must examine it a while. Ensure that it truly uses no magic that will come back to haunt us." He looked at me significantly. "Too many solutions to bramble have simply sought to use magic in some glancing way. To build a fire, for example, and then when the bramble is burned, it turns out that so much magic was used in the making of the fire that the bramble returns twice as strong."

"But the balanthast doesn't use magic," I protested.

Scacz looked at me. "You are a majister to know this, then? In some cases, a man will think he is not using magical principles, because he is ignorant. You yourself acknowledge that something unique is afoot with this device." He picked up the balanthast. "It's just for a little while, alchemist. Just to be sure."

The Mayor was watching me closely. "Don't worry, alchemist. We will not slight your due reward. But for us, the stakes are very high. If we invest our office in something which brings the doom of Takaz instead of the salvation of Mara... I'm sure you understand."

I wracked my mind, trying to find a reason to deny them, but my voice failed me, and at that moment, Jiala started to cough again. I glanced over at her, worried. It had the deep sound of cutting knives.

Scacz began to gather up the device. "Go on," he said. "See to your daughter's health. She is obviously tired. We will send for you quite soon."

Jiala's coughing worsened. The two most powerful men in the city looked down at her. "Poor thing," the Mayor murmured. "She seems to have the wasting cough."

I rushed to contradict. "No. It's something else. The cold is all. It starts the cough and makes it difficult to stop."

Scacz pried the balanthast away from me. "Go then. Take your daughter home and warm her. We will send for you, soon."

All the way home, Jiala coughed. Deep wracking seizures that folded her small body in half. By the time we arrived at our doorstep, her coughing was incessant. Pila took one look at Jiala and glared at me with astonished anger.

"The poor girl's exhausted. What took you so long?"

I shook my head. "They liked the device. And then they wanted to talk. And then to toast. And then to talk some more."

"And you couldn't bring the poor girl back?"

"What was I supposed to do?" I asked. "'Thank you so much, Mayor and Majister, I must leave, and no, the lost wines of Jhandpara are of no interest to me. Name a price and I will sell you the plans for my balanthast, good day'?"

Jiala's coughing worsened. Pila shot me a dark look and ushered her down the hall. "Come into the workshop, child. I've already lit the fire."

I watched the two of them go, feeling helpless and frustrated. What should have been a triumph had become something else. I didn't like the way Scacz behaved at the end. Everything he said had been perfectly reasonable, and yet his manner somehow disturbed me. And the way the Mayor spoke. All his words were correct. More than correct. And yet they filled me with unease.

I made my way up the stairs to my rooms, empty now except for piles of blankets and a chest of my clothes.

Was I turning paranoid? Into some sort of madman who looked beneath everyone's meaning to some darker intention? I had known a woman, once, when I was younger, who had gone mad like that. A glassblower who made wondrous jewel pendants that glittered with their own inner fire, seeming to burn from within. A genius with light. And yet there was something in her head that made her suspicious. She had suspected her husband, and then her children of plotting against her, and had finally thrown herself in the river, escaping demons from the Three Hundred Thirty-Three Halls that only she could see.

Was I now filled with the same suspicions? Was I going down her path?

Mayor and Majister had both spoken with fair words. I unbuttoned my vest, astounded at how threadbare it had become. The red and blue stitching was old and out of mode. How broken it was. As was everything except the balanthast. It, at least, had gleamed. I had put so much hope into this idea, had spent so many years...

A knock sounded on my door.

"Yes?"

Pila leaned in. "It's Jiala. Her coughing won't stop. She needs you."

"Yes. Of course. I'll come soon."

Pila hesitated. "Now, I think. It's very bad. There is blood. If you don't use your spells soon, she will be broken."

I stopped in the act of fixing my buttons. A thrill of fear coursed through me. "You know?"

Pila gave me a tight smile. "I've lived with you too long not to guess."

She motioned me out. "Don't worry about your fancy clothes. Your daughter doesn't care how you dress."

She hurried me down the stairs and into the workroom. We found Jiala beside the fire, curled on the flagstones, wracked by coughing. Her body contorted as another spasm took her. Blood pooled on the floor, red as roses, brighter than rubies.

"Papa..." she whispered.

I turned to find Pila standing beside me with the spellbook of Majister Arun in her hands.

"You know all my secrets?" I asked.

Pila looked at me sadly. "Only the ones that matter." She handed me the rest of my spell ingredients and ran to close the shutters so no sign of our magic would be visible, reportable to the outside world.

I took the ingredients and mixed them and placed the paste on Jiala's brow, bared her bony chest. Her breathing was like a bellows, labored and loud, rich with blood and the sound of crackling leaves. My hands shook as I finished the preparations and took up Majister Arun's hand.

I spoke the words and magic flowed from me and into my child.

Slowly, her breathing eased. Her face lost its fevered glare. Her eyes became her own again, and the rattle and scrape of her breath smoothed as the bloody rents closed themselves.

Gone. As quickly and brutally as it had come, it was gone, leaving nothing but the sulphur stink of magic in the room.

Pila was staring at me, astonished. "I knew," she whispered. "But I had not seen."

I blotted Jiala's brow. "I'm sorry to have involved you."

Jiala's breathing continued to ease. Pila knelt beside me, watching over my daughter. She was resting now, exhausted from what her body had used up in its healing.

"You mustn't be caught, Papa." Jiala whispered.

"It won't be much longer," I told her. "In no time at all, we'll be using magic just like the ancients and we won't have to hide a thing."

"Will we have a floating castle?"

I smiled gently. "I don't see why not. First we'll push back the bramble. Then we'll have a floating castle, and maybe one day we'll even grow wines on the slopes of Mount Sena." I tousled her hair. "But now I want you to rest and sleep and let the magic do its work."

Jiala looked up at me with her mother's dark eyes. "Can I dream of cloud castles?"

"Only if you sleep," I said.

Jiala closed her eyes, and the last tension flowed from her little body. To Pila, I said, "Open the windows, but just a little. Let the magic out slowly so no one has a chance to smell and suspect. If you are caught here, you will face the Executioner's great axe with me."

Pila went and opened one of the windows and began to air the room, while I covered Jiala with blankets. We met again at the far side of the workshop.

At one time, I had had chairs in this room, for talk and for thought, but those were long gone. We sat on the floor, together.

"And now you are part of my little conspiracy," I said sadly.

Pila smiled gently. "I guessed a long time ago. She clearly has the wasting cough, but she never wastes. Most children, by this time, they are dead. And yet Jiala runs through the streets and comes home without a cough for weeks at a time. At least before she fell into bramble. The cough seemed to stay at bay unnaturally."

"Why did you not call the guards?" I asked. "There is a fine reward for people like me. You could have lived well by selling your knowledge of my foolishness."

"You don't use this magic selfishly."

"Still. It curses the city. The Mayor is right about that much. The help I visit upon Jiala, means that hurt is visited upon Khaim. Some neighbor of ours may find a bit of bramble growing in his flagstones. A potato woman in the field will till up a new bramble root, attracted by my healing spells. The bramble wall marches ever closer, and cares not at all what intentions I have when I use magic. It only cares that there is magic to feed upon." I stood stiffly and went to squat by the fireplace, rolled a log so that it crackled and set up sparks. Pila watched me, I could feel her eyes on me. I glanced back at her. "I help my child and curse my neighbor. Simple truth."

"And many of your neighbors do the same," Pila said. "Simple truth. Now come and sit."

I rejoined her, and we both watched the fire and my sleeping daughter. "I'm afraid I cannot save her," I said, finally. "It will take great magic to make the cough go away, entirely. Her death is written in the dome of the

Judgment Hall, and I fear I cannot save her without great magic. Magic such as someone like Scacz wields. And he will not wield it for the sake of one little girl."

"And so you labor on the balanthast."

I shrugged. "If I can stop the bramble, then there's no reason not to use the great magics again. We can all be saved." I stared at the flames. Firewood had grown expensive since bramble started sprouting in the nearby forest. I grimaced. "We're caught in Halizak's Prison. Every move we make closes the walls down upon us."

"But the balanthast works," Pila reminded me. "You have found a solution."

I looked over at her. "I don't trust them."

"The Mayor?"

"Or the Majister. And now they have my balanthast. Another Halizakian box. I don't trust them, but they are the only ones who can save us."

Pila touched my shoulder. "I have watched you for more than fifteen years. You will discover a way."

I sighed. "When I add up the years, I feel sick. I was certain that I would have the balanthast perfected within a year or two. Within five. Within ten, for certain. In time to save Merali." I looked over at my sleeping daughter. "And now I can't help wondering if I'm too late to save even Jiala."

Pila smiled. "This time, I think you will succeed. I have never seen something like the balanthast. No one has. You have worked a miracle. What's one more, to save Jiala?"

She pushed her dark hair back, looking at me with her deep brown eyes. I started to answer, but lost my voice, struck suddenly by her proximity.

Pila...

With my work, I had never had time or moment to really look at her. Staring into her eyes, seeing the slight smile on her lips, I felt as if I was surfacing from some deep pool, suddenly breathing. Seeing Pila for the first time. Perhaps even seeing the world for the first time.

How long had I been gone? How long had I simply not paid attention to my growing daughter, or to Pila's care? In the firelight of the workshop, Pila was beautiful.

"Why did you stay?" I asked. "You could have gone on to other households. Could have made a family of your own. I pay you less than when you did little other than washing and cleaning, and now you run the household entire. Why not move on? I wouldn't begrudge it. Other households would welcome you. I would recommend you."

"You want to be rid of me just as you reach success?" Pila asked.

"No—" I stumbled on my own words. "I don't mean to say..." I fumbled. "I mean, others all pay more."

She snorted. "A great deal more, considering that I haven't taken pay for more than a year."

I looked at her, puzzled. "What do you mean?"

She gave me a sad smile. "It was a necessary economy, if we were to keep eating."

"Then why on earth didn't you leave?"

"You wished me to leave?"

"No!" All my words seemed to be wrong. "I'm in your debt. I owe you the moon. But you starve here—you can't think that I do not appreciate. It's just that you make no sense—"

"You poor fool," Pila said. "You truly can't see further than the bell of your balanthast."

She leaned close, and her lips brushed mine.

When she straightened, her dark eyes were deep with promise and knowledge. "I chose my place long ago," she said. "I watched you with Merali. When she was well, and when she fell ill. And I have watched you with Jiala. I would never leave one like you, one who never abandons others, even when it would be easy. You, I know."

"All my secrets," I whispered.

"All the ones that matter."

5

The next day, the Mayor again invited me to his great house on the hill, to demonstrate the mechanics of the balanthast.

Pila helped me with my finest once more, but now she leaned close, smiling as she did, our cheeks almost brushing, my mustaches quivering at the proximity of this woman who had suddenly come into view.

It was as if I had been peering through clouded glass, but now, had finally polished a clear lens. Our fingers met on the buttons of my vest and we laughed together, giddy with recognition, and Jiala watched us both, smiling a secret child's smile, the one that always touched her face when she thought she held some furtive bit of knowledge, but which showed as clearly on her expression as the fabled rocket blossoms of Jhandpara showed against the stars.

At the door, I hugged Jiala goodbye, then turned to Pila. I took a step toward her, then stopped, embarrassed at my forwardness, caught between past lives and new circumstance. Pila smiled at my uncertainty, then laughed and came to me, shaking her head. We embraced awkwardly. A new ritual. An acknowledgment that everything was different between us, and that new customs would write themselves over old habits.

I held Pila close and felt years falling away from me. And then Jiala crashed into us, hugging us both, together. Laughing and squeezing in between. Family. Finally, family again. After too long without. The Three Faces of Mara, all of us a little more whole, and grateful.

"I think she likes us this way," Pila murmured.

"Then never leave me."

"Never."

I left that empty house feeling more full of life than I had in years. Silly and full of laughter all at once. Thinking of weddings. Of Pila as a bride. A gift I had never hoped to find again. The weight of loneliness lifted from me. Even the bramble cutting crews didn't depress me. Men and women hacking bits of it from between the cobbles. Sweeping the city to make sure that vines didn't encroach. I smiled at them, instead. With the balanthast, people would at last be safe. Could at last live their lives as they saw fit.

In ancient Jhandpara, majisters imbued carpets with magic so that they could speed from place to place, arrowing across the skies. Great wide carpets, as big as a room, with silver tea services and glass smoking vessels all set out for their friends. Crossing the empire in the blink of an eye. Flying back and forth from their floating castles and their estates in the cool north, to their seasides in the gentle south. And children did not sicken and die, and there was no wasting cough. All things were possible, except that magic made bramble, and bramble dragged flying carpets from the sky.

But now I had the solution, and I had Pila's love, and I would have Jiala forever, or for at least as long any parent can hope for a child.

Not cursed at all. Blessed.

Out on the Sulong River, work was proceeding on the floating bridge. I couldn't help imagining what it would be like to have not just the one, but perhaps even three floating bridges. We could heat our homes in the winter with green magic flames. We could speed across the land. We could reclaim Jhandpara. I laughed in the sharp spring air. Anything was possible.

◆—✦—◆

As I entered Mayor's House, the steward greeted me with quick recognition, which put me more at ease. My fears of the night before had been erased by sleep and Pila's influence and the warming spring sunshine.

The steward ushered me into the audience gallery. I was surprised to find a number of notables also there, assembled in gold and finery: magistrates of the courts, clove merchants and diamond traders, generals and old nobility who traced their lineages back to Jhandpara. Even the three ancient Majisters of fallen Alacan. More people peered out from under the columned arches surrounding the gallery's marble and basalt flagstones. Much of Khaim's high and influential society, all gathered together.

I stopped, surprised.

"What's this?"

Majister Scacz strode toward me, smiling greeting. "We thought there should be a demonstration." He guided me over to a draped object in the center of the hall. From its shape, I guessed it was my balanthast.

"Is that my instrument?" I asked, concerned.

The Mayor joined us. "Of course it is. Don't be nervous, alchemist."

"It's a delicate device."

The Mayor nodded seriously. "And we have treated it with utmost respect." Scacz patted me on the back, trying to reassure me. "These people all around us are the ones whose support we need, if we are to effect your new balanthast workshop. We must raise taxes for the initial construction, and," he paused, delicately, "some of the old nobility may be interested in patronage, in return for ancient bramble lands reclaimed. I assure you, this is a very good thing. It's easier to gain support when people whiff profit than if they simply feel they are being taxed to no purpose." He motioned me to the balanthast. "Please, do not be nervous. All will be well. This is an opportunity for us all."

A servant brought in a huge pot, containing a cutting of bramble over seven feet tall. The thing seemed to fairly quiver in its pot, hunting malevolently for a new place to stretch its roots. They must have planted it the night before, immediately after I left, for it to have grown so large. Multiple branches sprouted from it, like great hairy tentacles.

The assembled dignitaries sucked in their breath at the sight of humanity's greatest enemy, sitting in the center of the gallery. In the light of day, with its hairy tendrils and milkweed-like pods dangling, it spoke of eldritch menace. Even the pot was frightening, carved with the faces of Takaz, the Demon Prince, his serpent heads making offers of escape that would never be honored.

The Mayor held up his hands to the assembled. "Fear not! This is but a demonstration. Necessary for you to grasp the significance of the alchemist's achievement." He waved a hand at the servants and they lifted the drapery from my instrument.

"Behold!" the Mayor said to the throng. "The balanthast!"

The man had the gift of showmanship, I had to grant him that. The instrument had been polished, and now with sunlight pouring down from the upper galleries, it fairly blazed. Its glass chambers refracted the light, sending off rainbows. The copper bell mouths of its vents and the belly of its combustion chamber reflected the people in strange and distorted glory.

The crowd gasped in amazement.

"Has it been tampered with?" I asked.

"Of course not," Scacz said. "Just polished. That's all. I examined the workings of the thing, but took nothing apart." He paused, concerned. "Is it damaged?"

"No." But still I studied it. "And did it satisfy you? That it does not use magic? That it is not some device of the majisters pressed into new form?"

Scacz almost grinned at that. "I apologize most profusely for my suspicions, alchemist. It seems to function entirely according to natural properties. A feat, truly. History can only bow to your singular genius." He nodded at the assembled people. "And now, will you demonstrate for our esteemed visitors?"

As I began assembling the ingredients, a general in the audience asked, "What is this instrument of yours, Scacz?"

"Salvation, war lord."

A fat merchant, out of the diamond quarter with thick mustaches from his many children called, "And what is the use of it?"

The Mayor smiled. "If we told you, it would spoil the astonishing surprise. You must see it as the Majister and I first did. Without preface or preamble."

I armed the balanthast, but then had to have the servants help me drag it over until it stood beside the huge bramble pot. Under the assembled gaze, it seemed to take forever to scrape the tripod over the flagstones. Despite my faith in my device, my heart was pounding. I pulled on a leather glove and pinched out a bit of the potted soil. Added it to the firing chamber. Plunged the delivery nozzles into the dirt. At last, I lit the match.

For a moment, we all watched, silent. The collected ingredients burned, and then were sucked into the combustion chamber. A pause.

I held my breath, thinking that Scacz and the Mayor had somehow broken the balanthast in their ignorance. Then the balanthast shook and the snake faces of the Demon Prince burst wide, spilling soil as the pot shattered. The bramble toppled and hit the marble. The crowd gasped.

Yellow smoke issued from the bramble's limbs. It writhed, smoking, twisting, boiling. Sap squealed and frothed as it effervesced, a dying howl from our ancient menace.

People covered their ears as the bramble thrashed. More smoke issued from its vines. Within a minute, the bramble lay still, leaving ash and tiny blackened threads floating in the sunlight. Yellow smoke billowed slowly over the assemblage, sending people coughing and wheezing, but as the clouds dispersed, a great murmuring rose at the sight of the scorched bramble corpse.

"Inspect it!" Scacz cried. "Come and see. You must see this to believe!"

Not many cared to come close, but the general did. Unafraid, he approached and knelt. He stared, thunderstruck. "There are no seeds." His wide-eyed gaze fell upon me. "There should be seeds."

His words carried through the crowds. No seeds. No seeds. The lightning strike of miracle.

The Mayor laughed, and servants arrived with goblets of wine for celebration. Scacz clapped me on the back and the men and women of the great merchant houses came to stare at the cleansed soil before them. And then Scacz called out again, "One further demonstration?"

The crowd clapped and stamped their feet. Again I primed the balanthast, eager to show off the wonder of our salvation. I looked around for another pot of bramble, but none was in evidence.

"How will I demonstrate?" I asked.

"It doesn't matter," Scacz said. "Let it ignite free."

I hesitated.

The Mayor said, "Don't be shy of a bit of showmanship. Let them see the glory."

"But it can't simply be fired. It must have something to attach to. Some bit of earth at least."

"Here." Scacz took something from his sleeve. "I have something else you might try this on." He said something under his breath and suddenly,

I smelled magic. The scent was different from the healing magic I had cast upon Jiala the night before. This was something special. Bright as bluebells in the summer sun, sticky as honey. He pressed a folded bit of parchment into my palm.

"Put this in your balanthast chamber," Scacz said. "It should burn well."

The whiff of bluebell honey magic clung to the paper.

I didn't want to. Didn't know what he was up to. But the Mayor was nodding, and I was surrounded by the assembled people, all those great names and powerful houses watching, and the Mayor motioned me to continue.

"Go on, alchemist. Show us your genius. The crowd loves you. Let us see this thing fire free."

And to my everlasting regret, I did.

I braced the delivery nozzles so they poked into the air, and lit my match. The spelled parchment and the neem and all the assembled ingredients disappeared into the belly of the balanthast, and it roared.

Blue flame erupted from the nozzles, a long streak of sparkling fire. Thick yellow smoke issued with it. And something else: the sticky breath of the magic-laced parchment Scacz had given me. Flower brightness, volatilized in the belly chamber of the balanthast, and now released as smoke.

Beside me, Scacz's body began to glow an unearthly aura of blue, sharp and defined. But not just him. The Mayor as well. His steward also. I stared at my hands. Myself, even.

The fumes of the expended balanthast billowed through the room and others began to glow as well. The general. The fat diamond merchant. His wife. More women in their skirts. Men in their fine embroidered vests. But Scacz's blue-limned features were brightest of all.

"You were right," the Mayor murmured. "Look at us all."

Everyone was staring at the many people who now glowed with spirit fire, gasping at the wonder of their unearthly beauty.

Scacz smiled at me. "You were right, alchemist. Neem loves magic. It clings to its memory like a child to her mother's skirts."

"What have you done?" I asked.

"Done?" Scacz looked around, amused. "Why, just added a bit of illumination to your neem essence. Your fine alchemy and my simple spellcraft, combined. A lovely effect, don't you think?"

Boots thudded and steel rang around the hall. Guards appeared from behind white columns and beneath the arches. Men in scaly armor, and the tramp of more boots behind them.

"Seize them!" Scacz shouted. "All the ones who burn with magic's use. Every one! If they are not of the Mayor's office, they are traitors."

A babble of protest rose. Already the people who did not glow were shrinking from those that did.

The general drew his sword. "Treachery?" he asked. "This is why you bring us here?" A few others drew steel with him.

The Mayor said, "Sadly, war lord, even you are not immune to law. You have used magic, when it is expressly forbidden. If you have some excuse, the magistrate will hear you..." He paused. "Oh dear, it appears the magistrate is also guilty." He waved to his guards. "Take them all, then."

The general roared. He raised his sword and charged for the Mayor. Guards piled atop him like wolves. Steel clashed. A man fell back. The general stumbled from within the tangle of steel. Blood streamed from half a dozen sword thrusts. For a moment, I thought he would reach us, but then he fell, sprawling on the marble. And yet still he tried to reach the Mayor. Scrabbling like a beetle, leaving a maroon streak behind him.

The Mayor watched the general's struggle with distaste.

"On second thought, kill them all now. We know what they've been up to."

The guards howled and the blue-glowing nobility shrank before them. Too few were armed. They scattered, running like sheep, scrambling about the gallery as the guards hunted them down and silenced their begging. At last, there were no more screams.

I stood in the midst of a massacre, clutching my balanthast.

The Mayor waved to the guards. "Drag the bodies out. Then go and seize their properties." In a louder voice he announced, "For those of you still standing, the holdings of the traitors will be sold at auction, as is custom. Your trustworthiness is proven, and you shall benefit."

He clapped Scacz on the back. "Well done, Majister. Inspired, even." His eyes fell on my own blue-glowing form. "Well. This is a pity. It seems the Majister was right in all respects. He told me he smelled magic on you when we first met, and I didn't believe him. But here you are, glowing like a lamp."

I backed away, cradling the balanthast. "You're the Demon Prince himself."

"Don't be absurd. Takaz would care not at all for stopping bramble."

The guards were grabbing bodies and dragging them into piles, leaving blood smears behind.

The Mayor eyed the stains. "Get someone in here to mop these tiles! Don't just leave this blood here." He glanced around. "Where's my steward disappeared to?"

Scacz cleared his throat. "I'm afraid he was caught up in the general slaughter."

"Ah." The Mayor frowned. "Inconvenient." He returned his attention to me. "Well, then. Let's have the device." He held out his hands.

"I would never—"

"Give it here."

I stared at him, filled with horror at what he had done. What I had been complicit in. In a rush, I lifted the balanthast over my head.

"No!" Scacz lunged forward.

But it was too late. I threw down the balanthast. Glass vacuum chambers shattered. Diamond fragments skittered across marble. Delicate copper and brass workings bent and snapped. I grabbed the largest part of the balanthast, and flung it from me, sending it sliding, breaking apart into even smaller parts before coming to rest in the blood of its victims.

"You fool." Scacz grabbed me. His hand closed on my throat and he forced me down. The blue glow about him intensified, magic flowing. My throat began to close, pinched tight by Scacz's hate and power.

"Join the rest of the traitors," he said.

My throat bound shut. I couldn't breathe. I couldn't even cry out. No air passed my lips. The man was powerful. He didn't even need an inked page to spell such evil.

Darkness.

And then, abruptly, sunlight.

I could breathe. I lay on the flagstones and sucked air through my suddenly unbound throat. Majister Scacz knelt over me.

His hand lay upon my chest, resting gently. And yet, at the same time, I could feel each of his five fingers beneath my ribs. Gripping my heart. I batted weakly at his hand, trying to push him away. Scacz's fingers tightened, constraining the beat of my blood. I gave up.

I realized that the Mayor was standing over us both, watching.

"The Mayor points out that you are much too talented to waste," Scacz said. Again he squeezed my heart. "I do hope his faith proves true."

Abruptly his grip relaxed. He straightened and waved for the guards. "Take our friend to the dungeon, until we have a suitable workshop for him." His eyes went to the broken balanthast. "He has many hours of labor ahead."

I found my voice. Croaked out words. "No. Not this bloodbath. I won't be a part of it."

Scacz shrugged. "You already are. And of course you will."

6

Should I tell you that I fought? That I didn't break? That I resisted torture and blandishment and took no part in the purge that followed? That I had no hand in the blood that gushed down Khaim's alleys and poured into the Sulong? Should I tell you that I was noble, while others pandered? That I was not party to the terror?

In truth, I refused once.

Then Scacz brought Jiala and Pila to visit. We all sat together in the chill of my cell, huddling under the water drip from stones, smelling the sweet damp rot of straw, and listening to the wet bellows of Jiala's lungs, the fourth participant in our stilted conversation.

Scacz himself said nothing at all. He simply let us sit together. He brought wooden stools, and had a guard provide cups of mint tea and at first I was relieved to see Jiala and Pila unharmed, but then Jiala's coughing started and wouldn't stop, and blood spackled her lips and she began to cry, and then I had to call the guard to take them away. And even though the man was fast in coming, it was still too slow.

The last vision I had of Jiala was of Pila carrying her small form, her wracking cough echoing against cold stones.

And then Scacz came down to visit me again. He leaned against the wall, studying my dishevelment through the bars.

"The cold of the dungeon disagrees with her lungs," he observed.

The repair of the first balanthast was the price of Jiala and Pila's well being, but Scacz and our Jolly Mayor were not finished with me. In Jiala they had the perfect lever. In return for the magic and healing that only Scacz could provide, I created the tools and instruments they desired. My devices purchased life for myself and my family, and death for everyone else.

Blood ran in the streets. Rumors in my prison said that the Mayor's halls were redder than a sunset. That bodies burned in bramble piles, the fat of their cooking twining with the yellow smoke of bramble to fill the skies with funeral pyres. The Executioner was so busy that on some days, a second and even a third were summoned to take over the efforts of the axeman who had grown exhausted with his work. Some days, they didn't even bother with the effort of a public spectacle.

Scacz had laughed at that.

"When we couldn't find these furtive little spell casters, we needed fear to keep the magic in check," he said. "Now that we can hunt them down, it's better to let them practice for a little while, and then seize everything."

As long as I furnished the tools of the hunt, I was not harmed. Scacz and the Mayor had so many uses for me. I was a prized hawk. Free enough, within certain confines. The dynamic between us was as taut as the strings on a violin. Each of us would pluck at those strings, seeking gain, testing the other's boundaries, trying the tenor of the note, the question of its strain. The workings of my mind and its creations tugging against the value of Jiala and Pila's well being. And so we each tugged and pulled at that catgut strand.

I was not a prisoner, precisely. More a scholar who worked all day and all night in a confined place, building better, more portable balanthasts. Constructing devices better tuned to sniffing out magic. Sometimes, I myself forgot my situation. When the work went well, I was as focused as I had ever been in my workshop.

I am ashamed to admit that there were even times when I reveled in the totality of focus that my cell provided. When there is nothing to do but work, a great deal of work can be done.

"Come now. I brought sweets. You like them," Pila urged. She sat outside the bars of my workshop, offering.

I sat, staring. "I'm not hungry anymore."

"I can see that. You're getting skinny."

"I was skinny before."

Pila watched me sadly. "Please. If you won't eat for yourself, then at least eat for me. For Jiala."

Unwillingly, I stood and shuffled over to her.

"You look unwell," she said.

I shrugged. Of late, I had been having nightmares. Oftentimes, I would dream of a river of my victims. Dreamed them pouring down the streets to where the Executioner stood waiting, the hooded butcher chopping off heads as they flowed past, his axe swinging like a scythe, heads spinning in all directions. And I stood at the source of that river, casting each person into the flow. Illuminating them in blue fire before tossing them into the current, sending them tumbling toward that final cataract of the axe.

Pila stretched her hand through the bars, and clasped my cold fingers. Her skin showed wrinkles and her palms showed surprising dryness. I thought that maybe those hands had been soft, that she had been young once, but I could hardly remember. She clasped my hand, and against all the promises I made myself, I collapsed against the bars, pressing her fingers to my cheek.

That I hungered for her warmth was something I could barely stand. Majister Scacz had offered us "relief" as he called it, but he did so with such a leer that after the first time, I could do it no more, and spat in his face when he next suggested the idea. Which enraged him so much that he barred Pila from visiting for nearly six months. Only when I threatened to cut my own throat with a bulb of glass did he finally relent and allow her visits again, if only through the bars. I kissed Pila's fingers, starved for her kindness and humanity in a place that I had turned brutish and bloody.

A few feet away, a guard sat, his body ostentatiously half-turned away from us, providing a semblance of privacy. This particular one was Jaiska. He had a family and his mustaches were long for his three sons, all of whom had followed him into the guards. Decent enough, and willing to give us a little privacy as we whispered to one another through the bars.

Not like Izaac, who loved to regale me with the executions he had seen, thanks to my inventions. Izaac said that within fifty miles of Khaim, no householder had passed untested by the balanthast. Heads not only decorated the city gates, but also the broad bridge that leaped the Sulong and now linked Khaim with its lesser kin. There were so many heads that the Mayor had gotten tired of mounting trophies and now simply ordered bodies tossed into the river to float to the sea.

"How is Jiala?" I asked.

"Better than you," Pila said. "She thrives. And grows. Scacz still refuses to let me bring her, but she is well. You can trust that. Scacz is evil but he loves your work and so he cares for us."

"Other people's heads in exchange for keeping our own." I stared at my workshop. "How many now have I killed? How much blood is on my hands?"

"It's no use thinking about. They were using magic, which was always forbidden. These are not guiltless people who go to the Executioner's axe."

"Don't forget that we were among them as well. Are among them, thanks to Scacz."

"There's no use thinking on it. It will only drive you mad."

I looked at her bitterly. "I've been here for two years already, and if I haven't found refuge in madness yet, I doubt I will."

She sighed. "In any case, it's slowing now. There are fewer who test the Mayor's powers of detection." She leaned close. "Some say that he now only finds magic on people who are too wealthy or powerful. Those ones he snuffs out, and confiscates their families and property."

"And no one fights?"

"A few. But he has supporters. The farmers near the bramble wall say the vines have slowed. In places, they even cut it back. For the first time in generations, they cut it back."

I scowled. "We could have cut back miles, if the Mayor had simply used the balanthast as it was intended."

"It's no use thinking on." She pushed a cloth-wrapped bundle of bread through the bars. "Here," she said. "Please. Eat a little."

But I shook my head and walked away from her offering. It was a petty thing. I knew it even as I did so. But there was no one else to lash out against. A petty rebellion for the real rebellion I had no stomach for.

Pila sighed. I heard a rustling and then her words to Jaiska. "Give these to him when he changes his mind. Some for you as well. Don't let him starve himself."

And then she was gone, leaving me with my workshop and my killing devices.

"Don't scorn her," Jaiska said. "She stands by you and your daughter when she could walk away easy. Old Scacz likes to bother her. Comes and bothers her."

I turned. "What do you mean?"

He shrugged. "Bothers her."

"She doesn't say so."

"Not to you. Wouldn't want you to do something stupid."

I sighed, feeling childish for my display. "I don't deserve her."

Jaiska laughed. "No one deserves anyone. You just win 'em and hope you can hang onto 'em." He offered me the bread. "Might as well eat while it's fresh."

I took the bread and cut a slice on a work table. Cut one for him as well. The scent of honey and rosemary, along with the reek of neem and mint and the burn of coals from my glass fire.

"It's a strange world we live in," I said, waving at my worktable. "All that time spent trying to find magic, and now, suddenly Scacz asks for balanthasts to kill bramble again. Maybe he'll finally decide to cut away the bramble wall."

Jaiska snorted. "Well. In a way." He took another bite of bread and spoke around the mouthful. "He cuts new lands into the bramble for his and the Mayor's friends. The people who inform for them. Their favored guards."

"Are you going to get new lands?"

Jaiska shrugged. "I'm just a sword. Keep my head down. Don't work magic when the hunters are out. Hope my sons all learn their sword swinging right. Don't need lands. Don't need honors. Don't do traffic with the Mayor."

I grimaced. "That's wisdom, there. I, on the other hand, thought I'd be a savior of our land."

"Bramble's mostly stopped." Jaiska said. "Hardly anyone except Scacz uses magic anymore. Not in any real way. Can't remember the last time I saw bramble sprouting in the city. We're saved. In a way."

"It isn't the way I hoped."

Jaiska laughed at that. "For being so clever with the devices, you're a damn silly-headed bastard."

"Pila said something similar to me, once."

"Because it's true, alchemist."

At the new voice, Jaiska leaped to his feet. "No offense, sir."

Scacz swept into view. "Go find something to do, guardsman."

"Grace." Jaiska touched his brow and fled.

Scacz sat down on the stool that Jaiska had vacated. His gaze came to rest on Pila's gift. "I'd ask you for some of that lovely bread, but I'm afraid you'd put bramble threads in it."

I shook my head. "Bramble threads would be too good for a creature like you."

"Ah. Yes. A creature. Indeed." He smiled. "A powerful creature, actually. Thanks to you. The most powerful majister in the land, now. The Majisters of Alacan all have their heads fitted to spikes." He sighed. "It really is an addiction. The feel of power flowing through... no one understands that. Siren song for those of us who have the knack. But then, you already knew that."

"I don't miss it," I said.

Scacz snorted. "Maybe. But the lure is certainly there. For many. For most. We could never allow the people to believe that your balanthast was actually a solution. False comfort there. As soon as they sipped a little magic from the pool, they would have demanded to drink deep. And then," he made a motion with his hands, "willy-nilly everyone would have been spelling here and there, charming and spelling and making flying carpets, and we'd all have a lovely time. Until the bramble overwhelmed us."

"It wouldn't have," I said. "We're not stupid."

Scacz laughed. "It's not as if the people of Jhandpara—of all the old empire—were unaware of magic's unfortunate effects. From the historical manuscripts, they tried mightily to hold back their base urges. But still they thirsted for magic. For the power, some. For the thrill. For the convenience. For the salvation. For the wonderful luxury."

He made a motion, and a castle appeared above his hand, glowing. It floated in clouds, with dragons of every color circling it.

"How could anyone give this up?" he asked. "The people of Jhandpara had no discipline. Even the ones who wished to control themselves lacked the necessary will. And so our Empire fell."

In Scacz's hand, the castle tumbled from its clouds, crashing into deep bramble forests below. Bramble spread over arched palaces, over coliseums, over temples to the Three Faces of Mara, growing tall and terrible. Dust and rubble clouds obscured the scene as more cloud castles fell.

Scacz brushed his hands together, obliterating the scene and knocking off a rain of dust that landed on his robes.

"Magic brings bramble," he said. "And even you, alchemist, hungered to use it."

"Only a little. To save my daughter."

"Every spell maker has a reasonable excuse. If we grant individual mercies, we commit collective suicide. A pretty puzzle for an ethical man like you."

"You think we're the same, then?"

"Magic is magic. Bramble is bramble. I couldn't care less what hairs a philosopher splits. Now, every night, I sleep knowing that bramble will no longer encroach. So I sleep very well indeed." He stood. Nodded at my new balanthast. "Hurry with your new device, alchemist. As always, your daughter's well-being depends upon it."

"Why not let me go?"

"Why would I do such a thing? Then you might go and carry this knowledge of balanthasts to some other city. Perhaps give others the illusion that discipline is no longer needed." He shook his head. "No. That would not do at all."

"Khaim is my home," I said. "I have no wish to leave. I could construct balanthasts. You say you want to cut back the bramble now. At last, our goals align."

"Our goals already align, alchemist." Scacz turned away. "Hurry with your tools. I have fiefs I wish to disburse."

"And if I refuse?"

Scacz turned back. "Then I simply will stop caring whether your daughter coughs up that river of blood of hers. The choice is yours. It always has been."

"You'll never let me go."

Scacz laughed. "I can't think why I would. You're far too useful."

That night I lay in my bed, surrounded by the weirdly comfortable smells and drips of my prison workshop, turning the problem of the Majister over in my head. I could not bargain with the dragon mind of Scacz. And despite his words, I suspected my time was running out.

Building balanthasts to create bramble fiefdoms was not the green grass of a new beginning, but the signal smoke of a bitter end. Once a brigade of balanthasts was prepared, there would be no more need of me.

I lay listening to the night guard's snores, and began to plan. Assembling pieces and components into a larger whole. Not a plan fully realized, but still...an intrigue. A tangle of misdirection, and at the end of its winding way, a path, perhaps, out of my Halizakian box. I considered the alleys and angles, testing chinks in the armor of my logic.

If I was honest, there were many.

But Pila, Jiala and I had already lived too long in the center of Khaim's bloody vortex. The storm would eventually tear us to pieces as well. Scacz might be a man of his word, but he was not a man of charity. The Mayor and Scacz thought in terms of trade, and when I had nothing left to offer, they would do away with me.

In the morning, I was up and constructing.

"Jaiska," I said. "Go find Scacz. Tell him I've had an inspiration."

When Scacz appeared, I made my proposal. "If you let me walk outside occasionally, I will make your detectors more powerful. I can extend their reach considerably, I think. And build them so that a man need not even handle them. They could run continuously, in market squares, all along the thoroughfares, at city gates."

Scacz looked at me suspiciously. "Why so amenable all of a sudden?"

"I want to live well. I want to see the sun and the sky, and I'm willing to bargain."

"You think to escape."

"From a great majister like you?" I shook my head. "I have no illusions. But I cannot live forever without fresh air." I held up an arm. "Look at me. I'm wasting away. Look how pale I become. Shackle me how you like, but I would breathe fresh air."

"How will you improve your design?"

"Here." I rolled out parchment and dipped my quill. Scratched out the bones of a design. "It would be a bit like a torch, standing. A sentry. It would issue a slow smoke from its boiler. Anyone who walked near would be caught." I pushed the rough sketch through the bars.

"You've been holding this back."

I met Scacz's gaze. "You should realize that keeping me alive and happy has benefits."

Scacz laughed at that, liking the bargain he thought we were making. "Does your hold on survival feel tenuous, alchemist?"

"I want assurances, Scacz. And a life. A life better than this."

"Oh? There's something else you desire?"

"I want Pila to be able to visit me again."

Scacz leered, then shook his head. "No. I think not."

"Then I will not improve your detectors."

"I could torture you."

I looked at him through the bars. "You have all the power, Majister. I ask for a favor and you return with threats. What else can I offer you? A better balanthast as well? Something that works faster and better than the ones you currently have? I can design ones that are light and portable. They could clear fields in days. Imagine the magics you could wield if bramble was hardly a threat at all."

And the hook was set. After all, what good is it to be the finest majister in the land when you cannot wield the finest, most impressive magics? Scacz's hunger to use his powers chafed against the natural limits that bramble imposed.

And so I set to work on my newly conceived balanthasts and my detectors. My workroom filled with supplies, with copper rolls, with bellows and tongs, with brass and nails, glass bulbs and vacuum tubes, and Scacz came to visit daily, eager for my promised improvements.

And Pila came to visit, as well.

In the darkness, we clutched close and I murmured in her ear.

"This cannot work," she whispered.

"If it does not, you must go without me," I said.

"I won't. It will do no good."

"Do you love Jiala?"

"Of course I do."

"Then you must trust me. Trust me as much as you did when I labored for so many years to get us into this mess."

"It's madness."

"A madness I created. And I must stop it. If I cannot, you must run. Take the spell for Jiala's health and go. Run as far as you can. For if I fail, Scacz will pursue you to the very ends of the earth."

In the morning, Pila left with a kiss and a copper token of my affection, bound around her wrist, a little bit of the workshop, leaving with her.

Over the course of weeks I worked, feverish. And at night, I met with Pila and whispered formulas and processes in her ear. She listened close, her long black hair tickling like feathers on my lips, the lustrous strands cloaking us as we played at intimacy and worked at salvation.

My detectors went up in the city, gouting out foul smoke and blanketing Khaim in their reactants, and once again blood ran in the streets. Scacz was well pleased. He granted me the privilege of letting me out of my cage.

I was so unfit that I ran out of breath simply walking up the stairs out of the dungeon. And then I gasped again when we reached the grounds and gazed over the city.

The flames of the detectors glowed here and there, blue fireflies sending out scented smoke that clung to anything magical at all. The bridge to Lesser Khaim blazed astonishingly bright, a beacon of magic in the thickening darkness.

"You have wrought something beautiful," Scacz said. "Khaim will always be known as the Blue City, now. And from now on, we will grow." He pointed into the sky, and I could see where the beginnings of a castle clung to wisps of accumulating clouds.

I sucked in my breath in astonishment.

"It's damnably difficult to summon and collect the clouds," Scacz said. "But it will be quite pretty when it's completed."

I felt as if I was staring at fabled Jhandpara. I could almost hear the music and taste the joy of the Mount Sena wine I had quaffed so long ago.

When I found my voice, I said, "You must bring the old balanthasts back to me so that I can adjust them. I will have to trade out their combustion chambers for the power that they will now wield."

Scacz smiled and rubbed his hands together. "And then I will truly be able to set to work on my castle. I won't have to check my powers at all."

"The Majister of the Blue City," I said.

"Indeed."

"I'd very much like to see it when it's done."

Scacz looked over at me, thoughtful. "If these balanthasts perform as you describe them, alchemist, then the very least I can do for you is to give you domicile above the earth."

"A prison in the air?"

"Better than one on the ground. You will have a most astonishing view."

I laughed at that. "I won't argue. In fact, I will hurry the moment." I turned to leave, but then paused, voicing an afterthought. "When the balanthasts arrive, I'll also need several pots of bramble. To test and make sure my designs are correct."

Scacz nodded, distracted, still staring up at the triumph of his castle. "What's that?"

"Bramble," I said patiently. "For the testing."

Scacz waved an acknowledgment, and the guards led me back down to my dungeon.

A few days later, I asked Jaiska to summon Scacz for the final demonstrations.

I had lined up a number of bramble plants in pots. "It would work better if we were at the bramble wall," I grumbled, "but this should suffice."

Along one wall, I had all the balanthasts of the city, lined up. Each one newly altered, its delivery tubes and chambers reshaped to their improved purpose. I took one of the gleaming instruments from its rank and plunged its nozzle into the bramble pot. The bramble's limbs quivered malevolently, as if it understood the evil I planned for it. The dry pods rattled as the pot shifted.

I lit the match, and pressed it into the new combustion chamber. Much faster and easier to ignite, now.

A low explosion. The plant thrashed briefly, and then disappeared in a puff of acrid smoke. There was simply nothing left of it at all.

I laughed, delighted.

"You see?"

Scacz and Jaiska stared, dumbfounded. I did it again, laughing, and now Scacz and Jaiska laughed as well.

"Well done, alchemist! Well done!"

"And it is prepared much more quickly now," I said. "These chambers on top mix the ingredients, so that they are always at the ready. Open this valve, and..." I lit another match. Explosion. Vented smoke. The potted bramble soaked up the balanthast's poison and disappeared in a squeal of burning sap and writhing smoke.

I grinned. Did it again and again, working something greater than magic in my workshop. Jaiska stamped his feet and whistled. Scacz's smile widened into a greedy astonished grin. And then I, laughing and in my folly, drunk on my success, grabbed a bramble with my bare hands.

A silly, reckless thing. A moment of inattention, and all my genius was destroyed.

I yanked my hands away as if the bramble was on fire, but its thread-like hairs clung already to my bare skin. The sleeping toxins numbed my hands, spreading like fire. I fell to my knees. Tried to stand. Stumbled and crashed into the balanthast, tumbling it and knocking it over, shattering it.

"Fool!" Scacz shouted.

I tried to get up once more, but fell back instead, tangling with bramble again. Its thorns pricked me, its threads clung to my skin, poisoning, clutching and hungry for me. Burrowing sleep into my heart, pressing down upon my lungs.

Darkness closed on my vision. It was terrifyingly fast. I crawled away, stupid with the toxins, reached through the bars. Scacz and Jaiska shied from my thread-covered hands.

"Please." I whispered. "Use your magic. Save me."

Scacz shook his head, staying well away from my touch. "No magic works against bramble's sleep."

"Please." I croaked. "Jiala. Please. Keep her well."

Scacz looked at me with contempt. "There's really no point, now, is there?"

My limbs turned to water. I slumped to the flagstones, still reaching through the bars as he went blurry and distant.

The Majister stared down at me with a bemused expression.

"It's probably better this way, alchemist. We would have had to chop your head off, eventually." He turned to Jaiska. "As soon as he's done thrashing, gather up the balanthasts. And don't be so stupid as he was."

"What about his body? Should I take him to his wife?"

"No. Dump it in the river with the rest."

I was too far gone to panic. Bramble stilled my heart.

7

Having your flesh burned with blue flame is not my preferred method to awaken, but it is a great improvement over death. Another gust of flame washed over me. It burned through my blood, blistered my lungs, tunneled about in my heart, and dragged me back to life. I writhed in the heat, trying to breathe. Another blast of flame.

And suddenly, I was coughing and wheezing. My skin burned, but I breathed.

"Stop," I croaked, waving weakly for mercy, praying I wouldn't be scoured again. I opened my eyes.

Pila crouched over me, a fantastic jeweled balanthast in her hands. Jiala stood beside her, worried, clutching at her skirt.

"Are you alive, Papa?" she asked.

I pushed myself upright, shaking bramble threads from my arms. Pila looked me over, brushed me with a gloved hand. "He's alive enough, child. Now hurry and get our things. It's time for us to run."

Jiala nodded obediently and ran out of my workroom. I stared after her, astonished. How she had grown! Not a small child at all, but tall and vital. So much change in the two years I had been imprisoned. Pila continued to brush away the singed bramble thread. I winced at her touch.

"Don't complain," she said. "Blisters mean you're alive."

I flinched away from another round of brushing. "You found my body, it seems."

"It was a near thing. I was expecting a coffin to arrive. If Jaiska hadn't been decent enough to send word of where you'd been dumped..." She shrugged. "You were nearly tossed into the water with the rest of the corpses before I found you."

"Help me stand."

With her support, I made it to my feet. My old familiar workshop, but altered under Pila's influence.

"I had to replace much of the equipment," Pila explained as she braced me upright. "Even with your instruction, it was an uncertain thing."

"I'm alive, though." I looked at her balanthast. My design but her construction, noticing places where she had made changes. She held it by a leather strap that she slung over her shoulder. "You've made it quite portable," I said, admiring.

"If we're to run, it's time we did."

"More than time."

In the hall, our last belongings were stuffed into wicker baskets with harnesses to hold them upon our backs. A tiny pile of essentials. So little of my old life. A few wool blankets, food and water jugs. And yet, there also, Pila and Jiala. More than any man had any right to ask for. We slung our baskets, and I groaned at the weight in mine.

"Easy living," Pila commented. "Jiala could carry more than you."

"Not quite that bad, I hope. In any case, nothing that a long walk won't fix."

We ducked out into the streets, the three of us together, winding through the alleys. We ran as quickly as we could for the gates of Khaim, making our way toward the open fields. Inside, I felt laughter and relief bubbling up. My skin was burned, my hair was matted and melted, but I was alive, maybe for the first time in almost twenty years.

And then the wind shifted and a cloud of smoke blew across us. One of my own infernal detectors, now standing sentry on every street.

Jiala lit up like an oil lamp.

Pila sucked in her breath. "She was only treated yesterday. The magic still shows. Normally I kept her in, after Scacz spelled her."

Quick as a cat, she swept a cloak over Jiala, smothering the blue glow. And yet still it leaked out. Jiala's face shone an unearthly shade. I picked her up and buried her face in my chest. She was heavy.

"Don't show your skin, child."

We slunk through the city and out into the fields as darkness fell. We went along the muddy road, trying to hide my daughter's fatal hue. But it was useless. Farmers on the road saw and gasped and dashed away, and even as we hurried forward, we heard cries behind. People who sought to profit from turning in a user of magic.

"We aren't going to make it," Pila said.

"Run then!"

And we did, galloping and stumbling. I panted at the unaccustomed exercise. I was not meant to run. Not after years in prison. In a minute, I was gasping. In two, spots swam before my vision and I was staggering. And still we ran, now with Jiala on her own, tugging at me, dragging me forward. Healthier by far than I.

Behind us, the shouts of guardsmen echoed. They gained.

Ahead, black bramble shadows rose.

"Halt! In the name of Khaim and the Mayor!"

On the run, Pila fired her balanthast. Lit its prime. Prepared to plunge it into the ground at the bracken root.

"No!" I gasped. "Not like that." I lifted the device so it pointed into the guts of the bracken. "Don't hurt the roots. Just the branches."

Pila glanced at me, puzzled, then nodded sharply. The balanthast roared. Blue flame lanced from the nozzle, igniting the branches. Bramble writhed and vaporized, opening a deep narrow corridor of smoking writhing vines. We plunged into the gap. Another shout came from behind.

"Halt!"

An arrow thudded into a bramble branch. Another creased my ear. I grabbed Jiala and forced her low as Pila fired the balanthast again.

Behind us, the guardsmen were stumbling across the tilled fields, splashing through irrigated trenches. Their swords gleamed in the moonlight.

Blue flame speared the night again, and a writhing bramble path opened before us.

I pulled out the spell book of Majister Arun. "A match, daughter."

I struck the flame and handed it to Jiala. In its flickering unsteady light, I read spidering text by the hand of that long dead majister. A spell for sweeping.

A dust devil formed in the bracken, swirling. I waved my hand and sent it spinning down the narrow way behind us. A simple spell. A bit of household magic for a servant or a child. Nothing in comparison to the great works of Jhandpara.

But to the bramble all around, that tiny spell was like meat tossed before a tiger. The vines shivered at magic's scent and clutched after my sweeping whirlwind. I cast more small spells as Pila opened a way ahead. Bramble closed in behind, starving for the magic that I scattered like breadcrumbs, ravenous for the nurturing flavors of magic cast so close to its roots. Vines erupted from the earth, filling the path and locking us in the belly of the bramble forest.

Behind us, the guards' shouts faded and became indistinct. A few more arrows plunged into the bramble, ricocheting and clattering, but already the vines were thick and tangled behind us. We might as well have been behind a wall of oak.

Pila fired the balanthast again and we moved deeper into the malevolent forest.

"We won't have long before they follow us," she said.

I shook my head. "No. We have time. Scacz's balanthasts will not work. I crippled them all before I left, when Scacz thought I was improving them. Only the one I used for my demonstration worked, and I made sure to shatter it."

"Where are we going, Papa?" Jiala asked.

I pulled Jiala close as I whispered another spell of dust and tidying. The little whirlwind whisked its way into the darkness, baiting bramble, closing the path behind us. When I was done, I smiled at my daughter and touched her under her chin. "Have I ever told you of the copper mines of Kesh?"

"No, Papa."

"They are truly wondrous. Not a bit of bramble populates the land, no matter how much magic is used. An island in a sea of bramble."

The blue fire of Pila's balanthast again lit the night, sending bramble writhing away from us, opening a corridor of flight. I picked up Jiala, amazed at how heavy she had become in my years away, but unwilling to let her leave my side even for a moment, welcoming her truth and weight. We started down the corridor that Pila had opened.

Jiala gave a little cough and wiped her lips on her sleeve. "Truly?" she asked. "There is a place where you can use magic? Even for my cough?"

"As sure as balanthasts," I told her, and hugged her tight. "We only have to get there."

Another blast of blue flame lit the night, and we all forged onward.

Sandmagic

Orson Scott Card

Orson Scott Card *is the bestselling author of more than forty novels, including* Ender's Game, *which was a winner of both the Hugo and Nebula awards. The sequel,* Speaker for the Dead, *also won both awards, making Card the only author to have captured science fiction's two most coveted prizes in consecutive years. His most recent books include another entry in the Enderverse,* Ender in Exile, *the first of a new young adult series,* Pathfinder, *and* The Lost Gates, *the first volume of a new fantasy series.*

THE GREAT DOMES of the city of Gyree dazzled blue and red when the sun shone through a break in the clouds, and for a moment Cer Cemreet thought he saw some of the glory his uncles talked about in the late night tales of the old days of Greet. But the capital did not look dazzling up close, Cer remembered bitterly. Now dogs ran in the streets and rats lived in the wreckage of the palace, and the King of Greet lived in New Gyree in the hills far to the north, where the armies of the enemy could not go. Yet.

The sun went back behind a cloud and the city looked dark again. A Nefyr patrol was riding briskly on the Hetterwee Road far to the north. Cer turned his gaze to the lush grass on the hill where he sat. The clouds meant rain, but probably not here, he thought. He always thought of something else when he saw a Nefyr patrol. Yes, it was too early in Hrickan for rains to fall here. This rain would fall to the north, perhaps in the land of the King of the High Mountains, or on the vast plain of Westwold where they said horses ran free but were tame for any man to ride at need. But no rain would fall in Greet until Doonse, three weeks from now. By then the wheat would all be stored and the hay would be piled in vast ricks as tall as the hill Cer sat on.

In the old days, they said, all during Doonse the great wagons from Westwold would come and carry off the hay to last them through the snow season. But not now, Cer remembered. This year and last year and the year before the wagons had come from the south and east, two-wheeled wagons with drivers who spoke, not High Westil, but the barbarian Fyrd language. Fyrd or firt, thought Cer, and laughed, for firt was a word he could not say in front of his parents. They spoke firt.

Cer looked out over the plain again. The Nefyr patrol had turned from the highway and was on the road to the hills.

The road to the hills. Cer leaped to his feet and raced down the track leading home. A patrol heading for the hills could only mean trouble.

He stopped to rest only once, when the pain in his side was too bad to bear. But the patrol had horses, and he arrived home only to see the horses of the Nefyrre gathered at his father's gate.

Where are the uncles? Cer thought. The uncles must come.

But the uncles were not there, and Cer heard a terrible scream from inside the garden walls. He had never heard his mother scream before, but somehow he knew it was his mother, and he ran to the gate. A Nefyr soldier seized him and called out, "Here's the boy!" in a thick accent of High Westil, so that Cer's parents could understand. Cer's mother screamed again, and now Cer saw why.

His father had been stripped naked, his arms and legs held by two tall Nefyrre. The Nefyr captain held his viciously curved short-sword, point up, pressing against Cer's father's hard-muscled stomach. As Cer and his mother watched, the sword drew blood, and the captain pushed it in to the hilt, then pulled it up to the ribs. Blood gushed. The captain had been careful not to touch the heart, and now they thrust a spear into the huge wound, and lifted it high, Cer's father dangling from the end. They lashed the spear to the gatepost, and the blood and bowels stained the gates and the walls.

For five minutes more Cer's father lived, his chest heaving in the agony of breath. He may have died of pain, but Cer did not think so, for his father was not the kind to give in to pain. He may have died of suffocation, for one lung was gone and every breath was excruciating, but Cer did not think so, for his father kept breathing to the end. It was loss of blood, Cer decided, weeks later. It was when his body was dry, when the veins collapsed, that Cer's father died.

He never uttered a sound. Cer's father would never let the Nefyrre hear him so much as sigh in pain.

Cer's mother screamed and screamed until blood came from her mouth and she fainted.

Cer stood in silence until his father died. Then when the captain, a smirk on his face, walked near Cer and looked in his face, Cer kicked him in the groin.

They cut off Cer's great toes, but like his father, Cer made no sound.

Then the Nefyrre left and the uncles came.

Uncle Forwin vomited. Uncle Erwin wept. Uncle Crune put his arm around Cer's shoulder as the servants bound his maimed feet and said, "Your father was a great, brave man. He killed many Nefyrre, and burned many wagons. But the Nefyrre are strong."

Uncle Crune squeezed Cer's shoulder. "Your father was stronger. But he was one, and they were many."

Cer looked away.

"Will you not look at your uncle?" Uncle Crune asked.

"My father," Cer said, "did not think that he was alone."

Uncle Crune got up and walked away. Cer never saw the uncles again.

He and his mother had to leave the house and the fields, for a Nefyr farmer had been given the land to farm for the King of Nefyryd. With no money, they had to move south, across the River Greebeck into the drylands near the desert, where no rivers flowed and so only the hardiest plants lived. They lived the winter on the charity of the desperately poor. In the summer, when the heat came, so did the Poor Plague, which swept the drylands. The cure was fresh fruits, but fresh fruits came from Yffyrd and Suffyrd and only the rich could buy them, and the poor died by the thousands. Cer's mother was one of them.

They took her out on the sand to burn her body and free her spirit. As they painted her with tar (tar, at least, cost nothing, if a man had a bucket), five horsemen came to the brow of a dune to watch. At first Cer thought they were Nefyrre, but no. The poor people looked up and saluted the strangers, which Greetmen never do the enemy. These, then, were desert men, the Abadapnur nomads, who raided the rich farms of Greet during dry years, but who never harmed the poor.

We hated them, Cer thought, when we were rich. But now we are poor, and they are our friends.

His mother burned as the sun set.

Cer watched until the flames went out. The moon was high for the second time that night. Cer said a prayer to the moonlady over his mother's bones and ashes and then he turned and left.

He stopped at their hut and gathered the little food they had, and put on his father's tin ring, which the Nefyrre had thought was valueless, but which Cer knew was the sign of the Cemreet family's authority since forever ago.

Then Cer walked north.

He lived by killing rats in barns and cooking them. He lived by begging at poor farmers' doors, for the rich farmers had servants to turn away beggars. That, at least, Cer remembered, his father had never done. Beggars always had a meal at his father's house.

Cer also lived by stealing when he could hunt or beg no food. He stole handfuls of raw wheat. He stole carrots from gardens. He stole water from wells, for which he could have lost his life in the rainless season. He stole, one time, a fruit from a rich man's food wagon.

It burned his mouth, it was so cold and the acid so strong. It dribbled down his chin. As a poor man and a thief, Cer thought, I now eat a thing so dear that even my father, who was called wealthy, could never buy it.

And at last he saw the mountains in the north. He walked on, and in a week the mountains were great cliffs and steep slopes of shale. The Mitherkame, where the king of the High Mountains reigned, and Cer began to climb.

He climbed all day and slept in a cleft of a rock. He moved slowly, for climbing in sandals was clumsy, and without his great toes Cer could not climb barefoot. The next morning he climbed more. Though he nearly fell one time when falling would have meant crashing a mile down into the distant plain, at last he reached the knifelike top of the Mitherkame, and heaven.

For of a sudden the stone gave way to soil. Not the pale sandy soil of the drylands, nor the red soil of the Greet, but the dark black soil of the old songs from the north, the soil that could not be left alone for a day or it would sprout plants that in a week would be a forest.

And there *was* a forest, and the ground was thick with grass. Cer had seen only a few trees in his life, and they had been olive trees, short and gnarled, and fig sycamores, that were three times the height of a man. These were twenty times the height of a man and ten steps around, and the young trees shot up straight and tall so that not a sapling was as small as Cer, who for twelve years old was not considered small.

To Cer, who had known only wheat and hay and olive orchards, the forest was more magnificent than the mountain or the city or the river or the moon.

He slept under a huge tree. He was very cold that night. And in the morning he realized that in a forest he would find no farms, and where there were no farms there was no food for him. He got up and walked deeper into the forest. There were people in the High Mountains, else there would be no king, and Cer would find them. If he didn't, he would die. But at least he would not die in the realms of the Nefyrre.

He passed many bushes with edible berries, but he did not know they could be eaten so he did not eat. He passed many streams with slow stupid fish that he could have caught, but in Greet fish were never eaten, because it always carried disease, and so Cer caught no fish.

And on the third day, when he began to feel so weak from hunger that he could walk no longer, he met the treemage.

He met him because it was the coldest night yet, and at last Cer tore branches from a tree to make a fire. But the wood did not light, and when Cer looked up he saw that the trees had moved. They were coming closer, surrounding him tightly. He watched them, and they did not move as he watched, but when he turned around the ones he had not been watching were closer yet. He tried to run, but the low branches made a tight fence he could not get through. He couldn't climb, either, because the branches all stabbed downward. Bleeding from the twigs he had scraped, Cer went back to his camping place and watched as the trees at last made a solid wall around him.

And he waited. What else could he do in his wooden prison?

In the morning he heard a man singing, and he called for help.

"Oh ho," he heard a voice say in a strange accent. "Oh ho, a tree cutter and a firemaker, a branch killer and a forest hater."

"I'm none of those," Cer said. "It was cold, and I tried to build a fire only to keep warm."

"A fire, a fire," the voice said. "In this small part of the world there are no fires of wood. But that's a young voice I hear, and I doubt there's a beard beneath the words."

"I have no beard," Cer answered. "I have no weapon, except a knife too small to harm you."

"A knife? A knife that tears sap from living limbs, Redwood says. A knife that cuts twigs like soft manfingers, says Elm. A knife that stabs bark till it bleeds, says Sweet Aspen. Break your knife," said the voice outside the trees, "and I will open your prison."

"But it's my only knife," Cer protested, "and I need it."

"You need it here like you need fog on a dark night. Break it or you'll die before these trees move again."

Cer broke his knife.

Behind him he heard a sound, and he turned to see a fat old man standing in a clear space between the trees. A moment before there had been no clear space.

"A child," said the man.

"A fat old man," said Cer, angry at being considered as young as his years.

"An illbred child at that," said the man. "But perhaps he knows no better, for from the accent of his speech I would say he comes from Greetland, and from his clothing I would say he was poor, and it's well known in Mitherwee that there are no manners in Greet."

Cer snatched up the blade of his knife and ran at the man. Somehow there were many sharp-pointed branches in the way, and his hand ran into a hard limb, knocking the blade to the ground.

"Oh, my child," said the man kindly. "There is death in your heart."

The branches were gone, and the man reached out his hands and touched Cer's face. Cer jerked away.

"And the touch of a man brings pain to you." The man sighed. "How inside out your world must be."

Cer looked at the man coldly. He could endure taunting. But was that kindness in the old man's eyes?

"You look hungry," said the old man.

Cer said nothing.

"If you care to follow me, you may. I have food for you, if you like."

Cer followed him.

They went through the forest, and Cer noticed that the old man stopped to touch many of the trees. And a few he pointedly snubbed, turning his back or taking a wider route around them. Once he stopped and spoke to a tree that had lost a large limb—recently, too, Cer thought, because the tar on the stump was still soft. "Soon there'll be no pain at all," the old man said to the tree. Then the old man sighed again. "Ah, yes, I know. And many a walnut in the falling season."

Then they reached a house. If it could be called a house, Cer thought. Stones were the walls, which was common enough in Greet, but the roof was living wood—thick branches from nine tall trees, interwoven and heavily leaved, so that Cer was sure no drop of rain could ever come inside.

"You admire my roof?" the old man asked. "So tight that even in the winter, when the leaves are gone, the snow cannot come in. But *we* can," he said, and led the way through a door into a single room.

The old man kept up a constant chatter as he fixed breakfast: berries and cream, stewed acorns, and thick slices of cornbread. The old man named all the foods for Cer, because except for the cream it was all strange to him. But it was good, and it filled him.

"Acorn from the Oaks," said the old man. "Walnuts from the trees of that name. And berries from the bushes, and neartrees. Corn, of course, comes from an untree, a weak plant with no wood, which dies every year."

"The trees don't die every year, then, even though it snows?" Cer asked, for he had heard of snow.

"Their leaves turn bright colors, and then they fall, and perhaps that's a kind of death," said the man. "But in Eanan the snow melts and by Blowan there are leaves again on all the trees."

Cer did not believe him, but he didn't disbelieve him either. Trees were strange things.

"I never knew that trees in the High Mountains could move."

"Oh ho," laughed the old man. "And neither can they, except here, and other woods that a treemage tends."

"A treemage? Is there magic then?"

"Magic. Oh ho," the man laughed again. "Ah yes, magic, many magics, and mine is the magic of trees."

Cer squinted. The man did not look like a man of power, and yet the trees had penned an intruder in. "You rule the trees here?"

"Rule?" the old man asked, startled. "What a thought. Indeed no. I serve them. I protect them. I give them the power in me, and they give me the power in them, and it makes us all a good deal more powerful. But rule? That just doesn't enter into magic. What a thought."

Then the old man chattered about the doings of the silly squirrels this year, and when Cer was through eating the old man gave him a bucket and they spent the morning gathering berries. "Leave a berry on the bush for every one you pick," the old man said. "They're for the birds in the fall and for the soil in the Kamesun, when new bushes grow."

And so Cer, quite accidentally, began his life with the treemage, and it was as happy a time as Cer ever had in his life, except when he was a child and his mother sang to him and except for the time his father took him hunting deer in the hills of Wetfell.

And after the autumn when Cer marveled at the colors of the leaves, and after the winter when Cer tramped through the snow with the treemage to tend to ice-splintered branches, and after the spring when Cer thinned the new plants so the forest did not become overgrown, the treemage began to think that the dark places in Cer's heart were filled with light, or at least put away where they could not be found.

He was wrong.

For as he gathered leaves for the winter's fires Cer dreamed he was gathering the bones of his enemies. And as he tramped the snow he dreamed he was marching into battle to wreak death on the Nefyrre. And as he thinned the treestarts Cer dreamed of slaying each of the uncles as his father had been slain, because none of them had stood by him in his danger.

Cer dreamed of vengeance, and his heart grew darker even as the wood was filled with the bright light of the summer sun.

One day he said to the treemage, "I want to learn magic."

The treemage smiled with hope. "You're learning it," he said, "and I'll gladly teach you more."

"I want to learn things of power."

"Ah," said the treemage, disappointed. "Ah, then, you can have no magic."

"You have power," said Cer. "I want it also."

"Oh, indeed," said the treemage. "I have the power of two legs and two arms, the power to heat tar over a peat fire to stop the sap flow from broken limbs, the power to cut off diseased branches to save the tree, the power to teach the trees how and when to protect themselves. All the rest is the power of the trees, and none of it is mine."

"But they do your bidding," said Cer.

"Because I do theirs!" the treemage said, suddenly angry. "Do you think that there is slavery in this wood? Do you think I am a king? Only men allow men to rule them. Here in this wood there is only love, and on that love and by that love the trees and I have the magic of the wood."

Cer looked down, disappointed. The treemage misunderstood, and thought that Cer was contrite.

"Ah, my boy," said the treemage. "You haven't learned it, I see. The root of magic is love, the trunk is service. The treemages love the trees and serve them and then they share treemagic with the trees. Lightmages love the sun and make fires at night, and the fire serves them as they serve the fire. Horsemages love and serve horses, and they ride freely whither they will because of the magic in the herd. There is field magic and plain magic, and the magic of rocks and metals, songs and dances, the magic of winds and weathers. All built on love, all growing through service."

"I must have magic," said Cer.

"Must you?" asked the treemage. "Must you have magic? There are kinds of magic, then, that you might have. But I can't teach them to you."

"What are they?"

"No," said the treemage, and he wouldn't speak again.

Cer thought and thought. What magic could be demanded against anyone's will?

And at last, when he had badgered and nagged the treemage for weeks, the treemage angrily gave in. "Will you know then?" the treemage snapped. "I will tell you. There is seamagic, where the wicked sailors serve the monsters of the deep by feeding them living flesh. Would you do that?" But Cer only waited for more.

"So that appeals to you," said the treemage. "Then you will be delighted at desert magic."

And now Cer saw a magic he might use. "How is that performed?"

"*I* know not," said the treemage icily. "It is the blackest of the magics to men of *my* kind, though your dark heart might leap to it. There's only one magic darker."

"And what is that?" asked Cer.

"What a fool I was to take you in," said the treemage. "The wounds in your heart, you don't want them to heal; you love to pick at them and let them fester."

"What is the darkest magic?" demanded Cer.

"The darkest magic," said the treemage, "is one, thank the moon, that you can never practice. For to do it you have to love men and love the love of men more than your own life. And love is as far from you as the sea is from the mountains, as the earth is from the sky."

"The sky touches the earth," said Cer.

"Touches, but never do they meet," said the treemage.

Then the treemage handed Cer a basket, which he had just filled with bread and berries and a flagon of streamwater. "Now go."

"Go?" asked Cer.

"I hoped to cure you, but you won't have a cure. You clutch at your suffering too much to be healed."

Cer reached out his foot toward the treemage, the crusty scars still a deep red where his great toe had been.

"As well you might try to restore my foot."

"Restore?" asked the treemage. "I restore nothing. But I staunch, and heal, and I help the trees forget their lost limbs. For if they insist on rushing sap to the limb as if it were still there, they lose all their sap; they dry, they wither, they die."

Cer took the basket.

"Thank you for your kindness," said Cer. "I'm sorry that you don't understand. But just as the tree can never forgive the ax or the flame, there are those that must die before I can truly live again."

"Get out of my wood," said the treemage. "Such darkness has no place here."

And Cer left, and in three days came to the edge of the Mitherkame, and in two days reached the bottom of the cliffs, and in a few weeks reached the desert. For he would learn desertmagic. He would serve the sand, and the sand would serve him.

On the way the soldiers of Nefyryd stopped him and searched him. Now all the farms were farmed by Nefyrre, men of the south who had never owned land before. They drove him away, afraid that he might steal. So he snuck back in the night and from his father's storehouse stole meat and from his father's barn stole a chicken.

He crossed the Greebeck to the drylands and gave the meat and the chicken to the poor people there. He lived with them for a few days. And then he went out into the desert.

He wandered in the desert for a week before he ran out of food and water. He tried everything to find the desertmage. He spoke to the hot sand and the burning rocks as the treemage had spoken to the trees. But the sand was never injured and did not need a healing touch, and the rocks could not be harmed and so they needed no protection. There was no answer when Cer talked, except the wind which cast sand in his eyes. And at last Cer lay dying on the sand, his skin caked and chafed and burnt, his clothing long since tattered away into nothing, his flagon burning hot and filled with sand, his eyes blind from the whiteness of the desert.

He could neither love nor serve the desert, for the desert needed nothing from him and there was neither beauty nor kindness to love.

But he refused to die without having vengeance. Refused to die so long that he was still alive when the Abadapnu tribesmen found him. They gave him water and nursed him back to health. It took weeks, and they had to carry him on a sledge from waterhole to waterhole.

And as they traveled with their herds and their horses, the Abadapnur carried Cer farther and farther away from the Nefyrre and the land of Greet.

Cer regained his senses slowly, and learned the Abadapnu language even more slowly. But at last, as the clouds began to gather for the winter rains, Cer was one of the tribe, considered a man because he had a beard, considered wise because of the dark look on his face that remained even on those rare times when he laughed.

He never spoke of his past, though the Abadapnur knew well enough what the tin ring on his finger meant and why he had only eight toes. And they, with the perfect courtesy of the incurious, asked him nothing.

He learned their ways. He learned that starving on the desert was foolish, that dying of thirst was unnecessary. He learned how to trick the desert into yielding up life. "For," said the tribemaster, "the desert is never willing that anything should live."

Cer remembered that. The desert wanted nothing to live. And he wondered if that was a key to desertmagic. Or was it merely a locked door that he could never open? How can you serve and be served by the sand that wants only your death? How could he get vengeance if he was dead? "Though I would gladly die if my dying could kill my father's killers," he said to his horse one day. The horse hung her head, and would only walk for the rest of the day, though Cer kicked her to try to make her run.

Finally one day, impatient that he was doing nothing to achieve his revenge, Cer went to the tribemaster and asked him how one learned the magic of sand.

"Sandmagic? You're mad," said the tribemaster. For days the tribemaster refused to look at him, let alone answer his questions, and Cer realized that here on the desert the sandmagic was hated as badly as the treemage hated it. Why? Wouldn't such power make the Abadapnur great?

Or did the tribemaster refuse to speak because the Abadapnur did not know the sandmagic?

But they knew it.

And one day the tribemaster came to Cer and told him to mount and follow.

They rode in the early morning before the sun was high, then slept in a cave in a rocky hill during the heat of the day. In the dusk they rode again, and at night they came to the city.

"Ettuie," whispered the tribemaster, and then they rode their horses to the edge of the ruins.

The sand had buried the buildings up to half their height, inside and out, and even now the breezes of evening stirred the sand and built little dunes against the walls. The buildings were made of stone, rising not to domes like the great cities of the Greetmen but to spires, tall towers that seemed to pierce the sky.

"Ikikietar," whispered the tribemaster, "Ikikiaiai re dapii. O ikikiai etetur o abadapnur, ikikiai re dapii."

"What are the 'knives'?" asked Cer. "And how could the sand kill them?"

"The knives are these towers, but they are also the stars of power."

"What power?" asked Cer eagerly.

"No power for you. Only power for Etetur, for they were wise. They had the manmagic."

Manmagic. Was that the darkest magic spoken of by the treemage?

"Is there a magic more powerful than manmagic?" Cer asked.

"In the mountains, no," said the tribemaster. "On the well-watered plain, in the forest, on the sea, no."

"But in the desert?"

"A huu par eiti ununura," muttered the tribemaster, making the sign against death. "Only the desert power. Only the magic of the sand."

"I want to know," said Cer.

"Once," the tribemaster said, "once there was a mighty empire here. Once a great river flowed here, and rain fell, and the soil was rich and red like the soil of Greet, and a million people lived under the rule of the King of Ettue Dappa. But not all, for far to the west there lived a few who hated Ettue and the manmagic of the kings, and they forget the tools that undid this city.

"They made the wind blow from the desert. They made the rains run off the earth. By their power the river sank into the desert sand, and the fields bore no fruit, and at last the King of Ettue surrendered, and half his kingdom was given to the sandmages. To the dapinur. That western kingdom became Dapnu Dap."

"A kingdom?" said Cer, surprised. "But now the great desert bears that name."

"And once the great desert was no desert, but a land of grasses and grains like your homeland to the north. The sandmages weren't content with half a kingdom, and they used their sandmagic to make a desert of Ettue, and they covered the lands of rebels with sand, until at last the victory of the desert was complete, and Ettue fell to the armies of Greet and Nefyryd—they were allies then—and we of Dapnu Dap became no-mads, living off that tiny bit of life that even the harshest desert cannot help but yield."

"And what of the sandmages?" asked Cer.

"We killed them."

"All?"

"All," said the tribemaster. "And if any man will practice sandmagic, today, we will kill him. For what happened to us we will let happen to no other people."

Cer saw the knife in the tribemaster's hand.

"I will have your vow," said the tribemaster. "Swear before these stars and this sand and the ghosts of all who lived in this city that you will seek no sandmagic."

"I swear," said Cer, and the tribemaster put his knife away.

The next day Cer took his horse and a bow and arrows and all the food he could steal and in the heat of the day when everyone slept he went out into the desert. They followed him, but he slew two with arrows and the survivors lost his trail.

Word spread through the tribes of the Abadapnur that a would-be sandmage was loose in the desert, and all were ready to kill him if he came. But he did not come.

For he knew now how to serve the desert, and how to make the desert serve him. For the desert loved death, and hated grasses and trees and water and the things of life.

So in service of the sand Cer went to the edge of the land of the Nefyrre, east of the desert. There he fouled wells with the bodies of diseased animals. He burned fields when the wind was blowing off the desert, a dry wind that pushed the flames into the cities. He cut down trees. He killed sheep and cattle. And when the Nefyrre patrols chased him he fled onto the desert where they could not follow.

His destruction was annoying, and impoverished many a farmer, but alone it would have done little to hurt the Nefyrre. Except that Cer felt his power over the desert growing. For he was feeding the desert the only thing it hungered for: death and dryness.

He began to speak to the sand again, not kindly, but of land to the east that the sand could cover. And the wind followed his words, whipping the sand, moving the dunes. Where he stood the wind did not touch him, but all around him the dunes moved like waves of the sea.

Moving eastward.

Moving into the lands of the Nefyrre.

And now the hungry desert could do in a night a hundred times more than Cer could do alone with a torch or a knife. It ate olive groves in an hour. The sand borne on the wind filled houses in a night, buried cities in a week, and in only three months had driven the Nefyrre across the Greebeck and the Nefyr River, where they thought the terrible sandstorms could not follow.

But the storms followed. Cer taught the desert almost to fill the river, so that the water spread out a foot deep and miles wide, flooding some lands that had been dry, but also leaving more water surface for the sun to drink from; and before the river reached the sea it was dry, and the desert swept across into the heart of Nefyryd.

The Nefyrre had always fought with the force of arms, and cruelty was their companion in war. But against the desert they were helpless. They could not fight the sand. If Cer could have known it, he would have gloried in the fact that, untaught, he was the most powerful sandmage who had ever lived. For hate was a greater teacher than any of the books of dark lore, and Cer lived on hate.

And on hate alone, for now he ate and drank nothing, sustaining his body through the power of the wind and the heat of the sun. He was utterly dry, and the blood no longer coursed through his veins. He lived on the energy of the storms he unleashed. And the desert eagerly fed him, because he was feeding the desert.

He followed his storms, and walked through the deserted towns of the Nefyrre. He saw the refugees rushing north and east to the high ground. He saw the corpses of those caught in the storm. And he sang at night the old songs of Greet, the war songs. He wrote his father's name with chalk on the wall of every city he destroyed. He wrote his mother's name in the sand, and where he had written her name the wind did not blow and the sand did not shift, but preserved the writing as if it had been incised on rock.

Then one day, in a lull between his storms, Cer saw a man coming toward him from the east. Abadapnu, he wondered, or Nefyrre? Either way he drew his knife, and fit the nock of an arrow on his bowstring.

But the man came with his hands extended, and he called out, "Cer Cemreet."

It had never occurred to Cer that anyone knew his name.

"Sandmage Cer Cemreet," said the man when he was close. "We have found who you are."

Cer said nothing, but only watched the man's eyes.

"I have come to tell you that your vengeance is full. Nefyryd is at its knees. We have signed a treaty with Greet and we no longer raid into Hetterwee. Driplin has seized our westernmost lands."

Cer smiled. "I care nothing for your empire."

"Then for our people. The deaths of your father and mother have been avenged a hundred thousand times, for over two hundred thousand people have died at your hands."

Cer chuckled. "I care nothing for your people."

"Then for the soldiers who did the deed. Though they acted under orders, they have been arrested and killed, as have the men who gave them those orders, even our first general, all at the command of the King so that your vengeance will be complete. I have brought you their ears as proof of it," said the man, and he took a pouch from his waist.

"I care nothing for the soldiers, nor for proof of vengeance," said Cer.

"Then what do you care for?" asked the man quietly.

"Death," said Cer.

"Then I bring you that, too," said the man, and a knife was in his hand, and he plunged the knife into Cer's breast where his heart should have been. But when the man pulled the knife out no blood followed, and Cer only smiled.

"Indeed you brought it to me," said Cer, and he stabbed the man where his father had been stabbed, and drew the knife up as it had been drawn through his father's body, except that he touched the man's heart, and he died.

As Cer watched the blood soaking into the sand, he heard in his ears his mother's screams, which he had silenced for these years. He heard her screams and now, remembering his father and his mother and himself as a child he began to cry, and he held the body of the man he had killed and rocked back and forth on the sand as the blood clotted on his clothing and his skin. His tears mixed with the blood and poured into the sand and Cer realized that this was the first time since his father's death that he had shed any tears at all.

I am not dry, thought Cer. There is water under me still for the desert to drink.

He looked at his dry hands, covered with the man's blood, and tried to scrub off the clotted blood with sand. But the blood stayed, and the sand could not clean him.

He wept again. And then he stood and faced the desert to the west, and he said, "Come."

A breeze began.

"Come," he said to the desert, "come and dry my eyes."

And the wind came up, and the sand came, and Cer Cemreet was buried in the sand, and his eyes became dry, and the last life passed from his body, and the last sandmage passed from the world.

Then came the winter rains, and the refugees of Nefyryd returned to their land. The soldiers were called home, for the wars were over, and now their weapons were the shovel and the plow. They redug the trench of the Nefyr and the Greebeck, and the river soon flowed deep again to the sea. They scattered grass seed and cleaned their houses of sand. They carried water into the ruined fields with ditches and aqueducts.

Slowly life returned to Nefyryd.

And the desert, having lost its mage, retreated quietly to its old borders, never again to seek death where there was life. Plenty of death already where nothing lived, plenty of dryness to drink where there was no water.

In a wood a little way from the crest of the Mitherkame, a treemage heard the news from a wandering tinker.

The treemage went out into the forest and spoke softly to the Elm, to the Oak, to the Redwood, to the Sweet Aspen. And when all had heard the news, the forest wept for Cer Cemreet, and each tree gave a twig to be burned in his memory, and shed sap to sink into the ground in his name.

The Road to Levinshir

Patrick Rothfuss

Patrick Rothfuss was born in Madison, Wisconsin. In April 2007, The Name of the Wind *was published and met with surprising success. In the years since, it has been translated into thirty languages, won all manner of awards, and become a bestseller in several countries. The sequel,* The Wise Man's Fear *came out in March 2011, immediately hitting #1 on the* New York Times *bestseller list. When not working on the third book of the series, Pat plays with his baby, makes mead, and runs Worldbuilders, a geek-centered charity that has raised more than a million dollars for Heifer International.*

Chapter 1: Wine and Water

I WAS WALKING one of those long, lonely stretches of road you only find in the low hills of eastern Vintas. I was, as my father used to say, on the edge of the map.

I had passed one or two travelers all day and not a single inn. The thought of sleeping outdoors wasn't particularly troubling, but I had been eating from my pockets for a couple days, and a warm meal would have been a welcome thing.

Night had nearly fallen, and I had given up hope of something decent in my stomach when I spotted a line of white smoke trailing into the twilight sky ahead of me. I took it for a farmhouse at first. Then I heard a faint strain of music and my hopes for a bed and a hearth-hot meal began to rise.

But as I came around a curve in the road I found a surprise better than any roadside inn. Through the trees I saw a tall campfire flickering between two achingly familiar wagons. Men and women lounged about, talking. One strummed a lute, while another tapped a small tabor idly against his leg. Others were pitching a tent between two trees while an older woman set a tripod over the fire.

Troupers. What's better, I recognized familiar markings on the side of one of the wagons. To me they stood out more brightly than the fire. Those signs meant these were true troupers. My family, the Edema Ruh.

As I stepped from the trees, one of the men gave a shout, and before I could draw breath to speak there were three swords pointing at me. The sudden stillness after the music and chatter was more than slightly unnerving.

A handsome man with a black beard and a silver earring took a slow step forward, never taking the tip of his sword off my eye. "Otto!" he shouted into the woods behind me. "If you're napping I swear on my mother's milk I'll gut you. Who the hell are you?"

The last was directed at me. But before I could respond, a voice came out of the trees. "I'm right here, Alleg, as... Who's that? How in the God's name did he get past me?"

When they'd drawn their swords on me, I'd raised my hands. It's a good habit to have when anyone points something sharp at you. Nevertheless I was smiling as I spoke. "Sorry to startle you, Alleg...."

"Save it," he said coldly. "You have one breath left to tell me why you were sneaking around our camp."

I had no need to talk, and instead turned so everyone by the fire could see the lutecase slung across my back.

The change in Alleg's attitude was immediate. He relaxed and sheathed his sword. The others followed suit as he smiled and approached me, laughing.

I laughed too. "One family."

"One family." He shook my hand and turned toward the fire, shouting, "Best behavior everyone. We have a guest tonight!" There was a low cheer, and everyone went busily back to whatever they had been doing before I arrived.

A thick-bodied man wearing a sword stomped out of the trees. "I'll be damned if he came past me, Alleg. He's probably from—"

"He's from our family," Alleg interjected smoothly.

"Oh," Otto said, obviously taken aback. He looked at my lute. "Welcome then."

"I didn't go past, actually," I lied. When it was dark, my shaed made me very difficult to see. But that wasn't his fault, and I didn't want to get him in trouble. "I heard the music and circled around. I thought you might be a different troupe, and I was going to surprise them."

Otto gave Alleg a pointed look, then turned and stomped back into the woods.

Alleg put his arm around my shoulders. "Might I offer you a drink?"

"A little water, if you can spare it."

"No guest drinks water by our fire," he protested. "Only our best wine will touch your lips."

"The water of the Edema is sweeter than wine to those who have been upon the road." I smiled at him.

"Then have water and wine, each to your desire." He led me to one of the wagons, where there was a water barrel.

Following a tradition older than time, I drank a ladle of water and used a second to wash my hands and face. Patting my face dry with the sleeve of my shirt, I looked up at him and smiled. "It's good to be home again."

He clapped me on the back. "Come. Let me introduce you to the rest of your family."

First were two men of about twenty, with scruffy beards. "Fren and Josh are our two best singers, excepting myself of course." I shook their hands.

Next were the two men playing instruments around the fire. "Gaskin plays lute. Laren does pipes and tabor." They smiled at me. Laren struck the head of the tabor with his thumb, and the drum made a mellow *tum.*

"There's Tim." Alleg pointed across the fire to a tall, grim man oiling a sword. "And you've already met Otto. They keep us from falling into danger on the road." Tim nodded, looking up briefly from his sword.

"This is Anne." Alleg gestured to an older woman with a pinched expression and a grey bun of hair. "She keeps us fed and plays mother to us all." Anne continued to cut carrots, ignoring both of us.

"And far from last is our own sweet Kete, who holds the key to all our hearts." Kete had hard eyes and a mouth like a thin line, but her expression softened a little when I kissed her hand.

"And that's everyone," Alleg said with a smile and a little bow. "Your name is?"

"Kvothe."

"Welcome, Kvothe. Rest yourself and be at your ease. Is there anything we can do for you?"

"A bit of that wine you mentioned earlier?" I smiled.

He touched the heel of his hand to his forehead. "Of course! Or would you prefer ale?"

I nodded, and he fetched me a mug.

"Excellent," I said after tasting it, seating myself on a convenient stump.

He tipped an imaginary hat. "Thank you. We were lucky enough to nick it on our way through Levinshir a couple days ago. How has the road been treating you of late?"

I stretched backwards and sighed. "Not bad for a lone minstrel." I shrugged. "I take advantage of what opportunities present themselves. I have to be careful since I'm alone."

Alleg nodded wisely. "The only safety we have is in numbers," he admitted, then nodded to my lute. "Would you favor us with a bit of a song while we're waiting for Anne to finish dinner?"

"Certainly," I said, setting down my drink. "What would you like to hear?"

"Can you play, 'Leave the Town, Tinker'?"

"Can I? You tell me." I lifted my lute from its case and began to play. By the chorus, everyone had stopped what they were doing to listen. I even caught sight of Otto near the edge of the trees as he left his lookout to peer toward the fire.

When I was done, everyone applauded enthusiastically. "You can play it," Alleg laughed. Then his expression became serious, and he tapped a finger to his mouth. "How would you like to walk the road with us for a while?" he asked after a moment. "We could use another player."

I took a moment to consider it. "Which way are you heading?"

"Easterly," he said.

"I'm bound for Severen," I said.

Alleg shrugged. "We can make it to Severen," he said. "So long as you don't mind taking the long way around."

"I have been away from the family for a long time," I admitted, looking at the familiar sights around the fire.

"One is a bad number for an Edema on the road," Alleg said persuasively, running a finger along the edge of his dark beard.

I sighed. "Ask me again in the morning."

He slapped my knee, grinning. "Good! That means we have all night to convince you."

I replaced my lute and excused myself for a call of nature. Coming back, I knelt next to Anne where she sat near the fire. "What are you making for us, mother?" I asked.

"Stew," she said shortly.

I smiled. "What's in it?"

Anne squinted at me. "Lamb," she said, as if daring me to challenge the fact.

"It's been a long while since I've had lamb, mother. Could I have a taste?"

"You'll wait, same as everyone else," she said sharply.

"Not even a small taste?" I wheedled, giving her my best ingratiating smile.

The old woman drew a breath, then shrugged it away. "Fine," she said. "But it won't be my fault if your stomach sets to aching."

I laughed. "No, mother. It won't be your fault." I reached for the long-handled wooden spoon and drew it out. After blowing on it, I took a bite. "Mother!" I exclaimed. "This is the best thing to touch my lips in a full year."

"Hmmmph," she said, squinting at me.

"It's the first truth, mother," I said earnestly. "Anyone who does not enjoy this fine stew is hardly one of the Ruh in my opinion."

Anne turned back to stir the pot and shooed me away, but her expression wasn't as sharp as it had been before.

After stopping by the keg to refill my mug, I returned to my seat.

Gaskin leaned forward. "You've given us a song. Is there anything you'd like to hear?"

"How about 'Piper Wit'?" I asked.

His brow furrowed. "I don't recognize that one."

"It's about a clever Ruh who outwits a farmer."

Gaskin shook his head. "I'm afraid not."

I bent to pick up my lute. "Let me. It's a song every one of us should know."

"Pick something else," Laren protested. "I'll play you something on the pipes. You've played for us once already tonight."

I smiled at him. "I forgot you piped. You'll like this one." I assured him, "Piper's the hero. Besides, you're feeding my belly, I'll feed your ears." Before they could raise any more objections, I started to play, quick and light.

They laughed through the whole thing. From the beginning when Piper kills the farmer, to the end when he seduces the dead man's wife and daughter. I left off the last two verses where the townsfolk kill Piper.

Laren wiped his eyes after I was done. "Heh. You're right, Kvothe. I'm better off knowing that one. Besides..." He shot a look at Kete where she sat across the fire. "It's an honest song. Women can't keep their hands off a piper."

Kete snorted derisively and rolled her eyes.

We talked of small things until Anne announced the stew was done. Everyone fell to, breaking the silence only to compliment Anne on her cooking.

"Honestly, Anne," Alleg asked after his second bowl, "did you lift a little pepper back in Levinshir?"

Anne looked smug. "We all need our secrets, dear," she said. "Don't press a lady."

I asked Alleg, "Have times been good for you and yours?"

"Oh certainly," he said between mouthfuls. "Three days ago Levinshir was especially good to us." He winked. "You'll see how good later."

"I'm glad to hear it."

"In fact," he leaned forward conspiratorially, "we've done so well that

I feel quite generous. Generous enough to offer you anything you'd like. Anything at all. Ask and it is yours." He leaned closer and said in a stage whisper, "I want you to know this is a blatant attempt to bribe you into staying on with us. We would make a thick purse off that lovely voice of yours."

"Not to mention the songs he could teach us," Gaskin chimed in.

Alleg gave a mock snarl. "Don't help him bargain, boy. I have the feeling this is going to be hard enough as it is."

I gave it a little thought. "I suppose I could stay...." I let myself trail off uncertainly.

Alleg gave a knowing smile. "But..."

"But I would ask for three things."

"Hmmmm, three things." He looked me up and down. "Just like in one of the stories."

"It only seems right," I urged.

He gave a hesitant nod. "I suppose it does. And how long would you travel with us?"

"Until no one objects to my leaving."

"Does anyone have any problem with this?" Alleg looked around.

"What if he asks for one of the wagons?" Tim asked. His voice startled me, harsh and rasping like two bricks grating together.

"It won't matter, as he'll be traveling with us," Alleg argued. "They belong to all of us anyway. And since he can't leave unless we say so..."

There were no objections. Alleg and I shook hands and there was a small cheer.

Kete held up her mug. "To Kvothe and his songs!" she said. "I have a feeling he'll be worth whatever he costs us."

Everyone drank, and I held up my own glass. "I swear on my mother's milk, none of you will ever make a better deal than the one you made with me tonight." This evoked a more enthusiastic cheer and everyone drank again.

Wiping his mouth, Alleg looked me in the eye. "So, what is the first thing you want from us?"

I lowered my head. "It's a little thing really. I don't have a tent of my own. If I'm going to be traveling with my family..."

"Say no more!" Alleg waved his wooden mug like a king granting a boon. "You'll have my own tent, piled with furs and blankets a foot deep!" He made a gesture over the fire to where Fren and Josh sat. "Go set it up for him."

"That's all right," I protested. "I can manage it myself."

"Hush, it's good for them. Makes them feel useful. Speaking of which..." He made another gesture at Tim. "Bring them out, would you?"

Tim stood and pressed a hand to his stomach, "I'll do it in a quick minute. I'll be right back." He turned to walk off into the woods. "I don't feel very good."

"That's what you get for eatin' like you're at a trough!" Otto called after him. He turned back to the rest of us. "Someday he'll realize he can't eat more'n me and not feel sick afterward."

"Since Tim's busy painting a tree, I'll go get them," Laren said with thinly veiled eagerness.

"I'm on guard tonight," Otto said. "I'll do it."

"*I'll* get them," Kete said, exasperated. She stared the other two back into their seats and walked behind the wagon on my left.

Josh and Fren came out of the other wagon with a tent, ropes, and stakes. "Where do you want it?" Josh asked.

"That's not a question you usually have to ask a man, is it, Josh?" Fren joked, nudging his friend with an elbow.

"I tend to snore," I warned them. "You'll probably want me a little away from everyone else." I pointed. "Over between those two trees would be fine."

"I mean, with a man, you normally know where they want it, don't you, Josh?" Fren continued as they wandered off and began to string up the tent.

Kete returned a minute later, leading a pair of lovely young girls. One had a lean body and face, with straight, black hair cut short like a boy's. The other was more generously rounded, with curling golden hair. Both wore hopeless expressions and looked to be about sixteen.

"Meet Krin and Ellie," Kete said, gesturing to the girls.

Alleg smiled. "They are one of the ways in which Levinshir was generous to us. Tonight, one of them will be keeping you warm. My gift to you, as the new member in our family." He made a show of looking them over. "Which one would you like?"

I looked from one to the other. "That's a hard choice. Let me think on it a little while."

Kete sat them near the edge of the fire and put a bowl of stew in each of their hands. The girl with the golden hair, Ellie, ate woodenly for a few bites, then slowed to a stop like a toy winding down. Her eyes looked almost blind, as if she were watching something none of us could see. Krin's eyes, on the other hand, were focused fiercely into the fire. She sat stiffly with her bowl in her lap.

"Girls," Alleg chided. "Don't you know that things will get better as soon as you start cooperating?" Ellie took another slow bite, then stopped. Krin stared into the fire, her back stiff, her expression hard.

From where she sat by the fire, Anne prodded at them with her wooden spoon. "Eat!" The response was the same as before. One slow bite. One tense rebellion. Scowling, Anne leaned closer and gripped the dark-haired girl firmly by the chin, her other hand reaching for the bowl of stew.

"Don't," I urged. "They'll eat when they get hungry enough." Alleg looked up at me curiously. "I know what I'm talking about. Give them something to drink instead."

The old woman looked for a moment as if she might continue anyway, then shrugged and let go of Krin's jaw. "Fine. I'm sick of force-feeding this one anyway. She's been nothing but trouble."

Kete sniffed in agreement. "Little bitch came at me when I untied her for her bath," she said, brushing her hair away from the side of her face to reveal scratch marks. "Almost took out my damn eye."

"Did a runner, too," Anne said, still scowling. "I've had to start doping her at night." She made a disgusted gesture. "Let her starve if she wants."

Laren came back to the fire with two mugs, setting them in the girls' unresisting hands.

"Water?" I asked.

"Ale," she said. "It'll be better for them if they aren't eating."

I stifled my protest. Ellie drank in the same vacant manner in which she had eaten. Krin moved her eyes from the fire, to the cup, to me. I felt an almost physical shock at her resemblance to Denna. Still looking at me, she drank. Her hard eyes gave away nothing of what was happening inside her head.

"Bring them over to sit by me," I said. "It might help me to make up my mind."

Kete brought them over. Ellie was docile. Krin was stiff.

"Be careful with this one," Kete said, nodding to the dark-haired girl. "She's a scratcher."

Tim came back looking a little pale. He sat by the fire where Otto nudged him with an elbow. "Want some more stew?" he asked maliciously.

"Sod off," Tim rasped weakly.

"A little ale might settle your stomach," I advised.

He nodded, seeming eager for anything that might help him. Kete fetched him a fresh mugful.

By this time the girls were sitting on either side of me, facing the fire. Closer, I saw things I had missed before. There was a dark bruise on the back of Krin's neck. The blonde girl's wrists were merely chafed from being tied, but Krin's were raw and scabbed. For all that, they smelled clean. Their hair was brushed and their clothes had been washed recently. Kete had been tending to them.

They were also much more lovely up close. I reached out to touch their shoulders. Krin flinched, then stiffened. Ellie didn't react at all.

From off in the direction of the trees Fren called out. "It's done. Do you want us to light a lamp for you?"

"Yes, please," I called back. I looked from one girl to the other and then to Alleg. "I cannot decide between the two," I told him honestly. "So I will have both."

Alleg laughed incredulously. Then, seeing I was serious, he protested, "Oh come now. That's hardly fair to the rest of us. Besides, you can't possibly...."

I gave him a frank look.

"Well," he hedged, "Even if you can. It..."

"This is the second thing I ask for," I said formally. "Both of them."

Otto made a cry of protest that was echoed in the expressions of Gaskin and Laren.

I smiled reassuringly at them. "Only for tonight."

Fren and Josh came back from setting up my tent. "Be thankful he didn't ask for you, Otto," Fren said to the big man. "That's what Josh would have asked for, isn't it, Josh?"

"Shut your hole, Fren," Otto said in an exasperated tone, "Now *I* feel ill."

I stood and slung my lute over one shoulder. Then I led both lovely girls, one golden and one dark, toward my tent.

Chapter 2: Black by Moonlight

Fren and Josh had done a good job with the tent. It was tall enough to stand in the center, but still crowded with me and both girls standing. I gave the golden haired one, Ellie, a gentle push toward the bed of thick blankets. "Sit down," I said gently.

When she didn't respond, I took her by the shoulders and eased her into a sitting position. She let herself be moved, but her blue eyes were wide and vacant. I checked her head for any signs of a wound. Not finding any, I guessed she was in deep shock.

I took a moment and dug through my travel sack, then shook some powdered leaf into my traveling cup and added some water from my waterskin. I set the cup into Ellie's hands, and she took hold of it absently. "Drink it," I encouraged, trying to capture the tone of voice Felurian had used to gain my thoughtless compliance from time to time.

It may have worked, or perhaps she was just thirsty. Whatever the reason, Ellie drained the cup to the bottom. Her eyes still held the same faraway look they had before.

I shook another measure of the powdered leaf into the cup, refilled it with water, and held it out for the dark-haired girl to drink.

We stayed there for several minutes, my arm outstretched, her arms motionless at her sides. Finally she blinked, her eyes focusing on me. "What did you give her?" she asked.

"Crushed velia," I said gently. "It's a counter-toxin. There was poison in the stew."

Her eyes told me she didn't believe me. "I didn't eat any of the stew."

"It was in the ale too. I saw you drink that."

"Good," she said. "I want to die."

I gave a deep sigh. "It won't kill you. It'll just make you miserable. You'll throw up and be weak with muscle cramps for a day or two." I raised the cup, offering it to her.

"Why do you care if they kill me?" she asked tonelessly. "If they don't do it now they'll do it later. I'd rather die...." She clenched her teeth before she finished the sentence.

"They didn't poison you. I poisoned them and you happened to get some of it. I'm sorry, but this will help you over the worst of it."

Krin's gaze wavered for a second, then became iron hard again. She looked at the cup, then fixed her gaze on me. "If it's harmless, you drink it."

"I can't," I explained. "It would put me to sleep, and I have things to do tonight."

Krin's eyes darted to the bed of furs laid out on the floor of the tent.

I smiled my gentlest, saddest smile. "Not those sorts of things."

She still didn't move. We stood there for a long while. I heard a muted retching sound from off in the woods. I sighed and lowered the cup. Looking down, I saw Ellie had already curled up and gone to sleep. Her face looked almost peaceful.

I took a deep breath and looked back up at Krin. "You don't have any reason to trust me," I said, looking straight into her eyes. "Not after what has happened to you. But I hope you will." I held out the cup again.

She met my eyes without blinking, then reached for the cup. She drank it off in one swallow, choked a little, and sat down. Her eyes stayed hard as marble as she stared at the wall of the tent. I sat down, slightly apart from her.

In fifteen minutes she was asleep. I covered the two of them with a blanket and watched their faces. In sleep they were even more beautiful than before. I reached out to brush a strand of hair from Krin's cheek. To my surprise, she opened her eyes and stared at me. Not the marble stare she had given me before, she looked at me with the dark eyes of a young Denna.

I froze with my hand on her cheek. We watched each other for a second. Then her eyes drew closed again. I couldn't tell if it was the drug pulling her under, or her own will surrendering to sleep.

I settled myself at the entrance of the tent and lay Caesura across my knees. I felt rage like a fire inside me, and the sight of the two sleeping girls was like a wind fanning the coals. I set my teeth and forced myself to think of what had happened here, letting the fire burn fiercely, letting the heat of it fill me. I drew deep breaths, tempering myself for what was to come.

I waited for three hours, listening to the sounds of the camp. Muted conversation drifted toward me, shapes of sentences with no individual words. They faded, mixing with cursing and sounds of people being ill. I took long, slow breaths as Vashet had shown me, relaxing my body, slowly counting my exhalations.

Then, opening my eyes, I looked at the stars and judged the time to be right. I slowly unfolded myself from my sitting position and made a long, slow stretch. There was a solid crescent of moon hanging in the sky, and everything seemed very bright.

I approached the campfire slowly. It had fallen to sullen coals that did little to light the space between the two wagons. Otto was there, his huge body slumped against one of the wheels. I smelled vomit. "Is that you, Kvothe?" he asked blurrily.

"Yes." I continued my slow walk toward him.

"That bitch Anne didn't let the lamb cook through," he moaned. "I swear to holy God I've never been this sick before." He looked up at me. "Are you all right?"

Caesura leapt, caught the moonlight briefly on her blade, and tore his throat. He staggered to one knee, then toppled to his side, his hands staining black as they clutched his neck. I left him bleeding darkly in the moonlight, unable to cry out, dying but not dead.

I tossed a piece of brittle iron into the coals of the fire and headed toward the other tents.

Laren startled me as I came around the wagon. He made a surprised noise as he saw me walk around the corner with my naked sword. But the poison had made him sluggish, and he had barely managed to raise his hands before Caesura took him in the chest. He choked a scream as he fell backward, writhing on the ground.

None of them had been sleeping soundly due to the poison, so Laren's cry set them pouring from the wagons and tents, staggering and looking around wildly. Two indistinct shapes that I knew must be Josh and Fren leapt from the open back of the wagon closest to me. I struck one in the eye before he hit the ground and tore the belly from the other.

Everyone saw, and now there were screams in earnest. Most of them began to run drunkenly into the trees, some falling as they went. But the tall shape of Tim hurled itself at me. The heavy sword he had been sharpening all evening glinted silver in the moonlight.

But I was ready. I slid a second long, brittle piece of sword-iron into my hand and muttered a binding. Then, just as he came close enough to strike I snapped the iron sharply between my fingers. His sword shattered with the sound of a broken bell, and the pieces tumbled and disappeared in the dark grass.

Tim was more experienced than me, stronger, and with longer reach. Even poisoned and with half a sword he made a good showing of himself. It took me nearly half a minute before I snuck past his guard with Lover Out the Window and severed his hand at the wrist.

He fell to his knees, letting out a raspy howl and clutching at the stump. I struck him high in the chest and headed for the trees. The fight hadn't taken long, but every second was vital, as the others were already scattering into the woods.

I hurried in the direction I'd seen one of the dark shapes stagger. I was careless, so when Alleg threw himself on me from the shadow of a tree he caught me unaware. He didn't have a sword, only a small knife flashing in the moonlight as he dove for me. But a knife is enough to kill a man. He stabbed me in the stomach as we rolled to the ground. I struck the side of my head against a root and tasted blood.

I fought my way to my feet before he did and cut the hamstring on his leg. Then I stabbed him in the stomach and left him cursing on the ground as I went to hunt the others. I held one hand tight across my stomach. I knew the pain would hit me soon, and after that I might not have long to live.

It was a long night, and I will not trouble you with any further details. I found all the rest of them as they made their way through the forest. Anne had broken her leg in her reckless flight, and Tim made it nearly half a mile despite the loss of his hand and the wound in his chest. They shouted and cursed and begged for mercy as I stalked them through the forest, but nothing they said could appease me.

It was a terrible night, but I found them all. There was no honor to it, no glory. But there was justice of a sort, and blood, and in the end I brought their bodies back.

I came back to my tent as the sky was beginning to color to a familiar blue. A sharp, hot line of pain burned a few inches below my navel, and I could tell from the unpleasant tugging when I moved that dried blood had matted my shirt to the wound. I ignored the feeling as best I could, knowing I could do nothing for myself with my hands shaking and no decent light to see by. I'd have to wait for dawn to see how badly I was hurt.

I tried not to dwell on what I knew from my work in the Medica. Any deep wound to the gut promises a long, painful trip to the grave. A skilled physicker with the right equipment could make a difference, but

I couldn't be farther from civilization. I might as well wish for a piece of the moon.

I wiped my sword, sat in the wet grass in front of the tent, and began to think.

Chapter 3: The Broken Circle

I had been busy for more than an hour when the sun finally peered over the tops of the trees and began to burn the dew from the grass. I had found a flat rock and was using it as a makeshift anvil to hammer a spare horseshoe into a different shape. Above the fire a pot of oats was boiling.

I was just putting the finishing touches on the horseshoe when I saw a flicker of movement from the corner of my eye. It was Krin peeking around the corner of the wagon. I guessed I'd woken her with the sound of hammering iron.

"Oh my God." Her hand went to her mouth and she took a couple stunned steps out from behind the wagon. "You killed them."

"Yes," I said simply, my voice sounding dead in my ears.

Krin's eyes ran up and down my body, staring at my torn and bloody shirt. "Are..." Her voice caught in her throat, and she swallowed. "Are you alright?"

I nodded silently. When I'd finally worked up the courage to examine my wound, I'd discovered that Felurian's cloak had saved my life. Instead of spilling open my guts, Alleg's knife had merely given me a long, shallow cut across my belly. He had also ruined a perfectly good shirt, but I had a hard time feeling bad about that, all things considered.

I examined the horseshoe, then used a damp leather strap to tie it firmly to one end of a long, straight branch. I pulled the kettle of oats off the fire and thrust the horseshoe into the coals.

Seeming to recover from some of her shock, Krin slowly approached, eyeing the row of bodies on the other side of the fire. I had done nothing other than lay them out in a rough line. It wasn't tidy. Blood stained the bodies, and their wounds gaped openly. Krin stared as if she were afraid they might start to move again.

"What are you doing?" she asked finally.

In answer, I pulled the now-hot horseshoe from the coals of the fire and approached the nearest body. It was Tim. I pressed the hot iron against the back of his remaining hand. The skin smoked and hissed and stuck to the metal. After a moment I pulled it away, leaving a black burn against his white skin. A broken circle. I moved back to the fire and began to heat the iron again.

Krin stood mutely, too stunned to react normally. Not that there could be a normal way to react in a situation like this, I suppose. But she didn't scream or run off as I thought she might. She simply looked at the broken circle and repeated, "What are you doing?"

When I finally spoke, my voice sounded strange to my own ears. "All of the Edema Ruh are one family," I explained. "Like a closed circle. It doesn't matter if some of us are strangers to others, we are still family, still close. We have to be this way, because we are always strangers wherever we go. We are scattered, and people hate us.

"We have laws. Rules we follow. When one of us does a thing that cannot be forgiven or mended, if he jeopardizes the safety or the honor of the Edema Ruh, he is killed and branded with the broken circle to show he is no longer one of us. It is rarely done. There is rarely a need."

I pulled the iron from the fire and walked to the next body. Otto. I pressed it to the back of his hand and listened to it hiss. "These were *not* Edema Ruh. But they made themselves out to be. They did things no Edema would do, so I am making sure the world knows they were not part of our family. The Ruh do not do the sort of things that these men did."

"But the wagons," she protested. "The instruments."

"They were not Edema Ruh," I said firmly. "They probably weren't even real troupers, just a group of thieves who killed a band of Ruh and tried to take their place."

Krin stared at the bodies, then back at me. "So you killed them for pretending to be Edema Ruh?"

"For pretending to be Ruh? No." I put the iron back in the fire. "For killing a Ruh troupe and stealing their wagons? Yes. For what they did to you? Yes."

"But if they aren't Ruh..." Krin looked at the brightly painted wagons. "How?"

"I am curious about that myself," I said. Pulling the broken circle from the fire again, I moved to Alleg and pressed it onto his palm.

The false trouper jerked and screamed himself awake.

"He isn't dead!" Krin exclaimed shrilly

I had examined the wound earlier. "He's dead," I said coldly. "He just hasn't stopped moving yet." I turned to look him in the eye. "How about it, Alleg? How did you come by a pair of Edema wagons?"

"Ruh bastard," he cursed at me with blurry defiance.

"Yes," I said, "I am. And you are not. So how did you learn my family's signs and customs?"

"How did you know?" he asked. "We knew the words, the handshake. We knew water and wine and songs before supper. How did you know?"

"You thought you could fool me?" I said, feeling my anger coiling inside me again like a spring. "This is my family! How could I not know? Ruh don't do what you did. Ruh don't steal, don't kidnap girls."

Alleg shook his head with a mocking smile. There was blood on his teeth. "Everyone knows what you people do...."

My temper exploded. "Everyone thinks they know! They think rumor is the truth! Ruh don't do this!" I gestured wildly around me. "People only think those things because of people like you!" My anger flared even hotter and I found myself screaming. "Now tell me what I want to know or God will weep when he hears what I've done to you!"

Alleg paled and had to swallow before he found his voice. "There was an old man and his wife and a couple other players. I traveled guard with them for half a year. Eventually they took me in." He ran out of breath and gasped a bit as he tried to get it back.

He'd said enough. "So you killed them."

Alleg shook his head vigorously. "No....were attacked on the road." He gestured weakly to the other bodies. "They surprised us. The other players were killed, but I was just...knocked out."

I looked over the line of bodies and felt the rage flare up, even though I'd already known. There was no other way these people could have come by a pair of Edema wagons with their markings intact.

Alleg was talking again. "I showed them afterward... How to act like a troupe." He swallowed against the pain. "...good life."

I turned away, disgusted. He was one of us, in a way. One of our adopted family. It made everything ten times worse knowing that. I pushed the horseshoe into the coals of the fire again, then looked to the girl as it heated. Her eyes had gone to flint as she watched Alleg.

Not sure if it was the right thing to do, I offered her the brand. Her face went hard and she took it.

Alleg didn't seem to understand what was about to happen until she had the hot iron against his chest. He shrieked and twisted but lacked the strength to get away as she pressed it hard against him. She grimaced as he struggled weakly against the iron, her eyes brimming with angry tears.

After a long minute she pulled the iron away and stood, crying quietly. I let her be.

Alleg looked up at her and somehow managed to find his voice. "Ah girl, we had some good times, didn't we?" She stopped crying and looked at him. "Don't—"

I kicked him sharply in the side before he could say anything else. He stiffened in mute pain and then spat blood at me. I landed another kick, and he went limp.

Not knowing what else to do, I took back the brand and began heating it again.

There was a long silence. "Is Ellie still asleep?" I asked.

Krin nodded.

"Do you think it would help for her to see this?"

She thought about it, wiping at her face with a hand. "I don't think so," she said finally. "I don't think she *could* see it right now. She's not right in her head."

"The two of you are from Levinshir?" I asked, to keep the silence at arm's length.

"My family farms just north of Levinshir," Krin said. "Ellie's father is mayor."

"When did these come into your town?" I asked as I set the brand to the back of another hand. The sweet smell of charred flesh was becoming thick in the air.

"What day is it?"

I counted in my head. "Felling."

"They came into town on Theden," she paused. "Five days ago?" Her voice was tinged with disbelief. "We were glad to have the chance to see a play and hear the news. Hear some music." She looked down. "They were camped on the east edge of town. When I came to get my fortune read they told me to come back that night. They seemed so friendly, so exciting."

Krin looked at the wagons. "When I showed up, they were all sitting around the fire. They sang me songs. The old woman gave me some tea. I didn't even think...I mean...she looked like my gran." Her eyes strayed to the body of the old woman, then away. "Then I don't remember what happened. I woke up in the dark, in one of the wagons. I was tied up and I..." Her voice broke a little, and she rubbed absentmindedly at her wrists. She glanced back at the tent. "I guess Ellie got an invitation too."

I finished branding the backs of their hands. I had been planning to do their faces too, but the iron was slow to heat in the fire, and I was quickly growing sick of the work. I hadn't slept at all, and the anger that had burned so hot for so long was in its final flicker, leaving me feeling cold and numb.

I made a gesture to the pot of oats I'd pulled off the fire. "Are you hungry?"

"Yes," she said, then darted a look toward the bodies. "No."

"Me neither. Go wake up Ellie and we can get you home."

Krin hurried off to the tent. After she disappeared inside, I turned to the line of bodies. "Does anyone object to my leaving the troupe?" I asked.

None of them did. So I left.

Chapter 4: Dreams

It was an hour's work to drive the wagons into a thick piece of forest and hide them. I destroyed their Edema markings and unhitched the horses. There was only one saddle, so I loaded the other two horses with food and whatever other portable valuables I could find.

When I returned with the horses, Krin and Ellie were waiting for me. More precisely, Krin was waiting. Ellie was merely standing nearby, her expression vacant, her eyes empty.

"Do you know how to ride?" I asked Krin.

She nodded and I handed her the reins to the saddled horse. She got one foot in the stirrup and stopped, shaking her head. She brought her foot back down slowly. "I'll walk."

"Do you think Ellie would stay on a horse?"

Krin looked over to where the blonde girl was standing. One of the horses nuzzled her curiously and got no response. "Probably. But I don't think it would be good for her. After..."

I nodded in understanding. "We'll all walk then."

"What is the heart of the Lethani?" I asked Vashet.

"Success and right action."

"Which is the more important, success or rightness?"

"They are the same. If you act rightly success follows."

"But others may succeed by doing wrong things," I pointed out.

"Wrong things never lead to success," Vashet said firmly. "If a man acts wrongly and succeeds, that is not the way. Without the Lethani there is no true success."

Sir? A voice called. "Sir?"

My eyes focused on Krin. Her hair was windblown, her young face tired. She looked at me timidly. "Sir? It's getting dark."

I looked around and saw twilight creeping in from the east. I was bone weary and had fallen into a walking doze after we had stopped for lunch at midday.

"Just call me Kvothe, Krin. Thanks for jogging my elbow. My mind was somewhere else."

Krin gathered wood and started a fire. I unsaddled the horses, then fed and rubbed them down. I took a few minutes to set up the tent, too. Normally I don't bother with such things, but there had been room for it on the horses, and I guessed the girls weren't used to sleeping out of doors.

After I finished with the tent, I realized I'd only brought one extra blanket from the troupe's supplies. There would be a chill tonight too, if I was any judge of such things.

"Dinner's ready," I heard Krin call. I tossed my blanket and the spare one into the tent and headed back to where she was finishing up. She'd done a good job with what was available. Potato soup with bacon and toasted bread. There was a green summer squash nestled into the coals as well.

Ellie worried me. She had been the same all day, walking listlessly, never speaking or responding to anything Krin or I said to her. Her eyes would follow things, but there was no thought behind them. Krin and I had discovered the hard way that if left to herself she would stop walking, or wander off the road if something caught her eye.

Krin handed me a bowl and spoon as I sat down. "It smells good." I complimented her.

She half-smiled and dished a second bowl for herself. She started to fill a third bowl, then hesitated, realizing Ellie couldn't feed herself.

"Would you like some soup, Ellie?" I asked in normal tones. "It smells good."

She sat blankly by the fire, staring into nothing.

"Do you want to share mine?" I asked as if it were the most natural thing in the world. I moved closer to her and blew on a spoonful to cool it. "Here you go."

Ellie ate it mechanically, turning her head slightly in my direction, toward the spoon. Her eyes reflected the dancing patterns of the fire. They were like the windows of an empty house.

I blew on another spoonful and held it out to the blonde girl. She opened her mouth only when the spoon touched her lips. I moved my head, trying to see past the dancing firelight in her eyes, desperately hoping to see something behind them. Anything.

"I bet you're an Ell, aren't you?" I said conversationally. I looked at Krin. "Short for Ellie?"

Krin shrugged helplessly. "We weren't friends, really. She's just Ellie Anwater. The mayor's daughter."

"It sure was a long walk today," I continued speaking in the same easy tone. "How do your feet feel, Krin?"

Krin continued to watch me with her serious dark eyes. "A little sore."

"Mine too. I can't wait to get my shoes off. Are your feet sore, Ell?"

No response. I fed her another bite.

"It was pretty hot too. It should cool off tonight, though. Good sleeping weather. Won't that be nice, Ell?"

No response. Krin continued to watch me from the other side of the fire. I took a bite of soup for myself. "This is truly fine, Krin." I said earnestly, then turned back to the vacant girl. "It's a good thing we have Krin to cook for us, Ell. Everything I cook tastes like horseshit."

On her side of the fire, Krin tried to laugh with a mouthful of soup with predictable results. I thought I saw a flicker in Ell's eyes. "If I had some horse apples I could make us a horse apple pie for dessert," I offered. "I could make some tonight if you want..." I trailed off, making it a question.

Ell gave the slightest frown, a small wrinkle creased her forehead.

"You're probably right," I said. "It wouldn't be very good. Would you like more soup instead?"

The barest nod. I gave her a spoonful.

"It's a little salty, though. You probably want some water."

Another nod. I handed her the waterskin and she lifted it to her own lips. She drank for a long, long minute. She was probably parched from our long walk today. I would have to watch her more closely tomorrow to make sure she drank enough.

"Would you like a drink, Krin?"

"Yes please," Krin said, her eyes fixed on Ell's face.

Moving automatically, Ell held the waterskin out toward Krin, holding it directly over the fire with the shoulder strap dragging in the coals. Krin grabbed it quickly, then added a belated, "Thank you, Ell."

I kept the slow stream of conversation going through the whole meal. Ell fed herself toward the end of it, and though her eyes were clearer, it was as if she were looking at the world through a sheet of frosted glass, seeing but not seeing. Still, it was an improvement.

After she ate two bowls of soup and half a loaf of bread, her eyes began to bob closed. "Would you like to go to sleep, Ell?" I asked.

A more definite nod.

"Should I carry you to the tent?"

Her eyes snapped open at this and she shook her head firmly.

"Maybe Krin would help you get ready for bed if you asked her."

Ell turned to look in Krin's direction. Her mouth moved in a vague way. Krin darted a glance at me and I nodded.

"Let's go and get tucked in then," Krin said, sounding every bit the older sister. She came over and took Ell's hand, helping her to her feet. As they went into the tent, I finished off the soup and ate a piece of bread that had been too badly burnt for either of the girls.

Before too long Krin came back to the fire. "Is she sleeping?" I asked.

"Before she hit the pillow. Do you think she will be all right?"

She was in deep shock. Her mind had stepped through the doors of madness to protect itself from what was happening. "It's probably just a matter of time," I said tiredly, hoping it was the truth. "The young heal quickly." I chuckled humorlessly as I realized she was probably only about a year younger than me. I felt every year twice tonight, some of them three times.

Despite the fact that I felt covered in lead, I forced myself to my feet and helped Krin clean the dishes. I sensed her growing unease as we finished cleaning up and re-picketing the horses to a fresh piece of grazing. The tension grew worse as we approached the tent. I stopped and held the flap open for her. "I'll sleep out here tonight."

Her relief was tangible. "Are you sure?"

I nodded. She slipped inside, and I let the flap fall closed behind her. Her head poked back out almost immediately, followed by a hand holding a blanket.

I shook my head. "You'll need them both. There'll be a chill tonight." I pulled my shaed around me and lay directly in front of the tent. I didn't want Ell wandering out during the night and getting lost or hurt.

"Won't you be cold?"

"I'll be fine," I said. I was tired enough to sleep on a running horse. I was tired enough to sleep *under* a running horse.

Krin ducked her head back into the tent. Soon I heard her nestling into the blankets. Then everything was quiet.

I remembered the startled look on Otto's face as I cut his throat. I heard Alleg struggle weakly and curse me as I dragged him back to the wagons. I remembered the blood. The way it had felt against my hands. The thickness of it.

I had never killed anyone like that before. Not coldly, not close up. I remembered how warm their blood had been. I remembered the way Kete had cried as I stalked her through the woods. "It was them or me!" she had screamed hysterically. "I didn't have a choice. It was them or me!"

I lay awake a long while. When I finally slept, the dreams were worse.

Chapter 5: The Road to Levinshir

We made poor time the next day, as Krin and I were forced to lead the three horses and Ell besides. Luckily, the horses were well-behaved, as Edema-trained horses tend to be. If they had been as wayward-witted as the poor mayor's daughter, we might never have made it to Levinshir at all.

Even so, the horses were almost more trouble than they were worth. The glossy roan in particular liked to wander off into the underbrush, foraging. Three times now I'd had to drag him out, and we were irritated with each other. I'd named him Burrback for obvious reasons.

The fourth time I had to pull him back onto the road, I seriously considered cutting him loose to save myself the trouble. I didn't, of course. A good horse is the same as money in your pocket. And it would be quicker to ride back to Severen than walk the whole way.

Krin and I did our best to keep Ell engaged in conversation as we walked. It seemed to help a bit. And by the time our noon meal came around she seemed almost aware of what was going on around her. Almost.

I had an idea as we were getting ready to set out again after lunch. I led our dappled grey mare over to where Ell stood. Her golden hair was one great tangle and she was trying to run one of her hands through it while her eyes wandered around in a distracted way, as if she didn't quite understand where she was.

"Ell." She turned to look. "Have you met Greytail?" I gestured to the mare.

A faint, confused shake of the head.

"I need your help leading her. Have you led a horse before?"

A nod.

"She needs someone to take care of her. Can you do it?" Greytail looked at me with one large eye, as if to let me know she needed leading as much as I needed wheels to walk. But then she lowered her head a bit and nuzzled Ell in a motherly way. The girl reached out a hand to pet her nose almost automatically, then took the reins from me.

"Do you think that's a good idea?" Krin asked when I came back to pack the other horses.

"Greytail is gentle as a lamb."

"Just because Ell is witless as a sheep," Krin said archly, "doesn't make them a good pairing."

I cracked a smile at that. "We'll watch them close for an hour or so. If it doesn't work, it doesn't. But sometimes the best help a person can find is helping someone else."

Since I had slept poorly I was twice weary today. My stomach was sour, and I felt gritty, like someone had sanded the first two layers of my skin away. I was almost tempted to doze in the saddle, but I couldn't bring myself to ride while the girls walked.

So I plodded along, leading my horse and nodding on my feet. But today I couldn't fall into the comfortable half-sleep I tend to use when walking. I was plagued with thoughts of Alleg, wondering if he were still alive.

I knew from my time in the Medica that the gut wound I'd given him was fatal. I also knew it was a slow death. Slow and painful. With proper care it might be a full span of days before he died. Even alone in the middle of nowhere he could live for days with such a wound.

Not pleasant days. He would grow delirious with fever as the infection set in. Every movement would tear the wound open again. He couldn't walk on his hamstrung leg, either. So if he wanted to move he'd have to crawl. He would be cramped with hunger and burning with thirst by now.

But not dead from thirst. No. I had left a full waterskin nearby. I had laid it at his side before we had left. Not out of kindness. Not to make his last hours more bearable. I had left it because I knew that with water he would live longer, suffer more.

Leaving him that waterskin was the most terrible thing I'd ever done, and now that my anger had cooled to ashes I regretted it. I wondered how much longer he would live because of it. A day? Two? Certainly no more than two. I tried not to think of what those two days would be like.

But even when I forced thoughts of Alleg from my mind, I had other demons to fight. I remembered bits and pieces of that night, the things the false troupers had said as I cut them down. The sounds my sword had made as it dug into them. The smell of their skin as I had branded them. I had killed two women. What would Vashet think of my actions? What would anyone think?

Exhausted from worry and lack of sleep, my thoughts spun in these circles for the remainder of the day. I set up camp from force of habit and kept up a conversation with Ell through an effort of sheer will. The time for sleep came before I was ready, and I found myself rolled in my shaed, lying in the front of the girls' tent. I was dimly aware that Krin had started giving me the same worried look she'd been giving Ell for the past two days.

I lay wide-eyed for an hour before falling asleep, wondering about Alleg.

When I slept I dreamt of killing them. In my dream I stalked the forest like grim death, unwavering.

But it was different this time. I killed Otto, his blood spattering my hands like hot grease. Then I killed Laren, and Josh, and Tim. They moaned and screamed, twisting on the ground. Their wounds were horrible, but I could not look away.

Then the faces changed. I was killing Taren, the bearded ex-mercenary in my troupe. Then I killed Trip. Then I was chasing Shandi through the forest, my sword naked in my hand. She was crying out, weeping in fear. When I finally caught her she clutched at me, knocking me to the ground, burying her face in my chest, sobbing. "No no no," she begged. "No no no."

I came awake. I lay on my back, terrified and not knowing where my dream ended and the world began. After a brief moment I realized the truth. Ell had crawled from the tent and lay curled against me. Her face pressed against my chest, her hand grasping desperately at my arm.

"No no," she choked out, "no no no no no." Her body shook with helpless sobs when she couldn't say it any more. My shirt was wet with hot tears. My arm was bleeding where she clutched it.

I made consoling noises and brushed at her hair with my hand. After a long while she quieted and eventually fell into an exhausted sleep, still clinging tightly to my chest.

I lay very still, not wanting to wake her by moving. My teeth were clenched. I thought of Alleg and Otto and all the rest. I remembered the blood and screaming and the smell of burning skin. I remembered it all and dreamed of worse things I could have done to them.

I never had the nightmares again. Sometimes I think of Alleg and I smile.

We made it to Levinshir the next day. Ell had come to her senses, but remained quiet and withdrawn. Still, things went more quickly now, especially as the girls decided they had recovered enough to take turns riding Greytail.

We covered six miles before we stopped at midday, with the girls becoming increasingly excited as they began to recognize parts of the countryside. The shape of hills in the distance. A crooked tree by the road.

But as we grew closer to Levinshir they grew quiet.

"It's just over the rise there," Krin said, getting down off the roan. "You ride from here, Ell."

Ell looked from her, to me, to her feet. She shook her head.

I watched them. "Are the two of you okay?"

"My father's going to kill me." Krin's voice was barely a whisper, her face full of serious fear.

"Your father will be one of the happiest men in the world tonight," I said, then thought it best to be honest. "He might be angry too. But that's only because he's been scared out of his mind for the last eight days."

Krin seemed slightly reassured, but Ell burst out crying. Krin put her arms around her, making gentle sounds.

"No one will marry me," Ell sobbed. "I was going to marry Jason Waterson and help him run his store. He won't marry me now. No one will."

I looked up to Krin and saw the same fear reflected in her wet eyes. But Krin's eyes were angry while Ell's held nothing but despair.

"Any man who thinks that way is a fool," I said, weighting my voice with all the conviction I could bring to bear. "And the two of you are too clever and too beautiful to be marrying fools."

It seemed to calm Ell somewhat, her eyes turning up at me as if looking for something to believe.

"It's the truth," I said. "And none of this was your fault. Make sure you remember that for these next couple days."

"I hate them!" Ell spat, surprising me with her sudden rage. "I hate men!" Her knuckles were white as she gripped Greytail's reins. Her face twisted into a mask of anger. Krin put her arms around Ell, but when she looked at me I saw the sentiment reflected quietly in her dark eyes.

"You have every right to hate them," I said, feeling more anger and helplessness than ever before in my life. "But I'm a man too. Not all of us are like that."

We stayed there for a while, not more than a half-mile from town. We had a drink of water and a small bite to settle our nerves. And then I took them home.

Chapter 6: Homecoming

Levinshir wasn't a big town. Two hundred people lived there, maybe three if you counted the outlying farms. It was mealtime when we rode in, and the dirt road that split the town in half was empty and quiet. Ell told me her house was on the far side of town. I hoped to get the girls there without being seen. They were worn down and distraught. The last thing they needed was to face a mob of gossipy neighbors.

But it wasn't meant to be. We were halfway through the town when I saw a flicker of movement in a window. A woman's voice cried out, *"Ell!"* and in ten seconds people began to spill from every doorway in sight.

The women were the quickest, and inside a minute a dozen of them had formed a protective knot around the two girls, talking and crying and hugging each other. The girls didn't seem to mind. Perhaps it was better this way. A warm welcome might do a lot to heal them.

The men held back, knowing they were useless in situations like this. Most watched from doorways or porches. Six or eight came down onto the street, moving slowly and eyeing up the situation. These were cautious men, farmers and friends of farmers. They knew the names of everyone within ten miles of their homes. There were no strangers in a town like Levinshir, except for me.

None of the men were close relatives to the girls. Even if they were, they knew they wouldn't get near them for at least an hour, maybe as much as a day. So they let their wives and sisters take care of things. With nothing else to occupy them, their attention wandered briefly past the horses and settled onto me.

I motioned over a boy of ten or so. "Go tell the mayor his daughter's back. Run!" He tore off in a cloud of road dust, his bare feet flying.

The men moved slowly closer to me, their natural suspicion of strangers made ten times worse by recent events. A boy of twelve or so wasn't as cautious as the rest and came right up to me, eyeing my sword, my cloak.

"What's your name?" I asked him.

"Pete."

"Can you ride a horse, Pete?"

He looked insulted. "S'nuf."

"Do you know where the Walker farm is?"

He nodded. "'Bout north two miles by the millway."

I stepped sideways and handed him the reins to the roan. "Go tell them their daughter's home. Then let them use the horse to come back to town."

He had a leg over the horse before I could offer him a hand up. I kept a hand on the reins long enough to shorten the stirrups so he wouldn't kill himself on the way there.

"If you make it there and back without breaking your head or my horse's leg, I'll give you a penny," I said.

"You'll give me two," he said.

I laughed. He wheeled the horse around and was gone.

The men had wandered closer in the meantime, gathering around me in a loose circle.

A tall, balding fellow with a scowl and a grizzled beard seemed to appoint himself leader. "So who're you?" he asked, his tone speaking more clearly than his words, *Who the hell are you?*

"Kvothe," I answered pleasantly. "And yourself?"

"Don't know as that's any of your business," he growled. "What are you doing here?" *What the hell are you doing here with our two girls?*

"God's mother, Seth," an older man said to him. "You don't have the sense God gave a dog. That's no way to talk to the..."

"Don't give me any of your lip, Benjamin," the scowling man bristled back. "We got a good right to know who he is." He turned to me and took a few steps in front of everyone else. "You one of those trouper bastards what came through here?"

I shook my head and attempted to look harmless. "No."

"I think you are. I think you look kinda like one of them Ruh. You got them eyes." The men around him craned to get a better look at my face.

"God, Seth," the old fellow chimed in again. "None of them had red hair. You remember hair like that. He ain't one of 'em."

"Why would I bring them back if I'd been one of the men who took them?" I pointed out.

His expression grew darker and he continued his slow advance. "You gettin' smart with me, boy? Maybe you think all us are stupid here? You think if you bring 'em back you'll get a reward or maybe we won't send anyone else out after you?" He was almost within arm's reach of me now, scowling furiously.

I looked around and saw the same anger lurking in the faces of all the men who stood there. It was the sort of anger that comes to a slow boil inside the hearts of good men who want justice, and finding it out of their grasp, decide vengeance is the next best thing.

I tried to think of a way to calm the situation, but before I could do anything I heard Krin's voice lash out from behind me. "Seth, you get away from him!"

Seth paused, his hands half-raised against me. "Now..."

Krin was already stepping toward him. The knot of women loosened to release her, but stayed close. "He saved us, Seth," she shouted furiously. "You stupid shit-eater, *he* saved us. Where the hell were all of you? Why didn't you come get us?"

He backed away from me as anger and shame fought their way across his face. Anger won. "We came," he shouted back. "After we found out what happened we went after 'em. They shot out Bil's horse from under him, and he got his leg crushed. Jim got his arm stabbed, and old Cup-per still ain't waked up from the thumping they give him. They almost killed us."

I looked again and saw anger on the men's faces. Saw the real reason for it. The helplessness they had felt, unable to defend their town from the false troupe's rough handling. Their failure to reclaim the daughters of their friends and neighbors had shamed them.

"Well it wasn't good enough!" Krin shouted back hotly, her eyes burning. "He came and got us because he's a real man. Not like the rest of you who left us to die!"

The anger leapt out of a young man to my left, a farmboy, about seventeen. "None of this would have happened if you hadn't been running around like some Ruh whore!"

I broke his arm before I quite realized what I was doing. He screamed as he fell to the ground.

I pulled him to his feet by the scruff of his neck. "What's your name?" I snarled into his face.

"My arm!" he gasped, his eyes showing me their whites.

I shook him like a rag doll. "Name!"

"Jason," he blurted. "God's mother, my arm..."

I took his chin in my free hand and turned his face toward Krin and Ell. "Jason," I hissed quietly in his ear. "I want you to look at those girls. And I want you to think about the hell they've been through in these past days, tied hand and foot in the back of a wagon. And I want you to ask yourself what's worse. A broken arm, or getting kidnapped by a stranger and raped four times a night?"

Then I turned his face toward me and spoke so quiet that even an inch away it was hardly a whisper. "After you've thought of that, I want you to pray to God to forgive you for what you just said. And if you mean it, Tehlu grant your arm heal straight and true." His eyes were terrified and wet. "After that, if you ever think an unkind thought about either of them, your arm will ache like there's hot iron in the bone. And if you ever say an unkind word, it will go to fever and slow rot and they'll have to cut it off to save your life." I tightened my grip on him, watching his eyes widen. "And if you ever do anything to either of them, I'll know. I will come here, and kill you, and leave your body hanging in a tree."

There were tears on his face now, although whether from shame or fear or pain I couldn't guess. "Now you tell her you're sorry for what you said." I let go of him after making sure he had his feet under him and pointed him in the direction of Krin and Ell. The women stood around them like a protective cocoon.

He clutched his arm weakly. "I shouldn'ta said that, Ellie," he sobbed, sounding more wretched and repentant than I would have thought possible, broken arm or no. "It was a demon talkin' out of me. I swear though, I been sick worryin'. We all been. And we did try to come get you, but they was a lot of them and they jumped us on the road, then we had to bring Bil home or he'd died from his leg."

Something tickled my memory about the boy's name. Jason? I suddenly suspected I had just broken Ell's boyfriend's arm. Somehow I couldn't feel bad for it just now. Best thing for him, really.

Looking around I saw the anger bleed out of the faces of the men around me, as if I'd used up the whole town's supply in a sudden, furious flash. Instead they watched Jason, looking slightly embarrassed, as if the boy were apologizing for the lot of them.

Then I saw a big, healthy looking man running down the street followed by a dozen other townsfolk. From the look on his face I guessed it was Ell's father, the mayor. He forced his way into the knot of women, gathered his daughter up in his arms, and swung her around.

You find two types of mayor in small towns like this. The first type are balding, older men of considerable girth who are good with money and tend to wring their hands a great deal when anything unexpected happens. The second type are tall, broad-shouldered men whose families have grown slowly prosperous because they had worked like angry bastards behind a plow for twenty generations. Ell's father was the second sort.

He walked over to me, keeping one arm around his daughter's shoulders. "I understand I have you to thank for bringing our girls back." He reached out to shake my hand and I saw his arm was bandaged. His grip was solid in spite of it. He smiled the widest smile I'd seen since I left Simmon at the University.

"How's the arm?" I asked, not realizing how it would sound. His smile faded a little, and I was quick to add. "I've had some training as a physicker. And I know that those sort of things can be tricky to deal with when you're away from home." *When you're living in a country that thinks mercury is medicine*, I thought to myself.

His smile came back, and he flexed his fingers. "It's stiff, but that's all. Just a little meat. They caught us by surprise. I got my hands on one of them, but he stuck me and got away. How did you end up getting the girls away from those Godless Ruh bastards?" He spat.

"They weren't Edema Ruh," I said, my voice sounding more strained than I would have liked. "They weren't even real troupers."

His smile began to fade again. "What do you mean?"

"They weren't Edema Ruh. We don't do the things they did."

"Listen," the mayor said plainly, his temper starting to rise a bit. "I know damn well what they do and don't do. They came in all sweet and nice, played a little music, made a penny or two. Then they started to make trouble around town. When we told them to leave they took my girl." He almost breathed fire as he said the last words.

"We?" I heard someone say faintly behind me. "Jim, he said *we*."

Seth scowled around the side of the mayor to get a look at me again. "I told you he looked like one," he said triumphantly. "I know 'em. You can always tell by them eyes."

"Hold on," the mayor said with slow incredulity. "Are you telling me you're one of *them*?" His expression grew dangerous.

Before I could explain myself. Ell had grabbed his arm. "Oh, don't make him mad, Daddy," she said quickly, holding onto his good arm as if to pull him away from me. "Don't say anything to get him angry. He's not with them. He brought me back, he saved me."

The mayor seemed somewhat mollified by this, but his congeniality was gone. "Explain yourself," he said grimly.

I sighed inside, realizing what a mess I'd made of this. "They weren't troupers, and they certainly weren't Edema Ruh. They were bandits who had killed some of my family and stolen their wagons. They were only pretending to be performers."

"Why would anyone pretend to be Ruh?" the mayor asked, as if the thought were incomprehensible.

"So they could do what they did," I snapped. "You let them into your town and they abused that trust. That's something no Edema Ruh would ever do."

"You never did answer my question," he said. "How did you get the girls away?"

"I took care of things," I said simply.

"He killed them," Krin said loudly enough for everyone to hear. "He killed them all."

I could feel everyone looking at me. Half of them were thinking, *All of them? He killed seven men?* The other half were thinking, *There were two women with them, did he kill them too?*

"Well, then." The mayor looked down at me for a long moment. "Good," he said as if he had just made up his mind. "That's good. The world's a better place for it."

I felt everyone relax slightly. "These are their horses." I pointed to the two horses that had been carrying our baggage. "They belong to the girls now. About forty miles east you'll find the wagons. Krin can show you where they're hidden. They belong to the girls too."

"They'll fetch a good price off in Temsford," the mayor mused.

"Together with the instruments and clothes and such, they'll fetch a heavy penny," I agreed. "Split two ways, it'll make a fine dowry, " I said firmly.

He met my eyes, nodded slowly in understanding. "That it will."

"What about the things they stole from us?" a stout man in an apron protested. "They smashed up my place and stole two barrels of my best ale!"

"Do you have any daughters?" I asked him calmly. The sudden, stricken look on his face told me he did. I met his eye, held it. "Then I think you came away from this pretty well."

The mayor finally noticed Jason clutching his broken arm. "What happened to you?"

Jason looked at his feet, and Seth spoke up for him, "He said some things he shouldn't."

The mayor looked around and saw that getting more of an answer would involve an ordeal. He shrugged and let it go.

"I could splint it for you," I said easily.

"No!" Jason said too quickly, then backpedaled. "I'd rather go to Gran."

I gave a sideways look to the mayor. "Gran?"

He gave a fond smile. "When we scrape our knees Gran patches us back up again."

"Would Bil be there?" I asked. "The man with the crushed leg?"

He nodded. "She won't let him out of her sight for another span of days if I know her."

"I'll walk you over," I said to the sweating boy who was carefully cradling his arm. "I'd like to watch her work."

As far from civilization as we were, I expected Gran to be a hunched old woman who treated her patients with leeches and wood alcohol.

That opinion changed when I saw the inside of her house. Her walls were covered with bundles of dry herbs and shelves lined with small, carefully labeled bottles. There was a small desk with three heavy leather books on it. One of them lay open, and I recognized it as *The Heroborica*. I could see handwritten notes scrawled in the margins, while some of the entries had been edited or crossed out entirely.

Gran wasn't as old as I'd thought she'd be, though she did have her share of grey hair. She wasn't hunched either, and actually stood taller than me, with broad shoulders and a round, smiling face.

She swung a copper kettle over the fire, humming gently to herself. Then she brought out a pair of shears and sat Jason down, prodding his arm gently. Pale and sweating, the boy kept up a constant stream of nervous chatter while she methodically cut his shirt away. In the space of a few minutes, without her even asking, he'd given her an accurate if somewhat disjointed version of Ell and Krin's homecoming.

"It's a nice clean break," she said at last, interrupting him. "How'd it happen?"

Jason's wild eyes darted to me, then away. "Nothin," he said quickly. Then realized he hadn't answered the question. "I mean..."

"I broke it," I said. "Figured the least I could do was come along and see if there's anything I could do to help set it right again."

Gran looked back at me. "Have you dealt with this sort of thing before?"

"I've studied medicine at the University," I said.

She shrugged. "Then I guess you can hold the splints while I wrap 'em. I have a girl who helps me, but she run off when she heard the commotion up the street."

Jason eyed me nervously as I held the wood tight to his arm, but it took Gran less than three minutes to bind up the splint with an air of bored competence. Watching her work, I decided she was worth more than half the students I could name in the Medica.

After we'd finished she looked down at Jason. "You're lucky," she said. "It didn't need to be set. You hold off using it for a month, it should heal up just fine."

Jason left as quickly as he was able, and after a small amount of persuasion Gran let me see Bil, who was laid up in her back room.

If Jason's arm was a clean break, then Bil's was messy as a break can be. Both the bones in his lower leg had broken in several places. I couldn't see under the bandages, but his leg was hugely swollen. The skin above the bandages was bruised and mottled, stretched as tight as an overstuffed sausage.

Bil was pale but alert, and it looked like he would probably keep the leg. How much use it would be was another matter. He might come away with nothing more than a heavy limp, but I wouldn't bet on him ever running again.

"What sort of folk shoot a man's horse?" he asked indignantly, his face covered in a sheen of sweat. "It ain't right."

It had been his own horse, of course. And this wasn't the sort of town where folk had horses to spare. Bil was a young man with a new wife and his own small farm, and he might never walk again because he'd tried to do the right thing. It hurt to think about.

Gran gave him two spoonfuls of something from a brown bottle, and it dragged his eyes shut. She ushered us out of the room and closed the door behind her.

"Did the bone break the skin?" I asked once the door was closed.

She nodded as she put the bottle back on the shelf.

"What have you been using to keep it from going septic?"

"Sour, you mean?" she asked. "Ramsburr."

"Really?" I asked. "Not arrowroot?"

"Arrowroot," she snorted as she added wood to the fire and swung the now-steaming kettle off of it. "You ever tried to keep something from going sour with arrowroot?"

"No," I admitted.

"Let me save you the trouble of killing someone, then." She brought out a pair of wooden cups. "Arrowroot is useless. You can eat it if you like, but that's about it."

"But a paste of arrowroot and bessamy is supposed to be ideal for this."

"Bessamy might be worth half a damn," she admitted. "But ramsburr is better. I'd rather have some redblade, but we can't always have what we want. A paste of motherleaf and ramsburr is what I use, and you can see he's doing just fine. Arrowroot is easy for folk to find, and it pulps smooth, but it hain't got any worthwhile properties."

She shook her head. "Arrowroot and camphor. Arrowroot and bessamy. Arrowroot and saltbine. Arrowroot hain't a palliative of any sort. It's just good at carrying around what works."

I opened my mouth to protest, then looked around her house, at her heavily annotated copy of *The Heroborica*. I closed my mouth.

Gran poured hot water from the kettle into two cups. "Sit yourself down for a bit," she said. "You look like you're on your last leg."

I looked longingly at the chair. "I should probably be getting back," I said.

"You've got time for a cup," she said, taking my arm and setting me firmly into the chair. "And a quick bite. You're pale as a dry bone, and I have a bit of sweet pudding here that hain't got anybody to give it a home."

I tried to remember if I'd eaten any lunch today. I remembered feeding the girls...."I don't want to put you to any more trouble," I said. "I've already made more work for you."

"About time somebody broke that boy's arm," she said conversationally. "Has a mouth on him like you wouldn't believe." She handed me one of the wooden cups. "Drink that down and I'll get you some of that pudding."

The steam coming off the cup smelled wonderful. "What's in it?" I asked.

"Rosehip. And some apple brandy I still up my own self." She gave a wide smile that crinkled the edges of her eyes. "If you like, I can put in some arrowroot, too."

I smiled and sipped. The warmth of it spread through my chest, and I felt myself relax a bit. Which was odd, as I hadn't realized I'd been tense before.

Gran bustled about a bit before setting two plates on the table and easing herself down into a nearby chair.

"You really kill those folk?" she asked plainly. There wasn't any accusation in her voice. It was just a question.

I nodded.

"You probably shouldn't have told anyone," she said. "There's bound to be a fuss. They'll want a trial and have to bring in the azzie from Temsford."

"I didn't tell them," I said. "Krin did."

"Ah," she said.

The conversation lulled. I drank the last swallow out of my cup, but when I tried to set it on the table my hands were shaking so badly that it knocked against the wood, making a sound like an impatient visitor at the door.

Gran sipped calmly from her cup.

"I don't care to talk about it," I said at last. "It wasn't a good thing."

"Some folk might argue that," she said gently. "I think you done the right thing."

Her words brought a sudden hot ache behind my eyes, as if I were about to burst into tears. "I'm not so sure about that," I said, my voice sounding strange in my own ears. My hands were shaking worse now.

Gran didn't seem surprised at this. "You've had the bit in your teeth for a couple days now, haven't you?" Her tone made it clear it wasn't really a question. "I know the look. You've been keeping busy. Looking after the girls. Not sleeping. Probably not eating much." She picked up the plate. "Eat your pudding. It will help to get some food in you."

I ate the pudding. Halfway through, I began to cry, choking a bit as it stuck in my throat.

Gran refilled my cup with more tea and poured another dollop of brandy in on top of it. "Drink that down," she repeated.

I took a swallow. I didn't mean to say anything, but I found myself talking anyway. "I think there might be something wrong with me," I said quietly. "A normal person doesn't have it in him to do the things I do. A normal person would never kill people like this."

"That may be," she admitted, sipping from her own cup. "But what would you say if I told you Bil's leg had gone a bit green and sweet smelling under that bandage?"

I looked up, startled. "He's got the rot?"

She shook her head. "No. I told you he's fine. But what if?"

"We'd have to cut the leg off," I said.

Gran nodded seriously. "That's right. And we'd have to do it quick. Today. No dithering about and hoping he'd fight his way through on his own. That wouldn't do a thing but kill him." She took a sip, watching me over the top of her cup, making it a question of sorts.

I nodded. I knew it was true.

"You've got some medicine," she said. "You know that proper doctoring means hard choices." She gave me an unflinching look. "We en't like other folk. You burn a man with an iron to stop his bleeding. You save the mother and lose the babe. It's hard, and nobody ever thanks you for it. But we're the ones that have to choose."

She took another slow drink of tea. "The first few times are the worst. You'll get the shakes and lose some sleep. But that's the price of doing what needs to be done."

"There were women too," I said, the words catching in my throat.

Gran's eyes flashed. "They earned it twice as much," she said, and the sudden, furious anger in her sweet face caught me so completely by surprise that I felt prickling fear crawl over my body. "A man who would do that to a girl is like a mad dog. He en't hardly a person, just an animal needs to be put down. But a woman who helps him do it? That's worse. She knows what she's doing. She knows what it means."

Gran put her cup down gently on the table, her expression composed again. "If a leg goes bad, you cut it off." She made a firm gesture with the flat of her hand, then picked up her slice of pudding and began to eat it with her fingers. "And some folk need killing. That's all there is to it."

By the time I got myself under control and made it back outside, the crowd in the street had swelled. The local tavern keeper had rolled a barrel onto his front landing and the air was sweet with the smell of beer.

Krin's father and mother had ridden back into town on the roan. Pete was there too, having run back. He offered up his unbroken head for my inspection and demanded his two pennies for services rendered.

I was warmly thanked by Krin's parents. They seemed to be good people. Most people are if given the chance. I caught hold of the roan's reins, and using him as a sort of portable wall I managed to get a moment of relatively private conversation with Krin.

Her dark eyes were a little red around the edges, but her face was bright and happy. "Make sure you get Lady Ghost," I said, nodding to one of the horses. "She's yours." The mayor's daughter would have a fair dowry no matter what, so I'd loaded Krin's horse with the more valuable goods, as well as most of the false troupers' money.

Her expression grew serious as she met my eyes, and again she reminded me of a young Denna. "You're leaving," she said.

I guess I was. She didn't try to convince me to stay, and instead surprised me with a sudden embrace. After kissing me on the cheek she whispered in my ear, "Thank you."

We stepped away from each other, knowing propriety would only allow so much. "Don't sell yourself short and marry some fool," I said, feeling as if I should say something.

"Don't you either," she said, her dark eyes mocking me gently.

I took Greytail's reins and led her over to where the mayor stood, watching the crowd in a proprietary way. He nodded as I approached.

I drew a deep breath. "Is the constable about?"

He raised an eyebrow at this, then shrugged and pointed off into the crowd. "That's him there. He was three-quarters drunk even before you brought our girls home, though. Don't know how much use he'll be to you now."

"Well," I said hesitantly. "I'm guessing someone is going to need to lock me up until you can get word to the azzie off in Temsford." I nodded to the small stone building in the center of town.

The mayor looked sideways at me, frowning a bit. "You *want* to be locked up?"

"Not particularly," I admitted.

"You can come and go as you please then," he said.

"The azzie won't be happy when he hears," I said. "I'd rather not have anyone else go up against the iron law because of something I've done. Aiding in the escape of a murderer can be a hanging offense."

The big man gave me a long looking over. His eyes lingered a bit on my sword, the worn leather of my boots. I could almost feel him noticing the lack of any serious wounds despite the fact that I'd just killed half a dozen armed men.

"So you'd let us just lock you up?" he asked. "Easy as that?"

I shrugged.

He frowned again, then shook his head as if he couldn't make sense of me. "Well aren't you just as gentle as a lamb?" he said wonderingly. "But no. I won't lock you up. You haven't done anything less than proper."

"I broke that boy's arm," I said.

"Hmmmm," he rumbled darkly. "Forgot about that." He reached into his pocket and brought out ha'penny. He handed it to me. "Much obliged."

I laughed as I put it in my pocket.

"Here's my thought," he said. "I'll head over and see if I can find the constable. Then I'll explain to him we've got to lock you up. If you've slipped off in the middle of this confusion, we wouldn't hardly be aiding in the escape, would we?"

"It would be negligence in maintenance of the law," I said. "He might take a few lashes for it, or lose his post."

"Shouldn't come to that," the mayor said. "But if it does, he'll be happy to do it. He's Ellie's uncle." He looked out at the crowd on the street. "Will fifteen minutes be enough for you to slip off in all the confusion?"

"If it's all the same to you," I said. "Could you say I disappeared in a strange and mysterious way when your back was turned?"

He laughed at this. "Don't see why not. You need more than fifteen minutes on account of it being mysterious and all?"

"Ten should be a great plenty," I said as I unpacked my lutecase and travelsack from Greytail and handed the mayor the reins. "You'd be doing me a favor if you took care of him until Bil is up and about," I said. "Or you could send it out to his farm, if he's got family tending it."

"You leaving your horse?" he asked.

"He's just lost his." I shrugged. "And we Ruh are used to walking. I wouldn't know what to do with a horse, anyway," I said half-honestly.

The big man gripped the reins and gave me a long look, as if he wasn't quite sure what to make of me. "Is there anything we can do for you?" he asked at last.

"Remember it was bandits that took them," I said as I turned to leave. "And remember it was one of the Edema Ruh who brought them back."

Rysn

Brandon Sanderson

Brandon Sanderson has published seven solo novels with Tor—Elantris, the Mistborn books, Warbreaker, *and* The Way of Kings—*as well as four books in the middle-grade* Alcatraz Versus the Evil Librarians *series from Scholastic. He was chosen to complete Robert Jordan's* Wheel of Time *series; 2009's* The Gathering Storm *and 2010's* Towers of Midnight *will be followed by the final book,* A Memory of Light, *in 2013. His newest Mistborn novel,* The Alloy of Law, *was released in November 2011, and his newest novel is* The Emperor's Soul. *Currently living in Utah with his wife and children, Brandon teaches creative writing at Brigham Young University.*

RYSN HESITANTLY STEPPED DOWN from the caravan's lead wagon. Her feet fell on soft, uneven ground that sank down a little beneath her. That made her shiver, particularly since the too-thick grass didn't move away as it should. Rysn tapped her foot a few times. The grass didn't so much as quiver.

"It's not going to move," Vstim said. "Grass here doesn't behave the way it does elsewhere. Surely you've heard that." The older man sat beneath the bright yellow canopy of the lead wagon. He rested one arm on the side rail, holding a set of ledgers with the other hand. One of his long white eyebrows was tucked behind his ear and he let the other trail down beside his face. He preferred stiffly starched robes—blue and red— and a flat-topped conical hat. It was classic Thaylen merchant's clothing: several decades out of date, yet still distinguished.

"I've heard of the grass," Rysn said to him. "But it's just so *odd*." She stepped again, walking in a circle around the lead wagon. Yes, she'd heard of the grass here in Shinovar, but she'd assumed that it would just be lethargic. That people said it didn't disappear because it moved too slowly.

But no, that wasn't it. It didn't move *at all*. How did it survive? Shouldn't it have all been eaten away by animals? She shook her head in wonder, looking up across the plain. The grass completely *covered* it. The blades were all crowded together, and you couldn't see the ground. What a mess it was.

"The ground is springy," she said, rounding back to her original side of the wagon. "Not just because of the grass."

"Hmm," Vstim said, still working on his ledgers. "Yes. It's called soil."

"It makes me feel like I'm going to sink down to my knees. How can the Shin stand living here?"

"They're an interesting people. Shouldn't you be setting up the device?"

Rysn sighed, but walked to the rear of the wagon. The other wagons in the caravan—six in all—were pulling up and forming a loose circle. She took down the tailgate of the lead wagon and heaved, pulling out a wooden tripod nearly as tall as she was. She carried it over one shoulder, marching to the center of the grassy circle.

She was more fashionable than her babsk; she wore the most modern of clothing for a young woman her age: a deep blue patterned silk vest over a light green long-sleeved shirt with stiff cuffs. Her ankle-length skirt—also green—was stiff and businesslike, utilitarian in cut but embroidered for fashion.

She wore a green glove on her left hand. Covering the safehand was a silly tradition, just a result of Vorin cultural dominance. But it was best to keep up appearances. Many of the more traditional Thaylen people—including, unfortunately, her babsk—still found it scandalous for a woman to go about with her safehand uncovered.

She set up the tripod. It had been five months since Vstim became her babsk and she his apprentice. He'd been good to her. Not all babsk were; by tradition, he was more than just her master. He was her father, legally, until he pronounced her ready to become a merchant on her own.

She did wish he wouldn't spend so much time traveling to such *odd* places. He was known as a great merchant, and she'd assumed that great merchants would be the ones visiting exotic cities and ports. Not ones who traveled to empty meadows in backward countries.

Tripod set up, she returned to the wagon to fetch the fabrial. The wagon back formed an enclosure with thick sides and top to offer protection against highstorms—even the weaker ones in the West could be dangerous, at least until one got through the passes and into Shinovar.

She hurried back to the tripod with the fabrial's box. She slid off the wooden top and removed the large heliodor inside. The pale yellow gemstone, at least two inches in diameter, was fixed inside a metal framework. It glowed gently, not as bright as one might expect of such a sizable gem.

She set it in the tripod, then spun a few of the dials underneath, setting the fabrial to the people in the caravan. Then she pulled a stool from the wagon and sat down to watch. She'd been astonished at what Vstim had paid for the device—one of the new, recently invented types that would give warning if people approached. Was it really so important?

She sat back, looking up at the gemstone, watching to see if it grew brighter. The odd grass of the Shin lands waved in the wind, stubbornly refusing to withdraw, even at the strongest of gusts. In the distance rose the white peaks of the Misted Mountains, sheltering Shinovar. Those mountains caused the highstorms to break and fade, making Shinovar one of the only places in all of Roshar where highstorms did not reign.

The plain around her was dotted with strange, straight-trunked trees with stiff, skeletal branches full of leaves that didn't withdraw in the wind. The entire landscape had an eerie feel to it, as if it were dead. Nothing moved. With a start, Rysn realized she couldn't see any spren. Not a one. No windspren, no lifespren, nothing.

It was as if the entire land were slow of wit. Like a man who was born without all his brains, one who didn't know when to protect himself, but instead just stared at the wall drooling. She dug into the ground with a finger, then brought it up to inspect the "soil," as Vstim had called it. It was dirty stuff. Why, a strong gust could uproot this entire field of grass and blow it away. Good thing the highstorms couldn't reach these lands.

Near the wagons, the servants and guards unloaded crates and set up camp. Suddenly, the heliodor began to pulse with a brighter yellow light. "Master!" she called, standing. "Someone's nearby."

Vstim—who had been going through crates—looked up sharply. He waved to Kylrm, head of the guards, and his six men got out their bows.

"There," one said, pointing.

In the distance, a group of horsemen was approaching. They didn't ride very quickly, and they led several large animals—like thick, squat horses—pulling wagons. The gemstone in the fabrial pulsed more brightly as the newcomers got closer.

"Yes," Vstim said, looking at the fabrial. "That is going to be *very* handy. Good range on it."

"But we knew they were coming," Rysn said, rising from her stool and walking over to him.

"This time," he said. "But if it warns us of bandits in the dark, it'll repay its cost a dozen times over. Kylrm, lower your bows. You know how they feel about those things."

The guards did as they were told, and the group of Thaylens waited. Rysn found herself tucking her eyebrows back nervously, though she didn't know why she bothered. The newcomers were just Shin. Of course, Vstim insisted that she shouldn't think of them as savages. He seemed to have great respect for them.

As they approached, she was surprised by the variety in their appearance. Other Shin she'd seen had worn basic brown robes or other worker's clothing. At the front of this group, however, was a man in what must be Shin finery: a bright, multicolored cloak that completely enveloped him, tied closed at the front. It trailed down on either side of his horse, drooping almost to the ground. Only his head was exposed.

Four men rode on horses around him, and they wore more subdued clothing. Still bright, just not *as* bright. They wore shirts, trousers, and colorful capes.

At least three dozen other men walked alongside them, wearing brown tunics. More drove the three large wagons.

"Wow," Rysn said. "He brought a lot of servants."

"Servants?" Vstim said.

"The fellows in brown."

Her babsk smiled. "Those are his guards, child."

"What? They look so dull."

"Shin are a curious folk," he said. "Here, warriors are the lowliest of men—kind of like slaves. Men trade and sell them between houses by way of little stones that signify ownership, and any man who picks up a weapon must join them and be treated the same. The fellow in the fancy robe? *He's* a farmer."

"A landowner, you mean?"

"No. As far as I can tell, he goes out every day—well, the days when he's not overseeing a negotiation like this—and works the fields. They treat all farmers like that, lavish them with attention and respect."

Rysn gaped. "But most villages are *filled* with farmers!"

"Indeed," Vstim said. "Holy places, here. Foreigners aren't allowed near fields or farming villages."

How strange, she thought. *Perhaps living in this place has affected their minds.*

Kylrm and his guards didn't look terribly pleased at being so heavily outnumbered, but Vstim didn't seem bothered. Once the Shin grew close, he walked out from his wagons without a hint of trepidation. Rysn hurried after him, her skirt brushing the grass below.

Bother, she thought. Another problem with its not retracting. If she had to buy a new hem because of this dull grass, it was going to make her very cross.

Vstim met up with the Shin, then bowed in a distinctive way, hands toward the ground. "*Tan balo ken tala,*" he said. She didn't know what it meant.

The man in the cloak—the *farmer*—nodded respectfully, and one of the other riders dismounted and walked forward. "Winds of Fortune guide you, my friend." He spoke Thaylen very well. "He who adds is happy for your safe arrival."

"Thank you, Thresh-son-Esan," Vstim said. "And my thanks to he who adds."

"What have you brought for us from your strange lands, friend?" Thresh said. "More metal, I hope?"

Vstim waved and some of the guards brought over a heavy crate. They set it down and pried off the top, revealing its peculiar contents. Pieces of scrap metal, mostly shaped like bits of shell, though some were formed like pieces of wood. It looked to Rysn like garbage that had—for some inexplicable reason—been Soulcast into metal.

"Ah," Thresh said, squatting down to inspect the box. "Wonderful!"

"Not a bit of it was mined," Vstim said. "No rocks were broken or smelted to get this metal, Thresh. It was Soulcast from shells, bark, or branches. I have a document sealed by five separate Thaylen notaries attesting to it."

"You needn't have done such a thing as this," Thresh said. "You have once earned our trust in this matter long ago."

"I'd rather be proper about it," Vstim said. "A merchant who is careless with contracts is one who finds himself with enemies instead of friends."

Thresh stood up, clapping three times. The men in brown with the downcast eyes lowered the back of a wagon, revealing crates.

"The others who visit us," Thresh noted, walking to the wagon. "All they seem to care about are horses. Everyone wishes to buy horses. But never you, my friend. Why is that?"

"Too hard to care for," Vstim said, walking with Thresh. "And there's too often a poor return on the investment, valuable as they are."

"But not with these?" Thresh said, picking up one of the light crates. There was something alive inside.

"Not at all," Vstim said. "Chickens fetch a good price, and they're easy to care for, assuming you have feed."

"We brought you plenty," Thresh said. "I cannot believe you buy these from us. They are not worth nearly so much as you outsiders think. And you give us metal for them! Metal that bears no stain of broken rock. A miracle."

Vstim shrugged. "Those scraps are practically worthless where I come from. They're made by ardents practicing with Soulcasters. They can't make food, because if you get it wrong, it's poisonous. So they turn garbage into metal and throw it away."

"But it can be forged!"

"Why forge the metal," Vstim said, "when you can carve an object from wood in the precise shape you want, *then* Soulcast it?"

Thresh just shook his head, bemused. Rysn watched with her own share of confusion. This was the *craziest* trade exchange she'd ever seen. Normally, Vstim argued and haggled like a crushkiller. But here, he freely revealed that his wares were worthless!

In fact, as conversation proceeded, the two both took pains to explain how worthless their goods were. Eventually, they came to an agreement—though Rysn couldn't grasp how—and shook hands on the deal. Some of Thresh's soldiers began to unload their boxes of chickens, cloth, and exotic dried meats. Others began carting away boxes of scrap metal.

"You couldn't trade me a soldier, could you?" Vstim asked as they waited.

"They cannot be sold to an outsider, I am afraid."

"But there was that one you traded me..."

"It's been nearly seven years!" Thresh said with a laugh. "And still you ask!"

"You don't know what I got for him," Vstim said. "And you gave him to me for practically nothing!"

"He was Truthless," Thresh said, shrugging. "He wasn't worth anything at all. You *forced* me to take something in trade, though to confess, I had to throw your payment into a river. I could not take money for a Truthless."

"Well, I suppose I can't take offense at that," Vstim said, rubbing his chin. "But if you ever have another, let me know. Best servant I ever had. I still regret that I traded him."

"I will remember, friend," Thresh said. "But I do not think it likely we will have another like him." He seemed to grow distracted. "Indeed, I should hope that we never do...."

Once the goods were exchanged, they shook hands again, then Vstim bowed to the farmer. Rysn tried to mimic what he did, and earned a smile from Thresh and several of his companions, who chattered in their whispering Shin language.

Such a long, boring ride for such a short exchange. But Vstim was right; those chickens would be worth good spheres in the East.

"What did you learn?" Vstim said to her as they walked back toward the lead wagon.

"That Shin are odd."

"No," Vstim said, though he wasn't stern. He never seemed to be stern. "They are simply different, child. Odd people are those who act erratically. Thresh and his kind, they are anything but erratic. They may be a little *too* stable. The world is changing outside, but the Shin seem determined to remain the same. I've tried to offer them fabrials, but they find them worthless. Or unholy. Or too holy to use."

"Those are rather different things, master."

"Yes," he said. "But with the Shin, it's often hard to distinguish among them. Regardless, what did you *really* learn?"

"That they treat being humble like the Herdazians treat boasting," she said. "You both went out of your way to show how worthless your wares were. I found it strange, but I think it might just be how they haggle."

He smiled widely. "And already you are wiser than half the men I've brought here. Listen. Here is your lesson. *Never* try to cheat the Shin. Be forthright, tell them the truth, and—if anything—undervalue your goods. They will love you for it. And they'll pay you for it too."

She nodded. They reached the wagon, and he got out a strange little pot. "Here," he said. "Use a knife and go cut out some of that grass. Be sure to cut down far and get plenty of the soil. The plants can't live without it."

"Why am I doing this?" she asked, wrinkling her nose and taking the pot.

"Because," he said. "You're going to learn to care for that plant. I want you to keep it with you until you stop thinking of it as odd."

"But why?"

"Because it will make you a better merchant," he said.

She frowned. Must he be so strange so much of the time? Perhaps that was why he was one of the only Thaylens who could get a good deal out of the Shin. He was as odd as they were.

She walked off to do as she was told. No use complaining. She did get out a rugged pair of gloves first, though, and roll up her sleeves. She was *not* going to ruin a good dress for a pot of drooling, wall-staring, imbecile grass. And that was that.

While the Gods Laugh

Michael Moorcock

Michael Moorcock is best known for his genre-redefining swords-and-sorcery series featuring the albino anti-hero Elric of Melniboné. Books featuring Elric include Stormbringer, The Bane of the Black Sword, and The Weird of the White Wolf, among many others. Other prominent works include the Eternal Champion series, the Warrior of Mars series, the Jerry Cornelius series, and the Hawkmoon series. Moorcock is a winner of numerous awards, including several career awards, such as being named a SFWA Grand Master and being inducted into the SF Hall of Fame, as well as being honored with the World Fantasy and Stoker lifetime achievement awards.

> *I, while the gods laugh, the world's vortex am;*
> *Maelstrom of passions in that hidden sea*
> *Whose waves of all-time lap the coasts of me,*
> *And in small compass the dark waters cram.*
> —Mervyn Peake, "Shapes and Sounds," 1941

One

ONE NIGHT, as Elric sat moodily drinking alone in a tavern, a wingless woman of Myyrrhn came gliding out of the storm and rested her lithe body against him.

Her face was thin and frail-boned, almost as white as Elric's own albino skin, and she wore flimsy pale-green robes which contrasted well with her dark red hair.

The tavern was ablaze with candle-flame and alive with droning argument and gusty laughter, but the words of the woman of Myyrrhn came clear and liquid, carrying over the zesty din.

"I have sought you twenty days," she said to Elric who regarded her insolently through hooded crimson eyes and lazed in a high-backed chair, a silver wine-cup in his long-fingered right hand and his left on the pommel of his sorcerous runesword Stormbringer.

"Twenty days," murmured the Melnibonéan softly, speaking as if to himself, mockingly rude. "A long time for a beautiful and lonely woman to be wandering the world." He opened his eyes a trifle wider and spoke to her directly: "I am Elric of Melniboné, as you evidently know. I grant no favours and ask none. Bearing this in mind, tell me why you have sought me for twenty days."

Equably, the woman replied, undaunted by the albino's supercilious tone. "You are a bitter man, Elric; I know this also—and you are grief-haunted for reasons which are already legend. I ask you no favours—but bring you myself and a proposition. What do you desire most in the world?"

"Peace," Elric told her simply. Then he smiled ironically and said: "I am an evil man, lady, and my destiny is hell-doomed, but I am not unwise, nor unfair. Let me remind you a little of the truth. Call this legend if you prefer—I do not care.

"A woman died a year ago, on the blade of my trusty sword." He patted the blade sharply and his eyes were suddenly hard and self-mocking. "Since then I have courted no woman and desired none. Why should I break such secure habits? If asked, I grant you that I could speak poetry to you, and that you have a grace and beauty which moves me to interesting speculation, but I would not load any part of my dark burden upon one as exquisite as you. Any relationship between us, other than formal, would necessitate my unwilling shifting of part of that burden." He paused for an instant and then said slowly: "I should admit that I scream in my sleep sometimes and am often tortured by incommunicable self-loathing. Go while you can, lady, and forget Elric for he can bring only grief to your soul."

With a quick movement he turned his gaze from her and lifted the silver wine-cup, draining it and replenishing it from a jug at his side.

"No," said the wingless woman of Myyrrhn calmly, "I will not. Come with me."

She rose and gently took Elric's hand. Without knowing why, Elric allowed himself to be led from the tavern and out into the wild, rainless storm which howled around the Filkharian city of Raschil. A protective and cynical smile hovered about his mouth as she drew him towards the sea-lashed quayside where she told him her name. Shaarilla of the Dancing Mist, wingless daughter of a dead necromancer—a cripple in her own strange land, and an outcast.

Elric felt uncomfortably drawn to this calm-eyed woman who wasted few words. He felt a great surge of emotion well within him, emotion he had never thought to experience again, and he wanted to take her finely moulded shoulders and press her slim body to his. But he quelled the urge and studied her marble delicacy and her wild hair which flowed in the wind about her head.

Silence rested comfortably between them while the chaotic wind howled mournfully over the sea. Here, Elric could ignore the warm stink of the city and he felt almost relaxed. At last, looking away from him towards the swirling sea, her green robe curling in the wind, she said: "You have heard, of course, of the Dead Gods' Book?"

Elric nodded. He was interested, despite the need he felt to disassociate himself as much as possible from his fellows. The mythical book was believed to contain knowledge which could solve many problems that had plagued men for centuries—it held a holy and mighty wisdom which every sorcerer desired to sample. But it was believed destroyed, hurled into the sun when the Old Gods were dying in the cosmic wastes which lay beyond the outer reaches of the solar system. Another legend, apparently of later origin, spoke vaguely of the dark ones who had interrupted the Book's sunward coursing and had stolen it before it could be destroyed. Most scholars discounted this legend, arguing that, by this time, the Book would have come to light if it did still exist.

Elric made himself speak flatly so that he appeared to be uninterested when he answered Shaarilla. "Why do you mention the Book?"

"I know that it exists," Shaarilla replied intensely, "and I know where it is. My father acquired the knowledge just before he died. Myself—and the Book—you may have if you will help me get it."

Could the secret of peace be contained in the Book? Elric wondered. Would he, if he found it, be able to dispense with Stormbringer?

"If you want it so badly that you seek my help," he said eventually, "why do you not wish to keep it?"

"Because I would be afraid to have such a thing perpetually in my custody—it is not a book for an ordinary mortal to own, but you are possibly the last mighty nigromancer left in the world and it is fitting that you should have it. Besides, you might kill me to obtain it—I would never be safe with such a volume in my hands. I need only one small part of its wisdom."

"What is that?" Elric enquired, studying her patrician beauty with a new pulse stirring within him.

Her mouth set and the lids fell over her eyes. "When we have the Book in our hands—then you will have your answer. Not before."

"This answer is good enough," Elric remarked quickly, seeing that he would gain no more information at that stage. "And the answer appeals to me." Then, half before he realized it, he seized her shoulders in his slim, pale hands and pressed his colourless lips to her scarlet mouth.

Elric and Shaarilla rode westwards, towards the Silent Land, across the lush plains of Shazaar where their ship had berthed two days earlier. The border country between Shazaar and the Silent Land was a lonely stretch of territory, unoccupied even by peasant dwellings; a no-man's land, though fertile and rich in natural wealth. The inhabitants of Shazaar had deliberately refrained from extending their borders further, for though the dwellers in the Silent Land rarely ventured beyond the Marshes of the Mist, the natural borderline between the two lands, the inhabitants of Shazaar held their unknown neighbours in almost superstitious fear.

The journey had been clean and swift, though ominous, with several persons who should have known nothing of their purpose warning the travelers of nearing danger. Elric brooded, recognizing the signs of doom but choosing to ignore them and communicate nothing to Shaarilla who, for her part, seemed content with Elric's silence. They spoke little in the day and so saved their breath for the wild love-play of the night.

The thud of the two horses' hoofs on the soft turf, the muted creak and clatter of Elric's harness and sword, were the only sounds to break the stillness of the clear winter day as the pair rode steadily, nearing the quaking, treacherous trails of the Marshes of the Mist.

One gloomy night, they reached the borders of the Silent Land, marked by the marsh, and they halted and made camp, pitching their silk tent on a hill overlooking the mist-shrouded wastes.

Banked like black pillows against the horizon, the clouds were ominous. The moon lurked behind them, sometimes piercing them sufficiently to send a pale tentative beam down on to the glistening marsh or its ragged, grassy frontiers. Once, a moonbeam glanced off silver, illuminating the dark silhouette of Elric, but, as if repelled by the sight of a living creature on that bleak hill, the moon once again slunk behind its cloud-shield, leaving Elric thinking deeply. Leaving Elric in the darkness he desired.

Thunder rumbled over distant mountains, sounding like the laughter of far-off gods. Elric shivered, pulled his blue cloak more tightly about him, and continued to stare over the misted lowlands.

Shaarilla came to him soon, and she stood beside him, swathed in a thick woolen cloak which could not keep out all the damp chill in the air.

"The Silent Land," she murmured. "Are all the stories true, Elric? Did they teach you of it in old Melniboné?"

Elric frowned, annoyed that she had disturbed his thoughts. He turned abruptly to look at her, staring blankly out of crimson-irised eyes for a moment and then saying flatly:

"The inhabitants are unhuman and feared. This I know. Few men ventured into their territory, ever. None have returned, to my knowledge. Even in the days when Melniboné was a powerful empire, this was one nation my ancestors never ruled—nor did they desire to do so. Nor did they make a treaty. The denizens of the Silent Land are said to be a dying race, far more selfish than my ancestors ever were, who enjoyed dominion over the Earth long before Melnibonéans gained any sort of power. They rarely venture beyond the confines of their territory, nowadays, encompassed as it is by marshland and mountains."

Shaarilla laughed, then, with little humour. "So they are unhuman are they, Elric? Then what of my people, who are related to them? What of me, Elric?"

"You're unhuman enough for me," replied Elric insouciantly, looking her in the eyes. She smiled.

"A compliment? I'll take it for one—until your glib tongue finds a better."

That night they slept restlessly and, as he had predicted, Elric screamed agonizingly in his turbulent, terror-filled sleep and he called a name which made Shaarilla's eyes fill with pain and jealousy. Wide-eyed in his grim sleep, Elric seemed to be staring at the one he named, speaking other words in a sibilant language which made Shaarilla block her ears and shudder.

The next morning, as they broke camp, folding the rustling fabric of the yellow silk tent between them, Shaarilla avoided looking at Elric directly but later, since he made no move to speak, she asked him, in a voice which shook somewhat, a question.

It was a question which she needed to ask, but one which came hard to her lips. "Why do you desire the Dead Gods' Book, Elric? What do you believe you will find in it?"

Elric shrugged, dismissing the question, but she repeated her words less slowly, with more insistence.

"Very well then," he said eventually. "But it is not easy to answer you in a few sentences. I desire, if you like, to know one of two things."

"And what is that, Elric?"

The tall albino dropped the folded tent to the grass and sighed. His fingers played nervously with the pommel of his runesword. "Can an ultimate god exist—or not? That is what I need to know, Shaarilla, if my life is to have any direction at all.

"The Lords of Law and Chaos now govern our lives. But is there some being greater than them?"

Shaarilla put a hand on Elric's arm. "Why must you know?" she said.

"Despairingly, sometimes, I seek the comfort of a benign god, Shaarilla. My mind goes out, lying awake at night, searching through black barrenness for something—anything—which will take me to it, warm me, protect me, tell me that there is order in the chaotic tumble of the universe; that it is consistent, this precision of the planets, not simply a brief, bright spark of sanity in an eternity of malevolent anarchy."

Elric sighed and his quiet tones were tinged with hopelessness. "Without some confirmation of the order of things, my only comfort is to accept anarchy. This way, I can revel in chaos and know, without fear, that we are all doomed from the start—that our brief existence is both meaningless and damned. I can accept, then, that we are more than forsaken, because there was never anything there to forsake us. I have weighed the proof, Shaarilla, and must believe that anarchy prevails, in spite of all the laws which seemingly govern our actions, our sorcery, our logic. I see only chaos in the world. If the book we seek tells me otherwise, then I shall gladly believe it. Until then, I will put my trust only in my sword and myself."

Shaarilla stared at Elric strangely. "Could not this philosophy of yours have been influenced by recent events in your past? Do you fear the consequences of your murder and treachery? Is it not more comforting for you to believe in deserts which are rarely just?"

Elric turned on her, crimson eyes blazing in anger, but even as he made to speak, the anger fled him and he dropped his eyes towards the ground, hooding them from her gaze.

"Perhaps," he said lamely. "I do not know. That is the only *real* truth, Shaarilla. *I do not know.*"

Shaarilla nodded, her face lit by an enigmatic sympathy; but Elric did not see the look she gave him, for his own eyes were full of crystal tears which flowed down his lean, white face and took his strength and will momentarily from him.

"I am a man possessed," he groaned, "and without this devil-blade I carry I would not be a man at all."

Two

They mounted their swift, black horses and spurred them with abandoned savagery down the hillside towards the marsh, their cloaks whipping behind them as the wind caught them, lashing them high into the air. Both rode with set, hard faces, refusing to acknowledge the aching uncertainty which lurked within them.

And the horses' hoofs had splashed into quaking bogland before they could halt.

Cursing, Elric tugged hard on his reins, pulling his horse back on to firm ground. Shaarilla, too, fought her own panicky stallion and guided the beast to the safety of the turf.

"How do we cross?" Elric asked her impatiently.

"There was a map—" Shaarilla began hesitantly.

"Where is it?"

"It—it was lost. I lost it. But I tried hard to memorize it. I think I'll be able to get us safely across."

"How did you lose it—and why didn't you tell me of this before?" Elric stormed.

"I'm sorry, Elric—but for a whole day, just before I found you in that tavern, my memory was gone. Somehow, I lived through a day without knowing it—and when I awoke, the map was missing."

Elric frowned. "There is some force working against us, I am sure," he muttered, "but what it is, I do not know." He raised his voice and said to her: "Let us hope that your memory is not too faulty, now. These marshes are infamous the world over, but by all accounts, only natural hazards wait for us." He grimaced and put his fingers around the hilt of his runesword. "Best go first, Shaarilla, but stay close. Lead the way."

She nodded, dumbly, and turned her horse's head towards the north, galloping along the bank until she came to a place where a great, tapering rock loomed. Here, a grassy path, four feet or so across, led out into the misty marsh. They could only see a little distance ahead, because of the clinging mist, but it seemed that the trail remained firm for some way. Shaarilla walked her horse on to the path and jolted forward at a slow trot, Elric following immediately behind her.

Through the swirling, heavy mist which shone whitely, the horses moved hesitantly and their riders had to keep them on short, tight rein. The mist padded the marsh with silence and the gleaming, watery fens around them stank with foul putrescence. No animal scurried, no bird shrieked above them. Everywhere was a haunting, fear-laden silence which made both horses and riders uneasy.

With panic in their throats, Elric and Shaarilla rode on, deeper and deeper into the unnatural Marshes of the Mist, their eyes wary and even their nostrils quivering for scent of danger in the stinking morass.

Hours later, when the sun was long past its zenith, Shaarilla's horse reared, screaming and whinnying. She shouted for Elric, her exquisite features twisted in fear as she stared into the mist. He spurred his own bucking horse forwards and joined her.

Something moved, slowly, menacingly in the clinging whiteness. Elric's right hand whipped over to his left side and grasped the hilt of Stormbringer.

The blade shrieked out of its scabbard, a black fire gleaming along its length and alien power flowing from it into Elric's arm and through his body. A weird, unholy light leapt into Elric's crimson eyes and his mouth was wrenched into a hideous grin as he forced the frightened horse further into the skulking mist.

"Arioch, Lord of the Seven Darks, be with me now!" Elric yelled as he made out the shifting shape ahead of him. It was white, like the mist, yet somehow *darker*. It stretched high above Elric's head. It was nearly ten feet tall and almost as broad. But it was still only an outline, seeming to have no face or limbs—only movement: darting, malevolent movement! But Arioch, his patron god, chose not to hear.

Elric could feel his horse's great heart beating between his legs as the beast plunged forward under its rider's iron control. Shaarilla was screaming something behind him, but he could not hear the words. Elric hacked at the white shape, but his sword met only mist and it howled angrily. The fear-crazed horse would go no further and Elric was forced to dismount.

"Keep hold of the steed," he shouted behind him to Shaarilla and moved on light feet towards the darting shape which hovered ahead of him, blocking his path.

Now he could make out some of its saliencies. Two eyes, the colour of thin, yellow wine, were set high in the thing's body, though it had no separate head. A mouthing, obscene slit, filled with fangs, lay just beneath the eyes. It had no nose or ears that Elric could see. Four appendages sprang from its upper parts and its lower body slithered along the ground, unsupported by any limbs. Elric's eyes ached as he looked at it. It was incredibly disgusting to behold and its amorphous body gave off a stench of death and decay. Fighting down his fear, the albino inched forward warily, his sword held high to parry any thrust the thing might make with its arms. Elric recognized it from a description in one of his grimoires. It was a Mist Giant—possibly the only Mist Giant, Bellbane. Even the wisest wizards were uncertain how many existed—one or many. It was a ghoul of the swamp-lands which fed off the souls and the blood of men and beasts. But the Marshes of this Mist were far to the east of Bellbane's reputed haunts.

Elric ceased to wonder why so few animals inhabited that stretch of the swamp. Overhead the sky was beginning to darken.

Stormbringer throbbed in Elric's grasp as he called the names of the ancient demon-gods of his people. The nauseous ghoul obviously recognized the names. For an instant, it wavered backwards. Elric made his legs move towards the thing. Now he saw that the ghoul was not white at all. But it had no colour to it that Elric could recognize. There was a suggestion of orangeness dashed with sickening greenish yellow, but he did not see the colours with his eyes—he only *sensed* the alien, unholy tinctures.

Then Elric rushed towards the thing, shouting the names which now had no meaning to his surface consciousness. "*Balaan—Marthim! Aesma! Alastor! Saebos! Verdelet! Nizilfkm! Haborym!* Haborym of the Fires Which Destroy!" His whole mind was torn in two. Part of him wanted to run, to hide, but he had no control over the power which now gripped him and pushed him to meet the horror. His sword blade hacked and slashed at the shape. It was like trying to cut through water—sentient, pulsating water. But Stormbringer had effect. The whole shape of the ghoul quivered as if in dreadful pain. Elric felt himself plucked into the air and his vision went. He could see nothing—do nothing but hack and cut at the thing which now held him.

Sweat poured from him as, blindly, he fought on.

Pain which was hardly physical—a deeper, horrifying pain, filled his being as he howled now in agony and struck continually at the yielding bulk which embraced him and was pulling him slowly towards its gaping maw. He struggled and writhed in the obscene grasp of the thing. With powerful arms, it was holding him, almost lasciviously, drawing him closer as a rough lover would draw a girl. Even the mighty power intrinsic in the runesword did not seem enough to kill the monster. Though its efforts were somewhat weaker than earlier, it still drew Elric nearer to the gnashing, slavering mouth-slit.

Elric cried the names again, while Stormbringer danced and sang an evil song in his right hand. In agony, Elric writhed, praying, begging and promising, but still he was drawn inch by inch towards the grinning maw.

Savagely, grimly, he fought and again he screamed for Arioch. A mind touched his—sardonic, powerful, evil—and he knew Arioch responded at last! Almost imperceptibly, the Mist Giant weakened. Elric pressed his advantage and the knowledge that the ghoul was losing its strength gave him more power. Blindly, agony piercing every nerve of his body, he struck and struck.

Then, quite suddenly, he was falling.

He seemed to fall for hours, slowly, weightlessly until he landed upon a surface which yielded beneath him. He began to sink.

Far off, beyond time and space, he heard a distant voice calling to him. He did not want to hear it; he was content to lie where he was as the cold, comforting stuff in which he lay dragged him slowly into itself.

Then, some sixth sense made him realize that it was Shaarilla's voice calling him and he forced himself to make sense out of her words.

"*Elric—the marsh! You're in the marsh. Don't move!*"

He smiled to himself. Why should he move? Down he was sinking, slowly, calmly—down into the welcoming marsh... *Had there been another time like this; another marsh?*

With a mental jolt, full awareness of the situation came back to him and he jerked his eyes open. Above him was mist. To one side a pool of unnamable colouring was slowly evaporating, giving off a foul odour. On the other side he could just make out a human form, gesticulating wildly. Beyond the human form were the barely discernible shapes of two horses. Shaarilla was there. Beneath him—

Beneath him was the marsh.

Thick, stinking slime was sucking him downwards as he lay spread-eagled upon it, half-submerged already. Stormbringer was still in his right hand. He could just see it if he turned his head. Carefully, he tried to lift the top half of his body from the sucking morass. He succeeded, only to feel his legs sink deeper. Sitting upright, he shouted to the girl.

"Shaarilla! Quickly—a rope!"

"There is no rope, Elric!" She was ripping off her top garment, frantically tearing it into strips.

Still Elric sank, his feet finding no purchase beneath them.

Shaarilla hastily knotted the strips of cloth. She flung the makeshift rope inexpertly towards the sinking albino. It fell short. Fumbling in her haste, she threw it again. This time his groping left hand found it. The girl began to haul on the fabric. Elric felt himself rise a little and then stop.

"It's no good, Elric—I haven't the strength."

Cursing her, Elric shouted: "The horse—tie it to the horse!"

She ran towards one of the horses and looped the cloth around the pommel of the saddle. Then she tugged at the beast's reins and began to walk it away.

Swiftly, Elric was dragged from the sucking bog and, still gripping Stormbringer, was pulled to the inadequate safety of the strip of turf.

Gasping, he tried to stand, but found his legs incredibly weak beneath him. He rose, staggered, and fell. Shaarilla knelt down beside him.

"Are you hurt?"

Elric smiled in spite of his weakness. "I don't think so."

"It was dreadful. I couldn't see properly what was happening. You seemed to disappear and then—then you screamed that—that name!" She was trembling, her face pale and taut.

"What name?" Elric was genuinely puzzled. "What name did I scream?"

She shook her head. "It doesn't matter—but whatever it was—it saved you. You reappeared soon afterwards and fell into the marsh..."

Stormbringer's power was still flowing into the albino. He already felt stronger.

With an effort, he got up and stumbled unsteadily towards his horse.

"I'm sure that the Mist Giant does not usually haunt this marsh—it was sent here. By what—or whom—I don't know, but we must get to firmer ground while we can."

Shaarilla said: "Which way—back or forward?"

Elric frowned. "Why, forward, of course. Why do you ask?"

She swallowed and shook her head. "Let's hurry, then," she said.

They mounted their horses and rode with little caution until the marsh and its cloak of mist was behind them.

Now the journey took on a new urgency as Elric realized that some force was attempting to put obstacles in their way. They rested little and savagely rode their powerful horses to a virtual standstill.

On the fifth day they were riding through barren, rocky country and a light rain was falling.

The hard ground was slippery so that they were forced to ride more slowly, huddled over the sodden necks of their horses, muffled in cloaks which only inadequately kept out the drizzling rain. They had ridden in silence for some time before they heard a ghastly cackling baying ahead of them and the rattle of hoofs.

Elric motioned towards a large rock looming to their right. "Shelter there," he said. "Something comes towards us—possibly more enemies. With luck, they'll pass us." Shaarilla mutely obeyed him and together they waited as the hideous baying grew nearer.

"One rider—several other beasts," Elric said, listening intently. "The beasts either follow or pursue the rider."

Then they were in sight—racing through the rain. A man frantically spurring an equally frightened horse—and behind him, the distance decreasing, a pack of what at first appeared to be dogs. But these were not dogs—they were half-dog and half-bird, with the lean, shaggy bodies and legs of dogs but possessing birdlike talons in place of paws and savagely curved beaks which snapped where muzzles should have been.

"The hunting dogs of the Dharzi!" gasped Shaarilla. "I thought that they, like their masters, were long extinct!"

"I, also," Elric said. "What are they doing in these parts? There was never contact between the Dharzi and the dwellers of this land."

"Brought here—by *something*," Shaarilla whispered. "Those devil-dogs will scent us to be sure."

Elric reached for his runesword. "Then we can lose nothing by aiding their quarry," he said, urging his mount forward. "Wait here, Shaarilla."

By this time, the devil-pack and the man they pursued were rushing past the sheltering rock, speeding down a narrow defile. Elric spurred his horse down the slope.

"Ho there!" he shouted to the frantic rider. "Turn and stand, my friend—I'm here to aid you!"

His moaning runesword lifted high, Elric thundered towards the snapping, howling devil-dogs and his horse's hoofs struck one with an impact which broke the unnatural beast's spine. There were some five or six of the weird dogs left. The rider turned his horse and drew a long sabre from a scabbard at his waist. He was a small man, with a broad ugly mouth. He grinned in relief.

"A lucky chance, this meeting, good master."

This was all he had time to remark before two of the dogs were leaping at him and he was forced to give his whole attention to defending himself from their slashing talons and snapping beaks.

The other three dogs concentrated their vicious attention upon Elric.

One leapt high, its beak aimed at Elric's throat. He felt foul breath on his face and hastily brought Stormbringer round in an arc which chopped the dog in two. Filthy blood spattered Elric and his horse and the scent of it seemed to increase the fury of the other dogs' attack. But the blood made the dancing black runesword sing an almost ecstatic tune and Elric felt it writhe in his grasp and stab at another of the hideous dogs. The point caught the beast just below its breastbone as it reared up at the albino. It screamed in terrible agony and turned its beak to seize the blade. As the beak connected with the lambent black metal of the sword, a foul stench, akin to the smell of burning, struck Elric's nostrils and the beast's scream broke off sharply.

Engaged with the remaining devil-dog, Elric caught a fleeting glimpse of the charred corpse. His horse was rearing high, lashing at the last alien animal with flailing hoofs. The dog avoided the horse's attack and came at Elric's unguarded left side. The albino swung in the saddle and brought his sword hurtling down to slice into the dog's skull and spill brains and blood on the wet and gleaming ground. Still somehow alive, the dog snapped feebly at Elric, but the Melnibonéan ignored its futile attack and turned his attention to the little man who had dispensed with one of his adversaries, but was having difficulty with the second. The dog had grasped the sabre with its beak, gripping the sword near the hilt.

Talons raked towards the little man's throat as he strove to shake the dog's grip. Elric charged forward, his runesword aimed like a lance to where the devil-dog dangled in mid-air, its talons slashing, trying to reach the flesh of its former quarry. Stormbringer caught the beast in its lower abdomen and ripped upwards, slitting the thing's underparts from crutch to throat. It released its hold on the small man's sabre and fell writhing to the ground. Elric's horse trampled it into the rocky ground. Breathing heavily, the albino sheathed Stormbringer and warily regarded the man he had saved. He disliked unnecessary contact with anyone and did not wish to be embarrassed by a display of emotion on the little man's part.

He was not disappointed, for the wide, ugly mouth split into a cheerful grin and the man bowed in the saddle as he returned his own curved blade to its scabbard.

"Thanks, good sir," he said lightly. "Without your help, the battle might have lasted longer. You deprived me of good sport, but you meant well. Moonglum is my name."

"Elric of Melniboné, I," replied the albino, but saw no reaction on the little man's face. This was strange, for the name of Elric was now infamous throughout most of the world. The story of his treachery and the slaying of his cousin Cymoril had been told and elaborated upon in taverns throughout the Young Kingdoms. Much as he hated it, he was used to receiving some indication of recognition from those he met. His albinism was enough to mark him.

Intrigued by Moonglum's ignorance, and feeling strangely drawn towards the cocky little rider, Elric studied him in an effort to discover from what land he came. Moonglum wore no armour and his clothes were of faded blue material, travel-stained and worn. A stout leather belt carried the sabre, a dirk and a woolen purse. Upon his feet, Moonglum wore ankle-length boots of cracked leather. His horse-furniture was much used but of obviously good quality. The man himself, seated high in the saddle, was barely more than five feet tall, with legs too long in proportion to the rest of his slight body. His nose was short and uptilted, beneath grey-green eyes, large and innocent-seeming. A mop of vivid red hair fell over his forehead and down his neck, unrestrained. He sat his horse comfortably, still grinning but looking now behind Elric to where Shaarilla rode to join them.

Moonglum bowed elaborately as the girl pulled her horse to a halt.

Elric said coldly, "The Lady Shaarilla—Master Moonglum of—?"

"Of Elwher," Moonglum supplied, "The mercantile capital of the East—the finest city in the world."

Elric recognized the name. "So you are from Elwher, Master Moonglum. I have heard of the place. A new city, is it not? Some few centuries old. You have ridden far."

"Indeed I have, sir. Without knowledge of the language used in these parts, the journey would have been harder, but luckily the slave who inspired me with tales of his homeland taught me the speech thoroughly."

"But why do you travel these parts—have you not heard the legends?" Shaarilla spoke incredulously.

"Those very legends were what brought me hence—and I'd begun to discount them, until those unpleasant pups set upon me. For what reason they decided to give chase, I will not know, for I gave them no cause to take a dislike to me. This is, indeed, a barbarous land."

Elric was uncomfortable. Light talk of the kind which Moonglum seemed to enjoy was contrary to his own brooding nature. But in spite of this, he found that he was liking the man more and more.

It was Moonglum who suggested that they travel together for a while. Shaarilla objected, giving Elric a warning glance, but he ignored it.

"Very well then, friend Moonglum, since three are stronger than two, we'd appreciate your company. We ride towards the mountains." Elric, himself, was feeling in a more cheerful mood.

"And what do you seek there?" Moonglum enquired.

"A secret," Elric said, and his new-found companion was discreet enough to drop the question.

Three

So they rode, while the rainfall increased and splashed and sang among the rocks with a sky like dull steel above them and the wind crooning a dirge about their ears. Three small figures riding swiftly towards the black mountain barrier which rose over the world like a brooding god. And perhaps it was a god that laughed sometimes as they neared the foothills of the range, or perhaps it was the wind whistling through the dark mystery of canyons and precipices and the tumble of basalt and granite which climbed towards lonely peaks. Thunder clouds formed around those peaks and lightning smashed downwards like a monster finger searching the earth for grubs. Thunder rattled over the range and Shaarilla spoke her thoughts at last to Elric; spoke them as the mountains came in sight.

"Elric—let us go back, I beg you. Forget the Book—there are too many forces working against us. Take heed of the signs, Elric, or we are doomed!"

But Elric was grimly silent, for he had long been aware that the girl was losing her enthusiasm for the quest she had started.

"Elric—please. We will never reach the Book. Elric, turn back."

She rode beside him, pulling at his garments until impatiently he shrugged himself clear of her grasp and said:

"I am intrigued too much to stop now. Either continue to lead the way—or tell me what you know and stay here. You desired to sample the Book's wisdom once—but now a few minor pitfalls on our journey have frightened you. What was it you needed to learn, Shaarilla?"

She did not answer him, but said instead: "And what was it you desired, Elric? Peace, you told me. Well, I warn you, you'll find no peace in those grim mountains—if we reach them at all."

"You have not been frank with me, Shaarilla," Elric said coldly, still looking ahead of him at the black peaks. "You know something of the forces seeking to stop us."

She shrugged. "It matters not—I know little. My father spoke a few vague warnings before he died, that is all."

"What did he say?"

"He said that He who guards the Book would use all his power to stop mankind from using its wisdom."

"What else?"

"Nothing else. But it is enough, now that I see that my father's warning was truly spoken. It was this guardian who killed him, Elric—or one of the guardian's minions. I do not wish to suffer that fate, in spite of what the Book might do for me. I had thought you powerful enough to aid me—but now I doubt it."

"I have protected you so far," Elric said simply. "Now tell me what you seek from the Book?"

"I am too ashamed."

Elric did not press the question, but eventually she spoke softly, almost whispering. "I sought my wings," she said.

"Your wings—you mean the Book might give you a spell so that you could grow wings!" Elric smiled ironically. "And that is why you seek the vessel of the world's mightiest wisdom!"

"If you were thought deformed in your own land—it would seem important enough to you," she shouted defiantly.

Elric turned his face towards her, his crimson-irised eyes burning with a strange emotion. He put a hand to his dead white skin and a crooked smile twisted his lips. "I, too, have felt as you do," he said quietly. That was all he said and Shaarilla dropped behind him again, shamed.

They rode on in silence until Moonglum, who had been riding discreetly ahead, cocked his overlarge skull on one side and suddenly drew rein.

Elric joined him. "What is it, Moonglum?"

"I hear horses coming this way," the little man said. "And voices which are disturbingly familiar. More of those devil-dogs, Elric—and this time accompanied by riders!"

Elric, too, heard the sounds, now, and shouted a warning to Shaarilla.

"Perhaps you were right," he called. "More trouble comes towards us."

"What now?" Moonglum said, frowning.

"Ride for the mountains," Elric replied, "and we may yet outdistance them."

They spurred their steeds into a fast gallop and sped towards the hills.

But their flight was hopeless. Soon a black pack was visible on the horizon and the sharp birdlike baying of the devil-dogs drew nearer. Elric stared backward at their pursuers. Night was beginning to fall, and visibility was decreasing with every passing moment but he had a vague impression of the riders who raced behind the pack. They were swathed in dark cloaks and carried long spears. Their faces were invisible, lost in the shadow of the hoods which covered their heads.

Now Elric and his companions were forcing their horses up a steep incline, seeking the shelter of the rocks which lay above.

"We'll halt here," Elric ordered, "and try to hold them off. In the open they could easily surround us."

Moonglum nodded affirmatively, agreeing with the good sense contained in Elric's words. They pulled their sweating steeds to a standstill and prepared to join battle with the howling pack and their dark-cloaked masters.

Soon the first of the devil-dogs were rushing up the incline, their beak-jaws slavering and their talons rattling on stone. Standing between two rocks, blocking the way between with their bodies, Elric and Moonglum met the first attack and quickly dispatched three of the animals. Several more took the place of the dead and the first of the riders was visible behind them as night crept closer.

"Arioch!" swore Elric, suddenly recognizing the riders. "These are the Lords of Dharzi—dead these ten centuries. We're fighting dead men, Moonglum, and the too-tangible ghosts of their dogs. Unless I can think of a sorcerous means to defeat them, we're doomed!"

The zombie-men appeared to have no intention of taking part in the attack for the moment. They waited, their dead eyes eerily luminous, as the devil-dogs attempted to break through the swinging network of steel with which Elric and his companion defended themselves. Elric was racking his brains—trying to dredge a spoken spell from his memory which would dismiss these living dead. Then it came to him, and hoping that the forces he had to invoke would decide to aid him, he began to chant:

> *"Let the Laws which govern all things*
> *Not so lightly be dismissed;*
> *Let the Ones who flaunt the Earth Kings*
> *With a fresher death be kissed."*

Nothing happened. "I've failed." Elric muttered hopelessly as he met the attack of a snapping devil-dog and spitted the thing on his sword.

But then—the ground rocked and seemed to *seethe* beneath the feet of the horses upon whose backs the dead men sat. The tremor lasted a few seconds and then subsided.

"The spell was not powerful enough," Elric sighed.

The earth trembled again and small craters formed in the ground of the hillside upon which the dead Lords of Dharzi impassively waited. Stones crumbled and the horses stamped nervously. Then the earth rumbled.

"Back!" yelled Elric warningly. "Back—or we'll go with them!" They retreated—backing towards Shaarilla and their waiting horses as the ground sagged beneath their feet. The Dharzi mounts were rearing and snorting and the remaining dogs turned nervously to regard their masters with puzzled, uncertain eyes. A low moan was coming from the lips of the living dead. Suddenly, a whole area of the surrounding hillside split into cracks, and yawning crannies appeared in the surface. Elric and his companions swung themselves on to their horses as, with a frightful multivoiced scream, the dead lords were swallowed by the earth, returning to the depths from which they had been summoned.

A deep unholy chuckle arose from the shattered pit. It was the mocking laughter of the earth elemental King Grome, taking his rightful subjects back into his keeping. Whining, the devil-dogs slunk towards the edge of the pit, sniffing around it. Then, with one accord, the black pack hurled itself down into the chasm, following its masters to whatever unholy doom awaited it.

Moonglum shuddered. "You are on familiar terms with the strangest people, friend Elric," he said shakily and turned his horse towards the mountains again.

⬅—✦—➡

They reached the black mountains on the following day and nervously Shaarilla led them along the rocky route she had memorized. She no longer pleaded with Elric to return—she was resigned to whatever fate awaited them. Elric's obsession was burning within him and he was filled with impatience—certain that he would find, at last, the ultimate truth of existence in the Dead Gods' Book. Moonglum was cheerfully skeptical, while Shaarilla was consumed with foreboding.

Rain still fell and the storm growled and crackled above them. But, as the driving rainfall increased with fresh insistence, they came, at last, to the black, gaping mouth of a huge cave.

"I can lead you no further," Shaarilla said wearily. "The Book lies somewhere beyond the entrance to this cave."

Elric and Moonglum looked uncertainly at one another, neither of them sure what move to make next. To have reached their goal seemed somehow anti-climactic—for nothing blocked the cave entrance—and nothing appeared to guard it.

"It is inconceivable," said Elric, "that the dangers which beset us were not engineered by something, yet here we are—and no-one seeks to stop us entering. Are you sure that this is the *right* cave, Shaarilla?"

The girl pointed upwards to the rock above the entrance. Engraved in it was a curious symbol which Elric instantly recognized.

"The sign of Chaos!" Elric exclaimed. "Perhaps I should have guessed."

"What does it mean, Elric?" Moonglum asked.

"That is the symbol of everlasting disruption and anarchy," Elric told him. "We are standing in territory presided over by the Lords of Entropy or one of their minions. So that is who our enemy is! This can only mean one thing—the Book is of extreme importance to the order of things on this plane—possibly all the myriad planes of the multiverse. It was why Arioch was reluctant to aid me—he, too, is a Lord of Chaos!"

Moonglum stared at him in puzzlement. "What do you mean, Elric?"

"Know you not that two forces govern the world—fighting an eternal battle?" Elric replied. "Law and Chaos. The upholders of Chaos state that in such a world as they rule, all things are possible. Opponents of Chaos—those who ally themselves with the forces of Law—say that without Law *nothing* material is possible.

"Some stand apart, believing that a balance between the two is the proper state of things, but we cannot. We have become embroiled in a dispute between the two forces. The Book is valuable to either faction, obviously, and I could guess that the minions of Entropy are worried what power we might release if we obtain this book. Law and Chaos rarely interfere directly in men's lives—that is why only adepts are fully aware of their presence. Now perhaps, I will discover at last the answer to the one question which concerns me—does an ultimate force rule over the opposing factions of Law and Chaos?"

Elric stepped through the cave entrance, peering into the gloom while the others hesitantly followed him.

"The cave stretches back a long way. All we can do is press on until we find its far wall," Elric said.

"Let's hope that its far wall lies not *downwards*," Moonglum said ironically as he motioned Elric to lead on.

They stumbled forward as the cave grew darker and darker. Their voices were magnified and hollow to their own ears as the floor of the cave slanted sharply down.

"This is no cave," Elric whispered, "it's a *tunnel*—but I cannot guess where it leads."

For several hours they pressed onwards in pitch darkness, clinging to one another as they reeled forward, uncertain of their footing and still aware that they were moving down a gradual incline. They lost all sense of time and Elric began to feel as if he were living through a dream. Events seemed to have become so unpredictable and beyond his control that he could no longer cope with thinking about them in ordinary terms. The tunnel was long and dark and wide and cold. It offered no comfort and the floor eventually became the only thing which had any reality. It was firmly beneath his feet. He began to feel that possibly he was not moving—that the floor, after all, was moving and he was remaining stationary. His companions clung to him but he was not aware of them. He was lost and his brain was numb. Sometimes he swayed and felt that he was on the edge of a precipice. Sometimes he fell and his groaning body met hard stone, disproving the proximity of the gulf down which he half-expected to fall.

All the while he made his legs perform walking motions, even though he was not at all sure whether he was actually moving forward. And time meant nothing—became a meaningless concept with relation to nothing.

Until, at last, he was aware of a faint, blue glow ahead of him and he knew that he had been moving forward. He began to run down the incline, but found that he was going too fast and had to check his speed.

There was a scent of alien strangeness in the cool air of the cave tunnel and fear was a fluid force which surged over him, something separate from himself.

The others obviously felt it, too, for though they said nothing, Elric could sense it. Slowly they moved downward, drawn like automatons towards the pale blue glow below them.

And then they were out of the tunnel, staring awe-struck at the unearthly vision which confronted them. Above them, the very air seemed of the strange blue colour which had originally attracted them. They were standing on a jutting slab of rock and, although it was still somehow *dark*, the eerie blue glow illuminated a stretch of glinting silver beach beneath them. And the beach was lapped by a surging dark sea which moved restlessly like a liquid giant in disturbed slumber. Scattered along the silver beach were the dim shapes of wrecks—the bones of peculiarly designed boats, each of a different pattern from the rest. The sea surged away into darkness and there was no horizon—only blackness. Behind them, they could see a sheer cliff which was also lost in darkness beyond a certain point. And it was cold—bitterly cold, with an unbelievable sharpness. For though the sea threshed beneath them, there was no dampness in the air—no smell of salt. It was a bleak and awesome sight and, apart from the sea, they were the only things that moved—the only things to make sound, for the sea was horribly silent in its restless movement.

"What now, Elric?" whispered Moonglum, shivering.

Elric shook his head and they continued to stand there for a long time until the albino—his white face and hands ghastly in the alien light said: "Since it is impracticable to return—we shall venture over the sea."

His voice was hollow and he spoke as one who was unaware of his words.

Steps, cut into the living rock, led down towards the beach and now Elric began to descend them. Staring around them, their eyes lit by a terrible fascination, the others allowed him to lead them.

Four

Their feet profaned the silence as they reached the silver beach of crystalline stones and crunched across it. Elric's crimson eyes fixed upon one of the objects littering the beach and he smiled. He shook his head savagely from side to side, as if to clear it. Trembling, he pointed to one of the boats, and the pair saw that it was intact, unlike the others. It was yellow and red—vulgarly gay in this environment and nearing it they observed that it was made of wood, yet unlike any wood they had seen. Moonglum ran his stubby fingers along its length.

"Hard as iron," he breathed. "No wonder it has not rotted as the others have." He peered inside and shuddered. "Well, the owner won't argue if we take it," he said wryly.

Elric and Shaarilla understood him when they saw the unnaturally twisted skeleton which lay at the bottom of the boat. Elric reached inside and pulled the thing out, hurling it on the stones. It rattled and rolled over the gleaming shingle, disintegrating as it did so, scattering bones over a wide area. The skull came to rest by the edge of the beach, seeming to stare sightlessly out over the disturbing ocean.

As Elric and Moonglum strove to push and pull the boat down the beach towards the sea, Shaarilla moved ahead of them and squatted down, putting her hand into the wetness. She stood up sharply, shaking the stuff from her hand.

"This is not water as I know it," she said. They heard her, but said nothing.

"We'll need a sail," Elric murmured. The cold breeze was moving out over the ocean. "A cloak should serve." He stripped off his cloak and knotted it to the mast of the vessel. "Two of us will have to hold this at either edge," he said. "That way we'll have some slight control over the direction the boat takes. It's makeshift—but the best we can manage."

They shoved off, taking care not to get their feet in the sea.

The wind caught the sail and pushed the boat out over the ocean, moving at a faster pace than Elric had at first reckoned. The boat began to hurtle forward as if possessed of its own volition and Elric's and

Moonglum's muscles ached as they clung to the bottom ends of the sail.

Soon the silver beach was out of sight and they could see little—the pale blue light above them scarcely penetrating the blackness. It was then that they heard the dry flap of wings over their heads and looked up.

Silently descending were three massive apelike creatures, borne on great leathery wings. Shaarilla recognized them and gasped.

"Clakars!"

Moonglum shrugged as he hurriedly drew his sword—"A name only—what are they?" But he received no answer for the leading winged ape descended with a rush, mouthing and gibbering, showing long fangs in a slavering snout. Moonglum dropped his portion of the sail and slashed at the beast but it veered away, its huge wings beating, and sailed upwards again.

Elric unsheathed Stormbringer—and was astounded. The blade remained silent, its familiar howl of glee muted. The blade shuddered in his hand and instead of the rush of power which usually flowed up his arm, he felt only a slight tingling. He was panic-stricken for a moment—without the sword, he would soon lose all vitality. Grimly fighting down his fear, he used the sword to protect himself from the rushing attack of one of the winged apes.

The ape gripped the blade, bowling Elric over, but it yelled in pain as the blade cut through one knotted hand, severing fingers which lay twitching and bloody on the narrow deck. Elric held tight to the side of the boat and hauled himself upright once more. Shrilling its agony, the winged ape attacked again, but this time with more caution. Elric summoned all his strength and swung the heavy sword in a two-handed grip, ripping off one of the leathery wings so that the mutilated beast flopped about the deck. Judging the place where its heart should be, Elric drove the blade in under the breast-bone. The ape's movements subsided.

Moonglum was lashing wildly at two of the winged apes which were attacking him from both sides. He was down on one knee, vainly hacking at random. He had opened up the whole side of a beast's head but, though in pain, it still came at him. Elric hurled Stormbringer through the darkness and it struck the wounded beast in the throat, point first. The ape clutched with clawing fingers at the steel and fell overboard.

Its corpse floated on the liquid but slowly began to sink. Elric grabbed with frantic fingers at the hilt of his sword, reaching far over the side of the boat. Incredibly, the blade was sinking with the beast; knowing Stormbringer's properties as he did, Elric was amazed. Now it was being dragged beneath the surface as any ordinary blade would be dragged. He gripped the hilt and hauled the sword out of the winged ape's carcass.

His strength was seeping swiftly from him. It was incredible. What alien laws governed this cavern world? He could not guess—and all he was concerned with was regaining his waning strength. Without the runesword's power, that was impossible!

Moonglum's curved blade had disemboweled the remaining beast and the little man was busily tossing the dead thing over the side. He turned, grinning triumphantly, to Elric.

"A good fight," he said.

Elric shook his head. "We must cross this sea speedily," he replied, "else we're lost—finished. My power is gone."

"How? Why?"

"I know not—unless the forces of Entropy rule more strongly here. Make haste—there is no time for speculation."

Moonglum's eyes were disturbed. He could do nothing but act as Elric said.

Elric was trembling in his weakness, holding the billowing sail with draining strength. Shaarilla moved to help him, her thin hands close to his, her deep-set eyes bright with sympathy.

"What *were* those things?" Moonglum gasped, his teeth naked and white beneath his back-drawn lips, his breath coming short.

"Clakars," Shaarilla replied. "They are the primeval ancestors of my people, older in origin than recorded time. My people are thought the oldest inhabitants of this planet."

"Whoever seeks to stop us in this quest of yours had best find some— original means." Moonglum grinned. "The old methods don't work." But the other two did not smile, for Elric was half-fainting and the woman was concerned only with his plight. Moonglum shrugged, staring ahead.

When he spoke again, sometime later, his voice was excited. "We're nearing land!"

Land it was, and they were traveling fast towards it. Too fast. Elric heaved himself upright and spoke heavily and with difficulty. "Drop the sail!" Moonglum obeyed him. The boat sped on, struck another stretch of silver beach and ground up it, the prow ploughing a dark scar through the glinting shingle. It stopped suddenly, tilting violently to one side so that the three were tumbled against the boat's rail.

Shaarilla and Moonglum pulled themselves upright and dragged the limp and nerveless albino on to the beach. Carrying him between them, they struggled up the beach until the crystalline shingle gave way to thick, fluffy moss, padding their footfalls. They laid the albino down and stared at him worriedly, uncertain of their next actions.

Elric strained to rise, but was unable to do so. "Give me time," he gasped. "I won't die—but already my eyesight is fading. I can only hope that the blade's power will return on dry land."

With a mighty effort, he pulled Stormbringer from its scabbard and he smiled in relief as the evil runesword moaned faintly and then, slowly, its song increased in power as black flame flickered along its length. Already the power was flowing into Elric's body, giving him renewed vitality. But even as strength returned, Elric's crimson eyes flared with terrible misery.

"Without this black blade," he groaned, "I am nothing, as you see. But what is it making of me? Am I to be bound to it for ever?"

The others did not answer him and they were both moved by an emotion they could not define—an emotion blended of fear, hate and pity—linked with something else...

Eventually, Elric rose, trembling, and silently led them up the mossy hillside towards a more natural light which filtered from above. They could see that it came from a wide chimney, leading apparently to the upper air. By means of the light, they could soon make out a dark, irregular shape which towered in the shadow of the gap.

As they neared the shape, they saw that it was a castle of black stone—a sprawling pile covered with dark green crawling lichen which curled over its ancient bulk with an almost sentient protectiveness. Towers appeared to spring at random from it and it covered a vast area. There seemed to be no windows in any part of it and the only orifice was a rearing doorway blocked by thick bars of a metal which glowed with dull redness, but without heat. Above this gate, in flaring amber, was the sign of the Lords of Entropy, representing eight arrows radiating from a central hub in all directions. It appeared to hang in the air without touching the black, lichen-covered stone.

"I think our quest ends here," Elric said grimly. "Here, or nowhere."

"Before I go further, Elric, I'd like to know what it is you seek," Moonglum murmured. "I think I've earned the right."

"A book," Elric said carelessly. "The Dead Gods' Book. It lies within those castle walls—of that I'm certain. We have reached the end of our journey."

Moonglum shrugged. "I might not have asked," he smiled, "for all your words mean to me. I hope that I will be allowed some small share of whatever treasure it represents."

Elric grinned, in spite of the coldness which gripped his bowels, but he did not answer Moonglum.

"We need to enter the castle, first," he said instead.

As if the gates had heard him, the metal bars flared to a pale green and then their glow faded back to red and finally dulled into non-existence. The entrance was unbarred and their way apparently clear.

"I like not *that*," growled Moonglum. "Too easy. A trap awaits us—are we to spring it at the pleasure of whoever dwells within the castle confines?"

"What else can we do?" Elric spoke quietly.

"Go back—or forward. Avoid the castle—do not tempt He who guards the Book!" Shaarilla was gripping the albino's right arm, her whole face moving with fear, her eyes pleading. "Forget the Book, Elric!"

"*Now?*" Elric laughed humourlessly. "Now—after this journey? No, Shaarilla, not when the truth is so close. Better to die than never to have tried to secure the wisdom in the Book when it lies so near."

Shaarilla's clutching fingers relaxed their grip and her shoulders slumped in hopelessness. "We cannot do battle with the minions of Entropy..."

"Perhaps we will not have to." Elric did not believe his own words but his mouth was twisted with some dark emotion, intense and terrible. Moonglum glanced at Shaarilla.

"Shaarilla is right," he said with conviction. "You'll find nothing but bitterness, possibly death, inside those castle walls. Let us, instead, climb yonder steps and attempt to reach the surface." He pointed to some twisting steps which led towards the yawning rent in the cavern roof.

Elric shook his head. "No. You go if you like."

Moonglum grimaced in perplexity. "You're a stubborn one, friend Elric. Well, if it's all or nothing—then I'm with you. But personally, I have always preferred compromise."

Elric began to walk slowly forward towards the dark entrance of the bleak and towering castle.

In a wide, shadowy courtyard a tall figure, wreathed in scarlet fire, stood awaiting them.

Elric marched on, passing the gateway. Moonglum and Shaarilla nervously followed.

Gusty laughter roared from the mouth of the giant and the scarlet fire fluttered about him. He was naked and unarmed, but the power which flowed from him almost forced the three back. His skin was scaly and of smoky purple colouring. His massive body was alive with rippling muscle as he rested lightly on the balls of his feet. His skull was long, slanting sharply backwards at the forehead and his eyes were like slivers of blue steel, showing no pupil. His whole body shook with mighty, malicious joy.

"*Greetings to you, Lord Elric of Melniboné—I congratulate you for your remarkable tenacity!*"

"Who are you?" Elric growled, his hand on his sword.

"*My name is Orunlu the Keeper and this is a stronghold of the Lords of Entropy.*" The giant smiled cynically. "*You need not finger your puny blade so nervously, for you should know that I cannot harm you now. I gained power to remain in your realm only by making a vow.*"

Elric's voice betrayed his mounting excitement. "You cannot stop us?"

"*I do not dare to—since my oblique efforts have failed. But your foolish endeavours perplex me somewhat, I'll admit. The Book is of importance to us—but what can it mean to you? I have guarded it for three hundred centuries and have never been curious enough to seek to discover why my Masters place so much importance upon it—why they bothered to rescue it on*" *its sunward course and incarcerate it on this boring ball of earth populated by the capering, briefly lived clowns called Men.*"

"I seek in it the Truth," Elric said guardedly.

"*There is no Truth but that of Eternal struggle,*" the scarlet-flamed giant said with conviction.

"What rules above the forces of Law and Chaos?" Elric asked. "What controls your destinies as it controls mine?"

The giant frowned.

"*That question, I cannot answer. I do not know. There is only the Balance.*"

"Then perhaps the Book will tell us who holds it." Elric said purposely. "Let me pass—tell me where it lies."

The giant moved back, smiling ironically. "*It lies in a small chamber in the central tower. I have sworn never to venture there, otherwise I might even lead the way. Go if you like—my duty is over.*"

Elric, Moonglum and Shaarilla stepped towards the entrance of the castle, but before they entered, the giant spoke warningly from behind them.

"*I have been told that the knowledge contained in the Book could swing the balance on the side of the forces of Law. This disturbs me—but, it appears, there is another possibility which disturbs me even more.*"

"What is that?" Elric said.

"*It could create such a tremendous impact on the multiverse that complete entropy would result. My Masters do not desire that—for it could mean the destruction of all matter in the end. We exist only to fight—not to win, but to preserve the eternal struggle.*"

"I care not," Elric told him. "I have little to lose, Orunlu the Keeper."

"*Then go.*" The giant strode across the courtyard into blackness.

Inside the tower, light of a pale quality illuminated winding steps leading upwards. Elric began to climb them in silence, moved by his own doom-filled purpose. Hesitantly, Moonglum and Shaarilla followed in his path, their faces set in hopeless acceptance.

On and upward the steps mounted, twisting tortuously towards their goal, until at last they came to the chamber, full of blinding light, many-coloured and scintillating, which did not penetrate outwards at all but remained confined to the room which housed it.

Blinking, shielding his red eyes with his arm, Elric pressed forward and, through slitted pupils, saw the source of the light lying on a small stone dais in the centre of the room.

Equally troubled by the bright light, Shaarilla and Moonglum followed him into the room and stood in awe at what they saw.

It was a huge book—the Dead Gods' Book, its covers encrusted with alien gems from which the light sprang. It gleamed, it *throbbed* with light and brilliant colour.

"At last," Elric breathed. "At last—the Truth!"

He stumbled forward like a man made stupid with drink, his pale hands reaching for the thing he had sought with such savage bitterness. His hands touched the pulsating cover of the Book and, trembling, turned it back.

"Now, I shall learn," he said, half-gloatingly.

With a crash, the cover fell to the floor, sending the bright gems skipping and dancing over the paving stones.

Beneath Elric's twitching hands lay nothing but a pile of yellowish dust.

"No!" His scream was anguished, unbelieving. "No!" Tears flowed down his contorted face as he ran his hands through the fine dust. With a groan which racked his whole being, he fell forward, his face hitting the disintegrated parchment. Time had destroyed the Book—untouched, possibly forgotten, for three hundred centuries. Even the wise and powerful gods who had created it had perished—and now its knowledge followed them into oblivion.

They stood on the slopes of the high mountain, staring down into the green valleys below them. The sun shone and the sky was clear and blue. Behind them lay the gaping hole which led into the stronghold of the Lords of Entropy.

Elric looked with sad eyes across the world and his head was lowered beneath a weight of weariness and dark despair. He had not spoken since his companions had dragged him sobbing from the chamber of the Book. Now he raised his pale face and spoke in a voice tinged with self-mockery, sharp with bitterness—a lonely voice: the calling of hungry seabirds circling cold skies above bleak shores.

"Now," he said, "I will live my life without ever knowing why I live it—whether it has purpose or not. Perhaps the Book could have told me. But would I have believed it, even then? I am the eternal skeptic—never *sure* that my actions are my own, never certain that an ultimate entity is not guiding me.

"I envy those who know. All I can do now is to continue my quest and hope, without hope, that before my span is ended, the truth will be presented to me."

Shaarilla took his limp hands in hers and her eyes were wet.

"Elric—let me comfort you."

The albino sneered bitterly. "Would that we'd never met, Shaarilla of the Dancing Mist. For a while, you gave me hope—I had thought to be at last at peace with myself. But, because of you, I am left more hopeless than before. There is no salvation in this world—only malevolent doom. Goodbye."

He took his hands away from her grasp and set off down the mountainside.

Moonglum darted a glance at Shaarilla and then at Elric. He took something from his purse and put it in the girl's hand.

"Good luck," he said, and then he was running after Elric until he caught him up.

Still striding, Elric turned at Moonglum's approach and despite his brooding misery said: "What is it, friend Moonglum? Why do you follow me?"

"I've followed you thus far, Master Elric, and I see no reason to stop," grinned the little man. "Besides, unlike yourself, I'm a materialist. We'll need to eat, you know."

Elric frowned, feeling a warmth growing within him. "What do you mean, Moonglum?"

Moonglum chuckled. "I take advantage of situations of any kind, where

I may," he answered. He reached into his purse and displayed something on his outstretched hand which shone with a dazzling brilliancy. It was one of the jewels from the cover of the Book. "There are more in my purse," he said, "And each one worth a fortune." He took Elric's arm.

"Come Elric—what new lands shall we visit so that we may change these baubles into wine and pleasant company?"

Behind them, standing stock still on the hillside, Shaarilla stared miserably after them until they were no longer visible. The jewel Moonglum had given her dropped from her fingers and fell, bouncing and bright, until it was lost amongst the heather. Then she turned—and the dark mouth of the cavern yawned before her.

Mother of All Russiya

Melanie Rawn

Melanie Rawn *received a B.A. in history from Scripps College and worked as a teacher and editor before becoming a full-time writer. Her work includes the Dragon Prince and Dragon Star trilogies, as well as the Exiles and Spellbinder series. Her latest novel,* Touchstone, *is the first in a new fantasy series. She lives in Flagstaff, Arizona.*

Kyiv, 946

SHE PACED THE STONES, her feet separated from the chill by sable-lined slippers. She was cold despite them, cold from her toes to her crown. Perhaps it was the vengeance of the fire, that she had not joined her husband in its embrace. Long ago, he had decided that he wished to be immolated in the manner of their ancestors. The Christ-folk had gawked and fled, horrified by what they saw as desecration to the body, but when Yvor's corpse was at last returned to her by the treacherous vassals who had killed him, she had done as he had asked. Better, yes, to send a soul instantly unto the gods, rather than bury the flesh in the ground for the worms to feed upon.

She could think of many Drevlianian souls she would see denied the flames and devoured by worms. They were the souls of murderers who had taken a father from his son, a prince from his people.

A husband from his wife...no, for that she cared not at all.

As she passed through the stone corridors, she was vaguely aware of the slaves and warriors and *druzhina*, her personal attendants, all bowing to her, their Grand Princess. So empty, the obeisances; meant for the woman others had made of her. Daughter of one Grand Prince, wife—widow now—of another, mother of yet a third. *A boy of five*, she thought, her frozen fingers twisting around each other as she walked unseeingly through her dead husband's stronghold on her way to she knew not where.

A boy of five. She had been twice his age when her father died and Yvor took dead Helgi's golden earring and golden daughter for his own. They had the jewels now, her husband's killers: two huge white lumps of pearl and a clot of blood-crimson ruby, the earring handed down since her people had come from the Dane-land to rule over the fractious Rus. The pearls: Tears of Freya. The ruby: a drop of Woden's Blood. These sanctified the Grand Princes of Kyiv. The Drevlianians had sent back Yvor's body but kept his symbol of power. Soon they would have more than the symbol. Those who had killed her husband would choose who would next wear the Tears and the Blood. It would not be her son.

Or perhaps it *would* be a son of her body—though certainly not the little boy now playing safely in his chamber. She was no longer young, but she was not yet too old for bearing. And suddenly through the frozen numbness of her fear there came fire's heat. She would sink her father's dagger into her own heart before any of the assassins took her to his bed to seed her body with a Grand Prince of Kyiv. Her son, her Sviatoslav, *was* the Grand Prince.

But they had the jewels. They would soon have her. Unless—

Grand Princess Olga swore loudly and violently, in words that would have made her father roar with laughter.

"Ah, I perceive you have awakened," murmured a soft, oddly cadenced voice.

Awakened, most certainly; she looked around and found she was in her own chambers, with no idea how she had arrived there. A fire blazed in the hearth, thick carpets softened her steps on the stone floor, and patterned woolen weavings flung bright colors across the walls. She strode to the bed and flung her sable cloak upon it, casting a sideways glance at the strange little man who had spoken from the shadows.

After all these years she was still unused to the angle of his eyes and the odd duskiness of his skin. In his youth, in his homeland, had this wizened creature been deemed handsome? Perhaps. She had no way of knowing if all the peoples of Serica looked like Master Cheng. She only felt his strangeness, down to her blood and bones. He was the only man allowed solitary speech with her—but only because he was not wholly a man.

"What do you recommend?" she asked bitterly. "They intend that before the summer I shall be either dead or wedded and bedded."

"This is undoubtedly in their minds, Most Gracious One." He preened himself like a tidy little bird, smoothing the heavily embroidered silk of his sleeves. His only concession to the climate was the sable lining of his boots.

"And?" she asked impatiently. She hated him when he breathed his cleverness at her.

"They will come. You know they will come. And you must be ready for them. May this unworthy one suggest...?"

She swore again in her own language, then returned to the Greek that was the only tongue she and the sage shared. "Tell me!"

"They deserve to die for what they have done. They know it. They will expect you to—"

"—to huddle in my bed, weeping and wailing, frightened and helpless—" She began to pace again, knowing how close she had come to doing exactly those things. Forever. "So I must do as they will *not* expect, Cheng. That is what you mean, yes? They will come as conquerors, and as men guilty of murder, to claim their prize—me." She choked to say the words, but knew they must be said. "And I am compelled to welcome them as honored and honorable guests."

"Excellent." Thin lips stretched in a smile. "A large feast is poor nourishment for suspicion."

She paused in her restless stalking about the carpeted room. Cold again; she felt so cold. Feasting put her in mind of—"Poison?" she enquired sharply. "So that they all die at the same time, and only they die? Or do you suggest I sacrifice a few spare members of my *druzhina* to make it all look reasonable? As if such a thing *could* look reasonable! I am not a fool, Cheng."

"No, Most High," he agreed. "Poison is a woman's weapon, in any case." A musing smile crossed his face. "Have I ever shared with you the tale of Livia, Empress of Rome, who—"

She interrupted impatiently. "Another time. But if in your learnings of history there is example for me to follow, tell me at once."

"Your situation is not unique—though you yourself are most certainly so. As I say, poison is a woman's weapon. Something they will expect. They will have guards, so the weapon cannot be a man's weapon of blade or cudgel, either. And all must die at the same time, in such a fashion as—"

"—as to encourage belief that it was an accident. Yes, I see. But how?"

He said nothing. He merely watched her, waiting for her to be clever.

"The weapon of neither woman nor man," she said slowly, "but of one who is neither."

Master Cheng bowed low. "Your husband, may your gods grant him glory, forbade my magic."

"Perhaps if he hadn't, he might have lived longer," she snapped. "But Yvor had greater faith in his own strength." Yvor, of course, had been a fool. She shrugged. "I will have you use your magic, then. By the snake that killed my father, I swear—" And she broke off, only to repeat more softly, "Snake." Memory took her back to that horrible day of her childhood, when her nurse had told her that her father was dead. Tall, golden, magnificent Grand Prince Helgi, who had hung his shield on the gates of mighty Mikligardur, who was clever and invincible, had been bitten by a deadly snake.

A soothsayer had told Helgi many years earlier that a certain horse would be the cause of his death. He had known instantly which horse the man had in mind. The stallion was a noble animal, fine in form and regal in manner, and Helgi loved him—so much that he could not order him killed. Instead, he commanded that the horse be properly fed and looked after, but never led into his presence. Occasionally, though, he would be out walking, or riding another horse, and glimpse the stallion at a distance, and after a few moments' sorrowful gazing would turn and move swiftly away. But eventually, after living many years and siring many foals almost—but not quite—as splendid as he, the horse died. Upon Helgi's return from another victory in battle, he went to the place where the skull and bare bones lay. He walked about in great distress, regretting the magnificent stallion, and by accident his boot crunched the whitened skull. It so happened that the skull lay atop the entrance to a snake's lair. The snake crawled forth from underground and sank its fangs into his flesh. And Helgi died.

Olga remembered imagining the snake in its lair deep in the earth, slithering out to strike down a noble prince. She had for years afterward dreamed of snakes, and been unable to enter the homes of any of her people: the wood dwellings were built above pits twice a man's height, and she was sure snakes waited there to kill her. Gradually she had conquered her dread of visiting her people's houses, but she had never overcome her terror of snakes.

Yet as she thought of the dreams, and of the houses, all at once she smiled. "Make me a magic, Master Cheng of Serica, as lethal and as cunning as a snake," she murmured almost sweetly. "The Drevlianians will come here, and die."

He looked puzzled—him, the great sage from the silk-lands where all other countries were sneered at and all other peoples were considered savages. She laughed softly, pleased that she had finally managed to out-think him.

"The history of the land that has become our land," said her father, "begins with three brothers and a sister."

"What was her name?" she asked. "Was it Olga, like me?"

"No, but that's no reason not to listen." He softened the reproof with a smile. He always did; he was always gentle with her, this fierce and fearsome warrior. She was ferociously proud of him, and of herself for being the only one who ever saw that particular smile.

"The first brother's name was Kyi, the second was Shchek, and the third was Khoriv." Her father paused, arching one heavy blond brow. She knew from his look that he was expecting, not another interruption, but instead some sign that she recognized the names. She did not. She hated it when she disappointed him. "And their sister, who was very beautiful—as all sisters in such tales must be—was named Lybyd. Their parents and all their folk had been killed by invaders from the East, and they were seeking a new place to live, safe from war."

Olga could not help but frown. Lybyd's desire to escape, she could understand; it was not a woman's business to make war. But war was the thing that all men who were true men lived for, the only way a man became rich and great and powerful. Her father was a perfect example. Yet here he was, telling her a story about three brothers who did not want to go to war—not even for vengeance against those who had murdered their parents and kindred.

"They came upon a beautiful river, and on its western banks saw seven green hills, lush with *kashtan* trees and carpeted with flowers. Kyi, Shchek, and Khoriv made for themselves a boat to cross the great river. Lybyd waited on the eastern shore, anxious for her brothers' safety. And what do you think happened? I'll tell you what happened. The boat—for it was not a mighty longship like ours, but a boat smaller than a *lodya*—it was caught in dangerous rapids. The three brothers fought bravely against the currents as water foamed all around them. What they did not know was that within the river lived spirits who enjoyed more than anything else playing with whatever boat might dare to cross. And because the local people knew of them, and avoided the river, they had not had anything to play with in a long, long time. These spirits were called Vesuppi, who warns the traveler 'do not sleep,' and Gjallandi, who warns by loudly ringing, and Eiforr ever-fierce, and Hlaejandi, who is always laughing— or maybe that spirit's name was Leandi who is always seething—"

"I think there must have been two of them—one laughing while the other seethed. Just like when Heirleif sees Ylwa talking to another man, and she giggles when he looks all daggery at her!"

"Entirely possible. And I am glad to know that even at your little age you can recognize a look that flashes daggers." Her father nodded his approval, and she glowed from the inside out. She could feel it, warmer than sables, brighter than summer sunlight. It was a vast thing, to have this man's praise.

"Where was I? Ah, yes. The three brothers in their little boat were tossed from one to the other like the toys the spirits considered them to be. Lybyd, back on shore, loudly wailed, sure that her brothers would be lost to her forever. But Kyi and Shchek and Khoriv fought back, for to them their lives were not toys to be played with by river spirits. Shchek and Khoriv wielded their oars as weapons, and though they were brave and strong, after a time they began to tire. Kyi struggled with the tiller, steering as best he could while his brothers battled the river spirits. He knew that if he let go, the little boat would veer even more madly and they would certainly all be killed. Finally, seeing that his brothers were exhausted, Kyi summoned the last of his strength and was able to swerve the boat away from the river spirits. It fetched up onto shore, and the three brothers dragged themselves out and onto dry land—soaked to the skin, tired unto death, but alive."

She waited, knowing there must be more, but at length could contain herself no longer. "What about Lybyd?"

"They called to her from the western bank of the river, and she left off her fear and weeping and called back joyously."

"But—how did she get across?"

"Because the three brothers had fought so long and valiantly, the river spirits were tired and so the waters were quiet. They went back across, picked up Lybyd, and soon all were safe on the western shore."

"But didn't she do anything? She only wept and waited for them to come back, and didn't *do* anything?"

"What was there to be done?"

Olga twisted her mouth to one side so her front teeth could chew on the inside of her cheek. It was a deplorable habit, according to her nurse, but it helped her to think. Once or twice she had gnawed hard enough to taste blood. "I don't know—she could have made another boat, couldn't she? If the river spirits were tired, then she could have gone across on her own."

"So it's your belief that there is always something to be done?" her father asked, grinning widely. "I believe the same! I have yet to encounter circumstances where there was absolutely nothing to be done. And I hope I never do!" He laughed his sharp, loud laugh and swung her up off his knees, holding her high in the air with his big hands strong and gentle around her shoulder bones. Olga giggled, and grabbed at the ends of her long golden braids to tickle her father's cheeks and nose. It was an old game with them, going back to her earliest memories, before her mother had died. He shook his head and twitched his face around in terrible contortions, which only made her laugh harder.

At length, exhausted with laughing, she settled back into his lap and asked, "What happened to the brothers—and their sister who didn't do anything?"

Another burst of laughter told her she had chosen exactly the right thing to say. "You don't approve of Lybyd, do you? I think that *you* would not weep and wail on the riverbank. As for Lybyd, she and Kyi and Shchek and Khoriv made a great city on the banks of the river. A smaller river that ran through the city was named for her. Each of the brothers chose a hill to live on, and so named them Shchekovitza, Khorivitza, and—ah, I see you have guessed!"

"The whole city was named for Kyi! Are you going there? Are you going to Kyiv? Will you take me with you?"

"One day. One day. For now, you must stay here at home in Novgorod, attend to your lessons, and be very good, for there is a place waiting for you in Kyiv, and to take it with honor you must become accomplished and wise." He kissed her forehead in blessing, and set her onto her feet. "And I do not think you will cower on the shore and wait to be rescued, the way Lybyd did."

Five years later, she took the place her father had promised.

She made the long journey from Novgorod to Kyiv in winter—for to travel at any other time was to risk becoming hopelessly mired in mud on roads that barely existed; the ice and snow stayed solid beneath the hooves of the horses and the runners of the sleighs. She went to Kyiv and married Yvor, grandson of the great Rurik, and if it had been many,

many years before she gave Yvor a son, it was the fault of Yvor and no one else. Had he spent more time in Kyiv instead of progressing through the tributary lands; had he stayed to rule instead of venturing out to battle the Pechenegs, the Khazars, the Greeks, the Drevlianians...

And, of course, if he had not beaten her bloody many, many times for being the daughter of a greater warrior than he, perhaps she would have borne more sons.

There was only the one little boy. Five years old. And the Drevlianians would kill him.

They came to Kyiv, the triumphant Drevlianians, but only twenty of them. She hid her furious disappointment and received them in the great hall. They were uneasy with the stone all around them—they who lived within wood and wattle, with packed dirt for flooring. Yet they understood the wealth that all this stone implied.

With great ceremony, they gave her the Tears and the Blood. She was surprised by this, and allowed it to show. She had expected one of them to be wearing the earring. Yet it seemed they had something else in mind.

"The Grand Prince Yvor," one of them said, their warchief, his darkness suiting the rain-clogged day as her own golden fairness did not, "while a great man in some ways, was unwise. This year he came as he always came each year to our city of Iskorosten. We presented him with our tribute. He demanded double. We spoke among ourselves, and decided thus: If a wolf comes among the sheep, he will take away the whole flock one by one, unless he be killed."

He paused, as if waiting for her to say something. To acknowledge his tribe's cumulative wisdom in murdering their Grand Prince, perhaps? She clamped her jaws shut over exclamations of outrage as he reviewed the events that had brought them all here. One did not shout at someone who merely told the truth, insulting as that truth might be. She kept her gaze on the sprays of flowers thickly embroidered on her silk-covered sleeve, and resisted the impulse to chew at her cheek.

"Now you are a woman without a husband, and a woman alone cannot rule. As Yvor, grandson of Rurik, married you and became Grand Prince in your father's stead, so now a Drevlianian will become your husband,

and Grand Prince, and rule long and wisely, and provide sons for the future glory and wealth of Russiya."

Stiff and formal in her crimson silk robes and heavy crown and looped necklaces of gold and amber, she said nothing.

"We invite you to choose among us," their warchief continued with an oily smile. "I have brought with me twelve fine, strong, proud young warriors. The best our land can offer." The promised twelve came forward; she did not even glance at them. "Only consider, good Lady, that with a Drevlianian as your husband, and a Drevlianian as your son, this land will be ruled by those who have belonged here since time began."

She stayed silent, not trusting herself to speak, for what she was thinking would have ruined all. *Those who "belong" here—by which you mean those descended of the three brothers who ran away from taking vengeance for their people's destruction! And let us not forget the sister who cringed and shivered on the riverbank! It is no wonderment to me that you pleaded with great Rurik to rule over you and give you laws and safety from your enemies, for you are all cowards and fools.*

It was her late husband's warchief, Sveneld, who spoke, taking one long stride from near the silk-draped chair that was her throne. "Dare you forget," Sveneld rumbled from deep within a chest the size of a wine cask, "that it was you who asked of us a prince to rule over you? We Varangians wanted only a secure route to Mikligardur, to the Silk Road of Serica, to the trading of sables. Prince Rurik you invited—begged!—to become your leader and your salvation from invaders. Prince Helgi made you great, proclaimed Kyiv the Mother of All Russiya—"

"Enough," Olga said softly. All eyes, wide with shock, were upon her. She would apologize to Sveneld later—and thank him for saying what she must not. Rising from her chair, she smoothed her robes and looked down on the Drevlianian warchief. "You must understand the disquiet of my spirit since—since—" She stopped and stared down at her hands again, as if unable to go on. Spies had reported to them, she was certain, about her pacing and her sleeplessness and her cold turmoil. She could not present them with a woman completely in control of herself and her emotions. If they thought her grief-stricken and terrified, so much the better. "You have given me a difficult choice, for all the young men you propose are worthy, I am sure, of the Tears and the Blood." Her fingers clenched around the earring in her palm. "Please, forgive me if I am unable to choose at this exact moment—"

"We never intended you to, gentle Lady," soothed the Drevlianian. "You may take as long as you like. We will wait."

Later, to Master Cheng, she gave voice to her fury. "Yes, wait! And while they do so they will devour my food, drown themselves in my drink, despoil my maids—"

"Peace, Most Gracious," the old man murmured. "Did we not hope for exactly this? They are here, and think you unbalanced by sorrow for the past and fear of the future. While they believe you to be wringing your hands in private over this choice, they will not think to see what is truly there to be seen."

Calming herself with an effort, she began removing the heavy amber jewelry from her neck. The crown she had taken off upon entering her rooms; it had given her a headache with the weight of its gold.

"All is prepared?" she asked.

"Of course."

A chain snagged on silken embroidery. She yanked at it, abruptly furious again. "Why did Yvor do it? Why did he demand double the tribute? Did he think himself so powerful that none would dare refuse? How rich did these Drevlianians appear, that Yvor demanded double?"

"Who can say what was in his mind?" Master Cheng folded his hands inside his sleeves. "Traveling to each vassal, collecting tribute, being feasted and entertained for a month or more—he considered the expense to them sufficient to deplete their resources, so that no armies might be raised against him. And indeed, you will note that a mere twenty men and their servitors have come to you. They are not the ones with an army. You are."

Finally freed of the offending necklace, she threw it onto the carpets. It was the hour when she went to see her son, and did not wish to frighten him by appearing in all her glittering golden finery. "An army," she observed, "is a man's weapon, Master Cheng."

"Of a certainty. And there are no men here." He smiled.

Only a mother, and one who could never be a father. It hovered on her lips to ask why he had lingered in Kyiv these many years; surely after experiencing the marvels of stately Athens and proud Rome and mighty Mikligardur in his travels with the silk trade, her city was pitiful in contrast. Those places blazed brighter than the sun; Kyiv was nothing more than a hearthfire by comparison—a fire likely to sputter and die if she did not guard it against the Drevlianians.

Yvor had asked Cheng once if he did not desire to go home to Serica. The old man shrugged, smiled, and replied that he feared he was too decrepit to survive the journey, and even if he did reach the Silk Lands, he had been hopelessly corrupted by his years in the vulgar West. Besides, he added with a twinkle in his tilting black eyes, he enjoyed looking at golden-haired women far too much never to look at one again.

"Tribute and armies," Cheng sighed, startling her from her thoughts. "An inconvenient and wasteful method of governing, if I may say so, Most Gracious. Building a nation from twigs and twine, when stone is required."

She shrugged. "It was always done that way. Is there a better?"

He only looked at her, amusement dancing in his black eyes. He had taken to watching her this way in the weeks since Yvor had been killed: watching her, waiting for her to be clever.

She thought of her first effort at such cleverness, and how he had actually laughed with glee and approval of her plan, and all at once tribute and armies and wood and stone came together and made elegant sense.

"From now on, keep them here," she heard herself say. "Let them go back to their own lands rarely, so they cannot make mischief. Root in them the desire to live as a prince does: in a house of stone, in a city encircled by stone, not cramped in a village of wood. They will build a city of stone for me, Cheng. They will spend their substance on that, and on pretty things to put inside their new houses, not on armies."

"The Most Gracious One is wise." He bowed to her, and once more she marveled at the satisfaction it gave her to earn his admiration. It was, she thought suddenly, even better than her father's smile.

She finished twisting her thick fair braids atop her head and secured them with a dragon-headed pin that had belonged to her husband's kinswoman, the Queen of Denmark. She composed her face into lines that spoke of happiness and humor, not anger and anxiety. "Come," she said to Master Cheng, "we'll go upset the nurses by keeping Sviatoslav awake late into the night. And you shall show him another magic." The prospect cheered her, and she wagged a finger playfully at the old man. "But not the one with the pigeons again!"

"They'd just fed," he protested, eyes dancing, "or they would not have messed the carpets."

"Your own master should have taught you how to make manure vanish," she teased. Then, grimly: "It would have been useful right now."

The fourth evening of the Drevlianians' stay, a feast was given. She had ordered constructed a large wooden hall, caparisoned in bright bolts of silk and warmed by iron braziers, and so thickly strewn with carpets that the floor of pine planks was completely covered. Sumptuous food was served by the prettiest of her pretty blonde slaves. Strong liquor flowed like spring snowmelt into immense silver-mounted drinking horns, and down the throats of her guests.

She had inspected the hall that morning. For so hasty a project, it was all quite beautifully built and decorated. She said this, exchanging glances with Master Cheng, and smiled.

As the guests feasted, she stayed upstairs watching her son wear himself out shrieking with delight as Master Cheng wielded magics complex enough to entertain a shrewd, clever child. At length the old man excused himself, much to the boy's dismay. She sat up late with Sviatoslav, soothing him to sleep in her lap, listening to the crackle of the hearthfire. There was a peace about it, despite the dread hovering nearby, for in these hours she was nothing grander or more elaborate than the mother of a beloved son. Other mothers sat near other fires tonight, rocking children to sleep throughout great Kyiv. And it seemed to her that she had been correct in her imaginings, and that the city was a hearthfire in itself, warmly glowing, as welcoming as a mother's gentle arms.

Mother Of All Russiya.

Gazing into the flames that defended her from cold and darkness, she turned her mind to the new wooden hall beyond her windows, and heard the music change from the old heroic ballads that always accompanied feasting to tunes suitable for dancing. The slaves would now be departing one by one, until only Drevlianians remained. They roared out drinking songs, fists pounding on tables, making plates and bowls skitter. Boots stomped on the pine planks beneath those tables and in the cleared spaces where agile young men danced off the excess energy of plenteous horns of wine. In her mind she saw it all. Saw, as well, just outside the wooden hall, an old man with strangely tilting black eyes making a gesture, and muttering a few words, and reaching most delicately with magic always young.

From her son's rooms she heard the screams begin. She heard the crack and splinter of a million flimsy kindling twigs beneath heavy boots as the flooring beneath the carpets lost its bewitchment and became what it truly was. She heard the crash of bodies and tables and benches and iron braziers as they all fell into a pit twice as tall as a man. She heard the hissing of ripped silks, the cracking of white skulls, and the final great sound like thunder as the walls woven of switches as slender as snakes collapsed atop the pit, smothering all within, burying them alive.

She smiled then, and nodded, and stared into the hearthfire, rocking her son in her arms.

But that night she dreamed of snakes.

"They are not all dead," she told Master Cheng the next day. "Some of those who killed my husband yet live."

He took some moments to respond to her words. "Short of attacking Iskorosten—"

"If I must." She paced, fingers fidgeting with the ends of her long golden braids. She did not feel clever. She could not command her brain to brilliance. She only knew that she could not use a man's weapons; she was no warleader to general an army. They would expect her to use a woman's weapon, and she was no Empress of Rome to wield poison. Magic stood before her in the shape of an old man—but she must be clever, and tell him how it ought to be done.

She stood before the hearthfire and stared into it, seeking among the identities others had provided her: daughter, wife, mother, Grand Princess. And she found her answers in all of them. In the fire.

There was only one way to be sure that a snake was dead.

Some weeks later, her envoy stood among the shocked and grieving Drevlianians and told them: "The Grand Princess is afraid, my lords. This horrible tragedy, this terrifying accident that took so many strong, proud lives—she is only a woman, my lords. Pity her in her solitude! Her father of glorious name is dead, her brave husband also, and her son is a child of but five summers. Therefore she begs that you send to her all your wisest men, the best men who govern Drevliania, for she is in dire need of your learned counsel."

They came. They actually came. She watched and hid her delight as they marched grimly into the stone-walled courtyard, fully a hundred of them, all in armor and all warriors. They were dark and stocky and full-bearded, and each possessed an axe, a sword, and a knife that never left him, not even when he slept. And they were angry. Gods, so angry.

Their new warchief, son of the old, stalked up to her on the steps of her residence where she stood ready to receive them. "We will stay here," he told her without preamble, "within stone walls. Your hall is large enough to house us. There will be no more accidents. We will stay here."

The clamor of their armor and weapons as they milled around her hall throbbed daily, nightly, in her brain. And in her dreams, while she slept and was vulnerable, their axes and swords and knives became yet more snakes, with iron fangs that sank into her son's small body.

"Highness," said Sveneld on the fifth afternoon, just before another session of "counsel" with her guests, "it has not escaped my notice that these assassins yet live."

She rounded on him furiously, ready to tear out his eyes with her fingernails. Nearby, Master Cheng folded his hands meekly within his sleeves and bent his head. She knew he was hiding a smile.

When she spoke, her voice emerged gentle as swansdown. "They will not be living much longer. They will pay tribute, Sveneld, believe me— and after this, the days of tribute are over." This one last tribute that would rid her of snakes.

For she had discovered a new weapon—not a man's or a woman's or a magician's, but the weapon of a mother. Master Cheng had done more than smile when she had told him of her plan. He had done something he had never done before, not even in her husband's honor: he went down on his knees, arms in their green silk sleeves spread wide as wings, and touched his forehead to the cold stone floor.

The great *lodya* in which her father had sailed to Mikligardur was brought by her command from its place of honor by the river. Made from the hollowed-out trunk of a single mighty oak, the *lodya*'s planking was as fresh as the day Grand Prince Helgi had stood among its oarsmen on his triumphant return home. The *lodya* had seemed huge to her when she was a little girl; she realized as she watched it being dragged carefully into the stone courtyard that it would of course appear smaller to her now, for she was a woman grown, with a whole country to worry over.

The mast was raised, the square sail unfurled. As the men worked, they sang the song of Grand Prince Helgi's great victory over proud Mikligardur, and how he had forced Emperors to pay for the food and shelter of every merchant of Russiya who came to the city thereafter. She waited, smiling, for her favorite part: The Emperors also had to provide as many baths as the Rus wished. It was always the hardest part to sing, for no one could keep from laughing: the lyric described hundreds of Greeks sweating and cursing as they hauled and heated water day and night for the gleefully fastidious Rus.

That night she stood on the steps of her home, arrayed in her finest silken robes and every jewel she owned, watching the commotion in the courtyard as all was readied for a celebration. Forty years it had been since Grand Prince Helgi's triumph over proud Mikligardur, and she intended to commemorate the occasion most impressively. These Drevlianians would be reminded that it had been a Varangian who had won such a great victory. They would remember why they had begged a Varangian to come and rule over them.

They were encouraged to climb onto the *lodya*, every one of them, and the pretty blonde slaves made sure each had a brimming horn of liquor. Sveneld had not been happy about allowing them access to the ship, but she merely shook her head and told him to have patience. He was especially disturbed that she gave orders for all the Kyivan soldiers to leave their weapons in their barracks. Again she was adamant. She was the Grand Princess, and it was her people's duty to obey.

She stood on the highest step, watching the Drevlianians drink and laugh. Master Cheng glided silently to her side. She glanced at him, and he smiled at her, and made a subtle gesture with his long, thin fingers.

Below them, every one of a hundred torches ranged about the courtyard sprang to fiery life.

And everyone in the courtyard gasped like a child taking its first breath.

She had seen Cheng do this before, but never on such a scale as this. The courtyard blazed bright as noonday. The Drevlianians' hands went to their sword hilts. She eyed Master Cheng sidelong. He gave her an innocent smile.

As she had planned, with the darkening of the sky and the lighting of the torches, a powerful male voice began to chant. On the gray stone walls of the courtyard, shadows began to flicker. They might have been cast by the torches. The dancers filed in and the warriors calmed down, leaning on the ship's railing to enjoy the show.

Prince Helgi, mighty in name, eternal in glory, forty springs are gone,
Yet we remember, will always remember, the splendor of your triumph.

It was difficult to watch Master Cheng at the same time she watched the courtyard. She felt rather than really saw his fingers twitch periodically, sensed rather than truly heard his voice whisper strange words.

Two thousand lodya *he sailed, only to find the harbor of Mikligardur*
Blocked by vast chains; the cunning Greeks thought victory theirs.
Yet Grand Prince Helgi was of a cunning even greater than the Greeks'.

The fire-lit dancers swarmed about the courtyard. The shadows on the
walls outlined brick towers bristling with warriors. No one believed the
shadows torch-flung now. Fear rippled through the arrogant Drevlianians
who had murdered a Grand Prince. But the fascination of it held all who
watched in silent thrall.

The warriors leaped from their lodya *like wolves leap from their lairs,*
Within sight of proud Mikligardur, beneath its very walls.
The Greeks came forth, soft sheep in their thousands,
To be slaughtered, devoured, only white bones left on the shore.

Suddenly a deafening roar went up from her own people, a bellow of
proud victory as Grand Prince Helgi's army destroyed the shadows of the
Greek host. At her side, Cheng trembled and whispered.

The warriors of Russiya knew not defeat, nor weariness, nor pain.
Prince Helgi hung his mighty shield on the gates of vanquished Mikligardur,
Then sailed him home with golden treasure and silver plunder
And gems enough to make a mountain; see them now,
Gracing his daughter's sweet white throat, her slender supple arms.

The shadows vanished, and all the torches save one were extinguished—
and that one lit only her as she stood on the steps, alone now. From her
neck and wrists and ears and fingers and body shimmered jewels of a
hundred different colors, set in gold or silver or stitched into her robes.
She stood unmoving, unsmiling. Nearby, out of the bright torchlight,
Master Cheng was breathing heavily with effort.

All glory to Grand Prince Helgi, he of the cunning and courage and might,
His word-fame will live forever among the hearthfires of Kyiv, Mother of
All Russiya!

Helgi's ship flared to light, spitting fire. Sparks caught and clung to
Drevlianian clothing. Thick dark hair burned. The wooden handles of
axes ignited; leather sword-sheaths blazed; embroidered sashes that held
long knives turned to searing belts of flame. All the fire in the world
devoured the screaming men in the *lodya*. The stench of charring flesh
was horrible. Olga watched, thinking that in their agony the men were

very like snakes—writhing, wicked snakes, burning alive. It was the only way to make sure they were really dead. Soon all that was left of Drevlianian strength and pride was the scorched metal of their axes, swords, and knives. Men's weapons, useless against the power of her fire. Great Mother Kyiv's warm hearth had become an inferno.

Master Cheng sank to the stones at her side. She knelt, taking his frail shoulders in her hands, and whispered his name. He smiled slightly, fingers daring to touch her hair.

"Living gold," he murmured.

And all at once she knew why the old man had lingered in Kyiv all these years. She knew, and suddenly his strange, wizened face with its tilting black eyes was beautiful.

By dawn the ship and the men trapped on it were ashes, and Master Cheng was dead.

For him, she used her army to destroy the Drevlianian city of Iskorosten. Her little son Sviatoslav accompanied her, guarded closely by the warchief Sveneld and the steward Asmund, who loved the boy dearly and together made a wiser and better father than Yvor could have been. Sviatoslav was allowed to cast the first spear against the enemy. The weapon of a man, wielded by a valiant little boy, put such fierce heart into the warriors that they forgot that it was a woman who had ordered them into battle.

Iskorosten was taken. Most of its citizens were killed, and the rest were handed over to Olga's *druzhina* as slaves. On the day Iskorosten fell, Olga put upon her ear the Tears and the Blood, and relinquished the jewels only when her son came of age. Sviatoslav then set out on his own wars of conquest, while his mother continued to rule. She was a wise and clever Grand Princess who reorganized the state and abolished the annual tribute. To Kyiv came the highest nobles of all the tribes, and until they built their own stone dwellings they slept in wooden houses—and flinched violently at sudden flames, at cracking twigs. She laughed to herself each time she heard of this, but she made sure that Kyiv became a city made more of stone than of wood: Mother of All Russiya, her hearthfire warm and welcoming.

Olga died in July of the year 969, having been twelve years baptized into the Christian faith—which, for her motherly care of her country and her guidance of her people to the Church, made of her the beloved Saint Olga of Kiev.

She never dreamed of snakes again.

Author's Note

Although Olga's methods are of my invention, she really did avenge her husband and protect her son by having the Drevlianian emissaries buried alive and burned alive. The detail of the trench beneath the houses is accurate, as is the description of the boat and the conquest of "Mikligardur"— Constantinople—by Olga's father. He died after stepping on a poisonous snake. The tale of the founding of Kyiv is one of the oldest historical legends of Russia. It probably stems from the mingling of three settlements, for which there is much archaeological evidence, that existed within the present-day city. At Iskorosten, Sviatoslav did throw the first spear. A contemporary account by an Arab chronicler made note of the earring he wore as an adult: pearls and a ruby. His son became the most celebrated of the Grand Princes of Kyiv: Saint Vladimir the Great. Through him, Olga was the ancestor of the kings of Poland, Hungary, France, Spain, and England.

Riding the Shore of the River of Death

Kate Elliott

*As a child in rural Oregon, **Kate Elliott** made up stories and drew maps of imaginary worlds because she longed to escape to a world of lurid adventure fiction. This dubious inclination led inexorably to a career as a fantasy writer. "Riding the Shore of the River of Death" takes places in the world of her seven-volume Crown of Stars fantasy series. The Spiritwalker Trilogy (Cold Magic and Cold Fire with Cold Steel forthcoming) is an Afro-Celtic post-Roman icepunk Regency adventure fantasy with swords, sharks, and lawyer dinosaurs. She has also written the Crossroads Trilogy (Spirit Gate, Shadow Gate, and Traitors' Gate), which features giant eagles, an examination of the old adage "power corrupts," and ghosts, as well as the science fiction Novels of the Jaran. While not writing, she lives not in lurid adventure fiction but in paradisiacal Hawaii.*

THIS WOODED WESTERN COUNTRY far from their tribal lands in the east smelled raw and unpalatable to Kereka, but the hawk that circled overhead had the same look as hawks in the grasslands. Some things were the same no matter where you went, even if you had to ride into the lands where foreigners made their homes to get what you wanted. Even if you had to journey far from your father's authority and your mother's tent to seize the glory of your first kill.

The reverberant thunk of an axe striking wood surprised her; she'd thought it was too early to hunt because they had yet to see any sign of habitation. Ahead, barely visible within the stretch of pine and beech through which they rode, her brother Belek unslipped his spear from its brace against his boot and urged his mare into a run. Kereka rose in her stirrups to watch him vanish into a clearing occluded by summer's leaves. Birds broke from cover, wings flashing. The clatter of weapons, a sharp shriek, and then a man's howl of pain chased off through the bright woodland.

Edek, riding in front of her, whipped his horse forward. His voice raised in a furious burst of words as he and Kereka broke out of the woods and into a clearing of grass, meadow flowers, bold green saplings, and a pair of sturdy young oak trees.

Belek's mare had lost her rider. She shied sideways and stood with head lifted and ears flat. Beside the oaks, two had fought. Belek's spear had thrust true, skewering the foreign man through the torso, but the farmer's axe had cut into the flesh below Belek's ribs before Belek had finally killed the man with a sword-thrust up under the ribs. Edek stood with mouth working soundlessly, watching as Belek sawed off the head of the dead man with his bloodied knife. Blood leaked from Belek's gut, trailing from under his long felt tunic and over the knees of his leather trousers, but he was determined to get that head.

If he could present the head to the *begh* before he died, then he would die as a man rather than a boy.

His teeth were gritted and his eyes narrowed, but he uttered no word that might betray how much he hurt. Even when he got the head detached so it rolled away from the body, blood spilling brightly onto the grass, he said nothing, only uttered a "gah" of pain as he toppled over to one side. His left hand clutched the hair of the dead man. With his gaze he tracked the sky, skipping from cloud to cloud, and fetched up on Kereka's face. He seemed about to speak but instead passed out.

Kereka stared. One of the young oaks had a gash in its side, but the farmer hadn't chopped deep enough to fell it. Bugs crawled among the chips of wood cut from the trunk. A cluster of white flowers had been crushed by the farmer's boots. His red blood mingled with Belek's, soaking into the grass. This could not be happening, could it?

Every year boys rode out of the clans to seek their first kill, and every year some did not return. Riding the shore of the river of death was the risk you took to become a man. Yet no lad rode out in the dawn's thunder thinking death would capture *him*.

Edek dismounted and knelt beside Belek to untie the heavy tunic, opening it as one might unfold the wings of a downed bird. Seeing the deep axe cut and the white flash of exposed rib, he swore softly. Kereka could not find words as she absorbed the death of her hopes.

"He'll never get home with this wound," said Edek. "We'll have to leave him." He started, hearing a crack, but it was only Belek's mare stepping on a fallen branch as it turned to move back toward the familiarity of its herd.

"We can't leave him." Kereka knew she had to speak quickly before she succumbed to the lure of Edek's selfish suggestion. "He is my brother. The *begh*'s son. It will bring shame on us if we abandon him."

Edek shrugged. "If we take him back, then you and I have no chance of taking a head. You must see that. He can't ride. He's dead anyway. Let's leave him and ride on. Others have done it."

She set her jaw against his tempting words. "Other boys who were left to die hadn't already taken a head. He's taken his head, so we must give him a chance to die as a man. We'll lose all honor if we leave him. Even if both of us took a head in our turn."

"I don't want to wait another season. I'm tired of being treated as a boy when I'm old enough to be a man."

"Go on alone if you wish, Edek the whiner." Kereka forced out the mocking words, and Edek's sullen frown deepened with anger. "You'll sour the milk with your curdling tongue. You can suckle on your grievances for another season. You'll get another chance to raid."

As she would not.

Last moon the *begh*'s son from the Pechanek clan had delivered six mares to her father, with the promise of twenty sheep, ten fleeces, two bronze cauldrons, a gilded saddle, three gold-embroidered saddle blankets, five felt rugs, and a chest of gold necklaces and bronze belt clasps as her bride price. Her father's wives and the mothers of the tribe had been impressed by the offer. They had been charmed by Prince Vayek's respectful manners and pleasing speeches. Perhaps most of all they had been dazzled by his handsome face and well-proportioned body displayed to good effect in several bouts of wrestling, all of which he had won against the best wrestlers of the Kirshat clan. Her father and uncles had praised his reputation as a mighty warrior, scourge of the Uzay and Torkay clans, and all the while their gazes had returned again and again to the deadly iron gleam of the griffin feathers he wore as his warrior's wings. Other warriors, even other *beghs* and their princely sons, wore ordinary wings, feathers fastened with wire to wooden frames that were riveted to an armored coat. Only a man who had slain a griffin could fly griffin wings. Such a man must be called a hero among men, celebrated, praised, and admired.

Her father had decreed she would wed Prince Vayek at the next full moon. Wed, and be marked as a woman forever, even unto death.

This was her last chance to prove her manhood.

When she spoke, her voice was as harsh as a crow's. "We'll weave a litter of sticks and drag him behind his horse."

Dismounting, she turned her back so Edek could not see her wipe away the hot tears. Honor did not allow her to cry. She wanted to be a man and live a man's life, not a woman's. But she could not abandon her dying brother.

Grass flattened under the weight of a litter as Belek's mare labored up a long slope. Kereka rode at a walk just in front of Belek's horse, its lead tied to her saddle. Her own mare, summer coat shiny in the hot sun, flicked an ear at a fly.

She glanced back at the land falling away to the west. She had lagged behind to shoot grouse in the brush that cloaked a stream, its banks marked at this distance by the crowd of trees and bushes flourishing alongside running water. She squinted into the westering sun, scanning the land for pursuers, but saw no movement. Yesterday they had left the broken woodland country behind. Out here under the unfenced sky, they'd flown beyond the range of the farmers and their stinking fields.

From ahead, Edek called her name. She whistled piercingly to let him know she was coming. The two birds she'd killed dangled from a line hooked to the saddle of Belek's horse. Belek himself lay strapped to the litter they had woven of sapling branches. He had drifted in and out of consciousness for four days. It was amazing he was still alive, but he had swallowed drips and drops of mare's blood, enough to keep breath in his body. Now, however, his own blood frothed at his lips. The end would come soon.

Maybe if he died now, before they reached the tents of the Kirshat clan, she and Edek could turn immediately around, ride back west, and take up their hunt in fresh territory. Yet even to think this brought shame; Belek deserved to die as a man, whatever it meant to her.

She topped the rise to see hills rolling all the way to the eastern horizon. Dropping smoothly away from her horse's hooves lay a long grassy hollow half in shadow with the late afternoon light. The ground bellied up again beyond the hollow like a pregnant woman's distended abdomen. Edek had dismounted partway up the farther slope. He'd stripped out of his tunic in the heat and crouched with the sun on his back as he examined the ground. Above him, thick blocks of stone stood like sentries at the height of the hill: a stone circle, dark and forbidding.

The sight of the heavy stones made her ears tingle, as though someone was trying to whisper a warning but couldn't speak loudly enough for her to hear. A hiss of fear escaped her, and at once she spat to avert spirits who might have heard that hiss and seek to capture her fear and use it against her. She whistled again, but Edek did not look up. With its reins dropped over its head, his mount grazed in a slow munch up the slope toward the looming stones. He had his dagger out and was digging at the dirt. His quiver shifted on his bare back as he hunkered forward. What was he doing, leaving himself vulnerable like that?

She nudged her mare forward. When the reins tightened and pulled, Belek's mare braced stubbornly, then gave in and followed. The litter bumped over a rough patch of ground. Belek grunted, whimpered. Eyes fluttering, he muttered spirit words forced out of him where he lay spinning between the living world and the world of the spirits. A bubble of blood swelled and popped on his lips. The head of the farmer he had slain bumped at his thigh. Its lank hair tangled in his fingers. The skin had gone gray, and it stank.

Edek did not look up when she halted behind him. She touched the hilt of the sword slung across her back. Once they reached the tribe, she would have to give it back to her uncle. Only men carried swords.

"What if I had been your enemy?" she asked. She drew the sword in a swift, practiced slide and lowered its tip to brush Edek between the shoulder blades.

He did not look up or even respond. He was trying to pry something out of the densely packed soil. The sun warmed his back as he strained. As the quiver shifted with each of his movements, the old Festival scars on his back pulled and retracted, displaying the breadth of his back to great advantage. She didn't like Edek much; he was good-looking enough to expect girls to admire him, but his family wasn't wealthy enough that he could marry where he pleased, and that had made him bitter, so in a way she understood his sulks and frowns. And she could still ogle his back, sweating and slick under the sun's weight.

Suddenly he hooked his dagger under an object and with a grunt freed it from an entangling root and the weight of moist soil. When he flipped it into plain view, she sucked in breath between teeth in astonishment.

The sun flashed in their eyes and she threw up a hand to shield herself from the flare. Edek cried out. From Belek came a horrible shriek more like the rasp of a knife on stone than a human cry. Only the horses seemed unmoved.

She lowered her hand cautiously. At first glance, the object seemed nothing more than an earth-encrusted feather, but as Edek cautiously wiped the vanes with the sleeve of his tunic, the cloth separated as though sliced. Where dirt flaked away, the feather glinted with a metallic sheen unlike that of any bird's feather.

"It's a griffin's feather!" said Edek.

Kereka was too amazed and humbled to speak, awed by its solidity, its beauty, its strength. Its sacred, powerful magic. Only shamans and heroes possessed griffin feathers.

He shifted in his crouch to measure her, eyes narrowed. "Even a humble clansman can aspire to wed a *begh*'s daughter if he brings a griffin's feather as her bride price."

Kereka snorted. "Even one you dug up from the dirt?"

"The gods give gifts to those they favor!"

"You'll set yourself against the mighty Vayek and the entire Pechanek clan? Who will listen to your bleating, even with a griffin feather in your hand to dazzle their eyes?"

"Who will listen? Maybe the one who matters most." How he stared! He'd never been so bold before! She shook a hand in annoyance, like swatting away a fly, and he flushed, mouth twisting downward.

The feather's glamour faded as the shadow of afternoon crept over their position. And yet, at the height of the hill to the east, a glimmer still brightened the air.

How could they see the setting sun's flash when they were facing east, not west?

"Look!" she cried.

A woman stood framed and gleaming within the western portal of stone and lintel. Sparks flowered above the stones in a pattern like the unfurling of wings sewn out of gold, the fading banner of a phoenix. So brief its passage; the last embers floating in the air snapped, winked bright, and vanished.

Edek stared, mouth agape.

The woman, not so very far away, watched them. She had black hair, bound into braids but uncovered, and a brown face and dark hands. She wore sandals bound by straps that wound up her calves over tight leggings suitable for riding. A close-fitting bodice of supple leather was laced over a white shirt. But she wore no decent skirts or heavy knee length tunic or long robe; her legs were gloved in cloth, but she might as well have been bare, for you could imagine her shape quite easily. She wore no other clothing at all unless one could count as clothing her wealth of necklaces. Made of gold and beads, they draped thickly around her shoulders like a collar of bright armor.

A woman of the Quman people who displayed herself so brazenly would have been staked down and had the cattle herd driven across her to obliterate her shame. But this woman seemed unaware of her own nakedness. Edek could not stop staring at that shapely bodice and those form-fitting trousers even as the woman hefted her spear and regarded them with no sign of fear.

"Chsst!" hissed Edek, warding himself with a gesture. "A witch!"

"A witch, maybe, but armed with stone like a savage," muttered Kereka in disgust. Anyway, even a woman who carried a spear was of no use to her.

A shape moved behind the foreigner: broad shoulders, long hair, sharp nose. Of course no woman would be traveling alone! Edek did not see the man because he was blinded by lust. Let him hesitate, and she would take the prize. This was her chance to take a head and never have to marry the Pechanek *begh*'s son.

Kereka sliced the halter rope that bound Belek's horse to her saddle, and drove her mare up the hill. A Quman warrior rode in silence, for he had wings to sing the song of battle for him. She had no wings yet—only men were allowed to wear armor and thereby fly the honored pennant of warrior's wings—but she clamped her lips tight down over a woman's trilling ululation, the goad to victory. She would ride in silence, like a man.

The horse was surefooted and the hill none too steep. Edek had only a moment in which to cry out an unheeded question before he scrambled for his mount. Ahead, the woman retreated behind one of the huge stones. The man had vanished. Kereka grinned, yanked her mare to the right, and swung round to enter the stone circle at a different angle so she could flank them.

"Sister! Beware!"

The words rasped at the edge of her hearing.

It was too late.

She hit the trap with all the force of her mare's weight and her own fierce desire for a different life than the one that awaited her. A sheet of pebbles spun under its hooves. A taut line of rope took her at the neck, and she went tumbling. She hit the ground so hard, head cracking against stone, that she could not move. The present world faded until she could see, beyond it, into the shimmering lights of the spirit world where untethered souls wept and whispered and danced. Belek reached out to her, his hand as insubstantial as the fog that swallows the valleys yet never truly possesses them. It was his spirit voice she heard, because he was strong enough in magic for his spirit to bridge the gap.

"Sister! Take my hand!"

"I will not go with you to the other side!" she cried, although no sound left her mouth. In the spirit world, only shamans and animals could speak out loud. "But I will drag you back here if it takes all my strength!"

She grasped his hand and *tugged*. A fire as fierce as the gods' anger rose up to greet her. She had to shield her eyes from its heat and searing power. She blinked back tears as the present world came into focus again.

It was night. Twilight had passed in what seemed to her only an instant while she had swum out of the spirit world.

Pebbles ground uncomfortably into her buttocks. A stalk of grass tickled the underside of one wrist. Tiny feet tracked on her forehead, then vanished as the creature flew. She sat propped against the rough wall of standing stones, wrists and ankles bound. How had this happened? She could not remember.

The scene before her lay in sullen colorless tones, lit by a grazing moon and by the blazing stars. Each point of light marked a burning arrow shot into the heavens by the warrior Tarkan, he who had bred with a female griffin and fathered the Quman people.

The flaring light of a campfire stung her eyes. The man crouched before it, raking red coals to one side. He had a thick beard, like the northern farmers, and skin pale enough that it was easy to follow his gestures as he efficiently scalded and plucked *her grouse* and roasted them over coals. Grease dripped and sizzled, the smell so sweet it was an insult thrown in her face.

Where were the others?

Edek lay well out of her reach, slumped against one of the giant stones. The horses stood hobbled just beyond the nimbus of light; she saw them only as shapes. Belek's litter lay at the edge of the harsh and restless flare of the fire. Still strapped to the litter, he moaned and shuddered. The woman appeared out of the darkness as abruptly as a shaman's evil dream. She crouched beside him with both hands extended. Lips moving but without sound, she sprinkled grains of dirt or flakes of herbs over his body.

Fear came on Kereka in the same way a spirit sickness does, penetrating the eyes first and sinking down to lodge in the throat and, at last, to grasp hold of her belly like an ailment. There are ways to animate dead flesh with sorcery. She had to stop the working, or Belek would be trapped by this creature's magic and never able to find his way past the spirit-lands to the ancient home of First Grandfather along the path lit by Tarkan's flaming arrows. But she could not move, not even to push her foot along the ground to kick the corpse and dislodge Belek's spirit.

Mist and darkness writhed between dying youth and foreign woman. With a powerful inhalation, the woman sucked in the cloud. Belek thrashed as foam speckled his lips. The witch rocked forward to balance so lightly on her toes that Kereka was sure she would fall forward onto Belek's unprotected chest. Instead, the woman exhaled, her breath loud in the silence; the air glittered with sparks expelled from her mouth. They dissolved into the youth's flesh as the witch settled smoothly back on her heels. She lifted her gaze to look directly at Kereka.

No matter how vulnerable she appeared, indecently clothed and armed only with a stone-pointed spear in the midst of the grasslands, she had power. As the *begh* Bulkezu, ancestor of Kereka's ancestors, had wrapped himself in an impenetrable coat of armor in his triumphant war against the westerners, this woman was armed with something more dangerous than a physical weapon. She was not the bearded man's wife or slave, but his master.

She nodded to mark Kereka's gaze, and spoke curtly in a language unlike any of those muttered by the tribe's slaves.

Kereka shook her head, understanding nothing. It would be better to kill the witch, but in the event, she had no choice except to negotiate from a position of weakness. "What do you want from us? My father will pay a ransom—"

As if her voice awakened him, Belek murmured as in a daze. "Kereka? Are you there?" Rope creaked as he fought with unexpected strength against his bonds. He looked up at the woman crouched above him. "Who are you? Where is my sister—?"

The witch rose easily to her feet and moved away into the gloom. The bearded man stood up and followed her. Kereka heard them speaking, voices trading back and forth in the manner of equals, not master and slave. Two warriors might converse in such tones, debating the best direction for a good hunt, or two female cousins or friendly co-wives unravel an obstacle tangling the weave of family life within their tents.

Belek tried again, voice spiking as he tried to control his fear. "Kereka? Edek?"

"Chsst!" Kereka spoke in a calming voice. She adored her brother, son of her father's third wife, but he was the kind of person who felt each least pebble beneath him when he slept, and although he never complained— what Quman child would and not get beaten for being weak?—he would shift and scoot and brush at the ground all night to get comfortable and thus disturb any who slept next to him. "We're here, Belek. We had to tie you down to keep you on the litter. You'd taken a wound. Now, we have been captured by foreigners."

"I feel a sting in my gut. Ah. Aah!" He grunted, bit back a curse, thapped his head against the litter, and yelped. These healthy noises, evidence of his return from the threshold of the spirit world, sang in her belly with joy. "I remember when I charged that dirty farmer, but nothing after it. Did I get his head?"

"Yes. We tied it to your belt."

His hand groped; he found the greasy hair. "Tarkan's blessings! But what happened to me?"

He deserved to know the worst. "The woman is a witch. She trapped us with sorcery. I think she must have healed you."

"Aie! Better dead than in her debt! If it's true, I am bound to her and she can take from me whatever she wants in payment."

His fretful tone irritated her. "No sense panicking! Best we get free of her, then."

"It's not so simple! The binding which heals has its roots in the spirit world and can't be so easily escaped. Her magic can follow me wherever I go—"

"Then it's best we get back to the tribe quickly and ask for the shamans to intercede. There's a knife at your belt. You should be able to cut yourself loose."

Obedient as always to her suggestions, he writhed under the confining ropes. "Eh! Fah! Knife's gone."

Night lay everywhere over them. The fattening moon grazed on its dark pastures. Kereka clenched her teeth in frustration. There must be some way to free themselves!

Only then did she see a stockpile of weapons—*their* good Kirshat steel swords, iron-pointed arrows, and iron-tipped spears—heaped beyond the campfire, barely visible in the darkness. A stubborn gleam betrayed the griffin's feather, resting atop the loot in the seat of honor.

The foreigners ceased speaking and walked back into the fire's aura. The witch still carried her primitive spear and she was now brandishing a knife that gleamed in black splendor, an ugly gash of obsidian chipped away to make one sharp edge. She had not even bothered to arm herself with the better weapons she had captured, although the bearded man wore a decent iron sword at his side, foreign in its heft and length.

The woman crouched again beside Belek.

Anything was better than pleading—that was a woman's duty, not a man's—but the knife's evil gleam woke such fear in Kereka's heart that she knew such distinctions no longer mattered.

"I beg you, listen to my words. Belek is the honored son of the Kirshat *begh*'s third wife. He has powerful magic. The shamans have said so. He has already entered the first tent of apprenticeship. To kill him would be to release his anger and his untrained power into the spirit world. You don't want that!"

Where there is no understanding there can be no response. And yet, the woman weighed her sorcerer's knife and, with a flicker of a smile, sheathed it. Instead, she slid a finger's length needle of bone from a pouch slung from her belt.

Leather cord bit into Kereka's skin, tightening as she wiggled her hands and only easing its bite when she stilled. She could do nothing to spare Belek whatever torture this creature meant to inflict on him. Witchcraft had bound her to the rock.

The woman caught hold of her own tongue. With exaggerated care she slid the fine needle point through thick pink flesh. Then, with a delicacy made more horrifying for the sight of her bland expression in the face of self-mutilation, she slid the needle back out of her tongue, leaned over Belek, and let those drops of blood mingle with the drying froth on Belek's lips.

He struggled, but he too was bound tight. He gasped, swallowed, grimaced; then he sighed as if his breath had been pulled out of him, and abruptly his head lolled back. He had fainted. Or been murdered.

"Tarkan's curse on you!" Kereka shouted. "I'll have my revenge in my brother's name and in the name of the Kirshat tribe! Our father will drive his warband against you even to the ends of the earth—"

The woman laughed, and Kereka sputtered to a halt, her mouth suddenly too dry to moisten words. The skin on her neck crawled as with warning of a storm about to blow down over the grass.

The witch gestured, and the bearded man came forward, knelt beside Belek, and dribbled water from a pouch into his mouth. Belek sputtered, choked, spat, eyes blinking furiously. The bearded man stoppered the pouch and dragged the litter over to rest in the lee of the great stone to Kereka's right. He offered water to Kereka, wordlessly, and she tipped back her head to let the cool liquid flow down her parched throat. She knew better than to refuse it. She needed time to think about that knowing laugh.

He returned to the fire. Tearing apart the grouse, he ate one, wrapped the rest of the meat in a woven grass mat, then curled up on the ground beneath a cloak. The woman settled down cross-legged to stare into the fire. Occasionally she fed it with dried pats of dung.

Night passed, sluggish and sleepy. Kereka dozed, woke, tried to worm her way out of her bonds but could not. No matter how hard she tried to roll away from the monolith, she could not separate herself from the stone. She hissed to get Belek's attention, saw his eyes roll and his mouth work, but no sound emerged except for a faint wordless groan.

The witch woman did not stir from her silent contemplation of the campfire. Now and again a bead of blood leaked from between her lips, and each time as it pearled on her lips she licked it away as if loathe to let even that droplet escape her. She did not speak to them, did not test the bonds that held them, only waited, tasting nothing except her own blood.

Very late a sword moon, thin and curved, rose out of the east. Soon after, the light changed, darkness lightening to gray and at last ceding victory to the pinkish tint of dawn.

The woman roused. Picking up the pouch, she trickled water into Belek's mouth; he gulped, obviously awake, but still he said nothing. She approached Kereka.

As she leaned in to offer water, Kereka caught the scent of her, like hot sand and bitter root. She tried to grab at her with her teeth, any way of fighting back, but the woman jumped nimbly back and grinned mockingly. The man chuckled and spoke words in their harsh foreign tongue as he flung off the cloak and stretched to warm his muscles.

The brilliant disc of the sun nosed above the horizon to paint the world in daylight colors.

From the bundle of gear heaped by a stone, the bearded man unearthed a shovel and set to work digging a shallow ditch just outside the limit of the stones. It was hard work, even though he was only scraping away enough of the carpet of grass and its dense tangle of roots to reveal the black earth. The woman joined him, taking a turn. The grasslands were tough, like its people, unwilling to yield up even this much. Both soon stripped down to shirt and trousers, their shirts sticking to their backs, wet through with sweat. It was slave's work, yet they tossed words back and forth in the manner of free men. And although the woman's form was strikingly revealed, breasts outlined by the shirt's fabric, nipples erect from the effort and heat, the bearded man never stared at her as men stared at women whose bodies they wanted to conquer. He just talked, and she replied, and they passed the shovel back and forth, sharing the work as the ditch steadily grew from a scar, to a curve, to a half-circle around the stones.

Kereka waited until they had moved out of sight behind her. "Hsst! Belek? Edek?"

Yet when there came no answer, she was afraid to speak louder lest she be overheard.

The sun crept up off the eastern horizon as the foreigners toiled.

Shadows shortened and shifted; the sloping land came clear as light swallowed the last hollows of darkness. It was a cloudless day, a scalding blue that hurt the eye. Kereka measured the sun's slow rise between squinted eyes: two hands; four hands. A pair of vultures circled overhead but did not land. The steady scrape of the shovel and the spatter of clumps of dirt sprayed on the ground serenaded her, moving on from behind her and around to her right, closing the circle.

The sound caught her ear first as a faint discordance beneath the noise of digging. She had heard this precious and familiar music all her life, marked it as eagerly as the ring of bells on the sheep she was set to watch as a little girl or the scuff of bare feet spinning in the dances of Festival time.

The wind sings with the breath of battle, the flight of the winged riders, the warriors of the Quman people. It whistles like the approach of griffins whose feathers, grown out of the metals of the earth, thrum their high calls in the air.

Kereka scrambled to get her feet under her, shoved up along the rough surface of the stone. She had to see, even if she couldn't escape the stone's grip. Their enemies heard Quman warriors before they saw them, and some stood in wonder, not knowing what that whirring presaged, while others froze in fear, knowing they could not run fast enough to outpace galloping horses.

Belek struggled against the ropes that bound him but gained nothing. Edek neither moved nor spoke.

The woman and bearded man had worked almost all the way around the stones. The woman spoke. The man stopped digging. They stood in profile, listening. She shook her head, and together, shoulders tense, they trotted back into the stones straight to Edek's limp body. The bearded man grabbed the lad by his ankles and dragged him down to the scar. The body lay tumbled there; impossible to say if he was breathing. The woman gestured peremptorily, and the bearded man leaped away from the bare earth and ran up to the nearest stone, leaning on the haft of the shovel, panting from the exertion as he watched her through narrowed eyes.

The obsidian blade flashed in the sun. She bent, grabbed Edek's hair, and tugged his head back to expose his throat. With a single cut she sliced deep.

Kereka yelped. Did the witch mean to take Edek's head as a trophy, as Quman lads must take a head to prove themselves as men?

Belek coughed, chin lifting, feet and hands twitching as he fought against his bonds. He could see everything but do nothing.

Blood pumped sluggishly from Edek's throat. The witch grabbed him by the ankles and, with his face in the dirt and his life's blood spilling onto the black earth, dragged him along the scar away around the circle. All the while her lips moved although Kereka heard no words.

The bearded man wiped his mustache and nose with the back of a grimy hand, shrugged his shoulders to loosen the strain of digging, and dropped the shovel beside their gear. With the casual grace of a man accustomed to fighting, he pulled on a quilted coat and over it a leather coat reinforced with overlapping metal plates. He set out two black crossbows, levering each back to hook the trigger and ready a bolt. After, he drew on gloves and strapped on a helm before gathering up a bow as tall as he was, a quiver of arrows, an axe, and his sword and trotting away out of Kereka's line of sight, again carrying the shovel.

The woman appeared at the other limit of the scar, still towing Edek's body. Where they had ceased digging, a gap opened, about five paces wide. He gestured with the shovel. She shook her head, with a lift of her chin seeming to indicate the now-obvious singing of wings. The two argued, a quick and brutal exchange silenced by two emphatic words she spat out. She arranged the body to block as much of the gap as possible. With a resigned shrug, the bearded man took up a defensive position behind one of the stones to line up on the gap.

Brushing her hands off on her trousers, the witch jogged over to the gear, hooked a quiver of bolts onto her belt, and picked up both crossbows. Women did not wear armor, of course; Kereka knew better than to expect that even this remarkable creature would ever have been fitted with a man's accoutrements. Yet when she sauntered to take a measure of cover behind the standing stone nearest the gap, her easy pace, her lack of any outward sign of nervousness, made her seem far more powerful than her companion, who was forced to rely on leather and metal to protect himself. She propped one crossbow against the stone and, holding the other, straightened. The sun illuminated her haughty face. As she surveyed the eastern landscape and the golden hills, she smiled, a half twist of scornful amusement that woke a traitorous admiration in Kereka's heart. Someday she, the *begh*'s daughter who wished to live a man's life, would look upon her enemies with that same lazy contempt.

A band of warriors topped a far rise, the sound of their wings fading as they pulled up behind their leader to survey the stones beyond. The captain wore the distinctive metal glitter of griffin feathers on his wings, their shine so bright it hurt the eyes. They carried a banner of deep night blue on which rose a sword moon, dawn's herald.

"Belek," Kereka whispered, sure he could not see them, "it's the Pechanek! Curse them!"

Belek coughed and moaned; turned his head; kicked his feet in frustration.

She, too, struggled. Bad as things were, they had just gotten worse. Belek was healed; if they could escape or talk their way free, they had a hope of riding out again to continue Kereka's hunt, or maybe tricking their captors into a moment's inattention that would allow Kereka to kill the bearded man. Tarkan's bones! How had the Pechanek come to this forsaken place? Only a man who had killed a griffin had earned the right to wear griffin's wings. The *begh* of the Pechanek clan was not such a man. But his son Vayek was.

No *begh*'s son of a rival tribe would be out looking for three youths who must, after all, make their own way home or be judged unworthy of manhood's privileges and a man's respect. Had all her attempts to train herself in secret with her brother's aid in weapons and hunting and bragging and running and wrestling and the crafts and knowledge reserved for men now come to nothing?

A bitter anger burned in Kereka's throat. Her eyes stung, and for an instant she thought she might actually burst out of her bonds from sheer fury, but the magic binding her was too powerful.

The leader raised his spear to signal the advance. They raced out, wings singing, and split to encircle the stones. Waiting at a distance, they watched as their leader trotted forward alone. He was that sure of himself. His gaze scanned the stones, the two foreigners, the corpse, and the prisoners. Spotting Kereka, he stiffened, shoulders taut. He bent slightly forward, as if after all he had not expected to find her in such a predicament.

He absorbed the shock quickly enough. He was a man who knew how to adapt when the tide of battle turned against him; his cunning retreat in the face of superior numbers that he had twisted into a flanking ambush as the enemy galloped in reckless pursuit had defeated the Torkay, a tale everyone knew. He swung his gaze away from Kereka and addressed the bearded man, punctiliously polite.

"Honored sir, I address you. I, who am Prince Vayek, son of the Pechanek *begh*, scourge of the Uzay and Torkay clans, defender of Tarkan's honor, Festival champion, slayer of griffins. If you please, surrender. Therefore, if you do so, we will be able to allow you to live as a slave among us, treated fairly as long as you work hard. If we are forced to fight you, then unfortunately we must kill you."

"You are not the man who arranged to meet me here," said the woman, her voice so resonant and clear that it seemed the wind spoke at her command. Had she always known their language? For unlike the foreigners enslaved by the clans, she spoke without accent, without mistake, as smoothly as if she had taken someone else's voice as her own.

Belek coughed again, and Kereka glanced his way as he opened and closed his mouth impotently. Was this the payment—or maybe only the first of many payments—the witch had ripped out of him? Had she stolen his voice?

"Women are consulted in private, not in public among men," Vayek continued, still looking toward the bearded man. "I do not wish to insult any woman by so boldly addressing her where any man could hear her precious words."

"Alas, my companion cannot speak your language, while I can. Where are my griffin feathers? For I perceive you have them with you, there, in that bundle." She gestured with the crossbow.

Kereka had all this time been staring at Vayek, not because the conical helm seemed shaped to magnify and enhance the shapely regularity of his features but rather as a dying person stares at the arrow of death flying to meet her. But now she looked in the direction of the gesture to see one horse whose rider was slung belly-down over the saddle, a bulky bundle of rolled-up hides strapped to his back.

Fool of a stupid girl! How was she to free herself if she could not pay attention, observe, and react? She was still on the hunt. She wasn't married yet.

Vayek's warband rode with a dead man. And it was this man, apparently, who the witch had been waiting for. Kereka and the others had merely had the bad fortune to stumble upon their meeting place.

"I am willing to pay you the same reward I offered to the man I first dealt with. I presume that the bundle on his back is what he was obliged to deliver to me."

Vayek struggled; he truly did. He was famous among the clans for his exceptional courtesy and honor, and he made now no attempt to hide his feelings of embarrassment and shame, because true warriors expressed rage and joy and grief in public so that others might live their own struggles through such manly display. He looked again toward the bearded man, but the bearded man made no effort to intercede.

"Very well." As unseemly as it was to engage in such a conversation, he accepted the battleground, as a warrior must. "I will speak. I pray the gods will pardon me for my rudeness. I discovered a Berandai man skulking westward through the land with this bundle of griffin feathers. It is forbidden to trade the holy feathers outside the clans. He has paid the penalty." He gestured toward the body draped over the horse. "How can it be that such a meeting transpired, between foreign people and a plainsman, even one of the lowly Berandai, who like to call themselves our cousins? How can any foreigner have convinced even one of them to dishonor himself, his clan, and the grass and sky that sustains us?"

"Have your ancestors' tales not reminded you of that time, long in the past, when the Quman clans as well as the Berandai and the Kerayit made an agreement with the western queen? When they sent a levy to guard her, so the sorcerers of their kind could weave paths between the stones?"

"Women do not rule over men. We clansmen do not send our warriors to serve foreigners as slaves."

But Kereka had seen the flash of light in the stones. Could it be true that the witch and her companion had used sorcery to weave a path into these stones from some other faraway place? That they could cross a vast distance with a single step? The old tales spoke of such sorcery, but she had never believed it because the Quman shamans said it could not be accomplished. Yet what if they had only meant that *they* could not weave such magic?

"Maybe *you* do not remember," the witch went on, "but some among you have not forgotten the old compact. This man had not. He was one among a levy sent into the west by his chiefs ten years ago. I saved his life, but that is another story. His debt I agreed could be repaid by him delivering to me what I needed most."

"But I have already declared that it is forbidden! Perhaps an explanation is necessary. Griffin feathers are proof and purchase against sorcery. They are too powerful to be handled by any man except a shaman or a hero. They cannot be allowed to leave the grasslands. Long ago, griffin feathers were stolen from our ancestors, but the fabled *begh* Bulkezu invaded the western lands and returned the stolen feathers to their rightful place."

"Bulkezu the Humbled?" Her laughter cut sharply. "I see your clans do not learn from the past, as ours do in our careful keeping of records."

"Bulkezu was the greatest of *beghs*, the most honored and respected! He conquered the western lands and trampled their riders beneath his feet, and all the people living in those days knelt before him with their faces in the dirt."

She snorted. "He died a hunted man, killed by the bastard prince, Sanglant of Wendar. How small your world is! What tales you tell yourself! You don't even know the truth!"

Belek squirmed and grimaced, looking at Kereka with that excitable gaze of his, full of the hidden knowledge he had gleaned from the shamans who favored him and had shared with the sister he loved so well that he had secretly taught her how to fight.

She was accustomed to silence in the camp, but the witch's confident tongue emboldened her: *how small your world is*. Her own voice was harsh, like a crow's, but she cawed nevertheless, just to show that not all Quman were ignorant and blind. "I heard a different tale! I heard the great *begh* Bulkezu was killed by a phoenix, with wings of flame!"

Vayek's bright gaze flashed to her, and maybe he was shocked or maybe he simply refused to contradict her publicly before his waiting men because such correcting words would shame them both. Maybe he just knew better than to reveal to his enemy that he knew their prisoners. No doubt he was waiting to attack only for fear of risking Kereka's life. He himself need not fear the witch's sorcery; with his griffin wings, he was protected against it.

"Lads," he said instead, pretending not to recognize Kereka in her male clothing, "where did the witch come from?"

"Prince Belek was already wounded." Kereka choose her words slowly. Through desperate and thereby incautious speech, she and her brother had already betrayed their chiefly lineage, so all that was left them was to conceal Vayek's interest in her specifically. Yet she could not bear for Vayek to think she had given up, that she was returning meekly to the clans having failed in her hunt. "He was wounded taking a head. We had to help him reach his father the *begh* so he could die as a man, not a boy. Any other path would have been dishonorable. When we were riding back, we saw a flash of light like the sun rising. After that, we saw the witch standing up among the stones. We didn't see where she came from."

"Prince Vayek!" the witch cried, laughing as would a man after victory in a wrestling bout. "And this lad, the one whose spirit is woven with magic, he too is a prince!" Her gaze skipped from Belek to Kereka, and as the woman stared, Kereka did not flinch; she met her gaze; she would not be the first one to look away! But the woman's lips curved upward, cold and deadly: she was no fool, she could weave together the strands lying before her. She looked back toward the *begh*'s son. "Why are you come, Prince Vayek, son of the *begh* of the Pechanek clan, scourge, defender, champion? How have you stumbled across my poor comrade who so dutifully gathered griffin feathers for me? Were you out here in the western steppe looking for *something else?*"

He could not answer in words: he was too intelligent to give Kereka away, too proud to show weakness in public, too honorable to reply to a charge cast into the air by a woman who by all proper custom and understanding must be deemed insane and her life therefore forfeit.

He was a hero of the clans, seeking his bride. He had a different answer for his enemies.

He signaled with his spear. His riders shifted from stillness to motion between one heartbeat and the next. His own horse broke forward into a charge.

But the witch had guessed what was coming. She flung a handful of dust outward. When the first grains pattered onto the scarred earth sown with Edek's blood, threads of twisting red fire spewed out of the ground. Their furious heat scorched the grass outside the stones, although within them the air remained cool and the breeze gentle. Within two breaths, her sorcery wove a palisade impossible to breach.

Except for a man wearing griffin wings.

He tossed his spear to the ground and, drawing his sword, rode for the gap, where Edek's body, encased in white fire, did not quite seal the sorcerous palisade.

The bearded man released an arrow, the shot flying through the narrow gap.

Vayek rose in his stirrups and twisted, feathers flashing, and the arrow shredded to bits in the metal wings. He settled back into the saddle, lashing the horse, and with a leap they cleared the opening between the fiery palisade and Edek's burning feet. Again, and again, the bearded man released arrows, and again Vayek's quick reflexes shielded him as the arrows shattered in the feathers. He pressed hard, slamming a sword stroke at the bearded man, who hastily flung up his wooden shield to protect himself, taking such a solid blow that his legs twisted away under him and he stumbled back. Yet he was a strong and canny fighter, not easily subdued; he threw himself behind one of the great standing stones for cover as Vayek pulled the weight of his horse around in the confined corral made by the stones and the ring of sorcerous fire. Carrying a crossbow, the witch ran down to Edek's body and with her stone knife scraped the drying dregs of his blood out from Edek's head toward the far end of the scar. She meant to close the circle.

Kereka tugged at her ropes, hating this helplessness. All her life she had hated the things that bound her, just as poor Belek had hated his warriors' training so much that their father had once joked angrily that it would have been better had they swapped spirits into the other's body. Now, too—of course!—Belek had given up trying to break free; he had even shut his eyes!

"Belek!" Kereka whispered, hard enough to jolt him. "Is there no magic the shamans taught you? Anything that might help us—?"

Hoofbeats echoed eerily off the stones. She heard the snorting of a horse and then the horse loomed beside her, Vayek himself leaning from the saddle with a griffin feather plucked from his own wings held in his gauntlet. His gaze captured hers; he smiled, the expression all the more striking and sweet for its brevity.

"Boldest among women!" he said admiringly. "You have a man's courage and a man's wit! You alone will stand first among my wives, now and always! This I promise!"

What promises he made, he would keep. How could it be otherwise? He was a hero.

And so he would rescue her, and the tale's fame and elaboration would grow in the telling to become one of the great romantic legends told among the clans: his story, and she, like his noble horse, attendant in it.

A bolt like a slap of awakening clattered on the stone's face above Kereka's head and tumbled down over her body: another arrow. He sliced with the feather toward her. Ropes and magic slithered away. As she collapsed forward, released from the stone, he reined his steed hard aside and clattered off at a new angle to continue the fight. Kereka's hands and shoulders hurt, prickling with agony, but she shoved up against the pain. She had to watch. Movement flashed as a spear thrust from behind a huge stone monolith standing off to her right; steel flashed in reply as Vayek parried with his sword.

Over by the fiery palisade, the witch cursed, rising with blood on her knife, the gap between Edek's head and the scar now sealed. She raised the crossbow and released a bolt, but the missile slammed into stone to the right of the two warriors as they kept moving. She cursed again and winched in another bolt, then spun around as a bold rider tried to push through the remaining gap but was driven back by the intensity of the sorcerous flames.

Vayek fought the bearded man through the stones, using the stones and his wings to protect himself while the bearded man, with the agility of a seasoned fighter, used the stones to protect himself, trying to get close enough to hook his axe into Vayek's armor and pull him off the horse.

But in the end, the foreign man was just that: a man. He was not a hero. He was already bleeding from several wounds. It was only a matter of time before Vayek triumphed, yet again, as victor. What glory he would gather then!

All for him, because that was how the gods had fashioned the world: hawks hunted; horses grazed; marmots burrowed; flies annoyed. A man hunted glory while a woman tended the fires.

So the elders and shamans said. Their word was truth among the clans. What tales they told themselves! How small was their world?

Legs burning as with a hundred pricking needles, Kereka staggered to the pile of gear and grabbed the haft of the griffin's feather Edek had found. Where her skin brushed the lower edge of a vane, blood welled at once. She grabbed the first leather riding glove that came to hand and shoved her bleeding hand into it, and even then the griffin feather bit through it; tugged on a gauntlet—Edek's—and at last she could grasp it without more blood spilling. She sliced Belek free and hauled him up, the farmer's head bumping against his thigh, still tied to his belt. She shoved him toward the flames consuming Edek's corpse.

"Run! Quickly!" She pushed him before her, and after a few clumsy steps he broke away from her and, clutching his belly, limped in a staggering run as he choked down cries of pain. Kereka easily kept pace beside him, and as the witch swung around, braids flying, bringing her crossbow to bear, Kereka leaped in front into the line of fire.

"Do not kill us!" she cried, "and in exchange for my brother's life and his debt to you, I will fetch you the griffin feathers you seek. I swear it on the bones of my father's father! I swear it on the honor of Tarkan's arrows."

A sword rang, striking stone, and sparks tumbled. A male voice shouted; a thump was followed by the straining howls of men grappling.

The witch stepped aside.

With the griffin feather held before her to cut away the searing heat of the palisade, Kereka dragged Belek through the breach. The cool breeze within the stones vanished and they ran through a haze of hot smoke and blackened grass to burst coughing and heaving into clearer air beyond. The sky throbbed with such a hollow blue like the taut inside of a drum that she wondered all at once what the sky within the stone circle had looked like. Had it even been the same sky? She looked back, but smoke and the weave of fire obscured the area.

The Pechanek men closed around them, spears bristling, faces grim.

"Don't harm us!" Belek cried. "I'm the son of the Kirshat *begh*!"

She gave Belek a shove that sent him sprawling in the grass. Waving the griffin's feather, she shouted in her crow's voice.

"The foreign witch is almost vanquished, but her magic must be smothered once and for all! I come at Prince Vayek's command to take to him the bundle of griffin feathers he captured. At once!"

Women did not command warriors. They sat beside their fathers, or brothers, or husbands, and a man knew he must listen to the advice they dispensed lest he suffer for having foolishly ignored female wisdom. Yet a *begh*'s daughter cannot be trifled with, however unseemly her behavior. Nor would a common warrior wish to offend the future wife of his future *begh*.

The horse with its corpse and cargo was brought swiftly, the thick bundle wrapped in leather cut free. She grabbed the cords and hoisted the bundle onto her back, its weight oddly light given the power of what lay concealed within. Brandishing the griffin feather to cut a path for herself through the witch's sorcery, she ran back into the smoke before they could think to question her, although which one would have the courage to speak directly to her, who was neither kin or wife, she could not imagine. Grass crackled beneath her feet; soot and ash flaked and floated everywhere; the tapestry of flames rose as if to touch the pastures of the heavens, but she did not hesitate. She plunged into the maelstrom of scalding magic. Stinging hot ash rained on her cheeks and forehead.

"Sister! Don't leave me!"

But her and Belek's lives had been severed on the day Prince Vayek had ridden into the Kirshat clan with her bride price. It was the only reason cautious Belek had agreed to let her hunt with him: he was more afraid of losing her than of being beaten for taking her along where no one intended her to go.

Blessed breathable air hit her chest so unexpectedly that she was gulping and hacking as tears flowed freely. She blinked hard until she could see.

At the far edge of the circle, Vayek had caught the bearded man and pinned his axe against stone with his spear. The witch, her back to Kereka, loosed a bolt toward his magnificent profile, but he could not be taken by surprise. He twisted to bring his wings around to shield himself, and with the motion cut his sword down on his hapless prey.

The bearded man crumpled.

The witch shrieked.

Kereka shoved the bundle against the woman's torso and, when the witch flinched back, grabbed the crossbow out of her hands.

"You're not warrior enough to defeat him!" she cried. "Even I am not that! And there's no glory for me in being dead! Here are your griffin feathers. If you want to escape, pretend to fall at my feet."

She tossed the crossbow to one side as she screamed in as loud a voice as she had ever used. "Husband! Husband! The witch weaves an evil sorcery even now. She means to wither my womb! Hurry! We must escape this wicked, evil trap or I will be barren forever, no sons born from your siring to join the Pechanek clan! Hurry!"

He reined his horse hard away from the stone, casting a glance as swift as an arrow toward her. The bearded man lay slumped along the base of the black megalith. It was too late for him. But not for Kereka.

The witch had not moved, caught in a choice between clutching the precious bundle of griffin feathers or lunging past Kereka for the crossbow.

Kereka tripped her neatly, using a wrestling move she'd learned from Belek, speaking fast as she released her. "If it's true there are paths between the stones, then open a way now with your sorcery. But wait for me! Remember that I have fulfilled a debt and I want payment in return. Remember to trust me."

She leaped back as if fleeing something she feared more deeply than death itself. Vayek thundered up behind her, sword raised for the running kill, but Kereka held her ground with the griffin's feather shielding the witch's body.

"I've killed her!" she shouted. "Your courage has emboldened me! Now it won't be said that you laid hands on a mere woman! Quickly, let us go before her sorcery sickens me! I am so frightened, husband!"

She bolted toward the fire like an arrow released from Tarkan's heavenly bow, praying that Vayek would dismiss the woman as not worthy of his warrior's prowess. She ran, and he followed.

The fire's hissing crackle, the horse's weight and speed and heavy hoof-falls as it plunged toward the wall of fire; the high thrumming atonal singing of the wings in the presence of powerful magic; all this perhaps distracted Vayek as she raced ahead and dashed through that flaming gap in front of him. Fire roared. The smoke poured up to greet her, and because she was only one small human on two small feet, she darted to one side even as the clothes on her back grew hot and began to curl and blacken. He galloped past like the fury of the heavens, not even seeing her step aside because he was blinded by the tale he had long since learned to believe was the only tale in all the world.

But it wasn't true. The world was not the same no matter where you went. She'd seen the truth of that today.

She could follow Vayek back onto the sea of grass into a life whose contours were utterly familiar and entirely honorable. Handsome, brave, strong, even-tempered, honorable, famous among the clans for his prowess, with two secondary wives already although he was not ten years a man, he would be the worst kind of husband. A woman could live her life tending the fire of such a man's life. Its heat was seductive, but in the end its glory belonged only to him.

She spun, feet light beneath her, and raced back through the gap.

To find the witch already in action. She had bound the bundle of griffin feathers to her own back. Now she had her arms under the bearded man's shoulders, trying to hoist him up and over a saddled horse. Kereka ran to help her, got her arms around his hips and her own body beneath him. Blood slicked her hands and dripped on her face, but his rattling breaths revealed that he still lived.

The woman spared her one surprised glance. Then, like a *begh*, she gestured toward the other horses before running to a patch of sandy soil churned by the battle and spotted with blood. She unsheathed her obsidian knife and began, as one might at the Festival dance with Tarkan's flaming arrows, to cut a pattern into the expectant air.

A distant howl of rage rang from beyond the sorcerous fire.

Kereka ran to fetch the three remaining foreign beasts who had come with the witch and the bearded man as well as her own mount. The other horses were already saddled and laded, obedient to the lead. She strung them on a line and mounted the lead mare as an arch of golden fire flowered into existence just beyond the obsidian blade. The witch grabbed the reins of the bearded man's horse and walked under the fulgent threads.

Into what she walked, Kereka could not see. But riding the shore of the river of death was the risk you took to find out what lay on the other side.

Wings sang. The shape of a winged man astride a horse loomed beyond the fire. Vayek burst back past the writhing white fire of Edek's corpse and into the circle. The complex weave that gave the arch form began to fray at the edges, flashing and shivering.

Griffin feathers are proof against sorcery.

She flung Edek's griffin feather away; it glittered, spinning as on a wind blowing out of the unseen land beyond the arch, while Edek's gauntlet fell with a thud to the dirt. Then she whipped her mount forward, and they charged into a mist that stank of burned and rotting corpses, of ash and grass, of blood and noble deeds.

Her eyes streamed stinging tears; heat burned in her lungs.

The foul miasma cleared, and she was trotting free down the slope of a hill with blackened grass flying away beneath the horses' hooves and the sun setting ahead of her, drawing long shadows over the grass. The witch had already reached a familiar-looking stream, and she was kneeling beside the body of her comrade as she cast handfuls of glittering dust over his limp form. Saplings and brush fluttered in a brisk wind out of the west.

Kereka twisted to see behind her the same stones, the very same stone circle, rising black and ominous exactly where they had stood moments before. Vayek and his warband had vanished.

Did the witch possess such powerful sorcery that she could pluck men from the present world and cast them into the spirit world?

No.

The carpet of burned grass had cooled; its ashy stubble had been disheveled by strong winds; green shoots had found the courage to poke their heads above the scorched ground. She dismounted, tossed the reins over her mount's head. Her mare nipped one of the pack horses, who kicked; she separated the steppe horse and hobbled her, then trudged on aching feet back up into the stones. The soles of her boots were almost burned away. Her clothes shed flakes of soot. Her hands oozed blood from a score of hairline cuts. Her chest stung with each breath she inhaled.

There lay what remained of Edek, flesh eaten away by the unearthly fire and skeleton torn and scattered by beasts. Cut ropes lay in heaps at the base of three stones; the litter had been mauled by animals but was mostly intact. Their gear was gone, picked up to the last knife and bridle and leather bottle. The ashes of the campfire were ground into the earth. The wind gentled as dusk sighed down over them.

The moon shouldered up out of the east, round and bright, the full moon on which she was to have been wed. The moon could not lie. Half a month had passed since the night of the sword moon. The witch had woven a path between that time and this time, and they had ridden down it.

A whistle shrilled. Standing at the edge of the stones, Kereka saw the witch, standing now and waving to catch her attention. Trusting fool! It might well be easy to kill her and take the bearded man's head while he was injured and weak, before the witch fully healed him, if he could be healed. She could then ride back to her mother's tent and her father's tribe and declare herself a man. She knew what to expect from a man's life, just as she knew what a woman's life entailed.

So what kind of life did these foreigners live, with their sorcery and their crossbows and the way they handed a shovel from one to the other, sharing the same work, maybe even sharing the same glory? It was a question for which she had no answer. Not yet.

She went back to the litter and grabbed the leather tow lines. Pulled them taut over her own shoulders and tugged. Like uncertainty, the burden was unwieldy, but she was stubborn and it was not too heavy for her to manage.

Could she trust a witch? Would a witch and a foreigner ever trust her?

Pulling the litter behind her, she walked across the charred earth and down through the tall grass to find out.

Bound Man

Mary Robinette Kowal

Mary Robinette Kowal is the author of Shades of Milk and Honey *and* Glamour in Glass. *In 2008, she won the Campbell Award for Best New Writer and in 2011 her story "For Want of a Nail" won the Hugo Award for Best Short Story. Her work has also been a finalist for the Nebula and Locus awards. Her stories have appeared in* Strange Horizons, Asimov's, *and several Year's Best anthologies, as well as in her collection* Scenting the Dark and Other Stories *from Subterranean Press. She served two terms as the Vice President of Science Fiction and Fantasy Writers of America. Mary lives in Chicago with her husband Rob and over a dozen manual typewriters.*

LIGHT DAPPLED through the trees in the family courtyard, painting shadows on the paving stones. Li Reiko knelt by her son to look at his scraped knee.

"I just scratched it." Nawi squirmed under her hands.

Her daughter, Aya, leaned over her shoulder studying the healing. "Maybe Mama will show you her armor after she heals you."

Nawi stopped wiggling. "Really?"

Reiko shot Aya a warning look, but her little boy's dark eyes shone with excitement. Reiko smiled. "Really." What did tradition matter? "Now let me heal your knee." She laid her hand on the shallow wound.

"Ow."

"Shush." Reiko closed her eyes and rose in the dark space behind them.

In her mind's eye, Reiko took her time with the ritual, knowing it took less time than it appeared. In a heartbeat, green fire flared out to the walls of her mind. She dissolved into it as she focused on healing her son.

When the wound closed beneath her hand, she sank to the surface of her mind.

"There." She tousled Nawi's hair. "That wasn't bad, was it?"

"It tickled." He wrinkled his nose. "Will you show me your armor now?"

She sighed. She should not encourage his interest in the martial arts. His work would be with the histories that men kept, and yet..."Watch."

Pulling the smooth black surface out of the ether, she manifested her armor. It sheathed her like silence in the night. Aya watched with obvious anticipation for the day when she earned her own armor. Nawi's face, full of sharp yearning for something he would never have, cut Reiko's heart like a new blade.

"Can I see your sword?"

She let her armor vanish into thought. "No." Reiko brushed his hair from his eyes. "It's my turn to hide, right?"

Halldór twisted in his saddle, trying to ease the kink in his back. When the questing party reached the Parliament, he could remove the weight hanging between his shoulders.

With each step his horse took across the moss-covered lava field, the strange blade bumped against his spine, reminding him that he carried a legend. None of the runes or sheep entrails he read before their quest had foretold the ease with which they fulfilled the first part of the prophecy. They had found the Chooser of the Slain's narrow blade wrapped in linen, buried beneath an abandoned elf-house. In that dark room, the sword's hard silvery metal—longer than any of their bronze swords—had seemed lit by the moon.

Lárus pulled his horse alongside Halldór. "Will the ladies be waiting for us, do you think?"

"Maybe for you, my lord, but not for me."

"Nonsense. Women love the warrior-priest. 'Strong and sensitive.'"

He snorted through his mustache. "Just comb your hair so you don't look like a straw man."

A horse screamed behind them. Halldór turned, expecting to see its leg caught in one of the thousands of holes between the rocks. Instead, armed men swarmed from the gullies between the rocks, hacking at the riders. Bandits.

Halldór spun his horse to help Lárus and the others fight them off.

Lárus shouted, "Protect the Sword."

At the Duke's command, Halldór cursed and turned his horse from the fight, galloping across the rocks. Behind him, men cried out as they protected his escape. His horse twisted along the narrow paths between stones. It stopped abruptly, avoiding a chasm. Halldór looked back.

Scant lengths ahead of the bandits, Lárus rode, slumped in his saddle. Blood stained his cloak. The other men hung behind Lárus, protecting the Duke as long as possible.

Behind them, the bandits closed the remaining distance across the lava fields.

Halldór kicked his horse's side, driving it around the chasm. His horse stumbled sickeningly beneath him. Its leg snapped, caught between rocks. Halldór kicked free of the saddle as the horse screamed. He rolled clear. The rocky ground slammed the sword into his back. His face passed over the edge of the chasm. Breathless, he recoiled from the drop.

As he scrambled to his feet, Lárus thundered up. Without wasting a beat, Lárus flung himself from the saddle and tossed Halldór the reins. "Get the Sword to Parliament!"

Halldór grabbed the reins, swinging into the saddle. If they died returning to Parliament, did it matter that they had found the sword? "We must invoke the Sword!"

Lárus's right arm hung, blood-drenched, by his side, but he faced the bandits with his left. "Go!"

Halldór yanked the sword free of its wrappings. For the first time in six thousand years, the light of the sun fell on the silvery blade bringing fire to its length. It vibrated in his hands.

The first bandit reached Lárus and forced him back.

Halldór chanted the runes of power, petitioning the Chooser of the Slain.

Time stopped.

Reiko hid from her children, blending into the shadows of the courtyard with more urgency than she felt in combat. To do less would insult them.

"Ready or not, here I come!" Nawi spun from the tree and sprinted past her hiding place. Aya turned more slowly and studied the courtyard. Reiko smiled as her daughter sniffed the air, looking for tracks. Her son crashed through the bushes, kicking leaves with each footstep.

As another branch cracked under Nawi's foot, Reiko stifled the urge to correct his appalling technique. She would speak with his tutor about what the woman was teaching him. He was a boy, but that was no reason to neglect his education.

Watching Aya find Reiko's initial footprints and track them away from where she hid, Reiko slid from her hiding place. She walked across the courtyard to the fountain. This was a rule with her children; to make up for the size difference, she could not run.

She paced closer to the sparkling water, masking her sounds with its babble. From her right, Nawi shouted, "Have you found her?"

"No, silly!" Aya shook her head and stopped. She put her tiny hands on her hips, staring at the ground. "Her tracks stop here."

Reiko and her daughter were the same distance from the fountain, but on opposite sides. If Aya were paying attention, she would realize her mother had retraced her tracks and jumped from the fountain to the paving stones circling the grassy center of the courtyard. Reiko took three more steps before Aya turned.

As her daughter turned, Reiko felt, more than heard, her son on her left, reaching for her. Clever. He had misdirected her attention with his noise in the shrubbery. She fell forward, using gravity to drop beneath his hands. Rolling on her shoulder, she somersaulted, then launched to her feet as Aya ran toward her.

Nawi grabbed for her again. With a child on each side, Reiko danced and dodged closer to the fountain. She twisted from their grasp, laughing with them each time they missed her. Their giggles echoed through the courtyard.

The world tipped sideways and vibrated. Reiko stumbled as pain ripped through her spine.

Nawi's hand clapped against her side. "I got her!"

Fire engulfed Reiko.

The courtyard vanished.

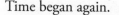

Time began again.

The sword in Halldór's hands thrummed with life. Fire from the sunset engulfed the sword and split the air. With a keening cry, the air opened and a form dropped through, silhouetted against a haze of fire. Horses and men screamed in terror.

When the fire died away, a woman stood between Halldór and the bandits.

Halldór's heart sank. Where was the Chooser of the Slain? Where was the warrior the sword had petitioned?

A bandit snarled a laughing oath and rushed toward them. The others followed him with their weapons raised.

The woman snatched the sword from Halldór's hands. In that brief moment, when he stared at her wild face, he realized that he *had* succeeded in calling Li Reiko, the Chooser of the Slain.

Then she turned. The air around her rippled with a heat haze as armor, dark as night, materialized around her body. He watched her dance with deadly grace, bending and twisting away from the bandits' blows. Without seeming thought, with movement as precise as ritual, she danced with death as her partner. Her sword slid through the bodies of the bandits.

Halldór dropped to his knees, thanking the gods for sending her. He watched the point of her sword trace a line, like the path of entrails on the church floor. The line of blood led to the next moment, the next and the next, as if each man's death was predestined.

Then she turned her sword on him.

Her blade descended, burning with the fire of the setting sun. She stopped as if she had run into a wall, with the point touching Halldór's chest.

Why had she stopped? If his blood was the price for saving Lárus, so be it. Her arm trembled. She grimaced, but did not move the sword closer.

Her face, half-hidden by her helm, was dark with rage. "Where am I?" Her words were crisp, more like a chant than common speech.

Holding still, Halldór said, "We are on the border of the Parliament lands, Li Reiko."

Her dark eyes, slanted beneath angry lids, widened. She pulled back and her armor rippled, vanishing into thought. Skin, tanned like the smoothest leather stretched over her wide cheekbones. Her hair hung in a heavy, black braid down her back. Halldór's pulse sang in his veins.

Only the gods in sagas had hair the color of the Allmother's night. Had he needed proof he had called the Chooser of the Slain, the inhuman black hair would have convinced him of that.

He bowed his head. "All praise to you, Great One. Grant us your blessings."

Reiko's breath hissed from her. He knew her name. She had dropped through a flaming portal into hell and this demon with bulging eyes knew her name.

She had tried to slay him as she had the others, but could not press her sword forward, as if a wall had protected him.

And now he asked for blessings.

"What blessings do you ask of me?" Reiko said. She controlled a shudder. What human had hair as pale as straw?

Straw lowered his bulging eyes to the demon lying in front of him. "Grant us, O Gracious One, the life of our Duke Lárus."

This Lárus had a wound deep in his shoulder. His blood was as red as any human's, but his face was pale as death.

She turned from Straw and wiped her sword on the thick moss, cleaning the blood from it. As soon as her attention seemed turned from them, Straw attended Lárus. She kept her awareness on the sounds of his movement as she sought balance in the familiar task of caring for her weapon. By the Gods! Why did he have her sword? It had been in her rooms not ten minutes before playing hide and seek with her children.

Panic almost took her. What had happened to her Aya and Nawi? She needed information, but displaying ignorance to an enemy was a weakness, which could kill surer than the sharpest blade. She considered.

Their weapons were bronze, not steel, and none of her opponents had manifested armor. They dressed in leather and felted wool, but no woven goods. So, then. That was their technology.

Straw had not healed Lárus, so perhaps they could not. He wanted her aid. Her thoughts checked. Could demons be bound by blood debt?

She turned to Straw.

"What price do you offer for this life?"

Straw raised his eyes; they were the color of the sky. "I offer my life unto you, O Great One."

She set her lips. What good would vengeance do? Unless... "Do you offer blood or service?"

He lowered his head again. "I submit to your will."

"You will serve me then. Do you agree to be my bound man?"

"I do."

"Good." She sheathed her sword. "What is your name?"

"Halldór Arnarsson."

"I accept your pledge." She dropped to her knees and pushed the leather from the wound on Lárus's shoulder. She pulled upon her reserves and, rising into the healing ritual, touched his mind.

He was human.

She pushed the shock aside; she could not spare the attention.

Halldór gasped as fire glowed around Li Reiko's hands. He had read of gods healing in the sagas, but bearing witness was beyond his dreams.

The glow faded. She lifted her hands from Lárus's shoulder. The wound was gone. A narrow red line and the blood-soaked clothing remained. Lárus opened his eyes as if he had been sleeping.

But her face was drawn. "I have paid the price for your service, bound man." She lifted a hand to her temple. "The wound was deeper..." Her eyes rolled back in her head and she slumped to the ground.

Lárus sat up and grabbed Halldór by the shoulder. "What did you do?"

Shaking Lárus off, Halldór crouched next to her. She was breathing. "I saved your life."

"By binding yourself to a woman? Are you mad?"

"She healed you. Healed! Look." Halldór pointed at her hair. "Look at her. This is Li Reiko."

"Li Reiko was a Warrior."

"You saw her. How long did it take her to kill six men?" He pointed at the carnage behind them. "Name one man who could do that."

Would moving her be a sacrilege? He grimaced. He would beg forgiveness if that were the case. "We should move before the sun sets and the trolls come out."

Lárus nodded slowly, his eyes still on the bodies around them. "Makes you wonder, doesn't it?"

"What?"

"How many other sagas are true?"

Halldór frowned. "They're all true."

The smell of mutton invaded her dreamless sleep. Reiko lay under sheepskin, on a bed of straw ticking. The straw poked through the wool fabric, pricking her bare skin. Straw. Her memory tickled her with an image of hair the color of straw. Halldór.

Long practice kept her breath even. She lay with her eyes closed, listening. A small room. An open fire. Women murmuring. She needed to learn as much as possible, before changing the balance by letting them know she was awake.

A hand placed a damp rag on her brow. The touch was light, a woman or a child.

The sheepskin's weight would telegraph her movement if she tried grabbing the hand. Better to open her eyes and feign weakness than to create an impression of threat. There was time for that later.

Reiko let her eyes flutter open. A girl bent over her, cast from the same demonic mold as Halldór. Her hair was the color of honey, and her wide blue eyes started from her head. She stilled when Reiko awoke, but did not pull away.

Reiko forced a smile, and let worry appear on her brow. "Where am I?"

"In the women's quarters at the Parliament grounds."

Reiko sat up. The sheepskin fell away, letting the cool air caress her body. The girl averted her eyes. Conversation in the room stopped.

Interesting. They had a nudity taboo. She reached for the sheepskin and pulled it over her torso. "What is your name?"

"Mara Halldórsdottir."

Her bound man had a daughter. And his people had a patronymic system—how far from home was she? "Where are my clothes, Mara?"

The girl lifted a folded bundle of cloth from a low bench next to the bed. "I washed them for you."

"Thank you." If Mara had washed and dried her clothes, Reiko must have been unconscious for several hours. Lárus's wound had been deeper than she thought. "Where is my sword?"

"My father has it."

Rage filled Reiko's veins like the fire that had brought her here. She waited for the heat to dwindle, then began dressing. As Reiko pulled her boots on, she asked, "Where is he?"

Behind Mara, the other women shifted as if Reiko were crossing a line. Mara ignored them. "He's with Parliament."

"Which is where?" The eyes of the other women felt like heat on her skin. Ah. Parliament contained the line she should not cross, and they clearly would not answer her. Her mind teased her with memories of folk in other lands. She had never paid much heed to these stories, since history had been men's work. She smiled at Mara. "Thank you for your kindness."

As she strode from the room she kept her senses fanned out, waiting for resistance from them, but they hung back as if they were afraid.

The women's quarters fronted on a narrow twisting path lined with low turf and stone houses. The end of the street opened on a large raised circle surrounded by stone benches.

Men sat on the benches, but women stayed below. Lárus spoke in the middle of the circle. By his side, Halldór stood with her sword in his hands. Sheltering in the shadow by a house, Reiko studied them. They towered above her, but their movements were clumsy and oafish like a trained bear. Nawi had better training than any here.

Her son. Sudden anxiety and rage filled her lungs, but rage invited rash decisions. She forced the anger away.

With effort, she returned her focus to the men. They had no awareness of their mass, only of their size and an imperfect grasp of that.

Halldór lifted his head. As if guided by strings his eyes found her in the shadows.

He dropped to his knees and held out her sword. In mid-sentence, Lárus looked at Halldór, and then turned to Reiko. Surprise crossed his face, but he bowed his head.

"Li Reiko, you honor us with your presence."

Reiko climbed onto the stone circle. As she crossed to retrieve her sword, an ox of a man rose to his feet. "I will not sit here, while a woman is in the Parliament's circle."

Lárus scowled. "Ingolfur, this is no mortal woman."

Reiko's attention sprang forward. What did they think she was, if not mortal?

"You darkened a trollop's hair with soot." Ingolfur crossed his arms. "You expect me to believe she's a god?"

Her pulse quickened. What were they saying? Lárus flung his cloak back, showing the torn and blood-soaked leather at his shoulder. "We were set upon by bandits. My arm was cut half off and she healed it." His pale face flushed red. "I tell you this is Li Reiko, returned to the world."

She understood the words, but they had no meaning. Each sentence out of their mouths raised a thousand questions in her mind.

"Ha." Ingolfur spat on the ground. "Your quest sought a warrior to defeat the Troll King."

This she understood. "And if I do, what price do you offer?"

Lárus opened his mouth but Ingolfur crossed the circle.

"You pretend to be the Chooser of the Slain?" Ingolfur reached for her, as if she were a doll he could pick up. Before his hand touched her shoulder, she took his wrist, pulling on it as she twisted. She drove her shoulder into his belly and used his mass to flip him as she stood.

She had thought these were demons, but by their actions they were men, full of swagger and rash judgment. She waited. He would attack her again.

Ingolfur raged behind her. Reiko focused on his sounds and the small changes in the air. As he reached for her, she twisted away from his hands and with his force, sent him stumbling from the circle. The men broke into laughter.

She waited again.

It might take time but Ingolfur would learn his place. A man courted death, touching a woman unasked.

Halldór stepped in front of Reiko and faced Ingolfur. "Great Ingolfur, surely you can see no mortal woman could face our champion."

Reiko cocked her head slightly. Her bound man showed wit by appeasing the oaf's vanity.

Lárus pointed to her sword in Halldór's hands. "Who here still doubts we have completed our quest?" The men shifted on their benches uneasily. "We fulfilled the first part of the prophecy by returning Li Reiko to the world."

What prophecy had her name in it? There might be a bargaining chip here.

"You promised us a mighty warrior, the Chooser of the Slain," Ingolfur snarled, "not a woman."

It was time for action. If they wanted a god, they should have one. "Have no doubt. I can defeat the Troll King." She let her armor flourish around her. Ingolfur drew back involuntarily. Around the circle, she heard gasps and sharp cries.

She drew her sword from Halldór's hands. "Who here will test me?"

Halldór dropped to his knees in front of her. "The Chooser of the Slain!"

In the same breath, Lárus knelt and cried, "Li Reiko!"

Around the circle, men followed suit. On the ground below, women and children knelt in the dirt. They cried her name. In the safety of her helm, Reiko scowled. Playing at godhood was a dangerous lie.

She lowered her sword. "But there is a price. You must return me to the heavens."

Halldór's eyes grew wider than she thought possible. "How, my lady?"

She shook her head. "You know the gods grant nothing easily. They say you must return me. You must learn how. Who here accepts that price for your freedom from the trolls?"

She sheathed her sword and let her armor vanish into thought. Turning on her heel, she strode off the Parliament's circle.

Halldór clambered to his feet as Li Reiko left the Parliament circle. His head reeled. She hinted at things beyond his training. Lárus grabbed him by the arm. "What does she mean, return her?"

Ingolfur tossed his hands. "If that is the price, I will pay it gladly.

Ridding the world of the Troll King and her at the same time would be a joy."

"Is it possible?"

Men crowded around Halldór, asking him theological questions of the sagas. The answers eluded him. He had not cast a rune-stone or read an entrail since they started for the elf-house a week ago. "She would not ask if it were impossible." He swallowed. "I will study the problem with my brothers and return to you."

Lárus clapped him on the back. "Good man." When Lárus turned to the throng surrounding them, Halldór slipped away.

He found Li Reiko surrounded by children. The women hung back, too shy to come near, but the children crowded close. Halldór could hardly believe she had killed six men as easily as carding wool. For the space of a breath, he watched her play peek-a-boo with a small child, her face open with delight and pain.

She saw him and shutters closed over her soul. Standing, her eyes impassive, she said, "I want to read the prophecy."

He blinked, surprised. Then his heart lifted; maybe she would show him how to pay her price. "It is stored in the church."

Reiko brushed the child's hair from its eyes, then fell into step beside Halldór. He could barely keep a sedate pace to the church.

Inside, he led her through the nave to the library beside the sanctuary. The other priests, studying, stared at the Chooser of the Slain. Halldór felt as if he were outside himself with the strangeness of this. He was leading Li Reiko, a Warrior out of the oldest sagas, past shelves containing her history.

Since the gods had arrived from across the sea, his brothers had recorded their history. For six-thousand unbroken years, the records of prophecy and the sagas kept their history whole.

When they reached the collections desk, the acolyte on duty looked as if he would wet himself. Halldór stood between the boy and the Chooser of the Slain, but the boy still stared with an open mouth.

"Bring me the Troll King prophecy, and the Sagas of Li Nawi, Volume I. We will be in the side chapel."

Still gaping, the boy nodded and ran down the aisles.

"We can study in here." He led the Chooser of the Slain to the side chapel. Halldór was shocked again at how small she was, not much taller than the acolyte. He had thought the gods would be larger than life.

He had hundreds of questions, but none of the words.

When the acolyte came back, Halldór sent a silent prayer of thanks. Here was something they could discuss. He took the vellum roll and the massive volume of sagas the acolyte carried and shooed him out of the room.

Halldór's palms were damp with sweat as he pulled on wool gloves to protect the manuscripts. He hesitated over another pair of gloves, then set them aside. Her hands could heal; she would not damage the manuscripts.

Carefully, Halldór unrolled the prophecy scroll on the table. He did not look at the rendering of entrails. He watched her.

She gave no hint of her thoughts. "I want to hear your explanation of this."

A cold current ran up his spine, as if he were eleven again, explaining scripture to an elder. Halldór licked his lips and pointed at the arc of sclera. "This represents the heavens, and the overlap here," he pointed at the bulge of the lower intestine, "means time of conflict. I interpreted the opening in the bulge to mean specifically the Troll King. This pattern of blood means—"

She crossed her arms. "You clearly understand your discipline. Tell me the prophecy in plain language."

"Oh." He looked at the drawing of the entrails again. What did she see that he did not? "Well, in a time of conflict—which is now—the Chooser of the Slain overcomes the Troll King." He pointed at the shining knot around the lower intestine. "See how this chokes off the Troll King. That means you win the battle."

"And how did you know the legendary warrior was—is me?"

"I cross-referenced with our histories and you were the one that fit the criteria."

She shivered. "Show me the history. I want to understand how you deciphered this."

Halldór thanked the gods that he had asked for Li Nawi's saga as well. He placed the heavy volume of history in front of Li Reiko and opened to the Book of Fire, Chapter I.

In the autumn of the Fire, Li Reiko, greatest of the warriors, trained Li Nawi and his sister Aya in the ways of Death. In the midst of the training, a curtain of fire split Nawi from Aya and when they came together again, Li Reiko was gone. Though they were frightened, they understood that the Chooser of the Slain had taken a rightful place in heaven.

Reiko trembled, her control gone. "What is this?"

"It is the Saga of Li Nawi."

She tried phrasing casual questions, but her mind spun in circles. "How do you come to have this?"

Halldór traced the letters with his gloved hand. "After the Collapse, when waves of fire had rolled across our land, Li Nawi came across the oceans with the other gods. He was our conqueror and our salvation."

The ranks of stone shelves filled with thick leather bindings crowded her. Her heart kicked wildly.

Halldór's voice seemed drowned out by the drumming of her pulse. "The Sagas are our heritage and charge. The gods have left the Earth, but we keep records of histories as they taught us."

Reiko turned her eyes blindly from the page. "Your heritage?"

"I have been dedicated to the service of the gods since my birth." He paused. "Your sagas were the most inspiring. Forgive my trespasses, may I beg for your indulgence with a question?"

"What?" Hot and cold washed over her in sickening waves.

"I have read your son Li Nawi's accounts of your triumphs in battle."

Reiko could not breathe. Halldór flipped the pages forward. "This is how I knew where to look for your sword." He paused with his hand over the letters. "I deciphered the clues to invoke it and call you here, but there are many—"

Reiko pushed away from the table. "You caused the curtain of fire?" She wanted to vomit her fear at his feet.

"I—I do not understand."

"I dropped through fire this morning." *And when they came together again, Li Reiko was no more.* What had it been like for Aya and Nawi to watch their mother ripped out of time?

Halldór said, "In answer to my petition."

"I was playing hide and seek with my children and you took me."

"You were in the heavens with the gods."

"That's something you tell a grieving child!"

"I—I didn't, I—" His face turned gray. "Forgive me, Great One."

"I am not a god!" She pushed him, all control gone. He tripped over a bench and dropped to the floor. "Send me back."

"I cannot."

Her sword flew from its sheath before she realized she held it. "Send me back!" She held it to his neck. Her arms trembled with the desire to run it through him. But it would not move.

She leaned on the blade, digging her feet into the floor. "You ripped me out of time and took me from my children."

He shook his head. "It had already happened."

"Because of you." Her sword crept closer, pricking a drop of blood from his neck. What protected him?

Halldór lay on his back. "I'm sorry. I didn't know...I was following the prophecy."

Reiko staggered. Prophecy. A wall of predestination. Empty, she dropped to the bench and cradled her sword. "How long ago...?"

"Six thousand years."

She closed her eyes. This was why he could not return her. He had not simply brought her from across the sea like the other "gods." He had brought her through time. If she were trapped here, if she could never see her children again, it did not matter if these were human or demons. She was banished in Hell.

"What do the sagas say about my children?"

Halldór rolled to his knees. "I can show you." His voice shook.

"No." She ran her hand down the blade of her sword. Its edge whispered against her skin. She touched her wrist to the blade. It would be easy. "Read it to me."

She heard him get to his feet. The pages of the heavy book shuffled.

Halldór swallowed and read, "This is from the Saga of Li Nawi, the Book of the Sword, Chapter Two. 'And it came to pass that Li Aya and Li Nawi were raised unto adulthood by their tutor.'"

A tutor raised them, because he, Halldór, had pulled their mother away. He shook his head. It had happened six thousand years ago.

"'But when they reached adulthood, each claimed the right of Li Reiko's sword.'"

They fought over the sword, with which he had called her, not out of the heavens, but from across time. Halldór shivered and focused on the page.

"'Li Aya challenged Li Nawi, saying Death was her birthright. But Nawi, on hearing this, scoffed and said he was a Child of Death. And saying so, he took Li Reiko's sword and the gods smote Li Aya with their fiery hand, thus granting Li Nawi the victory.'"

Halldór's entrails twisted as if the gods were reading them. He had read these sagas since he was a boy. He believed them, but he had not thought they were real. He looked at Li Reiko. She held her head in her lap and rocked back and forth.

For all his talk of prophecies, he was the one who had found the sword and invoked it. "'Then all men knew he was the true Child of Death. He raised an army of men, the First of the Nine Armies, and thus began the Collapse—'"

"Stop."

"I'm sorry." He would slaughter a thousand sheep if one would tell him how to undo his crime. In the Saga of Li Nawi, Li Reiko never appeared after the wall of fire. He closed the book and took a step toward her. "The price you asked...I can't send you back."

Li Reiko drew a shuddering breath and looked up. "I have already paid the price for you." Her eyes reflected his guilt. "Another hero can kill the Troll King."

His pulse rattled forward like a panicked horse. "No one else can. The prophecy points to you."

"Gut a new sheep, bound man. I won't help you." She stood. "I release you from your debt."

"But, it's unpaid. I owe you a life."

"You cannot pay the price I ask." She turned and touched her sword to his neck again. He flinched. "I couldn't kill you when I wanted to." She cocked her head, and traced the point of the blade around his neck, not quite touching him. "What destiny waits for you?"

"Nothing." He was no one.

She snorted. "How nice to be without a fate." Sheathing her sword, she walked toward the door.

He followed her. Nothing made sense. "Where are you going?" She spun and drove her fist into his midriff. He grunted and folded over the pain. Panting, Reiko pulled her sword out and hit his side with the flat of her blade. Halldór held his cry in.

She swung again, with the edge, but the wall of force stopped her; Halldór held still. She turned the blade and slammed the flat against his ribs again. The breath hissed out of him, but he did not move. He knelt in front of her, waiting for the next blow. He deserved this. He deserved more than this.

Li Reiko's lip curled in disgust. "Do not follow me."

He scrabbled forward on his knees. "Then tell me where you're going, so I will not meet you by chance."

"Maybe that is your destiny." She left him.

Halldór did not follow her.

Li Reiko chased her shadow out of the parliament lands. It stretched before her in the golden light of sunrise, racing her across the moss-covered lava. The wind, whipping across the treeless plain, pushed her like a child late for dinner.

Surrounded by the people in the Parliament lands, Reiko's anger had overwhelmed her and buried her grief. Whatever Halldór thought her destiny was, she saw only two paths in front of her—make a life here or join her children in the only way left. Neither were paths to choose rashly.

Small shrubs and grasses broke the green with patches of red and gold, as if someone had unrolled a carpet on the ground. Heavy undulations creased the land with crevices. Some held water reflecting the sky, others dropped to a lower level of moss and soft grasses, and some were as dark as the inside of a cave.

When the sun crossed the sky and painted the land with long shadows, Reiko sought shelter from the wind in one of the crevices. The moss cradled her with the warmth of the earth.

She pulled thoughts of Aya and Nawi close. In her memory, they laughed as they reached for her. Sobs pushed past Reiko's reserves. She wrapped her arms around her chest. Each cry shattered her. Her children were dead because Halldór had decided a disemboweled sheep meant he should rip her out of time. It did not matter if they had grown up; she had not been there. They were six-thousand years dead. Inside her head, Reiko battled grief. Her fists pounded against the walls of her mind. *No.* Her brain filled with that silent syllable.

She pressed her face against the velvet moss wanting the earth to absorb her.

She heard a sound.

Training quieted her breath in a moment. Reiko lifted her head from the moss and listened. Footsteps crossed the earth above her. She manifested her armor and rolled silently to her feet. If Halldór had followed her, she would play the part of a man and seek revenge.

In the light of the moon, a figure, larger than a man, crept toward her. A troll. Behind him, a gang of trolls watched. Reiko counted them and considered the terrain. It was safer to hide, but anger still throbbed in her bones. She left her sword sheathed and slunk out of the crevice in the ground. Her argument was not with them.

Flowing across the moss, she let the uneven shadows mask her until she reached a standing mound of stones. The wind carried the trolls' stink to her.

The lone troll reached the crevice she had sheltered in. His arm darted down like a bear fishing and he roared with astonishment.

The other trolls laughed. "Got away, did she?"

One of them said, "Mucker was smelling his own crotch is all."

"Yah, sure. He didn't get enough in the Hall and goes around thinking he smells more."

They had taken human women. Reiko felt a stabbing pain in her loins; she could not let that stand.

Mucker whirled. "Shut up! I know I smelled a woman."

"Then where'd she go?" The troll snorted the air. "Don't smell one now."

The other lumbered away. "Let's go, while some of 'em are still fresh."

Mucker slumped and followed the other trolls. Reiko eased out of the shadows. She was a fool, but would not hide while women were raped.

She hung back, letting the wind bring their sounds and scents as she tracked the trolls to their Hall.

The moon had sunk to a handspan above the horizon as they reached the Troll Hall. Trolls stood on either side of the great stone doors.

Reiko crouched in the shadows. The night was silent except for the sounds of revelry. Even with alcohol slowing their movement, there were too many of them.

If she could goad the sentries into taking her on one at a time she could get inside, but only if no other trolls came. The sound of swordplay would draw a crowd faster than crows to carrion.

A harness jingled.

Reiko's head snapped in the direction of the sound.

She shielded her eyes from the light coming out of the Troll Hall. As her vision adjusted, a man on horseback resolved out of the dark. He sat twenty or thirty horselengths away, invisible to the trolls outside the Hall. Reiko eased toward him, senses wide.

The horse shifted its weight when it smelled her. The man put his hand on its neck, calming it. Light from the Troll Hall hinted at the planes on his face. Halldór. Her lips tightened. He had followed her. Reiko warred with an irrational desire to call the trolls down on them.

She needed him. Halldór, with his drawings and histories, might know what the inside of the Troll Hall looked like.

Praying he would have sense enough to be quiet, she stepped out of the shadows. He jumped as she appeared, but stayed silent.

He swung off his horse and leaned close. His whisper was hot in her ear. "Forgive me. I did not follow you."

He turned his head, letting her breathe an answer in return. "Understood. They have women inside."

"I know." Halldór looked toward the Troll Hall. Dried blood covered the left side of his face.

"We should move away to talk," she said.

He took his horse by the reins and followed her. His horse's hooves were bound with sheepskin so they made no sound on the rocks. Something had happened since she left the Parliament lands.

Halldór limped on his left side. Reiko's heart beat as if she were running. The trolls had women prisoners. Halldór bore signs of battle. Trolls must have attacked the Parliament. They walked in silence until the sounds of the Troll Hall dwindled to nothing.

Halldór stopped. "There was a raid." He stared at nothing, his jaw clenched. "While I was gone...they just let the trolls—" His voice broke like a boy's. "They have my girl."

Mara. Anger slipped from Reiko. "Halldór, I'm sorry." She looked for other riders. "Who came with you?"

He shook his head. "No one. They're guarding the walls in case the trolls come back." He touched the side of his face. "I tried persuading them."

"Why did you come?"

"To get Mara back."

"There are too many of them, bound man." She scowled. "Even if you could get inside, what do you plan to do? Challenge the Troll King to single combat?" Her words resonated in her skull. Reiko closed her eyes, dizzy with the turns the gods spun her in. When she opened them, Halldór's lips were parted in prayer. Reiko swallowed. "When does the sun rise?"

"In another hour."

She turned to the Hall. In an hour, the trolls could not give chase; the sun would turn them to stone. She unbraided her hair.

Halldór stared as her long hair began flirting with the wind. She smiled at the question in his eyes. "I have a prophecy to fulfill."

Reiko stumbled into the torchlight, her hair loose and wild. She clutched Halldór's cloak around her shoulders.

One of the troll sentries saw her. "Hey. A dolly."

Reiko contorted her face with fear and whimpered. The other troll laughed. "She don't seem taken with you, do she?"

The first troll came closer. "She don't have to."

"Don't hurt me. Please, please..." Reiko retreated from him. When she was between the two, she whipped Halldór's cloak off, tangling it around the first troll's head. With her sword, she gutted the other. He dropped to his knees, fumbling with his entrails as she turned to the first. She slid her sword under the cloak, slicing along the base of the first troll's jaw.

Leaving them to die, Reiko entered the Hall. Women's cries mingled with the sounds of debauchery.

She kept her focus on the battle ahead. She would be out-matched in size and strength, but hoped her wit and weapon would prevail. Her mouth twisted. She knew she would prevail. It was predestined.

A troll saw her. He lumbered closer. Reiko showed her sword, bright with blood. "I have met your sentries. Shall we dance as well?"

The troll checked his movement and squinted his beady eyes at her. Reiko walked past him. She kept her awareness on him, but another troll, Mucker, loomed in front of her.

"Where do you think you're going?"

"I am the one you sought. I am Chooser of the Slain. I have come for your King."

Mucker laughed and reached for her, heedless of her sword. She dodged under his grasp and held the point to his jugular. "I have come for your King. Not for you. Show me to him."

She leapt back. His hand went to his throat and came away with blood.

A bellow rose from the entry. Someone had found the sentries. Reiko kept her gaze on Mucker, but her peripheral vision filled with trolls running. Footsteps behind her. She spun and planted her sword in a troll's arm. The troll howled, drawing back. Reiko shook her head. "I have come for your King."

They herded her to the Hall. She had no chance of defeating them, but if the Troll King granted her single combat, she might escape the Hall with the prisoners. When she entered the great Hall, whispers flew; the number of slain trolls mounted with each rumor.

The Troll King lolled on his throne. Mara, her face red with shame, serviced him.

Anger buzzed in Reiko's ears. She let it pass through her. "Troll King, I have come to challenge you."

The Troll King laughed like an avalanche of stone tearing down his Hall. "You! A dolly wants to fight?"

Reiko paid no attention to his words.

He was nearly twice her height. Leather armor, crusted with crude bronze scales, covered his body. The weight of feast hung about his middle, but his shoulders bulged with muscle. If he connected a blow, she would die. But he would be fighting gravity as well as her. Once he began a movement, it would take time for him to stop and begin another.

Reiko raised her head, waiting until his laughter faded. "I am the Chooser of the Slain. Will you accept my challenge?" She forced a smile to her lips. "Or are you afraid to dance with me?"

"I will grind you to paste, dolly. I will sweep over your lands and eat your children for my breakfast."

"If you win, you may. Here are my terms. If I win, the prisoners go free."

He came down from his throne and leaned close. "If you win, we will never show a shadow in human lands."

"Will your people hold that pledge when you are dead?"

He laughed. The stink of his breath boiled around her. He turned to the trolls packed in the Hall. "Will you?"

The room rocked with the roar of their voices. "Aye."

The Troll King leered. "And when you lose, I won't kill you till I've bedded you."

"Agreed. May the gods hear our pledge." Reiko manifested her armor.

As the night-black plates materialized around her, the Troll King bellowed, "What is this?"

"This?" She taunted him. "This is but a toy the gods have sent to play with you."

She smiled in her helm as he swung his heavy iron sword over his head and charged her. Stupid. Reiko stepped to the side, already turning as she let him pass.

She brought her sword hard against the gap in his armor above his boot. The blade jarred against bone. She yanked her sword free; blood coated it like a sheath.

The Troll King dropped to one knee, hamstrung. Without waiting, she vaulted up his back and wrapped her arms around his neck. *Like Aya riding piggyback*. He flailed his sword through the air, reaching for her. She slit his throat. His bellow changed to a gurgle as blood fountained in an arc, soaking the ground.

A heavy ache filled her breast. She whispered in his ear. "I have killed you without honor. I am a machine of the gods."

Reiko let gravity pull the Troll King down, as trolls shrieked. She leapt off his body as it fell forward.

Before the dust settled around him, Reiko pointed her sword at the nearest troll. "Release the prisoners."

Reiko led the women into the dawn. As they left the Troll Hall, Halldór dropped to his knees with his arms lifted in prayer. Mara wrapped her arms around his neck, sobbing.

Reiko felt nothing. Why should she, when the victory was not hers? She withdrew from the group of women weeping and singing her praises.

Halldór chased her. "Lady, my life is already yours but my debt has doubled."

He reminded her of a suitor in one of Aya's bedtime stories, accepting gifts without asking what the witchyman's price would be. She knelt to clean her sword on the moss. "Then give me your firstborn child."

She could hear his breath hitch in his throat. "If that is your price."

Reiko raised her eyes. "No. That is a price I will not ask."

He knelt beside her. "I know why you can not kill me."

"Good." She turned to her sword. "When you fulfill your fate let me know, so I can."

His blue eyes shone with fervor. "I am destined to return your daughter to you."

Reiko's heart flooded with pain and hope. She fought for breath. "Do not toy with me, bound man."

"I would not. I reviewed the sagas after you went into the Hall. It says 'and the gods smote Li Aya with their fiery hand.' I can bring Li Aya here."

Reiko sunk her fingers into the moss, clutching the earth. Oh gods, to have her little girl here—she trembled. Aya would not be a child. There would be no games of hide and seek. *When they reached adulthood, each claimed the right of Li Reiko's sword...*how old would Aya be?

Reiko shook her head. She could not do that to her daughter. "You want to rip Aya out of time as well. If Nawi had not won, the Collapse would not have happened."

Halldór brow furrowed. "But it already did."

Reiko stared at the women, and the barren landscape beyond them. Everything she saw was a result of her son's actions. Or were her son's actions the result of choices made here? She did not know if it mattered. The cogs in the gods' machine clicked forward.

"Are there any prophecies about Aya?"

Halldór nodded. "She's destined to—"

Reiko put her hand on his mouth as if she could stop fate. "Don't." She closed her eyes, fingers still resting on his lips. "If you bring her, promise me you won't let her know she's bound to the will of the gods."

He nodded.

Reiko withdrew her hand and pressed it to her temple. Her skull throbbed with potential decisions. Aya had already vanished into fire; if Reiko did not decide to bring her here, where would Aya go?

Her bound man knelt next to her, waiting for her decision. Aya would not forgive Reiko for yanking her out of time, anymore than Reiko had forgiven Halldór.

His eyes flicked over her shoulder and then back. Reiko turned to follow his gaze. Mara comforted another girl. What did the future hold for Halldór's daughter? In this time, women seemed to have no role.

But times could change. Watching Mara, Reiko knew which path to choose if she were granted free will.

"Bring Aya to me." Reiko looked at the sword in her hand. "My daughter's birthright waits for her."

The Narcomancer

N. K. Jemisin

N. K. Jemisin is a Brooklyn author whose short fiction and novels have been multiply nominated for the Hugo and the Nebula awards, and shortlisted for the Crawford and the Tiptree awards; she has won the Locus Award for Best First Novel and the Romantic Times *Reviewers' Choice Award for fantasy. She is also the first winner of the Speculative Literature Foundation's Gulliver Travel Research Grant, a graduate of the Viable Paradise workshop, and a current member of the Altered Fluid writers' group. Her epic fantasy novels include* The Hundred Thousand Kingdoms *and the other books in the Inheritance trilogy, as well as the Dreamblood series, which includes the novels* The Killing Moon *and* The Shadowed Sun. *The following story also takes place in that same milieu.*

IN THE LAND OF GUJAAREH it was said that trouble came by twos. Four bands of color marked the face of the Dreaming Moon; the great river split into four tributaries; there were four harvests in a year; four humours coursed the inner rivers of living flesh. By contrast, two of anything in nature meant inevitable conflict: stallions in a herd, lions in a pride. Siblings. The sexes.

Gatherer Cet's twin troubles came in the form of two women. The first was a farmcaste woman who had been injured by an angry bull-ox; half her brains had been dashed out beneath its hooves. The Sharers, who could work miracles with the Goddess' healing magic, had given up on her. "We can grow her a new head," said one of the Sharer-elders to Cet, "but we cannot put the memories of her lifetime back in it. Best to claim her dreamblood for others, and send her soul where her mind has already gone."

But when Cet arrived in the Hall of Blessings to see to the woman, he confronted a scene of utter chaos. Three squalling children struggled in the arms of a Sentinel, hampering him as he tried to assist his brethren. Nearer by, a young man fought to get past two of the Sharers, trying to reach a third Templeman—whom, clearly, he blamed for the woman's condition. "You didn't even try!" he shouted, the words barely intelligible through his sobs. "How can my wife live if you won't even try?"

He elbowed one of the Sharers in the chest and nearly got free, but the other flung himself on the distraught husband's back then, half dragging him to the floor. Still the man fought with manic fury, murder in his eyes. None of them noticed Cet until Cet stepped in front of the young man and raised his jungissa stone.

Startled, the young man stopped struggling, his attention caught by the stone. It had been carved into the likeness of a dragonfly; its gleaming black wings blurred as Cet tapped the stone hard with his thumbnail. The resulting sharp whine cut across the cacophony filling the Hall until even the children stopped weeping to look for the source of the noise. As peace returned, Cet willed the stone's vibration to soften to a low, gentle hum. The man sagged as tension drained out of his body, until he hung limp in the two Sharers' arms.

"You know she is already dead," Cet said to the young man. "You know this must be done."

The young man's face tightened in anguish. "No. She breathes. Her heart beats." He slurred the words as if drunk. "No."

"Denying it makes no difference. The pattern of her soul has been lost. If she were healed, you would have to raise her all over again, like one of your children. To make her your wife then would be an abomination."

The man began to weep again, quietly this time. But he no longer fought, and when Cet moved around him to approach his wife, he uttered a little moan and looked away.

Cet knelt beside the cot where the woman lay, and put his fore- and middle-fingers on her closed eyelids. She was already adrift in the realms between waking and dream; there was no need to use his jungissa to put her to sleep. He followed her into the silent dark and examined her soul, searching for any signs of hope. But the woman's soul was indeed like that of an infant, soft and devoid of all but the most simplistic desires and emotions. The merest press of Cet's will was enough to send her toward the land of dreams, where she would doubtless dissolve into the substance of that realm—or perhaps she would eventually be reborn, to walk the realm of waking anew and regain the experiences she had lost.

Either way, her fate was not for Cet to decide. Having delivered her soul safely, he severed the tether that had bound her to the waking realm, and collected the delicate dreamblood that spilled forth.

The weeping that greeted Cet upon his return to waking was of a different order from before. Turning, Cet saw with satisfaction that the farmcaste man stood with his children now, holding them as they watched the woman's flesh breathe its last. They were still distraught, but the violent madness was gone; in its place was the sort of grief that expressed itself through love and would, eventually, bring healing.

"That was nicely done," said a low voice beside him, and Cet looked up to see the Temple Superior. Belatedly he realized the Superior had been the target of the distraught husband's wrath. Cet had been so focused on the family that he had not noticed.

"You gave them peace without dreamblood," the Superior continued. "Truly, Gatherer Cet, our Goddess favors you."

Cet got to his feet, sighing as the languor of the Gathering faded slowly within him. "The Hall has still been profaned," he said. He looked up at the great shining statue of the Goddess of Dreams, who towered over them with hands outstretched in welcome and eyes shut in the Eternal Dream. "Voices have been raised and violence done, right here at Her feet."

"S-Superior?" A boy appeared at the Superior's shoulder, too young to be an acolyte. One of the Temple's adoptees from the House of Children, probably working a duty-shift as an errand runner. "Are you hurt at all? I saw that man..."

The Superior smiled down at him. "No, child; I'm fine, thank you. Go back to the House before your Teacher misses you."

Looking relieved, the boy departed. The Superior sighed, watching him leave. "Some chaos is to be expected at times like this. The heart is rarely peaceful." He gave Cet a faint smile. "Though, of course, you would not know that, Gatherer."

"I remember the time before I took my oath."

"Not the same."

Cet shrugged, gazing at the mourning family. "I have the peace and order of Temple life to comfort me now. It is enough."

The Superior looked at him oddly for a moment, then sighed. "Well, I'm afraid I must ask you to leave that comfort for a time, Cet. Will you come with me to my office? I have a matter that requires the attention of a Gatherer—one with your unique skill at bestowing peace."

And thus did Cet's second hardship fall upon him.

The quartet that stood in the Superior's office were upriver folk. Cet could see that in their dingy clothing and utter lack of makeup or jewelry; not even the poorest city dweller kept themselves so plain. And no city dweller went unsandaled on the brick-paved streets, which grew painfully hot at midday. Yet the woman who stood at the group's head had the proud carriage of one used to the respect and obedience of others, finery or no finery. The three men all but cowered behind her as the Superior and Cet entered the room.

"Cet, this is Mehepi," said the Superior, gesturing to the woman. "She and her companions are from a mining village some ways to the south, in the foothills that border the Empty Thousand. Mehepi, I bring you Cet, one of the Temple's Gatherers."

Mehepi's eyes widened in a way that would have amused Cet, had he been capable of amusement. Clearly she had expected something more of Gujaareh's famed Gatherers; someone taller, perhaps. But she recovered quickly and gave him a respectful bow. "I greet you in peace, Gatherer," she said, "though I bring unpeaceful tidings."

Cet inclined his head. "Tidings of—" But he trailed off, surprised, as his eyes caught a slight movement in the afternoon shadows of the room.

Some ways apart from Mehepi and the others, a younger woman knelt on a cushion. She was so still—it was her breathing Cet had noticed—that Cet made no wonder he had overlooked her, though now it seemed absurd that he had. Wealthy men had commissioned sculptures with lips less lush, bones less graceful; sugared currants were not as temptingly black as her skin. Though the other upriver folk were staring at Cet, her eyes remained downcast, her body unmoving beneath the faded-indigo drape of her gown. Indigo: the mourning color. Mehepi wore it too.

"What is this?" Cet asked, nodding toward the younger woman.

Was there unease in Mehepi's eyes? Defensiveness, certainly. "We were told the Temple offers its aid only to those who follow the ways of the Dream Goddess," she said. "We have no money to tithe, Gatherer, and none of us has offered dreams or goods in the past year..."

All at once Cet understood. "You brought her as payment."

"No, not payment—" But even without the hint of a stammer in Mehepi's voice, the lie was plain in her manner.

"Explain, then." Cet spoke more sharply than was, perhaps, strictly peaceful. "Why does she sit apart from the rest of you?"

The villagers looked at one another. But before any of them could speak, the young woman said, "Because I am cursed, Gatherer."

The Temple Superior frowned. "Cursed? Is that some upriver superstition?"

Cet had thought the younger woman broken in spirit, to judge by her motionlessness and fixed gaze at the floor. But now she lifted her eyes, and Cet realized that whatever was wrong with her, she was not broken. There was despair in her, strong enough to taste, but something more as well.

"I was a lapis merchant's wife," she said. "When he died, I was taken by the village headman as a secondwife. Now the headman is dead, and they blame me."

"She is barren!" said one of the male villagers. "Two husbands and no children yet? And Mehepi here, she is the firstwife—"

"All of my children had been stillborn," said Mehepi, touching her belly as if remembering the feel of them inside her. That much was truth, as was her pain; some of Cet's irritation with her eased. "That was why my husband took another wife. Then my last child was born alive. The whole village rejoiced! But the next morning, the child stopped breathing. A few days later the brigands came." Her face tightened in anger. "They killed my husband while she slept beside him. And they had their way with her, but even despite that there is no child." Mehepi shook her head. "For so much death to follow one woman, and life itself to shun her? How can it be anything but a curse? That is why..." She darted a look at Cet, then drew herself up. "That is why we thought you might find value in her, Gatherer. Death is your business."

"Death is not a Gatherer's business," Cet said. Did the woman realize how greatly she had insulted him and all his brethren? For the first time in a very long while, he felt anger stir in his heart. "*Peace* is our business. Sharers do that by healing the flesh. Gatherers deal with the soul, judging those which are too corrupt or damaged to be salvaged and granting them the Goddess' blessing—"

"If you had learned your catechisms better you would understand that," the Superior interjected smoothly. He threw Cet a mild look, doubtless to remind Cet that they could not expect better of ignorant country folk. "And you would have known there was no need for payment. In a situation like this, when the peace of many is under threat, it is the Temple's duty to offer aid."

The men looked abashed; Mehepi's jaw tightened at the scolding. With a sigh, the Superior glanced down at some notes he'd taken on a reedleaf sheet. "So, Cet; these brigands she mentioned are the problem. For the past three turns of the greater moon, their village and others along the Empty Thousand have suffered a curious series of attacks. Everyone in the village falls asleep—even the men on guard duty. When they wake, their valuables are gone. Food stores, livestock, the few stones of worth they gather from their mine; their children have been taken too, no doubt sold to those desert tribes who traffic in slaves. Some of the women and youths have been abused, as you heard. And a few, such as the village headman and the guards, were slain outright, perhaps to soften the village's defenses for later. No one wakes during these assaults."

Cet inhaled, all his anger forgotten. "A sleep spell? But only the Temple uses narcomancy."

"Impossible to say," the Superior said. "But given the nature of these attacks, it seems clear we must help. Magic is fought best with magic." He looked at Cet as he spoke.

Cet nodded, suppressing the urge to sigh. It would have been within his rights to suggest that one of his other Gatherer-brethren—perhaps Liyou, the youngest—handle the matter instead. But after all his talk of peace and righteous duty, that would have been hypocritical. And... in spite of himself, his gaze drifted back to the younger woman. She had lowered her eyes once more, her hands folded in her lap. There was nothing peaceful in her stillness.

"We will need a soul-healer," Cet said softly. "There is more to this than abuse of magic."

The Superior sighed. "A Sister, then. I'll write the summons to their Matriarch." The Sisters were an offshoot branch of the faith, coexisting with the Servants of Hananja in an uneasy parallel. Cet knew the Superior had never liked them.

Cet gave him a rueful smile. "Everything for Her peace." He had never liked them either.

They set out that afternoon: the five villagers, two of the Temple's warrior Sentinels, Cet, and a Sister of the Goddess. The Sister, who arrived unescorted at the river docks just as they were ready to push off, was worse than even Cet had expected—tall and commanding, clad in the pale gold robes and veils that signified high rank in their order. That meant this Sister had mastered the most difficult techniques of erotic dreaming, with its attendant power to affect the spirit and the subtler processes of flesh. A formidable creature. But the greatest problem in Cet's eyes was that the Sister was male.

"Did the messenger not explain the situation?" Cet asked the Sister at the first opportunity. He kept his tone light. They rode in a canopied barge more than large enough to hold their entire party and the pole-crew besides. It was not large enough to accommodate ill feelings between himself and the Sister.

The Sister, who had given his name as Ginnem, stretched out along the bench he had claimed for himself. "Gatherers; so tactful."

Cet resisted the urge to grind his teeth. "You cannot deny that a different Sister—a female Sister—would have been better-suited to deal with this matter."

"Perhaps," Ginnem replied, with a smile that said he thought no one better-suited than himself. "But look." He glanced across the aisle at the villagers, who had occupied a different corner of the barge. The three men sat together on a bench across from the firstwife. Three benches back, the young woman sat alone.

"That one has suffered at the hands of both men and women," Ginnem said. "Do you think my sex makes any difference to her?"

"She was raped by men," Cet said.

"And she is being destroyed by a woman. That firstwife wants her dead, can you not see?" Ginnem shook his head, jingling tiny bells woven into each of his braids. "If not for the need to involve the Temple in the brigand matter, no doubt the firstwife would've found some quiet way to do her in already. And why do you imagine only a woman could know of rape?"

Cet started. "Forgive me. I did not realize—"

"It was long ago." Ginnem shrugged his broad shoulders. "When I was a soldier; another life."

Cet's surprise must have shown on his face, for a moment later Ginnem laughed. "Yes, I was born military caste," he said. "I earned high rank before I felt the calling to the Sisterhood. And I still keep up some of my old habits." He lifted one flowing sleeve to reveal a knife-sheath strapped around his forearm, then flicked it back so quickly that no one but Cet noticed. "So you see, there is more than one reason the Sisterhood sent me."

Cet nodded slowly, still trying and failing to form a clear opinion of Ginnem. Male Sisters were rare; he wondered if all of them were this strange. "Then we are four fighters and not three. Good."

"Oh, don't count me," Ginnem said. "My soldier days are over; I fight only when necessary now. And I expect I'll have my hands full with other duties." He glanced at the young woman again, sobering. "Someone should talk to her."

And he turned his kohl-lined eyes to Cet.

Night had fallen, humid and thick, by the time Cet went to the woman. Her companions were already abed, motionless on pallets the crew had lain on deck. One of the Sentinels was asleep; the other stood at the prow with the ship's watchman.

The woman still sat on her bench. Cet watched her for a time, wondering if the lapping water and steadily passing palm trees had lulled her to sleep, but then she lifted a hand to brush away a persistent moth. Throwing a glance at Ginnem—who was snoring faintly on his bench—Cet rose and went to sit across from the woman. Her eyes were lost in some waking dream until he sat down, but they sharpened very quickly.

"What is your name?" he asked.

"Namsut." Her voice was low and warm, touched with some southlands accent.

"I am Cet," he replied.

"Gatherer Cet."

"Does my title trouble you?"

She shook her head. "You bring comfort to those who suffer. That takes a kind heart."

Surprised, Cet smiled. "Few even among the Goddess' most devout followers see anything other than the death I bring. Fewer still have ever called me kind for it. Thank you."

She shook her head, looking into the passing water. "No one who has known suffering would think ill of you, Gatherer."

Widowed twice, raped, shunned... He tried to imagine her pain and could not. That inability troubled him, all of a sudden.

"I will find the brigands who hurt you," he said, to cover his discomfort. "I will see that their corruption is excised from the world."

To his surprise, her eyes went hard as iron though she kept her voice soft. "They did nothing to me that two husbands had not already done," she said. "And wife-brokers before that, and my father's creditors before that. Will you hunt down all of them?" She shook her head. "Kill the brigands, but not for me."

This was not at all the response that Cet had expected. So confused was he that he blurted the first question that came to his mind. "What shall I do for you, then?"

Namsut's smile threw him even further. It was not bitter, that smile, but neither was it gentle. It was a smile of anger, he realized at last. Pure, politely restrained, tooth-grinding rage.

"Give me a child," she said.

In the morning, Cet spoke of the woman's request to Ginnem.

"In the upriver towns, the headman's wife rules if the headman dies," Cet explained as they broke their fast. "That is tradition, according to Namsut. But a village head must prove him or herself favored by the gods, to rule. Namsut says fertility is one method of proof."

Ginnem frowned, chewing thoughtfully on a date. A group of women on the passing shore were doing laundry at the riverside, singing a rhythmic song while they worked. "That explains a great deal," he said at last. "Mehepi has proven herself at least able to conceive, but after so many dead children the village must be wondering if she too is cursed. And since having a priest for a lover might also connote the gods' favor, I know now why Mehepi has been eying me with such speculation."

Cet started, feeling his cheeks heat. "You think she wants—" He took a date to cover his discomfort. "From you?"

Ginnem grinned. "And why not? Am I not fine?" He made a show of tossing his hair, setting all the tiny bells a-tinkle.

"You know full well what I mean," Cet said, glancing about in embarrassment. Some of the other passengers looked their way at the sound of Ginnem's hair-bells, but no one was close enough to overhear.

"Yes, and it saddens me to see how much it troubles you," Ginnem said, abruptly serious. "*Sex*, Gatherer Cet. That is the word you cannot bring yourself to say, isn't it?" When Cet said nothing, Ginnem made an annoyed sound. "Well, I will not let you avoid it, however much you and your stiff-necked Servant brethren disapprove. I am a Sister of the Goddess. I use narcomancy—and yes, my body when necessary—to heal those wounded spirits that can be healed. It is no less holy a task than what you do for those who cannot be healed, Gatherer, save that my petitioners do not die when I'm done!"

He was right. Cet bent at the waist, his eyes downcast, to signal his contrition. The gesture seemed to mollify Ginnem, who sighed.

"And no, Mehepi has not approached me," Ginnem said, "though she's hardly had time, with three such devoted attendants..." Abruptly he caught his breath. "Ahh—yes, *now* I understand. I first thought this was a simple matter of a powerful senior wife plotting against a weaker secondwife. But more than that—this is a race. Whichever woman produces a healthy child first will rule the village."

Cet frowned, glancing over at the young woman again. She had finally allowed herself to sleep, leaning against one of the canopy-pillars and drawing her feet up onto the bench. Only in sleep was her face peaceful, Cet noticed. It made her even more beautiful, though he'd hardly imagined that possible.

"The contest is uneven," he said. He glanced over at the headwoman Mehepi—acting headwoman, he realized now, by virtue solely of her seniority. She was still asleep on one of the pallets, comfortable between two of her men. "Three lovers to none."

"Yes." Ginnem's lip curled. "That curse business was a handy bit of cleverness on Mehepi's part. No man will touch the secondwife for fear of sharing the curse."

"It seems wrong," Cet said softly, gazing at Namsut. "That she should have to endure yet another man's lust to survive."

"You grew up in the city, didn't you?" When Cet nodded, Ginnem said, "Yes, I thought so. My birth-village was closer to the city, and surely more fortunate than these people's, but some customs are the same in every backwater. Children are wealth out here, you see—another miner, another strong back on the farm, another eye to watch for enemies. A woman is honored for the children she produces, and so she should be. But make no mistake, Gatherer: this contest is for power. The secondwife could leave that village. She could have asked asylum of your Temple Superior. She returns to the village by choice."

Cet frowned, mulling over that interpretation for a moment. It did not feel right.

"My father was a horse-trader," he said. Ginnem raised an eyebrow at the apparent non-sequitur; Cet gave him a faint shrug of apology. "Not a very good one. He took poor care of his animals, trying to squeeze every drop of profit from their hides."

Even after so many years it shamed Cet to speak of his father, for anyone who listened could guess what his childhood had been like. A man so neglectful of his livelihood was unlikely to be particularly careful of his heirs. He saw this realization dawn on Ginnem's face, but to Cet's relief Ginnem merely nodded for Cet to continue.

"Once, my father sold a horse—a sickly, half-starved creature—to a man so known for his cruelty that no other trader in the city would serve him. But before the man could saddle the horse, it gave a great neigh and leapt into the river. It could have swum back to shore, but that would have meant recapture. So it swam in the opposite direction, deeper into the river, where finally the current carried it away."

Ginnem gave Cet a skeptical look. "You think the secondwife *wants* the village to kill her?"

Cet shook his head. "The horse was not dead. When last I saw it, it was swimming with the current, its head above the water, facing whatever fate awaited it downriver. Most likely it drowned or was eaten by predators. But what if it survived the journey, and even now runs free over some faraway pasture? Would that not be a reward worth so much risk?"

"Ah. All or nothing; win a better life or die trying." Ginnem's eyes narrowed as he gazed contemplatively at Cet. "You understand the secondwife well, I see."

Cet drew back, abruptly unnerved by the way Ginnem was looking at him. "I respect her."

"You find her beautiful?"

He said it with as much dignity as he could: "I am not blind."

Ginnem looked Cet up and down in a way that reminded Cet uncomfortably of his father's customers. "You are fine enough," Ginnem said, with more than a hint of lasciviousness in his tone. "Handsome, healthy, intelligent. A tad short, but that's no great matter if she does not mind a small child—"

"'A Gatherer belongs wholly to the Goddess,'" Cet said, leaning close so that the disapproval in his voice would not be heard by the others. "That is the oath I swore when I chose this path. The celibacy—"

"Comes second to your primary mission, Gatherer," Ginnem said in an equally stern voice. "It is the duty of any priest of the Goddess of Dreams to bring peace. There are two ways we might create peace in this village, once we've dealt with the brigands. One is to let Mehepi goad the villagefolk into killing or exiling the secondwife. The other is to give the secondwife a chance to control her own life for the first time. Which do you choose?"

"There are other choices," Cet muttered, uneasily. "There must be."

Ginnem shrugged. "If she has any talent for dreaming, she could join my order. But I see no sign of the calling in her."

"You could still suggest it to her."

"Mmm." Ginnem's tone was noncommittal. He turned to gaze at Namsut. "That horse you spoke of. If you could have helped it on its way, would you have? Even if that earned you the wrath of the horse's owner and your father?"

Cet flinched back, too startled and flustered to speak. Ginnem's eyes slid back to him.

"How did the horse break free, Cet?"

Cet set his jaw. "I should rest while I can. The rest of the journey will be long."

"Dream well," Ginnem said. Cet turned away and lay down, but he felt Ginnem's eyes on him for a long while afterward.

When Cet slept, he dreamt of Namsut.

The land of dreams was as infinite as the mind of the Goddess who contained it. Though every soul traveled there during sleep, it was rare for two to meet. Most often, the people encountered in dreams were phantoms—conjurations of the dreamer's own mind, no more real than the palm trees and placid oasis which manifested around Cet's dreamform now. But real or not, there sat Namsut on a boulder overlooking the water, her indigo veils wafting in the hot desert wind.

"I wish I could be you," she said, not turning from the water. Her voice was a whisper; her mouth never moved. "So strong, so serene, the kind-hearted killer. Do your victims feel what you feel?"

"You do not desire or require death," Cet said.

"True. I'm a fool for it, but I want to live." Her image blurred for a moment, superimposed by that of a long-legged girlchild with the same despairing, angry eyes. "I was nine when a man first took me. My parents were so angry, so ashamed. I made them feel helpless. I should have died then."

"No," Cet said quietly. "Others' sins are no fault of yours."

"I know that." Abruptly something large and dark turned a lazy loop under the water—a manifestation of her anger, since oases did not have fish. But like her anger, the monster never broke the surface. Cet found this at once fascinating and disturbing.

"The magic that I use," he said. "Do you know how it works?"

"Dreamichor from nonsense-dreams," she said. "Dreamseed from wet dreams, dreambile from nightmares, dreamblood from the last dream before death. The four humours of the soul."

He nodded. "Dreamblood is what Gatherers collect. It has the power to erase pain and quiet emotions." He stepped closer then, though he did not touch her. "If your heart is pained, I can share dreamblood with you now."

She shook her head. "I do not want my pain erased. It makes me strong." She turned to look up at him. "Will you give me a child, Gatherer?"

He sighed, and the sky overhead seemed to dim. "It is not our way. The Sister...dreamseed is his specialty. Perhaps..."

"Ginnem does not have your kind eyes. Nor do your Sentinel brethren. You, Gatherer Cet. If I must bear a child, I want yours."

Clouds began to race across the desert sky, some as tormented abstractions, some forming blatantly erotic shapes. Cet closed his eyes against the shiver that moved along his spine. "It is not our way," he said again, but there was a waver in his voice that he could not quite conceal.

He heard the smile in her voice just as keenly. "These are your magic-quieted emotions, Gatherer? They seem loud enough."

He forced his mind away from thoughts of her, lest they disturb his inner peace any further. What was wrong with him? By sheer will he stilled the unrest in his heart, and gratifyingly the sky was clear again when he opened his eyes.

"Forgive me," he murmured.

"I will not. It comforts me to know that you are still capable of feeling. You should not hide it; people would fear Gatherers less if they knew." She looked thoughtful. "Why do you hide it?"

Cet sighed. "Even the Goddess' magic cannot quiet a Gatherer's emotions forever. After many years, the feelings inevitably break free... and they are very powerful then. Sometimes dangerous." He shifted, uncomfortable on many levels. "As you said, we frighten people enough as it is."

She nodded, then abruptly rose and turned to him. "There are no other choices," she said. "I have no desire to serve the Goddess as a Sister. There is none of Her peace in my heart, and there may never be. But I mean to live, Gatherer—*truly* live, as more than a man's plaything or a woman's scapegoat. I want this for my children as well. So I ask you again: Will you help me?"

She was a phantom. Cet knew that now, for she could not have known of his conversation with Ginnem otherwise. He was talking to himself, or to some aspect of the Goddess come to reflect his own folly back at him. Yet he felt compelled to answer. "I cannot."

The dreamscape transformed, becoming the inside of a room. A gauze-draped low bed, wide enough for two, lay behind Namsut.

She glanced at it, then at him. "But you want to."

That afternoon they disembarked at a large trading-town. There Cet used Temple funds to purchase horses and supplies for the rest of the trip. The village, said Mehepi, was on the far side of the foothills, beyond the verdant floodplain that made up the richest part of Gujaareh. It would take at least another day's travel to get there.

They set out as soon as the horses were loaded, making good time along an irrigation road which ran flat through miles of barley, hekeh, and silvercape fields. As sunset approached they entered the low, arid foothills—Gujaareh's last line of defense against the ever-encroaching desert beyond. Here Cet called a halt. The villagers were nervous, for the hills were the brigands' territory, but with night's chill already setting in and the horses weary, there was little choice. The Sentinels split the watch while the rest of them tended their mounts and made an uneasy camp.

Cet had only just settled near a large boulder when he saw Ginnem crouched beside Namsut's pallet. Ginnem's hands were under her blanket, moving over her midsection in some slow rhythmic dance. Namsut's face had turned away from Cet, but he heard her gasp clearly enough, and saw Ginnem's smile.

Rage blotted out thought. For several breaths Cet was paralyzed by it, torn between shock, confusion, and a mad desire to walk across camp and beat Ginnem bloody.

But then Ginnem frowned and glanced his way, and the anger shattered.

Goddess... Shivering with more than the night's chill, Cet lifted his eyes to the great multihued face of the Dreaming Moon. What had that been? Now that the madness had passed, he could taste magic in the air: the delicate salt-and-metal of dreamseed. Ginnem had been healing the girl, nothing more. But even if Ginnem had been pleasuring her, what did it matter? Cet was a Gatherer. He had pledged himself to a goddess, and goddesses did not share.

A few moments later he heard footsteps and felt someone settle beside him. "Are you all right, Gatherer Cet?" Ginnem.

Cet closed his eyes. The Moon's afterimage burned against his eyelids in tilted stripes: red for blood, white for seed, yellow for ichor, black for bile.

"I do not know," he whispered.

"Well." Ginnem kept his voice light, but Cet heard the serious note underneath it. "I know jealousy when I sense it, and shock and horror too. Dreamseed is more fragile than the other humours; your rage tore my spell like a rock through spidersilk."

Horrified, Cet looked from him to Namsut. "I'm sorry. I did not mean—is she—"

"She is undamaged, Gatherer. I was done by the time you wanted to throttle me. What concerns me more is that you wanted to throttle me at all." He glanced sidelong at Cet.

"Something is...wrong with me." But Cet dared not say what that might be. Had it been happening all along? He thought back and remembered his anger at Mehepi, the layers of unease that Namsut stirred in him. Yes. Those had been the warnings.

Not yet, he prayed to Her. *Not yet. It is too soon.*

Ginnem nodded and fell silent for a while. Finally he said, very softly, "If I could give Namsut what she wants, I would. But though those parts of me still function in the simplest sense, I have already lost the ability to father a child. In time, I will only give pleasure through dreams."

Cet started. The Sisters were a secretive lot—as were Cet's own fellow Servants, of course—but he had never known what price they paid for their magic. Then he realized Ginnem's confession had been an offering. Trust for trust.

"It...begins slowly with us," Cet admitted, forcing out the words. It was a Gatherer's greatest secret, and greatest shame. "First surging emotions, then dreaming awake, and finally we...we lose all peace, and go

mad. There is no cure, once the process begins. If it has begun for me..."
He trailed off. It was too much, on top of everything else. He could not
bear the thought. He was not ready.

Ginnem put a hand on his shoulder in silent compassion. When Cet
said nothing more, Ginnem got to his feet. "I will help all I can."

This made Cet frown. Ginnem chuckled and shook his belled head.
"I am a healer, Gatherer, whatever you might think of my bedroom
habits—"

He paused suddenly, his smile fading. A breath later Cet felt it too—
an intense, sudden desire to sleep. With it came the thin, unmistakable
whine of a jungissa stone, wafting through the camp like a poisoned
breeze.

One of the Sentinels cried an alarm. Cet scrambled to his feet,
fumbling for his ornaments. Ginnem dropped to his knees and began
chanting something, his hands held outward as if pushing against some
invisible force. The Sentinels had gone back to back in the shadow of a
boulder, working some kind of complicated dance with their knives to
aid their concentration against the spell. Mehepi and one of the men
were already asleep; as Cet looked around for the source of the spell, the
other two men fell to the ground. Namsut made a sound like pain and
stumbled toward Cet and Ginnem. Her eyes were heavy and dull, Cet
saw, her legs shaking as if she walked under a great weight, but she was
awake. She fought the magic with an almost visible determination.

He felt fear and longing as he gazed at her, a leviathan rising beneath
the formerly placid waters of his soul.

So he snatched forth his own jungissa and struck it with a fingernail.
Its deeper, clearer song rang across the hills, cutting across the atonal
waver of the narcomancer's stone. Folding his will around the shape
of the vibrations, Cet closed his eyes and flung forth the only possible
counter to the narcomancer's sleep-spell: one of his own.

The Sentinels dropped, their knives clattering on the rocky soil.
Namsut moaned and collapsed, a dark blur among the moonlit stones.
Ginnem caught his breath. "Cet, what...are you..." Then he, too, sagged.

There was a clatter of stones from a nearby hill as the narcomancer's
jungissa-song faltered. Cet caught a glimpse of several dark forms moving

among the stones there, some dragging others who had fallen, and abruptly the narcomancer's jungissa began to fade as with distance. They were running away.

Cet kept his jungissa humming until the last of the terrible urge to sleep had passed. Then he sagged onto a saddle and thanked the Goddess, over and over again.

"A jungissa," Cet said. "No doubt."

It was morning. The group sat around a fire eating travel-food and drinking bitter, strong coffee, for none of them had slept well once Cet awakened them from the spell.

The villagers looked at each other and shook their heads at Cet's statement, uncomprehending. The Sentinels looked grim. "I suspected as much," Ginnem said with a sigh. "Nothing else has that sound."

For the villagers, Cet plucked his own jungissa stone from the belt of his loinskirt and held it out for them to see. It sat in his hand, a delicately carved dragonfly in polished blue-black. He tapped it with his thumbnail, and they all winced as it shivered and sent forth its characteristic whine.

"The jungissa itself has no power," Cet said to reassure them. He willed the stone silent; it went instantly still. "It amplifies magic only for those who have been trained in narcomantic techniques. This jungissa is the child of a stone which fell from the sky many centuries ago. There are only fifteen other ornaments like it in all the world. Three have cracked or broken over time. One was given to the House of the Sisters; one is used by the Temple for training and healing purposes; but only I and my three brother-Gatherers carry and use the stones on a regular basis. The remainder of the stones are kept in the Temple vault under guard." He sighed. "And yet, somehow, these brigands have one."

Ginnem frowned. "I saw the Sisters' queen-bee stone in our House just before I left for this journey. Could someone have stolen a stone from the Temple?"

One of the Sentinels drew himself up at that, scowling in affront. "No one could get past my brothers and I to do so."

"You said these stones fall from the sky?" asked Namsut. She looked thoughtful. "There was sun's seed in the sky a few months ago, on the night of the Ze-kaari celebration. I saw many streaks cross the stars; there was a new Moon that night. Most faded to nothing, but one came very near, and there was light in the hills where it fell."

"Another jungissa?" It was almost too astounding and horrible to contemplate—another of the Goddess' gifts, lying unhallowed in a pit somewhere and pawed over by ruffians? Cet shuddered. "But even if they found such a thing, the rough stone itself would be useless. It must be carved to produce a sound. And it takes years of training to use that sound."

"What difference does any of that make?" Ginnem asked, scowling. "They have one and they've used it. We must capture them and take it."

Military thinking; Cet almost smiled. But he nodded agreement.

"How did you see sun's seed?" Mehepi demanded suddenly of Namsut. "Our husband had you with him that night—or so I believed 'til now. Did you slip out to meet some other lover?"

Namsut smiled another of her polite, angry smiles. "I often went outside after a night with him. The fresh air settled my stomach."

Mehepi caught her breath in affront, then spat on the ground at Namsut's feet. "Nightmare-spawned demoness! Why our husband married a woman so full of hate and death, I will never understand!"

Ginnem threw a stern look at Mehepi. "Your behavior is offensive to our goddess, headwoman."

Mehepi looked sullen for a moment, but then mumbled an apology. No hint of anger showed on Namsut's face as she inclined her head first to Ginnem, then to Mehepi. That done, she rose, brushed off her gown, and walked away.

But Cet had seen something which made him frown. Nodding to the others to excuse himself, he rose and trotted after her. Though Namsut must have heard him, she kept walking, and only when he caught her in the lee of the hill did she turn to face him.

He took her hands and turned them over. Across each of the palms was a row of dark crusted crescents.

"So that was how you fought the spell," he said.

Namsut's face was as blank as a stone. "I told you, Gatherer. Pain makes me strong."

He almost flinched, for that conversation had taken place in dreaming. But within the mind of the Goddess everything was possible, and desires often called forth the unexpected.

To encourage that desire was dangerous. Yet the compulsion to brush a thumb across her small wounds was irresistible, as was the compulsion to do something about them. Namsut's eyelids fluttered as Cet willed her into a waking dream. In it she looked down to see that her hands were whole. When he released the dream, she blinked, then looked down. Cet rubbed away the lingering smears of dried blood with his thumb; the wounds were gone.

"A simple healing is within any Servant's skill," he said softly. "And it is a Gatherer's duty to fight pain."

Her lips thinned. "Yes, I had forgotten. Pain makes me strong, and you will do nothing that actually helps me. I thank you, Gatherer, but I must wash before we begin the day's travels."

She pulled away before he could think of a reply, and as he watched her leave he wondered how a Gatherer could fight pain in himself.

By afternoon the next day they reached their destination. According to Mehepi, the brigands had attacked the village repeatedly to claim the mined lapis-stones, and the result was devastation on a scale that Cet had never seen. They passed an empty standing granary and bare fields. Several of the village's houses were burned-out shells; the eyes and cheeks of the people they saw were nearly as hollow. Cet could not imagine why anyone would vie to rule such a place.

Yet here he saw for the first time that not all the village was arrayed against Namsut. Two young girls with warm smiles came out to tend her horse when she dismounted. A toothless old man hugged her tightly, and threw an ugly glare at Mehepi's back. "That is the way of things in a small community like this one," Ginnem murmured, following Cet's gaze. "Often it takes only a slight majority—or an especially hateful minority—to make life a nightmare for those in disfavor."

Here Mehepi took over, leading them to the largest house in the village, built of sun-baked brick like the rest, but two stories high. "See to our guests," she ordered Namsut, and without a word Namsut did as she was told. She led Cet, Ginnem, and the two Sentinels into the house.

"Mehepi's room," Namsut said as they passed a room which bore a handsome wide bed. It had probably been the headman's before his death. "My room." To no one's surprise her room was the smallest in the house. But to Cet's shock he saw that her bed was low and gauze-draped—the same bed he'd seen in his dream.

A true-seeing: a dream of the future sent by the Goddess. He had never been so blessed, or so confused, in his life.

He distracted himself by concentrating on the matter at hand. "Stay nearby," he told the Sentinels as they settled into the house's two guestrooms. "If the brigands attack again, I'll need to be able to wake you." They nodded, looking sour; neither had forgiven Cet for putting them to sleep before.

"And I?" asked Ginnem. "I can create a kind of shield around myself and anyone near me. Though I won't be able to hold it if you fling a sleep spell at my back again."

"I'll try not to," Cet said. "If my narcomancy is overwhelmed, your shield may be our only protection."

That evening the villagefolk threw them a feast, though a paltry one. One of the elders drew out a battered double-flute, and with a child clapping a menat for rhythm they had weak, off-key entertainment. The food was worse: boiled grain porridge, a few vegetables, and roasted horsemeat. Cet had made a gift of the horses to Mehepi and her men, and they'd promptly butchered one of them. It was likely the first meat the village had seen in months.

"Stopping the brigands will not save this place," Ginnem muttered under his breath. He was grimly chewing his way through the bland porridge, as were all of them. To refuse the food would have been an insult. "They are too poor to survive."

"The mine here produces lapis, I heard," one of the Sentinels said. "That's valuable."

"The veins are all but depleted," said the other. "I talked to one of the elders awhile this afternoon. They have not mined good stone here in years. Even the nodes the brigands take are poor quality. With new tools and more men they might dig deeper, find a new vein, but..." He looked about the room and sighed.

"We must ask the Temple Superior to send aid," Ginnem said.

Cet said nothing. The Temple had already given the villagers a phenomenal amount of aid just by sending a Gatherer and two Sentinels; he doubted the Superior would be willing to send more. More likely the village would have to dissolve, its people relocating to other settlements to survive. Without money or status in those places, they would be little better than slaves.

Almost against his will, Cet looked across the feast-table at Namsut, who sat beside Mehepi. She had eaten little, her eyes wandering from face to face around the table, seemingly as troubled by the sorry state of her village as the Templefolk. When her eyes fell on Cet, she frowned in wary puzzlement. Flustered, Cet looked away.

To find Ginnem watching him with a strange, sober look. "So, not just jealousy."

Cet lowered his eyes. "No. No doubt it is the start of the madness."

"A kind of madness, yes. Maybe just as dangerous in its own way, for you."

"What are you talking about?"

"Love," Ginnem said. "I'd hoped it was only lust, but clearly you care about her."

Cet set his plate down, his appetite gone. Love? He barely knew Namsut. And yet the image of her fighting the sleep spell danced through his mind over and over, a recurring dream that he had no power to banish. And yet the thought of leaving her to her empty fate filled him with anguish.

Ginnem winced, then sighed. "Everything for Her peace."

"What?"

"Nothing." Ginnem did not meet Cet's eyes. "But if you mean to help her, do it tomorrow, or the day after. That will be the best time."

The words sent a not-entirely-unpleasant chill along Cet's spine. "You've healed her?"

"She needed no healing. She's as fertile as river soil. I can only assume she hasn't conceived yet because the Goddess wanted her child fathered by a man of her choosing. A blessing, not a curse."

Cet looked down at his hands, which trembled in his lap. How could a blessing cause him such turmoil? He wanted Namsut; that he could no longer deny. Yet being with her meant violating his oath. He had never questioned that oath in the sixteen years of his service as a Gatherer. For his faithfulness he had been rewarded with a life of such peace and fulfillment as most people could only imagine. But now that peace was gone, ground away between the twin inexorabilities of duty and desire.

"What shall I do?" he whispered. But if the Sister heard him, he made no reply.

And when Cet looked up, a shadow of regret was in Namsut's eyes.

Ginnem and the Sentinels, who had some ability to protect themselves against narcomancy, took the watch, with Ginnem to remain in the house in case of attack. Exhausted from the previous night's battle and the day's travels, Cet went to sleep in the guestroom as soon as the feast ended. It came as no great surprise that his hours in the land of dreams were filled with faceless phantoms who taunted him with angry smiles and inviting caresses. And among them, the cruelest phantom of all: a currant-skinned girlchild with Cet's kind eyes.

When he woke just as the sky began to lighten with dawn, he missed the sound of the jungissa, so distracted was he by his own misery. The urge to sleep again seemed so natural, dark and early as it was, that he did not fight it. Perhaps if he slept again, his dreams would be more peaceful.

"Gatherer!"

Perhaps if he slept again...

A foot kicked Cet hard in his side. He cried out and rolled to a crouch, disoriented. Ginnem sat nearby, his hands raised in that defensive gesture again, his face tight with concentration. Only then did Cet notice the high, discordant whine of the narcomancer's jungissa, startlingly loud and nearby.

"The window," Ginnem gritted through his teeth. The narcomancer was right outside the house.

There was a sudden scramble of footsteps outside. The window was too small for egress, so Cet ran through the house, bursting out of the front door just as a fleet shadow ran past. In that same instant Cet passed beyond range of Ginnem's protective magic, and stumbled as the urge to sleep came down heavy as stones. Lifting his legs was like running through mud; he groaned in near pain from the effort. He was dreaming awake when he reached for his own jungissa. But he was a Gatherer and dreams were his domain, so he willed his dream-self to strike the ornament against the doorsill, and it was his waking hand that obeyed.

The pure reverberation of the dragonfly jungissa cleared the lethargy from his mind, and his own heart supplied the righteous fury to replace it. Shaping that fury into a lance of vibration and power, Cet sent it at the fleeing figure's back with all the imperative he could muster. The figure stumbled, and in that instant Cet caught hold of the narcomancer's soul.

There was no resistance as Cet dragged him into dream; whatever training the brigands' narcomancer had, it went no further than sleep-spells. So they fell, blurring through the land of dreams until their shared minds snagged on a commonality. The Temple appeared around them as a skewed, too-large version of the Hall of Blessings, with a monstrous statue of the Dream Goddess looming over all. The narcomancer cried out and fell to his knees at the sight of the statue, and Cet took the measure of his enemy at last.

He was surprised to see how young the man was—twenty at the most, thin and ragged with hair in a half-matted mix of braids and knots. Even in the dream he stank of months unwashed. But despite the filth, it was the narcomancer's awe of the statue which revealed the truth.

"You were raised in the Temple," Cet said.

The narcomancer crossed his arms over his breast and bent his head to the statue. "Yes, yes."

"You were trained?"

"No. But I saw how the magic was done."

And he had taught himself, just from that? But the rest of the youth's tale was easy enough to guess. The Temple raised orphans and other promising youngsters in its House of Children. At the age of twelve those children chose whether to pursue one of the paths to service, or leave for a life among the laity. Most of the latter did well, for the Temple found apprenticeships or other vocations for them, but there were always a few who suffered from mistakes or misfortune and ended badly.

"Why?" Cet asked. "You were raised to serve peace. How could you turn your back on the Goddess' ways?"

"The brigands," whispered the youth. "They stole me from my farm, used me, beat me. I, I tried to run away. They caught me, but not before I'd found the holy stone, taken a piece for myself. They said I wasn't worthy to be one of them. I showed them, showed them. I showed them I could make the stone work. I didn't want to hurt anyone but it had been so long! So long. It felt so good to be strong again."

Cet cupped his hands around the young man's face. "And look what you have become. Are you proud?"

"...No."

"Where did you find the jungissa?"

The dreamscape blurred in response to the youth's desire. Cet allowed this, admiring the magic in spite of himself. The boy was no true narcomancer, not half-trained and half-mad as he was, but what a Gatherer he could have been! The dream re-formed into an encampment among the hills: the brigands, settled in for the night, eighteen or twenty snoring lumps that had caused so much suffering. Through the shared underpinnings of the dream Cet understood at once where to find them. Then the dream flew over the hills to a rocky basin. On its upper cliff-face was an outcropping shaped like a bird of prey's beak. In a black-burned scar beneath this lay a small, pitted lump of stone.

"Thank you," Cet said. Taking control of the dream, he carried them from the hills to a greener dreamscape. They stood near the delta of a great river, beyond which lay an endless sea. The sky stretched overhead in shades of blue, some lapis and some as deep as Namsut's mourning gown. In the distance a small town shone like a gemstone amid the carpet of green. Cet imagined it full of people who would welcome the youth when they met him.

"Your soul will find peace here," Cet said.

The youth stared out over the dreamscape, lifting a hand as if the beauty hurt his eyes. When he looked at Cet he was weeping. "Must I die now?"

Cet nodded, and after a moment the youth sighed.

"I never meant to hurt anyone," he said. "I just wanted to be free."

"I understand," Cet said. "But your freedom came at the cost of others' suffering. That is corruption, unacceptable under the Goddess' law."

The narcomancer bowed his head. "I know. I'm sorry."

Cet smiled and passed a hand over the youth's head. The grime and reek vanished, his appearance becoming wholesome at last. "Then She will welcome your return to the path of peace."

"Thank you," said the youth.

"Thank Her," Cet replied. He withdrew from the dream then, severing the tether and collecting the dreamblood. Back in waking, the boy's body released one last breath and went still. As shouts rang out around the village, Cet knelt beside the body and arranged its limbs for dignity.

Ginnem and one of the Sentinels ran up. "Is it done?" the Sentinel asked.

"It is," Cet said. He lifted the jungissa stone he'd taken from the boy's hand. It was a heavy, irregular lump, its surface jagged and cracked. Amazing the thing had worked at all.

"And are you well?" That was Ginnem. Cet looked at the Sister and understood then that the question had nothing to do with Cet's physical health.

So Cet smiled to let Ginnem see the truth. "I am very well, Sister Ginnem."

Ginnem blinked in surprise, but nodded.

More of the villagers arrived. One of them was Namsut, breathless, with a knife in one hand. Cet admired her for a moment, then bowed his head to the Goddess' will.

"Everything for Her peace," he said.

The Sentinels went into the hills with some of the armed village men, after Cet told them where the brigands could be found. He also told the villagefolk where they could find the parent-stone of the narcomancer's jungissa.

"A basin marked by a bird's beak. I know the place," said Mehepi with a frown. "We'll go destroy the thing."

"No," Namsut said. Mehepi glared at her, but Namsut met her eyes. "We must fetch it back here. That kind of power is always valuable to someone, somewhere."

Cet nodded. "The Temple would indeed pay well for the stone and any pieces of it."

This set the villagers a-murmur, their voices full of wonder and, for the first time since Cet had met them, hope. He left them to their speculations and returned to the guestroom of the headman's house, where he settled himself against a wall and gazed through the window at passing clouds. Presently, as he had known she would, Namsut came to find him.

"Thank you," she said. "You have saved us in more ways than one."

He smiled. "I am only Her servant."

She hesitated and then said, "I...I should not have asked you for what I did. It seemed a simple matter to me, but I see how it troubles you."

He shook his head. "No, you were right to ask it. I had forgotten: my duty is to alleviate suffering by any means at my disposal." His oath would have become meaningless if he had failed to remember that. Ginnem had been right to remind him.

It took her a moment to absorb his words. She stepped forward, her body tense. "Then you will do it? You will give me a child?"

He gazed at her for a long while, memorizing her face. "You understand that I cannot stay," he said. "I must return to the Temple afterward, and never see the daughter we make."

"Daugh—" She put a hand to her mouth, then controlled herself. "I understand. The village will care for me. After all their talk of a curse they must, or lose face."

Cet nodded and held out a hand to her. Her face wavered for a moment beneath a mix of emotions—sudden doubt, fear, resignation, and hope—and then she crossed the room, took his hand, and sat down beside him.

"You must...show me how," he said, ducking his eyes. "I have never done this thing."

Namsut stared at him, then blessed him with the first genuine, untainted smile he had ever seen on her face. He smiled back, and in a waking dream saw a horse running, running, over endless green.

"I have never *wanted* to do this thing before now," she said, abruptly shy. "But I know the way of it." And she stood.

Her mourning garments slipped to the floor. Cet fixed his eyes on them, trying not to see the movements of her body as she stripped off her headcloth and undergarments. When she knelt straddling his lap, he trembled as he turned his face away, his breath quickening and heart pounding fast. *A Gatherer belongs wholly to the Goddess*, that was the oath. He could hardly think as Namsut's hands moved down the bare skin of his chest, sliding towards the clasp of his loinskirt, yet he forced his mind to ponder the matter. He had always taken the oath to mean celibacy, but that was foolish, for the Goddess had never been interested in mere flesh. He loved Namsut and yet his duty, his calling, was still first in his heart. Was that not the quintessence of a Gatherer's vow?

Then Namsut joined their bodies, and he looked up at her in wonder.

"H-holy," he gasped. She moved again, a slow undulation in his lap, and he pressed his head back against the wall to keep from crying out. "This is holy."

Her breath was light and quick on his skin; dimly he understood that she had some pleasure of him as well. "No," she whispered, cupping his face between her hands. Her lips touched his; for a moment he thought he tasted sugared currants before she licked free. "But it will get better."

It did.

They returned to the Temple five days later, carrying the narcomancer's jungissa as a guarantee of the villagers' good faith. The Superior immediately dispatched scribes and tallymen to verify the condition of the parent stone and calculate an appropriate price. The payment they brought for the narcomancer's jungissa alone was enough to buy a year's food for the whole village.

Ginnem bid Cet farewell at the gates of the city, where a party of green- and gold-clad women waited to welcome him home. "You made the hard choice, Gatherer," he said. "You're stronger than I thought. May the Goddess grant your child that strength in turn."

Cet nodded. "And you are wiser than I expected, Sister. I will tell this to all my brothers, that perhaps they might respect your kind more."

Ginnem chuckled. "The gods will walk the earth before that happens!" Then he sobered, the hint of sadness returning to his eyes. "You need not do this, Gatherer Cet."

"This is Her will," Cet replied, reaching up to grip Ginnem's shoulder. "You see so much, so clearly; can you not see that?"

Ginnem gave a slow nod, his expression troubled. "I saw it when I realized you loved that woman. But..."

"We will meet again in dreams," Cet said softly.

Ginnem did not reply, his eyes welling with tears before he turned sharply away to rejoin his Sisters. Cet watched in satisfaction as they surrounded Ginnem, forming a comforting wall. They would take good care of him, Cet knew. It was the Sisterhood's gift to heal the soul.

So Cet returned to the Temple, where he knelt before the Superior and made his report—stinting nothing when it came to the tale of Namsut. "Sister Ginnem examined her before we left," he said. "She is healthy and should have little trouble delivering the child when the time comes. The firstwife did not take the news happily, but the elder council vowed that the first child of their reborn village would be cared for, along with her mother who so clearly has the gods' favor."

"I see," said the Temple Superior, looking troubled. "But your oath... that was a high price to pay."

Cet lifted his head and smiled. "My oath is unbroken, Superior. I still belong wholly to Her."

The Superior blinked in surprise, then looked hard at Cet for a long moment. "Yes," he said at last. "Forgive me; I see that now. And yet..."

"Please summon one of my brothers," Cet said.

The Superior started. "Cet, it may be weeks or months before the madness—"

"But it will come," Cet said. "That is the price of Her magic; that is what it means to be a true narcomancer. I do not begrudge the price, but I would rather face a fate of my choosing." The horse was in his mind again, its head lunging like a racer's against the swift river current. Sweet Namsut; he yearned for the day he would see her again in dreams. "Fetch Gatherer Liyou, Superior. Please."

The Superior sighed, but bowed his head.

When young Liyou arrived and understood what had to be done, he stared at Cet in shock. But Cet touched his hand and shared with him a moment of the peace that Namsut had given him, and when it was done Liyou wept. Afterward Cet lay down ready, and Liyou put his fingertips over Cet's closed eyes.

"Cetennem," Cet said, before sleep claimed him for the final time. "I heard it in a dream. My daughter's name shall be Cetennem."

Then with a joyful heart, Cet—Gatherer and narcomancer, servant of peace and justice and the Goddess of Dreams—ran free.

Strife Lingers in Memory

Carrie Vaughn

Carrie Vaughn *is the author of the bestselling series about a werewolf named Kitty who hosts a talk radio advice show. She's also written for young adults (*Steel, Voices of Dragons*), the novels* Discord's Apple *and* After the Golden Age, *many short stories, and she's a contributor to George R. R. Martin's* Wild Cards *series. When she isn't writing, she collects hobbies and enjoys the great outdoors in Colorado, where she makes her home.*

MY FATHER WAS A WISE MAN to whom many came seeking advice. During his audiences I'd lurk behind his chair or fetch his cup, and they called me fair, even when I was little. I grew to be golden-haired and wary. I was destined for—something.

War overwhelmed us. The Heir to the Fortress was dead—no, in exile, nearly the same. The evil rose, broke the land over an iron knee, and even my father went into hiding.

Then he came.

I was eighteen. The stranger was—hard to say. He looked young but carried such a weight of care, he might have lived many lifetimes already. He came to ask my father how he might make his way along the cursed paths that led to the ancient fortress now held by the enemy.

My father proclaimed, "That way is barred to any who are not of the Heir's blood, but that line is dead. It is useless."

Our gazes met, mine and that stranger's, and I saw in him a shuttered light waiting to blaze forth. I gripped the back of my father's chair to steady myself.

The stranger and I knew in that moment what was destined to be, though our elders needed a bit more persuading.

So it came to pass that the stranger, Evrad—Heir to the Fortress, the true-blooded prince himself—took the cursed paths and led an army to overthrow the stronghold of his enemy and claim the ancient fortress as his own. He married the wizard's daughter and made her—me—his Queen. Happily, the land settled into a long-awaited peace.

The night after the day of his coronation and of our wedding we had alone and to ourselves. When the door closed, we looked at one another for a long time, not believing that this moment had come at last, remembering all the moments we believed it would not come at all. Then, all at once, we fell into each other's arms.

He made love to me as if the world were ending. I drowned in the fury of it, clinging to him like he was a piece of splintered hull after a shipwreck. Exhausted, we rested in each other's arms. I sang him to sleep and, running my fingers through his thick hair, fell asleep myself.

I had dreamed of this, sleeping protected by him. I had dreamed of waking in his arms, sunlight through the window painting our chamber golden, drawing on his warmth in the chill of morning.

Instead, I awoke to the sound of a scream. Evrad's scream. He thrashed, kicking me. I backed away, arms covering my head. Our blankets twisted, pulling away from the bed as he fought with them. When I dared to look, he had curled up, drawing his limbs close. He was trembling so hard I felt it through the bed.

"Evrad?" I whispered. He remained hunched over and shaking, so I reached for him. "Evrad. Please."

I touched his shoulder, the slope of it glowing pale in moonlight shining through the window. It was damp with sweat.

He flinched at the touch and looked at me, his eyes wide and wild. My stomach clenched—he did not seem to see me.

Then, "Alida?"

He came to life, returned to himself, and pulled me close in an embrace. I held him as tightly as I could, but my grip seemed so weak compared to his.

"Oh, my love," he said over and over. "I thought it was a dream: you, peace—you. I dreaded waking to find you weren't real."

"Hush. Oh, please hush. You're safe."

I said those words to him many times, on many nights. I kept hoping he would believe me.

Strife lingered in the memory of what we had suffered. He defeated an army of horrors, but the demons may yet overcome him.

He kept the nightmares well-hidden. He always appeared to his men, his guards, his people as the hero, the savior, the King. He looked the part, standing tall, smiling easily and accepting gracefully the adoration of hardened warriors and toddling children alike.

He turned his best face toward the people, keeping his secret soul hidden. But he could not hide it from me. So it fell to me to keep my best face toward him, to be strong for him, and hide my secret soul away.

One night, he came to our chamber carrying an arcane-looking bottle covered with dust, the cap sealed with wax.

"I will sleep through the night," he said in much the same way he'd once said he would defeat the dark army that threatened to overrun him. Liquid sloshed in the bottle when he set it on the table.

"What is it? Rare potion?"

"Rare whiskey," he said with a grunt. "Perhaps it will make me forget the shadows."

I pursed my lips, making a wry smile. "That will inspire sweet dreams, and not the comfort of my arms?"

"Oh, my love." He touched my cheek with all the tenderness I could hope for, though his face was lined with worry. I took his hands, locking their anxious movements in mine.

Once, we needed no words, but I could not read the thoughts that clouded his expression. During the war, he had been proud, his look keen and determined. I had never seen him so careworn.

He kissed my hands and went out of our chambers. At least he left the whiskey behind.

A month passed, then came the night I awoke alone.

Perhaps the stillness woke me. Midnight—the dark chill of night when he usually began sweating, trembling as if all the fears he had kept at bay during the war came on him at once—had passed and no screams woke me. I sat up, felt all around the bed, looked when my sight adjusted to the dark. I was alone.

I searched for him. Wrapping my cloak tight around me, I went along the battlements where I could see half the realm across the plains. I searched the stables, where he might have sought the calm influence of sleeping horses. I carried a lantern through stone corridors where no one had walked since Evrad claimed the fortress.

I found him crouched in a forgotten corner, arms wrapped around his head, face turned to the wall. He had managed to tie a cloak around his middle, but it was slipping off his shoulders.

A guard walking his post from the other end of the corridor found him at the same time. "My liege!" the man cried and rushed toward him.

I interposed, stopping him with a raised hand. "Please. Stay back." Turning to Evrad I said, "My lord? My lord, are you awake?"

I touched his shoulder. He looked at me. The lantern light showed his cheeks wet with tears. "Come, my lord. Let's go to bed." I helped him to his feet, like he was an old man or a child.

To the guard I said, "You will not speak of this. You will keep this secret." And what of the next night? And what of the night the guards found him before I did? I was a wizard's daughter but I still needed sleep. I needed more eyes. "You will help me keep this secret, yes?"

"Yes, my Queen. Oh yes." Wonder and pity filled his gaze. I remembered his face, learned his name, Petro. If I ever heard rumor of the King's illness, this man would answer for it.

We had fair nights. Some nights, he only whimpered in his sleep, in the throes of visions I did not want to imagine. Some nights, drunk on wine, we threw logs on the fire until it blazed, making the room hot, and we played until we wore each other out.

Other nights, I wore my cloak, took another in case he had lost his, and searched deserted corridors by lantern light. I always waited until I had put him back to bed and he slept before I sat by the fire and cried.

STRIFE LINGERS IN MEMORY | 447

At last, weary and despairing, I departed in the shrouded hour before dawn. I used craft that my father taught me: how to move without sound, how to turn aside the curious gaze, how to not leave tracks. I left my own horse behind and took one from the couriers that would not be so quickly missed. I rode hard, turned off the main way, and found the forested path that led through ravine and glen to my father's valley.

After the war, he secluded himself in a valley beyond the line of hills where the city lay, a day's journey away. He said he wished to be out of reach of peaceful folk who would trouble him with petty complaints now that the great matters were over. He said he was finished dispensing wisdom for people simply because they asked for it.

What a gentle place. I had traveled with him when he came to live here, but my heart had been so full of the times, of the ache of war and separation from my beloved, that I hadn't looked around me. Water ran frothing down a rocky hillside and became a stream that flowed through a meadow of tall grass scattered with the color of wildflowers. Late sun shining through pollen turned the air golden. I could smell the light, fresh and fertile.

I made a mistake. I shouldn't have run away. Or better, I should have brought Evrad here, to this place.

The whitewashed cottage sat where the grass ended and trees began. Smoke rose from a hole in the roof.

My horse, breathing hard and soaked with sweat, sighed deeply and lowered her head to graze. I pulled off her tack, brushed her, and let her roam free. I left my gear by the cottage's door and went inside.

A fire burned at the hearth in the back of the cottage's one room. Near it were a kettle and all manner of cooking implements. A cot occupied one corner, a table and chair another, and the rest of the walls had shelves and shelves of books. My father sat in a great stuffed chair near the fire, wrapped in a blanket, gazing into a shallow bowl of water he held in his lap.

Quietly, I sat at his feet as I had when I was little.

"My Queen, is it?" he said. A smile shifted the wrinkles of his face. He was bald, but for a fringe of white hair.

"Your daughter still."

"No, I gave you away."

"Father—"

He sighed. "Why have you come here? What trouble drives you from your home?"

"Perhaps I only wish to visit you."

"I still have sight, girl." He touched the surface of the water in the basin and flicked his fingers at me, sprinkling me. I flinched, then hugged my knees.

He shook his head. "I was supposed to be able to leave the keeping of the world to its heirs."

"If you have your sight, then you know what is wrong."

"Tell me. I want to hear what you think is wrong."

I was Queen of this land, the destined love of the greatest of heroes, fortunate and blessed beyond reason, and he made me feel like a hapless child. Perhaps that was why the heroes in the stories were almost always orphans.

"The war haunts him," I said. "He has nightmares. He cannot sleep. He buries all this deep in his heart, but it is festering there. How long can he survive like this? I am afraid, more afraid than I ever was when he carried his sword against the enemy. I try to comfort him. I don't know what to do."

Grunting with the effort, he leaned over the arm of his chair to set the basin on the floor. "So, are you looking for a potion or a spell that will set all to rights?"

I hadn't thought of that, when I decided to come here. If there were such a thing I would gladly take it. But my coming here was selfish. I wanted to rest in the shelter of another, as tired as I was of *being* shelter for another.

"Or do you simply flee from what you do not understand?"

I could have cried, but I pretended to be strong. In a world where fate had ordered all our actions and brought us all to this point, I was terrified that it should leave us now. "The evil lingers. I thought he had defeated it for all time."

"He is battle weary. That is no surprise. As for a cure? Time and care. I know no magic to speed it along. We must be vigilant. Each of us has a role in the war. Now, yours has come."

"But he is the warrior and King, I am just a—" I almost said any of a dozen things: woman, child, pawn, symbol. None of the stories prepared me to be anything else.

"He is King, so he must hide his fears. It falls to you, then, to keep him sane."

"This has been a mistake. Would the true Heir of the Fortress suffer so?"

"Would one who was not the Heir have survived to suffer so?"

"I cannot do this," I said, tears falling at last.

My father smiled and touched my hair with his arthritic hand. "He said the same thing to me before he departed for the last battle. I will tell you what I told him." He held my hand. His was warm and dry. "'That may be true,' I said. 'But you must try, because no one else will.'"

I pressed his hand to my face, wishing I was a child again, able to hide behind his chair and take no part in the worries of the world.

He continued, "You may have the hardest battle of all. No one victory will defeat this enemy. This is not a beast to slay and be done with."

"And no one will sing of my battles."

I slept curled in a blanket near the hearth that night—the first night in many I had not been awakened by sleepwalking or nightmare cries. I treasured the peace of the valley. In the morning, I sat in the meadow by the stream. Since settling at the fortress and into my life as Queen, I had seldom touched living earth or smelled grass and wildflowers warmed by the sun. Here, I could pretend none of it had happened.

My father joined me. He spent a long time settling to the ground, leaning on his cane. He'd never used a cane before. Too late, I reached to help him, to give him my arm to lean on. He'd never needed help before, so I didn't think of it. He spent time arranging his cane and robes around him, gazing over the dancing water.

"When will you return to him?" he said at last.

"I don't know." I had to gather my strength. I could spend the rest of my life gathering strength and still not have enough.

"Make it soon."

I'd been picking at grass, weaving something of a tangled wreath. I threw the mess of it into the stream. "If you don't wish me to stay, I can go elsewhere."

"I want you to go to your home. Your child should know his father."

"My—" I flushed, my whole body burning from my scalp to my bare toes. Then the expected movement: I put my hand on my belly. "You don't mean—"

He smiled, a cat-wise smile of secrets. "I still have sight. You—are still learning."

A child. Me—a child. My child. *His* child. Oh, have mercy. Forgive me.

"Father, I must go."

"Yes, you must."

I caught my horse, saddled her quickly, and fled in a whirlwind. I had galloped a mile when I pulled up suddenly—I was carrying a child. I should be more careful.

What would Evrad say? Perhaps he would sleep well, with a child in his arms.

Halfway back to the fortress, a thunder of hoofbeats galloped toward me. I waited for the rider to appear around the curve in the road. The horse was a snow-white charger, with a gold breastplate and gold fixings on his tack, tail flying, mane rippling. His rider pulled up hard, and his hooves raised dust as he skidded in the road.

I knew this stallion, and I knew the rider who jumped from the saddle and ran toward me.

As I dismounted I stumbled, my grip on the saddle keeping me upright. Here was my hero, my King, face uplifted, striding with strength and determination. Grim and fierce, as I had seen him ride to battle, as I had not seen him in weeks. I had not lost him to the war.

I would have run to meet him, but I had moved just a few steps away from my horse when he reached me. He caught me in his arms and held tight. His leather doublet pressed my flesh, his rough cheek brushed mine.

"I'm sorry," I cried again and again, weeping on his shoulder.

He made soothing noises. "Hush. It's enough that you're safe. I guessed where you had gone, and I meant to go and beg you to return. I meant to make promises—to tie myself to the bed so you wouldn't have to search after me at midnight anymore. To have my guards knock me unconscious every evening so I might sleep through the night."

I laughed. "No guard of yours would even try, my lord."

He touched my cheeks, wiping away tears. "I know you are a wizard's daughter. Your spirit is wild, free as the wind, and your will is strong. I have nothing that can bind you—but tell me you will never leave me again. Promise me."

Oh, how such words would bind me. Did he not know that words are nearly all that will bind a wizard, or his daughter?

"I promise," I said.

Men fight for symbols: a crown, a throne, lines on a map.

When he reclaimed the fortress and we married, our story ended but our lives didn't. None of the old stories prepared me for the battles I now fought.

I remembered the night he left my father's hall to meet the last battle, when all but I believed he was marching to his death.

I held him as long as I could. "I wish I could go with you. I wish I could do more than wait here for news."

"But you're already doing so much."

"What? What am I doing?" I said, smiling with wonder.

"You are the symbol of what we fight for: all that is beautiful."

Men fight for symbols. What do women fight for?

Again I wandered nighttime passages, my way lit by a dim lantern, searching. I moved slowly, some seven months along my child's time. I wore two cloaks and fur boots, because winter was upon us. On bad nights, when the terrors wrenched Evrad to immobility, he found dark passages and shivered there in the cold, fighting demons in his mind. I walked every corridor in the fortress and could not find him. Petro had not seen him either.

On bad nights, he hid in dark passages. This night was worse.

I found him on the battlements of the highest tower. A spire jutting above the sheer wall of the fortress, it served as a watchtower and a place for message fires. He leaned on the stone wall, gazing straight down, a hundred feet to hard earth.

I caught my breath and swallowed a scream.

"My lord? Evrad," I said softly, my voice shaking. "What are you doing?"

He climbed to sit on the lip of the wall. He looked at me; his eyes were feral, shining. He trembled. Sweat matted his hair, and his face was pale, drained of blood. He wore only breeches and gooseflesh covered his arms.

If I reached for him, the gesture might push him over.

"Go back to bed. Why must you follow me?"

Because I loved him. Because I worried about him. Because it was my duty, and I must do it so the secret of his nighttime terrors did not spread. But I didn't say those things.

"I will follow you to the end of the world, over cliffs into fiery rifts that split the earth if I must. But I will follow you."

"Like the demons."

"I'm faster than demons. They will not reach you before I do."

"Will you follow me there?" He nodded over the wall to the long drop.

The moon shone near full, low in the sky, painting the land with shadows. Lurking behind each house and tower and city wall, stretching away from every rise in the land, every tree on the plain, black shapes reached toward the fortress.

"They whisper in my ear, *jump*. Oh Alida."

My knees gave way and I sat on the stone, lurching with my swollen weight. I couldn't shutter the moon, to chase away the shadows.

"Evrad. What did you fight for? Did you fight for this, to cast yourself off a tower? Then they've won. The enemy is dead and gone, but will still win the war. It was all for nothing. What did you fight for?"

"I don't know anymore—"

"Me, Evrad! You fought for me! Now I am yours. You don't have to fight anymore. You've won."

He shook his head. "I'm not worthy of you. You deserve better. Someone who doesn't have nightmares."

I laughed, clapping my hand over my mouth because the sound was so acrid. "I deserve better? Evrad—you are the hero of the age, the king of legends. And I deserve *better?* Who do you think I am?"

He looked at me. His frown was long, unmovable. "You are everything."

I crawled toward him. "Come down from there, Evrad. Come to me." I stretched my hand to him. I had to be stronger than the shadows. My voice had to be more alluring. "Touch me. Just touch me."

A small goal, an easy quest, well within his reach. A slender hand, poised in the dark. He leaned, lips parted in an expression of longing.

He fell off the lip of the wall and into my arms.

"I don't want better. I don't want the hero and king. I want you." We sat for many hours, hugging each other against the cold.

I brought him to bed and wrapped myself around him. He shivered. I was not blanket enough against the cold.

"Do you see them? In the shadows on the wall," he said. Candle flames flickered in a draft. The warped shadows of a cup, a candlestick, a comb danced and trembled all around.

"It's only light and dark."

"I know that—but I see memories. I see a thousand goblin warriors throwing themselves against the burning ramparts of the city. I see them pulling my men into the flames. And there's nothing I can do. I didn't destroy them. They're still here, watching us."

Almost I could see their red eyes and clawed hands. For all his army had saved, ten thousand men had perished in the war. Goblins shook spears which rippled like ocean waves above their heads. I had not been there, yet I could almost see. He lived with such visions in his waking mind. How did he endure?

I got up and blew out the candle, banishing the shadows. Returning to bed, I pressed myself against his back and whispered in his ear. "They're gone now."

He was crying.

Over time, we learned what sparked the grim memories. Bonfires. Shadows under a full moon. Then, our sons in armor. Oh, were his nightmares fierce after Biron's first day in armor. If I could have changed the world, altered the course of sun and moon, rewritten tales of destiny that had been put down by great unseen hands, our children would never have learned to fight. But they were the children of a King and must learn the ways of arms. Evrad insisted on this. Even after waking in the night and telling me that the faces of his men dying over and over in his dreams had changed, and were now the faces of our children.

Over time, nights became easier. With children to occupy him—first a son, then two daughters, and two more sons—he went to bed happy and weary. He did not notice the shadows so much.

Thus peace ruled the land for our children's time, and our children's children's time, and will rule beyond. Just like in the stories.

I sit by a window, my gray hair braided behind me, my withered hands resting on a worn blanket. Evrad is also old, but he wears his age, his gray, and his wrinkles like a prize. He still rides out, straight as a statue in the saddle, and I still wait for him.

Behind me, a door opens and closes softly. Our youngest son, Perrin, attempts to not disturb me. I don't have to look; I am my father's daughter, and I have acquired some of his sight over the years. My father is long dead.

Perrin comes to my chair and kneels on the rug. This puts him at the

—

height he was as a boy. I look on him as if he is a boy come to beg a favor. But he is a man, with a beard and his father's bold eyes.

"Mother? I've almost finished. But I have one last question."

My other children have become warriors, diplomats, husbands, wives, parents, leaders and healers. Perrin, while he dutifully learned swordplay and manners along with his siblings, has become none of these. He is a scholar, historian, chronicler. A bard.

He has been writing an account of the great War of the Fortress and the turning of the age. I've read parts of it—what he has seen fit to show me—and hardly recognize the events and trials I lived through. It reads like the old stories.

"Oh?" I say. "Why not just invent an answer? It won't sound any more outlandish than what's there already."

"I've written no lies—"

"No, of course not. But you've painted the truth with bold colors indeed." Gah, that's something my father might have said.

He looks away, smirking. Like I might have done, kneeling at my father's chair. "I have a question about a thing I am not sure even happened."

He paused, wincing in difficult thought, trying to speak—my son the bard, tongue tied. I might have laughed, but he looked to be in pain. Finally, he said,

"When I was young, quite small, a noise woke me, and I was afraid. I thought to go to your chamber to seek comfort. The passages were very dark. I crept along the walls like a mouse, fearful of losing my way in my own home. Then, I heard crying. I turned a corner and saw a lantern. In the circle of light I saw you and Father sitting on the floor. You held him in your arms, and he was crying. I thought his heart would break. And I realized—he was afraid of something, more afraid than I was or had ever been. That sight...terrified me. I ran back to my own bed. I trembled under my blankets until dawn, and never spoke of it until now.

"Tell me: What I saw—was it real? Did it happen?"

Evrad and I have even managed to keep our troubles from our children. Mostly. He walks in his sleep rarely these days. No reason anyone should know.

"Yes. It happened that night and many others. The horrors of that war have haunted him for many years. It may be that the enemy left him with such visions as revenge, as a final defiance. Or perhaps it is the price for victory." I shake my head. I have invented many excuses, but the simplest is probably the truest: his memory haunts him, and there is no one to blame.

I lean forward and rest my hand on Perrin's shoulder. "You must not write of this. You must not add this to your chronicle."

"But—it means the hero's journey is not ended. It adds all the more to his victory, that he has continued to struggle and continued to win—"

"The hero must be strong, more than human, and when he becomes King, his struggles should be over. *That* is the end of the story. That is the law of stories, Perrin, however else the rest of us must live. If people saw him any different—some spirit would go out of the world, I think. People would believe in him less." I sit back and take a tired breath.

"Believe in him less because he is human?"

"Just so."

I watch Perrin thinking. As a child, his questions went on longer than any of the others' did. He was the one who wanted to know why different birds had different songs, and why water could not flow uphill. He exhausted my ability to make answers. Even now, I hope he has no more questions.

"I understand, I think," he says at last. "The war ends, the age ends, the story ends."

"So the children can make their own stories."

He nods, and wonder of wonders I think he does understand. "One more question," he says, and I brace. "Which was harder? The battles leading into the new age, or the ones after?"

Strange. Looking back now, I only remember the ones after. The ones before happened to someone else, in another age.

I click my tongue and think of what my father might have said. "That's not a fair question. It doesn't matter which is harder, because no one will ever know of the battles after."

Shadows writhe across the floor and climb to the ceiling. They swim around the bed and my sleeping lord. One is like a laughing mouth, another like a reaching hand that touches the slope of his shoulder.

"Get away from him." I have drunk too much wine and my vision is spinning. I throw the cup. Wine flies in a spray of droplets across the floor. The silver cup drops with a ringing noise. The sound of swords striking or inhuman teeth gnashing in a cry of victory.

"He is mine!" I cry, standing. "You cannot have him."

Blood rushes in my ears like laughter. I want to scream, I open my mouth to scream, and then—

"Dear heart? What are you doing?" Sitting up, he rubs sleep from his eyes, his brow furrowed with curiosity.

"It's the light," I say in a fey mood. "You were right all along. The demons have come for us."

He searches the room, his eyes gold in the candle's glow. His face is calm, but he takes a trembling breath before saying, "It's only light. Come to bed."

"I must win you back. You fought a war and won. Now it's my turn. I will win you back!"

I clench my fists at my sides. My jaw trembles with an unsounded scream. My King watches me. Soon, the wrinkled brow eases, the tired face softens into a smile. To see him smile so, at night—but then, I must look amusing, in a rage, wine spilled around me, shift falling off my shoulders.

He says, simply as grass in summer, "I know you will. Come to bed, love."

I go to him, wrap my arms around him and kiss him, deeply, longingly. His hands press against me, inviting and warm. So warm.

He pulls away for just a moment. "I know how to chase away the shadows," he says, and blows out the candle.

The Mad Apprentice:
A Black Magician Story

Trudi Canavan

Trudi Canavan lives in Melbourne, Australia. She has been making up stories about people and places that don't exist for as long as she can remember. Her first short story, "Whispers of the Mist Children," received an Aurealis Award for Best Fantasy Short Story in 1999. When she recovered from the surprise, she went on to finish the fantasy novel-that-became-three, the bestselling Black Magician Trilogy: The Magicians' Guild, The Novice, and The High Lord, followed by another trilogy, Age of the Five. Last year the prequel to the Black Magician Trilogy, The Magician's Apprentice, was released and she is now working on the sequel, the Traitor Spy Trilogy. One day she will write a series that doesn't contain three books.

THE SUMI POT rose in the air seemingly of its own volition, tilted and poured the hot drink into her cup. Indria looked at her brother. He grinned, and she rolled her eyes.

"I see your magic training is coming along well, Tagin," she observed.

Tagin waved dismissively at the pot as it settled on the table again. "That was nothing. First year exercises. Boring."

Sipping the hot drink, Indria considered her brother over the rim of her cup. His eyes were bright and he had fidgeted constantly since arriving. This usually meant he was in a good mood. When he was hunched and glowering she had to be doubly careful what she said and did, as his temper was much easier to spark. But something was different about him today. Though he was cheerful, there was a hint of tension in his movements, and his eyes kept darting about the room.

"Is what you're learning now more interesting?"

"With Magician Herrol teaching me?" He sniffed derisively and looked away. "Hardly."

Indria suppressed a sigh and put down her cup. Tagin had been an apprentice magician for over two years but, like with most of his obsessions, he had grown impatient with his training and teacher. Usually he found something new to engage his brilliant mind. But magic was no hobby or pastime. It was supposed to become the source of his income and place in society. If he ended his apprenticeship, rather than remaining until his master taught him higher magic and granted him independence, he would not receive income from the king, or attract work from the Houses.

"Perhaps if Magician Herrol moved back to the city—to the Guild—it would be better. You'd have a greater variety of teachers."

Tagin sneered. "He suggested it, but what's the point? All the Guild magicians are like him: stuffy old men. I'd rather be away from them, but close enough to visit you." He smiled. "You wouldn't want me to leave you all alone with *Demrel* for company, would you?"

Indria grimaced. Lord Demrel was an excellent husband, according to her family. He'd improved their connections among the Houses, earning them valuable favours in trade. He was wealthy and generous. But he was also a boorish, possessive man, and old enough to be her father. Growing up with her volatile brother had taught her how to handle difficult men, and Demrel was a lot less troublesome than Tagin. But she hated how Demrel treated her like a child and an idiot.

Tagin may be a handful, but he doesn't think I'm stupid, she thought. *And at least he loves me—in his way.*

"When we rule the world, I'll build us a palace in the city," Tagin said, his eyes flashing. "We'll get rid of Demrel and all the boring, old magicians."

She smiled at this familiar game. They had played it since they were children.

"When we rule the world, Demrel and the Guild will search all the lands for gifts to lay at our feet," she replied.

He grinned. "When we rule the world..." He paused as his attention was drawn elsewhere, toward the windows. Indria listened, and heard the sound of galloping horses.

"Visitors," she said. "I wonder who it could— "

She faltered as Tagin leapt to his feet and hurried to the windows, stopping a few steps short and peering down at the courtyard below.

"Ah. Rot them," he said in a sullen, resigned tone. "I have to go."

"What is it?" Standing up, she moved to one of the panes of glass. Directly below them three horses milled. Their riders—wearing the uniforms of higher magicians—were handing their reins to the servants who had greeted them. One looked up at the house and saw her. In the corner of her eye she saw Tagin duck back out of sight. She glanced at him, then down at the magicians, and felt her stomach sink.

They're here for Tagin, she guessed. *And this is no social visit.* But she knew from long experience not to speak such thoughts aloud. If she was right, Tagin might jump to the conclusion that she had already known they were coming, and perhaps even betrayed him to them.

"Who are they?" she asked.

"Magicians," he told her.

"I can see that from their robes," she said crossly. "What are their names? Why are they here? Do they want to see Demrel?"

"They want me. They want to kill me."

As she turned to stare at him, he smiled crookedly. Sometimes Tagin believed everyone wanted to do him harm. Even herself. She shook her head.

"Why are they here, really?"

His smile faded. "I did something bad." He turned away and strode toward the door.

Indria rolled her eyes. "What this time?"

"I killed Magician Herrol," he told her, without looking back.

She stared at his back. *He's joking.* Tagin might have a temper, and a cruel sense of humour, but he was no killer. He had beaten servants and horses and, when a boy, had been inclined to torment their mother's pets, but he'd never *killed* anything.

He opened the door. From beyond came the sound of voices and footsteps, growing louder. He closed the door and cast about, his gaze suddenly flat with terror. "Help me, Indria," he said helplessly. "I've got to get out of here!"

Her heart twisted. He truly believed they meant him harm. And when he was in this mood it was better to let him run away and hide than try to reason with him. He'd calm down and return later. If the magicians believed Tagin to be a murderer they might try to kill him before he had a chance to calm down, explain himself and prove his innocence.

She beckoned and started toward a side door. As they passed through it into a narrow corridor she considered whether she'd be punished for helping him. Surely not. If she claimed to be too frightened to do otherwise, the Guild would see her as more of a victim than an accomplice.

But is there still some truth to that? she wondered. *Am I still scared of Tagin?* She thought of the bruises he'd given her, before she'd learned to avoid rousing his temper or to calm him down. After she'd married he hadn't dared hurt her, lest Demrel notice and stop him from seeing her.

Yet if I thought I could turn him over without either of us getting hurt, would I?

Probably not. He was her brother. Beneath the temper there was a fragile, lonely boy with a clever mind. She would not want to see him imprisoned. He'd go mad—madder than he already was—if he was ever locked away.

They reached the door to her husband's study. Tagin's footsteps were loud behind her as they entered the room.

"You're lucky Demrel's away. He'd never let you in here," she told Tagin as she moved to a large wooden cupboard. "Open this for me, will you?"

He narrowed his eyes at the lock and she heard it click open. She pulled the doors apart and slid aside the bolt locking the inner doors. Cold air rushed in from the narrow cavity beyond. "There's a ladder. I don't know where it comes out—and I don't want to know—but it must be safe or Demrel wouldn't use it."

His eyebrows rose. "Why doesn't it surprise me that your husband has a secret way out of his own house?"

"I only know about it because he got stuck one day and nobody else heard him shouting for help. He wouldn't let me get any of the servants. I had to pull him out all by myself."

Tagin's lip curled in disgust. "You should leave him and come with me."

She shook her head.

"But you hate him."

"Yes, but I'd also hate being homeless and hunted." She gave him a serious look. "And I'd slow you down. I'll be more able to help you if I stay here."

He stared at her and opened his mouth to speak, but the sound of footsteps in the main corridor outside the room reached them. "Hurry!" she hissed. "Get inside and lock the door behind you."

As he climbed in she felt her heart starting to pound. She closed the doors and heard the lock click. A scuffling inside the cupboard followed. The footsteps outside the room grew ever louder. Her heart raced. If Tagin didn't stop making noise soon the magicians would hear him and investigate the cupboard. A knock came from the study door and hear heart lurched.

The sounds inside the cupboard finally stopped. Taking a deep breath, Indria wiped sweaty hands on the sides of her dress and walked slowly across the room. Opening the study door, she forced herself not to flinch at the wall of masculine, uniformed power that stood before her.

"Welcome, my lords," she said, with as much dignity as she could muster. "If you are after my husband I'm afraid he is absent. Is there anything I can help you with?"

The magicians stepped into the room. The first was tall and quite handsome—nothing like the way Tagin had described the magicians he'd encountered. The second was as grey and stooped with age as her brother had described. The third was of an age somewhere between his companions and wore an expression of disapproval and disappointment.

"I am Lord Arfon," the tall magician said. "This is Lord Towin and Magician Beller. Is your brother, Apprentice Tagin, here?"

"He was, but he has left."

Arfon frowned down at her. "Do you know where he is now?"

"No. What is this about?"

"He has committed a terrible crime. He has murdered Magician Herrol."

She feigned shock and surprise. "Murdered?"

"Yes. You brother told you nothing of this, I gather."

"No." She looked away. "He said something about being in trouble. He didn't explain." *That is close enough to the truth.* She turned to regard him closely. "Are you sure Tagin is the murderer?"

"Yes," he replied, returning her gaze steadily. "I read the mind of a servant who witnessed the crime—and other, earlier, crimes. Did you know your brother had learned higher magic in secret, against the king's law?"

Indria shook her head, not having to fake her shock this time.

"He's been taking magical strength from the servants for months, no doubt in preparation for dispatching his master," the scowling magician said with unconcealed disgust.

"But..." Indria finally managed. "Tagin wouldn't do that. Well, I can imagine him learning something forbidden out of boredom. But he's not the murdering type."

Lord Arfon's eyebrows rose. "Are you saying you've known enough murdering types to be able to tell them from non-murdering types?"

"Don't mock me." She raised her chin and met his gaze. "He's my brother. I know him better than anyone."

He pursed his lips thoughtfully, then nodded. "Forgive me. That was tactless, and this is a serious matter. Can you guess where your bother may have gone? A simple read of your brother's mind would confirm or disprove his guilt."

"No," she said, honestly.

He nodded. "Then I'm afraid we're going to have to take you with us."

Record of the 235th Year.

News arrived today of the death of Magician Herrol, family Agyll, House Parin, and of a terrible crime. A mind-read of the servant who reported the death revealed that Magician Herrol had been murdered, the strength drained from him with the use of higher magic, by his very own apprentice, Tagin. How this apprentice came upon the knowledge is unknown, but it appears he was able to overcome his master by first strengthening himself by draining servants, who were kept silent through threats. His crimes are threefold: first in learning higher magic before being granted independence by his master, second in applying it to commoners to strengthen himself, and third in using it to kill.

Lord Arfon has been given the task of finding Tagin. He has taken Tagin's sister, Indria, into custody as the siblings are close and the apprentice may emerge from hiding in an attempt to free her. He has informed me that she is cooperating with efforts to detain her brother.

Gilken, family Balen, House Sorrel, Record-keeper of the Magicians' Guild.

Gilken wiped the nib of his pen and set it down next to the old leather book. Moving over to the tower window, he looked out over Imardin, capital city of Kyralia. The high wall of the Royal Palace rose to the left, facing down the mansions of the rich and powerful Houses. He could not see the King's Parade leading down from the palace to Market Square and the docks, but his memory supplied images of it willingly, along with the remembered smells and sounds of the busiest parts of the city.

If he listened, he could hear a constant hum, but a wide stretch of gardens separated him from the bustling metropolis, keeping the noise and hustle at a distance. Two hundred years ago, after the magicians of Kyralia had defeated invading forces from Sachaka, King Errik had granted them a generous area of land and ordered a Guildhall to be built to house their newly formed Magicians' Guild. The Record-keeper's room, Gilken's domain and responsibility for the last twenty-three years, was in the highest room of the southwest tower.

While he had never grown tired of the view, he was liking the long climb up to it a lot less as the years passed. He had never gained the mental control necessary to levitate himself around and around and up the staircase, and the only way he could have gone straight up—on the outside of the building, then somehow crawling in through a window— would hardly be a dignified way for a magician to behave.

There are worse things for a magician to be guilty of than being undignified, he thought, and his mind turned back to the ill news he had recorded that day. *Murder. Blackmail. The unauthorised learning and use of higher magic. Surely no apprentice would abandon his training and future by committing such crimes without good reason. What could have driven him to do it?*

Gilken knew little about the apprentice. Only that Tagin had a sister and that his family was of a weaker, less favoured House. It was unusual for the only son and heir of a family to be given magical training, since magicians were forbidden, by law, to act as head of a family in political matters. The law was meant to stop power in Kyralia shifting entirely into magicians'—and the Guild's—hands, though it was by no means entirely successful. By allowing Tagin to become a magician, his father had put future control of the family and its assets into the hands of his daughter's husband.

Lord Herrol must have known this when he took on the young man as his apprentice. Gilken considered what he knew of the magician. Herrol's wife had died ten years ago, and his five children were grown and married. He had been a good-humoured, intelligent man.

Having grown up in the country, Herrol had returned there a few years ago. His home was a day's ride from the city. And a few hours' ride from Tagin's sister's home. Herrol, knowing how close the siblings were, may have taken that into account when he made his decision to move.

If he had, then Tagin chose a terrible way to repay that favour.

Gilken looked out over the Guild grounds to the city again. Herrol had been well liked in the Guild. Many were upset at his death, especially his ex-apprentices. Magicians had been alerted across the country. The docks and borders were being watched day and night.

Wherever Tagin is, he'll not evade the Guild and justice for long.

Lord Arfon lifted a glass jug and poured clear liquid into a matching goblet. He handed the goblet to Indria. She sniffed at the contents, then sipped.

"Water?" she said, surprised and a little disappointed. She'd expected an exotic and expensive liquor that only royalty or the Guild could afford.

"There's a spring in the Guild grounds," he told her. "The water from it is the purest you'll ever drink. It is piped only to this building and to the Royal Palace—and in the palace it goes first to the king's rooms."

Taking a larger sip, she swirled the water around in her mouth, then swallowed. It had almost no taste to it. Perhaps a faint suggestion of stone and rock. Arfon poured himself a glass.

"Tell me more about your brother."

She shrugged. "What haven't I told you already?"

He gave her a level look. "The servants at your family home say he was prone to violent tantrums, and that he often struck you."

She looked away. "Not often," she corrected, figuring there was no point denying the truth when it could be confirmed by a mind-read. "Just...when he was frustrated. He's smart, you see. Too smart. People don't understand him, and he's not good at explaining himself in a way ordinary people understand."

"Did you understand him?"

"Not always. That's why he loses his temper with me." She waved a hand. "But I see his frustration and his..." *His loneliness*, she was going to say. But Tagin would not have liked her to speak of him as if he was weak or pitiful.

"You want to protect him?" Arfon observed.

"Of course. I'm his sister."

"Would you still want to, if you knew he'd murdered Lord Herrol? Would you still hide his location, if you knew it?"

She looked at him and smiled crookedly. "Probably."

"Why?"

She sighed and turned away. "He's the only one who ever cared about me. Mother and Father never did. And Demrel certainly doesn't."

Arfon said nothing. The silence stretched between them and eventually drew her eyes back to him. He was looking at her intently. His expression was not disapproving. It was unfathomable, and yet it sent a shiver up her spine.

Stop it, she told herself. *It's not right to fancy the man who wants to catch and possibly execute your own brother.* Then, belatedly, she added to that, *and you're a married woman.*

She could not help liking Arfon, though. He'd treated her so differently than her husband—as if he not only saw that she had a mind but was interested in its contents. He had been gentle and apologetic the few times he'd had to physically force her to cooperate. The only time she'd seen him angry, it had fascinated her to see how he'd held the anger back, and how quickly it had faded away.

And it doesn't help that he's so good looking. She sighed. *I guess that's part of the Guild's ploy to get information out of me. I might give more away if I wanted to impress that person. Fortunately I don't have any information to give.*

Arfon drew in a deep breath and stood up. "It's late. I'll take you back to your room."

My "room"? she thought as she followed him up the stairs. *My "prison" is more accurate.* Though the little bedroom the Guild had set up for her in one of the Guildhall towers was comfortable, she had not left it and the room below it for two weeks.

Arfon left her as soon as she was safely locked away. It did not take her long to change into her nightclothes, and she fell asleep as soon as her head touched the pillow. The next thing she was aware of was the patterns of light and shadow the moon had cast on the ceiling.

Then she frowned. *I'm awake and it's still night. Why am I awake?*

Something interrupted the pattern. She raised her head and stared at the window. A shadowed face was pressed up to the glass.

That's impossible. This room is three floors up and there are guards outside. She let her head drop back onto the pillow. *I must be dreaming.*

"Indria!" a muffled voice hissed. "Get up! It's me. Tagin."

Her heart skipped. She wasn't dreaming. Someone really was there, and that someone was Tagin. *The fool! They'll catch him for sure!* She scrambled out of the bed and stumbled to the window. Cold air surrounded her. The paper screens had been pushed aside and the frame of mullioned glass hinged outward. Tagin was outside. Below his feet was something flat, hovering in the chill air. It looked suspiciously like a piece of the paving from the Guild gardens.

"How are you...?" she asked.

"Same way I move a pot of sumi," he said. "Only this time I'm standing on it. Took some practise to keep my balance, though. Don't worry. I'm used to it now. I won't drop you."

"Drop me?"

He grinned. "I've come to rescue you. Can't have my sister in prison because of something she didn't do."

"I don't need rescuing," she told him. "When they realise you're not coming to get me they'll give up and let me go."

"But I *have* come to get you."

"And take me where?"

"Away from here."

She shook her head. "They'll find us, Tagin. Listen, I believe they won't harm you if you give yourself up. They'll give you a chance to prove that you're innocent. Once they read your mind they'll know you didn't kill anyone, and they'll let you go."

He smiled crookedly. "But I *did* kill Herrol. And most of his servants. And..." he looked down and shrugged.

She followed his gaze, past the floating stone beneath his feet, and caught her breath. Three men lay on the ground below, their eyes open and staring. Dead. Had Tagin killed them? *Of course he had. To save me.* She felt guilt welling up, but pushed it away. The Guild had set a trap for him. If it had gone badly then it was hardly her fault.

But it did mean her brother had killed. And once again admitted to killing his master.

"Oh, Tagin," she heard herself say. "They'll definitely execute you now. And me, if I come with you."

"They won't find us," he told her, extending a hand.

"But..." *But I don't want to leave and become a fugitive,* she wanted to say. His eyes narrowed. She could see the first signs of suspicion and anger. His anger was always worst when he thought he'd been betrayed. *Only this time he's killed people. But he won't kill me.*

Still he might take his anger out on others. He'll blame the Guild and my husband for turning me against him. She felt her heart sink. *If I go with him, I might be able to persuade him otherwise. Steer him away from further trouble. From murdering people.*

It would mean leaving her life of comfort and safety.

But he's my brother. I'm the only one who can save him.

Sighing, knowing that he did not comprehend what he asked her to sacrifice, she climbed up onto the window sill and took his hand. His face was transformed by a grin. Pulling her forward, he steadied her as she stepped onto the slab. She looked down as they began to descend.

Lord Arfon was going to be so disappointed in her.

Record of the 235th Year.

The rogue apprentice has rescued his sister, killing two guards and Lord Towin in the process. Lord Towin's death is a shock and loss to both his family and the Guild. He had so much potential, and his innovative study of the application of magic in shaping metals will be left unfinished.

Towin's death has roused and united the Guild. Apprentice Tagin has shown himself to have little moral character, willing to use higher magic as cruelly as the Sachakans did before the War. We cannot leave him to roam the world unchecked and unpunished. Lord Arfon believes that we must capture him and find out how he learned higher magic without the assistance of a teacher, but many of the others feel Tagin is too dangerous, and must be killed at the soonest oppor

Gilken let his pen hover over the page for a moment, listening to the expectant silence that came after the knock at his door. Then he finished the sentence, wiped the pen and set it aside. Rising from his chair, he sent a little magic out to the door to nudge the latch open, and then tug the door inward.

Lord Arfon nodded politely at him. "Record-keeper Gilken, may I speak with you?"

"Of course, Lord Arfon," Gilken replied, waving to the comfortable chairs he kept in the room for visitors. "Would you like a drink of water?"

"No, thank you." Arfon sat down, his gaze distracted and a crease deepening between his brows. "I thought you should know that Lord Valin, Magician Loral and Lord Greyer haven't been seen since last night's meeting. You know they volunteered to search for Tagin, but I didn't choose them?"

"Yes." Gilken nodded to show he understood Arfon's alarm. The young magicians had been friends of Lord Towin, the magician who had been guarding Indria, and were so outraged at the murder it was clear to all that if they'd found Tagin it was unlikely there'd be an apprentice alive to question and put to trial.

Would that be so terrible? he asked himself. He considered how conflicted his feelings had been the previous night, at the meeting. While he felt the same sense of loss and anger at the murders as many of the magicians, he had been disturbed by the fierce, unquestioning drive for revenge raging among the magicians. *We are supposed to be examples of calm and reason. And justice. Tagin deserves a trial.*

"You fear they will kill Tagin," Gilken said.

Arfon looked at him. "Or in attempting their own search they will upset our arrangements for capturing him."

Gilken nodded again. *He wants me to put something in the record, so that if the trio upset his plans and Tagin gets away, Arfon and his helpers won't be blamed. It is a pity that he feels the Guild might react that way, but he is no fool. If things go very wrong, people always look for someone to blame, and leaders always fall first.*

"I should make note of their absence," Gilken said, rising from this chair.

Taking the hint, Arfon stood up. "Thank you. I will distract you no longer."

Gilken smiled. "Receiving information for the record is more necessity than distraction. And you are always welcome, Lord Arfon."

The young magician bent at the waist in a half bow, then left the room. Gilken sat down at his desk again and considered the last sentence he had written. Then he picked up his pen and resumed writing.

Though she wanted to look away, to flee from the scene before her, Indria forced herself to look at the five bodies. Three magicians and two apprentices lay sprawled around the campfire—three men and two boys a few years older than Tagin. They looked as if they had fallen into a drunken sleep, but she knew better. Each bled from a small cut, through which her brother had taken their magic and their lives while they had been drugged. She wrapped her arms around the simple commoner's tunic Tagin had brought for her as part of her rescue and disguise, and shivered.

It had been her idea to let the magicians catch her, convince them she had been Tagin's prisoner, then drug them so she and Tagin could gain some distance or even get them off their trail. She had bought the tincture at a market, pretending to be suffering from insomnia and women's pains but wanting something that didn't taste foul. As the herbalist had recommended, Indria had mixed it into the magicians' wine, taking care not to make it too strong and risk poisoning them.

But Tagin had decided it was too great an opportunity to pass up. He'd taken their power, and in doing so he'd killed them. And now he was dancing around the fire, crowing with triumph.

"Too easy!" he exclaimed. "And all it took was *this*." He slipped a hand into the pocket of his jacket and brought out the little bottle containing the drug. "Not a bit of magic wasted—none of mine, none of theirs, and now it's all mine!"

He grabbed her hands and whirled her about. Her foot caught on a fallen branch and she stumbled, so he stopped and steadied her. "Did you hear me?" he asked. "Do you understand?"

She nodded. "Not a bit wasted," she repeated. "And now they're off our trail. We've gained...how many days? How long do you think it'll take before they're found or missed?"

"A few days." He shrugged. "More if I burn their bodies."

"Long enough for us to make it to the border, if we take their horses. We'll have to hope the Elynes aren't waiting for us." She looked at the dead magicians again and forced herself to see the situation with cold practicality. "Are they carrying any money? We could buy passage on a ship. Head for Vin. Or Lonmar."

Tagin shook his head. A familiar mad gleam came into his eyes. "We're not going to Vin, sister. Or Lonmar. Or Elyne. We're going to Imardin."

"The city? But..."

His grip on her hands tightened. "Think of all the times we pretended we'd rule the world one day..." He laughed as she opened her mouth to protest. "Yes, I know it was a game, but I think...I think it's possible. We *could* change the world. We could make the Guild see that their rules and restrictions are wrong." He looked at her and his expression became serious. "It would be a way to make up for what I did. Which is all their fault, really."

"But..."

His face darkened suddenly, and he flung her hands away. "You don't know what it was like, Indria. Every night, Herrol taking all my strength so I could barely do anything he'd taught me." Tagin flushed and turned from her, his head dropping so she could not see his face.

"That's the secret, you know," he said in a quieter voice. "The secret of higher magic. Masters take the strength from the apprentices, supposedly in exchange for their teaching. It seems fair at first. Strength in exchange for knowledge. But Herrol kept holding me back. When I started teaching myself—things in his own books—he was angry. He started taking extra power so I couldn't try anything. I couldn't learn anything." Tagin looked up at her, his gaze tortured and his face older than it had ever appeared before. "It doesn't have to take ten years for an apprentice to become a higher magician. They hold us back—stop us from learning at our natural pace—so that they can take magic from us for longer."

Indria felt her heart twist. That might not be so bad for any ordinary apprentice, but for Tagin it would have been intolerable. He was clever. He learned quickly, and grew bored even faster. Herrol should have realised that. Should have rewarded Tagin for his initiative, not punished him.

"But I'm going to reveal the lie," Tagin continued, straightening as determination filled him. "I'm going to make the Guild tell everyone the truth." His gaze shifted to the distance and he was silent a moment. Then his eyes snapped to her and he smiled. "We're going to change world, Indria, and this time it's not a game. It's real."

Record of the 235th Year.

We now know that the three burned corpses found yesterday are the remains of Lord Valin, Magician Loral and Lord Greyer. They were identified by the charred scraps of their clothing brought back to the city.

Today our minds have been buzzing with mental communications as magicians here and there have reported more terrible news. Nine of Arfon's searchers and two apprentices had stopped at a Stayhouse for the evening. By the morning they, their servants, the Stayhouse owner and his wife, and many of the staff and customers at the Stayhouse, had perished. Most died in the fire that burned the building to the ground, but we suspect the magicians were first killed by Tagin and his sister, as the pair were identified by those lucky enough to escape the blaze.

All here are shocked by this tragic loss of life.

Gilken paused. His mind crowded with questions, but he always tried (and often failed) to keep speculation to a minimum in his reporting. Records should be strictly factual. Had the searchers come upon Tagin and his sister, and if so, was their attempt to capture them a catastrophic failure? Why did none of them report the encounter to the Guild via mental communication before they died? He could not help but think the location of the two groups of perished magicians was significant. The bodies of the three young magicians were found further from the city than the Stayhouse. Instead of fleeing after the first encounter, Tagin and Indria had turned and headed toward the city.

Almost as though Tagin is hunting magicians, not the other way around.

But he couldn't write that in the record. With a shudder, he wiped his pen, set it down and went to bed hoping for a night uninterrupted by mental calls reporting ill news, or nightmares.

When Indria had turned herself in to the first three magicians, they'd decided not to tell the Guild in case Tagin heard their mental conversation and their intention to sneak up on him. It had surprised her to learn that any mental communication could be overheard by all other magicians. She'd wondered why they bothered to use it at all.

The second group had no reason to contact other magicians—they had fallen asleep from the drug Tagin had forced the innkeeper to add to their drinks, and never knew they'd just eaten their last meal.

However, the third lot of magicians to fall foul of Tagin's grand plan did not die silently.

To Indria's relief, Tagin hadn't told her to approach and drug the four magicians they'd seen at the village. Instead they'd watched the men buy food and a bottle of wine, then followed them at a distance. The four did not have any apprentices with them, she'd noted. As dusk greyed the landscape, the magicians had stopped to eat their meal, though they remained on their horses. Tagin and Indria had tied their horses to a fence post out of sight, then crept closer, hidden by a stone wall.

Bringing out the bottle of poison, Tagin had somehow taken a large drop of it out of the bottle with magic. The drop floated up in the air to hover above the magicians. Indria had watched, heart racing and wondering how they could not have noticed it.

Then one of the magicians had brought out wine to share around. The droplet had shot downward and into the wine bottle so fast that none of them had seen it. The magicians had begun taking it in turns to drink straight from the bottle.

It had seemed a needless risk to keep peering over the wall at the men, so Tagin and Indria had slipped away to reclaim their mounts. That had been their mistake, Indria realised. The magicians had ridden on for several minutes before the drug began to take effect. As they began to fall from their saddles, Tagin confidently rode up to them, grinning widely. But one magician did not fall. One magician hadn't drunk from the bottle, or else had drunk too little, and that magician had attacked Tagin. The strike had knocked Tagin from his horse, and the animal had raced off down the road. "Get out of range!" Tagin had shouted to Indria, so she'd raced off to shelter behind a copse of trees.

It was hard to tell what was happening, watching the battle from a distance. Night was advancing, and she caught flashes of light and booming noises, but only glimpses of her brother and the magician. Her heart pounded, and she felt sick.

Don't kill him, she pleaded silently at the magician.

Suddenly all went black. For a long moment there was only darkness and silence, then a figure appeared, lit by his own magic. It waved at her, beckoning. She felt a rush of relief as she recognised it. Guilt followed as she realised the magician must be dead. Then something else stirred. Something darker.

Dread.

Tagin was alive and well, but so were his plans. Until she could talk him out of them, more people would die. Sighing, she urged her horse out of the copse toward the site of the battle. The dust was settling now. Tagin was crouching beside one of the unconscious men. Perhaps she could talk him into letting them live.

But before she had moved far from the trees a flame suddenly shot up from the ground, twice as high as the trees, and she felt heat on her skin. Her horse started and she clung to its back, heart pounding. *What was that?* Tagin shouted—though it sounded more like a curse than surprise or pain. Another flash of light burned the night. She felt her horse tense, ready to leap into a run, and quickly hauled on the reins. It danced in a circle, slowly settling at she talked to it soothingly. She looked toward Tagin to see him standing near where the flames had come from. He turned away and started toward her.

When he reached her, he frowned up at her.

"Are you sure that's the same poison you bought last time?"

She nodded, then shrugged. "It smells the same."

Tagin scowled. "Two of them died from it before I got a chance to take their power. That's what the light was—the last of their magic released from their bodies when they died. Good thing I was shielding."

A shock went through Indria, despite knowing that he would have killed them anyway. She thought of the size of the drop of poison Tagin had put into the wine. Much bigger than the single drop per person she'd used before. Had he used too much?

"Maybe it's stronger," she suggested. "Maybe the ones we drugged before this would have died too, if you'd been delayed this long." *The herbalist was very insistent that I not use too much.*

He nodded. "I've used too much power in the fight." He looked up at her, his expression thoughtful. "I'm a strong magician, so as my sister it's possible you have strong powers, too."

She frowned. "But I'm not a magician."

He smiled. "No, but you have the potential. You can't use any of your magic, but I can." He beckoned. "Get down."

Reluctantly, she dismounted. He took her hands and looked into her eyes earnestly. "I know I said that having power taken from you is awful, but it isn't if it's done gently. If you aren't drained dry you hardly know the difference. Will you let me take your strength?"

She stared back at him. He wanted her to endure the same thing that he'd killed Lord Herrol for.

"We need to do this," he told her. "Or the next time we meet any magicians they'll kill us."

After what he's done, of course they will. But his expression was so direct and anxious. Not a hint of crazed ambition, or deception. He looked far more sane than she'd seen him in weeks.

She nodded. He smiled briefly in thanks, then became serious again. From somewhere in his clothing he produced a knife. The blade touched each of her palms. She felt a pressure, then a slowly growing sting. Covering her hands in his, he closed his eyes.

First she went a bit wobbly as a feeling of weakness spread through her, but somehow she stayed on her feet. Then she felt languid and passive. After a time the feeling eased, and she felt normal but for a tingle in her palms. Tagin grinned and let her hands go. The cuts he'd made were gone, healed away with magic. He reached out to touch her cheek, his eyes warm with affection.

"Thank you. How do you feel?" he asked.

She considered. "Fine. It was a bit draining, at first."

He nodded. "Took me a while to judge the speed of it. I'm not used to having to do it slowly."

"How do *you* feel?" she asked.

He frowned and looked at the ground, then he shook his head. "You're strong, but you're only one person. I need more magic." He turned around, stopping as he faced the road to the village they'd just left. Tiny lights glinted in the distance.

"Stay here, hidden behind the wall," he said, taking the reins of her horse. "I'll be back in an hour or so."

Record of the 235th Year.

Our worst fears have come to pass. Apprentice Tagin, now being called "The Mad Apprentice" has turned on the common man and woman in his pursuit of power. Lord Telkan, on his way to the city after a visit to Elyne, found the entire village of Whiteriver dead and left to rot. All victims had been killed with higher magic. Even the locals' enka, gorin and reber had perished. Only small children were spared.

After informing the Guild of the tragedy, Lord Telkan continued on his way only to encounter signs of a magical battle, and the bodies of Lord Purwe and Lord Horet. The two deceased were not even on Tagin's trail, instead, misfortune brought them in contact with their killer. Fortunately Lord Telkan was not so unlucky, and has this evening reached the Guild safely.

Looking down at his entry, Gilken shook his head in disbelief.

"Nearly a quarter of Kyralian magicians have died at Tagin's hands. I'm beginning to find my opinion swaying toward those who believe he should be killed as soon as possible, rather than risk further lives in the attempt to catch him."

Lord Arfon sighed. "You are not the only one, if whispers in the Guildhall corridors are any indication."

"But you still feel strongly that we must find out how he came to learn higher magic without assistance?"

"Yes. And it is less likely Indria will be harmed if we capture him."

Gilken looked at Arfon closely. The man had spent several nights talking to Indria while she had been held at the Guildhall. Had he grown fond of her? While the general opinion of the magicians was that Tagin's sister was guilty of helping a murderer, Arfon had pointed out many times that she may not have any choice. But when her husband, who had been found in Lonmar visiting his trading partners, was told of her involvement in her brother's crimes he had all but disowned her, and many in the Guild had taken that as proof of her bad character.

"What will you do now?" Gilken asked.

Arfon frowned as he considered. "He's so unpredictable. First he runs, now he attacks. I've instructed the searchers to report his position if they see him, but to avoid approaching or confronting him. Once we know where he is, we can gather together and decide how best to corner him."

"You don't have any idea how strong he is, do you?"

"No." Arfon's expression was grim. "Only that, now he has taken to attacking commoners, he will grow rapidly stronger. The longer it takes for us to find and subdue him, the stronger he will get."

"Do you need my help?"

The younger magician looked at Gilken in surprise and gratitude, and shook his head. "The Guild needs a record of these events," he said. "Hopefully only as a warning to those who come after us. But thank you for offering."

Gilken smiled and shrugged, feeling a mixture of relief and frustration. If only there was something he could do to help. But he was old, and perhaps the best he could do was the task already in his hands.

Exhausted, Indria sat down on a low wall and stared at the ground. She did not want to see the bodies of the villagers around her. Despair and guilt would only drain the last of her energy—though deliberately avoiding the sight brought a wave of shame anyway.

Every night Tagin took magical energy from her. He said it not only kept them strong and safe, but it would help her sleep. He was right: she all but fell unconscious and only woke when he shook her the next day. She would have been grateful for the lack of dreams, if her waking hours had not become so nightmarish.

He insisted she come with him each time he attacked a village, afraid that the magicians would find her and use her against him. When she had seen what he did to the people, she had protested, too tired to care what he might do to her. But she had been too worn out to argue convincingly, and he had obviously been expecting and preparing for her reaction. He wore her down with his reasoning.

Or maybe it was the sheer madness of his reasoning that left her unable to speak or resist. *He has gone so far past the point of ordinary human boundaries, so beyond my reach, that there is no use in me arguing with him.*

Still, she clung to hope. Perhaps he would return from his delusion. If he did, she must be there to steer him back to sanity. The right word at the right time, and she might persuade him to flee Kyralia and hide somewhere remote and safe from the Guild.

Either that, or turn him in. But even now, that was unthinkable.

A movement caught her eye and she reluctantly looked up. A figure was approaching her. Tagin.

"We'll have magical company soon," he told her.

She frowned. "What do you mean?"

"I saw it in the mind of the village leader. The local Lord told him to send a messenger if we turned up. Once he knows we're here, he'll call on five other country magicians for help. They'll come after us."

"Oh." She stood up with an effort.

"Rest, sister," Tagin said, his voice growing gentle for a moment. "We're not going anywhere."

"We aren't running away?"

"No."

"Are we going to poison them?"

"No. No more poison. No more tricks. It is time for good, honest battle."

She felt her heart start to beat faster, and suddenly felt a little more awake. It was not a pleasant sensation. "How many magicians did the man say there were?"

"Six."

"But...you're...one."

"Yes, but they are weaker."

"How do you know? Don't they take power from their apprentices?"

"Yes. One apprentice, once a day. I have taken magic from many hundreds, and you would not believe how many commoners have as much latent power as a trained magician. I can see why the Sachakans have slaves..." His voice faded, then he shook his head. "Guild magicians aren't allowed to take magic from anyone but their apprentices. Not unless there's a war."

"Do...do you know anything about fighting?"

He smiled. "A lot more than they do. It's been over two hundred years since the Sachakan War. Kyralian magicians have forgotten how to fight. There's been no reason to, since the wasteland ruined Sachaka." He frowned. "Herrol had a big library, most of it inherited, and I don't think he'd read all of it. I found books on strategy. Books all about fighting and planning battles. I've practised as much as I could, trying different kinds of barriers and strikes. It wasn't as good as real fighting practise, but it was more than what the Guild teaches."

"But...if you attack them...does that make it war?"

He looked at her and smiled. "They're already in a war, they just don't know it yet. And by the time they realise it, it will be too late."

Record of the 235th Year.

It is difficult to believe that any man could be capable of such acts of needless violence. Yesterday's attempt to subdue him appears to have sent him into a passion. The last reports say he has slaughtered all in the villages of Tenker and Forei. He is beyond all controlling and I fear for the future of us all. I am amazed that he has not turned on us yet—but perhaps this is his preparation for that final strike.

Gilken, family Balen, House Sorrel, Record-keeper of the Magicians' Guild.

I definitely should not include my suspicions in my entries, Gilken thought as he finished rereading his previous entry. *Whenever I do, they prove to be correct in the most unpleasant way.*

He sighed and dipped his pen into the bottle of ink.

It is looking more and more likely that the confrontation between Tagin and the country magicians was a deliberate move. Most here now believe he was ridding himself of the threat of attack from the rear in preparation for his advance toward the city.

Today, reports have been arriving every hour of villages and towns emptied of life, the luckier citizens having fled on Tagin's arrival, and of country magicians found dead in their homes or searchers perishing on the road.

The only benefit to this is that Tagin is no longer hiding. Today Lord Arfon left with twenty-three magicians with orders to kill, not capture, the Mad Apprentice and his sister, Indria.

A sound in the stairwell leading to his room made his heart skip. Had Lord Arfon returned? Had he been successful?

The steps were slow and dragged with weariness. Gilken wiped his pen, set it down, and hurried to the door. As he opened it, the man climbing the stairs looked up. Arfon's expression was grim, but it softened as he saw Gilken. By the time he had entered the room and collapsed into a chair his face was drawn and strained.

"It's not good news, is it?" Gilken said, taking the other chair.

"No." Arfon covered his face with his hands, drew in a deep breath and shook his head. He looked up at Gilken. "He defeated us. I only survived because...Indria suggested Tagin let me return to the Guild to deliver the news and suggest we surrender."

Gilken felt his heart sink down low in his chest. "How is that possible? How could we have got to this point in a few short months. How can we fall to one crazed apprentice?"

"Because we have underestimated him," Arfon replied. "He is no apprentice; he knows higher magic, therefore we should have treated him as a higher magician. And because we are fools, too slow and arrogant to consider we could ever be challenged, too split by politics to cooperate when we were, and too proud to foresee that one of our own might turn on us one day."

"You could not have predicted any of this," Gilken protested. "How could anyone have guessed that Tagin would dare to attack us?"

"We should have considered it." Arfon shook his head. "I should have considered it. But there is no point arguing about it now. We can argue all we want, but it won't undo our mistakes."

Gilken regarded the young magician with dismay. He'd never seen Arfon so resigned and hopeless.

"What will your next move be?"

Arfon shook his head. "The hunt has been taken out of my hands."

Gilken stared at Arfon in disbelief. There was little wonder Arfon looked so defeated. "But surely Tagin has been weakened by the fight. He is just one magician. Another attack will surely—"

"If anyone wants to gather a force to confront Tagin now it has to be at their own arranging," Arfon told him. "But the Guild may not approve it. When I left the meeting room talk had turned to bargaining and negotiation."

"Do you think Tagin will be willing to negotiate?" he found himself asking, not quite ready to abandon the future he'd always assumed would come to pass.

Arfon shrugged. "I've given up guessing what he will do. Maybe there will be no Guild left to negotiate with. I suspect those of a less optimistic outlook will have gathered their most valued possessions and found somewhere else to be by tomorrow morning."

"Can't we...can't we call upon the people of Imardin to give us their strength?"

"That was also discussed, but I have to agree with the prevailing opinion: the people are unlikely to agree to it. This has happened too fast for them to comprehend the danger. There is no army at the gates—no foreign enemy. There is one man. One of our own members, who we are responsible for dealing with. They don't understand how one apprentice could be such a threat. Even if we tried to explain...they don't trust magicians like they used to, and this king is hardly the type to stir love from his people."

Gilken looked away. *So they weren't even going to try to persuade the people to help? Or confront Tagin one more time, while he was weak?* He pushed himself to his feet.

"I'm going down to this meeting. There are other options they may not have considered."

Arfon looked up at him in surprise, then nodded.

"I'll come with you," he said.

Gilken smiled in gratitude, then led the way out of the Record-keeper's room to talk some sense into what was left of the Guild.

Indria had lost all sense of feeling, apart from a numbness that frightened her. It had been hard to justify the deaths of the magicians that had pursued Tagin, but she'd managed it. Watching her brother strip the life from one person after another, sparing only the youngest of the children, she had found she could not reason it away, so she stopped reasoning at all.

He is a monster. My brother. A monster, the shreds of her conscience told her.

But if he is, then the Guild made him so.

They may have used their apprentices badly, but did they deserve this in return?

She ignored the question. Once more she told herself that, once all this was over, the monster in her brother would go and the old Tagin would return. It was madness to hold onto this hope, but she did. Stupidly, stubbornly. There was nothing left but that hope. It was all out of her hands. Never had been in them to start with.

He never listened to me before all this started. Why did I think he would if I came with him?

She had been a fool to think she could keep him out of trouble and stop him from killing more people. Nothing she had said or did had turned him from this path.

But at least she had tried.

Not hard enough. You could have refused to go with him. You could have neglected to slip the poison in the wine that first time. Look at what your cowardice has brought about.

She looked up. The road before her was littered with the bodies of magicians.

As the last of the magicians fell, Tagin turned to grin at her. He beckoned. Obediently she followed him into the city. The people of Imardin shrank back, watching the lone figure and his sister. Indria thought back to the apprentices who had sought her brother out, traitors seeking to join him and thereby save themselves.

"You would give your lives to my cause?" he'd asked.

"Yes," they'd assured him. So he'd taken what they offered, wiping their blood from his knife onto their robes.

As he turned into King's Parade a chill of foreboding shivered through her. He was not heading for the Guild, he was heading for the palace. Somehow that realisation stirred up an emotion deep within the emptiness and she faltered. It briefly pushed away the numbness and after a moment of confusion she realised what she felt was anger.

"When you and I rule the world..." he had said to her, playing their familiar game. *This was his plan all along. All the talk of changing the Guild has been a lie.*

No. He was merely heading to the palace because he knew that was where the magicians would be. Tagin looked over his shoulder at her. His eyes gleamed with mad eagerness, but as he looked at her it faded and changed to concern.

"Are you well, sister? Am I walking too fast for you?"

She felt her heart lift a little. There was still good in him. She managed a smile. "I'm fine."

As he turned back she let the chill in her heart numb her doubts and held onto a hope that had shrivelled and shrunk, but somehow refused to wither away entirely.

Record of the 235th Year.

My worst fears have come to life. Today Tagin killed Lord Gerin, Lord Dirron, Lord Winnel and Lady Ella. Will it end only when all magicians are dead, or will he not be satisfied until all life has been drained from the world? The view from my window is ghastly. Thousands of gorin, enka and reber rot in the fields, their strength given to the defence of Kyralia. Too many to eat, even.

Thousands of people are leaving the city while Tagin is too occupied with establishing control in the palace to stop them. The Guild is all but empty. Aside from a few brave magicians, we have all fled to safer locations to wait and observe. Some are planning to leave Kyralia. I am undecided. Should I leave the country and take this record with me, or stay and continue in my duty to document these events? Some would reason that the Guild is finished so there is nothing more to record. But we are not all dead yet.

Gilken, family Balen, House Sorrel, Record-keeper of the Magicians' Guild.

The carriage bounced and swayed as Gilken put aside the record book. The driver had been instructed to get them all as far away from the city as possible, as quickly as possible so, once the vehicle had passed all the people fleeing the city on foot or in carts, it had sped up. The combination of speed and the rougher country roads made writing impossible.

His fellow passengers, two female magicians and one male apprentice, were silent. *Along with me, a grey-haired old man, we are hardly a formidable force.* He thought of the rest of the Guild members, now scattering across the country: mostly the older or younger magicians, a handful of women—and far more apprentices than magicians, since so many had lost their masters.

Though two hundred years had passed since the Sachakan War, the Guild's Kyralian membership hadn't reached the number of magicians that had existed before the war. Now, even if Tagin was somehow defeated and all surviving magicians returned to the Guild, it would take many more years to replace those that had been lost to the Mad Apprentice.

Not to forget the emptied villages and towns. And however many Imardians Tagin killed in future to keep himself in charge of the country. *But I suppose he'll have to keep some alive, otherwise he'll run out of people to take power from. He'll keep the ones with the greatest latent magic as slaves, most likely.* Gilken shuddered. *Maybe it is better that I am leaving. I'm not sure I'd be able to bear recording it all.*

"They have *what?*"

The old servant flinched at Tagin's anger.

"Left, my lord."

"Where did they go?"

"I don't know. They took carriages and headed in different directions. Some to the south, some to th—"

"Good," Tagin declared. "If they've split up, they won't be coming back to fight me any time soon." He moved back to the throne and sat down. "I want a list of all the magicians that left." Tagin narrowed his eyes at the man. "I know you'll try to hide some. For every magician I learn you've left off the list I'll...I'll kill a member of your family."

The man nodded. "I understand."

Tagin looked away, his expression thoughtful. "I also want everyone in Kyralia to know that any magicians that are found are to be sent to me. And their apprentices. Let it be known that no magician is allowed to use higher magic to strengthen themselves."

"I will summon the street callers," the man murmured.

"Thirdly, I want all the books in the Guild sent here." Tagin pointed to one of the courtiers he'd selected, after reading their minds, to serve him. "My assistant will go with you to make sure you don't hide any." He waved a hand. "Go."

The man bowed and backed away. Tagin ignored him, reaching for his glass of water.

Indria watched from a chair that had been placed beside the throne for her. As Tagin drank, a memory flashed into her mind of a glass goblet full of clear water that had tasted faintly of rocks. Of Lord Arfon.

"*There's a spring in the Guild grounds,*" he told her. "*The water from it is the purest you'll ever drink. It is piped only to this building and to the Royal Palace—and in the palace it goes first to the king's rooms.*" She had told Tagin about the spring, but not about its location in the Guild, and he had decided to only drink from this safe source.

"Oh, that's right." Tagin looked up at the retreating man. "Stop! I have another instruction. Send me the Guild records. I want to know what's been said about me."

The servant bowed again, then hurried out of the entrance to the audience chamber. Indria felt a pang of sympathy and sighed.

"Are you well, sister? You look pale."

Indria looked up to find Tagin looking at her, and shrugged. "Just tired."

He considered her thoughtfully. Since taking over the palace he had insisted she stay by his side. She told herself he was being protective, but sometimes she detected an old, familiar mood of suspicion and distrust. Worry grew like a tangled knot inside her. She knew that mood. It had always been a dangerous one. In the past it had led to accusations of imagined slights against him and, when she was younger, beatings. Now that he had grown accustomed to killing with little hesitation, what would he do if he imagined she was betraying him?

Suddenly he smiled. "Go on, sister. This has all been exhausting for you. Rest and return when you feel better."

Somehow she forced her weary legs to take her to the rooms Tagin had chosen for her. The beauty of the decorations and furnishings within the palace only made her more melancholy. As she reached the door to her apartment a guard held it open for her. She all but staggered through to the greeting room, relieved when the door clicked shut behind her. Then she froze.

A man stood in the centre of the room. She blinked at him stupidly for a moment. He was not a servant. He was familiar, but for a moment she didn't recognise him because he wasn't wearing his robes.

"Lord Arfon?"

He nodded. She glanced back at the door. Had the guard noticed the intruder? Surely if he had, he would have said or done something. Or did the guard know Lord Arfon was here and was helping the magician?

"Tagin will kill you if he sees you," she warned.

Arfon nodded again. He gazed back at her, saying nothing but looking hesitant. As if he wanted to say something, but didn't know where to start.

"Why are you here?" she asked.

He swallowed. "To find out if there is anything that can be done."

She looked down at the floor, realising only as the feeling faded that the sight of Arfon had lightened her heart a little.

"Nothing. Even if there was, it's too late."

"He trusts you."

She looked at him. His eyebrows rose suggestively, even while his expression remained grim.

"I can't do that," she told him. "I can't kill someone. Least of all my own brother."

Arfon nodded, then sighed and sat down on the edge of one of the chairs. All the determination fell from him and he shook his head.

"I wish the world could have heard you say that. It is such a strange thing, that the sibling of the worst killer in history has the gentlest of natures. It is too hard to believe, for most people."

She frowned. "What do they believe?"

He looked away. "That you are his ally. You are, aren't you?" His gaze returned, and his eyes were now hard and judgemental.

I tried to stop him, she wanted to say. But that was a lie.

"I was never able to stop him, once he got something into his head," she said instead. "Not when we were children. Not now."

Arfon nodded, then rose and walked to one of the large paintings. To her astonishment, it hinged away from the wall like a door. Behind was a square opening. He paused and looked back at her.

"If you decide to do something, I will help you."

Then he stepped into the hole, reached back and pulled the painting-door closed behind him.

Indria stared at the painting. She felt a strange disappointment. *I wanted him to stay and argue with me,* she realised. *He accepted my excuse too easily.*

But she *had* tried to stop Tagin. In her mind she heard the argument begin again. *No. You haven't,* the quiet voice in the back of her mind replied. *You could have stopped him many times. But you were afraid of what he'd do if you failed, or he escaped. You were a coward.*

But he was her brother.

And your responsibility. What would have been worse: Betraying him to the Guild when he had only murdered a few, or letting him kill again and again until he became the monster he is now?

Her head spun. There was no point acting now. It was too late. Tagin was on the throne. Things could not get any worse.

Oh, yes they can.

He would have to keep killing to stay strong enough to repel attempts by the Guild to rescue the city. Or else he would enslave people so that he could take power from them, over and over.

Slaves. We'll end up like the Sachakans. Only there'll be just one master, my brother, and all Kyralians will be slaves.

There was nothing she could do.

Oh, yes there is.

Her mouth went dry as she thought of it. The solution had been there right from the start. She only needed the courage to use it. She walked slowly to the cabinet that held the few possessions she had carried these last months, and took out a small vial, paper, ink and a pen.

Nothing stopped her. She resolved to keep going until her nerve failed, or her conscience stopped arguing with her, and stilled her hands.

Some time later she found Tagin digging through a chest of dusty books in the middle of the audience chamber.

"Look!" he said as she approached. "Books from the Guild."

She grimaced. "They smell old."

"They are," he told her. "This one is a record of the Guild magicians who ruled Sachaka after the war." As he dug through them dust billowed up and he coughed. He waved a hand. "Get me a drink, sister."

Her spine tingled as she picked up the goblet beside the throne and moved to the back of the room. The spring water was clear and cold. She filled the vessel and returned to Tagin's side. As he watched, she raised the goblet to her lips and sipped.

Satisfied, he took the glass, drained it and handed it back to her. He selected a book and returned to the throne. She watched as he began to read. Then, as his eyes closed and his head began to nod she set her glass aside.

Moving to the throne, she leaned close as if to look at the pages. He swayed as he looked up at her.

"Sister," he said, his eyes slowly closing and opening again. He let the book drop. "I am very tired."

"Brother," she replied. "I am, too. Lean on me. Don't worry. I'll take care of you."

She caught him as he fell and held him as his eyes closed. Slowly his breathing slowed and his lips turned blue. Reaching out to take her glass and drain it, she marvelled at how the taste of the drug was barely noticeable in the clear water, even when strong enough to kill.

Then her eyes were assailed by a flash of intense white, and a sensation too brief to register as pain.

A few weeks' absence had not made the tower steps any easier to climb. This time Gilken had a burden to carry, too. The record book and writing equipment felt heavier than they had when he'd taken them out of the room. Finally he reached the last step, and the platform before the door. He stopped to gaze at the plain wood, and the plaque stating that this room was for the "Record-keeper of the Magicians' Guild." For a moment he was overwhelmed by emotion.

Taking a deep breath, he pushed into the room beyond.

There were a few signs of disturbance. Cupboards had been opened. A glass water jug had been smashed. The bed was at an angle, suggesting it had been moved. But the small, high table on which he always worked remained whole and in place.

He put his burden down on the table, then moved to the window. What he saw made his breath catch.

Though he had seen the ruins of the city as his carriage had passed through to the Guild, it had been a confusing jumble of stone and wood. Now, from the higher position, he could see patterns in the devastation. The explosion that had levelled so many buildings had fanned out from the palace. It had missed the Guild, instead smashing everything between the throne room and the docks. It was a terrible sight, but it stirred a guilty relief.

Tagin was dead.

So were thousands of people. Magicians and non-magicians. Lords and servants. Men and women. Adults and children. Either murdered by the Mad Apprentice, or killed when all the magic he had stolen had been released on his death.

Gilken stared at the view for a long time, until he could no longer bear the sight. He turned from the window and moved back to the high table. Taking the record book out of its wrappings, he placed it on the sloped surface. He returned the inkpot to its place and removed his pen from its carry case.

He wet the nib.

And began writing.

Record of the 235ᵗʰ Year.

It is over. When Alyk told me the news I dared not believe it, but an hour ago I climbed the stairs of the Lookout and saw the truth with my own eyes. It is true. Tagin is dead. Only he could have created such destruction in his final moments.

Lord Eland called us together and read a letter sent from Indria, Tagin's sister. She told of her intention to poison him. We can only assume that she succeeded.

Did she know that killing him would release the power he contained? Did she know it would blast the palace and much of the city to rubble? Why did she support him despite all he did, only to turn on him at the end?

We will never know. It is likely we will see more stringent rules governing apprentices and the teaching of higher magic. Some have even suggested higher magic be banned altogether, though that would leave us foolishly vulnerable to attack. Still, Sachaka is no longer a threat and we are on friendly terms with our other neighbours.

One suggestion gaining support is to encourage magicians to dedicate themselves to learning and using magic for fighting and warfare in the same way that some of us do with magical healing. Perhaps then we'll be ready for the next threat, and not repeat the many mistakes we made in dealing with the Mad Apprentice.

Change is certain. I suspect the effects of this tragic story will haunt us for many years to come, but I am starting to believe that we will grow stronger and wiser as a result.

Good things can come from awful events, so long as we learn from our mistakes, and record what we have learned for future generations.

Gilken, family Balen, House Sorrel, Record-keeper of the Magicians' Guild.

Otherling

Juliet Marillier

*Juliet Marillier was born and brought up in Dunedin, New Zealand, and now lives
in Western Australia. Her historical fantasy novels for adults and young adults have
been translated into many languages and have won a number of awards including
the Aurealis, the American Library Association's Alex Award, the Sir Julius Vogel
Award and the Prix Imaginales. Her lifelong love of folklore, fairy tales and mythology is a major influence on her writing. Juliet is currently working on the third book
in the Shadowfell series, a story of tyranny and rebellion set in a magical version
of ancient Scotland. When not busy writing, she tends to a small pack of waifs and
strays.*

IT WAS A HARSH WINTER, a season of slicing winds and ice-fettered wa-
terways, of hunger and endurance. The days were always short in the
shadow season, but this year dark seemed hungry to devour light. Bellies
yearned for fresh meat; hearts ached for the sun's blessing. The Songs told
of the coming of seals, and sanctioned the killing of three: sufficient for a
good feast for every man, woman and child of the Folk. Bard's Singing set
out how the hunting must be done. The men went masked, their leader
garbed in the hunt cloak, soft and grey, shining and supple as if he himself
were a seal. The spearing was prefaced by apologies and words of gratitude.
Afterwards there was feasting, and oil for lamps, and the Folk took new
heart. Now they might endure until the days began to lengthen again, and
the first cautious leaf-swellings appeared on the wind-battered trees.

But Bard felt the rasping in his chest, his cough like a stick drawn over
wattles, and he knew he had seen his last spring. He watched his student.
She had been apt to learn: she could draw forth the pipe's piercing keen,

and conjure the subtle rhythm of the bones. By candlelight she summoned the voice of the small harp strung with the gut of winter hares. Its melody hung bittersweet in air: call and echo, substance and shadow. The girl had endured the days of fasting, the sleepless nights, the necessary trials by water and fire and deep earth. She had heard the Songs; had held within her the voices of the ancestors, a burden precious as an unborn child. All this she had learned. But she was young: perhaps too young.

"Tonight's lesson is grave indeed." Bard spoke quietly as the harpsong ended. "You know already that Bard is born only from a twinning; that in the way of things there will be one such birth amongst the Folk in each generation. This allows time for one Bard to pass on the mysteries to the next, as I have done to you. If the cycle were broken, and Bard died before his student was ready, the Singing would be lost, and without it the Folk would perish. The Songs reveal the great pattern that must be followed. They are our true map and pathway: our balance and our lodestar."

The girl nodded, saying nothing.

"Our calling cannot be denied. It is a sacred trust. But..." He faltered. How could her mind encompass the desolation of a life spent without human touch? She was but half grown: barely a woman. "There is a darker side. The Songs must be taken unsullied from their source, and passed on pure and strong to the Folk. Bard must devote every scrap of will, every fibre of spirit, every last corner of mind to that. It will be long; you will bear the burden until your student is ready to take your place. There is no room for other things. So we remain alone; apart. But it is not enough. Bard must be stronger than an ordinary man or woman; strong enough to endure the power of the Singing and not splinter into madness; true enough to form unbreakable link and pure conduit from spirit to man." His sigh scraped like a blade on ice. "That is why Bard must be twinborn. That is why we have the Choosing."

"What is the Choosing?" The girl's small features were frost-white in the dimness of the stone hut, and her eyes had darkened to shadows. Outside, the wind roared across the thatch; the rope-hung weights knocked against the walls.

"If you had lived amongst the Folk, you would know a little of this already," the old man said wearily. "I have kept it from you; it is a mystery darker than any you have yet learned. Now you must know it, and begin to harden your will towards it. You may be lucky; for you the Choosing may come late, when you are practised in the disciplines of the mind. Have you asked yourself what becomes of the twin who is not Bard? How this choice is made?"

She pondered a moment. "I suppose one seems more apt. Perhaps the other is sent away. I have seen no likeness of myself amongst the Folk."

"Indeed not. Your brother died long ago, when you were no more than babes; mine met the same fate in a time before my memory. We hold their strength as well as our own, and are ourselves doubly strong: two in one. Without this, no man or woman has the endurance, the fortitude, the clear head and unsullied spirit a Bard must possess. You could not hear the Songs, you could not draw the voice of power from the harp, or sway the minds of the Folk, without your Otherling."

"My Otherling?" she breathed.

"Your twin; the one who was sacrificed so that you could become Bard."

Her eyes were mirrors of darkness. "They killed him?" she whispered.

The old man nodded, his features calm. He was still Bard; if he felt compassion, he did not let it show. "Soon after birth. It is always thus. A choice is made. The stronger, the more suitable, is preserved. The Otherling dies before he sees a second dawn, and his spirit flows into the brother or sister. That way, Bard becomes strong enough for the Singing. It is necessary, child."

"Bard?" Her voice was very faint in the half-dark, and not quite steady. "Who makes the choice? Who performs the—the sacrifice?"

The old man looked at the girl, and she looked back at him. He needed no words to answer her; she read the truth in his eyes.

It was as well he told her when he did. Next morning when she arose, shivering, to make up the fire and heat some gruel for the old man's breakfast, she found him calm-faced and cold on his bed. She laid white shells on his eyelids, and touched his shaven head with her fingertips. When a boy passed by, trudging to the outer field with a bucket of oats, she called her message from behind closed shutters. Before nightfall the elders came with a board and took the old man away. Now she was Bard. Later, she stood dry-eyed by the pyre as he burned hot and pungent in the freezing air of the solstice.

At her first Singing, she told the old man's life and his passing, and she told a good season to come, for all the harsh winter. Seed could be planted early; mackerel would be plentiful. The sea would take no men this spring, as long as they were careful. When she was done the people made their reverences and departed. Some lived close by in the settlement of Storna, but others had far to travel, across the island to Grimskaill, Settersby or distant Frostrim. They boarded their sledges and whipped on wiry dog or sturdy pony; they strapped bone skates to their boots and made their way by frozen stream and lake path. They would return for the great Singings Bard must give at each season's turning. At these times new Songs would be given: new wisdom from ancient voices. The Singings had names: Waking, Ripening, Reaping, Sleeping. But she had her own names for them, which she did not tell. Longing, Knowing, Sacrifice, Silence.

They said she was a good Bard in those days. She kept aloof, as she should. She'd greet them when she must, and withdraw inside her hut like a ghost-woman. Days and nights she waited at the stones, silent in their long shadows, listening. They said if you dared to speak to her at such a time, she would not hear you, though her eyes were open. All that she could hear was the silence of the Song.

One long winter a man brought a load of wood and stayed to chop it for her. She watched him from behind the shutters, marvelling at the strength and speed of it. When he was done, he did not simply go away as he should, but used his fist to play a firm little dance-beat on her door. She opened it the merest crack, looked out with her shadowy eyes, her face pale with knowledge.

"All finished," said the young man, his grin dimpled and generous, his hair standing on end, fair as ripe barley. "Stacked in the corner to keep dry for you. Cold up here."

"Thank you," she whispered, looking into his eyes: merry, kind eyes the colour of rock pools under a summer sky. "Thank you." The door began slowly to creak shut.

"Lonely life," said the young man.

Bard nodded, and looked again, and closed the door.

After that he would come up from time to time, not often, but perhaps more often than the natural pattern of things would allow. He would mend leaking thatch, or unblock a drain; she would watch him from behind the door, or through the chinks of a shutter, and thank him. There was never more than a word or two in it, but after a while she found she was looking for him in the crowd whenever she ventured into Storna. She found she was peering from her window when folk passed on the road, in case she might see him go by, and turn his head towards her shutters, and smile just for her. She learned his name: Ekka, a warrior's name, though a man with such a smile was surely no fighter, for all his strong arms that hewed the iron-hard logs as if cleaving through rounds of fresh cheese.

She found her attention wandering, and brought it sharply back. Under the stones, sitting cross-legged in silent pose of readiness, she waited for the Songs, and they did not come. Instead of their powerful voices, their ancient, binding truths, all she could hear was a faint fragment of melody, a little tinkling thing like the tunes played by the band of travelling folk who went about the island in summer, entertaining the crowds with tricks and dancing. It was the first time the Songs had ever eluded her, and when she came down to her hut, empty of the wisdom whose telling was her life's only purpose, she knew the old man's teaching had been sound. She must shut down those parts of herself that belonged to the spring season: the Longing. Bard must move forward quite alone.

From that time on her door was closed to him. Once or twice he called through fastened shutters, knowing she was there, and she set her jaw and held her silence. She went out hooded, and kept her eyes on the ground. He could not be totally avoided, for he was a leader in the settlement, with a part to play in the gatherings. Bard taught herself to greet him and feel nothing. She taught herself to look at him as she looked at all the others: as if the space between them were as wide and as unbridgeable as the great bowl of the star-studded sky. She watched him withdraw, the blue eyes darkened, the smile quite gone. Later, she watched him fall in love and marry, and she kept her thoughts in perfect order. Sleep was another matter. Even Bard's training cannot teach the mastery of dreams.

Time passed. Ekka's young wife had a tiny daughter. There were bountiful seasons and harsh ones. In times of trouble, the Songs cannot of themselves make things good. They cannot calm stormy seas, or cure sheep of the murrain, or bring sunshine in place of endless drenching rain. But they do bring wisdom. A warning of bad times enables preparation: the mending of thatch, the strengthening of walls, the shepherding of stock into barns and the conservation of supplies. Such a warning makes it possible to get through the hard times. The Folk kept a careful balance, each decision governed by the pattern she gave them, an ancient pattern in which wind and tide, fire and earth, man and beast were all part of the one great dance. One year the Ripening Song told of raiders in high ships, vessels with names like *Dragonflight* and *Sea Queen* and *Whalesway*. The Folk moved north to Frostrim, driving their stock before them. The raiders came and passed the island by; a shed or two was burned, a boat taken. At Reaping the Folk returned, and Bard sang their safety and a mild winter. Another year the Songs told of death. That season an ague took Storna, and twelve good folk perished, man, woman and babe. Ekka's wife was gravely ill, and Bard performed a Telling by the bedside. In a Telling one did not exactly ask the ancestors a favour. One simply set out a possible course of events, then hoped. Bard told how Sifri would bear more children: fine, bonny girls like her little daughter there, strong sons, blue-eyed and merry. She told the laughter of these children through the narrow ways of Storna and out across the fields, as they chased one another under the sun of an endless summer day. She finished, pulled the hood up over her shaven head, and left. The next morning Sifri was sitting up and drinking barley broth. By springtime her belly was swollen with child again, her small, sweet features flushed and mysterious with inner life.

At Reaping that year, Bard stood beneath the watchstone and heard the Song, and felt her heart grow cold, for all the discipline she laid on herself. One did not ask the ancestors, *Are you sure?* Before the first frost

Sifri gave birth to twins, a pair of boys each the image of the other. They were named, though neither would keep his name for long: Halli and Gelli. It was time for the Choosing.

She came down the hill, each step a thudding heartbeat. The Folk watched silent and solemn-eyed as if she herself were the sacrifice. Outside the Choosing place, the elders waited. Sifri and Ekka stood hand in hand, faces ash-white with grief and pride. They would lose both sons today, though one they might keep for a little while. The small girl stood at Sifri's skirts, thumb in mouth. Bard nodded gravely, acknowledging their courage; and then she went in.

The noise was deafening. Her own hut was always quiet. No hearthside cat or watchful dog disturbed her days, no servant muttered greetings, no child yelled fit to split her head apart as these two did. But wait. Only one babe screamed thus, one lusty child turned his face red with wailing and beat his tiny fists helplessly in air, seeking the comfort of touch, the return to warmth and love. This babe struggled; the other was quiet, so quiet one might have thought him already dead. She moved closer. The crying set her teeth on edge; it made her own eyes water. The children were in rush baskets, the lids set each to the side. Between them a stool had been set, and on it lay a dagger, its hilt an ornate masterpiece of gilded wire and small red gems, its blade sturdy, sharp, purpose-made. The children were naked, washed clean of the residue of birth. Perhaps they were cold. Perhaps that was why one screamed so. Soon one would be warm again, and the other colder still. It would only take a moment. Grasp, thrust, turn the eyes away. It would be over quickly, so quickly. There was no doubt which must be chosen: the stronger, the more fit. The fighter.

She moved forward again. The screams went on. This lad would have a powerful voice for the Singing. As for the other...she looked down. There in the woven basket, still as some small woodland creature discovered by a sudden predator, he lay gazing up at her. His round eyes were the colour of rock pools under a summer sky. His hair was a fuzz of pure gold. He smiled, and a dimple showed in his infant cheek. He was the image of his father. She turned to the other, her heart lurching, her hands shaking so violently she could surely scarcely lift the knife, let alone use it. As if in recognition of the moment, the first twin fell suddenly quiet, though his small chest still heaved from the effort of his outcry. His face was blotched with crying. His hands clutched the air, eager for life.

Now that the sobbing was hushed, sounds filtered in from outside: the creak of cart wheels, children's voices, the lilt of a whistle. Her mind showed her the travelling folk passing by, motley in their ragged cavalcade, their faces painted in bizarre patterns of red and black and white, their hair knotted and plaited, feathered and ribboned. Even their children looked like a flock of exotic birds. The whistle played a small arch of melody, and ceased abruptly. Someone had told them this was no time for music. And her decision was made. With steady hand, now, Bard reached down and grasped the knife.

There was a form of ritual to be observed, a pattern for the right doing of things. She came out of the small hut, basket in arms. The rush lid now covered the still form that lay within. Atop this lay the knife, its iron blade gaudy with fresh blood. The mother, the father, they did not ask to look or touch. This was not the way of it. The Otherling was gone to shadow; become a part of the great Song which would one day sound from his brother's lips.

"Go to your child," Bard told them softly. "Comfort him well. In three years bring him to me, and I will teach him."

"Thank you," said Ekka, blue eyes deep and solemn.

"Thank you," said Sifri, her voice a very thread of grief, and the two of them went into the hut. Their son's voice called them; now that it was over, he had set to yelling again with double vigour.

Bard bore the little basket up to her own hut, where it lay quiet, encircled by candles, until dusk fell. Her hand was bleeding. She tore a strip of linen from an old shift and bound it around palm and fingers, using her teeth to pull the knot tight. Later, the elders came for the basket and put it on the pyre, and they burned the Otherling with due ceremony. It did not take long, for he was quite small.

It seemed she had chosen well. Halli was apt. He grew sturdy and strong, broad shouldered and fair haired like his father, and with a fierce determination to master all he must know. By day she might show a new pattern on the bones, a more challenging mode of harpsong. At night she would lie awake to the endless repetitions, the long struggle for perfection. She need not use discipline; her student's own discipline was more rigorous than any she might devise.

For him patience was a far harder lesson, and without patience there can be no listening. At twelve he underwent the trials and showed himself strong enough. That did not surprise her; it was what came after that made her belly tighten with unease, her mind cloud with misgiving.

They stood beneath the watchstone in summer dawn, Bard and student.

"You know what must be done," she said.

There was a shallow depression below the great monolith, a hollow grave-like in its proportions, lined with soft grasses as if to encourage sleep. At summer solstice this place of listening caught the sun, and was a vessel of gold light on the green hill. At midwinter the shadow of the watchstone stretched out across the circle, shrouding the small hollow in profound, mysterious darkness.

Today there were clouds. Halli sat cross-legged, silent. Even so had she waited once, while the old Bard stood by the stones as still and patient as if he were himself one of these guardians of ancient truth; as if the lichens, pyre-red, sun-gold, corn-yellow, might in time grow up across his grey-cloaked form and make a gentle cap for his close-shaven skull. Even so had she waited, and emptied her mind of thought, and willed her breathing slow and slower. Then the Song had come to her, pure and certain, welling in the heart, sounding in the spirit, flooding the receptive mind with truth. It was the voice of the ancestors, ringing forth from the stones themselves, from the deep earth where they stood rooted firm, from the wind and the light and the unfathomable depth of the sky. She still held it within her somewhere: that first transcendent moment of joy.

Time passed. It could be long, a day and a night, maybe more. She knew the boy's strength. He would sit there immobile as long as he must, to hear it. And yet, as the sky darkened to rose and violet and pigeon grey, she wondered. He was apt, anyone could see that. Clever, quick, dedicated. Why was it so long? Inside her, memory stirred and shivered.

At dawn she spoke softly, breaking into his trance, bidding him cease. Another time, she told him. Next time. Halli was angry: with her, with the ancestors, with himself.

"You must learn patience," Bard said.

He clamoured to try again. Tomorrow. Tomorrow. Not yet, she said. If the ancestors would not speak, it was not time. His eyes narrowed with resentment, his mouth twisted with frustration.

"You must learn calm," Bard said.

He played the bones like a dance of death. He sounded the pipe in a piercing wail of need. His fingers dragged notes of aching emptiness from the small harp. She made him wait.

The season passed. At Reaping the travelling folk came through Storna with juggling and dances, with coloured streamers and performing dogs. A whistle tune floated up the hill, clean and innocent on the easterly breeze: a tune wrought untutored and free, yet exquisite in its form and feeling. The melody made its way in at her window and tugged at Bard's memory. Behind a closed door Halli played his own pipe, his music intricate, tangled on itself. She heard the two tunes meet and mingle, and she put her hands over her ears and used a technique long practised to shut out unwelcome thoughts. When she emerged from her trance, all was quiet. At last her student slept, his sturdy form relaxed as a child's, his strong features wan with exhaustion. The pipe had slipped from his fingers to the earthen floor. She laid the blanket over him.

Three Ripenings passed before he began to hear the Songs, and before she let him sing one he was already a man. Halli chafed against her restrictions. Why did she hold him back thus? He could do it, he knew he could. Didn't she trust him?

"You must learn humility," Bard said. "We are vessels, no more." His anger troubled her. Dreams came, and left her weary.

In his eighteenth summer Halli gave the Folk his first Singing. Bard listened as he told of early frost and the coming of whales; of a far shore where green fields and fruitful vines might be discovered; of the building of boats. His Singing was like the call of a war horn, deep and resonant.

By the end of it, the young men's eyes were alight with excitement: here was a challenge beyond any yet imagined. Did not the ancestors bid them set forth on a great adventure? In the crowd Sifri stood quiet, her three fair daughters by her. There had been no more sons.

Before the turning of the season they made a fine ship of wattles and skins, tarred for seaworthiness, with oars of larch wood. On the prow they set the great skull of a whale. They called the vessel *Seaskimmer*, and in her the young men of the island journeyed forth one sparkling dawn in search of the fruitful land to the west, a land where one day they might all live and prosper under a smiling sun. They did not return at Reaping. The women, the old people, the children cut the barley and stacked the straw. They did not return as the year moved on and the days began to shorten. It was in the shadow time that they came back to the island, those bold venturers of the Folk. A boy and his dog wandered the cold beach of Grimskaill, gathering driftwood. Shrouded in weed, cloaked in ribbons of sea wrack, the young men of Storna and Settersby, Grimskaill and far Frostrim lay quiet under the winter sky. For seven long days the Folk stood there by the water as the ocean delivered up their sons, each at his own time, each riding his own last wave. Then there was a burning such as the island had not seen in many a long year. The people looked at Bard with doubt in their eyes.

"This was wrong," she told him afterwards.

Halli lifted his fair brows. "How can the Singing be wrong? I told only the Song the ancestors gave me."

"It was wrong. The Songs help us avoid such acts of foolish waste, such harvests of anguish. It could not be meant thus."

"Why not?" her student said. "Who can say what the ancestors intend?"

"Surely not the wiping out of a full generation of young men. Who will father sons here? Who will fish and hunt? How will the Folk survive this?"

He smiled: his father's sunny, dimpled smile. "Perhaps the ancestors see a short future for us. Perhaps raiders will come and beget children. Who knows? I cannot answer your questions. You said yourself, we are no more than vessels."

That winter grandmothers and grandfathers swept floors and tended infants and stirred pots of thin gruel, while women cleared snow from thatch and broke ice from fishing holes. The few men of middle years slaughtered stock and hauled up the boats. It was a harsh season, but wisdom was remembered from times past, and they survived. At Waking, when the air held a deceptive whisper of new season's warmth, she would not let him listen for the Song.

"I am Bard," she told him, "and I will do it. You are not yet ready. You must learn something more."

"What?" Halli demanded fiercely. "What?"

But Bard gave no answer, for she had none.

The Song was an anthem to the lost ones, and a warning. The Folk must keep the balance or perish. Their children had survived the savage winter. Now all must be watchful. Bard thought the ancestors' message was not without hope. But she was tired, so tired that she stumbled as she went to stand before the Folk in the ritual place; so weak that she could scarcely summon the breath for the Singing. Afterwards her mind felt drained, her thoughts scattered. She could hardly remember what she had told them.

The weariness continued. Maybe she was sick. Maybe she should get a potion from the travelling folk, ever renowned for their elixirs. There was wisdom amongst that colourful, elusive band of wanderers: they had sent no sons voyaging across the ocean to return in a tumble of bleached and broken bone. But she was too tired to seek them out.

Halli was solicitous. He brought her warm infusions. He ensured the fire was made up and the floor swept clean. It was he who performed the Singing at midsummer, telling of fine shoals of fish south of Storna Bay, and favourable winds. Before the season's end deer might be taken and the meat smoked for winter.

The few men left on the island were not over-keen to put to sea, but the Singing removed any choice. They came to her afterwards with questions. How many deer? How many days may we fish in safety? With our young men gone, who will lead the hunt? She could not answer them. She had not heard this Song, for the stones were far, a weary distance up the hill. It was Halli who answered.

"Since the Singing did not tell of this, take what you will," he said.

There were some men of middle years, too old to sail for new horizons, still young enough for work. They found mackerel in great numbers and, thinking of winter, brought in netful after shining netful. The salting huts were crammed to bursting, and still there were more, a bountiful harvest. They went for deer, and found them in wooded valleys beyond Settersby. They were gone seven days; they returned bearing two great antlered carcases and the body of a fine, fair-haired man. Ekka was dead, slipped from an outcrop as he readied his spear to take the stag cleanly. Bard could hear the sound of Sifri's grieving all the way up the hill and through the shutters. She looked into her student's clear blue eyes, reading the iron there, and something shivered deep inside her. This was her doing. This was her Choosing. The boy had killed his own father. A Telling came to her mind as she lay shivering under her thick blankets, a Telling of times to come: of a spring with no mackerel, a spring where the young of puffin and albatross starved on the cliffs for lack of nourishment. In the season after, their numbers were less, and less again next Waking. Then weasel and fox, wolf and bear grew bolder, and neither chicken nor goose, young lamb nor younger babe in cradle was safe. The men grew old and feeble, the women gaunt and weary. Children were few. The Telling turned Bard's bones to ice. In such a time, all it would take was one hard winter to finish the Folk.

"You look tired," Halli observed. "You must rest. Leave everything to me." And indeed, there seemed a great urge in her to sleep; to melt into darkness, and let it all slip away. After all, what could she do? She had made her choice long years ago. All stemmed from that, and there was no changing it.

On the edge of slumber she heard again the sweet voice of a whistle, played somewhere out in the night, as deep and subtle, for all its simplicity, as the voices of the ancestors themselves. Bard slid out of bed, careful to make no sound. From Halli's chamber the small harp rang out. Still he drilled his fingers, the patterns ever more complex, as if he would never be satisfied. The sound of it frightened her. He frightened her. Unchecked, he would be the end of them all. But she felt so weak. The Folk no longer trusted her. Ekka was dead. She was alone, all alone...

A long time she knelt there on the earthen floor, shivering in her worn nightrobe. The old learning seemed almost forgotten: how to empty the mind and slow the breath, how to calm the body and control the will, how to listen. Somehow it had almost slipped away from her. She had forgotten she was Bard.

Of course you are alone, she thought fiercely. Bard is always alone. Have you let even that most basic lesson escape you?

"Not quite. But you have misremembered."

Her head jerked upwards. For a moment she thought—but no, the harp still sounded from the far chamber, servant of his will. The figure which stood before her was another entirely, and yet as familiar as the image she saw when she bent over the water trough to cup hands and drink. This wraith with hollow eyes and pallid cheeks, with shaven head, with ragged cloak and long hands apt for the making of music, this phantom was...herself. And yet...and yet...

"You know me," said her visitor, moving closer. She reached out a hand to touch, scarcely believing what she saw, and her fingers moved though him, cloak, flesh, bone all nebulous as shadow.

"You are my brother," she whispered, her eyes sliding fearful towards the inner door.

"He will not hear us."

"Why have you come? Why journey from—from death to seek me out?"

"You are afraid. You see no answers. Yet you hold the key to this yourself, Bard." His voice was grave and quiet. "The pattern is gone awry; that is your doing. It is for you to weave it straight and even once more."

"Why didn't you come before?" she asked him urgently. "I needed help. Why not come before good folk died, before he did what he did? Where were you?"

"You have carried me within you all this time, sister. If not for your error, you could have heard my voice, stronger as the years passed. Bard is never truly alone; always she has her Otherling. But you disobeyed the ancestors. Your choice was flawed. Now its influence spreads dark over you."

Bard stared at him, aware once more of her leaden limbs, her burdened heart. "The Folk will perish. Maybe not this year, maybe not next, but in time all will be lost. I've seen it."

The Otherling gazed back. His eyes seemed empty sockets, yet full of light. He was both old and young: an infant in a rush basket, a strong man in his prime, an ancient wise in spirit. "You made it so," he said quietly. "Now unmake it. Do what you could not do, long years ago. One does not lightly disregard the wisdom of the ancestors. Since the day you did so the Folk have walked under a shadow, a darkness that will in time engulf them. You hold their very future at the point of your knife."

"But—"

"The Otherling must die, Bard. There is no avoiding it. He cannot live in the light; he cannot be left to walk the land and whisper his stories in the ear of farmer and fisherwoman, merchant and seamstress. And Bard cannot do her work without him. The two must be one, for they are reality and reflection, light and dark, substance and shadow."

Bard shivered. "You mean the Otherling is—evil? That if he lives he must inevitably work destruction?"

"Ah, no. It is not so simple. The two are halves of the one whole: complement and completion of each other. Can day exist without night, light without shade, waking without sleeping? Can the Folk survive without the death of the mackerel in the net, the spear in the seal's heart, the hen's surrender of her unborn children? The Otherling must stand behind, in darkness, to make the balance. Only then can Bard sing truth. Now go, do what you must do before it is too late."

"I'm so tired."

"I will help you." He moved to embrace her; his encircling arms were as insubstantial as vapour. She felt a shudder like a cool breath through her, and he was gone.

The travellers were encamped by the seafront, children gathering shells under a blood-red dawn, the smoke of campfires rising sluggishly. There was a rumble of approaching storm, its deep music a counterpoint to the whistle's plangent tone. The young man sat watching the sky, as if his tune might coax the sun to show himself between the rain-heavy clouds. As Bard approached him the melody faltered and ceased.

She had not known how she would speak to him. How can you say, *Come with me, I will tell you whose brother you are, and then you will die?* Ah, those eyes, those fine, merry eyes she had seen gazing up at her once, open and guileless. He had been so quiet. He had been so good. Never a sound from him, as she had borne him forth, basket closed tight, all the way up the hill to her hut. Never a peep out of him, as she bribed the little girls to take him, the little girls with plaited crests to their hair, and faces all painted in spirals and dots of red and white. What was one more infant amongst so many? Who would know, when every one of them wore a guise of rainbow colours, a cloak of dazzling anonymity? She had paid handsomely; the women would feed him and care for him. They were a generous kind, and made their own rules. The rush basket, weighted with the carcase of a fat goose, had burned to nothing. Nobody had known. Nobody but Bard, whose heart shivered every time the travellers came by, whose eyes filled with tears to hear the voice of the whistle, so sad, so pure. What had she done to him? What had she done to them both?

"Come with me. I want to show you something."

He had no questions as they walked together under dark skies, up the hill to the place of the stones. She asked his name; he said, Sam.

"Were you at the last Singing?" she asked him.

He nodded and said nothing. At the old water trough they halted.

"Wash your face," Bard told him. Washed clean, the two of them, naked and clean.

The young man, Sam, looked at her a moment, eyes wide. His features were daubed with spiral and link, dot and line. His hair stood in rows of hedgehog prickles, waxed honey-dark. He bent to the water and splashed his face, washing the markings away. The water clouded.

"Wait," Bard said.

The water cleared. The sun pierced the cloud for one bright moment.

"Now look," she said.

The image was murky; specks of coloured clay floated across his mirrored features. But it was plain enough. He glanced up at her.

"I did wrong," Bard said. "He is your brother. I saved you, because—because—no matter. Now all is awry because of what I did not do." In its way, it was an apology.

There were no desperate denials, no protests.

"Can I see him?" Sam asked. "I'd like to see him first." It was as if he knew. Clouds rolled across, heavy with rain. The sky growled like a wild beast.

"Come, then," said Bard.

Halli was by the watchstone, hands outstretched, eyes shut in pose of meditation. Often before a storm she had found him thus; the soughing of the wind, the uneasy movement of trees, the air's strange pungent smell excited him. At such times of danger, he said, who knew what powerful voices might speak from the stones?

They stood by the hollow's rim, Bard and the young man Sam. Under the dark folds of her long cloak, her fingers touched cold iron.

"He is your brother," she said again, and Halli's blue eyes snapped open. No need for explanations. The two stood frozen, one in astonished wonderment, the other in sudden furious realisation. There was a moment of silence. Then Halli drew ragged breath.

"You saved him!" he whispered, accusatory, furious. "No wonder I was never good enough, no wonder I could not hear them! You saved the Otherling! Why? Why?"

Because of love, Bard answered, but not aloud. *I did wrong, and now he must die.*

"Brother, well met indeed!" Sam's dimpled smile was generous. Below the bizarre spiked hair his blue eyes spoke a bright welcome. He took a step forward, hand outstretched in friendship. Now she was behind him. Halli's agonised eyes met hers over his twin's shoulder, their message starkly clear. *Do it now. Do what you could not do before. Make it right again.* Perhaps it was her own Otherling who spoke these words: the shadow within. She drew out the knife. She saw the dimple appear in Halli's cheek, the curve of his mouth as he watched her. Sam went very still. He did not turn. Bard raised her hand.

A great blade speared down from above; there was a thunderous crack like the very ending of the world, and a sudden rending. It was not her own small weapon that set the earth shuddering, and came like a wave through the damp air, hurtling her head over heels to land sprawling, gasping, face down in wet grass with her two hands clutching for purchase and her ears ringing, deafened by the immense voice that had spoken. Her heart thudded; her head swam. Slowly she got to her knees. The knife lay on the ground at her feet, its blade clean as a new-washed babe. She looked up. The watchstone was split asunder, its monumental form chiselled in two pieces by the force of the blast. One part still stood tall, reaching its lichen-crusted head to touch the storm-tossed sky. The other part lay prone now, like shadow given substance: dark testament to the sky's ferocity. This slab would never be lifted, not should all the Folk of the island come with ropes and oxen. It was grave and cradle; ending and beginning. After all, she had not had to choose. The ancestors had spoken, and the choice was made.

"You're weeping," she said. "Bard does not weep."

"How can I not weep?" he asked her. "He was my brother."

"Come, Halli," said Bard gently. "There is no more to be done here. And it's starting to rain." She unfastened her cloak and reached to put it around his shoulders.

He stared at her, face ashen with the shock of finding, and losing, and finding again. "I have so much to learn," he whispered, and she saw that he had recognised her meaning. "So much."

Bard nodded. "I am not so old yet that I cannot teach you what you must know. Already you are rich in understanding. Already you hear the Songs and tell them, unaware. He will help you. His fingers know the harp, his lips the pipe. The heart that beats new wisdom into the Songs belongs now to the two of you."

He bowed his head, looking towards the gentle hollow, now hidden beneath the huge slab of stone. Rain fell like tears on its fresh-hewn surface, making a pattern of spiral and curve, dot and line.

"Best put that hood up," she said, "until I attend to that hair of yours. No student of mine goes unshaven. Now come. There's work to be done."

The Mystery Knight

George R. R. Martin

George R. R. Martin is the wildly popular author of the A Song of Ice and Fire epic fantasy series, and many other novels, such as Dying of the Light *and* The Armageddon Rag. *His short fiction—which has appeared in numerous anthologies and in most if not all of the genre's major magazines—has garnered him four Hugos, two Nebulas, the Stoker, and the World Fantasy Award. Martin is also known for editing the* Wild Cards *series of shared world superhero anthologies, and for his work as a screenwriter on such television projects as the 1980s version of* The Twilight Zone *and* Beauty and the Beast. *A TV series based on A Song of Ice and Fire debuted on HBO in 2011.*

A LIGHT SUMMER RAIN was falling as Dunk and Egg took their leave of Stoney Sept.

Dunk rode his old warhorse Thunder, with Egg beside him on the spirited young palfrey he'd named Rain, leading their mule Maester. On Maester's back were bundled Dunk's armor and Egg's books, their bedrolls, tent, and clothing, several slabs of hard salt beef, half a flagon of mead, and two skins of water. Egg's old straw hat, wide-brimmed and floppy, kept the rain off the mule's head. The boy had cut holes for Maester's ears. Egg's new straw hat was on his own head. Except for the ear holes, the two hats looked much the same to Dunk.

As they neared the town gates, Egg reined up sharply. Up above the gateway a traitor's head had been impaled upon an iron spike. It was fresh from the look of it, the flesh more pink than green, but the carrion crows had already gone to work on it. The dead man's lips and cheeks were torn and ragged; his eyes were two brown holes weeping slow red tears as raindrops mingled with the crusted blood. The dead man's mouth sagged open, as if to harangue travelers passing through the gate below.

Dunk had seen such sights before. "Back in King's Landing when I was a boy, I stole a head right off its spike once," he told Egg. Actually it had been Ferret who scampered up the wall to snatch the head, after Rafe and Pudding said he'd never dare, but when the guards came running he'd tossed it down, and Dunk was the one who'd caught it. "Some rebel lord or robber knight, it was. Or maybe just a common murderer. A head's a head. They all look the same after a few days on a spike." He and his three friends had used the head to terrorize the girls of Flea Bottom. They'd chase them through the alleys, and make them give the head a kiss before they'd let them go. That head got kissed a lot, as he recalled. There wasn't a girl in King's Landing who could run as fast as Rafe. Egg was better off not hearing that part, though. Ferret, Rafe, and Pudding. *Little monsters, those three, and me the worst of all.* His friends and he had kept the head until the flesh turned black and began to slough away. That took the fun out of chasing girls, so one night they burst into a pot shop and tossed what was left into the kettle. "The crows always go for the eyes," he told Egg. "Then the cheeks cave in, the flesh turns green..." He squinted. "Wait. I know that face."

"You do, ser," said Egg. "Three days ago. The hunchbacked septon we heard preaching against Lord Bloodraven."

He remembered then. *He was a holy man sworn to the Seven, even if he did preach treason.* "His hands are scarlet with a brother's blood, and the blood of his young nephews too," the hunchback had declared to the crowd that had gathered in the market square. "A shadow came at his command to strangle brave Prince Valarr's sons in their mother's womb. Where is our Young Prince now? Where is his brother, sweet Matarys? Where has Good King Daeron gone, and fearless Baelor Breakspear? The grave has claimed them, every one, yet he endures, this pale bird with bloody beak who perches on King Aerys's shoulder and caws into his ear. The mark of hell is on his face and in his empty eye, and he has brought us drought and pestilence and murder. Rise up, I say, and remember our true king across the water. Seven gods there are, and seven kingdoms, and the Black Dragon sired seven sons! Rise up, my lords and ladies. Rise up, you brave knights and sturdy yeomen, and cast down Bloodraven, that foul sorcerer, lest your children and your children's children be cursed forevermore."

Every word was treason. Even so, it was a shock to see him here, with holes where his eyes had been. "That's him, aye," Dunk said, "and another good reason to put this town behind us." He gave Thunder a touch of the spur, and he and Egg rode through the gates of Stoney Sept, listening to the soft sound of the rain. *How many eyes does Lord Bloodraven have?* the riddle ran. *A thousand eyes, and one.* Some claimed the King's Hand was a student of the dark arts who could change his face, put on the likeness of a one-eyed dog, even turn into a mist. Packs of gaunt gray wolves hunted down his foes, men said, and carrion crows spied for him and whispered secrets in his ear. Most of the tales were only tales, Dunk did not doubt, but no one could doubt that Bloodraven had informers everywhere.

He had seen the man once with his own two eyes, back in King's Landing. White as bone were the skin and hair of Brynden Rivers, and his eye—he only had the one, the other having been lost to his half-brother Bittersteel on the Redgrass Field—was red as blood. On cheek and neck he bore the winestain birthmark that had given him his name.

When the town was well behind them Dunk cleared his throat and said, "Bad business, cutting off the heads of septons. All he did was talk. Words are wind."

"Some words are wind, ser. Some are treason." Egg was skinny as a stick, all ribs and elbows, but he did have a mouth.

"Now you sound a proper princeling."

Egg took that for an insult, which it was. "He might have been a septon, but he was preaching lies, ser. The drought wasn't Lord Bloodraven's fault, nor the Great Spring Sickness either."

"Might be that's so, but if we start cutting off the heads of all the fools and liars, half the towns in the Seven Kingdoms will be empty."

Six days later, the rain was just a memory.

Dunk had stripped off his tunic to enjoy the warmth of sunlight on his skin. When a little breeze came up, cool and fresh and fragrant as a maiden's breath, he sighed. "Water," he announced. "Smell it? The lake can't be far now."

"All I can smell is Maester, ser. He stinks." Egg gave the mule's lead a savage tug. Maester had stopped to crop at the grass beside the road, as he did from time to time.

"There's an old inn by the lake shore." Dunk had stopped there once when he was squiring for the old man. "Ser Arlan said they brewed a fine brown ale. Might be we could have a taste while we waited for the ferry."

Egg gave him a hopeful look. "To wash the food down, ser?"

"What food would that be?"

"A slice off the roast?" the boy said. "A bit of duck, a bowl of stew? Whatever they have, ser."

Their last hot meal had been three days ago. Since then, they had been living on windfalls and strips of old salt beef as hard as wood. *It would be good to put some real food in our bellies before we started north. That Wall's along way off.*

"We could spend the night as well," suggested Egg.

"Does m'lord want a featherbed?"

"Straw will serve me well enough, ser," said Egg, offended.

"We have no coin for beds."

"We have twenty-two pennies, three stars, one stag, and that old chipped garnet, ser."

Dunk scratched at his ear. "I thought we had two silvers."

"We did, until you bought the tent. Now we have the one."

"We won't have any if we start sleeping at inns. You want to share a bed with some peddler and wake up with his fleas?" Dunk snorted. "Not me. I have my own fleas, and they are not fond of strangers. We'll sleep beneath the stars."

"The stars are good," Egg allowed, "but the ground is hard, ser, and sometimes it's nice to have a pillow for your head."

"Pillows are for princes." Egg was as good a squire as a knight could want, but every so often he would get to feeling princely. *The lad has dragon blood, never forget.* Dunk had beggar's blood himself...or so they used to tell him back in Flea Bottom, when they weren't telling him that he was sure to hang. "Might be we can afford some ale and a hot supper, but I'm not wasting good coin on a bed. We need to save our pennies for the ferryman." The last time he had crossed the lake, the ferry only cost a few coppers, but that had been six years ago, or maybe seven. Everything had grown more costly since then.

"Well," said Egg, "we could use my boot to get across."

"We could," said Dunk, "but we won't." Using the boot was dangerous. *Word would spread. Word always spreads.* His squire was not bald by chance. Egg had the purple eyes of old Valyria, and hair that shone like beaten gold and strands of silver woven together. He might as well wear a three-headed dragon as a brooch as let that hair grow out. These were perilous times in Westeros, and...well, it was best to take no chances. "Another word about your bloody boot, and I'll clout you in the ear so hard you'll *fly* across the lake."

"I'd sooner swim, ser." Egg swam well, and Dunk did not. The boy turned in the saddle. "Ser? Someone's coming up the road behind us. Hear the horses?"

"I'm not deaf." Dunk could see their dust as well. "A large party. And in haste."

"Do you think they might be outlaws, ser?" Egg raised up in the stirrups, more eager than afraid. The boy was like that.

"Outlaws would be quieter. Only lords make so much noise." Dunk rattled his sword hilt to loosen the blade in its scabbard. "Still, we'll get off the road and let them pass. There are lords and lords." It never hurt to be a little wary. The roads were not as safe as when Good King Daeron sat the Iron Throne.

He and Egg concealed themselves behind a thorn bush. Dunk unslung his shield and slipped it onto his arm. It was an old thing, tall and heavy, kite-shaped, made of pine and rimmed with iron. He had bought it in Stoney Sept to replace the shield the Longinch had hacked to splinters when they fought. Dunk had not had time to have it painted with his elm and shooting star, so it still bore the arms of its last owner: a hanged man swinging grim and gray beneath a gallows tree. It was not a sigil that he would have chosen for himself, but the shield had come cheap.

The first riders galloped past within moments: two young lordlings mounted on a pair of coursers. The one on the bay wore an open-faced helm of gilded steel with three tall feathered plumes, one white, one red, one gold. Matching plumes adorned his horse's crinet. The black stallion beside him was barded in blue and gold. His trappings rippled with the wind of his passage as he thundered past. Side by side the riders streaked on by, whooping and laughing, their long cloaks streaming behind.

A third lord followed more sedately, at the head of a long column. There were two dozen in the party, grooms and cooks and serving men, all to attend three knights, plus men-at-arms and mounted crossbowmen, and a dozen drays heavy-laden with their armor, tents, and provisions. Slung from the lord's saddle was his shield, dark orange and charged with three black castles.

Dunk knew those arms, but from where? The lord who bore them was an older man, sour-mouthed and saturnine, with a close-cropped salt-and-pepper beard. *He might have been at Ashford Meadow*, Dunk thought. *Or maybe we served at his castle when I was squiring for Ser Arlan.* The old hedge knight had done service at so many different keeps and castles through the years that Dunk could not recall the half of them.

The lord reined up abruptly, scowling at the thorn bush. "You. In the bush. Show yourself." Behind him two crossbowmen slipped quarrels into the notch. The rest continued on their way.

Dunk stepped through the tall grass, his shield upon his arm, his right hand resting on the pommel of his longsword. His face was a red-brown mask from the dust the horses had kicked up, and he was naked from the waist up. He looked a scruffy sight, he knew, though it was like to be the size of him that gave the other pause. "We want no quarrel, m'lord. There's only the two of us, me and my squire." He beckoned Egg forward.

"Squire? Do you claim to be a knight?"

Dunk did not like the way the man was looking at him. *Those eyes could flay a man.* It seemed prudent to remove his hand from his sword. "I am a hedge knight, seeking service."

"Every robber knight I've ever hanged has said the same. Your device may be prophetic, ser...if *ser* you are. A gallows and a hanged man. These are your arms?"

"No, m'lord. I need to have the shield repainted."

"Why? Did you rob it off a corpse?"

"I bought it, for good coin." Three castles, black on orange...where have I seen those before? "I am no robber."

The lord's eyes were chips of flint. "How did you come by that scar upon your cheek? A cut from a whip?"

"A dagger. Though my face is none of your concern, m'lord."

"I'll be the judge of what is my concern."

By then the two younger knights had come trotting back to see what had delayed their party. "There you are, Gormy," called the rider on the black, a young man lean and lithe, with a comely clean-shaved face and fine features. Black hair fell shining to his collar. His doublet was made of dark blue silk edged in gold satin. Across his chest an engrailed cross had been embroidered in gold thread, with a golden fiddle in the first and third quarters, a golden sword in the second and the fourth. His eyes caught the deep blue of his doublet, and sparkled with amusement. "Alyn feared you'd fallen from your horse. A palpable excuse, it seems to me, I was about to leave him in my dust."

"Who are these two brigands?" asked the rider on the bay.

Egg bristled at the insult: "You have no call to name us brigands, my lord. When we saw your dust we thought you might be outlaws, that's the only reason that we hid. This is Ser Duncan the Tall, and I'm his squire."

The lordlings paid no more heed to that than they would have paid the croaking of a frog. "I believe that is the largest lout I have ever seen," declared the knight of three feathers. He had a pudgy face beneath a head of curly hair the color of dark honey. "Seven feet if he's an inch, I'd wager. What a mighty crash he'll make when he comes tumbling down."

Dunk felt color rising to his face. *You'd lose your wager*, he thought. The last time he had been measured, Egg's brother Aemon pronounced him an inch shy of seven feet.

"Is that your warhorse, Ser Giant?" said the feathered lordling. "I suppose we could butcher it for the meat."

"Lord Alyn oft forgets his courtesies," the black-haired knight said.

"Please forgive his churlish words, ser. Alyn, you will ask Ser Duncan for his pardon."

"If I must. Will you forgive me, ser?" He did not wait for reply, but turned his bay about and trotted down the road.

The other lingered. "Are you bound for the wedding, ser?"

Something in his tone made Dunk want to tug his forelock. He resisted the impulse and said, "We're for the ferry, m'lord."

"As are we...but the only lords hereabouts are Gormy and that wastrel who just left us, Alyn Cockshaw. I am a vagabond hedge knight like yourself. Ser John the Fiddler, I am called." That was the sort of name a hedge knight might choose, but Dunk had never seen any hedge knight garbed or armed or mounted in such splendor. *The knight of the golden hedge*, he thought. "You know my name. My squire is called Egg."

"Well met, ser. Come, ride with us to Whitewalls and break a few lances to help Lord Butterwell celebrate his new marriage. I'll wager you could give a good account of yourself."

Dunk had not done any jousting since Ashford Meadow. *If I could win a few ransoms, we'd eat well on the ride north*, he thought, but the lord with the three castles on his shield said, "Ser Duncan needs to be about his journey, as do we."

John the Fiddler paid the older man no mind. "I would love to cross swords with you, ser. I've tried men of many lands and races, but never one your size. Was your father large as well?"

"I never knew my father, ser."

"I am sad to hear it. Mine own sire was taken from me too soon." The Fiddler turned to the lord of the three castles. "We should ask Ser Duncan to join our jolly company."

"We do not need his sort."

Dunk was at a loss for words. Penniless hedge knights were not oft asked to ride with highborn lords. *I would have more in common with their servants*. Judging from the length of their column, Lord Cockshaw and the Fiddler had brought grooms to tend their horses, cooks to feed them, squires to clean their armor, guards to defend them. Dunk had Egg.

"His sort?" The Fiddler laughed. "What sort is that? The big sort?

Look at the size of him. We want strong men. Young swords are worth more than old names, I've oft heard it said."

"By fools. You know little and less about this man. He might be a brigand, or one of Lord Bloodraven's spies."

"I'm no man's spy," said Dunk. "And m'lord has no call to speak of me as if I were deaf or dead or down in Dorne."

Those flinty eyes considered him. "Down in Dorne would be a good place for you, ser. You have my leave to go there."

"Pay him no mind," the Fiddler said. "He's a sour old soul, he suspects everyone. Gormy, I have a good feeling about this fellow. Ser Duncan, will you come with us to Whitewalls?"

"M'lord..." How could he share a camp with such as these? Their serving men would raise their pavilions, their grooms would curry their horses, their cooks would serve them each a capon or a joint of beef, whilst Dunk and Egg gnawed on strips of hard salt beef. "I couldn't."

"You see," said the lord of the three castles. "He knows his place, and it is not with us." He turned his horse back toward the road. "By now Lord Cockshaw is half a league ahead."

"I suppose I must chase him down again." The Fiddler gave Dunk an apologetic smile. "Perchance we'll meet again some day. I hope so. I should love to try my lance on you."

Dunk did not know what to say to that. "Good fortune in the lists, ser," he finally managed, but by then Ser John had wheeled about to chase the column. The older lord rode after him. Dunk was glad to see his back. He had not liked his flinty eyes, nor Lord Alyn's arrogance. The Fiddler had been pleasant enough, but there was something odd about him as well. "Two fiddles and two swords, a cross engrailed," he said to Egg as they watched the dust of their departure. "What house is that?"

"None, ser. I never saw that shield in any roll of arms."

Perhaps he is a hedge knight after all. Dunk had devised his own arms at Ashford Meadow, when a puppeteer called Tanselle Too-Tall asked him what he wanted painted on his shield. "Was the older lord some kin to House Frey?" The Freys bore castles on their shields, and their holdings were not far from here.

Egg rolled his eyes. "The Frey arms are two blue towers connected by a bridge, on a gray field. Those were three castles, black on orange, ser. Did you see a bridge?"

"No." *He just does that to annoy me.* "And next time you roll your eyes at me, I'll clout you on the ear so hard they'll roll back into your head for good."

Egg looked chastened. "I never meant—"

"Never mind what you meant. Just tell me who he was."

"Gormon Peake, the Lord of Starpike."

"That's down in the Reach, isn't it? Does he really have three castles?"

"Only on his shield, ser. House Peake did hold three castles once, but two of them were lost."

"How do you lose two castles?"

"You fight for the black dragon, ser."

"Oh." Dunk felt stupid. *That again.*

For two hundred years the realm had been ruled by the descendants of Aegon the Conqueror and his sisters, who had made the Seven Kingdoms one and forged the Iron Throne. Their royal banners bore the three-headed dragon of House Targaryen, red on black. Sixteen years ago, a bastard son of King Aegon IV named Daemon Blackfyre had risen in revolt against his trueborn brother. Daemon had used the three-headed dragon on his banners too, but he reversed the colors, as many bastards did. His revolt had ended on the Redgrass Field, where Daemon and his twin sons died beneath a rain of Lord Bloodraven's arrows. Those rebels who survived and bent the knee were pardoned, but some lost land, some titles, some gold. All gave hostages to ensure their future loyalty.

Three castles, black on orange. "I remember now. Ser Arlan never liked to talk about the Redgrass Field, but once in his cups he told me how his sister's son had died." He could almost hear the old man's voice again, smell the wine upon his breath. "Roger of Pennytree, that was his name. His head was smashed in by a mace wielded by a lord with three castles on his shield." *Lord Gormon Peake. The old man never knew his name. Or never wanted to.* By that time Lord Peake and John the Fiddler and their party were no more than a plume of red dust in the distance. *It was sixteen years ago. The pretender died, and those who followed him were exiled or forgiven. Anyway, it has nought to do with me.*

For a while they rode along without talking, listening to the plaintive cries of birds. Half a league on, Dunk cleared his throat and said, "Butterwell, he said. His lands are near?"

"On the far side of the lake, ser. Lord Butterwell was the master of coin when King Aegon sat the Iron Throne. King Daeron made him Hand, but not for long. His arms are undy green and white and yellow, ser." Egg loved showing off his heraldry.

"Is he a friend of your father?"

Egg made a face. "My father never liked him. In the Rebellion, Lord Butterwell's second son fought for the pretender and his eldest for the king. That way he was certain to be on the winning side. Lord Butterwell didn't fight for anyone."

"Some might call that prudent."

"My father calls it craven."

Aye, he would. Prince Maekar was a hard man, proud and full of scorn. "We have to go by Whitewalls to reach the kingsroad. Why not fill our bellies?" Just the thought was enough to cause his guts to rumble. "Might be that one of the wedding guests will need an escort back to his own seat."

"You said that we were going north."

"The Wall has stood eight thousand years, it will last a while longer. It's a thousand leagues from here to there, and we could do with some more silver in our purse." Dunk was picturing himself atop Thunder, riding down that sour-faced old lord with the three castles on his shield. That would be sweet. *"It was old Ser Arlan's squire who defeated you,"* I *could tell him when he came to ransom back his arms and armor. "The boy who replaced the boy you killed." The old man would like that.*

"You're not thinking of entering the lists, are you, ser?"

"Might be it's time."

"It's not, ser."

"Maybe it's time I gave you a good clout in the ear." *I'd only need to win two tilts. If I could collect two ransoms and pay out only one, we'd eat like kings for a year.* "If there was a melee, I might enter that." Dunk's size and strength would serve him better in a melee than in the lists.

"It's not customary to have a melee at a marriage, ser."

"It's customary to have a feast, though. We have a long way to go. Why not set out with our bellies full for once?"

The sun was low in the west by the time they saw the lake, its waters glimmering red and gold, bright as a sheet of beaten copper. When they glimpsed the turrets of the inn above some willows, Dunk donned his sweaty tunic once again and stopped to splash some water on his face. He washed off the dust of the road as best he could, and ran wet fingers through his thick mop of sun-streaked hair. There was nothing to be done for his size, or the scar that marked his cheek, but he wanted to make himself appear somewhat less the wild robber knight.

The inn was bigger than he'd expected, a great gray sprawl of a place, timbered and turreted, half of it built on pilings out over the water. A road of rough-cut planks had been laid down over the muddy lake shore to the ferry landing, but neither the ferry nor the ferrymen were in evidence. Across the road stood a stable with a thatched roof. A dry stone wall enclosed the yard, but the gate was open. Within, they found a well and a watering trough. "See to the animals," Dunk told Egg, "but see that they don't drink too much. I'll ask about some food."

He found the innkeep sweeping off the steps. "Are you come for the ferry?" the woman asked him. "You're too late. The sun's going down, and Ned don't like to cross by night unless the moon is full. He'll be back first thing in the morning."

"Do you know how much he asks?"

"Three pennies for each of you, and ten for your horses."

"We have two horses and a mule."

"It's ten for mules as well."

Dunk did the sums in his head, and came up with six-and-thirty, more than he had hoped to spend. "Last time I came this way it was only two pennies, and six for horses."

"Take that up with Ned, it's nought to me. If you're looking for a bed, I've none to offer. Lord Shawney and Lord Costayne brought their retinues. I'm full to bursting."

"Is Lord Peake here as well?" *He killed Ser Arlan's squire.* "He was with Lord Cockshaw and John the Fiddler."

"Ned took them across on his last run." She looked Dunk up and down. "Were you part of their company?"

"We met them on the road, is all." A good smell was drifting out the windows of the inn, one that made Dunk's mouth water. "We might like some of what you're roasting, if it's not too costly."

"It's wild boar," the woman said, "well peppered, and served with onions, mushrooms, and mashed neeps."

"We could do without the neeps. Some slices off the boar and a tankard of your good brown ale would do for us. How much would you ask for that? And maybe we could have a place on your stable floor to bed down for the night?"

That was a mistake. "The stables are for horses. That's why we call them stables. You're big as a horse, I'll grant you, but I only see two legs." She swept her broom at him, to shoo him off. "I can't be expected to feed all the Seven Kingdoms. The boar is for my guests. So is my ale. I won't have lords saying that I run short of food or drink before they were surfeit. The lake is full of fish, and you'll find some other rogues camped down by the stumps. Hedge knights, if you believe them." Her tone made it quite clear that she did not. "Might be they'd have food to share. It's nought to me. Away with you now, I've work to do." The door closed with a solid thump behind her, before Dunk could even think to ask where he might find these stumps.

He found Egg sitting on the horse trough, soaking his feet in the water and fanning his face with his big floppy hat. "Are they roasting pig, ser? I smell pork."

"Wild boar," said Dunk in a glum tone, "but who wants boar when we have good salt beef?"

Egg made a face. "Can I please eat my boots instead, ser? I'll make a new pair out of the salt beef. It's tougher."

"No," said Dunk, trying not to smile. "You can't eat your boots. One more word and you'll eat my fist, though. Get your feet out of that trough." He found his greathelm on the mule, and slung it underhand at Egg. "Draw some water from the well and soak the beef." Unless you soaked it for a good long time, the salt beef was like to break your teeth. It tasted best when soaked in ale, but water would serve. "Don't use the trough either, I don't care to taste your feet."

"My feet could only improve the taste, ser," Egg said, wriggling his toes. But he did as he was bid.

The hedge knights did not prove hard to find. Egg spied their fire flickering in the woods along the lake shore, so they made for it, leading the animals behind them. The boy carried Dunk's helm beneath one arm, sloshing with each step he took. By then the sun was a red memory in the west. Before long the trees opened up, and they found themselves in what must once have been a weirwood grove. Only a ring of white stumps and a tangle of bone-pale roots remained to show where the trees had stood, when the children of the forest ruled in Westeros.

Amongst the weirwood stumps, they found two men squatting near a cookfire, passing a skin of wine from hand to hand. Their horses were cropping at the grass beyond the grove, and they had stacked their arms and armor in neat piles. A much younger man sat apart from the other two, his back against a chestnut tree. "Well met, sers," Dunk called out in a cheerful voice. It was never wise to take armed men unawares. "I am called Ser Duncan, the Tall. The lad is Egg. May we share your fire?"

A stout man of middling years rose to greet them, garbed in tattered finery. Flamboyant ginger whiskers framed his face. "Well met, Ser Duncan. You are a large one...and most welcome, certainly, as is your lad. Egg, was it? What sort of name is that, pray?"

"A short one, ser." Egg knew better than to admit that Egg was short for Aegon. Not to men he did not know.

"Indeed. What happened to your hair?"

Rootworms, Dunk thought. Tell him it was rootworms, boy.

That was the safest story, the tale they told most often...though some-times Egg took it in his head to play some childish game.

"I shaved it off, ser. I mean to stay shaven until I earn my spurs."

"A noble vow. I am Ser Kyle, the Cat of Misty Moor. Under yonder chestnut sits Ser Glendon, ah, Ball. And here you have the good Ser Maynard Plumm."

Egg's ears pricked up at that name. "Plumm...are you kin to Lord Viserys Plumm, ser?"

"Distantly," confessed Ser Maynard, a tall, thin, stoop-shouldered man with long straight flaxen hair, "though I doubt that his lordship would admit to it. One might say that he is of the sweet Plumms, whilst I am of the sour." Plumm's cloak was as purple as his name, though frayed about the edges and badly dyed. A moonstone brooch big as a hen's egg fastened it at the shoulder. Elsewise he wore dun-colored roughspun and stained brown leather.

"We have salt beef," said Dunk.

"Ser Maynard has a bag of apples," said Kyle the Cat. "And I have pickled eggs and onions. Why, together we have the makings of a feast! Be seated, ser. We have a fine choice of stumps for your comfort. We will be here until midmorning, unless I miss my guess. There is only the one ferry, and it is not big enough to take us all. The lords and their tails must cross first."

"Help me with the horses," Dunk told Egg. Together the two of them unsaddled Thunder, Rain, and Maester.

Only when the animals had been fed and watered and hobbled for the night did Dunk accept the wineskin that Ser Maynard offered him. "Even sour wine is better than none," said Kyle the Cat. "We'll drink finer vintages at Whitewalls. Lord Butterwell is said to have the best wines north of the Arbor. He was once the King's Hand, as his father's father was before him, and he is said to be a pious man besides, and very rich."

"His wealth is all from cows," said Maynard Plumm. "He ought to take a swollen udder for his arms. These Butterwells have milk running in their veins, and the Freys are no better. This will be a marriage of cattle thieves and toll collectors, one lot of coin clinkers joining with another. When the Black Dragon rose, this lord of cows sent one son to

Daemon and one to Daeron, to make certain there was a Butterwell on the winning side. Both perished on the Redgrass Field, and his youngest died in the spring. That's why he's making this new marriage. Unless this new wife gives him a son, Butterwell's name will die with him."

"As it should." Ser Glendon Ball gave his sword another stroke with the whetstone. "The Warrior hates cravens."

The scorn in his voice made Dunk give the youth a closer look. Ser Glendon's clothes were of good cloth, but well-worn and ill-matched, with the look of hand-me-downs. Tufts of dark brown hair stuck out from beneath his iron halfhelm. The lad himself was short and chunky, with small, close-set eyes, thick shoulders, and muscular arms. His eyebrows were shaggy as two caterpillars after a wet spring, his nose bulbous, his chin pugnacious. And he was young. *Sixteen, might be. No more than eighteen.* Dunk might have taken him for a squire if Ser Kyle had not named him with a *ser*. The lad had pimples on his cheeks in place of whiskers.

"How long have you been a knight?" Dunk asked him.

"Long enough. Half a year when the moon turns. I was knighted by Ser Morgan Dunstable of Tumbler's Falls, two dozen people saw it, but I have been training for knighthood since I was born. I rode before I walked, and knocked a grown man's tooth out of his head before I lost any of my own. I mean to make my name at Whitewalls, and claim the dragon's egg."

"The dragon's egg? Is that the champion's prize? Truly?" The last dragon had perished half a century ago. Ser Arlan had once seen a clutch of her eggs, though. *They were hard as stone, but beautiful to look upon,* the old man had told Dunk. "How could Lord Butterwell come by a dragon's egg?"

"King Aegon presented the egg to his father's father after guesting for a night at his old castle," said Ser Maynard Plumm.

"Was it a reward for some act of valor?" asked Dunk.

Ser Kyle chuckled. "Some might call it that. Supposedly old Lord Butterwell had three young maiden daughters when His Grace came calling. By morning, all three had royal bastards in their little bellies. A hot night's work, that was."

Dunk had heard such talk before. Aegon the Unworthy had bedded half the maidens in the realm and fathered bastards on the lot of them, supposedly. Worse, the old king had legitimized them all upon his deathbed; the baseborn ones born of tavern wenches, whores, and shepherd girls, and the Great Bastards whose mothers had been highborn. "We'd all be bastard sons of old King Aegon if half these tales were true."

"And who's to say we're not?" Ser Maynard quipped.

"You ought to come with us to Whitewalls, Ser Duncan," urged Ser Kyle. "Your size is sure to catch some lordling's eye. You might find good service there. I know I shall. Joffrey Caswell will be at this wedding, the Lord of Bitterbridge. When he was three I made him his first sword. I carved it out of pine, to fit his hand. In my greener days, my sword was sworn to his father."

"Was that one carved from pine as well?" Ser Maynard asked.

Kyle the Cat had the grace to laugh. "That sword was good steel, I assure you. I should be glad to ply it once again in the service of the centaur. Ser Duncan, even if you do not choose to tilt, do join us for the wedding feast. There will be singers and musicians, jugglers and tumblers, and a troupe of comic dwarfs."

Dunk frowned. "Egg and I have a long journey before us. We're headed north to Winterfell. Lord Beron Stark is gathering swords to drive the krakens from his shores for good."

"Too cold up there for me," said Ser Maynard. "If you want to kill krakens, go west. The Lannisters are building ships to strike back at the ironmen on their home islands. That's how you put an end to Dagon Greyjoy. Fighting him on land is fruitless, he just slips back to sea. You have to beat him on the water."

That had the ring of truth, but the prospect of fighting ironmen at sea was not one that Dunk relished. He'd had a taste of that on the *White Lady*, sailing from Dorne to Oldtown, when he'd donned his armor to help the crew repel some raiders. The battle had been desperate and bloody, and once he'd almost fallen in the water. That would have been the end of him.

"The throne should take a lesson from Stark and Lannister," declared Ser Kyle the Cat. "At least they fight. What do the Targaryens do? King

Aerys hides amongst his books, Prince Rhaegel prances naked through the Red Keep's halls, and Prince Maekar broods at Summerhall."

Egg was prodding at the fire with a stick, to send sparks floating up into the night. Dunk was pleased to see him ignoring the mention of his father's name. *Perhaps he's finally learned to hold that tongue of his.*

"Myself, I blame Bloodraven," Ser Kyle went on. "He is the King's Hand, yet he does nothing, whilst the krakens spread flame and terror up and down the sunset sea."

Ser Maynard gave a shrug. "His eye is fixed on Tyrosh, where Bittersteel sits in exile, plotting with the sons of Daemon Blackfyre. So he keeps the king's ships close at hand, lest they attempt to cross."

"Aye, that may well be," Ser Kyle said, "but many would welcome the return of Bittersteel. Bloodraven is the root of all our woes, the white worm gnawing at the heart of the realm."

Dunk frowned, remembering the hunchbacked septon at Stoney Sept. "Words like that can cost a man his head. Some might say you're talking treason."

"How can the truth be treason?" asked Kyle the Cat. "In King Daeron's day, a man did not have to fear to speak his mind, but now?" He made a rude noise. "Bloodraven put King Aerys on the Iron Throne, but for how long? Aerys is weak, and when he dies it will be bloody war between Lord Rivers and Prince Maekar for the crown, the Hand against the heir."

"You have forgotten Prince Rhaegel, my friend," Ser Maynard objected, in a mild tone. "He comes next in line to Aerys, not Maekar, and his children after him."

"Rhaegel is feeble-minded. Why, I bear him no ill will, but the man is good as dead, and those twins of his as well, though whether they will die of Maekar's mace or Bloodraven's spells..."

Seven save us, Dunk thought, as Egg spoke up shrill and loud. "Prince Maekar is Prince Rhaegel's brother. He loves him well. He'd never do harm to him or his."

"Be quiet, boy," Dunk growled at him. "These knights want none of your opinions."

"I can talk if I want."

"No," said Dunk. "You can't." *That mouth of yours will get you killed some day. And me as well, most like.* "That salt beef's soaked long enough, I think. A strip for all our friends, and be quick about it."

Egg flushed, and for half a heartbeat Dunk feared the boy might talk back. Instead he settled for a sullen look, seething as only a boy of eleven years can seethe. "Aye, ser," he said, fishing in the bottom of Dunk's helm. His shaved head shone redly in the firelight as he passed out the salt beef.

Dunk took his piece and worried at it. The soak had turned the meat from wood to leather, but that was all. He sucked on one corner, tasting the salt and trying not to think about the roast boar at the inn, crackling on its spit and dripping fat.

As dusk deepened, flies and stinging midges came swarming off the lake. The flies preferred to plague their horses, but the midges had a taste for man flesh. The only way to keep from being bitten was to sit close to the fire, breathing smoke. *Cook or be devoured,* Dunk thought glumly, *now there's a beggar's choice.* He scratched at his arms and edged closer to the fire.

The wineskin soon came round again. The wine was sour and strong. Dunk drank deep, and passed along the skin, whilst the Cat of Misty Moor began to talk of how he had saved the life of the Lord of Bitterbridge during the Blackfyre Rebellion. "When Lord Armond's banner-bearer fell, I leapt down from my horse with traitors all around us—"

"Ser," said Glendon Ball. "Who were these traitors?"

"The Blackfyre men, I meant."

Firelight glimmered off the steel in Ser Glendon's hand. The pockmarks on his face flamed as red as open sores, and his every sinew was wound as tight as a crossbow. "My father fought for the black dragon."

This again. Dunk snorted. *Red or black?* was not a thing you asked a man. It always made for trouble. "I am sure Ser Kyle meant no insult to your father."

"None," Ser Kyle agreed. "It's an old tale, the red dragon and the black. No sense for us to fight about it now, lad. We are all brothers of the hedges here."

Ser Glendon seemed to weigh the Cat's words, to see if he was being mocked. "Daemon Blackfyre was no traitor. The old king gave *him* the sword. He saw the worthiness in Daemon, even though he was born bastard. Why else would he put Blackfyre into his hand in place of Daeron's? He meant for him to have the kingdom too. Daemon was the better man."

A hush fell. Dunk could hear the soft crackle of the fire. He could feel midges crawling on the back of his neck. He slapped at them, watching Egg, willing him to be still. "I was just a boy when they fought the Redgrass Field," he said, when it seemed that no one else would speak, "but I squired for a knight who fought with the red dragon, and later served another who fought for the black. There were brave men on both sides."

"Brave men," echoed Kyle the Cat, a bit feebly.

"Heroes." Glendon Ball turned his shield about, so all of them could see the sigil painted there, a fireball blazing red and yellow across a night-black field. "I come from hero's blood."

"You're *Fireball's* son," Egg said.

That was the first time they saw Ser Glendon smile.

Ser Kyle the Cat studied the boy closely. "How can that be? How old are you? Quentyn Ball died—"

"—before I was born," Ser Glendon finished, "but in me, he lives again." He slammed his sword back into its scabbard. "I'll show you all at Whitewalls, when I claim the *dragon's egg*."

The next day proved the truth of Ser Kyle's prophecy. Ned's ferry was nowise large enough to accommodate all those who wished to cross, so Lords Costayne and Shawney must go first, with their tails. That required several trips, each taking more than an hour. There were the mudflats to contend with, horses and wagons to be gotten down the planks, loaded on the boat, and unloaded again across the lake. The two lords slowed matters even further when they got into a shouting match over precedence. Shawney was the elder, but Costayne held himself to be better born.

There was nought that Dunk could do but wait and swelter. "We could go first if you let me use my boot," Egg said.

"We could," Dunk answered, "but we won't. Lord Costayne and Lord Shawney were here before us. Besides, they're lords."

Egg made a face. "Rebel lords."

Dunk frowned down at him. "What do you mean?"

"They were for the black dragon. Well, Lord Shawney was, and Lord Costayne's father. Aemon and I used to fight the battle on Maester Melaquin's green table with painted soldiers and little banners. Costayne's arms quarter a silver chalice on black with a black rose on gold. That banner was on the left of Daemon's host. Shawney was with Bittersteel on the right, but he died."

"Old dead history. They're here now, aren't they? So they bent the knee, and King Daeron gave them pardon."

"Yes, but—"

Dunk pinched the boy's lips shut." Hold your tongue."

Egg held his tongue.

No sooner had the last boatload of Shawney men pushed off than Lord and Lady Smallwood turned up at the landing with their own tail, so they must needs wait again.

The fellowship of the hedge had not survived the night, it was plain to see. Ser Glendon kept his own company, prickly and sullen. Kyle the Cat judged that it would be midday before they were allowed to board the ferry, so he detached himself from the others to try and ingratiate himself with Lord Smallwood, with whom he had some slight acquaintance. Ser Maynard spent his time gossiping with the innkeep.

"Stay well away from that one," Dunk warned Egg. There was something about Plumm that troubled him. "He could be a robber knight, for all we know."

The warning only seemed to make Ser Maynard more interesting to Egg. "I never knew a robber knight. Do you think he means to rob the dragon's egg?"

"Lord Butterwell will have the egg well guarded, I'm sure." Dunk scratched the midge bites on his neck. "Do you think he might display it at the feast? I'd like to get a look at one."

"I'd show you mine, ser, but it's at Summerhall."

"Yours? Your dragon's egg?" Dunk frowned down at the boy, wondering if this was some jape. "Where did it come from?"

"From a dragon, ser. They put it in my cradle."

"Do you want a clout in the ear? There are no dragons."

"No, but there are eggs. The last dragon left a clutch of five, and they have more on Dragonstone, old ones from before the Dance. My brothers all have them too. Aerion's looks as though it's made of gold and silver, with veins of fire running through it. Mine is white and green, all swirly."

"Your dragon's egg." *They put it in his cradle.* Dunk was so used to Egg that sometimes he forgot Aegon was a prince. *Of course they'd put a dragon egg inside his cradle.* "Well, see that you don't go mentioning this egg where anyone is like to hear."

"I'm not *stupid*, ser." Egg lowered his voice. "Some day the dragons will return. My brother Daeron's dreamed of it, and King Aerys read it in a prophecy. Maybe it will be my egg that hatches. That would be *splendid.*"

"Would it?" Dunk had his doubts.

Not Egg. "Aemon and I used to pretend that our eggs would be the ones to hatch. If they did, we could fly through the sky on dragonback, like the first Aegon and his sisters."

"Aye, and if all the other knights in the realm should die, I'd be the Lord Commander of the Kingsguard. If these eggs are so bloody precious, why is Lord Butterwell giving his away?"

"To show the realm how rich he is?"

"I suppose." Dunk scratched his neck again and glanced over at Ser Glendon Ball, who was tightening the cinches on his saddle as he waited for the ferry. *That horse will never serve.* Ser Glendon's mount was a swaybacked stot, undersized, and old. "What do you know about his sire? Why did they call him Fireball?"

"For his hot head and red hair. Ser Quentyn Ball was the master-at-arms at the Red Keep. He taught my father and my uncles how to fight. The Great Bastards too. King Aegon promised to raise him to the Kingsguard, so Fireball made his wife join the silent sisters, only by the time a place came open King Aegon was dead and King Daeron named

Ser Willam Wylde instead. My father says that it was Fireball as much as Bittersteel who convinced Daemon Blackfyre to claim the crown, and rescued him when Daeron sent the Kingsguard to arrest him. Later on, Fireball killed Lord Lefford at the gates of Lannisport and sent the Gray Lion running back to hide inside the Rock. At the crossing of the Mander he cut down the sons of Lady Penrose one by one. They say he spared the life of the youngest one as a kindness to his mother."

"That was chivalrous of him," Dunk had to admit. "Did Ser Quentyn die upon the Redgrass Field?"

"Before, ser," Egg replied. "An archer put an arrow through his throat as he dismounted by a stream to have a drink. Just some common man, no one knows who."

"Those common men can be dangerous when they get it in their heads to start slaying lords and heroes." Dunk saw the ferry creeping slowly across the lake. "Here it comes."

"It's slow. Are we going to go to Whitewalls, ser?"

"Why not? I want to see this dragon's egg." Dunk smiled. "If I win the tourney, we'd *both* have dragon's eggs."

Egg gave him a doubtful look.

"What? Why are you looking at me that way?"

"I could tell you, ser," the boy said solemnly, "but I need to learn to hold my tongue."

They seated the hedge knights well below the salt, closer to the doors than to the dais.

Whitewalls was almost new as castles went, having been raised a mere forty years ago by the grandsire of its present lord. The smallfolk hereabouts called it the Milkhouse, for its walls and keeps and towers were made of finely dressed white stone, quarried in the Vale and brought over the mountains at great expense. Inside were floors and pillars of milky white marble veined with gold; the rafters overhead were carved from the bone-pale trunks of weirwoods. Dunk could not begin to imagine what all of that had cost.

The hall was not so large as some others he had known, though. *At least we were allowed beneath the roof,* Dunk thought, as he took his place on the bench between Ser Maynard Plumm and Kyle the Cat. Though uninvited, the three of them had been welcomed to the feast quick enough; it was ill luck to refuse a knight hospitality on your wedding day.

Young Ser Glendon had a harder time, however. "Fireball never had a son," Dunk heard Lord Butterwell's steward tell him, loudly. The stripling answered heatedly, and the name of Ser Morgan Dunstable was mentioned several times, but the steward had remained adamant. When Ser Glendon touched his sword hilt, a dozen men-at-arms appeared with spears in hand, but for a moment it looked as though there might be bloodshed. It was only the intervention of a big blond knight named Kirby Pimm that saved the situation. Dunk was too far away to hear, but he saw Pimm clasp an arm around the steward's shoulders and murmur in his ear, laughing. The steward frowned, and said something to Ser Glendon that turned the boy's face dark red. *He looks as if he's about to cry,* Dunk thought, watching. *That, or kill someone.* After all of that, the young knight was finally admitted to the castle hall.

Poor Egg was not so fortunate. "The great hall is for the lords and knights," an understeward had informed them haughtily when Dunk had tried to bring the boy inside. "We have set up tables in the inner yard for squires, grooms, and men-at-arms."

If you had an inkling who he was, you would seat him on the dais on a cushioned throne. Dunk had not much liked the look of the other squires. A few were lads of Egg's own age, but most were older, seasoned fighters who long ago had made the choice to serve a knight rather than become one. *Or did they have a choice?* Knighthood required more than chivalry and skill at arms; it required horse and sword and armor too, and all of that was costly. "Watch your tongue," he told Egg before he left him in that company. "These are grown men, they won't take kindly to your insolence. Sit and eat and listen, might be you'll learn some things."

For his own part, Dunk was just glad to be out of the hot sun, with a wine cup before him and a chance to fill his belly. Even a hedge knight grows weary of chewing every bite of food for half an hour. Down here below the salt, the fare would be more plain than fancy, but there would be no lack of it. Below the salt was good enough for Dunk.

But peasant's pride is lordling's shame, the old man used to say. "This cannot be my proper place," Ser Glendon Ball told the understeward hotly. He had donned a clean doublet for the feast, a handsome old garment with gold lace at the cuffs and collar and the red chevron and white plates of House Ball sewn across the chest. "Do you know who my father was?"

"A noble knight and mighty lord, I have no doubt," said the understeward, "but the same is true of many here. Please take your seat or take your leave, ser. It is all the same to me."

In the end, the boy took his place below the salt with the rest of them, his mouth sullen. The long white hall was filling up as more knights crowded onto the benches. The crowd was larger than Dunk had anticipated, and from the looks of it some of the guests had come a very long way. He and Egg had not been around so many lords and knights since Ashford Meadow, and there was no way to guess who else might turn up next. *We should have stayed out in the hedges, sleeping under trees. If I am recognized...*

When a serving man placed a loaf of black bread on the cloth in front of each of them, Dunk was grateful for the distraction. He sawed the loaf open lengthwise, hollowed out the bottom half for a trencher, and ate the top. It was stale, but compared to his salt beef it was custard. At least it did not have to be soaked in ale or milk or water to make it soft enough to chew.

"Ser Duncan, you appear to be attracting a deal of attention," Ser Maynard Plumm observed, as Lord Vyrwel and his party went parading past them toward places of high honor at the top of the hall. "Those girls up on the dais cannot seem to take their eyes off you. I'll wager they have never seen a man so big. Even seated, you are half a head taller than any man in the hall."

Dunk hunched his shoulders. He was used to being stared at, but that did not mean he liked it. "Let them look."

"That's the Old Ox down there beneath the dais," Ser Maynard said. "They call him a huge man, but seems to me his belly is the biggest thing about him. You're a bloody giant next to him."

"Indeed, ser," said one of their companions on the bench, a sallow man, saturnine, clad in gray and green. His eyes were small and shrewd, set close together beneath thin, arching brows. A neat black beard framed his mouth, to make up for his receding hair. "In such a field as this, your size alone should make you one of the most formidable competitors."

"I had heard the Brute of Bracken might be coming," said another man, further down the bench.

"I think not," said the man in green and gray. "This is only a bit of jousting to celebrate his lordship's nuptials. A tilt in the yard to mark the tilt between the sheets. Hardly worth the bother for the likes of Otho Bracken."

Ser Kyle the Cat took a drink of wine. "I'll wager my lord of Butterwell does not take the field either. He will cheer on his champions from his lord's box in the shade."

"Then he'll see his champions fall," boasted Ser Glendon Ball, "and in the end, he'll hand his egg to me."

"Ser Glendon is the son of Fireball," Ser Kyle explained to the new man. "Might we have the honor of your name, ser?"

"Ser Uthor Underleaf. The son of no one of importance." Underleaf's garments were of good cloth, clean and well cared for, but simply cut. A silver clasp in the shape of a snail fastened his cloak. "If your lance is the equal of your tongue, Ser Glendon, you may even give this big fellow here a contest."

Ser Glendon glanced at Dunk as the wine was being poured. "If we meet, he'll fall. I don't care how big he is."

Dunk watched a server fill his wine cup. "I am better with a sword than with a lance," he admitted, "and even better with a battleaxe. Will there be a melee here?" His size and strength would stand him in good stead in a melee, and he knew he could give as good as he got. Jousting was another matter.

"A melee? At a marriage?" Ser Kyle sounded shocked. "That would be unseemly."

Ser Maynard gave a chuckle. "A marriage is a melee, as any married man could tell you."

Ser Uthor chuckled. "There's just the joust, I fear, but besides the dragon's egg, Lord Butterwell has promised thirty golden dragons for the loser of the final tilt, and ten each for the knights defeated in the round before."

Ten dragons is not so bad. Ten dragons would buy a palfrey, so Dunk would not need to ride Thunder save in battle. Ten dragons would buy a suit of plate for Egg, and a proper knight's pavilion sewn with Dunk's tree and falling star. *Ten dragons would mean roast goose and ham and pigeon pie.*

"There are ransoms to be had as well, for those who win their matches," Ser Uthor said as he hollowed out his trencher, "and I have heard it rumored that some men place wagers on the tilts. Lord Butterwell himself is not fond of taking risks, but amongst his guests are some who wager heavily."

No sooner had he spoken than Ambrose Butterwell made his entrance, to a fanfare of trumpets from the minstrel's gallery. Dunk shoved to his feet with the rest as Butterwell escorted his new bride down a patterned Myrish carpet to the dais, arm in arm. The girl was fifteen and freshly flowered, her lord husband fifty and freshly widowed. She was pink and he was gray. Her bride's cloak trailed behind her, done in undy green and white and yellow. It looked so hot and heavy that Dunk wondered how she could bear to wear it. Lord Butterwell looked hot and heavy too, with his heavy jowls and thinning flaxen hair.

The bride's father followed close behind her, hand in hand with his young son. Lord Frey of the Crossing was a lean man elegant in blue and gray, his heir a chinless boy of four whose nose was dripping snot. Lords Costayne and Risley came next, with their lady wives, daughters of Lord Butterwell by his first wife. Frey's daughters followed with their own husbands. Then came Lord Gormon Peake; Lords Smallwood, Vyrwel, and Shawney; various lesser lords and landed knights. Amongst them Dunk glimpsed John the Fiddler and Alyn Cockshaw. Lord Alyn looked to be in his cups, though the feast had not yet properly begun.

By the time all of them had sauntered to the dais, the high table was as crowded as the benches. Lord Butterwell and his bride sat on plump downy cushions in a double throne of gilded oak. The rest planted themselves in tall chairs with fancifully carved arms. On the wall behind them two huge banners hung from the rafters: the twin towers of Frey, blue on gray, and the green and white and yellow undy of the Butterwells.

It fell to Lord Frey to lead the toasts. *"The king!"* he began, simply. Ser Glendon held his wine cup out above the water basin. Dunk clanked his cup against it, and against Ser Uthor's and the rest as well. They drank.

"Lord Butterwell, our gracious host," Frey proclaimed next.

"May the Father grant him long life and many sons."

They drank again.

"Lady Butterwell, the maiden bride, my darling daughter. May the Mother make her fertile." Frey gave the girl a smile. "I shall want a grandson before the year is out. Twins would suit me even better, so churn the butter well tonight, my sweet."

Laughter rang against the rafters, and the guests drank still once more. The wine was rich and red and sweet.

Then Lord Frey said, "I give you the King's Hand, Brynden Rivers. May the Crone's lamp light his path to wisdom." He lifted his goblet high and drank, together with Lord Butterwell and his bride and the others on the dais. Below the salt, Ser Glendon turned his cup over to spill its contents to the floor.

"A sad waste of good wine," said Maynard Plumm.

"I do not drink to kinslayers," said Ser Glendon. "Lord Bloodraven is a sorcerer and a bastard."

"Born bastard," Ser Uthor agreed mildly, "but his royal father made him legitimate as he lay dying." He drank deep, as did Ser Maynard and many others in the hall. Near as many lowered their cups, or turned them upside down as Ball had done. Dunk's own cup was heavy in his hand. *How many eyes does Lord Bloodraven have?* the riddle went. *A thousand eyes, and one.*

Toast followed toast, some proposed by Lord Frey and some by others. They drank to young Lord Tully, Lord Butterwell's liege lord, who had begged off from the wedding. They drank to the health of Leo Longthorn, Lord of Highgarden, who was rumored to be ailing. They drank to the memory of their gallant dead. Aye, thought Dunk, remembering. *I'll gladly drink to them.*

Ser John the Fiddler proposed the final toast. "*To my brave brothers!* I know that they are smiling tonight!"

Dunk had not intended to drink so much, with the jousting on the morrow, but the cups were filled anew after every toast, and he found he had a thirst. "Never refuse a cup of wine or a horn of ale," Ser Arlan had once told him, "it may be a year before you see another." *It would have been discourteous not to toast the bride and groom*, he told himself, *and dangerous not to drink to the king and his Hand, with strangers all about.*

Mercifully, the Fiddler's toast was the last. Lord Butterwell rose ponderously to thank them for coming and promise good jousting on the morrow. "Let the feast begin!"

Suckling pig was served at the high table; a peacock roasted in its plumage; a great pike crusted with crushed almonds. Not a bite of that made it down below the salt. Instead of suckling pig they got salt pork, soaked in almond milk and peppered pleasantly. In place of peacock they had capons, crisped up nice and brown and stuffed with onions, herbs, mushrooms, and roasted chestnuts. In place of pike they ate chunks of flaky white cod in a pastry coffyn, with some sort of tasty brown sauce that Dunk could not quite place. There was pease porridge besides, buttered turnip, carrots drizzled with honey, and a ripe white cheese that smelled as strong as Bennis of the Brown Shield. Dunk ate well, but all the while wondered what Egg was getting in the yard. Just in case, he slipped half a capon into the pocket of his cloak, with some hunks of bread and a little of the smelly cheese.

As they ate, pipes and fiddles filled the air with spritely tunes, and the talk turned to the morrow's jousting. "Ser Franklyn Frey is well regarded along the Green Fork," said Uthor Underleaf, who seemed to know these local heroes well. "That's him upon the dais, the uncle of the bride. Lucas Nayland is down from Hag's Mire, he should not be discounted. Nor should Ser Mortimer Boggs, of Crackclaw Point. Elsewise, this should be a tourney of household knights and village heroes. Kirby Pimm and Galtry the Green are the best of those, though neither is a match for Lord Butterwell's good-son, Black Tom Heddle. A nasty bit of business, that one. He won the hand of his lordship's eldest daughter by killing three of her other suitors, it's said, and once unhorsed the Lord of Casterly Rock."

"What, young Lord Tybolt?" asked Ser Maynard.

"No, the old Gray Lion, the one who died in the spring." That was how men spoke of those who had perished during the Great Spring Sickness. *He died in the spring.* Tens of thousands had died in the spring, among them a king and two young princes.

"Do not slight Ser Buford Bulwer," said Kyle the Cat. "The Old Ox slew forty men upon the Redgrass Field."

"And every year his count grows higher," said Ser Maynard. "Bulwer's day is done. Look at him. Past sixty, soft and fat, and his right eye is good as blind."

"Do not trouble to search the hall for the champion," a voice behind Dunk said. "Here I stand, sers. Feast your eyes."

Dunk turned to find Ser John the Fiddler looming over him, a half-smile on his lips. His white silk doublet had dagged sleeves lined with red satin, so long their points drooped down past his knees. A heavy silver chain looped across his chest, studded with huge dark amethysts whose color matched his eyes. *That chain is worth as much as everything I own,* Dunk thought.

The wine had colored Ser Glendon's cheeks and inflamed his pimples. "Who are you, to make such boasts?"

"They call me John, the Fiddler."

"Are you a musician or a warrior?"

"I can make sweet song with either lance or resined bow, as it happens. Every wedding needs a singer, and every tourney needs a mystery knight. May I join you? Butterwell was good enough to place me on the dais, but I prefer the company of my fellow hedge knights to fat pink ladies and old men." The Fiddler clapped Dunk upon the shoulder. "Be a good fellow and shove over, Ser Duncan."

Dunk shoved over. "You are too late for food, ser."

"No matter. I know where Butterwell's kitchens are. There is still some wine, I trust?" The Fiddler smelled of oranges and limes, with a hint of some strange eastern spice beneath. Nutmeg, perhaps. Dunk could not have said. What did he know of nutmeg?

"Your boasting is unseemly," Ser Glendon told the Fiddler.

"Truly? Then I must beg for your forgiveness, ser. I would never wish to give offense to any son of Fireball."

That took the youth aback. "You know who I am?"

"Your father's son, I hope."

"Look," said Ser Kyle the Cat. "The wedding pie."

Six kitchen boys were pushing it through the doors, upon a wide wheeled cart. The pie was brown and crusty and immense, and there were noises coming from inside it, squeaks and squawks and thumps. Lord and Lady Butterwell descended from the dais to meet it, sword in hand. When they cut it open, half a hundred birds burst forth to fly around the hall. In other wedding feasts Dunk had attended, the pies had been filled with doves or songbirds, but inside this one were blue jays and skylarks, pigeons and doves, mockingbirds and nightingales, small brown sparrows and a great red parrot. "One-and-twenty sorts of birds," said Ser Kyle.

"One-and-twenty sorts of bird droppings," said Ser Maynard.

"You have no poetry in your heart, ser."

"You have shit upon your shoulder."

"This is the proper way to fill a pie," Ser Kyle sniffed, cleaning off his tunic. "The pie is meant to be the marriage, and a true marriage has in it many sorts of things—joy and grief, pain and pleasure, love and lust and loyalty. So it is fitting that there be birds of many sorts. No man ever truly knows what a new wife will bring him."

"Her cunt," said Plumm, "or what would be the point?"

Dunk shoved back from the table. "I need a breath of air." It was a piss he needed, truth be told, but in fine company like this it was more courteous to talk of air. "Pray excuse me."

"Hurry back, ser," said the Fiddler. "There are jugglers yet to come, and you do not want to miss the bedding."

Outside, the night wind lapped at Dunk like the tongue of some great beast. The hard-packed earth of the yard seemed to move beneath his feet...or it might be that he was swaying.

The lists had been erected in the center of the outer yard. A three-tiered wooden viewing stand had been raised beneath the walls, so

Lord Butterwell and his highborn guests would be well shaded on their cushioned seats. There were tents at both ends of the lists where the knights could don their armor, with racks of tourney lances standing ready. When the wind lifted the banners for an instant, Dunk could smell the whitewash on the tilting barrier. He set off in search of the inner ward. He had to hunt up Egg and send the boy to the master of the games to enter him in the lists. That was a squire's duty.

Whitewalls was strange to him, however, and somehow Dunk got turned around. He found himself outside the kennels, where the hounds caught scent of him and began to bark and howl. *They want to tear my throat out,* he thought, *or else they want the capon in my cloak.* He doubled back the way he'd come, past the sept. A woman went running past, breathless with laughter, a bald knight in hard pursuit. The man kept falling, until finally the woman had to come back and help him up. *I should slip into the sept and ask the Seven to make that knight my first opponent,* Dunk thought, but that would have been impious. *What I really need is a privy, not a prayer.* There were some bushes near at hand, beneath a flight of pale stone steps. *Those will serve.* He groped his way behind them and unlaced his breeches. His bladder had been full to bursting. The piss went on and on.

Somewhere above, a door came open. Dunk heard footfalls on the steps, the scrape of boots on stone. "....beggar's feast you've laid before us. Without Bittersteel..."

"Bittersteel be buggered," insisted a familiar voice. "No bastard can be trusted, not even him. A few victories will bring him over the water fast enough."

Lord Peake. Dunk held his breath...and his piss.

"Easier to speak of victories than win them." This speaker had a deeper voice than Peake, a bass rumble with an angry edge to it. "Old Milkblood expected the boy to have it, and so will all the rest. Glib words and charm cannot make up for that."

"A dragon would. The prince insists the egg will hatch. He dreamed it, just as he once dreamed his brothers dead. A living dragon will win us all the swords that we would want."

"A dragon is one thing, a dream's another. I promise you, Bloodraven is not off dreaming. We need a warrior, not a dreamer. Is the boy his father's son?"

"Just do your part as promised, and let me concern myself with that. Once we have Butterwell's gold and the swords of House Frey, Harrenhal will follow, then the Brackens. Otho knows he cannot hope to stand..."

The voices were fading as the speakers moved away. Dunk's piss began to flow again. He gave his cock a shake, and laced himself back up. "His father's son," he muttered. *Who were they speaking of? Fireball's son?*

By the time he emerged from under the steps, the two lords were well across the yard. He almost shouted after them, to make them show their faces, but thought better of it. He was alone and unarmed, and half drunk besides. *Maybe more than half.* He stood there frowning for a moment, then marched back to the hall.

Inside, the last course had been served and the frolics had begun. One of Lord Frey's daughters played "Two Hearts That Beat As One" on the high harp, very badly. Some jugglers flung flaming torches at each other for a while, and some tumblers did cartwheels in the air. Lord Frey's nephew began to sing "The Bear and the Maiden Fair" while Ser Kirby Pimm beat out time upon the table with a wooden spoon. Others joined in, until the whole hall was bellowing, *"A bear! A bear! All black and brown, and covered with hair!"* Lord Caswell passed out at the table with his face in a puddle of wine, and Lady Vyrwel began to weep, though no one was quite certain as to the cause of her distress.

All the while the wine kept flowing. The rich Arbor reds gave way to local vintages, or so the Fiddler said; if truth be told, Dunk could not tell the difference. There was hippocras as well, he had to try a cup of that. *It might be a year before I have another.* The other hedge knights, fine fellows all, had begun to talk of women they had known. Dunk found himself wondering where Tanselle was tonight. He knew where Lady Rohanne was—abed at Coldmoat Castle, with old Ser Eustace beside her, snoring through his mustache—so he tried not to think of her. *Do they ever think of me?* he wondered.

His melancholy ponderings were rudely interrupted when a troupe of painted dwarfs came bursting from the belly of a wheeled wooden pig to chase Lord Butterwell's fool about the tables, walloping him with inflated pig's bladders that made rude noises every time a blow was struck. It was the funniest thing Dunk had seen in years, and he laughed with all the rest. Lord Frey's son was so taken by their antics that he joined in, pummeling the wedding guests with a bladder borrowed from a dwarf. The child had the most irritating laugh Dunk had ever heard, a high shrill hiccup of a laugh that made him want to take the boy over a knee, or throw him down a well. *If he hits me with that bladder, I may do it.*

"There's the lad who made this marriage," Ser Maynard said, as the chinless urchin went screaming past.

"How so?" The Fiddler held up an empty wine cup, and a passing server filled it.

Ser Maynard glanced toward the dais, where the bride was feeding cherries to her husband. "His lordship will not be the first to butter that biscuit. His bride was deflowered by a scullion at the Twins, they say. She would creep down to the kitchens to meet him. Alas, one night that little brother of hers crept down after her. When he saw them making the two-backed beast, he let out a shriek, and cooks and guardsmen came running and found milady and her pot boy coupling on the slab of marble where the cook rolls out the dough, both naked as their name day and floured up from head to heel."

That cannot be true, Dunk thought. Lord Butterwell had broad lands, and pots of yellow gold. Why would he wed a girl who'd been soiled by a kitchen scullion, and give away his dragon's egg to mark the match? The Freys of the Crossing were no nobler than the Butterwells. They owned a bridge instead of cows, that was the only difference. Lords. Who can ever understand *them*? Dunk ate some nuts and pondered what he'd overheard whilst pissing. *Dunk the drunk, what is it that you think you heard?* He had another cup of hippocras, since the first had tasted good. Then he lay his head down atop his folded arms and closed his eyes just for a moment, to rest them from the smoke.

When he opened them again, half the wedding guests were on their feet and shouting, "Bed them! Bed them!" They were making such an uproar that they woke Dunk from a pleasant dream involving Tanselle Too-Tall and the Red Widow. "Bed them! Bed them!" the calls rang out. Dunk sat up and rubbed his eyes.

Ser Franklyn Frey had the bride in his arms and was carrying her down the aisle, with men and boys swarming all around him. The ladies at the high table had surrounded Lord Butterwell. Lady Vyrwel had recovered from her grief and was trying to pull his lordship from his chair, while one of his daughters unlaced his boots and some Frey woman pulled up his tunic. Butterwell was flailing at them ineffectually, and laughing. He was drunk, Dunk saw, and Ser Franklyn was a deal drunker...so drunk he almost dropped the bride. Before Dunk quite realized what was happening, John the Fiddler had dragged him to his feet. "Here!" he cried out. "Let the giant carry her!"

The next thing he knew, he was climbing a tower stair with the bride squirming in his arms. How he kept his feet was beyond him. The girl would not be still and the men were all around them, making ribald japes about flouring her up and kneading her well whilst they pulled off her clothes. The dwarfs joined in as well. They swarmed around Dunk's legs, shouting and laughing and smacking at his calves with their bladders. It was all he could do not to trip over them.

Dunk had no notion where Lord Butterwell's bedchamber was to be found, but the other men pushed and prodded him until he got there, by which time the bride was red-faced, giggling, and nearly naked, save for the stocking on her left leg, which had somehow survived the climb. Dunk was crimson too, and not from exertion. His arousal would have been obvious if anyone had been looking, but fortunately all eyes were on the bride. Lady Butterwell looked nothing like Tanselle, but having the one squirming half-naked in his arms had started Dunk thinking about the other. *Tanselle Too-Tall, that was her name, but she was not too tall for me.* He wondered if he would ever find her again. There had been some nights when he thought he must have dreamed her. *No, lunk, you only dreamed she liked you.*

Lord Butterwell's bedchamber was large and lavish, once he found it.

Myrish carpets covered the floors, a hundred scented candles burned in nooks and crannies, and a suit of plate inlaid with gold and gems stood beside the door. It even had its own privy set into a small stone alcove in the outer wall.

When Dunk finally plopped the bride onto her marriage bed, a dwarf leapt in beside her and seized one of her breasts for a bit of a fondle. The girl let out a squeal, the men roared with laughter, and Dunk seized the dwarf by his collar and hauled him kicking off m'lady. He was carrying the little man across the room to chuck him out the door when he saw the dragon's egg.

Lord Butterwell had placed it on a black velvet cushion atop a marble plinth. It was much bigger than a hen's egg, though not so big as he'd had imagined. Fine red scales covered its surface, shining bright as jewels by the light of lamps and candles. Dunk dropped the dwarf and picked up the egg, just to feel it for a moment. It was heavier than he'd expected. *You could smash a man's head with this, and never crack the shell.* The scales were smooth beneath his fingers, and the deep, rich red seemed to shimmer as he turned the egg in his hands. *Blood and flame,* he thought, but there were gold flecks in it as well, and whorls of midnight black.

"Here, you! What do you think you're doing, ser?" A knight he did not know was glaring at him, a big man with a coal-black beard and boils, but it was the voice that made him blink; a deep voice, thick with anger. *It was him, the man with Peake,* Dunk realized, as the man said, "Put that down. I'll thank you to keep your greasy fingers off his lordship's treasures, or by the Seven, you shall wish you had."

The other knight was not near as drunk as Dunk, so it seemed wise to do as he said. He put the egg back on its pillow, very carefully, and wiped his fingers on his sleeve. "I meant no harm, ser." *Dunk the lunk, thick as a castle wall.* Then he shoved past the man with the black beard and out the door.

There were noises in the stairwell, glad shouts and girlish laughter. The women were bringing Lord Butterwell to his bride. Dunk had no wish to encounter them, so he went up instead of down, and found himself on the tower roof beneath the stars, with the pale castle glimmering in the moonlight all around him.

He was feeling dizzy from the wine, so he leaned against a parapet. *Am I going to be sick?* Why did he go and touch the dragon's egg? He remembered Tanselle's puppet show, and the wooden dragon that had started all the trouble there at Ashford. The memory made Dunk feel guilty, as it always did. *Three good men dead, to save a hedge knight's foot.* It made no sense, and never had. *Take a lesson from that, lunk. It is not for the likes of you to mess about with dragons or their eggs.*

"It almost looks as if it's made of snow."

Dunk turned. John the Fiddler stood behind him, smiling in his silk and cloth-of-gold. "What's made of snow?"

"The castle. All that white stone in the moonlight. Have you ever been north of the Neck, Ser Duncan? I'm told it snows there even in the summer. Have you ever seen the Wall?"

"No, m'lord." *Why he is going on about the Wall?* "That's where we were going, Egg and me. Up north, to Winterfell."

"Would that I could join you. You could show me the way."

"The way?" Dunk frowned. "It's right up the kingsroad. If you stay to the road and keep going north, you can't miss it."

The Fiddler laughed. "I suppose not...though you might be surprised at what some men can miss." He went to the parapet and looked out across the castle. "They say those northmen are a savage folk, and their woods are full of wolves."

"M'lord? Why did you come up here?"

"Alyn was seeking for me, and I did not care to be found. He grows tiresome when he drinks, does Alyn. I saw you slip away from that bedchamber of horrors, and slipped out after you. I've had too much wine, I grant you, but not enough to face a naked Butterwell." He gave Dunk an enigmatic smile. "I dreamed of you, Ser Duncan. Before I even met you. When I saw you on the road, I knew your face at once. It was as if we were old friends."

Dunk had the strangest feeling then, as if he had lived this all before. *I dreamed of you*, he said. *My dreams are not like yours, Ser Duncan. Mine are true.* "You dreamed of me?" he said, in a voice made thick by wine. "What sort of dream?"

"Why," the Fiddler said, "I dreamed that you were all in white from head to heel, with a long pale cloak flowing from those broad shoulders. You were a White Sword, ser, a Sworn Brother of the Kingsguard, the greatest knight in all the Seven Kingdoms, and you lived for no other purpose but to guard and serve and please your king." He put a hand on Dunk's shoulder. "You have dreamed the same dream, I know you have."

He had, it was true. *The first time the old man let me hold his sword.* "Every boy dreams of serving in the Kingsguard."

"Only seven boys grow up to wear the white cloak, though. Would it please you to be one of them?"

"Me?" Dunk shrugged away the lordling's hand, which had begun to knead his shoulder. "It might. Or not." The knights of the Kingsguard served for life, and swore to take no wife and hold no lands. *I might find Tanselle again someday. Why shouldn't I have a wife, and sons?* "It makes no matter what I dream. Only a king can make a Kingsguard knight."

"I suppose that means I'll have to take the throne, then. I would much rather be teaching you to fiddle."

"You're drunk." And the crow once called the raven black.

"Wonderfully drunk. Wine makes all things possible, Ser Duncan. You'd look a god in white, I think, but if the color does not suit you, perhaps you would prefer to be a lord?"

Dunk laughed in his face. "No, I'd sooner sprout big blue wings and fly. One's as likely as t'other."

"Now you mock me. A true knight would never mock his king." The Fiddler sounded hurt. "I hope you will put more faith in what I tell you when you see the dragon hatch."

"A dragon will hatch? A *living* dragon? What, here?"

"I dreamed it. This pale white castle, you, a dragon bursting from an egg, I dreamed it all, just as I once dreamed of my brothers lying dead. They were twelve and I was only seven, so they laughed at me, and died. I am two-and-twenty now, and I trust my dreams."

Dunk was remembering another tourney, remembering how he had walked through the soft spring rains with another princeling. *I dreamed of you and a dead dragon*, Egg's brother Daeron said to him. *A great beast, huge, with wings so large they could cover this meadow. It had fallen on top of you, but you were alive and the dragon was dead. And so he was, poor*

Baelor. Dreams were a treacherous ground on which to build. "As you say, m'lord," he told the Fiddler. "Pray excuse me."

"Where *are* you going, ser?"

"To my bed, to sleep. I'm drunk as a dog."

"Be my dog, ser. The night's alive with promise. We can howl together, and wake the very gods."

"What do you want of me?"

"Your sword. I would make you mine own man, and raise you high. My dreams do not lie, Ser Duncan. You shall have that white cloak, and I *must* have the dragon's egg. I *must*, my dreams have made that plain. Perhaps the egg will hatch, or else..."

Behind them, the door banged open violently. "*There he is, my lord.*" A pair of men-at-arms stepped onto the roof. Lord Gormon Peake was just behind them.

"*Gormy*," the Fiddler drawled. "Why, what are you doing in my bedchamber, my lord?"

"It is a roof, ser, and you have had too much wine." Lord Gormon made a sharp gesture, and the guards moved forward. "Allow us to help you to that bed. You are jousting on the morrow, pray recall. Kirby Pimm can prove a dangerous foe."

"I had hoped to joust with good Ser Duncan here."

Peake gave Dunk an unsympathetic look. "Later, perhaps. For your first tilt, you have drawn Ser Kirby Pimm."

"Then Pimm must fall! So must they all! The mystery knight prevails against all challengers, and wonder dances in his wake." A guardsman took the Fiddler by the arm. "Ser Duncan, it seems that we must part," he called, as they helped him down the steps.

Only Lord Gormon remained upon the roof with Dunk. "Hedge knight," he growled, "did your mother never teach you not to reach your hand into the dragon's mouth?"

"I never knew my mother, m'lord."

"That would explain it. What did he promise you?"

"A lordship. A white cloak. Big blue wings."

"Here's my promise: three feet of cold steel through your belly, if you speak a word of what just happened."

Dunk shook his head to clear his wits. It did not seem to help. He bent double at the waist, and retched.

Some of the vomit spattered Peake's boots. The lord cursed. "Hedge knights," he exclaimed in disgust. "You have no place here. No true knight would be so discourteous as to turn up uninvited, but you creatures of the hedge…"

"We are wanted nowhere and turn up everywhere, m'lord." The wine had made Dunk bold, else he would have held his tongue. He wiped his mouth with the back of his hand.

"Try and remember what I told you, ser. It will go ill for you if you do not." Lord Peake shook the vomit off his boot. Then he was gone. Dunk leaned against the parapet again. He wondered who was madder, Lord Gormon or the Fiddler.

By the time he found his way back to the hall, only Maynard Plumm remained of his companions. "Was there any flour on her teats when you got the smallclothes off her?" he wanted to know.

Dunk shook his head, poured himself another cup of wine, tasted it, and decided that he had drunk enough.

Butterwell's stewards had found rooms in the keep for the lords and ladies, and beds in the barracks for their retinues. The rest of the guests had their choice between a straw pallet in the cellar, or a spot of ground beneath the western walls to raise their pavilions. The modest sailcloth tent Dunk had acquired in Stoney Sept was no pavilion, but it kept the rain and sun off. Some of his neighbors were still awake, the silken walls of their pavilions glowing like colored lanterns in the night. Laughter came from inside a blue pavilion covered with sunflowers, and the sounds of love from one striped in white and purple. Egg had set up their own tent a bit apart from the others. Maester and the two horses were hobbled nearby, and Dunk's arms and armor had been neatly stacked against the castle walls. When he crept into the tent, he found his squire sitting cross-legged by a candle, his head shining as he peered over a book.

"Reading books by candlelight will make you blind." Reading remained a mystery to Dunk, though the lad had tried to teach him.

"I need the candlelight to see the words, ser."

"Do you want a clout in the ear? What book is that?" Dunk saw bright colors on the page, little painted shields hiding in amongst the letters.

"A roll of arms, ser."

"Looking for the Fiddler? You won't find him. They don't put hedge knights in those rolls, just lords and champions."

"I wasn't looking for him. I saw some other sigils in the yard...Lord Sunderland is here, ser. He bears the heads of three pale ladies, on undy green and blue."

"A Sisterman? Truly?" The Three Sisters were islands in the Bite. Dunk had heard septons say that the isles were sinks of sin and avarice. Sisterton was the most notorious smuggler's den in all of Westeros. "He's come a long way. He must be kin to Butterwell's new bride."

"He isn't, ser."

"Then he's here for the feast. They eat fish on the Three Sisters, don't they? A man gets sick of fish. Did you get enough to eat? I brought you half a capon and some cheese." Dunk rummaged in the pocket of his cloak.

"They fed us ribs, ser." Egg's nose was deep in the book. "Lord Sunderland fought for the black dragon, ser."

"Like old Ser Eustace? He wasn't so bad, was he?"

"No, ser," Egg said, "but..."

"I saw the dragon's egg." Dunk squirreled the food away with their hardbread and salt beef. "It was red, mostly. Does Lord Bloodraven own a dragon's egg as well?"

Egg lowered his book. "Why would he? He's baseborn."

"Bastard born, not baseborn." Bloodraven had been born on the wrong side of the blanket, but he was noble on both sides. Dunk was about to tell Egg about the men he'd overhead when he noticed his face. "What happened to your lip?"

"A fight, ser."

"Let me see it."

"It only bled a little. I dabbed some wine on it."

"Who were you fighting?"

"Some other squires. They said—"

"Never mind what they said. What did I tell you?"

"To hold my tongue and make no trouble." The boy touched his broken lip. "They called my father a *kinslayer*, though."

He is, lad, though I do not think he meant it. Dunk had told Egg half a hundred times not to take such words to heart. *You know the truth. Let that be enough.* They had heard such talk before, in wine sinks and low taverns, and around campfires in the woods. The whole realm knew how Prince Maekar's mace had felled his brother Baelor Breakspear at Ashford Meadow. Talk of plots was only to be expected. "If they knew Prince Maekar was your father, they would never have said such things." *Behind your back, yes, but never to your face.* "And what did you tell these other squires, instead of holding your tongue?"

Egg looked abashed. "That Prince Baelor's death was just a mishap. Only when I said Prince Maekar loved his brother Baelor, Ser Addam's squire said he loved him to death, and Ser Mallor's squire said he meant to love his brother Aerys the same way. That was when I hit him. I hit him good."

"I ought to hit you good. A fat ear to go with that fat lip. Your father would do the same if he were here. Do you think Prince Maekar needs a little boy to defend him? What did he tell you when he sent you off with me?"

"To serve you faithfully as your squire, and not flinch from any task or hardship."

"And what else?"

"To obey the king's laws, the rules of chivalry, and you."

"And what else?"

"To keep my hair shaved or dyed," the boy said, with obvious reluctance, "and tell no man my true name."

Dunk nodded. "How much wine had this boy drunk?"

"He was drinking barley beer."

"You see? The barley beer was talking. Words are wind, Egg. Just let them blow on past you."

"Some words are wind." The boy was nothing if not stubborn. "Some words are treason. This is a traitor's tourney, ser."

"What, all of them?" Dunk shook his head. "If it was true, that was a long time ago. The black dragon's dead, and those who fought with him are fled or pardoned. And it's not true. Lord Butterwell's sons fought on both sides."

"That makes him *half* a traitor, ser."

"Sixteen years ago." Dunk's mellow winey haze was gone. He felt angry, and near sober. "Lord Butterwell's steward is the master of the games, a man named Cosgrove. Find him and enter my name for the lists. No, wait...hold back my name." With so many lords on hand, one of them might recall Ser Duncan the Tall from Ashford Meadow. "Enter me as the Gallows Knight." The smallfolk loved it when a mystery knight appeared at a tourney.

Egg fingered his fat lip. "The Gallows Knight, ser?"

"For the shield."

"Yes, but..."

"Go do as I said. You have read enough for one night." Dunk pinched the candle out between his thumb and forefinger.

The sun rose hot and hard, implacable.

Waves of heat rose shimmering off the white stones of the castle. The air smelled of baked earth and torn grass, and no breath of wind stirred the banners that drooped atop the keep and gatehouse, green and white and yellow.

Thunder was restless, in a way that Dunk had seldom seen before. The stallion tossed his head from side to side as Egg was tightening his saddle cinch. He even bared his big square teeth at the boy. It is so hot, Dunk thought, too hot for man or mount. A warhorse does not have a placid disposition even at the best of times. The Mother herself would be foul-tempered in this heat.

In the center of the yard the jousters began another run. Ser Harbert rode a golden courser barded in black and decorated with the red and white serpents of House Paege, Ser Franklyn a sorrel whose gray silk trapper bore the twin towers of Frey. When they came together, the red and white lance cracked clean in two and the blue one exploded into splinters, but neither man lost his seat. A cheer went up from the viewing stand and the guardsmen on the castle walls, but it was short and thin and hollow. *It is too hot for cheering.* Dunk mopped sweat from his brow. It is too hot for jousting. His head was beating like a drum. *Let me win this tilt and one more, and I will be content.*

The knights wheeled their horses about at the end of the lists and tossed down the jagged remains of their lances, the fourth pair they had broken. *Three too many.* Dunk had put off donning his armor as long as he dared, yet already he could feel his smallclothes sticking to his skin beneath his steel. *There are worse things than being soaked with sweat*, he told himself, remembering the fight on the *White Lady*, when the ironmen had come swarming over her side. He had been soaked in blood by the time that day was done.

Fresh lances in hand, Paege and Frey put their spurs into their mounts once again. Clods of cracked dry earth sprayed back from beneath their horses' hooves with every stride. The crack of the lances breaking made Dunk wince. *Too much wine last night, and too much food.* He had some vague memory of carrying the bride up the steps, and meeting John the Fiddler and Lord Peake upon a roof. *What was I doing on a roof?* There had been talk of dragons, he recalled, or dragon's eggs, or something, but...

A noise broke his reverie, part roar and part moan. Dunk saw the golden horse trotting riderless to the end of the lists, as Ser Harbert Paege rolled feebly on the ground. *Two more before my turn.* The sooner he unhorsed Ser Uthor, the sooner he could take his armor off, have a cool drink, and rest. He should have at least an hour before they called him forth again.

Lord Butterwell's portly herald climbed to the top of the viewing stand to summon the next pair of jousters. "Ser Argrave the Defiant," he called, "a knight of Nunny, in service to Lord Butterwell of Whitewalls.

Ser Glendon Flowers, the Knight of the Pussywillows. Come forth and prove your valor." A gale of laughter rippled through the viewing stands.

Ser Argrave was a spare, leathery man, a seasoned household knight in dinted gray armor riding an unbarded horse. Dunk had known his sort before; such men were tough as old roots, and knew their business. His foe was young Ser Glendon, mounted on his wretched stot and armored in a heavy mail hauberk and open-faced iron halfhelm. On his arm his shield displayed his father's fiery sigil. *He needs a breastplate and a proper helm,* Dunk thought. *A blow to the head or chest could kill him, clad like that.*

Ser Glendon was plainly furious at his introduction. He wheeled his mount in an angry circle and shouted, "I am Glendon *Ball*, not Glendon Flowers. Mock me at your peril, herald. I warn you, I have hero's blood." The herald did not deign to reply, but more laughter greeted the young knight's protest. "Why are they laughing at him?" Dunk wondered aloud. "Is he a bastard, then?" *Flowers* was the surname given to bastards born of noble parents in the Reach. "And what was all that about pussywillows?"

"I could find out, ser," said Egg.

"No. It is none of our concern. Do you have my helm?" Ser Argrave and Ser Glendon dipped their lances before Lord and Lady Butterwell. Dunk saw Butterwell lean over and whisper something in his bride's ear. The girl began to giggle.

"Yes, ser." Egg had donned his floppy hat, to shade his eyes and keep the sun off his shaved head. Dunk liked to tease the boy about that hat, but just now he wished he had one like it. Better a straw hat than an iron one, beneath this sun. He pushed his hair out of his eyes, eased the greathelm down into place with two hands, and fastened it to his gorget. The lining stank of old sweat, and he could feel the weight of all that iron on his neck and shoulders. His head throbbed from last night's wine.

"Ser," Egg said, "it is not too late to withdraw. If you lose Thunder and your armor..."

I would be done as a knight. "Why should I lose?" Dunk demanded. Ser Argrave and Ser Glendon had ridden to opposite ends of the lists. "It is not as if I faced the Laughing Storm. Is there some knight here like to give me trouble?"

"Almost all of them, ser."

"I owe you a clout in the ear for that. Ser Uthor is ten years my senior and half my size." Ser Argrave lowered his visor. Ser Glendon did not have a visor to lower.

"You have not ridden in a tilt since Ashford Meadow, ser."

Insolent boy. "I've trained." Not as faithfully as he might have, to be sure. When he could, he took his turn riding at quintains or rings, where such were available. And sometimes he would command Egg to climb a tree and hang a shield or barrel stave beneath a well-placed limb for them to tilt at.

"You're better with a sword than with a lance," Egg said. "With an axe or a mace there's few to match your strength."

There was enough truth in that to annoy Dunk all the more. "There is no contest for swords or maces," he pointed out, as Fireball's son and Ser Argrave the Defiant began their charge. "Go get my shield."

Egg made a face, then went to fetch the shield.

Across the yard, Ser Argrave's lance struck Ser Glendon's shield and glanced off, leaving a gouge across the comet. But Ball's coronal found the center of his foe's breastplate with such force that it burst his saddle cinch. Knight and saddle both went tumbling to the dust. Dunk was impressed despite himself. *The boy jousts almost as well as he talks.* He wondered if that would stop them laughing at him.

A trumpet rang, loud enough to make Dunk wince. Once more the herald climbed his stand. "Ser Joffrey of House Caswell, Lord of Bitterbridge and Defender of the Fords. Ser Kyle, the Cat of Misty Moor. Come forth and prove your valor."

Ser Kyle's armor was of good quality, but old and worn, with many dents and scratches. "The Mother has been merciful to me, Ser Duncan," he told Dunk and Egg, on his way to the lists. "I am sent against Lord Caswell, the very man I came to see."

If any man upon the field felt worse than Dunk this morning it had to be Lord Caswell, who had drunk himself insensible at the feast. "It's a wonder he can sit a horse, after last night," said Dunk. "The victory is yours, ser."

"Oh, no." Ser Kyle smiled a silken smile. "The cat who wants his bowl of cream must know when to purr and when to show his claws, Ser Duncan. If his lordship's lance so much as scrapes against my shield, I shall go tumbling to the earth. Afterward, when I bring my horse and armor to him, I will compliment his lordship on how much his prowess has grown since I made him his first sword. That will recall me to him, and before the day is out I shall be a Caswell man again, a knight of Bitterbridge."

There is no honor in that, Dunk almost said, but he bit his tongue instead. Ser Kyle would not be the first hedge knight to trade his honor for a warm place by the fire. "As you say," he muttered. "Good fortune to you. Or bad, if you prefer."

Lord Joffrey Caswell was a weedy youth of twenty, though admittedly he looked rather more impressive in his armor than he had last night when he'd been face down in a puddle of wine. A yellow centaur was painted on his shield, pulling on a longbow. The same centaur adorned the white silk trappings of his horse, and gleamed atop his helm in yellow gold. *A man who has a centaur for his sigil should ride better than that.* Dunk did not know how well Ser Kyle wielded a lance, but from the way Lord Caswell sat his horse it looked as though a loud cough might unseat him. *All the Cat need do is ride past him very fast.*

Egg held Thunder's bridle as Dunk swung himself ponderously up into the high, stiff saddle. As he sat there waiting, he could feel the eyes upon him. *They are wondering if the big hedge knight is any good.* Dunk wondered that himself. He would find out soon enough.

The Cat of Misty Moor was true to his word. Lord Caswell's lance was wobbling all the way across the field, and Ser Kyle's was ill-aimed. Neither man got his horse up past a trot. All the same, the Cat went tumbling when Lord Joffrey's coronal chanced to whack his shoulder. *I thought all cats landed gracefully upon their feet,* Dunk thought, as the hedge knight rolled in the dust. Lord Caswell's lance remained unbroken. As he brought his horse around, he thrust it high into the air repeatedly, as if he'd just unseated Leo Longthorn or the Laughing Storm. The Cat pulled off his helm and went chasing down his horse.

"My shield," Dunk said to Egg. The boy handed it up. He slipped his left arm through the strap and closed his hand around the grip.

The weight of the kite shield was reassuring, though its length made it awkward to handle, and seeing the hanged man once again gave him an uneasy feeling. *Those are ill-omened arms.* He resolved to get the shield repainted as soon as he could. *May the Warrior grant me a smooth course and a quick victory,* he prayed, as Butterwell's herald was clambering up the steps once more. "*Ser Uthor Underleaf,*" his voice rang out. "*The Gallows Knight. Come forth and prove your valor.*"

"Be careful, ser," Egg warned as he handed Dunk a tourney lance, a tapered wooden shaft twelve feet long ending in a rounded iron coronal in the shape of a closed fist. "The other squires say Ser Uthor has a good seat. And he's quick."

"Quick?" Dunk snorted. "He has a snail on his shield. How quick can he be?" He put his heels into Thunder's flanks and walked the horse slowly forward, his lance upright. *One victory, and I am no worse than before. Two will leave us well ahead. Two is not too much to hope for, in this company.* He had been fortunate in the lots, at least. He could as easily have drawn the Old Ox or Ser Kirby Pimm or some other local hero. Dunk wondered if the master of games was deliberately matching the hedge knights against each other, so no lordling need suffer the ignominy of losing to one in the first round. It does not matter. *One foe at a time, that was what the old man always said. Ser Uthor is all that should concern me now.*

They met beneath the viewing stand where Lord and Lady Butterwell sat on their cushions in the shade of the castle walls. Lord Frey was beside them, dandling his snot-nosed son on one knee. A row of serving girls was fanning them, yet Lord Butterwell's damask tunic was stained beneath the arms, and his lady's hair was limp from perspiration. She looked hot, bored, and uncomfortable, but when she saw Dunk she pushed out her chest in a way that turned him red beneath his helm. He dipped his lance to her and her lord husband. Ser Uthor did the same. Butterwell wished them both a good tilt. His wife stuck out her tongue.

It was time. Dunk trotted back to the south end of the lists. Eighty feet away, his opponent was taking up his position as well. His gray stallion was smaller than Thunder, but younger and more spirited. Ser Uthor wore green enamel plate and silvery chain mail. Streamers of green and gray silk flowed from his rounded bascinet, and his green shield bore a silver snail. *Good armor and a good horse means a good ransom, if I unseat him.*

A trumpet sounded.

Thunder started forward at a slow trot. Dunk swung his lance to the left and brought it down, so it angled across the horse's head and the wooden barrier between him and his foe. His shield protected the left side of his body. He crouched forward, legs tightening as Thunder drove down the lists. *We are one. Man, horse, lance, we are one beast of blood and wood and iron.*

Ser Uthor was charging hard, clouds of dust kicking up from the hooves of his gray. With forty yards between them, Dunk spurred Thunder to a gallop, and aimed the point of his lance squarely at the silver snail. The sullen sun, the dust, the heat, the castle, Lord Butterwell and his bride, the Fiddler and Ser Maynard, knights, squires, grooms, smallfolk, all vanished.

Only the foe remained. The spurs again. Thunder broke into a run. The snail was rushing toward them; growing with every stride of the gray's long legs...but ahead came Ser Uthor's lance with its iron fist. *My shield is strong, my shield will take the blow. Only the snail matters. Strike the snail and the tilt is mine.*

When ten yards remained between them, Ser Uthor shifted the point of his lance upwards.

A *crack* rang in Dunk's ears as his lance hit. He felt the impact in his arm and shoulder, but never saw the blow strike home. Uthor's iron fist took him square between his eyes, with all the force of man and horse behind it.

Dunk woke upon his back, staring up at the arches of a barrel-vaulted ceiling. For a moment he did not know where he was, or how he had arrived there. Voices echoed in his head, and faces drifted past him;

old Ser Arlan, Tanselle Too-Tall, Dennis of the Brown Shield, the Red Widow, Baelor Breakspear, Aerion the Bright Prince, mad sad Lady Vaith. Then all at once the joust came back to him: the heat, the snail, the iron fist coming at his face. He groaned, and rolled onto one elbow. The movement set his skull to pounding like some monstrous war drum.

Both of his eyes seemed to be working, at least. Nor could he feel a hole in his head, which was all to the good. He was in some cellar, he saw, with casks of wine and ale on every side. *At least it is cool here*, he thought, *and drink is close at hand.* The taste of blood was in his mouth. Dunk felt a stab of fear. If he had bitten off his tongue, he would be dumb as well as thick. "Good morrow," he croaked, just to hear his voice. The words echoed off the ceiling. Dunk tried to push himself onto his feet, but the effort set the cellar spinning.

"Slowly, slowly," said a quavery voice, close at hand. A stooped old man appeared beside the bed, clad in robes as gray as his long hair. About his neck was a maester's chain of many metals. His face was aged and lined, with deep creases on either side of a great beak of a nose. "Be still, and let me see your eyes." He peered in Dunk's left eye, and then the right, holding them open between his thumb and forefinger.

"My head hurts."

The maester snorted. "Be grateful it still rests upon your shoulders, ser. Here, this may help somewhat. Drink."

Dunk made himself swallow every drop of the foul potion, and managed not to spit it out. "The tourney," he said, wiping his mouth with the back of his hand. "Tell me. What's happened?"

"The same foolishness that always happens in these affrays. Men have been knocking each other off horses with sticks. Lord Smallwood's nephew broke his wrist and Ser Eden Risley's leg was crushed beneath his horse, but no one has been killed thus far. Though I had my fears for you, ser."

"Was I unhorsed?" His head still felt as though it was stuffed full of wool, else he would never have asked such a stupid question. Dunk regretted it the instant the words were out.

"With a crash that shook the highest ramparts. Those who had wagered good coin on you were most distraught, and your squire was beside himself. He would be sitting with you still if I had not chased him off. I need no children underfoot. I reminded him of his duty."

Dunk found that he needed reminding himself. "What duty?"

"Your mount, ser. Your arms and armor."

"Yes," Dunk said, remembering. The boy was a good squire; he knew what was required of him. *I have lost the old man's sword and the armor that Steely Pate forged for me.*

"Your fiddling friend was also asking after you. He told me you were to have the best of care. I threw him out as well."

"How long have you been tending me?" Dunk flexed the fingers of his sword hand. All of them still seemed to work. *Only my head's hurt, and Ser Arlan used to say I never used that anyway.*

"Four hours, by the sundial."

Four hours was not so bad. He had once heard tell of a knight struck so hard that he slept for forty years, and woke to find himself old and withered. "Do you know if Ser Uthor won his second tilt?" Maybe the Snail would win the tourney. It would take some sting from the defeat if Dunk could tell himself that he had lost to the best knight in the field.

"That one? Indeed he did. Against Ser Addam Frey, a cousin to the bride, and a promising young lance. Her ladyship fainted when Ser Addam fell. She had to be helped back to her chambers."

Dunk forced himself to his feet, reeling as he rose, but the maester helped to steady him. "Where are my clothes? I must go. I have to...I must..."

"If you cannot recall, it cannot be so very urgent." The maester made an irritated motion. "I would suggest that you avoid rich foods, strong drink, and further blows between your eyes...but I learned long ago that knights are deaf to sense. Go, go. I have other fools to tend."

Outside, Dunk glimpsed a hawk soaring in wide circles through the bright blue sky. He envied him. A few clouds were gathering to the east, dark as Dunk's mood. As he found his way back to the tilting ground, the sun beat down on his head like a hammer on an anvil. The earth seemed to move beneath his feet...or it might just be that he was swaying. He had almost fallen twice climbing the cellar steps. *I should have heeded Egg.*

He made his slow way across the outer ward, around the fringes of the crowd. Out on the field, plump Lord Alyn Cockshaw was limping off between two squires, the latest conquest of young Glendon Ball. A third squire held his helm, its three proud feathers broken. "*Ser John the Fiddler,*" the herald cried. "*Ser Franklyn of House Frey, a knight of the Twins, sworn to the Lord of the Crossing. Come forth and prove your valor.*"

Dunk could only stand and watch as the Fiddler's big black trotted onto the field in a swirl of blue silk and golden swords and fiddles. His breastplate was enameled blue as well, as were his poleyns, couter, greaves, and gorget. The ringmail underneath was gilded. Ser Franklyn rode a dapple gray with a flowing silver mane, to match the gray of his silks and the silver of his armor. On shield and surcoat and horse trappings he bore the twin towers of Frey. They charged and charged again. Dunk stood watching, but saw none of it. *Dunk the lunk, thick as a castle wall,* he chided himself. *He had a snail upon his shield. How could you lose to a man with a snail upon his shield?*

There was cheering all around him. When Dunk looked up, he saw that Franklyn Frey was down. The Fiddler had dismounted, to help his fallen foe back to his feet. *He is one step closer to his dragon's egg,* Dunk thought, *and where am I?*

As he approached the postern gate, Dunk came upon the company of dwarfs from last night's feast preparing to take their leave. They were hitching ponies to their wheeled wooden pig, and a second wayn of more conventional design. There were six of them, he saw, each smaller and more malformed than the last. A few might have been children, but they were all so short that it was hard to tell. In daylight, dressed in horsehide breeches and roughspun hooded cloaks, they seemed less jolly than they had in motley. "Good morrow to you," Dunk said, to be courteous. "Are you for the road? There's clouds to the east, could mean rain."

The only answer that he got was a glare from the ugliest dwarf. *Was he the one I pulled off Lady Butterwell last night?* Up close, the little man smelled like a privy. One whiff was enough to make Dunk hasten his steps.

The walk across the Milkhouse seemed to take Dunk as long as it had once taken him and Egg to cross the sands of Dorne. He kept a wall beside him, and from time to time he leaned on it. Every time he turned his head the world would swim. *A drink*, he thought. *I need a drink of water, or else I'm like to fall.*

A passing groom told him where to find the nearest well. It was there that he discovered Kyle the Cat, talking quietly with Maynard Plumm. Ser Kyle's shoulders were slumped in dejection, but he looked up at Dunk's approach.

"Ser Duncan? We had heard that you were dead, or dying."

Dunk rubbed his temples. "I only wish I were."

"I know that feeling well." Ser Kyle sighed. "Lord Caswell did not know me. When I told him how I carved his first sword, he stared at me as if I'd lost my wits. He said there was no place at Bitterbridge for knights as feeble as I had shown myself to be." The Cat gave a bitter laugh. "He took my arms and armor, though. My mount as well. What will I do?"

Dunk had no answer for him. Even a freerider required a horse to ride; sellswords must have swords to sell. "You will find another horse," Dunk said, as he drew the bucket up. "The Seven Kingdoms are full of horses. You will find some other lord to arm you." He cupped his hands, filled them with water, drank.

"Some other lord. Aye. Do you know of one? I am not so young and strong as you. Nor as big. Big men are always in demand. Lord Butterwell likes his knights large, for one. Look at that Tom Heddle. Have you seen him joust? He has overthrown every man he's faced. Fireball's lad has done the same, though. The Fiddler as well. Would that he had been the one to unhorse me. He refuses to take ransoms. He wants no more than the dragon's egg, he says...that, and the friendship of his fallen foes. The flower of chivalry, that one."

Maynard Plumm gave a laugh. "The fiddle of chivalry, you mean. That boy is fiddling up a storm, and all of us would do well to be gone from here before it breaks."

"He takes no ransoms?" said Dunk. "A gallant gesture."

"Gallant gestures come easy when your purse is fat with gold," said Ser Maynard. "There is a lesson here, if you have the sense to take it, Ser Duncan. It is not too late for you to go."

"Go? Go where?"

Ser Maynard shrugged. "Anywhere. Winterfell, Summerhall, Asshai by the Shadow. It makes no matter, so long as it's not here. Take your horse and armor and slip out the postern gate. You won't be missed. The Snail's got his next tilt to think about, and the rest have eyes only for the jousting."

For half a heartbeat, Dunk was tempted. So long as he was armed and horsed, he would remain a knight of sorts. Without them he was no more than a beggar. *A big beggar, but a beggar all the same.* But his arms and armor belonged to Ser Uthor now. So did Thunder. *Better a beggar than a thief.* He had been both in Flea Bottom, when he ran with Ferret, Rafe, and Pudding, but the old man had saved him from that life. He knew what Ser Arlan of Pennytree would have said to Plumm's suggestions. Ser Arlan being dead, Dunk said it for him. "Even a hedge knight has his honor."

"Would you rather die with honor intact, or live with it besmirched? No, spare me, I know what you will say. Take your boy and flee, gallows knight. Before your arms become your destiny."

Dunk bristled. "How would you know my destiny? Did you have a dream, like John the Fiddler? What do you know of Egg?"

"I know that eggs do well to stay out of frying pans," said Plumm. "Whitewalls is not a healthy place for the boy."

"How did you fare in your own tilt, ser?" Dunk asked him.

"Oh, I did not chance the lists. The omens had gone sour. Who do you imagine is going to claim the dragon's egg, pray?"

Not me, Dunk thought. "The Seven know. I don't."

"Venture a guess, ser. You have two eyes."

He thought a moment. "The Fiddler?"

"Very good. Would you care to explain your reasoning?"

"I just...I have a feeling."

"So do I," said Maynard Plumm. "A bad feeling, for any man or boy unwise enough to stand in our Fiddler's way."

Egg was brushing Thunder's coat outside their tent, but his eyes were far away. *The boy has taken my fall hard.* "Enough," Dunk called. "Any more and Thunder will be as bald as you."

"Ser?" Egg dropped the brush. "I *knew* no stupid snail could kill you, ser." He threw his arms around him.

Dunk swiped the boy's floppy straw hat and put it on his own head. "The maester said you made off with my armor."

Egg snatched back his hat indignantly. "I've scoured your mail and polished your greaves, gorget, and breastplate, ser, but your helm is cracked and dinted where Ser Uthor's coronal struck. You'll need to have it hammered out by an armorer."

"Let Ser Uthor have it hammered out. It's his now." No horse, no sword, no armor. *Perhaps those dwarfs would let me join their troupe. That would be a funny sight, six dwarfs pummeling a giant with pig bladders.* "Thunder is his too. Come. We'll take them to him and wish him well in the rest of his tilts."

"Now, ser? Aren't you going to ransom Thunder?"

"With what, lad? Pebbles and sheep pellets?"

"I thought about that, ser. If you could borrow—"

Dunk cut him off. "No one will lend me that much coin, Egg. Why should they? What am I, but some great oaf who called himself a knight until some snail with a stick near stove his head in?"

"Well," said Egg, "you could have Rain, ser. I'll go back to riding Maester. We'll go to Summerhall. You can take service in my father's household. His stables are full of horses. You could have a destrier and a palfrey too."

Egg meant well, but Dunk could not go cringing back to Summerhall. Not that way, penniless and beaten, seeking service without so much as a sword to offer. "Lad," he said, "that's good of you, but I want no crumbs from your lord father's table, or from his stables neither. Might be it's time we parted ways." Dunk could always slink off to join the City Watch in Lannisport or Oldtown, they liked big men for that. *I've bumped my bean on every beam in every inn from Lannisport to King's Landing, might be it's time my size earned me a bit of coin instead of just a lumpy head.* But watchmen did not have squires. "I've taught you what I could, and that was little enough. You'll do better with a proper master-at-arms to see to your training, some fierce old knight who knows which end of the lance to hold."

"I don't want a proper master-at-arms," Egg said. "I want you. What if I used my—"

"No. None of that, I will not hear it. Go gather up my arms. We will present them to Ser Uthor with my compliments. Hard things only grow harder if you put them off."

Egg kicked the ground, his face as droopy as his big straw hat. "Aye, ser. As you say."

From the outside Ser Uthor's tent was very plain; a large square box of dun-colored sailcloth staked to the ground with hempen ropes. A silver snail adorned the center pole above a long gray pennon, but that was the only decoration.

"Wait here," Dunk told Egg. The boy had hold of Thunder's lead. The big brown destrier was laden with Dunk's arms and armor, even his new old shield. *The Gallows Knight. What a dismal mystery knight I proved to be.* "I won't be long." He ducked his head and stooped to shoulder through the flap.

The tent's exterior left him ill prepared for the comforts he found within. The ground beneath his feet was carpeted in woven Myrish rugs, rich with color. An ornate trestle table stood surrounded by camp chairs. The featherbed was covered with soft cushions, and an iron brazier burned perfumed incense.

Ser Uthor sat at the table, a pile of gold and silver before him and a flagon of wine at his elbow, counting coins with his squire, a gawky fellow close in age to Dunk. From time to time the Snail would bite a coin, or set one aside. "I see I still have much to teach you, Will," Dunk heard him say. "This coin has been clipped, t'other shaved. And this one?" A gold piece danced across his fingers. "*Look* at the coins before taking them. Here, tell me what you see." The dragon spun through the air. Will tried to catch it, but it bounced off his fingers and fell to the ground. He had to get down on his knees to find it. When he did, he turned it over twice before saying, "This one's good, m'lord. There's a dragon on the one side and a king on t'other..."

Underleaf glanced toward Dunk. "The Hanged Man. It is good to see you moving about, ser. I feared I'd killed you. Will you do me a kindness and instruct my squire as to the nature of dragons? Will, give Ser Duncan the coin."

Dunk had no choice but to take it. *He unhorsed me, must he make me caper for him too?* Frowning, he hefted the coin in his palm, examined both sides, tasted it. "Gold, not shaved nor clipped. The weight feels right. I'd have taken it too, m'lord. What's wrong with it?"

"The king."

Dunk took a closer look. The face on the coin was young, clean-shaved, handsome. King Aerys was bearded on his coins, the same as old King Aegon. King Daeron, who'd come between them, had been clean-shaved, but this wasn't him. The coin did not appear worn enough to be from before Aegon the Unworthy. Dunk scowled at the word beneath the head. *Six letters.* They looked the same as he had seen on other dragons. *Daeron*, the letters read, but Dunk knew the face of Daeron the Good, and this wasn't him. When he looked again, he saw something odd about the shape of the fourth letter, it wasn't... "*Daemon*," he blurted out. "It says *Daemon*. There never was any King Daemon, though, only—"

"—the pretender. Daemon Blackfyre struck his own coinage during his rebellion."

"It's gold, though," Will argued. "If it's gold, it should be just as good as them other dragons, m'lord."

The Snail clouted him along the side of the head. "Cretin. Aye, it's gold. Rebel's gold. Traitor's gold. It's treasonous to own such a coin, and twice as treasonous to pass it. I'll need to have this melted down." He hit the man again. "Get out of my sight. This good knight and I have matters to discuss."

Will wasted no time in scrambling from the tent. "Have a seat," Ser Uthor said politely. "Will you take wine?" Here in his own tent, Underleaf seemed a different man than at the feast.

A snail hides in his shell, Dunk remembered. "Thank you, no." He flicked the gold coin back to Ser Uthor. Traitor's gold. Blackfyre gold. *Egg said this was a traitor's tourney, but I would not listen. He owed the boy an apology.*

"Half a cup," Underleaf insisted. "You sound in need of it." He filled two cups with wine, and handed one to Dunk. Out of his armor, he looked more a merchant than a knight. "You've come about the forfeit, I assume."

"Aye." Dunk took the wine. Maybe it would help to stop his head from pounding. "I brought my horse, and my arms and armor. Take them, with my compliments."

Ser Uthor smiled. "And this is where I tell you that you rode a gallant course."

Dunk wondered if *gallant* was a chivalrous way of saying *clumsy*. "That is good of you to say, but—"

"I think you misheard me, ser. Would it be too bold of me to ask how you came to knighthood, ser?"

"Ser Arlan of Pennytree found me in Flea Bottom, chasing pigs. His old squire had been slain on the Redgrass Field, so he needed someone to tend his mount and clean his mail. He promised he would teach me sword and lance and how to ride a horse if I would come and serve him, so I did."

"A charming tale...though if I were you I would leave out the part about the pigs. Pray, where is your Ser Arlan now?"

"He died. I buried him."

"I see. Did you take him home to Pennytree?"

"I didn't know where it was." Dunk had never seen the old man's Pennytree. Ser Arlan seldom spoke of it, no more than Dunk was wont to speak of Flea Bottom. "I buried him on a hillside facing west, so he could see the sun go down." The camp chair creaked alarmingly beneath his weight.

Ser Uthor resumed his seat. "I have my own armor, and a better horse than yours. What do I want with some old done nag and a sack of dinted plate and rusty mail?"

"Steely Pate made that armor," Dunk said, with a touch of anger. "Egg has taken good care of it. There's not a spot of rust on my mail, and the steel is good and strong."

"Strong and heavy," Ser Uthor complained, "and too big for any man of normal size. You are uncommon large, Duncan the Tall. As for your horse, he is too old to ride and too stringy to eat."

"Thunder is not as young as he used to be," Dunk admitted, "and my armor is large, as you say. You could sell it, though. In Lannisport and King's Landing there are plenty of smiths who will take it off your hands."

"For a tenth of what it's worth, perhaps," said Ser Uthor, "and only to melt down for the metal. No. It's sweet silver I require, not old iron. The coin of the realm. Now, do you wish to ransom back your arms, or no?"

Dunk turned the wine cup in his hands, frowning. It was solid silver, with a line of golden snails inlaid around the lip. The wine was gold as well, and heady on the tongue. "If wishes were fishes, aye, I'd pay. Gladly. Only—"

"—you don't have two stags to lock horns."

"If you would...would lend my horse and armor back to me, I could pay the ransom later. Once I found the coin."

The Snail looked amused. "Where would you find it, pray?"

"I could take service with some lord, or..." It was hard to get the words out. They made him feel a beggar. "It might take a few years, but I would pay you. I swear it."

"On your honor as a knight?"

Dunk flushed. "I could make my mark upon a parchment."

"A hedge knight's scratch upon a scrap of paper?" Ser Uthor rolled his eyes. "Good to wipe my arse. No more."

"You are a hedge knight too."

"Now you insult me. I ride where I will and serve no man but myself, true...but it has been many a year since I last slept beneath a hedge. I find that inns are far more comfortable. I am a *tourney* knight, the best that you are ever like to meet."

"The best?" His arrogance made Dunk angry. "The Laughing Storm might not agree, ser. Nor Leo Longthorn, nor the Brute of Bracken. At Ashford Meadow no one spoke of snails. Why is that, if you're such a famous tourney champion?"

"Have you heard me name myself a champion? That way lies renown. I would sooner have the pox. Thank you, but no. I shall win my next joust, aye, but in the final I shall fall. Butterwell has thirty dragons for the knight who comes second, that shall suffice for me...along with some goodly ransoms and the proceeds of my wagers." He gestured at the piles of silver stags and golden dragons on the table. "You seem a healthy fellow, and very large. Size will always impress the fools, though it means little and less in jousting. Will was able to get odds of three to one against me. Lord Shawney gave five to one, the fool." He picked up a silver stag and set it to spinning with a flick of his long fingers. "The Old Ox will be the next to tumble. Then the Knight of the Pussywillows, if he survives that long. Sentiment being what it is, I should get fine odds against them both. The commons love their village heroes."

"Ser Glendon has hero's blood," Dunk blurted out.

"Oh, I do hope so. Hero's blood should be good for two to one. Whore's blood draws poorer odds. Ser Glendon speaks about his purported sire at every opportunity, but have you noticed that he never makes mention of his mother? For good reason. He was born of a camp follower. Jenny, her name was. Penny Jenny, they called her, until the Redgrass Field. The night before the battle, she fucked so many men that thereafter she was known as Redgrass Jenny. Fireball had her, I don't doubt, but so did a hundred other men. Our friend Glendon presumes quite a lot, it seems to me. He does not even have red hair."

Hero's blood, thought Dunk. "He says he is a knight."

"Oh, that much is true. The boy and his sister grew up in a brothel, called the Pussywillows. After Penny Jenny died, the other whores took care of them and fed the lad the tale his mother had concocted, about him being Fireball's seed. An old squire who lived nearby gave the boy his training, such that it was, in trade for ale and cunt, but being but a squire he could not knight the little bastard. Half a year ago, however, a party of knights chanced upon the brothel and a certain Ser Morgan Dunstable took a drunken fancy to Ser Glendon's sister. As it happens, the sister was still virgin and Dunstable did not have the price of her maidenhead. So a bargain was struck. Ser Morgan dubbed her brother a knight, right there in the Pussywillows in front of twenty witnesses, and afterward little sister took him upstairs and let him pluck her flower. And there you are."

Any knight could make a knight. When he was squiring for Ser Arlan, Dunk had heard tales of other men who'd bought their knighthood with a kindness or a threat or a bag of silver coins, but never with a sister's maidenhead. "That's just a tale," he heard himself say. "That can't be true."

"I had it from Kirby Pimm, who claims that he was there, a witness to the knighting." Ser Uthor shrugged. "Hero's son, whore's son, or both, when he faces me the boy will fall."

"The lots may give you some other foe."

Ser Uthor arched an eyebrow. "Cosgrove is as fond of silver as the next man. I promise you, I shall draw the Old Ox next, then the boy. Would you care to wager on it?"

"I have nothing left to wager." Dunk did not know what distressed him more: learning that the Snail was bribing the master of the games to get the pairings he desired, or realizing the man had desired *him*. He stood. "I have said what I came to say. My horse and sword are yours, and all my armor."

The Snail steepled his fingers. "Perhaps there is another way. You are not entirely without your talents. You fall most splendidly." Ser Uthor's lips glistened when he smiled. "I will lend you back your steed and armor...if you enter my service."

"Service?" Dunk did not understand. "What sort of service? You have a squire. Do you need to garrison some castle?"

"I might, if I had a castle. If truth be told I prefer a good inn. Castles cost too much to maintain. No, the service I would require of you is that you face me in a few more tourneys. Twenty should suffice. You can do that, surely? You shall have a tenth part of my winnings, and in future I promise to strike that broad chest of yours and not your head."

"You'd have me travel about with you to be unhorsed?"

Ser Uthor chuckled pleasantly. "You are such a strapping specimen, no one will ever believe that some round-shouldered old man with a snail on his shield could put you down." He rubbed his chin. "You need a new device yourself, by the way. That hanged man is grim enough, I grant you, but...Well, he's *hanging*, isn't he? Dead and defeated. Something fiercer is required. A bear's head, mayhaps. A skull. Or three skulls, better still. A babe impaled upon a spear. And you should let your hair grow long and cultivate a beard, the wilder and more unkempt the better. There are more of these little tourneys than you know. With the odds I'd get we'd win enough to buy a dragon's egg before—"

"—it got about that I was hopeless? I lost my armor, not my honor. You'll have Thunder and my arms, no more."

"Pride ill becomes a beggar, ser. You could do much worse than ride with me. At the least I could teach you a thing or two of jousting, about which you are pig ignorant at present."

"You'd make a fool of me."

"I did that earlier. And even fools must eat."

Dunk wanted to smash that smile off his face. "I see why you have a snail on your shield. You are no true knight."

"Spoken like a true oaf. Are you so blind you cannot see your danger?" Ser Uthor put his cup aside. "Do you know why I struck you where I did, ser?" He got to his feet, and touched Dunk lightly in the center of his chest. "A coronal placed here would have put you on the ground just as quickly. The head is a smaller target, the blow is more difficult to land... though more likely to be mortal. I was paid to strike you there."

"Paid?" Dunk backed away from him. "What do you mean?"

"Six dragons tendered in advance, four more promised when you died. A paltry sum for a knight's life. Be thankful for that. Had more been offered, I might have put the point of my lance through your eye slit."

Dunk felt dizzy again. *Why would someone pay to have me killed? I've done no harm to any man at Whitewalls.* Surely no one hated him that much but Egg's brother Aerion, and the Bright Prince was in exile across the narrow sea. "Who paid you?"

"A serving man brought the gold at sunrise, not long after the master of the games nailed up the pairings. His face was hooded, and he did not speak his master's name."

"But why?" said Dunk.

"I did not ask." Ser Uthor filled his cup again. "I think you have more enemies than you know, Ser Duncan. How not? There are some who would say you were the cause of all our woes."

Dunk felt a cold hand on his heart. "Say what you mean."

The Snail shrugged. "I may not have been at Ashford Meadow, but jousting is my bread and salt. I follow tourneys from afar as faithfully as the maesters follow stars. I know how a certain hedge knight became the cause of a Trial of Seven at Ashford Meadow, resulting in the death of Baelor Breakspear at his brother Maekar's hand." Ser Uthor seated himself, and stretched his legs out. "Prince Baelor was well loved. The Bright Prince had friends as well, friends who will not have forgotten the cause of his exile. Think on my offer, ser. The snail may leave a trail of slime behind him, but a little slime will do a man no harm...but if you dance with dragons, you must expect to burn."

——✦——

The day seemed darker when Dunk stepped from the Snail's tent. The clouds in the east had grown bigger and blacker, and the sun was sinking to the west, casting long shadows across the yard. Dunk found the squire Will inspecting Thunder's feet.

"Where's Egg?" he asked of him.

"The bald boy? How would I know? Run off somewhere."

He could not bear to say farewell to Thunder, Dunk decided. He'll be back at the tent with his books.

He wasn't, though. The books were there, bundled neatly in a stack beside Egg's bedroll, but of the boy there was no sign. Something was wrong here. Dunk could feel it. It was not like Egg to wander off without his leave.

A pair of grizzled men-at-arms were drinking barley beer outside a striped pavilion a few feet away. "....well, bugger that, once was enough for me," one muttered. "The grass was green when the sun come up, aye..." He broke off when the other man gave him a nudge, and only then took note of Dunk. "Ser?"

"Have you seen my squire? Egg, he's called."

The man scratched at the gray stubble underneath one ear. "I remember him. Less hair than me, and a mouth three times his size. Some o' the other lads shoved him about a bit, but that was last night. I've not seen him since, ser."

"Scared him off," said his companion.

Dunk gave that one a hard look. "If he comes back, tell him to wait for me here."

"Aye, ser. That we will."

Might be he just went to watch the jousts. Dunk headed back toward the tilting grounds. As he passed the stables he came on Ser Glendon Ball, brushing down a pretty sorrel charger. "Have you seen Egg?" he asked him.

"He ran past a few moments ago." Ser Glendon pulled a carrot from his pocket and fed it to the sorrel. "Do you like my new horse? Lord Costayne sent his squire to ransom her, but I told him to save his gold. I mean to keep her for my own."

"His lordship will not like that."

"His lordship said that I had no right to put a fireball upon my shield. He told me my device should be a clump of pussywillows. His lordship can go bugger himself."

Dunk could not help but smile. He had supped at that same table himself, choking down the same bitter dishes as served up by the likes of the Bright Prince and Ser Steffon Fossoway. He felt a certain kinship with the prickly young knight. *For all I know, my mother was a whore as well.* "How many horses have you won?"

Ser Glendon shrugged. "I lost count. Mortimer Boggs still owes me one. He said he'd rather eat his horse than have some whore's bastard riding her. And he took a hammer to his armor before sending it to me. It's full of holes. I suppose I can still get something for the metal." He sounded more sad than angry. "There was a stable by the...the inn where I was raised. I worked there when I was a boy, and when I could I'd sneak the horses off while their owners were busy. I was always good with horses. Stots, rounseys, palfreys, drays, plough horses, war horses, I rode them all. Even a Dornish sand steed. This old man I knew taught me how to make my own lances. I thought if I showed them all how good I was, they'd have no choice but to admit I was my father's son. But they won't. Even now. They just won't."

"Some never will," Dunk told him. "It doesn't matter what you do. Others, though...they're not all the same. I've met some good ones." He thought a moment. "When the tourney's done, Egg and I mean to go north. Take service at Winterfell, and fight for the Starks against the ironmen. You could come with us." The north was a world all its own, Ser Arlan always said. *No one up there was like to know the tale of Penny Jenny and the Knight of the Pussywillows. No one will laugh at you up there. They will know you only by your blade, and judge you by your worth.*

Ser Glendon gave him a suspicious look. "Why would I want to do that? Are you telling me I need to run away and hide?"

"No. I just thought...two swords instead of one. The roads are not as safe as they once were."

"That's true enough," the boy said grudgingly, "but my father was once promised a place amongst the Kingsguard. I mean to claim the white cloak that he never got to wear."

You have as much chance of wearing a white cloak as I do, Dunk almost said. *You were born of a camp follower, and I crawled out of the gutters of Flea Bottom. Kings do not heap honor on the likes of you and me.* The lad would not have taken kindly to that truth, however. Instead he said, "Strength to your arm, then."

He had not gone more than a few feet when Ser Glendon called after him. "Ser Duncan, wait....I should not have been so sharp. A knight must needs be courteous, my mother used to say." The boy seemed to be struggling for words. "Lord Peake came to see me, after my last joust. He offered me a place at Starpike. He said there was a storm coming the likes of which Westeros had not seen for a generation, that he would need swords and men to wield them. Loyal men, who knew how to obey."

Dunk could hardly believe it. Gormon Peake had made his scorn for hedge knights plain, both on the road and on the roof, but the offer was a generous one. "Peake is a great lord," he said, wary, "but...but not a man that I would trust, I think."

"No." The boy flushed. "There was a price. He'd take me into his service, he said...but first I would have to prove my loyalty. He would see that I was paired against his friend the Fiddler next, and he wanted me to swear that I would lose."

Dunk believed him. He should have been shocked, he knew, and yet somehow he wasn't. "What did you say?"

"I said I might not be able to lose to the Fiddler even if I were trying, that I had already unhorsed much better men than him, that the dragon's egg would be mine before the day was done." Ball smiled feebly. "It was not the answer that he wanted. He called me a fool, then, and told me that I had best watch my back. The Fiddler had many friends, he said, and I had none."

Dunk put a hand upon his shoulder, and squeezed. "You have one, ser. Two, once I find Egg."

The boy looked him in the eye, and nodded. "It is good to know there are some true knights still."

Dunk got his first good look at Ser Tommard Heddle whilst searching for Egg amongst the crowds about the lists. Heavy-set and broad, with a chest like a barrel, Lord Butterwell's good-son wore black plate over boiled leather, and an ornate helm fashioned in the likeness of some demon, scaled and slavering. His horse was three hands taller than Thunder and two stone heavier, a monster of a beast armored in a coat of ringmail. The weight of all that iron made him slow, so Heddle never got up past a canter when the course was run; but that did not prevent him making short work of Ser Clarence Charlton. As Charlton was borne from the field upon a litter, Heddle removed his demonic helm. His head was broad and bald, his beard black and square. Angry red boils festered on his cheek and neck.

Dunk knew that face. Heddle was the knight who'd growled at him in the bedchamber when he touched the dragon's egg, the man with the deep voice that he'd heard talking with Lord Peake.

A jumble of words came rushing back to him...beggar's feast you've laid before us...is the boy his father's son...Bittersteel...need the sword... Old Milkblood expects...is the boy his father's son...I promise you, Bloodraven is not off dreaming...is the boy his father's son?

He stared at the viewing stand, wondering if somehow Egg had contrived to take his rightful place amongst the notables. There was no sign of the boy, however. Butterwell and Frey were missing too, though Butterwell's wife was still in her seat, looking bored and restive. That's queer, Dunk reflected. This was Butterwell's castle, his wedding, and Frey was father to his bride. These jousts were in their honor. Where would they have gone?

"Ser Uthor Underleaf," the herald boomed. A shadow crept across Dunk's face as the sun was swallowed by a cloud. "Ser Theomore of House Bulwer, the Old Ox, a knight of Blackcrown. Come forth and prove your valor."

The Old Ox made a fearsome sight in his blood-red armor, with black bull's horns rising from his helm. He needed the help of a brawny squire to get onto his horse, though, and the way his head was always turning as he rode suggested that Ser Maynard had been right about his eye. Still, the man received a lusty cheer as he took the field.

Not so the Snail, no doubt just as he preferred. On the first pass, both knights struck glancing blows. On the second, the Old Ox snapped his lance on Ser Uthor's shield, while the Snail's blow missed entirely. The same thing happened on the third pass, and this time Ser Uthor swayed as if about to fall. *He is feigning*, Dunk realized. *He is drawing the contest out to fatten the odds for next time. He had only to glance around to see Will at work, making wagers for his master. Only then did it occur to him that he might have fattened his own purse with a coin or two upon the Snail. Dunk the lunk, thick as a castle wall.*

The Old Ox fell on the fifth pass, knocked sideways by a coronal that slipped deftly off his shield to take him in the chest. His foot tangled in his stirrup as he fell, and he was dragged forty yards across the field before his men could get his horse under control. Again the litter came out, to bear him to the maester. A few drops of rain began to fall as Bulwer was carried away, darkened his surcoat where they fell. Dunk watched without expression. He was thinking about Egg. *What if this secret enemy of mine has got his hands on him?* It made as much sense as anything else. *The boy is blameless. If someone has a quarrel with me, it should not be him who answers for it.*

Ser John the Fiddler was being armed for his next tilt when Dunk found him. No fewer than three squires were attending him, buckling on his armor and seeing to the trappings of his horse, whilst Lord Alyn Cockshaw sat nearby drinking watered wine and looking bruised and peevish. When he caught sight of Dunk, Lord Alyn sputtered, dribbling wine upon on his chest. "How is it that you're still walking about? The Snail stove your face in."

"Steely Pate made me a good strong helm, m'lord. And my head is hard as stone, Ser Arlan used to say."

The Fiddler laughed. "Pay no mind to Alyn. Fireball's bastard knocked him off his horse onto that plump little rump of his, so now he has decided that he hates all hedge knights."

"That wretched pimpled creature is no son of Quentyn Ball," insisted Alyn Cockshaw. "He should never have been allowed to compete. If this were my wedding, I should have had him whipped for his presumption."

"What maid would marry you?" Ser John said. "And Ball's presumption is a deal less grating than your pouting. Ser Duncan, are you perchance a friend of Galtry the Green? I must shortly part him from his horse."

Dunk did not doubt it. "I do not know the man, m'lord."

"Will you take a cup of wine? Some bread and olives?"

"Only a word, m'lord."

"You may have all the words you wish. Let us adjourn to my pavilion." The Fiddler held the flap for him. "Not you, Alyn. You could do with a few less olives, if truth be told."

Inside, the Fiddler turned back to Dunk. "I knew Ser Uthor had not killed you. My dreams are never wrong. And the Snail must face me soon enough. Once I've unhorsed him, I shall demand your arms and armor back. Your destrier as well, though you deserve a better mount. Will you take one as my gift?"

"I...no...I couldn't do that." The thought made Dunk uncomfortable. "I do not mean to be ungrateful, but..."

"If it is the debt that troubles you, put the thought from your mind. I do not need your silver, ser. Only your friendship. How can you be one of my knights without a horse?" Ser John drew on his gauntlets of lobstered steel and flexed his fingers.

"My squire is missing."

"Ran off with a girl, perhaps?"

"Egg's too young for girls, m'lord. He would never leave me of his own will. Even if I were dying, he would stay until my corpse was cold. His horse is still here. So is our mule."

"If you like, I could ask my men to look for him."

My men. Dunk did not like the sound of that. *A tourney for traitors,* he thought. "You are no hedge knight."

"No." The Fiddler's smile was full of boyish charm. "But you knew that from the start. You have been calling me m'lord since we met upon the road, why is that?"

"The way you talk. The way you look. The way you act." *Dunk the lunk, thick as a castle wall.* "Up on the roof last night, you said some things..."

"Wine makes me talk too much, but I meant every word. We belong together, you and I. My dreams do not lie."

"Your dreams don't lie," said Dunk, "but you do. John is not your true name, is it?"

"No." The Fiddler's eyes sparkled with mischief.

He has Egg's eyes.

"His true name will be revealed soon enough, to those who need to know." Lord Gormon Peake had slipped into the pavilion, scowling. "Hedge knight, I warn you—"

"Oh, stop it, Gormy," said the Fiddler. "Ser Duncan is with us, or will be soon. I told you, I dreamed of him." Outside, a herald's trumpet blew. The Fiddler turned his head. "They are calling me to the lists. Pray excuse me, Ser Duncan. We can resume our talk after I dispose of Ser Galtry the Green."

"Strength to your arm," Dunk said. It was only courteous.

Lord Gormon remained after Ser John had gone. "His dreams will be the death of all of us."

"What did it take to buy Ser Galtry?" Dunk heard himself say. "Was silver sufficient, or does he require gold?"

"Someone has been talking, I see." Peake seated himself in a camp chair. "I have a dozen men outside. I ought to call them in and have them slit your throat, ser."

"Why don't you?"

"His Grace would take it ill."

His Grace. Dunk felt as though someone had punched him in the belly. Another black dragon, he thought. Another Blackfyre Rebellion. And soon another Redgrass Field. The grass was not red when the sun came up. "Why this wedding?"

"Lord Butterwell wanted a new young wife to warm his bed, and Lord Frey had a somewhat soiled daughter. Their nuptials provided a plausible pretext for some like-minded lords to gather. Most of those invited here fought for the black dragon once. The rest have reason to resent Bloodraven's rule, or nurse grievances and ambitions of their own. Many of us had sons and daughters taken to King's Landing to vouchsafe our future loyalty, but most of the hostages perished in the Great Spring Sickness. Our hands are no longer tied. Our time is come. Aerys is weak. A bookish man, and no warrior. The commons hardly know him, and what they know they do not like. His lords love him even less. His father was weak as well, that is true, but when his throne was threatened he had sons to take the field for him. Baelor and Maekar, the hammer and the anvil...but Baelor Breakspear is no more, and Prince Maekar sulks at Summerhall, at odds with king and Hand."

Aye, thought Dunk, and now some fool hedge knight has delivered his favorite son into the hands of his enemies. How better to ensure that the prince never stirs from Summerhall? "There is Bloodraven," he said. "He is not weak."

"No," Lord Peake allowed, "but no man loves a sorcerer, and kinslayers are accursed in the sight of gods and men. At the first sign of weakness or defeat, Bloodraven's men will melt away like summer snows. And if the dream the prince has dreamed comes true, and a living dragon comes forth here at Whitewalls..."

Dunk finished for him. "...the throne is yours."

"His," said Lord Gormon Peake. "I am but a humble servant." He rose. "Do not attempt to leave the castle, ser. If you do, I will take it as a proof of treachery, and you will answer with your life. We have gone too far to turn back now."

The leaden sky was spitting down rain in earnest as John the Fiddler and Ser Galtry the Green took up fresh lances at opposite ends of the lists. Some of the wedding guests were streaming off toward the great hall, huddled under cloaks.

Ser Galtry rode a white stallion. A drooping green plume adorned his helm, a matching plume his horse's crinet. His cloak was a patchwork of many squares of fabric, each a different shade of green. Gold inlay made his greaves and gauntlet glitter, and his shield showed nine jade mullets upon a leek green field. Even his beard was dyed green, in the fashion of the men of Tyrosh across the narrow sea.

Nine times he and the Fiddler charged with levelled lances, the green patchwork knight and the young lordling of the golden swords and fiddles, and nine times their lances shattered. By the eighth run, the ground had begun to soften, and big destriers splashed through pools of rainwater. On the ninth, the Fiddler almost lost his seat, but recovered before he fell. "Well struck," he called out, laughing. "You almost had me down, ser."

"Soon enough," the green knight shouted through the rain.

"No, I think not." The Fiddler tossed his splintered lance away, and a squire handed him a fresh one.

The next run was their last. Ser Galtry's lance scraped ineffectually off the Fiddler's shield, whilst Ser John's took the green knight squarely in the center of his chest and knocked him from his saddle, to land with a great brown splash. In the east Dunk saw the flash of distant lightning.

The viewing stands were emptying out quickly, as smallfolk and lordlings alike scrambled to get out of the wet. "See how they run," murmured Alyn Cockshaw, as he slid up beside Dunk. "A few drops of rain and all the bold lords go squealing for shelter. What will they do when the real storm breaks, I wonder?"

The real storm. Dunk knew Lord Alyn was not talking about the weather. *What does this one want? Has he suddenly decided to befriend me?*

The herald mounted his platform once again. "Ser Tommard Heddle, a knight of Whitewalls, in service to Lord Butterwell," he shouted, as thunder rumbled in the distance. "Ser Uthor Underleaf. Come forth and prove your valor."

Dunk glanced over at Ser Uthor in time to see the Snail's smile go sour. *This is not the match he paid for.* The master of the games had crossed him up, but why? *Someone else has taken a hand, someone Cosgrove esteems more than Uthor Underleaf.* Dunk chewed on that for a moment. *They do not know that Uthor does not mean to win*, he realized all at once. *They see him as a threat, so they mean for Black Tom to remove him from the Fiddler's path.* Heddle himself was part of Peake's conspiracy, he could be relied on to lose when the need arose. Which left no one but...

And suddenly Lord Peake himself was storming across the muddy field to climb the steps to the herald's platform, his cloak flapping behind him. "*We are betrayed*," he cried. "Bloodraven has a spy amongst us. The dragon's egg is stolen!"

Ser John the Fiddler wheeled his mount around. "My egg? How is that possible? Lord Butterwell keeps guards outside his bedchamber night and day."

"Slain," Lord Peake declared, "but one man named his killer before he died."

Does he mean to accuse me? Dunk wondered. A dozen men had seen him touch the dragon's egg last night, when he'd carried Lady Butterwell to her lord husband's bed.

Lord Gormon's finger stabbed down in accusation. "There he stands. The whore's son. Seize him."

At the far end of the lists, Ser Glendon Ball looked up in confusion. For a moment he did not appear to comprehend what was happening, until he saw men rushing at him from all directions. Then the boy moved more quickly than Dunk could have believed. He had his sword half out of its sheath when the first man threw an arm around his throat. Ball wrenched free of his grip, but by then two more of them were on him. They slammed into him and dragged him down into the mud. Other men swarmed over them, shouting and kicking. *That could have been me*, Dunk realized. He felt as helpless as he had at Ashford, the day they'd told him he must lose a hand and a foot.

Alyn Cockshaw pulled him back. "Stay out of this, you want to find that squire of yours."

Dunk turned on him. "What do you mean?"

"I may know where to find the boy."

"Where?" Dunk was in no mood for games.

At the far end of the field, Ser Glendon was yanked roughly back onto his feet, pinioned between two men-at-arms in mail and halfhelms. He was brown with mud from waist to ankle, and blood and rain washed down his cheeks. *Hero's blood*, thought Dunk, as Black Tom dismounted before the captive. "Where is the egg?"

Blood dribbled from Ball's mouth. "Why would I steal the egg? I was about to win it."

Aye, thought Dunk, and that they could not allow.

Black Tom slashed Ball across the face with a mailed fist. "Search his saddlebags," Lord Peake commanded. "We'll find the dragon's egg wrapped up and hidden, I'll wager."

Lord Alyn lowered his voice, "And so they will. Come with me if you want to find your squire. There's no better time than now, whilst they're all occupied." He did not wait for a reply.

Dunk had to follow. Three long strides brought him abreast of the lordling. "If you have done Egg any harm—"

"Boys are not to my taste. This way. Step lively now."

Through an archway, down a set of muddy steps, around a corner, Dunk stalked after him, splashing through puddles as the rain fell around them. They stayed close to the walls, cloaked in shadows, finally stopping in a closed courtyard where the paving stones were smooth and slick. Buildings pressed close on every side. Above were windows, closed and shuttered. In the center of the courtyard was a well, ringed with a low stone wall.

A lonely place, Dunk thought. He did not like the feel of it. Old instinct made him reach for his sword hilt, before he remembered that the Snail had won his sword. As he fumbled at his hip where his scabbard should have hung, he felt the point of a knife poke his lower back. "Turn on me, and I'll cut your kidney out and give it to Butterwell's cooks to fry up for the feast." The knife pushed in through the back of Dunk's jerkin, insistent. "Over to the well. No sudden moves, ser."

If he has thrown Egg down that well, he will need more than some little toy knife to save him. Dunk walked forward slowly. He could feel the anger growing in his belly.

The blade at his back vanished. "You may turn and face me now, hedge knight."

Dunk turned. "M'lord. Is this about the dragon's egg?"

"No. This is about the dragon. Did you think I would stand by and let you steal him?" Ser Alyn grimaced. "I should have known better than to trust that wretched Snail to kill you. I'll have my gold back, every coin."

Him? Dunk thought. *This plump, pasty-faced, perfumed lordling is my secret enemy?* He did not know whether to laugh or weep. "Ser Uthor earned his gold. I have a hard head, is all."

"So it seems. Back away."

Dunk took a step backwards.

"Again. Again. Once more."

Another step, and he was flush against the well. Its stones pressed against his lower back.

"Sit down on the rim. Not afraid of a little bath, are you? You cannot get much wetter than you are right now."

"I cannot swim." Dunk rested a hand on the well. The stones were wet. One moved beneath the pressure of his palm.

"What a shame. Will you jump, or must I prick you?"

Dunk glanced down. He could see the raindrops dimpling the water, a good twenty feet below. The walls were covered with a slime of algae. "I never did you any harm."

"And never will. Daemon's mine. I will command his Kingsguard. You are not worthy of a white cloak."

"I never claimed I was." *Daemon.* The name rang in Dunk's head. *Not John. Daemon, after his father. Dunk the lunk, thick as a castle wall.* "Daemon Blackfyre sired seven sons. Two died upon the Redgrass Field, twins..."

"Aegon and Aemon. Wretched witless bullies, just like you. When we were little, they took pleasure in tormenting me and Daemon both. I wept when Bittersteel carried him off to exile, and again when Lord Peake told me he was coming home. But then he saw you upon the road, and forgot that I existed." Cockshaw waved his dagger threateningly. "You can go into the water as you are, or you can go in bleeding. Which will it be?"

Dunk closed his hand around the loose stone. It proved to be less loose than he had hoped. Before he could wrench it free, Ser Alyn lunged. Dunk twisted sideways, so the point of the blade sliced through the meat of his shield arm. And then the stone popped free. Dunk fed it to his lordship, and felt his teeth crack beneath the blow.

"The well, is it?" He hit the lordling in the mouth again, then dropped the stone, seized Cockshaw by the wrist, and twisted until a bone snapped and the dagger clattered to the stones. "After you, m'lord." Sidestepping, Dunk yanked at the lordling's arm and planted a kick in the small of his back. Lord Alyn toppled headlong into the well. There was a splash.

"Well done, ser,"

Dunk whirled. Through the rain, all he could make out was a hooded shape and a single pale white eye. It was only when the man came forward that the shadowed face beneath the cowl took on the familiar features of Ser Maynard Plumm, the pale eye no more than the moonstone brooch that pinned his cloak at the shoulder.

Down in the well, Lord Alyn was thrashing and splashing and calling for help. "*Murder!* Someone help me."

"He tried to kill me," Dunk said.

"That would explain all the blood."

"Blood?" He looked down. His left arm from shoulder to elbow, his tunic clinging to his skin. "Oh."

Dunk did not remember falling, but suddenly he was on the ground, with raindrops running down his face. He could hear Lord Alyn whimpering from the well, but his splashing had grown feebler. "We need to have that arm bound up." Ser Maynard slipped his own arm under Dunk. "Up now. I cannot lift you by myself. Use your legs."

Dunk used his legs. "Lord Alyn. He's going to drown."

"He shan't be missed. Least of all by the Fiddler."

"He's not," Dunk gasped, pale with pain, "a fiddler."

"No. He is Daemon of House Blackfyre, the Second of His Name. Or so he would style himself, if ever he achieves the Iron Throne. You would be surprised to know how many lords prefer their kings brave and stupid. Daemon is young and dashing, and looks good on a horse."

The sounds from the well were almost too faint to hear. "Shouldn't we throw his lordship down a rope?"

"Save him now to execute him later? I think not. Let him eat the meal that he meant to serve to you. Come, lean on me." Plumm guided him across the yard. This close, there was something queer about the cast of Ser Maynard's features. The longer Dunk looked, the less he seemed to see. "I did urge you to flee, you will recall, but you esteemed your honor more than your life. An honorable death is well and good, but if the life at stake is not your own, what then? Would your answer be the same, ser?"

"Whose life?" From the well came one last splash. "Egg? Do you mean Egg?" Dunk clutched at Plumm's arm. "*Where is he?*"

"With the gods. And you will know why, I think."

The pain that twisted inside Dunk just then made him forget his arm. He groaned. "He tried to use the boot."

"So I surmise. He showed the ring to Maester Lothar, who delivered him to Butterwell, who no doubt pissed his breeches at the sight of it and started wondering if he had chosen the wrong side and how much Bloodraven knows of this conspiracy. The answer to that last is 'quite a lot.'" Plumm chuckled.

"Who are you?"

"A friend," said Maynard Plumm. "One who has been watching you, and wondering at your presence in this nest of adders. Now be quiet, until we get you mended."

Staying in the shadows, the two of them made their way back to Dunk's small tent. Once inside, Ser Maynard lit a fire, filled a bowl with wine, and set it on the flames to boil. "A clean cut, and at least it is not your sword arm," he said, slicing through the sleeve of Dunk's bloodstained tunic. "The thrust appears to have missed the bone. Still, we will need to wash it out, or you could lose the arm."

"It doesn't matter." Dunk's belly was roiling, and he felt as if he might retch at any moment. "If Egg is dead—"

"—you bear the blame. You should have kept him well away from here. I never said the boy was dead, though. I said that he was with the gods. Do you have clean linen? Silk?"

"My tunic. The good one I got in Dorne. What do you mean, he's with the gods?"

"In good time. Your arm first."

The wine soon began to steam. Ser Maynard found Dunk's good silk tunic, sniffed at it suspiciously, then slid out a dagger and began to cut it up. Dunk swallowed his protest.

"Ambrose Butterwell has never been what you might call decisive," Ser Maynard said, as he wadded up three strips of silk and dropped them in the wine. "He had doubts about this plot from the beginning, doubts that were inflamed when he learned that the boy did not bear the sword. And this morning his dragon's egg vanished, and with it the last dregs of his courage."

"Ser Glendon did not steal the egg," Dunk said. "He was in the yard all day, tilting or watching others tilt."

"Peake will find the egg in his saddlebags all the same." The wine was boiling. Plumm drew on a leather glove and said, "Try not to scream." Then he pulled a strip of silk out of the boiling wine, and began to wash the cut.

Dunk did not scream. He gnashed his teeth and bit his tongue and smashed his fist against his thigh hard enough to leave bruises, but he did not scream. Ser Maynard used the rest of his good tunic to make a bandage, and tied it tight around his arm. "How does that feel?" he asked when he was done.

"Bloody awful." Dunk shivered. "*Where's Egg?*"

"With the gods. I told you."

Dunk reached up and wrapped his good hand around Plumm's neck. "Speak plain. I am sick of hints and winks. Tell me where to find the boy, or I will snap your bloody neck, friend or no."

"The sept. You would do well to go armed." Ser Maynard smiled. "Is that plain enough for you, Dunk?"

His first stop was Ser Uthor Underleaf's pavilion.

When Dunk slipped inside, he found only the squire Will bent over a washtub, scrubbing out his master's smallclothes. "You again? Ser Uthor is at the feast. What do you want?"

"My sword and shield."

"Have you brought the ransom?"

"No."

"Then why would I let you take your arms?"

"I have need of them."

"That's no good reason."

"How about, try and stop me and I'll kill you."

Will gaped. "They're over there."

Dunk paused outside the castle sept. *Gods grant I am not too late.* His sword-belt was back in its accustomed place, cinched tight about his waist. He had strapped the gallows shield to his wounded arm, and the weight of it was sending throbs of pain through him with every step. If anyone brushed up against him, he feared that he might scream. He pushed the doors open with his good hand.

Within, the sept was dim and hushed, lit only by the candles that twinkled on the altars of the Seven. The Warrior had the most candles burning, as might be expected during a tourney; many a knight would have come here to pray for strength and courage before they chanced the lists. The Stranger's altar was shrouded in shadow, with but a single candle burning. The Mother and the Father each had dozens, the Smith and Maiden somewhat fewer. And beneath the shining lantern of the Crone knelt Lord Ambrose Butterwell, head bowed, praying silently for wisdom.

He was not alone. No sooner had Dunk started for him than two men-at-arms moved to cut him off, faces stern beneath their halfhelms. Both wore mail, beneath surcoats striped in the green, white, and yellow undy of House Butterwell. "Hold, ser," one said. "You have no business here."

"Yes, he does. I *warned* you he would find me."

The voice was Egg's.

When he stepped out from the shadows beneath the Father, his shaved head shining in the candlelight, Dunk almost rushed to the boy, to pluck him up with a glad cry and crush him in his arms. Something in Egg's tone made him hesitate. *He sounds more angry than afraid, and I have never seen him look so stern. And Butterwell on his knees. Something is queer here.*

Lord Butterwell pushed himself back to his feet. Even in the dim light of the candles, his flesh looked pale and clammy. "Let him pass," he told his guardsmen. When they stepped back, he beckoned Dunk closer. "I have done the boy no harm. I knew his father well, when I was the King's Hand. Prince Maekar needs to know, none of this was my idea."

"He shall," Dunk promised. *What is happening here?*

"Peake. This was all his doing, I swear it by the Seven." Lord Butterwell put one hand on the altar. "May the gods strike me down if I am false. He told me who I must invite and who must be excluded, and he brought this boy pretender here. I never wanted to be part of any treason, you must believe me. Tom Heddle now, he urged me on, I will not deny it. My good-son, married to my eldest daughter, but I will not lie, he was part of this."

"He is your champion," said Egg. "If he was in this, so were you."

Be quiet, Dunk wanted to roar. *That loose tongue of yours will get us killed.* Yet Butterwell seemed to quail. "My lord, you do not understand. Heddle commands my garrison."

"You must have some loyal guardsmen," said Egg.

"These men here," Lord Butterwell said. "A few more. I've been too lax, I will allow, but I have never been a traitor. Frey and I harbored doubts about Lord Peake's pretender since the beginning. *He does not bear the sword!* If he were his father's son, Bittersteel would have armed him with Blackfyre. And all this talk about a dragon...madness, madness and folly." His lordship dabbed the sweat from his face with his sleeve. "And now they have taken the egg, the dragon's egg my grandsire had from the king himself as a reward for leal service. It was there this morning when I woke, and my guards swear no one entered or left the bedchamber. It may be that Lord Peake bought them, I cannot say, but *the egg is gone.* They must have it, or else..."

Or else the dragon's hatched, thought Dunk. If a living dragon appeared again in Westeros, the lords and smallfolk alike would flock to whichever prince could lay claim to it. "My lord," he said, "a word with my...my squire, if you would be so good."

"As you wish, ser." Lord Butterwell knelt to pray again.

Dunk drew Egg aside, and went down upon one knee to speak with him face to face. "I am going to clout you in the ear so hard your head will turn around backwards, and you'll spend the rest of your life looking at where you've been."

"You should, ser." Egg had the grace to look abashed. "I'm sorry. I just meant to send a raven to my father."

So I could stay a knight. The boy meant well. Dunk glanced over to where Butterwell was praying. "What did you do to him?"

"Scared him, ser."

"Aye, I can see that. He'll have scabs on his knees before the night is done."

"I didn't know what else to do, ser. The maester brought me to them, once he saw my father's ring."

"Them?"

"Lord Butterwell and Lord Frey, ser. Some guards were there as well. Everyone was upset. Someone stole the dragon's egg."

"Not you, I hope?"

Egg shook his head. "No, ser. I knew I was in trouble when the maester showed Lord Butterwell my ring. I thought about saying that I'd stolen it, but I didn't think he would believe me. Then I remembered this one time I heard my father talking about something Lord Bloodraven said, about how it was better to be frightening than frightened, so I told them that my father had sent us here to spy for him, that he was on his way here with an army, that his lordship had best release me and give up this treason, or it would mean his head." He smiled a shy smile. "It worked better than I thought it would, ser."

Dunk wanted to take the boy by the shoulders and shake him until his teeth rattled. *This is no game, he might have roared. This is life and death.* "Did Lord Frey hear all this as well?"

"Yes. He wished Lord Butterwell happiness in his marriage and announced that he was returning to the Twins forthwith. That was when his lordship brought us here to pray."

Frey could flee, Dunk thought, but Butterwell does not have that option, and soon or late he will begin to wonder why Prince Maekar and his army have not turned up. "If Lord Peake should learn that you are in the castle—"

The sept's outer doors opened with a crash. Dunk turned to see Black Tom Heddle glowering in mail and plate, with rainwater dripping off his sodden cloak to puddle by his feet. A dozen men-at-arms stood with him, armed with spears and axes. Lightning flashed blue and white across the sky behind them, etching sudden shadows across the pale stone floor. A gust of wet wind set all the candles in the sept to dancing.

Oh, seven bloody hells was all that Dunk had time enough to think before Heddle said, "There's the boy. Take him."

Lord Butterwell had risen to his feet. "No. Halt. The boy's not to be molested. Tommard, what is the meaning of this?"

Heddle's face twisted in contempt. "Not all of us have milk running in our veins, your lordship. I'll have the boy."

"You do not understand." Butterwell's voice had turned into a high thin quaver. "We are undone. Lord Frey is gone, and others will follow. Prince Maekar is coming with an army."

"All the more reason to take the boy as hostage."

"No, no," said Butterwell, "I want no more part of Lord Peake or his pretender. I will not fight."

Black Tom looked coldly at his lord. "Craven." He spat. "Say what you will. You'll fight or die, my lord." He pointed at Egg. "A stag to first man to draw blood."

"No, no." Butterwell turned to his own guards. "Stop them, do you hear me? I command you. Stop them." But all the guards had halted in confusion, at a loss as to who they should obey.

"Must I do it myself, then?" Black Tom drew his longsword.

Dunk did the same. "Behind me, Egg."

"Put up your steel, the both of you!" Butterwell screeched. "I'll have no bloodshed in the sept! Ser Tommard, this man is the prince's sworn shield. He'll kill you!"

"Only if he falls on me." Black Tom showed his teeth in a hard grin. "I saw him try to joust."

"I am better with a sword," Dunk warned him.

Heddle answered with a snort, and charged.

Dunk shoved Egg roughly backwards and turned to meet his blade. He blocked the first cut well enough, but the jolt of Black Tom's sword biting into his shield and the bandaged cut behind it sent a jolt of pain crackling up his arm. He tried a slash at Heddle's head in answer, but Black Tom slid away from it and hacked at him again. Dunk barely got his shield around in time. Pine chips flew and Heddle laughed, pressing his attack, low and high and low again. Dunk took each cut with his shield, but every blow was agony, and he found himself giving ground.

"Get him, ser," he heard Egg call. "Get him, get him, he's *right there*." The taste of blood was in Dunk's mouth, and worse, his wound had opened once again. A wave of dizziness washed over him. Black Tom's blade was turning the long kite shield to splinters. *Oak and iron guard me well, or else I'm dead and doomed to hell,* Dunk thought, before he remembered that this shield was made of pine. When his back came up hard against an altar, he stumbled to one knee, and realized he had no more ground left to give.

"You are no knight," said Black Tom. "Are those tears in your eyes, oaf?"

Tears of pain. Dunk pushed up off his knee, and slammed shield-first into his foe.

Black Tom stumbled backward, yet somehow kept his balance. Dunk bulled right after him, smashing him with the shield again and again, using his size and strength to knock Heddle halfway across the sept. Then he swung the shield aside and slashed out with his longsword, and Heddle screamed as the steel bit through wool and muscle deep into his thigh. His own sword swung wildly, but the blow was desperate and clumsy. Dunk let his shield take it one more time and put all his weight into his answer.

Black Tom reeled back a step and stared down in horror at his forearm flopping on the floor beneath the Stranger's altar. "You," he gasped, "you, you..."

"I told you." Dunk stabbed him through the throat. "I'm better with a sword."

Two of the men-at-arms fled back into the rain as a pool of blood spread out from Black Tom's body. The others clutched their spears and hesitated, casting wary glances toward Dunk as they waited for their lord to speak.

"This...this was ill done," Butterwell finally managed. He turned to Dunk and Egg. "We must be gone from Whitewalls before those two bring word of this to Gormon Peake. He has more friends amongst the

guests than I do. The postern gate in the north wall, we'll slip out there...
come, we must make haste."

Dunk slammed his sword into its scabbard. "Egg, go with Lord
Butterwell." He put an arm around the boy, and lowered his voice. "Don't
stay with him any longer than you need to. Give Rain his head and get
away before his lordship changes sides again. Make for Maidenpool, it's
closer than King's Landing."

"What about you, ser?"

"Never mind about me."

"I'm your squire."

"Aye," said Dunk, "and you'll do as I tell you, or you'll get a good clout
in the ear."

A group of men were leaving the great hall, pausing long enough to
pull up their hoods before venturing out into the rain. The Old Ox was
amongst them, and weedy Lord Caswell, once more in his cups. Both
gave Dunk a wide berth. Ser Mortimer Boggs favored him with a curious
stare, but thought better of speaking to him. Uthor Underleaf was not
so shy. "You come late to the feast, ser," he said, as he was pulling on his
gloves. "And I see you wear a sword again."

"You'll have your ransom for it, if that's all that concerns you." Dunk
had left his battered shield behind, and draped his cloak across his
wounded arm to hide the blood. "Unless I die. Then you have my leave
to loot my corpse."

Ser Uthor laughed. "Is that gallantry I smell, or just stupidity? The
two scents are much alike, as I recall. It is not too late to accept my offer,
ser."

"It is later than you think," Dunk warned him. He did not wait for
Underleaf to answer, but pushed past him, through the double doors.
The great hall smelled of ale and smoke and wet wool. In the gallery
above, a few musicians played softly. Laughter echoed from the high

tables, where Ser Kirby Pimm and Ser Lucas Nayland were playing a drinking game. Up on the dais, Lord Peake was speaking earnestly with Lord Costayne, while Ambrose Butterwell's new bride sat abandoned in her high seat.

Down below the salt, Dunk found Ser Kyle drowning his woes in Lord Butterwell's ale. His trencher was filled with a thick stew made with food left over from the night before. *A bowl o' brown*, they called such fare in the pot shops of King's Landing. Ser Kyle plainly had no stomach for it. Untouched, the stew had grown cold, and a film of grease glistened atop the brown.

Dunk slipped onto the bench beside him. "Ser Kyle."

The Cat nodded. "Ser Duncan. Will you have some ale?"

"No." Ale was the last thing that he needed.

"Are you unwell, ser? Forgive me, but you look—"

—better than I feel. "What was done with Glendon Ball?"

"They took him to the dungeons." Ser Kyle shook his head. "Whore's get or no, the boy never struck me as a thief."

"He isn't."

Ser Kyle squinted at him. "Your arm...how did..."

"A dagger." Dunk turned to face the dais, frowning. He had escaped death twice today. That would suffice for most men, he knew. *Dunk the lunk, thick as a castle wall*. He pushed to his feet. "Your Grace," he called.

A few men on nearby benches put down their spoons, broke off their conversations, and turned to look at him.

"*Your Grace*," Dunk said again, more loudly. He strode up the Myrish carpet toward the dais. "*Daemon*."

Now half the hall grew quiet. At the high table, the man who'd called himself the Fiddler turned to smile at him. He had donned a purple tunic for the feast, Dunk saw. *Purple, to bring out the color of his eyes*. "Ser Duncan. I am pleased that you are with us. What would you have of me?"

"Justice," said Dunk, "for Glendon Ball."

The name echoed off the walls, and for half a heartbeat it was if every man, woman, and boy in the hall had turned to stone. Then Lord Costayne slammed a fist upon a table and shouted, "It's death that one deserves, not justice." A dozen other voices echoed his, and Ser Harbert

Paege declared, "He's bastard born. All bastards are thieves, or worse. Blood will tell."

For a moment Dunk despaired. *I am alone here.* But then Ser Kyle the Cat pushed himself to his feet, swaying only slightly. "The boy may be a bastard, my lords, but he's *Fireball's* bastard. It's like Ser Harbert said. Blood will tell."

Daemon frowned. "No one honors Fireball more than I do," he said. "I will not believe this false knight is his seed. He stole the dragon's egg, and slew three good men in the doing."

"He stole nothing and killed no one," Dunk insisted. "If three men were slain, look elsewhere for their killer. Your Grace knows as well as I that Ser Glendon was in the yard all day, riding one tilt after t'other."

"Aye," Daemon admitted. "I wondered at that myself. But the dragon's egg was found amongst his things."

"Was it? Where is it now?"

Lord Gormon Peake rose cold-eyed and imperious. "Safe, and well guarded. And why is that any concern of yours, ser?"

"Bring it forth," said Dunk. "I'd like another look at it, m'lord. T'other night, I only saw it for a moment."

Peake's eyes narrowed. "Your Grace," he said to Daemon, "it comes to me that this hedge knight arrived at Whitewalls with Ser Glendon, uninvited. He may well be part of this."

Dunk ignored that. "Your Grace, the dragon's egg that Lord Peake found amongst Ser Glendon's things was the one he placed there. Let him bring it forth, if he can. Examine it yourself. I'll wager you it's no more than a painted stone."

The hall erupted into chaos. A hundred voices began to speak at once, and a dozen knights leapt to their feet. Daemon looked near as young and lost as Ser Glendon had when he had been accused. "Are you drunk, my friend?"

Would that I were. "I've lost some blood," Dunk allowed, "but not my wits. Ser Glendon has been wrongfully accused."

"Why?" Daemon demanded, baffled. "If Ball did no wrong, as you insist, why would his lordship say he did and try to prove it with some painted rock?"

"To remove him from your path. His lordship bought your other foes with gold and promises, but Ball was not for sale."

The Fiddler flushed. "That is not true."

"It is true. Send for Ser Glendon, and ask him yourself."

"I will do just that. Lord Peake, have the bastard fetched up at once. And bring the dragon's egg as well. I wish to have a closer look at it."

Gormon Peake gave Dunk a look of loathing. "Your Grace, the bastard boy is being questioned. A few more hours, and we will have a confession for you, I do not doubt."

"By *questioned*, m'lord means tortured," said Dunk. "A few more hours, and Ser Glendon will confess to having killed Your Grace's father, and both your brothers too."

"*Enough!*" Lord Peake's face was almost purple. "One more word, and I will rip your tongue out by the roots."

"You lie," said Dunk. "That's two words."

"And you will rue the both of them," Peake promised. "Take this man and chain him in the dungeons."

"No." Daemon's voice was dangerously quiet. "I want the truth of this. Sunderland, Vyrwel, Smallwood, take your men and go find Ser Glendon in the dungeons. Bring him up forthwith, and see that no harm comes to him. If any man should try and hinder you, tell him you are about the king's business."

"As you command," Lord Vyrwel answered.

"I will settle this as my father would," the Fiddler said. "Ser Glendon stands accused of grievous crimes. As a knight, he has a right to defend himself by strength of arms. I shall meet him in the lists, and let the gods determine guilt and innocence."

Hero's blood or whore's blood, Dunk thought, when two of Lord Vyrwel's men dumped Ser Glendon naked at his feet, *he has a deal less of it than he did before.*

The boy had been savagely beaten. His face was bruised and swollen, several of his teeth were cracked or missing, his right eye was weeping blood, and up and down his chest his flesh was red and cracking where they'd burned him with hot irons.

"You're safe now," murmured Ser Kyle. "There's no one here but hedge knights, and the gods know that we're a harmless lot." Daemon had given them the maester's chambers, and commanded them to dress any hurts Ser Glendon might have suffered and see that he was ready for the lists.

Three fingernails had been pulled from Ball's left hand, Dunk saw, as he washed the blood from the boy's face and hands. That worried him more than all the rest. "Can you hold a lance?"

"A lance?" Blood and spit dribbled from Ser Glendon's mouth when he tried to speak. "Do I have all my fingers?"

"Ten," said Dunk, "but only seven fingernails."

Ball nodded. "Black Tom was going to cut my fingers off, but he was called away. Is it him that I'm to fight?"

"No. I killed him."

That made him smile. "Someone had to."

"You're to tilt against the Fiddler, but his real name—"

"—is Daemon, aye. They told me. The Black Dragon." Ser Glendon laughed. "My father died for his. I would have been his man, and gladly. I would have fought for him, killed for him, died for him, but I could not lose for him." He turned his head, and spat out a broken tooth. "Could I have a cup of wine?"

"Ser Kyle, get the wineskin."

The boy drank long and deep, then wiped his mouth. "Look at me. I'm shaking like a girl."

Dunk frowned. "Can you still sit a horse?"

"Help me wash, and bring me my shield and lance and saddle," Ser Glendon said, "and you will see what I can do."

It was almost dawn before the rain let up enough for the combat to take place. The castle yard was a morass of soft mud, glistening wetly by the light of a hundred torches. Beyond the field a gray mist was rising, sending ghostly fingers up the pale stone walls to grasp the castle battlements. Many of the wedding guests had vanished during the intervening hours, but those who remained climbed the viewing stand again and settled themselves on planks of rain-soaked pine. Amongst them stood Ser Gormon Peake, surrounded by a knot of lesser lords and household knights.

It had only been a few years since Dunk had squired for old Ser Arlan. He had not forgotten how. He cinched the buckles on Ser Glendon's ill-fitting armor, fastened his helm to his gorget, helped him mount, and handed him his shield. Earlier contests had left deep gouges in the wood, but the blazing fireball could still be seen. *He looks as young as Egg,* Dunk thought. *A frightened boy, and grim. His sorrel mare was unbarded, and skittish as well. He should have stayed with his own mount. The sorrel may be better bred and swifter, but a rider rides best on a horse that he knows well, and this one is a stranger to him.*

"I'll need a lance," Ser Glendon said. "A war lance."

Dunk went to the racks. War lances were shorter and heavier than the tourney lances that had been used in all the earlier tilts; eight feet of solid ash ending in an iron point. Dunk chose one and pulled it out, running his hand along its length to make sure it had no cracks.

At the far end of the lists, one of Daemon's squires was offering him a matching lance. He was a fiddler no more. In place of swords and fiddles, the trapping of his warhorse now displayed the three-headed dragon of House Blackfyre, black on a field of red. The prince had washed the black dye from his hair as well, so it flowed down to his collar in a cascade of silver and gold that glimmered like beaten metal in the torchlight. *Egg would have hair like that if he ever let it grow,* Dunk realized. He found it hard to picture him that way, but one day he knew he must, if the two of them should live so long.

The herald climbed his platform once again. "Ser Glendon the Bastard stands accused of theft and murder," he proclaimed, "and now comes forth to prove his innocence at the hazard of his body. Daemon of House

Blackfyre, the Second of His Name, rightborn Kin of the Andals and the Rhoynar and the First Men, Lord of the Seven Kingdoms and Protector of the Realm, comes forth to prove the truth of the accusations against the bastard Glendon."

And all at once the year fell away, and Dunk was back at Ashford Meadow once again, listening to Baelor Breakspear just before they went forth to battle for his life. He slipped the war lance back in place, plucked a tourney lance from the next rack; twelve feet long, slender, elegant. "Use this," he told Ser Glendon. "It's what we used at Ashford, at the Trial of Seven."

"The Fiddler chose a war lance. He means to kill me."

"First he has to strike you. If your aim is true, his point will never touch you."

"I don't know."

"I do."

Ser Glendon snatched the lance from him, wheeled about, and trotted toward the lists. "Seven save us both, then."

Somewhere in the east, lightning cracked across a pale pink sky. Daemon raked his stallion's side with golden spurs, and leapt forward like a thunderclap, lowering his war lance with its deadly iron point. Ser Glendon raised his shield and raced to meet him, swinging his own longer lance across his mare's head to bear upon the young pretender's chest. Mud sprayed back from their horses' hooves, and the torches seemed to burn the brighter as the two knights went pounding past.

Dunk closed his eyes. He heard a *crack*, a shout, a thump. "No," he heard Lord Peake cry out, in anguish. "*Noooooo.*" For half a heartbeat, Dunk almost felt sorry for him. He opened his eyes again. Riderless, the big black stallion was slowing to a trot. Dunk jumped out and grabbed him by the reins. At the far end of the lists, Ser Glendon Ball wheeled his mare and raised his splintered lance. Men rushed onto the field, to where the Fiddler lay unmoving, face down in the mud. When they helped him to his feet, he was mud from head to heel.

"The Brown Dragon," someone shouted. Laughter rippled through the yard, as the dawn washed over Whitewalls.

It was only a few heartbeats later, as Dunk and Ser Kyle were helping

Glendon Ball off his horse, that the first trumpet blew, and the sentries on the walls raised the alarum. An army had appeared outside the castle, rising from the morning mists.

"Egg wasn't lying after all," Dunk told Ser Kyle, astonished.

From Maidenpool had come Lord Mooton, from Raventree Lord Blackwood, from Duskendale Lord Darklyn. The royal demesnes about King's Landing sent forth Hayfords, Rosbys, Stokeworths, Masseys, and the king's own sworn swords, led by three knights of the Kingsguard and stiffened by three hundred Raven's Teeth with tall white weirwood bows. Mad Danelle Lothston herself rode forth in strength from her haunted towers at Harrenhal, clad in black armor that fit her like an iron glove, her long red hair streaming.

The light of the rising sun glittered off the points of five hundred lances and ten times as many spears. The night's gray banners were reborn in half a hundred gaudy colors. And above them all flew two regal dragons on night-black fields: the great three-headed beast of King Aerys I Targaryen, red as fire, and a white winged fury breathing scarlet flame.

Not Maekar after all, Dunk knew, when he saw those banners. The banners of the Prince of Summerhall showed four three-headed dragons, two and two, the arms of the fourth-born son of the late King Daeron II Targaryen. A single white dragon announced the presence of the King's Hand, Lord Brynden Rivers.

Bloodraven himself had come to Whitewalls.

The First Blackfyre Rebellion had perished on the Redgrass Field in blood and glory. The Second Blackfyre Rebellion ended with a whimper. "They cannot cow us," Young Daemon proclaimed from the castle battlements, after he had seen the ring of iron that encircled them, "for our cause is just. We'll slash through them and ride hellbent for King's Landing! Sound the trumpets!"

Instead, knights and lords and men-at-arms muttered quietly to one another, and a few began to slink away, making for the stables or a postern gate or some hideyhole they hoped might keep them safe. And when Daemon drew his sword and raised it above his head, every man of them could see it was not Blackfyre. "We'll make another Redgrass Field today," the pretender promised.

"Piss on that, fiddle boy," a grizzled squire shouted back at him. "I'd sooner live."

In the end, the second Daemon Blackfyre rode forth alone, reined up before the royal host, and challenged Lord Bloodraven to single combat. "I will fight you, or the coward Aerys, or any champion you care to name." Instead, Lord Bloodraven's men surrounded him, pulled him off his horse, and clasped him into golden fetters. The banner he had carried was planted in the muddy ground and set afire. It burned for a long time, sending up a twisted plume of smoke that could be seen for leagues around.

The only blood that was shed that day came when a man in service to Lord Vyrwel began to boast he had been one of Bloodraven's eyes and would soon be well rewarded. "By the time the moon turns I'll be fucking whores and drinking Dornish red," he was purported to have said, just before one of Lord Costayne's knights slit his throat. "Drink that," he said, as Vyrwel's man drowned in his own blood. "It's not Dornish, but it's red."

Elsewise it was a sullen, silent column that trudged through the gates of Whitewalls to toss their weapons into a glittering pile before being bound and led away to await Lord Bloodraven's judgment. Dunk emerged with the rest of them, together with Ser Kyle the Cat and Glendon Ball. They had looked for Ser Maynard to join them, but Plumm had melted away sometime during the night.

It was late that afternoon before Ser Roland Crakehall of the Kingsguard found Dunk among the other prisoners. "Ser Duncan. Where in seven hells have you been hiding? Lord Rivers has been asking for you for hours. Come with me, if you please."

Dunk fell in beside him. Crakehall's long cloak flapped behind him with every gust of wind, as white as moonlight on snow. The sight of it made him think back on the words the Fiddler had spoken, up on the roof. *I dreamed that you were all in white from head to heel, with a long pale cloak flowing from those broad shoulders.* Dunk snorted. *Aye, and you dreamed of dragons hatching from stone eggs. One is likely as t'other.*

The Hand's pavilion was half a mile from the castle, in the shade of a spreading elm tree. A dozen cows were cropping at the grass nearby. *Kings rise and fall,* Dunk thought, *and cows and smallfolk go about their business.* It was something the old man used to say. "What will become of all of them?" he asked Ser Roland, as they passed a group of captives sitting on the grass.

"They'll be marched back to King's Landing for trial. The knights and men-at-arms should get off light enough. They were only following their liege lords."

"And the lords?"

"Some will be pardoned, so long as they tell the truth of what they know and give up a son or daughter to vouchsafe their future loyalty. It will go harder for those who took pardons after the Redgrass Field. They'll be imprisoned or attainted. The worst will lose their heads."

Bloodraven had made a start on that already, Dunk saw when they came up on his pavilion. Flanking the entrance, the severed heads of Gormon Peake and Black Tom Heddle had been impaled on spears, with their shields displayed beneath them. *Three castles, black on orange. The man who slew Roger of Pennytree.*

Even in death, Lord Gormon's eyes were hard and flinty. Dunk closed them with his fingers. "What did you do that for?" asked one of the guardsmen. "The crows'll have them soon enough."

"I owed him that much." If Roger had not died that day, the old man would never have looked twice at Dunk when he saw him chasing that pig through the alleys of King's Landing. *Some old dead king gave a sword to one son instead of another, that was the start of it. And now I'm standing here, and poor Roger's in his grave.*

"The Hand awaits," commanded Roland Crakehall.

Dunk stepped past him, into the presence of Lord Brynden Rivers, bastard, sorcerer, and Hand of the King.

Egg stood before him, freshly bathed and garbed in princely raiment, as would befit a nephew of the king. Nearby, Lord Frey was seated in a camp chair with a cup of wine to hand and his hideous little heir squirming in his lap. Lord Butterwell was there as well...on his knees, pale-faced and shaking.

"Treason is no less vile because the traitor proves a craven," Lord Rivers was saying. "I have heard your bleatings, Lord Ambrose, and I believe one word in ten. On that account I will allow you to retain a tenth part of your fortune. You may keep your wife as well. I wish you joy of her."

"And Whitewalls?" asked Butterwell, with quavering voice.

"Forfeit to the Iron Throne. I mean to pull it down stone by stone, and sow the ground that it stands upon with salt. In twenty years, no one will remember it existed. Old fools and young malcontents still make pilgrimages to the Redgrass Field to plant flowers on the spot where Daemon Blackfyre fell. I will not suffer Whitewalls to become another monument to the black dragon." He waved a pale hand. "Now scurry away, roach."

"The Hand is kind." Butterwell stumbled off, so blind with grief that he did not even seem to recognize Dunk as he passed. "You have my leave to go as well, Lord Frey," Rivers commanded. "We will speak again later."

"As my lord commands." Frey led his son from the pavilion.

Only then did the King's Hand turn to Dunk.

He was older than Dunk remembered him, with a lined hard face, but his skin was still as pale as bone, and his cheek and neck still bore the ugly winestain birthmark that some people thought looked like a raven. His boots were black, his tunic scarlet. Over it he wore a cloak the color of smoke, fastened with a brooch in the shape of an iron hand. His hair fell to his shoulders, long and white and straight, brushed forward so as to conceal his missing eye, the one that Bittersteel had plucked from him on the Redgrass Field. The eye that remained was very red. *How many eyes has Bloodraven? A hundred eyes, and one.*

"No doubt Prince Maekar had some good reason for allowing his son to squire for a hedge knight," he said, "though I cannot imagine it included delivering him to a castle full of traitors plotting rebellion. How is that I come to find my cousin in this nest of adders, ser? Lord Butterbutt would have me believe that Prince Maekar sent you here, to sniff out this rebellion in the guise of a mystery knight. Is that the truth of it?"

Dunk went to one knee. "No, m'lord. I mean, yes, m'lord. That's what Egg told him. Aegon, I mean. Prince Aegon. So that part's true. It isn't what you'd call the true truth, though."

"I see. So the two of you learned of this conspiracy against the crown and decided you would thwart it by yourselves, is that the way of it?"

"That's not it either. We just sort of...blundered into it, I suppose you'd say."

Egg crossed his arms. "And Ser Duncan and I had matters well in hand before you turned up with your army."

"We had some help, m'lord," Dunk added.

"Hedge knights."

"Aye, m'lord. Ser Kyle the Cat, and Maynard Plumm. And Ser Glendon Ball. It was him unhorsed the Fidd...the pretender."

"Yes, I've heard that tale from half a hundred lips already. The Bastard of the Pussywillows. Born of a whore and a traitor."

"Born of *heroes*," Egg insisted. "If he's amongst the captives, I want him found and released. And rewarded."

"And who are you to tell the King's Hand what to do?"

Egg did not flinch. "You know who I am, cousin."

"Your squire is insolent, ser," Lord Rivers said to Dunk. "You ought to beat that out of him."

"I've tried, m'lord. He's a prince, though."

"What he is," said Bloodraven, "is a *dragon*. Rise, ser."

Dunk rose.

"There have always been Targaryens who dreamed of things to come, since long before the Conquest," Bloodraven said, "so we should not be surprised if from time to time a Blackfyre displays the gift as well. Daemon dreamed that a dragon would be born at Whitewalls, and it was. The fool just got the color wrong." Dunk looked at Egg. *The ring*, he saw. *His father's ring. It's on his finger, not stuffed up inside his boot.*

"I have half a mind to take you back to King's Landing with us," Lord Rivers to Egg, "and keep you at court as my...guest."

"My father would not take kindly to that."

"I suppose not. Prince Maekar has a...prickly...nature. Perhaps I should send you back to Summerhall."

"My place is with Ser Duncan. I'm his squire."

"Seven save you both. As you wish. You're free to go."

"We will," said Egg, "but first we need some gold. Ser Duncan needs to pay the Snail his ransom."

Bloodraven laughed. "What happened to the modest boy I once met at King's Landing? As you say, my prince. I will instruct my paymaster to give you as much gold as you wish. Within reason."

"Only as a loan," insisted Dunk. "I'll pay it back."

"When you learn to joust, no doubt." Lord River flicked them away with his fingers, unrolled a parchment, and began to tick off names with a quill.

He is marking down the men to die, Dunk realized. "My lord," he said, "we saw the heads outside. Is that...will the Fiddler...Daemon...will you have his head as well?"

Lord Bloodraven looked up from his parchment. "That is for King Aerys to decide...but Daemon has four younger brothers, and sisters as well. Should I be so foolish as to remove his pretty head, his mother will mourn, his friends will curse me for a kinslayer, and Bittersteel will crown his brother Haegon. Dead, young Daemon is a hero. Alive, he is an obstacle in my half-brother's path. He can hardly make a third Blackfyre king whilst the second remains so inconveniently alive. Besides, such a noble captive will be an ornament to our court, and a living testament to the mercy and benevolence of His Grace King Aerys."

"I have a question too," said Egg.

"I begin to understand why your father was so willing to be rid of you. What more would you have of me, cousin?"

"Who took the dragon's egg? There were guards at the door, and more guards on the steps, no way anyone could have gotten into Lord Butterwell's bedchamber unobserved."

Lord Rivers smiled. "Were I to guess, I'd say someone climbed up inside the privy shaft."

"The privy shaft was too small to climb."

"For a man. A child could do it."

"Or a dwarf," Dunk blurted. A thousand eyes, and one. Why shouldn't some of them belong to a troupe of comic dwarfs?

Acknowledgements

Many thanks to the following:

Jacob Weisman and Jill Roberts, for publishing the book, and to the rest of the team at Tachyon Publications.

John Coulthart for the cover.

My agent, Joe Monti, for being awesome and supportive, and for finding homes for all of my projects. To any writers reading this: you'd be lucky to have Joe in your corner.

My editorial colleagues Scott Andrews, Douglas Cohen, Howard Andrew Jones, and John O'Neill, for their many recommendations, and to all of the people who entered suggestions into my epic fantasy recommendations database.

Peter Ahlstrom, Deborah Beale, Kathleen Bellamy, Blanche Brown, Fran Bryson, Kristine Card, Gail Cross, Kaolin Imago Fire, Ty Franck, Russ Galen, Vaughne Lee Hansen, Kat Lemmer, Chris Lotts, Howard Morhaim, Eric Raab, William Schafer, Shawn Speakman, Matt Staggs, Jonathan Strahan, and Simon Taylor for helping me (or trying to!) arrange reprint permissions and/or helping me get my hands on electronic copies of the manuscripts I needed.

David Carani, Caleb Jordan Schulz, LaShawn Wanak, Data Watson, and Moshe Siegel for providing feedback on the stories during the editorial process.

Gordon Van Gelder, my friend and mentor.

My amazing wife, Christie, and my mom, Marianne, for all their love and support, and their endless enthusiasm for all my new projects.

My dear friends Robert Bland, Desirina Boskovich, Christopher M. Cevasco, Doug Cohen, Jordan Hamessley, Andrea Kail, David Barr Kirtley, and Matt London.

The readers and reviewers who loved my other anthologies, making it possible for me to do more.

And last, but certainly not least: a big thanks to all of the authors who appear in this anthology.

Copyrights

About the Editor

John Joseph Adams is the bestselling editor of many anthologies, such as *Other Worlds Than These*, *Armored*, *Under the Moons of Mars: New Adventures on Barsoom*, *Brave New Worlds*, *Wastelands*, *The Living Dead*, *The Living Dead 2*, *By Blood We Live*, *Federations*, *The Improbable Adventures of Sherlock Holmes*, and *The Way of the Wizard*. Forthcoming work includes *The Mad Scientist's Guide to World Domination*, *Dead Man's Hand*, and *Robot Uprisings* (co-edited with Daniel H. Wilson).

John is a four-time finalist for the Hugo Award and a four-time finalist for the World Fantasy Award. He has been called "the reigning king of the anthology world" by Barnes & Noble, and his books have been lauded as some of the best anthologies of all time.

In addition to his anthology work, John is also the editor of *Lightspeed Magazine* and *Nightmare Magazine*, and he is the co-host of Wired.com's *The Geek's Guide to the Galaxy* podcast.

For more information, visit his website at johnjosephadams.com, and you can find him on Twitter @johnjosephadams.